THE

CHICAGO

DOCTORS

DOCTOR TAYLOR

DOCTOR I DO

DOCTOR GRAY

SHARON WOODS

To everyone starting something new. Trust the magic of the beginning.

DOCTOR TAYLOR

SHARON WOODS

CHAPTER 1

ALICE

"READY TO PRETEND YOU'RE a millionaire?" Blake says as we exit the Uber.

My heels click on the concrete pavement as we take a few steps toward the entry for Luxe, the hottest new club in the city. Blake, from my course at college, has been begging me to join him for weeks, and I finally caved. It's been a really long week of finishing my final exams, and though my eyes feel heavy, and I have a constant throbbing pain in my temples from the constant late nights, nothing will stop me from celebrating the completion of my nursing degree with my three best friends.

I'm so excited I'm bouncing on my toes while waiting to get inside. I love the light-hearted pleasure of a club. The mix of dancing and drinking gets me feeling more relaxed and self-confident. Tonight's club is even better; it's a club I haven't been to before, but I'm now a member of.

Luxe is a club for the elite. Only the most successful and disgustingly rich men and women secure a membership to Luxe. It's a secret club where you must earn a minimum of a million dollars a year—with proof—in order to get a membership. But Blake scored us all one from his dad's work connections. His dad worked on the construction of this club, which has allowed us to take advantage of the perks of a lifetime membership.

They hid the club off the main road, and you wouldn't know it's here unless you're a member, as only members get the address. Shuffling up to the front of the line, I rub my hands together, trying to warm myself up, but it's not working. The fresh air on my skin raises goosebumps all over my body. I stopped by the local department store to pick up a new dress on my way home from work today. It's different from my usual style of jeans and a top. My wardrobe is usually a mixture of sweats or jeans, along with the occasional dress. I have my regular clubbing dresses, but I needed a statement dress for Luxe.

I feel super sexy for a change, and I love the way I am feeling tonight. I have been getting a few eyes raking over my body, just while standing in the line, so I know it was the right choice of outfit—the little black dress, paired with black strappy heels that wrap delicately around my calf, adding height to my small frame. Smoky gray eye shadow makes my blue eyes pop, and pinning all my hair back in a sleek high pony completes the outfit.

I never wear this much makeup; I'm usually a mascara-only girl. But thanks to YouTube, I have slain my makeup game tonight and look older than my twenty-three years. We strut past the two suited bouncers and step through the doors into the moodiest club I have ever been to. I take in the packed crowd. There are men in three-piece suits and a woman for every man, who are all dressed in designer gowns. I tug nervously at my dress, wishing it was an inch longer after seeing all the elegantly dressed women in the room.

Blake grabs my upper arm with his soft fingers. "Leave it, Alice. You look hot as fuck. If you had a dick, I'd totally fuck you."

I bring my hand up to stifle my giggles.

I had a few vodka, lemon, and lime drinks with Blake back at my house, so we already have a warm buzz coursing through our veins. The alcoholic drinks at clubs are too pricey for us students, and I barely make enough money at the coffee shop to pay my share of the rent.

Blake's hand drops from my arm. "My treat. Let's find the bar!" he shouts above the loud music blaring all around us.

On the right, just behind the crowd, the abstract gunmetal bar with servers in suits comes into clear view. We amble over the white stone floor to the front of the bar to order.

"This is incredible, Blake. I have never seen a club like this. Check out this bar. It's so luxurious." I skim my hands along the smooth surface. It's cool to the touch and completely opposite to how the alcohol is warming me.

Blake orders our drinks while I finally take in the whole club. It's a lot bigger than I had imagined. The dark-gray walls are softly lit by down lights; 3D sculptures are popping from the ceiling, and there are white couches lining the walls, leaving a large dance floor in the middle. Men and women already occupy every seat, so we have no choice but to stand. There are no fluorescent lights or nasty sticky floors in sight. Everything here is in immaculate condition.

When I turn back to the bar, the server is putting a peach-colored shot in front of each of us. I frown, touching the glass between my fingers, and shout, "Blake, what is this shot?"

"Just shoot it." And with that, he taps the shot on the bar and downs it.

Without giving it a second thought, I lift the cold shot glass to my bottom lip, and closing my eyes, I chase mine back. The shot burns my throat, making my eyes pop open, reminding me why I detest shots, but the aftertaste from this one is scrumptious. I lick my lips to pick up any remaining residue.

"Oh, peach. Yummy. What are these, Blake?" I question.

Before Blake can answer, the bartender speaks up. "Wet pussies." He winks and I flush, but he collects our empty glasses from the bar and takes them away before I can respond.

I turn to Blake. "Let's wait until the girls get here to order more drinks. I've got a good buzz going already, and I don't want to be drunk too early, especially since we had a few at home." I hiccup. We're waiting on my two roommates, Maddison and Tahlia, to get here. Tahlia had to work later than usual today, so they should join us soon.

He shakes his head. "No chance. They take forever getting ready. We are ordering now."

I giggle at his impatience. He swivels slowly on his heel and orders another round of our favorite—vodka, lemon, and lime. Blake hands his credit card across the bar to the flirty bartender to pay for our drinks.

The bartender shakes his head. "A fellow patron has already paid for these. Enjoy."

My lips shut into a flat, thin line. *What?* "By whom?" I ask.

Blake and I stand frozen before spinning around, trying to find the person responsible for paying for our drinks and, more importantly, why? The bar is full, and everyone is either in groups chatting among themselves, dancing on the crowded dance floor, or waiting in lines at the bar to be served. None of them are by themselves or seem to be paying attention to Blake and me. *Weird.*

"Who the fuck cares? Thank you to whoever paid for these." He picks up his drink and toasts the air.

I shake my head, reaching for the glass. Clutching it in one hand, I stir the alcohol with the black straw in the other. Wild doesn't begin to describe Blake. Meeting Blake three years ago was like finding another sibling. He sat down in the empty chair next to me in our first biology class for our nursing degree, and he kept distracting me with his constant outbursts. We both got warnings that very first day for disrupting the class, but we still achieved the top marks out of the entire class by the end of the three years. He always keeps the girls and me laughing at his weekend antics. It's like living in a real-life episode of *The Bold and the Beautiful.*

"You're crazy. We can't accept them. The person could be a weirdo."

"Honey, have you looked around the club? He would be a rich, successful weirdo. Drink his money. I'm sure he's swimming in it." He drinks it without a care and pushes off the bar, nodding to the dance floor. "Come on."

I peer down at the drink, thinking and watching the lemon bob around on the surface. *No one has ever bought me a drink before.* It sends a slight chill through me, but I shake off the feeling and walk over to stand beside Blake, taking a swig of my drink. No words leave either of our mouths, both of us happy just to peer at the patrons dancing on the floor in front of us. We have a good view of the entire dance floor from where we are standing. The music blaring from the speakers is R&B and the latest pop.

I take my last sip and drain the glass. My stare lands on a man standing across the dance floor directly opposite us, leaning his large frame against the arm of a white couch full of men. My gaze meets his and I let out a shocked gasp. My grip on the glass loosens and the smooth surface slides straight through my fingers to land on the stone floor, where it smashes into tiny fragments with a popping sound.

"Shit." I crouch down, but Blake pulls my arm, preventing me from picking up the glass.

"Alice, don't. You will cut yourself. The cleaners are heading over now."

Allowing Blake to help me up, I push up on my heels to straighten myself out. I spot a cleaner in a suit holding a dustpan and brush strolling over in our direction. I swallow and glance down at my twisted hands.

Remembering why I dropped the glass, I raise my head and look around for the handsome man with scorching blue eyes, but he's no longer standing there. I close my eyes, squeezing them shut for a moment, wishing I hadn't been so clumsy in front of him. He is probably used to elegant women, not a clumsy mess like me.

I have never had a reaction like that to a man. His eyes and the way he stared at me set my whole body on fire. Then the sexy smirk at the corner of his lip that rose when I dropped my glass sent chills down my spine. He must have seen what effect he had on me. I open my eyes, grimace, and hurry to the bathroom to clear my head. I need to forget about that man and focus on having a good night.

I hurry through the crowd of people, weaving in and out as I make my way toward the ladies' room. Not paying attention and keeping my gaze on the sign above the door with the word 'bathroom,' I collide with a hard chest. I bounce backward, stumbling on my heels. The stranger reaches out, grabbing on to the back of my arms to steady me, saving me from falling flat on my ass.

"Shit, I'm so sorry." The voice is smooth and rich, making me take a step back.

My eyes flick up and I meet the same magnificent blue eyes from before. I smile to myself as he stares, feeling heat spread across my cheeks. He stands there, devilishly handsome, his brown hair gleaming in the club lights. His lips part in a dazzling display of straight white teeth. He holds an air of authority and has the appearance of one who demands instant obedience.

I nod, fighting the overwhelming need to be close to him, to feel his tongue tangled with mine.

My tongue slides out between my lips, and I skim it across the lower one, moistening it. He makes no attempt to hide the fact that he's watching me with a heated stare. The air around us crackles with electricity.

"Can I buy you a drink?" The double meaning in his gaze is obvious.

I stand frozen, and my heart jolts inside my chest.

But as I stand there staring into his glowing eyes, I give in, and I lean forward and kiss him. He kisses me back, and it's a slow, all-consuming kiss. Not the hungry kiss I expected. I can taste the liquor on his tongue and the delicious sensation of the touch of his lips. When we pull away, I'm panting, staring up at him under heavy, hooded eyes.

The air becomes thick, overwhelming me. Clearing my constricting throat, I try to suck some much-needed air into my lungs. "I have to go to the bathroom. I'll catch up with you later," I whisper before I rush off to the ladies' room.

After using the bathroom, I collect myself. My breathing is now regulated, and my body temperature seems to be returning to normal. I wander back out and stand by the entrance to the bathroom. Scanning the club, I can't see him in the sea of faces. My heart constricts as I look around a few minutes more before giving up and walking to meet Blake. I spot him, so I quicken my pace. I notice my roommates, Tahlia and Maddison, have arrived, and they are standing around talking.

"Hey, girls," I yell, moving between them. Draping one arm around each of their shoulders, I squeeze them closer in a hug.

Chuckling at my affection, Maddison asks, "Where did you go? You sound happy."

"That's because you girls are finally here, so we can dance now." Just as I finish the sentence, my skin prickles. I glance toward the spot the man had been standing in before, and he is back in the exact same position. He's staring at me, but this time he is clutching a glass of amber liquid that he brings to his lips. I watch his Adam's apple bob when he takes a sip. His eyes don't falter; they drink me down with it. A delicious shudder heats my body, and before I can register what's happening, Maddison squeals.

"O.M.G. Yes! I love this song! Come on, let's go dance!"

"This Is How We Do It" by Montell Jordan plays, and I lose eye contact with him when Maddison drags me by the hand to the dance floor, pushing through the crowd of people to get to the middle. I'm almost tripping over my feet, trying to keep up with her. My tight dress only allows me to take short, quick steps.

Maddison, Tahlia, and I met during high school. Tahlia and I were working in a local coffee shop as waitresses after school. Maddison would come every day after lessons to have coffee and study. After a few months, I began talking to Maddison about college applications and she offered to assist me in the research and also with applying to my top three preferences—which I accepted. We hung out every weekend, all becoming fast friends before moving to the city and renting a house together. Blake was the final piece that completed our friendship group.

"Maddy, slow down. I'm going to break my neck in these stupid heels!" I shout.

She stops suddenly in the center of the dance floor, and, spinning my body to face her, she dances. The entire floor is packed with sweaty bodies touching and grinding against each other. I can't see past the people dancing to see if the man has moved or if he is still standing there. I'm strangely flattered and intrigued by his interest.

A few songs later, the crowd surrounding us has thinned. I'm having a blast. My knees ache and the balls of my feet are burning with pain from all our dancing, but I'm too buzzed to care. Tahlia and Blake join us, and we all dance together. I can't remember the last time I had this much fun. Recently, my life has consisted only of work or study. To be so carefree in this moment makes my heart sing. I sway my hips from side to side to the beat. I look around again for the sexy stranger and I note he is standing near the bar. A woman with rich, long brown hair, and wearing a black sequined dress, is engaged in conversation with him, her fingers wrapped around his bicep. They are standing relatively close to each other, and she is whispering in his ear.

My heart sinks at the sight of them, so I tear my gaze away. I'm about to ask if the others want to call an Uber soon, when I feel a body slide up behind me. A masculine arm snakes around my waist to pull me back flush against his hard torso, and he rocks our hips slowly to the beat.

The body hugging mine is tall and seems to be built of solid muscle. I can smell his deep sandalwood and caramel scent, which is intoxicating. I sigh audibly at the memory of when I was last being held in a man's embrace. I feel his breath tickle the tip of my ear, pulling me from the memory as we continue to sway into the next song. I close my eyes and get lost in this moment, forgetting everything and just enjoying his warmth.

He whispers, "You're incredible. I couldn't resist." His tone is soft and sensual, totally different from the smooth, rich voice of the man I kissed earlier in the night. I grin from ear to ear at the memory. The warm embrace is pulling a deep longing from me that I don't want to lose. I don't reply, but I continue to dance with him.

"Turn around, beautiful." I stop and turn in a circle, curious to see what this man looks like. Raising my arms, I lay them on his shoulders and step back, leaving a decent gap.

His eyes close and his hands are on my hips, moving them to the sound of the beat. I seize the opportunity to take him in—he has short brown hair, tanned skin, and his jeans, t-shirt, and blazer are all black. My lips lift at his classically handsome features. As I finish scanning him from head to toe, his eyes suddenly pop open and his blue eyes meet mine.

He is beaming, which makes me grin back. However, his beauty and presence don't hold the same power and control over me as the other man's did. It doesn't stroke the deep desires and feelings that have awoken in me. My gaze drops to his solid chest. And I sigh. *I'm not feeling it.*

Before I have the chance to speak, he leans forward, closing the gap until his lips meet mine. I gently push on his chest and take a step back, which breaks the seal of our lips.

I swallow hard, with a soft shake of my head. "I'm sorry," I whisper.

Then, in the corner of my eye, I see *him*. His fine tailored suit and crisp white shirt with no tie stand out in the crowd of dark clothes. He stands motionless, a dark, angry expression on his face, his hands deep in his pockets. The brunette is still talking to him, but his icy gaze is focused entirely on me. My eyes widen and I turn away to gaze back at the man in front of me. An easy smile plays at the corners of his mouth. He hasn't noticed the other man or my sudden loss of focus.

"I didn't intro—" he begins.

Tahlia comes over, her presence cutting into his speech. "Hey, Alice, can we head home soon? I'm pretty tanked and I have work in the morning." Her smile widens in approval as she glances between me and the man I had just been dancing with. A lump forms in my throat because my mind was elsewhere, and I couldn't get into him.

I twist to face her. "Sure, T." I swing back to face the man in front of me. "We have to go. Thanks, err, nice to meet you, I guess."

His posture is relaxed as he stands there, chuckling. "Yes, and I'm Alex, by the way. It was my pleasure. Are you going to be okay getting home, or do you need me to call you girls a cab or an Uber?" He is being so nice, making me feel a twinge of guilt in the pit of my stomach. I almost wish I had felt a small connection to Alex, but I shouldn't be surprised at my lack of interest. After all, I was with my ex for two years without feeling real love for him.

"No, thank you. I already called an Uber, and there are another two people coming with us. Thanks anyway."

"Okay. Well, if you're sure. It was lovely to meet you both. I'd better head off now to find my group of friends before I'm left here. Hope to see you here again sometime. Bye." He nods at Tahlia, and the beginning of a smile tips the corners of his mouth before he moves away.

I let out a shaky breath. I was petrified he was going to ask for my number, and I would have had to turn him down in front of Tahlia, but he didn't, so maybe he read the same signals I did. Even though he was nice, there was no spark.

Oh well. I won't have to see him ever again, except maybe when I come back here, so I don't have anything to worry about.

Linking my arm through Tahlia's, we slowly wander off the dance floor. "Let's find the other two and get out of here. My feet are killing me," I moan.

"Me too. What a great night, though, celebrating the end of your studies."

My smile widens. "The *best* night. Thank you."

CHAPTER 2

ALICE

SIX MONTHS LATER

It's midmorning and Blake is driving me into the city. Both of us need to pick up our parking passes for our graduate year. We decided to do it together and make a day of it. Neither of us has work today and we want to do a test run of driving into work to see how long it will take. Blake didn't get placed at the same hospital, but he is around the corner, within walking distance.

I gaze down at my Google Maps, noticing the hospitals are close by. "Let's park here," I say and point to the parking spots along the curb.

"Good idea," he mutters as he pulls in and parks.

I dressed in my comfortable clothes—jeans, a cream crewneck, and sneakers. My hair is thrown up in a sleek pony, opting to pin all my fringe back. We exit the car and peer around before I throw my phone inside my bag, then walk up to read the sign. "It's free all-day parking and we can walk up. Your building is farther away, so let's do yours first and then mine."

"Sweet. Let's get to it. I just need to find the information desk. They should have the pass ready."

I nod and we walk along the sidewalk. I link my arm through his, and we walk in sync as I peer around, admiring the trees and tall city buildings. The buzz of the people and cars surrounding us has me grinning wide.

"I still can't get over the fact we have finished our studies. All that hard work is finally paying off," I exclaim.

"I know, right? No more exams or studying, thank fuck. Here we are." He motions to the entry to his glass building.

I scale my eyes up and down the tall building, noting people standing outside smoking and others talking on their phones.

"You go inside. I will wait here." I point over to a spare bench outside the building.

"I'll just be a minute."

I watch him enter the doors before I walk over and take a seat, then I take out my phone to send a picture to Mom.

My phone vibrates after I hit send.

I smile and answer. "Mom."

"Hi, love. Are you at work today?"

"No. Blake and I are picking up our parking passes."

"Oh, how nice. Say hi to Blake for me."

I watch as Blake comes out, waving his pass in victory. I laugh loudly.

"Mom, I gotta run. I will call you tonight. Love you."

"Okay, have fun. I love you too."

I end the call and stand up.

"Ready?" Blake asks, nudging his head in the direction of my building.

"Yeah, let's go." We link arms and wander slowly down the path. "Mom called to see what I was doing. I sent her a picture. She said hi."

He throws his spare hand on his heart. "Aw, I love her. Let's go get your pass now before we find somewhere for a drink—I'm parched."

I giggle. "Okay."

Blake waits outside on the sidewalk while I enter the building, locating the information desk on my phone.

It takes me a minute to get mine, and when I exit the building, Blake jumps up.

"Drink time?" I ask.

"Are you talking alcohol?" He winks.

"No chance." I look around us and locate a shop across the road. "Hey, there is a smoothie bar across the road. Let's go there."

"This could be dangerous. I could waste all my money here when I'm working so close."

I nod in agreement and loop my arm through his. We cross at the lights and enter the smoothie shop. It is surprisingly quiet, with only a few patrons inside.

"Let's sit there in the booth," Blake says, motioning toward the brown leather booth in the corner. We walk over and slide into the seats, across from each other. I shiver from the cold leather before I pick up the menu and scan it.

"What are you thinking?" I ask Blake.

"Mango dream."

"Oh, that sounds good. I'll order them. Stay here. I will only be a minute."

Blake smiles and pulls out his phone. I round the booth and walk to the counter, then order two mango dreams.

I stand to the side and wait for them to be ready.

The door chimes, signaling people entering. I peer up and watch as a group of four men in tailored suits walk through.

But it's the last one that walks through the door that catches my eye. *Fuck.* He is taller and broader than the others, but that's not what captures my breath. It's the eyes I haven't been able to forget and the lips. His gaze holds mine and his jaw is tight from him clenching.

The black suit, fit to perfection, shows off his large shoulders and lean body. I shudder at the memory of his soft, controlled lips on mine and the taste. How I would love a taste again. My mouth dries. *Where the hell is my order? Did they pick the mangos off a tree themselves?*

He owns the room and I stare after him as he takes a seat opposite me. The guys around him are talking, clearly oblivious to his distraction.

He leans on the table, brows furrowed, rubbing his jaw—staring at me. The electricity in the room crackles, and the heat level makes my crewneck sweater feel restrictive. I bring my finger up and pull on the neck of it, trying to get more air.

"Two mango dreams."

I jump with a squeak. I spin around, breaking my intense eye contact with the sexy suit guy, and scoop up the drinks. I turn to see him still watching me. I dip my head with a flush and suck the drink up through the straw immediately, and his eyes darken. The cold sweet drink hitting my tongue helps to cool me down.

I reach our table and peer at Blake as I slide his drink to him.

"Thanks, hon."

I nod, just sucking the drink as I squeeze back in the booth. I peek over. He is still staring. I tear my gaze away again, overwhelmed by his presence.

"What's the plan tonight?" Blake asks.

"Let's grab something for—" I lose my train of thought as I hear the screech of a chair dragging on the floor. I look over and watch *him* on the phone, practically running out of the shop. Once he is out of my sight, I drop my head, sadness washing over me.

Twice I have missed out on finding out *his* name.

Chapter 3

Alice

I come to an abrupt stop, my heart jumping inside my chest as I arrive at the hospital for the first day of my new career in nursing. It's impossible to steady my erratic pulse as I walk through the doors on shaky feet.

The advisor was the one to find the rotation and thought I should apply. I didn't think I had a hope being young and fresh out of college, but the advisor said that is exactly what they wanted.

I managed to not give up on mine or Dad's dream. He would have been so proud to hear about this. My stomach knots at the memory. I've worked hard these last few years, sacrificing nights out, having fun, or traveling the world, like most women my age. Instead of doing any of those things, I kept my head stuck in my books. The sacrifices were worth it because I got the top grades out of the entire class and then was accepted for this once-in-a-lifetime opportunity.

I remember playing "doctors and nurses" with my family all the time when I was growing up. My mom constantly reminds me how I used to bandage my sister up and tend to her care. Claire, my younger sister by eighteen months, let me do whatever I wanted. I used to be the nurse and make her play the patient. I would bandage her arm or leg, and she would happily let me, often lying like that for over an hour. I'm so lucky to have always had the most supportive and loving family.

Just thinking of them makes me feel lighter, so I inhale deeply and step through the doors of the hospital. My jaw drops and my heart quickens inside my chest as I look around. The size of the hospital is bigger than I remember, making me feel bewildered at the sheer size. I dressed with a confidence I don't feel, but at least I can look it. I smooth down the scratchy fabric of my black-and-white-checked skirt with my hands, straighten my spine, and pop out my chest before taking off down the hall.

I open my handbag to grab the directions and the name of the person I need to meet today. As I pull the papers out, a few other pages fall to the floor. When I crouch down to pick them up, a pair of large masculine hands reach in to help me. I lift my head too quickly, and my head hits the chin of the helper. *Ouch.* I reach for my head to rub the painful area.

"Oh, shit. I'm so sorry," I say.

My eyes meet with a familiar pair of soft blues—Alex, the guy I danced with at the club. Recognizing him immediately, I drop my gaze to the papers on the floor and begin fixing the ones in front of me. *Shit, shit, shit.* Hopefully, he doesn't recognize me. I know I look different, so if I can make this conversation short, I'll be fine.

I quickly notice an overdue phone bill lying on the floor that I don't want him to see, and I panic. Quickly grabbing it, I stuff it in my handbag and stand back up. He follows.

"It's okay," he says. "I noticed the papers falling and wanted to help, but maybe next time I should talk to give you warning." His cheeky smile and words make my lips turn up.

"Thank you. You really didn't have to. I'm sorry I hurt you. It was unintentional." I watch him rub his chin with his hand.

"I know," he replies.

Standing here gazing properly at him, I take my time, noticing how different he looks compared to when we met at the club. Today he is dressed in a tailored, pin-striped suit with no tie, and he has a slight five-o'clock shadow across his jaw. He is still handsome and charming, looking more like he belongs in a catalog of a magazine than at a hospital, but slightly rougher. I can't see any recognition in his face, so I need to leave right now before he works out who I am.

"I must be going. I am so sorry about your chin," I apologize.

Alex's lips turn up. "Don't worry about it. I hope you have a good day."

He is still staring at me, but before he can put two and two together, I spin and take off down the hall, quickly waving at him as I call out, "Bye."

I quicken my pace to put some much-needed distance between us. My breathing has increased in pace, and I feel tightening in my chest. I ride the elevator up and pull the paper with directions out and concentrate on where I need to go, counting to ten to calm my heart rate down.

I exit the elevator and arrive at a set of doors marked Fracture and Emergency. They are ID swipe access only, so I stand and wait to grab a passerby, because I don't have any ID yet. I will need to ask about that today.

The doors open, and I turn when a nurse pops out. She doesn't stop me when I walk straight in through the same doors. Down the corridor, I find the row of offices I'm looking for, just before I reach the nurses' desk. I focus on finding the door with the name "Kate Irwin." After I locate her door, I stand directly in front of it and take a few deep breaths. My hand trembles, and my throat gets dry before I raise my fist and knock..

Waiting for an answer to my knock feels like years when it's only been a few minutes.

The door flies open, and a middle-aged woman, wearing a bright-red shade of lipstick and the warmest of smiles, greets me. "Hi there. You must be Alice Winters."

"Hi." My voice cracks so I clear my throat and start again. "Sorry about that, and yes. Hello, Kate. I am Alice Winters. It's very nice to meet you." I hold out my hand for her to shake. She looks at my hand and smiles, clearly impressed with my manners.

She shakes my hand, and it's a nice, soft shake. She lets go and opens the door wider, waving her arm in the direction of her office. "Come in."

I step into the office, which is light and airy, with neat bookshelves lining both sides of the room. Kate treads over to a white desk, which sits in front of a large window. Following close behind, I wander directly over to the leather chair in front of the desk and take a seat. Kate then sits down directly opposite me.

"So, Alice, first, I would like to formally welcome you to The Chicago Hospital. I hope you will enjoy your graduate year here in the fracture and emergency department. I can tell you that I, for one, am excited for the year ahead. This is an exciting opportunity we have never offered before."

My mouth hangs open, and I shift my body forward in my seat with delight. I feel so honored to have been chosen for this role. I don't know if it was my application letter or my test scores that made her choose me, but I am forever grateful for the opportunity.

"The role will involve you working part time on the ward, and part time with our top orthopedic surgeon. You will have the opportunity to watch him perform surgeries, assist him with notes, attend interstate conferences, and do a little bit of PA work. He was awarded the Best Surgeon in the Country award this month. This year will have lots of new opportunities for both you and him. But pick his brain, because he is one intelligent man. Please don't tell him that. I am sure he has a big enough head as it is with that award." We both laugh. Kate is so kind; she gives me the feeling of being wrapped in a warm blanket. I am so glad she is the manager. I will work hard to impress Kate and the surgeon to show them my gratitude.

Wow. I rub my hands together. He sounds impressive with all his high credentials, and I start feeling as though the walls are closing in on me again. Her eyebrows rise a fraction, waiting for my answer.

"I'm still shocked, to be honest, Kate, but I'm so grateful for the opportunity. I won't let you down."

"I have no doubt, Alice. I'll organize your roster and ID today. Now, just to let you know, the contract is fixed for the three-month rotation, so neither you nor he can change it. After three months, I will decide if we should continue or change your rotation. Does that make sense?"

I nod. "Yes, it does, thank you." Three months is a short amount of time, so I'm sure there will be no issues. Working with the middle-aged doctor won't be difficult. *At least, I hope it won't.*

"Dr. Taylor is running late, so I'll show you around the ward and let you grab a tea or coffee. I'll come find you when he arrives."

I nod, and she stands, then walks around her desk toward her door. I get up and follow her out of the office. On the way to the break room, she gives me a tour of the ward. I take in all my surroundings, trying to memorize the layout. She passes the nurses' desk and ushers me into the empty break room. I see a coffee station, which I instantly gravitate to.

"Have a tea or coffee and relax for a bit. I will be back as soon as he arrives. Do you have any questions for now?"

"Umm, not right now. Thank you, Kate. But I will let you know if I do. I will make a coffee and sit here," I say as I move toward an empty table near the window.

"Okay, I'll come grab you soon. You know where my office is if you need me."

Kate exits the break room. After five minutes, I finally figure out how to use the fancy coffee machine to make my drink and sit down at the table to enjoy it. I'm savoring the peace and quiet of the room while hugging the warm cup between my palms, when two nurses come barging in, talking loudly as if I don't exist.

"Did you see Mike arrive? He was rushing to his office in his gym gear."

"Oh, no, I didn't. No way. What a sight that would have been. He is so hot. Did you hear he kissed Monica in the elevator the other day?"

"What? No, no way. You have to be kidding."

"Yes, way. I overheard the mechanic telling Kate there was nothing wrong with the elevator, so he must have stopped it midway to make out with her in the elevator or fuck her." *Whoa!*

The girl gasps. "How lucky is she? Maybe I should head into his office now and see if he is keen for a quickie. Do I look okay?"

My eyes nearly pop out of their sockets, and my jaw hits the floor as I watch her flick her long, blond hair over her shoulder and straighten her uniform with the palms of her hands.

"You're a bombshell, Rachel. As if he could say no."

I watch the exchange out of the corner of my eye. One is a brunette whose back is to me, so I cannot get a good view of her, but I can see Rachel clearly, and I'm speechless. I have to agree that Rachel is a bombshell—tall, probably about my age, slim but with killer curves, and green eyes.

Keeping my head down, I busy myself with drinking my coffee. I cradle the mug tighter in my hands and stare down at the milky brown liquid. After a few minutes, the girls exit, leaving me to melt back into the chair in the room by myself again. My brain is ticking over and absorbing what I just heard, and I make a mental note to stay clear of that doctor.

After a while, Kate comes hurrying back through the doors, out of breath. "Hi, I'm so sorry, Alice. I had an emergency conference call that overran. Let's go to my office and we can call Dr. Taylor in."

I rise from my chair, put my paper cup in the trash and follow her out. My pulse has picked up and my palms sweat.

When we arrive at her office, I expect to find him sitting in one of the chairs, but the room is empty. I sigh and take a deep breath, waiting for direction from her.

"Please take a seat." She points to the same chair as before. I nod and sink back into the cold leather seat. It feels good against my back and thighs that are now burning hot. She picks up her desk phone and dials a number. "We are ready," she says into the phone before carefully hanging up.

A knock on the timber door sounds behind me less than a minute later, and then it creaks open. I turn in my seat, twisting my body to see the doctor as he enters. When he comes into view, the air is knocked out of my lungs, and I'm grateful that I am sitting. I grip the arms of the chair tightly and mentally count to ten to calm my breathing down.

Staring back at me are a startlingly familiar pair of piercing blue eyes that send chills down my spine.

CHAPTER 4

MIKE

My heart stops in my chest, and I turn to stone when I see the same set of blue eyes peeking up at me behind her thick black lashes. I inhale the rich vanilla scent that is wafting toward me and my lips purse into a thin line.

I'm taken aback by her. She looks so youthful today. My eyes roam up and down her body, taking in all her natural beauty and stamping it in my brain for later when I'm alone. She has minimal makeup on, her hair is down, fanning over her shoulders, and she now has a cute fringe covering her forehead.

She's sitting there peeking up at me so innocently, which I know is far from the truth. Her eyes still have the power to destroy me, to bring me to my knees, and I can clearly see the recognition written across her face, answering the question that's circling in my head. *She kissed my brother Alex at Luxe seven months ago.*

"Dr. Mike Taylor, please meet the graduate nurse, Miss Alice Winters." Kate's voice cuts through my thoughts, and I shake my head to clear it.

"Hi." I nod at Alice and take the seat beside her, clenching my jaw. *Alice.*

Her jaw drops at my name, and her mouth hangs wide open.

"You're drooling," I mumble so only she can hear. I wink at her, and her eyes pop further out of her head, making me chuckle out loud.

"Now that you're both here, let's get started," Kate begins.

I lean back in the chair and keep my eyes firmly on Kate. I'm trying not to make any glances in Alice's direction, but her sweet scent is so strong now that I'm this close. So, I breathe through my mouth and just listen to Kate.

"First, I'd like to congratulate you, Alice, on your placement here. As you both are aware, this is a new role that we have only introduced this year. You've both signed your contracts, so here is your ID and your uniform that we had ordered prior to today." Kate leans forward, holding out a bag for Alice to take.

"Thank you," Alice replies and reaches forward to collect the bag before settling back into the chair.

Her voice is angelic, sending goosebumps rising all over my body. I have had dreams about her and how she sounds, and upon hearing her voice again, it is even better now than in my memory. It makes all the hair on my body stand up.

I'm regretting signing that contract right now. *It's going to be a really long three months.*

"Your time will be split, so half the week is spent with Mike, and then the other half will be on the ward. And your pay will be double the standard rate." I notice she sits up in her seat and I stare at her, noting her eyes have lightened up at the mention of pay. She nods at Kate but doesn't say a word. Kate continues. "There is ample opportunity for overtime, as I'm sure you know emergency surgeries happen at all hours, and once Mike starts an operation, he can't leave until it's finished. And Mike, I expect you to call Alice with any exciting surgeries. She is here to learn and observe everything."

"Understood," I grunt.

"There will be opportunities for you to attend interstate conferences, but I don't plan to send you on too many, as one or two would be enough. Now, I must get to my next meeting, so I will have to cut this off here."

"Thank you," Alice responds.

"Okay, well, you two go and get started now. Tomorrow will be another day with Mike, but then the rest of the week you will be on the ward. And, Alice, I'm here anytime you need me. I will catch up with you soon to see how you're settling in."

My body has tensed up. I now have to go into my office and work with her, like right fucking now. I stand. "Thanks, Kate."

I round the chair, passing Alice and not bothering to glance her way. I walk out and march straight to my office, closing my door behind me. I just need a second to collect myself. *Fuck!* I rake my hands through my hair and drop myself into my office chair and thump my arms on the desk with my head in my arms. I'm royally fucked. To work this close to her is going to test me.

A tap on the door has my head whipping back up. "What?" I bark loudly. It comes out a little more harshly than I meant.

I sit up and the door slowly opens. Alice is standing there, her chest rising and falling quickly, and I take my time to take another good look at her. She hasn't moved an inch. She is still standing in my office doorway, nervously grasping the handle. She looks like every man's wet dream...and my fucking nightmare.

CHAPTER 5

ALICE

THE ICY LOOK IN Dr. Taylor's eyes stops me in my tracks. I stand still, unable to move.

My breathing is becoming more rapid, and I count down in my head to calm myself. *Ten, nine, eight, seven... I do not want to pass out in front of him.* His elbows are on his desk, his hands clasped together, and his eyes haven't moved. Neither of us speaks.

I clear my throat. "Hi, Dr. Taylor. I'm sorry to interrupt, but Kate said I'm with you for the rest of today." He doesn't reply; he just continues to stare. I wish he would just speak because the anger rolling off him is confusing me. I decide to try again. "What would you like me to do?"

Letting go of the door handle, I step inside and shut the door. I shake my hand to get the blood flowing properly again and then clasp them in front of me. I stand close to the door and wait for his instructions.

"Just... get me a coffee and it will give me some time to think of a task for you." He stands abruptly, reminding me how tall he is. His hand dives into his pocket and I watch as he grabs his wallet, opens it to pull out a bill, and thrusts it in my direction. "Get me a long black and buy whatever you want," he snaps.

He shakes it at me again, his eyebrows raised, so I quickly move forward and grab the bill, nodding my understanding as I can't seem to speak. My words are stuck in my throat. He drops back down in his chair and carries on shuffling the papers in front of him, silently dismissing me. My mind races, searching for an explanation for his cold demeanor, but coming up empty, I shrug and spin around to leave. I exit his office, giving him the time that he requested. However, he didn't give a specific time to return by, so I roam my way through the corridors, taking in the old building and all the areas I haven't yet had the chance to explore.

I notice up ahead the elevator doors have opened, and as people begin to enter, I rush forward and just make it before the doors close. I arrive on the ground floor and follow everyone out. Spotting a few shops, I mosey around until I arrive at the important one—the coffee shop.

I had a coffee back in the break room earlier, so I don't order anything for myself. I just order the long black for Dr. Taylor. It only takes them a few minutes to make his scorching hot coffee, so I trek back upstairs carrying his takeaway cup. On the ride back up, I think about how he was acting. He has had a giant stick up his ass since he met me in Kate's office and has been nothing but a cold prick to me. He barely knows me. I have been through worse than this at other jobs, and I didn't come this far to let him scare me off. I reach his closed door, and after a moment of staring at the timber barrier, I inhale a large breath and knock with my free hand before pushing the door open.

I let out a shaky breath, and my shoulders relax because he isn't here. I walk over to his desk, inspecting the room. Dr. Taylor's office is laid out in the same way as Kate's, except with dark furnishings—*dark and moody, just like him*. The bookshelves on either side of the room are full of books and his dark wood desk is piled high with papers. Unlike Kate's office, there is no window. I sniff the air, breathing in his intoxicating, musky spice scent. I smelled it briefly in Kate's office, but in here it's everywhere and it's almost suffocating, reminding me of the first time I met him. I will never forget a single detail about that night.

I wander over to the desk, moving some papers aside so I can find a coaster to place the coffee on, adding his change beside it. Wringing my hands together, I wonder what I should do next, since he's not here. I'm unsure, so I decide to sit in the chair opposite his desk and wait. A few minutes later, I hear the door creak open. I jerk my head around to peer over my shoulder and see him entering with a file hooked under his armpit. I turn away without a word.

He walks past the desk to sink into his black leather chair. He doesn't acknowledge me, just picks up the coffee and sips it. "You took your sweet time. Did you get lost?" he asks in a mocking tone.

I stare at him, baffled how I've earned such anger from him. I bite my tongue until I taste the metallic tang of blood. *He isn't worth it.* The connection I had with Mike has vanished. This man in front of me is obnoxious.

"No, I didn't get lost," I reply sweetly, refusing to bite back and enable his smart mouth.

"Right, well, I need to get home. I have just come back from an interstate conference and I'm exhausted. I don't have the energy for this shit today. You can sort out all of this until the end of your shift." He flaps his hands over the papers covering the desk. I blink rapidly at his attitude, watching in shock as he picks up his coffee and a briefcase that was tucked underneath the desk and storms out.

Sitting still, I try to absorb what's just occurred in this office. He clearly doesn't remember me, so I'll have to act like I don't either. On a positive note, day one is done. I hurtle back to earth as reality strikes, and pushing up out of my chair, I step around his desk, pondering.

I contemplate where these papers should belong, opening cupboards only to find them mostly bare, besides a few golf products and a family picture. The most impressive thing about his office is the book collection.

I browse along the spines of the books and notice a mix of true stories, fiction, and medical books. After a lot of snooping, I decide to see what the paperwork consists of so I can then plan a system for filing them—clearly, he needs one. I pile them up in one neat stack, then sit down in his office chair and sort them into categories. I realize there are a few different types. I also think he would benefit from a desk planner and diary. I decide to finish up for the day and head to the store to grab the supplies I need. I'll finish the organizing tomorrow.

In the car on the way home, I dial Blake.

"Hey, love, how was your first day?" he exclaims.

"A fucking disaster." I sigh. "Can you come over for dinner tonight, so I can fill you in?"

"Of course, I'll bring wine."

I chuckle. "Okay, I'll catch you later." I hang up and drive to the store to buy the stationery for Mike's office before driving home.

Blake, Tahlia, Maddison, and I are sitting around the dinner table enjoying pizza and wine. I haven't said much yet. I'm still trying to process my day. Hopefully, they can shed some light on my situation.

"Are you going to tell us what made you call me over midweek?" Blake questions.

Inspecting my half-eaten Margherita pizza, I inhale deeply and decide to speak before finishing the rest. "Where do I start? It was awful."

"From the beginning. It's okay, just tell us. I'm sure it's not that bad."

I laugh at Maddison's comment. "Okay, well, you know that first night we went to Luxe?"

"Mm-hmm." They all nod and murmur.

"Well, there was something I never told you." I shuffle in my seat, poking my pizza around on my plate. "I dropped my glass because I was sharing this weird eye fuck with a guy across the room."

Cutlery falls with a loud bang on a plate, making me jump, and I glance up at Tahlia.

"Sorry," she mouths.

"Then, when I was heading to the bathroom, I bumped into him and had the hottest kiss of my life. I got flustered and ran off to the bathroom." I swallow the lump that's formed in my throat, as they all laugh. When they recover, I continue with the story. "Then when we were all dancing, I spotted him talking with this tall, stunning brunette. She was draped on his arm. So, when that random guy came up to me grinding, and he pecked me, I let him, but when I stopped, I saw *him* staring at me again. It was so weird. I have never had a connection like that before, especially not with a stranger." I pick my pizza back up and take a large bite.

"Sounds hot," Blake says.

"I agree." Maddison's fanning herself with her hand, which turns my mouth up mid-chew.

"Well, I saw him again when we went to the smoothie bar, but he ran out on his phone."

"Okay, but what's that got to do with the problem you had today?" Tahlia frowns, looking at me for answers.

"Well, it started when I overheard two nurses describing a doctor called Mike, and how he had stopped the elevator to make out with another nurse."

"No fucking way," Blake says.

"You're kidding, how?" Maddison asks mid-chew.

"I don't know, but then I go into my meeting to meet the surgeon I'll be working with and guess who the doctor is?"

"The doctor from the elevator, surely," Maddison chirps, bouncing up and down in her chair.

I laugh at her enthusiasm. "Well, partially correct, the nightclub guy, the doctor, and now my supervisor is the exact same person."

"You're pulling my leg here, right?" Blake's mouth is hanging open.

I shake my head. "I wish. It was bad. He barely acknowledged me, so I don't think he remembers the moment we shared at the club. And then when we were alone in his office, he sent me to get him coffee so he could think. When I returned, he proceeded to leave me to clean his office while he went home for the day!" I huff.

"Oh, hopefully the hot doc pulls the stick out of his ass," Blake states.

"I'm sorry your first day wasn't better," Tahlia says.

"He is a piece of shit. You're not a damn cleaner," Maddison spits.

"Now I'm stuck with him for a minimum of three months because of our contract. But the money is too good. I can't say no." I glance down at my plate, wishing I knew what to do.

"Just keep turning up and do your best. You know what doctors are like. They always think they are above you," Blake reassures.

I sigh. "Thanks for listening to me complain. I guess I just needed to vent."

For the rest of the evening, Blake and the girls discuss their days at work and school. I can't concentrate on anything they are saying, because my mind is still racing with thoughts of Mike. Why do I have to be attracted to him? Why, when he is around, do I want to feel his lips on mine again?

I yawn and rub my heavy eyes, tired from the eventful first day. Excusing myself from the table, I plod to my room and throw my body down and drift off into a state of unconsciousness.

CHAPTER 6

ALICE

THE DOOR BURSTS OPEN as I hum a tune to myself. I'm sorting through the piles of paperwork in his chair. When I hear the thump of footsteps as Dr. Taylor approaches. I glance up and abruptly stand, stepping back around his desk so I am out of his way. I watch his face as he inspects his office, taking in what I have done. His eyes roam the room as he continues his walk around. His jaw is tight, but his eyes are brighter than they were yesterday. The cupboards are all open and the shelves lined with trays that I labeled, and most of the piles of paperwork now have a home.

"Have you had a break?" he asks gruffly, walking toward his desk. He puts his case underneath and presses the button to turn his computer on before he drops down in his office chair.

"No, I haven't yet," I say directly to his face, but he doesn't bother to meet my gaze. My gaze travels over his outfit choice today, and I am unable to tear my eyes away. I notice it's another suit, but this time without the jacket and tie, and his shirt sleeves are pushed up to his elbows, showing off his toned, tanned forearms.

There is something about him. I can't help it; my heart beats faster. *What am I doing?*

I glance away before he notices me checking him out and I get back to filing the papers into their assigned trays. The space feels like it's ten times smaller whenever he is in the room with me. The sexual tension is evident. We work in comfortable silence, the typing of his keyboard, the clicking of his mouse, and the rustling of paper being the only sounds in the room. When I'm finished filing the last paper and softly close the cupboard, I turn around to face him.

"I'll have my break now. See you in half an hour."

He nods at me, but otherwise doesn't respond, just continues to type away on his computer. Retrieving my handbag from the floor, I amble out the door and head toward the break room. When I enter, I halt in the doorway and stare at the back of Rachel. *Great! Just who I need.*

She spins with a cup handle in one hand and bobbing a tea bag in and out with the other. Even when making tea, the woman is a knockout. *So unfair!*

When she spots me, she offers me a dazzling smile. "Hi there. Who are you?"

"Uh, hi. I'm Alice, a new nurse graduate."

"Oh, nice! Well, I'm Rachel. It's nice to meet you. I work on this ward full time." She tilts her head in the direction of the ward.

"Oh, that's great. I'll be there part time."

"Have you met Dr. Taylor yet? Some lucky nurse is getting to work up close and personal with him. I wonder when she will start. I'll be trying to steal her job." She laughs, but I know she isn't kidding. "Why did *she* get it anyway?" My eyes bulge and my mouth drops open at her brash comment and bitter tone.

"Yeah, no idea." My stomach drops at the lie, but I don't want to get into it with her when it's only my second day. I decide to ignore her and stroll over to the fridge to retrieve my lunch, sitting down in the same chair as yesterday and focusing on eating my sandwich. When I've finished my half-hour break, I drag myself slowly back to Dr. Taylor's office. As I open the door, I see him speaking on the phone in the middle of a conversation. I've got no idea to whom, but it sounds like he is being as abrupt to them as he's been with me. I can't wrap my head around his cold attitude, but what really baffles me is that for some reason Rachel wants to fight for this role. I can't understand why she would want to. *What am I missing?*

"I'm not interested in hearing what you have to say. Just stop calling. I'll see you Sunday," he barks, slamming down the phone, and I'm sure the ears of the person on the other end will be ringing afterward. He cradles his head in his hands and stares down at his desk. My heart cracks at the sight. He clearly hasn't noticed me come in.

I clear my throat. "Hi. I'm back."

He whips his head up and his gaze meets mine. The pure hatred in his expression makes me take a step back. Then the look settles a bit. When he glances back at his monitor, I realize it wasn't being directed at me. "Okay."

What the hell am I going to do? This is bullshit. I march over to the cupboard underneath one of the bookshelves, yanking it open. "I have organized the paperwork into categories. Each tray is labeled with what each one is... like here." I point at one of the trays I've labeled. "This contains patient notes..." Then I move my finger to the tray beside it. "Correspondence..." I move my finger again to the next tray. "Bills... I'm sure you get the point." I straighten up, wrapping my fingers around the door that's open for something to lean on. I don't glance in his direction, instead keeping my gaze focused on my handiwork.

I don't know if he was even watching as I was explaining or whether he kept his gaze fixed to his monitor, but then he speaks, letting me know he was listening. "Right."

My lips purse up into a thin line. It wouldn't hurt him to say a simple "thanks," but I guess I would be asking for a miracle. *Asshole.*

"What's the plan for this afternoon?" I ask through gritted teeth. Closing the door, I swivel around to face him. I'm still standing near the bookshelf, not really knowing if I should sit or stand. I cross my arms over my chest to keep from fidgeting.

He eyes me suspiciously. "I need to discuss basics with you, and I'm assuming you don't know anything about orthopedics?" His brow raises in question.

"I have studied procedures, but no, I haven't physically worked on this type of ward."

"Right, okay then," he mumbles, scanning around for something. "Come, sit." He demands, before returning his gaze to the computer. He gestures for me to sit down in front of him.

I can't be bothered arguing with him, so I walk over, pull the chair out, and sit down.

He finds a spare notepad and a pen, passing both to me, and then pushes his chair back and stands and strolls over to the bookshelf. I watch as he grabs one from the top shelf, allowing my eyes to roam over his body. His shirt is tucked into his suit pants, which I'm sure are expensive by the way they are tailored to show off his fit, muscular body. His pants are so tight around his ass, I shift in my seat to try and ease the sudden throb.

He pulls it down, and I spin around, quickly glancing away, hoping to not get caught checking him out. I bite my lip and he steps over to stand next to me and I freeze. As if sensing his body near mine, the throb turns into an ache and I shuffle again in my seat.

He places the book down next to me with a heavy thud. I lift my gaze up, meeting his, and I notice that his jaw is clenched, but he doesn't utter a word.

CHAPTER 7

MIKE

STATIC IS BOUNCING BETWEEN us, so I move back quickly to my office chair, putting some much-needed distance between us.

Looking around my office, I can see that it isn't going to be an easy ride. Alice has completely organized my mess. I can actually see my mahogany desk now that there are no papers scattered on it. After her break, she begins explaining her filing system to me, showing me how she has filed and labeled where everything is. All my paperwork is inside the cupboards and will be completely out of sight. I notice there are multiple new trays, which she must have purchased herself. How is she this organized for someone so young? Normally, women her age are more worried about their social media, clubbing, and getting drunk. Working and careers always seem to be the last thing on their minds... but clearly that's not the case for Alice. It's refreshing and a huge turn-on.

Her passion for being a nurse was evident from her application letter and test scores. However, when I agreed to offer this position to a graduate, I didn't expect to be attracted to the applicant.

She is keen to help and eager to learn, so I decide to help prepare her for surgery. I step over to the books I keep in my office for teaching. Feeling heat on my back, I can tell she is staring at me, and when I turn around from grabbing the book from the shelf, I catch her checking me out. My lip twitches. I don't want her to know she's been caught, so I say nothing, instead acting as if I didn't notice. My cock gets excited at the prospect of her liking what she saw. It may be fun to torture her for a few months; it may even make this nightmare more bearable to know she's suffering too. *Let's see how she does.*

She is in her uniform today, and not the sexy little clothes that show off her body, but the ill-fitting scrubs. I'm not complaining, though. I would struggle to concentrate on my job if her tight body was in my face every day. Most people wouldn't realize how sexy Alice really is unless they have seen her out of this navy uniform. Thinking of her has made my workouts at the gym intense, and I'm so wound up I feel like I want to snap all the time. Every time she is near me, I stiffen and am forced to put a mental wall up to hide my attraction to her. The more she is around me, though, the harder it is to hold up.

I need to focus on the work at hand, and today I'm tasked with giving her a glimpse into nursing from an orthopedic perspective. I found a new notebook and pen and grabbed my old Tabner's book. I'm sure she'll already have a copy, but I would like to expand on certain areas while she is here. Knowledge is power, and she'll need a recap on some basics before entering an operating room with me.

I stare at her intently, but she hardly glances my way, so I just get on with what I have to say. "I assume you have this book at home, probably the newer release?"

She nods. "Yes."

"Don't you mean, 'Yes, Doctor Taylor'?" My voice commands her attention.

She lifts her head immediately, her eyes widening with surprise, and I watch as she swallows before mimicking, "Yes, Doctor Taylor." *Better.*

"I will list a few surgeries I do in my position, and what I want you to study. After that we will run through them. I need your basic knowledge to be immaculate. I need to help you get up to speed, ready for surgery next week."

I scan her critically. I see no expression on her face. *Should I be concerned?* "Are you okay with that?" I ask, raising a brow.

Her gaze meets mine and the glow of appreciation in them makes me glance away to the computer, pretending to be distracted by something other than her.

"Yes, Doctor Taylor," she repeats in a low composed voice.

I watch her from the corner of my eye as she opens the notepad with a shaky hand and grabs the pen, ready to take notes.

"Obviously, the main surgeries I perform are arthroscopy, knee replacement, specifically ACL repair, as well as shoulder and hip repairs.

There are a few more, but I'd like you to focus on those first. I need you to study these in detail today, make notes, and write down any questions you have, and I will answer them next week when I see you. I have a patient booked for surgery next week, so you will be able to see one of these performed. It will help you understand what I do and will give you an idea what before and aftercare the nurses carry out. It should benefit you and your future patients. I have a good relationship with everyone on this floor because they understand exactly what I like and how I like things done."

A frown begins to form between her eyebrows, and her mouth tightens.

My jaw ticks and I thrust my hand through my hair. I shift, staring at her closely, trying to understand why she has reacted that way. I can't shake it off, so I ask her, "I assumed going into surgery would make you happy, not make you angry. Why are you angry?"

Her head snaps up to face me and she stares at me with wide eyes, her mouth falling open. My eyebrow lifts with interest, waiting for her to reply.

"No, it's an amazing opportunity, thank you. I'm not angry. I'm just..." She glances away.

"Just what?" I snap back. I'm so over the way she constantly talks in riddles, and I don't trust her responses. *Three months is going to seem like an awfully long time.*

Her gaze flies back to mine. "Nothing. I'm happy."

Her dull eyes tell a different story.

"I don't believe you, but I don't care enough to continue this conversation. I need to write some notes on here and see some patients, so you may as well study at home." I dismiss her and continue scanning through my notes on the monitor, not glancing in her direction again even though I sense her glare on my face.

"Why are you being like this? I know you know who I am. Why are you so rude to me? I just don't get it?" she huffs.

My jaw ticks. I knew this would come up at some point. The electricity in the room is messing with my head. I don't look away from my computer as I respond tiredly, "Yes, I'm aware. Just go home and study. I will see you next week."

She stands up, grabs her bag and the book, and walks out the door, closing it behind her. As soon as I hear the door click, a deep sigh leaves my chest and I sit back in my chair and close my eyes for a moment. *She can't know how fucking attracted to her I am or how much I want her.*

I finish my ward round and arrive in my office, then I shut down my computer before I leave the hospital to drive home. Just as I am pulling my briefcase out, my phone rings. I remove it from my pocket, dump the briefcase on the desk, and check the screen. It's Ryan.

"Hey, what's up?" I answer.

"Not much. Driving home from the office and just checking in. You still at work?"

"Yeah, still here, but I'm just about to head home and watch the game. You want to come over to watch it?"

"I'm going to my parents' for dinner, so I can't, but did you want to come to Luxe again this weekend?"

"I would because it's been a hell of a week, but I'm on call," I groan.

"No big deal. Is everything okay? Just work shit? Or are we talking about your dad or your ex Amanda?"

Laughing, I answer, "Nah, none of them this time. However, my old man keeps blowing up my phone on a regular basis."

"Hear him out. It's been years."

"Maybe." I give him the same answer I always do. I zone out and stare at where the young and beautiful Alice sat today. I take a deep breath, clearing my thoughts. "I've got to go, man. I'll give you a call soon. Enjoy Luxe."

"I will. Let me know if anything changes and you can come."

"Will do." I hang up, stuffing the phone in my suit pocket, then open my briefcase and toss my unfinished papers inside before closing it and walking out. I take the elevator down to the staff parking lot. I've just exited the elevator and started walking to my car when I spot Alice. She's sitting on the hood of her car, slumped over, talking on her phone. *Shit.* I wish I could pretend I hadn't seen her, but I can't, and after what she did with my office, I owe it to her to ask if she is okay.

I turn and march toward her, and when she hears my shoes thundering along the concrete approaching, she leans back and lifts her eyes from the phone in her hand. Her eyes bulge as I stand over her, one hand clenching the briefcase and the other on my hip.

I tilt my head. "Alice, are you okay? Shouldn't you be home already?"

She hangs up the phone, shoving it inside her pocket. Pushing off the hood, she spins on her heel to face me, adjusting the bag on her shoulder. She slowly shakes her head. "Yeah, I know. I went and studied for a bit in the cafeteria and then came down here, but Lady here decided she didn't want to start. So, here I am, waiting until one of my friends answers their damn phone, so I can ask if they'll come pick me up."

I smirk and raise my eyebrows. "Your car has a name?" Her cheeks flush and it reminds me of how she looked at the club, so pretty and youthful.

"Yes, I named her Lady, like ladybug-red car. Please tell me you get what I mean because I'm rambling now." Her eyes drop down toward the concrete and my stomach clenches.

"Let me take a quick look. Give me your keys." Her head whips up in my direction and her face is etched with a perplexed expression. I hold my palm out in front of me and repeat, louder, "Keys?"

She examines my palm then snaps out of her daze, sliding her handbag from her shoulder and fishing in the bag to find the keys. When she finally finds them, she pulls them out and places them in my waiting hand. I grip the cold metal, place my briefcase down on the concrete, and walk over to the door. I rip the heavy beat-up door wide open, and leaning over, I push the lever down that controls the chair so I can slide it as far back as it can go, making room for my long legs. I climb in her car, noticing that it's a very old Toyota Corolla. Putting the keys in the ignition, I turn the key to try to start it. It doesn't work so I repeat, but it still doesn't work. I pop the hood lever and exit the car.

I stalk over to the front of the car, and once I've located the latch, I click it and lift up the hood with my other hand. I hook up the stand to keep it open while I inspect the motor. I check the oil and water levels, which are both full, then inspect the engine itself, but I'm unable to pinpoint any obvious issues. She is standing off to the side, giving me space to inspect, and as I close the hood, I notice she is chewing her lip and shuffling her feet, but I shrug it off.

"Nothing is sticking out to me; your oil and water levels look good. It's going to need a mechanic to look over it. I will take you home. Get all your stuff and let's go."

She stiffens momentarily before answering, "No, it's fine. I'm sure one of my friends will call me back soon."

"And how long have you already been waiting?" Her cheeks turn crimson. "Don't bother answering. Come on, I'll take you home," I fire back.

"Are you sure?" she whispers.

"Please hurry up. I'd like to get home tonight too."

Without waiting to see if she's following, I swing around, pick up my case, and take off in the direction of my car.

I hear her hurried footsteps on the pavement behind me as she tries to catch up. I stiffen as soon as she is near me, but don't say a word. When we arrive at my car, I open her door and her brows crease, but she hops in. I close it gently behind her and walk around to the driver's side. Yanking it open, I throw my briefcase in the back and climb in. I watch as she examines the car. Her mouth opens wide as she reaches out and touches the dash with her hands.

"Wow," she whispers.

I chuckle at her reaction with a knowing grin. *I do love this car.*

"What type of car is this?" she asks, still checking it out. Her eyes fill with awe as I turn the car on.

"Aston Martin, but it doesn't have a name," I cheekily mock.

"Marty," she whispers under her breath; I manage to just catch it. She has gone back to stroking the dash and I turn away, laughing and shaking my head.

I point to the monitor that's set into the dash between us. "Marty needs your address, so type it in here, please." I hear her small gasp, and then watch as she proceeds to enter her details into the GPS. When it has mapped out the route, I reverse out of my spot and drive out of the parking lot onto the main road.

We drive in comfortable silence with only the radio playing tunes through the car speakers, and her phone rings, startling us. She arches her back, trying to dig inside her pocket to retrieve her phone. I watch her from the corner of my eye as heat floods through me. She manages to pull it free.

"Ah-ha!" She waves it in the air.

An easy smile plays at the corners of my mouth as she answers it. I move my heated gaze to the road.

"Hi. I was just ringing about Lady. She wouldn't start after work today, and I just wanted to see if you could pick me up from work, but I'm on my way home now... Yes, I'm fine... I will see you soon," she whispers and hangs up.

"One of your friends, I take it?" I blurt. I don't know why that just came out, but I want to know more about her.

"Yeah, it was one of my roommates." She shrugs.

"So, you don't live with your parents?" My nose wrinkles. I know I shouldn't pry, but I can't help it.

"No, I live with my two of my best friends," she answers matter-of-factly.

Nodding slowly, I process the information. She didn't say anything about having a boyfriend and didn't say she was waiting for him to call her back, so I assume that she must be single. I really don't know why the fuck I even care. She is far too young for me. I'm her supervisor, and she danced with my brother shortly after we shared an intense kiss. I don't speak another word during the remainder of the drive. I pull up outside her house, which is a nice, white, weathered, older-looking home. The manicured front garden is full of blooming roses and luscious green grass. I park at the end of the driveway, behind another car, which I assume belongs to the roommate who called earlier.

She turns to me in her seat, her hands twisting in front of her. "Thanks for the drive home. I really appreciate it. You didn't have to do this. I know you're busy."

I shake my head. "It's fine. I was heading home anyway, so it's not a big deal. Would you like me to arrange a tow truck?"

"Oh no, I'll figure it out. Thanks for the offer, though."

"Let me know if you change your mind. I'll see you next week," I add.

She nods and reaches for the handle, pushing the door wide open, and steps out, closing the door after her. I watch her trek up the path, and as she reaches the front porch, she pauses, spins around, and waves at me with a small smile curving her lips. My jaw clenches, and as I continue to watch her, she swivels back around and heads into her house.

When she is safely inside, I take off down the road, deciding to drive back to the hospital to finish the last bit of paperwork. It's not like anyone is waiting for me at home. I dial a tow truck service to tow Alice's car back to her house. Money pays when it comes to service, so Alice should have her car back at her house by the time I get home tonight. Then she can figure out what to do with it. Although, if you ask me, it deserves to go straight to the scrap yard, but I didn't get the feeling she was willing to part with it.

CHAPTER 8

ALICE

I STEP INSIDE AFTER waving like a dickhead. *Sometimes I could just kick myself.* I walk into the kitchen, dump my handbag on the countertop, and go to the fridge to grab the bottle of Moscato. Pouring myself a glass, I fill it all the way to the top, then take a large sip. *Ahh, so good.*

Standing here in the kitchen, my hand on the cold stone counter, my other hand clutching the wineglass, I stare out the window and my thoughts drift over the day I've spent with the insufferable Mike. I hear light footsteps hit the tiles and I glance over as Maddison joins me in the kitchen with a towel wrapped around her hair and wearing her sleepwear. She drags out a stool and plops down on it. Her eyebrows draw together as she inspects my beverage choice.

"Whoa, Alice. It's only a Monday." Her eyes are wide as she looks me over.

"I had the worst day today. My head is all over the place, and I'm officially fucked." I sigh, enjoying another sip of the sweet wine.

"It can't be that bad. What happened?"

"The doctor I am working with is still being a moody asshole. It's like he barely wants me around, and ugh, I really don't know what to do. He hardly talks to me, but then when I tried to call you for a lift—"

She cuts me off. "I'm so sorry about that. I was stuck at school."

I shake my head. "Don't be sorry. It's fine, really. Here is the weird part. So, I'm waiting on top of Lady when *he* comes walking over to *help* me." My chest burns at the memory.

"No way. And then what?"

I lift my glass of wine and take another sip before I continue. "Well, I don't know if he knows much about cars, but he tried to see if he could start her. She wouldn't start for him, obviously, but then he popped the hood, and I nearly had a fit. He is leaning over in his suit pants and shirt, looking at my oil and water levels, or at least that's what he said he checked. He is so hot, Maddy, like his body is crazy fit. He must work out—a lot."

"Oh, that's so fucking hot." She starts fanning herself with her hand, and I chuckle.

"You have no idea. That image is seared into my brain forever. And that's not the only thing. Then he insisted on dropping me home. He drives this sexy gray sports car—I can't remember what model—but I named it Marty." I rub my brow, trying to think of the model, my mind coming up blank.

Her mouth drops open, and she shakes her head in denial. "No! You didn't name his car?"

My brows pinch together. "Err, why? Is that bad?"

She nods her head. "Oh, God, you make me laugh."

"I'm guessing I should be embarrassed based on your reaction, but he really didn't seem to mind. Anyway, back to my story. So, when he dropped me home, he asked if I wanted him to arrange towing Lady. I said no, of course. How embarrassing would it be to have him paying for that? He's my boss. I would never ask him that. Could you imagine? I plan to ask T when she gets home from work. When did she say she would be home?"

Glancing down at her wristwatch, she mumbles, "She should be here any minute."

"Oh, okay. I will start dinner then." I push off the counter, lift my drink, and down the rest of the wine. I don't usually drink during the week, but I just felt like one tonight. Moving to the sink, I lower the empty glass before roaming over to the fridge and scanning it for ingredients. I spot hamburger and decide to make tacos.

Tahlia arrives a little while later as I'm about to serve dinner. "Hey, girls. What a day." She blows out an audible breath.

Both Maddison and I laugh at her passing comment before I ask her, "What happened?"

She sighs, standing near the table. "It was just so busy. I barely managed to squeeze in a break."

Tahlia still works in the coffee shop, much to her parents' disgust. She is still trying to figure out what she wants to study, and the shop gives her the money she needs to not depend on her parents.

"Oh, one of those shit shifts. At least the time passes quickly. Well, dinner is almost ready. Did you want to have a quick shower and I'll dish it up?"

She lets out an appreciative moan. "That would be amazing. I won't be long." She saunters off in the direction of her room.

A little while later, she joins us at the table. Maddy and I have already begun to eat. I peer over at Tahlia, who starts to prepare her own taco. I clear the lump that's formed in my throat.

"T, would you mind if I borrowed some money until I get my first paycheck?"

Her gaze flicks to mine. "Of course not. What do you need it for, and how much?"

I glance over to Maddison, who is grinning like a Cheshire cat, and I roll my eyes before moving my gaze back to Tahlia. "Well, let's say I had a very interesting day with—"

"Doctor Dreamy!" Maddy yells out, cutting me off.

My eyes widen in horror, and I glare at Maddison. "Don't call him that!"

"Did you not describe him as hot to me earlier?" She smirks. *Bitch got me there!*

"Hey, is someone going to fill me in here?" Tahlia questions.

I laugh, shaking my head. I reach out to take a sip of water, needing something to soothe my dry throat. "I'm trying. It's Maddy's fault."

Maddison scoffs in the background, but I ignore her and keep my gaze on Tahlia. "So, the doctor was being his moody-ass self at work today, and at the end of the day, when it was time to drive home, Lady wouldn't start. So, I was sitting on the hood of the car, messing about on my phone, when he must have spotted me. He came over to check why I was still there and not at home already. I explained my car wouldn't start. So, he insisted on looking at the engine, oil, and water, but couldn't work it out, so he offered to take me home and wouldn't take no for an answer."

"And she named his car," Maddy adds.

I shoot her a hard glare. *Shut the fuck up!*

Her face splits into a knowing grin before I look back at Tahlia, who has an arched eyebrow in surprise.

"Hey! What is so wrong with that? He didn't laugh at me," I protest.

"I'm sure he did, just not out loud or openly like we are." She smirks.

I groan and slide down in my chair. "I need the money for a tow truck. I need to arrange one tomorrow."

A flash of humor crosses her face.

"What?" I ask.

"Lady is out front." She rolls her lips, suppressing a smile.

"What are you talking about?" I furrow my brows and peek over at Maddy. I don't understand, so I slide my chair back and march over to the front door, reaching the metal handle and yanking the wooden door wide open. My eyes blink rapidly. Sure enough, Lady is sitting outside of our house. *What. The. Fuck!*

"I told you," I hear her say from behind me.

I can't respond to Tahlia. My body is frozen in place, my hand still gripping the metal handle, my mouth hanging open.

"Now what will you do?" Maddy asks.

"I don't know," I whisper.

I hear the light patter of footsteps fading away. I'm alone at the door when a cool breeze hits my skin, causing goosebumps to rise on my body. It wakes me from my trance. I close the door, cross my arms over my chest, and wander back to the kitchen. My mind is racing. I don't understand what this means or what I should do.

The girls are packing the dishes away as I re-enter the kitchen. Uncrossing my arms, I slump over the counter and drop my head into my hands, massaging my temples.

"T, I definitely need the money now. I just need to figure out how much it cost to have her towed. I can't believe he did that." I groan.

"Yeah, of course. I think it's thoughtful. What a great boss," Tahlia coos.

My forearms slap down on the counter as I drop my hands to flick my tired gaze to her. "Oh, you don't know the whole story. He keeps fucking with my head. One minute I'm to call him Doctor Taylor, next he helps tow my car. I can't keep up. But this conversation is bringing on a headache. Can we go chill out and watch some Netflix?"

I ask as I press my hands onto the counter to straighten up and begin to wander over to the living room. Curling up in one of the chairs, I'm more than ready to relax for the evening.

I managed to drift off to sleep last night easier than I thought I would. I dreamed of Mike—well, more about Mike's hands on my body and his smart mouth consuming mine. Maddison offered me a lift into work today, and as we sit in silence for the drive, I stare out the window in a daze. My mind is on the ward and how I'll manage working there with the constant need between my legs that doesn't seem to want to let up, reminding me constantly of Mike's attractiveness.

I sink my teeth into my bottom lip as the hospital comes into view. Maddison pulls over into the loading zone so I can climb out. I hesitate for a second before I shove open the car door, and as I'm about to shut it, she barks, "Wait."

Reaching out with my hand, I stop the door from closing and peer down into the car. "Yeah?"

"I didn't say good luck on your first day on the ward. Knock 'em dead." She beams.

I chuckle. "Maybe not the greatest term to use near a hospital, Mads, but I get you. Thanks." I lean back and thrust the door the rest of the way shut with a bang. I roll my shoulders back, draw in a breath, and take off inside.

I arrive on the ward and store my bag in my assigned locker and arrive for morning handover. I'm assigned to follow a fellow nurse named Sarah.

Unlike Rachel, Sarah is very similar to me, wearing only minimal makeup, her hair tied up in a high ponytail, and wearing navy-blue scrubs. I watch Sarah work, from the beginning of the shift, when she's writing up her day plan, to her finishing the day handing over to the next member of staff. I'll be following nurses for the first two weeks before I'm on my own.

I'm standing next to Sarah at the nurses' station while she is completing some patient notes before filing them away.

Closing the folder, she spins to face me. "You ready to eat lunch now?"

I nod. "I'm starving."

She giggles. "Me too. It's all the walking we do."

We move away from the desk and walk toward the break room. We don't get far when Sarah gets stuck chatting with another nurse, so I walk ahead. When I spot a male doctor in scrubs leaning over a patient's bed talking, I pause outside the doorway to watch. The patient is an elderly woman with wild gray hair. Her face is flushed, and she is grinning widely at him in awe. I can see him shaking his head and his shoulders bouncing from a laugh. A warm tingle runs up my spine as I watch their exchange. I sigh, wishing Mike was as warm as this guy. Unable to see his face, I step forward and lean my shoulder against the frame to get a better view. It's nice to see a doctor who cares, but when the doctor rotates and gapes directly at me, I gasp in recognition. *Oh my, it's the god himself—Mike. Fuck.*

I thrust myself off the frame, suddenly feeling hot and flustered. I step back, bumping into Sarah, whom I didn't hear approach. Sarah's cheeks turn red.

"Sorry," I mumble, trying to focus anywhere but him, wishing my body would calm down. My heart is beating erratically in my chest, and I get a buzzing sensation before I hear the heavy footsteps of *him* approaching. I jerk my chin up, my gaze landing on his brilliant blues as he comes to stand right in front of us.

"Hi, Doctor Taylor, how are you?" Sarah speaks with a slight hitch in her voice.

His gaze briefly lands on hers as he answers, "I'm wonderful. Thanks for asking." His voice is seductive, and for once, his mouth is turned upward and his cold demeanor is nowhere in sight. I cross my arms tightly over my chest.

His gaze flicks back to mine. "Good morning, Alice."

I meet his stare, frowning at how brightly his eyes are shining. "Err, hi, Doctor Taylor."

Sarah looks between Mike and I, arching a brow, but not saying a word.

"Are you caring for Mary in room five?" He inclines his head to the room we are outside of.

"Yes, we are, Doctor. Did you want something for Mary?" Sarah is beaming, eagerly waiting for his reply.

He gives her a curt nod. "I just wrote up her discharge papers, her prescription, and explained them all to her. I'll be calling her daughter to give her an update, but it looks like she can go home. If you don't mind, could you please organize her medications from the pharmacy and file the release paperwork? I'll be in my office if you need me." He steps toward me and thrusts me the file.

As I reach out to take the file, our hands touch, sending a violent rush of heat between my thighs and a warm flush to my cheeks. I clutch the file tight, slamming it into my chest. As I watch him pivot and walk in the direction of his office, I have to restrain myself to keep from following him in there and demanding to find out. Shaking my head in dismay, I scold myself for my reaction toward him. I need to be acting professional, not like a schoolgirl with a crush.

Sarah and I begin speaking at the exact same time. "Go for it," I say, smiling at Sarah. I don't want to ask first, in case she didn't notice anything. But of course, I'm not that lucky.

"You two seem familiar with each other. I can tell that he already knows you because he knew your name." She moseys slowly over to Mary's room so we can have a quick chat before getting there.

A flush creeps across my cheeks. "I'm the selected graduate student this year chosen to work closely with him. This is the first time they have offered this, but I spend half the week with him and the other half here on the ward."

Tugging my arm gently, she stops me before we get too close to Mary. "No way. I'm so jealous."

"Yes, way." I laugh and continue, shrugging it off. "I applied while at college last year, and between the letter and test scores, I got it."

"That's amazing! He is the best surgeon, very intelligent, and you will learn so much. Plus, he is great eye candy." She wiggles her brows suggestively.

I chuckle. "I hope so. Is he... umm... is he that nice to everyone?"

"Oh, yeah. He is well respected around here. The patients love him, and the staff idolizes him. Just watch out for a few of the gold diggers. They've been throwing themselves at him since he became single a little over a year ago." My eyebrows shoot up in surprise as she tips her head toward me and begins whispering into my ear. "Rachel, for example, wants to bag a doctor so she can keep up her expensive lifestyle. It's so blatantly obvious, and most of them won't go near her because she reeks of desperation."

My mouth hangs open at her confession. "Ohhh, okay. Yeah, I can see what you mean. I haven't had much to do with her, but I have overheard her conversations, and I did get that vibe from her."

"Well, we better get Mary sorted so she can go home." She starts to wander off and I follow behind.

I want to go and talk to Mike about my car, but I'll be taking my lunch break next, so I'll do it after work.

After Mary leaves an hour later, we have only three patients left, so I take the opportunity to study from Mike's list and book. I haven't seen Mike on the ward again, which disappoints me as I enjoy catching glimpses of him without him realizing. Now that my shift is over, I walk up to his office with my stomach in knots, my heart rate up and my palms sweating.

I stand at his door, shuffling my feet, delaying knocking because I don't know which version of Mike I will get, but I need to pay him back. I pray for the warm Mike I witnessed earlier on the ward today. I suck in a breath and knock hard, mentally preparing myself with a pep talk. *You've got this. Just go in and do what you need to do.*

"Come in!" I hear him call out.

I gently push open the door and see him sitting at his desk, writing on papers that are once again sprawled out over his desk. When he peers up and sees me, he smirks, leaning back in his chair. *Beautiful bastard.*

The air in the room feels as though it's been sucked out and replaced with fireworks and steam, and I don't know if I want to slap him or fuck him more in this moment. I step in and close the door, and as I make my way toward his desk, he watches my every move. His eyes seem darker and his eyelids heavy, sending a shiver running down my spine from his intense scrutiny.

He pops a brow. "And to what do I owe this pleasure?" His tone holds a note of mockery.

"You arranged the towing of my car, didn't you?" I ask, my body vibrating with tension.

"Maybe." His smirk turns to a grin that reaches his eyes and shows off his stunning white teeth.

He moves one of his hands from the arm of the chair to under his chin and stares directly at me for a change. *He is actually really looking at me.* I feel my sex throb, so I switch feet, trying to discreetly rub it out. It doesn't work, which only annoys me more. *Fuck!*

"Please, Doctor Taylor. I know you did and thank you for the lift and the tow, but... It's too much and I need to pay you back. Could you tell me how much it was so I can give you the money for it?" I plead.

"No." His eyes don't move from mine, and he doesn't say anything else.

I take a deep breath and try again. "Please, tell me how much."

He shakes his head. "You brought the trays, planner, and the files." His hand thrusts in the direction of the newly organized system.

"Yeah, but... it's not the same," I huff.

"It's fine, I can afford it."

Excuse me? "And so can I!" I snap, raising my voice in frustration from the combination of the aching between my legs and the annoyance at him not telling me. I don't want to feel like a charity case. I try to keep my personal issues to myself and work hard.

"Alice, I know you can. But I have more than enough—"

"Knock, knock," I hear a woman say as she walks in, so I turn to put a face to the voice, and I recognize her straightaway at just one glance. *The woman from the club.*

"Amanda, I'm busy, so you need to leave!" he shouts, pointing to the hall and glaring at her with curled lips and a crease in his brows.

I didn't realize she would be older than me. She's a lot closer to his age of late thirties than I am. Sucker punch to the stomach, I'm just the young dumb student. I'm mortified that I was so close to jumping him, and now? Now, I just want to get away from here, to put some distance between us, give myself some time to think and sort out my head and heart. There's a mindfuck of emotions running through my body. All the sexual tension evaporates, and I'm left empty and heavyhearted.

"No, it's fine, I'm leaving." I storm out of the room.

"Alice, wait!" he shouts urgently, and I hear the thud of his chair hitting the wall as he stands.

Without looking back, I leave through the open door, slamming it shut behind me. Leaning back on it, I close my eyes, taking some much-needed deep breaths to slow down my speeding heart. *Him and all these girls. Paying for my tow, what is he into?* Thank God, I don't have to see him for a whole week.

CHAPTER 9

ALICE

I LEFT HIS OFFICE shaking and emotionally spent, wanting to get home as soon as possible. These mixed signals of his are giving me whiplash. The worst part is I want him; my body and mind crave him like a drug, but there are so many reasons why it can't work. Plus, I don't even know if he genuinely wants me, or if he is playing with me like every other nurse that he fucked around here.

Clearly, he doesn't take me seriously because he keeps treating me with disrespect and insisting on not telling me how much the tow service is. *I'm not a charity case for fuck's sake.*

I'm frustrated by his kindness. It feels like I'm struggling to breathe; it's too much—besides, he hardly knows me. The only people who know about my financial struggles are Tahlia, Blake, and Maddison. I don't need the world knowing how my family has struggled paying the bills since my dad passed away. I'm still visibly shaking from being so wound up, but thankfully I have two days off away from the hospital. I have homework to do, which is handy because I will have something *other* than Mike to stimulate and occupy my brain with.

I call Blake who is waiting to pick me up after my shift. "Hey, I'm ready. I'm just coming down now," I huff. I move quickly in case Mike decides to follow me... or am I just hoping he does? I know he won't, but I can't seem to convince my heart of that.

"Yeah, perfect. I'm just down in the loading zone," he answers.

I hang up the phone and ride the elevator. When the doors open, I rush out of the hospital. I spot Blake's car and walk up, tugging the car door open when I reach it. Climbing inside his car, I sink into the seat as Blake pulls out into the traffic and drives off in the direction of my house before I've had the chance to buckle up.

"What a day. Seriously, Blake, I have the worst headache starting and I hope it doesn't turn into a migraine. I cannot wait to get home, order some takeout, and chill out on the couch," I groan, closing my eyes and lying back onto the headrest.

"Sounds perfect, hon. Did you have a bad day with sex-on-legs?" My eyes pop open, and I tilt my head as he turns to face me, a wicked grin on his lips.

I choke out a laugh at his nickname for Mike. "Ha! Nice, but seriously. I went to chat with him in his office about paying him back for the tow, but he insists on not telling me how much it is, saying he has enough money to pay for it. Like, ugh, he fucking annoys me. I hate when people insinuate that I'm poor. It pisses me off. He doesn't know me."

He shrugs. "Yeah, but who cares. If he has the money and he is happy to pay for it, then I say, fuck it. Let him pay." His tone is nonchalant.

I sit forward, rotating to face him. "No, Blake. I just don't want to owe him anything. I want to be treated like we are on a level playing field. Could you imagine the rumors?"

"Yeah, I get you. And it's hard if he is a known player at the hospital. Do you think he is trying to say that he's sorry for being a dick?"

"Hmm, I doubt it. But as I'm talking to him, this woman walked in, and I recognized her straightaway. It was the woman from the nightclub."

His eyebrows shoot up in surprise. "I don't remember there being a woman."

"So, after using the bathroom at Luxe, I came out. Don't you remember, he had a brunette draped over his arm?"

He shakes his head. "No, sorry, I don't, but continue on."

I take a deep breath. "Well, in the middle of me arguing about him telling me how much I owe him, she walks in."

"Oh, shit." He sucks in and whistles.

My shoulders drop. "Yeah, he was shouting at her, trying to kick her out. Her name is Amanda."

"Ahh, so you think that she's a woman he is seeing?"

"No idea. He is a man-whore, so I'm sure she may be one of many. All of his female colleagues at work gush about him nonstop. They think he is smart, rich, and gorgeous." I roll my eyes.

"Well, hon, he is all that, but in your own words, he is a massive player. Clearly you don't want a fling. That's what you're saying."

"I don't want him at all. I think I'm just really sexually attracted to him, like I want to fuck him. He *is* hot, I can't deny that. But I work with him, and he doesn't really give me any vibes he is keen on me."

"I wish I had this problem on my ward. Seriously, all the hot doctors are straight. I just wish one was interested. I would be in heaven having these issues." He sighs.

We turn off the main road and start approaching my street. "You could have anyone you want. Your looks and personality are killer, Blake. I really wish I were you right now. I don't need this drama. I want a quiet life."

"Aww, honey, I love you. You're a beautiful person. Don't let those other girls make you forget that." I know Blake genuinely means that and I feel so lucky to have my friend's support.

"Thanks, Blake." I sit quietly for the last few minutes of the drive, deep in thought. I have two days off before I have to see Mike again. I have *got* to calm down and figure this out—and also study my ass off so I am ready for next week. *Bring it on.*

CHAPTER 10

MIKE

IT'S A MONDAY MORNING and I'm sitting in my office organizing the day ahead. I'm working with Alice, so I have decided to prepare all the patient notes prior to her arrival. I have just finished answering the few emails that arrived overnight—being on call all weekend enabled me to keep up to date with them.

My stomach has been in knots since Friday afternoon after the way Amanda barged in last week, right in the middle of Alice getting upset over the tow service money. I can tell there was more irritability from her than that. I just didn't get the time to figure out exactly what. It seems I really offended her, which was never my intent. I really can afford it, and I want to help her, like she helped me here in this office. I get a nagging suspicion that she needs it, but doesn't want to feel like I'm buying her, or that she didn't earn it.

Amanda can't seem to get the message that I don't want anything to do with her. She barges into my life when it suits her, disregarding all my feelings. It pisses me off, and it doesn't seem to matter how long it has been. She still insists on trying to talk to me. *Like I will ever forgive her and magically want her back after what she did to me.*

I'm not mentally or physically attracted to her anymore, and I wish she would understand that. No apology can make me forget the past. My feelings toward her will not change, and the way I feel toward Alice, with how strong the pull and desire for her when she is around, I know that Amanda did me a favor.

I click send with the mouse for the final email and am just twisting to file the paperwork in a neat pile when I hear tapping on my office door.

I bite my lips together to suppress a smile and answer, "Come in."
Even though I know it has to be Alice, I inhale deeply as I peer up from
my papers at her as she gently pushes the door open. Our gazes lock.
"Good morning."

"Good morning, Doctor Taylor," she mumbles softly, barely louder than a whisper, clicking the door closed behind her.

My body instantly warms at her voice and her calling me "Doctor
Taylor" stirs something inside of me. It makes me hard, and I'm glad
for now that I'm sitting behind my desk so she can't see what she does
to me. I run my fingers through my hair, and I try to keep my cold
attitude down and replace it with a professional one. She begins to
walk toward my desk, her eyes staring with purpose.

I stare back. "Did you want to join me for a coffee? I thought we
could discuss the morning's surgery."

"Sure." She sounds a little hesitant, but still agrees.

Knowing how important work is to her, I guessed correctly that she
would find it hard to turn down my offer. I think the fact that I'm
only going to discuss work with her, not the topic of her car again,
only helped her decision. I need her to be warm and calm around me.
I need to be my softer, gentle self to get her to open up to me more.

"Okay, then, let's go." I step around the desk and reach for the
door, holding it open for her to pass me, and when she does, her rich
vanilla scent wafts through my nostrils causing them to flare. I swallow
hard, closing the door, and walk with her to the elevator. While we
wait for it to arrive, I decide to probe her with questions to break the
awkwardness that is swirling around us.

"How was your weekend, Alice?" I ask.

I hear her audible intake of breath. "Pretty quiet really. I just studied
and hung out with friends. What about you?"

My brows crease at her answer. "Studied?" I question.

"Just the topics you gave me." She is looking down at her joined
hands, and I see her cheeks turn slightly pink.

She is so serious for someone so young, and her maturity is very
alluring. "Wow, if we had more dedicated nurses like you, the hospital
would run so much smoother."

Her cheeks deepen in color as she shyly peeks up at me from under
her dark lashes. "Thanks... I guess."

"Considering that you spent the weekend studying, I should quiz you. Let's see if all your studying paid off." I wink at her, trying to be playful in an attempt to get Alice to relax around me.

"Okay," she replies, unimpressed by my teasing.

We arrive at the cafeteria and line up to order our coffees from the barista. I order a long black for myself while Alice orders herself a latte. I hand over my card to pay, and get no resistance from Alice, and I raise my eyebrows when she doesn't complain about it.

"I'm shocked."

"Why, what happened?" She looks around to see if something has happened.

I chuckle out loud. "No, nothing has happened. You just didn't fight me about paying." I smirk at her. I have to resist the urge to touch her, even though I really want to hold her against me. While we wait for our drinks, she shuffles from side to side.

"You're weird, and I'm not keen on having another disagreement with you. Start quizzing, mister."

I find myself smiling broadly at her cheeky attitude.

Her cheeks glow, and a small smirk forms on her lips. I enjoy the more relaxed side to this work relationship she seems to be bringing out of me. Hopefully, it will be a good few days, with no further arguments.

I use my index finger to point to my temple, and I ask, "Hmm, where should I start? Do you want it easy or hard?"

She clears her throat, and the blush is returning to her cheeks. Realizing what I said and why she is blushing, I smile back at her with a knowing look. *Such a dirty mind.*

"Start with hard," she says with no hesitation, and I instantly harden.

To drive this direction to where it's going, I reply, "Just how I like it." My eyes bore into hers and I watch her swallow as she processes my words.

She doesn't say anything back, though, just watches and waits for the question. Our order is called, and she dives for it, breaking our intense eye contact, which makes me laugh.

I quickly and subtly rearrange myself in my pants, so she doesn't notice. I don't need to scare her away just yet. We are only just warming up.

She hands over my coffee without looking at me, and our fingers brush. The spark of electricity hits me hard and my dick strains in my pants further, almost to the point of pain. She bites her lip, clearly nervous, so I continue in my attempt to get her to relax and feel more at ease with me as we walk back to the elevator, by redirecting the questions back to her comfort zone.

"You've studied ACL surgery. Can you tell me who I'm most likely to perform this surgery on?" I question.

"I wouldn't say that's hard, but to answer your question: women over forty and people who play sports."

I nod. "Correct. And what does the general recovery look like?" I ask.

"Patients should be able to walk unassisted between two to four weeks, and after ten to twelve weeks, they can return to brisk walking or light jogging, but the full recovery takes approximately six to twelve months with the help of physiotherapy."

I sip my coffee, listening to her and nodding in approval. I could listen to her all day. She spent her weekend studying and not partying—what young woman does that? I'm in awe of her.

"Seriously, Alice, you have shocked me with your dedication. Thank you for caring enough to learn what I set out for you. I hope you're aware it's all for your benefit and I'm glad you're doing it. Your hard work and diligence will pay off."

Her eyes flick to mine and they are filled with an inner glow. "Thank you. I'm actually enjoying it, I never thought orthopedics would pique my interest, but it has."

A jolt is felt in my chest at hearing those words. "I'm glad to hear that. Well, we need to drink these, and then I have paperwork on my desk we need to read through, and then it's surgery time."

"Sounds great. I'm looking forward to witnessing a surgery. I have never seen one before," she gushes, offering me a shy smile.

"Well, I look forward to breaking you in." There is heat behind my words. All this talk is like foreplay in my brain. I'm going to have to straighten myself out before surgery so I can fully concentrate on the patient.

There her cheeks go again, pink rising to the surface.

Back at the office, we read through the papers concerning the patient. I answer any questions I can for Alice before we must leave to arrive in the operating room at the scheduled time.

In the operating room, I show Alice around before I leave her with Sarah to introduce herself to the patient, get into operating room scrubs, and meet me inside the operating suite. She won't be scrubbed in as she will only be observing today, but she will get a good view of what I am doing. I plan to teach her step by step of how things are done in my world.

I approach the sinks after getting into scrubs, and I begin the handwashing process. My usual flutters appear in my stomach and my heartbeat accelerates from the adrenaline that will not ease until after the completion of the surgery.

I have Doctor Paul Jenkins assisting me in the operating room today. He's five years older than me, making him forty-three, but he's still a great surgeon—although I'm more skilled in this area, despite being younger.

I exit the washroom, keeping my hands up and using my back to push open the door to protect my sterile hands. When I enter my OR, I pivot, scanning the room until my gaze lands on Alice. My lips turn up in acknowledgment before stepping slowly up to my sterile field. Paul is scrubbing up and will be inside the OR at any moment to join me, so I slowly begin the double-glove process.

When I'm ready, I peer across the room at Alice. I can see her wide grin and her eyes shining brightly with interest. I can already feel the air getting thicker and my desire returning.

Paul enters the operating room, the squeaking of the door breaking the silence of the room. I introduce Paul and Alice, and I notice how Paul takes her in, his eyes lighting up with interest as he studies her. I shake off the feelings the sight raises and refocus my concentration on the patient who needs my help.

As I perform the surgery, I talk Alice through the process of repairing the ACL. The patient is a forty-seven-year-old woman who played long-term netball, which has resulted in this injury. During the operation, Paul is talking and flirting constantly with Alice, and I wish he would stop. My annoyance is creeping back up the longer he continues. *She is mine, so he better fucking stop.* I feel my body growing more and more tense, and I need to relax in order to finish this surgery successfully. I can't afford for my hands to be tight.

I can feel the sweat dripping down my back from trying to hold inside all the anger I'm feeling toward Paul. *I need to concentrate.* When I glance up, she is watching me intently with her wide, bright eyes, and I notice she is looking only at me and not at Paul. I feel my shoulders relaxing, and with a slight perk of my lip, I finish the rest of the surgery with ease.

The patient heads to recovery, and I wash up with Paul. Paul finishes first and when I turn around, he is flirting with Alice again.

My body starts burning with rage and I can't stop myself from snapping. "Alice, what are you doing? We need to go and check on our patient," I huff.

I storm off without turning around to check if Alice has followed. I run my hand through my hair and smile when I hear the steady pattering of her light footsteps behind me. *Take that, Paul.*

CHAPTER 11

ALICE

I FOLLOW MIKE DOWN the hall, watching his tense body radiating with rage. His hands are balled into fists down beside him. I don't know what his issues are, but if I had to guess... I would say he is jealous. Which makes me smile.

When I catch up to him, I'm breathless and my lungs are burning. I tug on his arm, and he spins. His cold stare is back.

"Not now," he spits through clenched teeth.

"Yes. Now!"

"No, we need to work," he argues, walking off to the recovery room.

I watch his broad back leave before I follow. Walking into the room, I watch as he approaches the patient's husband. He offers his hand, and the husband slips his hand in his and shakes it. After the handshake, Mike guides him to take a seat, and he drags a chair to sit in front of him. I quietly tiptoe toward them and stand behind Mike, my mouth hanging open as I watch him speak.

"Your wife's operation was successful. She is very healthy. She should have a quick recovery. I will check on her tomorrow before she can go home. Do you have any questions?" He is so humble and caring.

"No questions, but thank you for taking care of my wife, Doctor Taylor." His eyes are bright with relief and awe.

Mike pushes off the chair to stand, offering a warm smile back. "I'll see you tomorrow." He nods and strolls out of recovery, and I trail behind.

"Get changed and meet me back in the office," he orders. Without waiting for a response, he takes off into the male changing rooms.

I change back into my uniform and walk inside his office. I step slowly up to the desk and drop down into the chair opposite him. He is slumped over, writing, and I note that the earlier tension has gone from his posture.

When he finishes writing, he glances up and pops a brow. "Did you want to have a go at the ward notes?" he asks nonchalantly.

I nod. "Yes, please."

He scoops two pages and hands them over the desk. I take them and scan through the details as he talks.

"Just write what you can next to each heading. Any you don't understand leave blank, and I'll run through them with you at the end."

"Okay."

I take a pen off the desk and begin filling in notes as he completes the medical bill claims. When I finish, I sit back and admiring how I left no blank spaces, pleased with how I managed it all on my own.

I glance up and Mike is staring at me, the beginning of a smile tipped at the corners of his mouth. His hand is stretched out to take my papers. I hand them over and watch as his smile widens with approval.

He nods. "Well done. Let's take the notes to the ward. The patient should be back there now. And afterward we need to do a ward round. I'll get you to write the notes into each of their files as I talk to the patients."

"Yep. Got it."

We walk out of the office and when we arrive at the ward, I follow behind Mike as he places the notes in the recent patient's folder and wanders off to visit his other patients. Visiting all his patients takes us an hour, but I managed to write in each of their files while he talked to the patients. It's an easy and enjoyable task. We seem to have a good system going.

Back in the office, I reach for my bag when Mike speaks. "So, how are you getting home today?"

I freeze and glance up. "My friend Blake is picking me up."

I watch his body stiffen and his lips press into a thin line. I can't help but laugh at the way he is looking at me with hurt and confusion before I quickly reassure him. "Blake is gay."

I watch as his shoulders sag, and he relaxes, all the tension leaving his solid body. I grin. *Maybe my feelings aren't one-sided.* His jealousy today is next level, and I secretly love every minute of his protectiveness.

Throwing my bag onto my shoulder, I yawn and roll my neck as we wander out of the office and walk silently to the elevator.

To fill the quiet, I ask, "What are your plans tonight?"

His walk falters, and it seems I've caught him off guard. "Huh? I'm just... ugh... heading home to watch football. Nothing exciting, really. What about you?"

I shuffle my feet from side to side while we wait for the elevator to reach our floor. I hold my handbag with both hands at the strap on my shoulder, feeling the fabric rub against my skin. "Probably just watch Netflix with my roommates. Nothing exciting either, to be honest."

The doors slide open, and it's empty. He waits, letting me step in first. I gaze down at the elevator floor when Mike reaches over in front of me to press the button for the ground floor. I completely forgot to press it. Standing inside the elevator with just him is intense. The air is crackling between us, warmth is building, and my stomach is on fire with the desire swirling around inside me.

I hear the words "Fuck it" leave his lips, and I lift my head just in time to catch the onslaught of Mike as he grabs my head with both of his hands, kissing me with enough passion to make me dizzy.

His kiss is so hungry, like he has been starved for days. I lose all sense of control and I can't stop him. My will just caves in, and I simply enjoy the moment, meeting his kiss with my own furious passion for him. His powerful, toned body presses against me as he walks me backward until my back hits the wall. This is enough to shake some sense into me.

"Mike, what are you doing?"

I shove at his chest with both hands, and he stumbles back until he grips the rail to steady himself. We are both panting heavily, trying to catch our breath after our shared moment of weakness. Mike's captivating gaze is sparkling blue under his heavily hooded lids.

My mouth opens and closes, but just then the elevator doors open, breaking the moment, and for a brief second, neither of us moves. Mike steps over to me, staring at me seductively, and I watch as he peels my hand off my swollen lip and lays his large hand on top of mine and links our fingers together. My heart flips in response, but before I can stop him, he stalks out of the elevator onto the ground floor, dragging me along behind him.

"Mike. No!" I have to fight my overwhelming urge to be close to him. I scan around, looking for any familiar faces, and not seeing any, I sigh in relief before my gaze lands back on him.

I tug my hand from his, unlinking our fingers. My hand feels cold and empty, so I cross my arms over my chest to prevent me from snatching his hand back. His eyebrows raise and his mouth forms an *O* at my move.

After clearing my throat, I speak up. "We can't do this here. I can't. I'm sorry."

Tears well within my eyes, and swallowing hard, I smother a sob and flee. Once I'm outside, I peer around for Blake's car. Eventually I spot it, and I move on shaky legs as I dive for the door, tearing the handle open with force and flopping into the seat before opening the dam to the flood of tears. The deep sobs violently rack my body, and the hot tears slip down my cheeks. The last week's emotions pour out of me, and when my sobs ease and I resettle, I look up to see Blake stroking my hair as he peers at me with a quiet concern.

"What happened, hon? Am I going to have to fuck up that pretty fucker's face?"

I snort, trying to laugh during a sob, so I shake my head vigorously. My voice breaks as I say, "No, please don't."

"Let's get you home so you can tell us what happened and what has got you in this state." His tone is cool and authoritative.

Inclining my head in a small gesture of thanks, I close my eyes, settling into the seat for the drive home.

I walk inside the house, heading straight to the pantry and tearing the door open to scan the contents for comfort food. Pulling the fresh block of milk chocolate out and ripping it open, I shove a few pieces inside my mouth. The chocolate melts on my tongue and I blink my eyes closed at the sweet taste. When I exit the kitchen, Blake,

Maddison, and Tahlia are all sitting at the table waiting and staring at me.

"Is this an intervention?" The amusement quickly dies when none of them react. I let out a shaky breath before dragging a chair out and sitting down, dumping the chocolate on the table with a thud. "It's really not that bad. I-I think there have been a lot of new feelings—good and bad—and I didn't have enough time to process."

Tahlia reaches over and places her dainty hands over mine and tightens for reassurance. "Talk to us, please."

I lean my head back to gaze into her green eyes, and I take a deep breath. "He kissed me in the elevator at work today."

"Holy shit!" Maddison says.

"Fuck me!" Blake shouts.

"If it's not wanted, then you need to report—" Tahlia begins to say before I rip my hand out from under hers and wave my arms in front of me.

"No, no, no, it's not that! I want it. Trust me! That's one of the issues. I feel overwhelmed. I have never had this compelling reaction. It's like he has unlocked something inside me." I reach over and snap off another piece of chocolate and stuff it in my mouth.

"I'm confused. What's the issue? Go jump his bones." Blake shrugs.

"Now he wants me, and even though I want him badly... my job. I worked so fucking hard to get that position. I'm not losing it over him, or to a meaningless office hook-up. I love it, I really do. My dad would be so proud."

"But I am sure you can have both, if that's what you want," Maddison says.

"How? And the other problem is, he sleeps with every nurse. I'm not going to be just another nurse on his bedpost." I sigh, shaking my head.

"Just take it one day at a time. I'm certain you won't lose your position, but you should tread carefully and don't do anything at work," Blake suggests.

I shiver at the memory of his mouth on mine. I lean on the table with my elbows and touch my lips with my fingers.

"Find out his motives for wanting you before you do anything," Tahlia cautiously offers.

"So, what was the kiss like?" Blake asks.

My cheeks flush a deep crimson. I bite my lip between my teeth before gazing at Blake. "Honestly? Hungry and dominating."

"Fucking hell, just from a kiss?" He pops a brow, and he drags his chair out. "I need some water. It's hot in here. You lucky bitch." I stare at him and then burst out laughing.

I feel so light and open after the cry and the discussion with my friends. I manage to have a deep, solid sleep that night and wake up the next day with a spring in my step.

I march into the hospital corridors with a determination that I haven't felt before. I stand straight with my shoulders back, ready to hash it out with Mike. My shoulders drop when I find his office empty, but shaking the disappointment off, I march over to his desk and throw my bag underneath it and go about starting the day.

I have my head buried in the planner, ticking off items on my to-do list, when my stomach grumbles. I glance at the clock. Nine a.m. My brows crease with worry. *Where is Mike?*

My stomach growls again, and I decide to get our usual coffees and some food from the downstairs cafeteria. I'm sure he will be here when I get back. I squat down to retrieve my wallet from my bag and wander down the hall to the elevator. When I step inside, a spark of excitement courses through me as I think back to yesterday. If this is the effect the slightest kiss has on me, I would love to know what would happen if he touched me properly. I'm pretty sure I would melt into a puddle.

I walk in the direction of the barista and restrain myself from contemplating acting on the urge that's demanding me to find out.

I carry the two scalding hot coffees in each hand, a bag with blueberry muffins, and my wallet tucked under my arm as I wait for the elevator back up to Mike's office. The bell dings and I watch the doors slide open. My skin prickles and my gaze lands on Mike's compelling blue eyes, the firm features of his handsome face, and the confident set of his broad shoulders.

I swallow hard and set my shoulders back and saunter into the elevator and stand beside him. *You can do this. Show him you are not like every other nurse.*

"Good morning, Mike," I say eagerly.

"Good morning," he mumbles before his mouth sets in a firm, straight line.

"Here you go, your long black."

His head tilts to the side and with his free hand he reaches out to grab the coffee. His hand grazes mine, causing the skin on my arms to shudder and the scalding coffee to leak on my hand.

"Shit," I yell as the burn sinks in.

His other hand immediately drops his briefcase with a thud on the floor, and he takes the coffee cup from my grip. I draw my hand to my mouth and wrap my lips around the skin, wetting the skin with saliva from my tongue. It calms the burning sensation somewhat. He watches intently with his lips parted and his eyes shining.

"Are you okay, Alice?" he grunts in a strained tone.

I remove my hand from my mouth with a pop and saliva coats the slight red mark on my skin, but thankfully the burn was superficial and hardly stings now. "Yes." My voice comes out breathy, and I stare down at my own coffee, embarrassed by my response, and take a large sip. The ache between my legs becomes a heavy throb. I need some distance to clear my head.

When the elevator doors open, I burst through the door and rush to his office. I suck in the fresh air, trying to cleanse his spicy masculine scent out of my nose. I hear his heavy footsteps becoming louder, signaling his approach. My back is on fire from his gaze. I pause at the door, but then enter, walking to his desk to dump my coffee cup and muffins, and then ease into the chair in front of his desk.

He inhales deeply before stepping around his desk and setting his coffee down, then he sits directly across from me in his chair. He stares at me as I reach out for my cup and take a long sip before putting it back on the desk. We both begin talking at the same time.

He laughs and waves. "You first." His stare is uncomfortably intense.

I twitch in my seat, trying to rub the ache out. It's not helping. If anything, it is adding friction and causing an even deeper throb in my core.

The attraction between us is palpable. Am I attracted to him? *Yes.* Do I want him right now? *Yes.* Does he want me? *I don't know.* Or is he playing with me like all of the other nurses he's fucked around with at the hospital?

Spit it out, Alice.

"We need to talk about yesterday. That cannot happen between us under any circumstances. This job is everything to me. I worked too hard for you to fuck it up!" I yell. He slumps back in his chair and crosses his arms as I continue my rant. "I refuse to lose my job because of you. I'm not just another nurse you can fuck, and I will not be a toy in a sick and twisted game to get me into bed." I point at him. The frustration of my longing and the gratification of my honesty is leaving me breathless.

"Are you done?" His voice is tight, and there is an expression I haven't seen on his face before. I refuse to apologize for my outburst, because it needed to be addressed.

I lean back in the chair and offer a curt nod.

"Do you want to attend a conference in New York next week, or would that be part of some sick game?" His expression is mocking.

I cross my leg over my knee. "Mike, I am serious about this. It's important to me. And to answer your question, I would love to. I saw that on your planner, but I didn't think I was included," I say.

He sits up straight and swivels to face his computer, banging on his keyboard and clicking on his mouse. "Did you forget about the contract? Kate will have my balls if I leave you here. I'll print our booking passes now."

I smirk and peer up at him from under my thick, dark lashes. I rake my assessing gaze over his blue tailored suit, white shirt, and his matching blue tie. The suit against his blue eyes and brown hair is intoxicating. I finish my coffee that's gone cold, which is refreshing rather than disgusting, and the complete opposite to the warmth that is tingling between my thighs.

A Week Later

Sitting in the back of the car on the way to the airport, my leg is bouncing on the spot and I get an empty feeling in the pit of my stomach as the car parks along the curb. The door opens and Mike climbs out first. I remove my seat belt and slide myself across and gaze up at Mike's hand. Without thinking, I clasp it and step out. I don't let go of his hand. His brow arches and I quickly yank my hand back to my side, gripping my bag handle. My hand starts to sweat as my gaze takes in the enormity of the airport. It's larger than I imagined.

"Is everything okay, Alice?" he questions, gazing down at me.

I clear my throat. "Ah, well, confession time... I have never been on a plane before."

An irresistible grin of amusement lights his face. "Well, I'm honored to be the first to take you and break you in." His double meaning lightens some of my tension.

"Come on, you'll be fine. I promise to look after you." He spins and saunters inside, and I trail behind, taking the chance to openly study him. Wearing his tailored suit, he looks like a hunky model. Looking down at my plain uniform, I cringe, wishing I didn't have to wear this ugly navy attire.

"Alice, you look great. No matter how shitty the clothes are," he drawls.

I didn't notice him pause. I must have been too slow for him, so he decided to wait for me. My muscles tense and my nipples harden. This is going to be a torturous day. *Why did I have to work with him?*

The flight is smooth, helped by being in business class for the two-hour-and-two-minute flight from Chicago to New York. The leg room and service were a dream. I have never felt so spoiled. They even offered me a warm washcloth to wash my hands when I boarded. I must admit, the downfall of flying was on takeoff and landing. I held on to the arms of the seat in a vise-like grip, and the way my stomach dropped felt so unnatural I was close to being sick on the plane.

Mike warned me on the plane that we weren't visiting New York, and that as soon as the conference was over, we would need to leave to catch the flight home. Entering the enormous red brick building, Mike is stopped every five minutes for a "congratulations" or a surgery discussion. He would ask how their wives or children are, but I notice that not one person has asked how Mike is, or anything about his personal life.

What is in Mike's personal life? He has never mentioned a family or after-work activities apart from watching football. All I really know about him is his work. My chest becomes tight, and I bite my lip as I stare at his profile. *Who is the real Mike?*

We enter the large hall lined with chairs, and a mic is positioned on the stage in front. We take our allocated seats and the middle-aged gentleman seated next to Mike sparks up a conversation. He asks question after question. Mike, as always, is proper and polite. He has never once been disinterested or rude.

I watch in fascination as the speakers come on stage and discuss a surgery or a case study.

The announcement of the next speaker is called. "I would like to call to the stage, Doctor Mike Taylor."

My lips part in surprise, and I straighten in my seat, swiveling around to gape at him. Mike grins and places his hand on my knee, squeezing it gently before he stands up, taking long strides up the steps and onto the stage. After introducing himself to the crowd, he discusses the new techniques he has been using, including the robotic machine. Images of him using the robots to perform surgeries appear on the screen behind him, and I'm in awe. His talent is moving and inspiring, and his passion for orthopedics radiates through him with every word he speaks while on the stage.

I take a peek around and everyone's gazes are fixated on Mike. The respect circulating is evident. I settle my eyes back on Mike who is roaming the stage, demonstrating different techniques, and the power radiating off him and the way he owns the stage is breathtaking.

He thanks the crowd, who erupts in an onslaught of cheers and clapping, and I beam. I feel like I'm a spectator at a football game and we've won. I rise on shaky legs and watch Mike closely. His eyes find mine in the sea of faces and he winks before sauntering off the stage. I feel a flush of warmth enter my body.

A tug on my upper arm has me tearing my eyes from the stage, and I tilt my head to see a middle-aged man trying to gain my attention. "You're a very lucky woman." His lips turn up in a smile.

I open and close my mouth. The words, *He is just my boss*, don't seem to want to leave my throat. The man walks off, and I stand frozen on the spot. *What just happened?*

"You ready, Alice?" Mike's tone is gentle and breaks my trance. I didn't even hear him approach.

"Yes." I spin and follow him out of the room. It takes a long time because he is stopped multiple times and engaged in conversation. I grin, enjoying the chance to catch glimpses of him without him realizing.

When we reach the taxi, he collapses inside, and I break into a wide smile. "Mike, that was incredible! The robotic system was cool, but I admire the way you spoke in the room. You owned that stage. You are the most hardworking person I have ever met, and you still managed to stop and kindly speak to every single person with a genuine smile. You make them feel so comfortable. I'm in awe of you."

He stares at me intently, the smoldering flame I see in his eyes startling me. My cheeks glow with an almost uncomfortable heat.

"I'm so sorry. I should shut up. How embarrassing," I mutter under my breath and tear my gaze away to my clasped hands in my lap.

I see a movement out of the corner of my eye, and he reaches out, caressing my joined hands. My gaze lands on his face, where an unreadable expression is etched.

"Alice." He shakes his head, so I tear my gaze back to my lap. "That means everything to me. Thank you. No one has ever said such kind and thoughtful words to me." His voice cracks.

My brows furrow and I stay silent, waiting for him to finish.

"Yes, they compliment my work, but they have never, not once, complimented me as a person. You just complimented *me*." His voice is strained, and his hand leaves mine to run through his hair.

My heart drops at his admission and I shuffle closer, my body aching for his touch again. His gaze travels over my face and he searches my eyes.

"You're different, Alice. You're not some toy, and I'm not playing any game with you," he admits honestly.

Wetting my lips with my tongue, I'm unable to hold back my craving for him. I tilt my head, my heated gaze focused on his darkened blues. My hand reaches out and thrusts roughly into his hair, tugging his head down toward mine. I hear him growl as I plant my lips on top of his and our mouths move together in a slow and sensual kiss. My lips part in a sigh, and he takes the opportunity to explore my mouth with his tongue. My nipples harden and I wish the hand he's resting on my thigh would move toward my sex, or the hand holding my head in place would drift down over my breast.

The car suddenly stops, and I pull back, breaking the seal of our lips. I glance out the window. We've arrived at the airport. We fly back in silence and when we arrive at the employee parking lot. The sight of it feels like someone just poured a bucket of ice over us, instantly cooling the heated exchange we shared earlier.

Mike grabs my hand and guides me out of the car toward Marty.

"Alice, you're coming to my house."

"Mike—"

"No, Alice, I cannot handle another second of this. I need you. I want you, and I crave you. I want to pull you apart and put you back together. I want to destroy you so no other man will please you like I can, ever again. No one will ever compare to me. You will only crave me, my touch, my kiss, my *fuck*."

Decision time. I stare up at him with lust-filled eyes that are begging me to accept. Exposing my heart, I give him my blessing with a nod.

He rushes to open the passenger door of his car, so I climb in. After buckling up, I quickly get my phone out of my pocket and send Blake a text.

> **Alice:** *Change of plans. No need to pick me up tonight. I'm hanging out with Mike. I will fill you in tomorrow.*

> **Blake:** *Get it, girl! Enjoy that fine as hell man.*

I stuff the phone back in my pocket as we drive in silence. I should be scared by Mike's words, but I'm not. I'm just intrigued, and so turned on... I need more of the intense passion and connection shared back in the cab.

Before we can arrive at his house, he drives his car at a crawl through a set of automatic gates, which slowly open to reveal a modern house. Mike's house is a concrete gray two-story, with four rectangle windows at the top and bottom. An attached garage with a simple green garden and lots of trees surrounding it.

"This is your house?" My eyes bulge at the sight.

"Yes, it is. Is it a problem?" He turns to me with a look of concern etched on his face.

"No, it's just... Wow, Mike, I have never seen anything so nice."

I hear him sigh in relief. "Oh, well, thank you."

He parks in the garage and then steps around the car to open my door. He grabs my hand to pull me out of the car and pecks me on the lips before locking the car and leading me down the path to the front door. Once we get to the front door, my legs start to wobble and my heartbeat picks up. I'm less experienced than him. He is older and most likely way more experienced with women. I doubt I can please him. I'm probably going to embarrass myself, so I should just ask to go home.

But before I can say anything, he has opened the front door, and as he leads me inside to what I presume is the kitchen, he asks, "Would you like a glass of water or wine or a cup of tea?"

"No, I am okay, thanks. Maybe I should just go..." I glance at him and then down to the floor sheepishly.

He walks over to me and stands directly in front of me, and putting his finger under my chin, he lifts my face up so I'm staring directly into his blue eyes.

"What's going on in that pretty little head of yours? You're pulling away, I can feel it." He is gazing down at me with a worried expression on his face.

I need to tell him my fears, but I don't want to sound like a whiny schoolgirl. The way he is looking at me makes my stomach feel as though it is full of butterflies. "Mike, how do I say this... I'm not experienced like you..." I bite my lip.

"Fuck, are you a virgin?" His eyes widen and he looks mortified.

"No! But I have only done it a few times, and it's been ages since my last..." *God, this is embarrassing.*

He instantly relaxes and takes a deep breath. "It doesn't matter about our previous experiences. All that matters is what happens now and how you feel about me. I want to please you. There will be no comparing scorecards."

I sigh and while my heart is still beating fast inside my chest, at least I'm feeling less flustered. "Okay."

He grabs my hand, moving me into the kitchen. Before I can take a good look around, he wraps his hands around my waist and lifts me up onto the kitchen island, spreading my legs wide to stand in between them. My jaw goes slack with shock, but I'm also instantly aroused, feeling my apex thud and my sex getting wet.

"Are you sure you don't want a drink?" I shake my head and grab his jacket lapels, pulling him down to me so I can kiss him. I don't know when I became so bold, but I like it. *Maybe it's because I'm so aroused.*

His lips are so soft and pillowy, I could kiss him forever. I moan into his mouth, and when his tongue starts to push against my lips, I open them so our tongues can glide all over each other. I want to climb him, but I can't, so I reach up and put my hands through his hair to try to bring him even closer to me. Tugging at his bottom lip with my teeth, I pull away, smirking at him.

"And you say you are less experienced. Fuck, babe, you're wicked... pure sin." I laugh as he tries to rearrange himself in his pants, and I get a glimpse of his huge bulge. Fuck me, my body is on fire, and my panties are soaked. *I need him.*

"Let's go."

He picks me up from the counter and I wrap my legs tightly around his waist. He carries me around the corner, then up the stairs to his room. My heart is beating so fast and I'm grinning widely at him. But I have a question playing havoc in my mind that I need an answer to before I can let this go any further. "Do you bring all the nurses back here?"

He frowns. "I have never brought a woman here before. You're my first."

The answer makes my heart sing and I cuddle in closer, sinking into his grip. I inhale his neck, getting a good sniff of his spicy, masculine scent. Knowing he hasn't brought anyone else here makes me feel good. I don't feel disgusting, or like I'm going to be just another notch on his bedpost. Once we get to his room, he sits on the end of his bed, still holding me so I'm straddling him. I can feel him through my clothes, and I rub up and down on him, which he rewards with a very low groan.

"See? Pure wicked. You're killing me."

I push his suit jacket from his shoulders, and he helps me shrug it off before flicking it across the room where it lands with a soft thump. My laugh ripples through the air. I feel cheeky with Mike, full of a new sense of confidence, but at that exact moment, something snaps in Mike and he stares at me with hungry eyes.

"Mike?" I whisper.

He stands up and drops me to my feet. Grabbing my top, he rips it up and over my head, then pushes my pants down over my hips. He stops, staring at me in my black cotton bra and matching panties.

His eyes are hooded and laced with desire. "So beautiful, so delectable... and all mine. Take my clothes off," he instructs.

My eyes sparkle and my pulse beats faster, vibrating in my chest, I cannot wait to see what's under his clothes. I have imagined him many times since I have seen him in scrubs and suit attire, and I already know he's broad and muscular. I start with his white shirt. I pull his shirt out of his slacks and unfasten all the buttons. I can feel him watching my hands move and I can hear his breathing slow. Once they are all unbuttoned, I push my hands underneath the shirt and push it off his shoulders and down his arms. The shirt falls to the floor—fuck, he is perfect. I take in his lightly tanned skin with muscles everywhere, a six-pack with a deep *V* that's prominently leading to the real prize.

He breaks through my thoughts, saying what I was thinking of anyway. "Take the rest off." I don't seem to be doing it fast enough and he becomes impatient. "Now," he commands.

I nod and unbutton his blue slacks and undo the zipper, pushing them down his hips so they drop to the floor. He steps out of them and kicks them to the side, leaving him standing in Calvin Klein undies like a model.

I try to suppress a giggle and fail. "You're kidding, right?"

"What's so funny?" His tone is full of confusion and hurt.

"Of course, you're wearing Calvin Kleins. You look like you model for them." I shake my head, laughing.

He laughs too. "I take it that's a compliment?"

"Yes, it is. Mike, a big one." Smirking, I put my hands in his briefs and slide them down. My jaw slacks and I nearly faint at the size of him—that's got to be the biggest cock I have ever seen. *Fuck me.*

Realizing what I'm probably thinking, he strokes my cheek with his thumb and whispers, "I'll take care of you. It will still hurt until you get used to my size, but I'll make you feel good... I promise." His mouth curves into a smile as he puts his hands on my shoulders and gently pushes my bra straps down my arms. He then turns me around and unclips my bra, peeling it off and dropping it to the floor. Slowly, he starts kissing my neck, starting just below my ear and down to my shoulder. It's so soft that I find myself closing my eyes and leaning back against him. *This feels so good.*

The dusty kisses are so sexy.

"I want to see you," he murmurs in my ear. I turn around slowly and gaze into his eyes, which have gone straight to my creamy breasts that I know are a good handful each. A hiss leaves his lips. "Perfect, you're perfect."

I offer him a small, shy smile and he grips the edge of my black panties, taking them down over my hips and revealing my bare pussy. He takes a sharp breath and inhales my scent, which I can't help finding extremely erotic. He grabs my hips and throws me onto the bed. I let out a giggle as he prowls up the bed and opens my legs wide. I lie back down, trying to close my legs.

"Relax, babe, you're beautiful... perfect... I'll make you feel good," he coos in a soothing voice.

I take a few calming breaths, but my heart is still racing with anticipation and nerves. When I finally feel a long, slow lick on my pussy as he drags his tongue up to my clit, I scream in both shock and pleasure. Not knowing what to do with my hands, I drive them straight into his perfect hair. He keeps licking up and down before he concentrates on my nub, and I can feel the pressure building.

Seeking release and also trying to escape the intensity of it, I try to wiggle away, but he uses his arms and hands to trap my legs. After a few more strokes of his tongue and a tug of his teeth on my nub, I convulse, screaming his name over and over in a chant until I come hard against his mouth. My body relaxes onto the bed, but he is still licking me slowly. I loosen my grip on his hair—I was pulling it so hard during my climax that I'm surprised he didn't complain.

Once I'm down from my high, I hear Mike mumble, "Beautiful, sweet pussy." His words turn me on even more. I feel one of his arms move and he strokes his fingers at my entrance before he pushes one in. "So tight, oh so tight. You're going to have to come again just so I can loosen you up enough for me to fuck you without hurting you."

He starts to pump his finger in and out, and it feels so good that I sink further into the bed. By the time he enters a second finger, I'm getting fire growing in my belly again. "Don't hold back," he grunts through his teeth. He leans up and sucks my nipples, lapping each one in time with the perfect strokes and pressure of his fingers, and after a few minutes I can feel my climax building, and my walls tightening.

"Mike! I can't take much more."

"It's okay. Come, babe."

Between sucking my nipples and his fingers deep inside, a minute later I'm screaming again. I shudder as I come down from the high, and when I finally open my eyes, his blue ones are glimmering back at me. He seems to be enjoying this just as much as I am. He crawls up over my body and kisses me. I'm weirdly turned on by the taste of my pleasure on his lips and tongue. He pulls back and starts to play with my tits, squeezing and playing with my nipples again, bringing me up again. Then I feel him at my entrance.

"Condom?"

"Are you on the pill?" I nod between kisses as he continues. "I'm clean, so we're good."

I don't think about anything else. I just nod again, and he lines himself up before he slides in, pausing and waiting for my body to adjust until, eventually, he is all the way in. I cry out and cling to his shoulders. He holds still, waiting for me to nod for him to start, before moving his hips back, pulling out so, so, slowly, and then sliding back inside. He does this over and over until I'm begging to come.

"Please, I need to come," I groan, my eyes closing in pleasure.

"Don't you dare come yet. We are going to come together. Hold it," he commands. He continues to pump a few more times. We both have a light sheen of sweat over our bodies, and I'm holding back with everything I have when I hear his order in my ear. "Come now."

I let go, coming so hard I see little spots in front of my eyes, and I feel his dick pump inside me over and over, until he is done and slowly backs away, pulling himself out.

Relaxing, I sigh contentedly, and he laughs before pulling me over him, so I'm draped across his body.

"How are you feeling?" he asks.

"Good, I have never come so many times in one night. This is a record."

My eyes are already closing, and just as I'm drifting off to sleep, I hear him say, "This is only the start."

CHAPTER 12

MIKE

I HEAR HER SOFT slow breaths and I realize she has fallen asleep on me. I'm in a state of bliss. She is a total dream, perfect body, smart, and courageous—she could totally ruin me. I stare at her for a while until a heaviness comes over me and I drift off too.

The next morning, I wake up to a warm body and I smile, remembering Alice slept here. She is still asleep, so I reach over to grab my phone and check the time and some emails. It's seven a.m. which is a sleep-in for me, as I usually hit the gym in the mornings. I lie here and reply to a few emails until I feel a flutter of movement on my chest and I know she is waking up.

"Good morning, beautiful."

"Mmm, good morning. What time is it?" Her voice is groggy.

"Half past seven," I say softly and put my phone down on the bedside table. I cuddle her to me. "Are you feeling sore?"

"Just a little, not bad though, considering." She giggles which makes me grin from ear to ear.

"Do you want to have a shower? Afterward, I will make you some coffee and breakfast." I kiss the top of her head.

"Yeah, that sounds wonderful, but I need you to give me a minute. This feels too good. I just want to stay like this for a bit longer."

I chuckle. "Okay, well, when you're ready, we will shower. I'd be happy to lie here with you all day, though."

Five minutes later, she raises her head and smiles up at me, and I lift my hand to touch her face, tracing my thumb along her bottom lip before dragging it down. Her eyes lock with mine and I can see the desire building behind them.

"Are you sure?" I ask.

She nods and hops up, holding her hand out for me to take. I grasp her hand and stand, guiding her into my bathroom where I turn one of the two showerheads on. I have two, but I don't want her using the other shower—I want to share, have her close to me, and wash her. Once the water is warm enough, I guide her under the spray. I pick up the bodywash and squirt a generous amount on my palm and gently massage her shoulders.

"This feels like heaven," Alice mumbles.

I smile as her body goes loose underneath my fingertips. Her moans turn me on again, and I don't think I'll ever get enough of her.

I keep massaging her for a while until the knots in both her shoulders are out. Then I get more bodywash and start rubbing her breasts and stomach from behind, before touching between her legs. She is wet with water and her arousal. I suck in a hard breath.

"Soaked," I say gruffly. I'm ready to go, but I need to be gentle, so I don't hurt her, especially as she is already a little sore.

She is moaning and writhing as I gently stroke her, my other hand touching her breast while she leans back against me. I ease a finger into her, and she moans louder. I slowly pump in and out of her and tug on her nipple with my fingers, and when I put a second finger in, she tightens around them.

"God, Mike. Ah, it feels so good. Don't stop," she pants.

Chuckling, I whisper, "Never. Come, babe. Give yourself to me."

I feel her clenching and she's riding my hand so hard and fast I know she must be close, so I turn her to face me. Picking her up, I push her against the shower wall and guide myself into her, slowly. I want to go hard, but I can't because she is already sore from last night, so with everything I have, I restrain my urges and take my time. I gently ease into her, letting her stretch around me. I grunt and groan, feeling the overwhelming tightness, and I have to hold myself back from coming too soon.

Once I am fully seated, I kiss her with a slightly open mouth and let her relax before moving torturously slowly—out and then back in, driving her mad in between kisses.

"Fuck me hard, Mike. Come on. Please... please." I pull out slowly, one more time, before filling her to the brim with one quick stroke. "Oh, mmm," she moans into me.

I fuck her hard against the shower wall until we are both about to blow, and I move my mouth to her ear and say, "Come." Then I bite her earlobe.

"Ahh, Mike!" She shivers in my arms.

We both come hard, and I hold her steady when I feel her go limp in my arms. Letting her recover for a minute, I lower her legs so she can stand, and I kiss her softly again.

"Wow, it just keeps getting better and better." Her voice is breathless, and her cheeks are pink.

"That's only the start. There's more if you keep begging me like that. But first, let me actually wash you."

She smiles at me slowly with hazy eyes before turning around. Grabbing the shampoo, I massage her scalp and wash her hair.

"I could almost fall asleep again. This feels amazing."

Laughing at her reaction, I tell her, "Not yet, Alice. You need to eat and drink first."

"Yeah, that's a very good idea."

I finish washing her hair before we get out and I head to my wardrobe to get dressed and come back with loungewear for Alice, who is smiling as she dries herself.

"Thanks."

"I'll start breakfast. Get dressed up here and I'll see you downstairs whenever you're ready." I kiss her lips and head downstairs to prepare some eggs, bacon, and muffins.

I put some music on the television quietly in the background and cook. The music is soft enough that I'm able to hear her footsteps coming down the stairs.

"How can I help you?" She wraps her arms around my waist, hugging me and looking around at the pans.

"No, I'm good. I have got it all under control. Thanks anyway. What did you want to drink?" I ask.

"I'll have water and a coffee, please."

I nod and step over to the fridge to retrieve a bottle of water and hand it to her.

She takes it from me. "Thanks." I plate up our food and hand her a plate before setting out to make our coffees.

I tilt my chin in the direction of the stool. "Now, eat that before I eat you." I say it, knowing it'll make her blush even more.

She smirks, walking over to the stools. She puts her plate down and drags one out from under the counter, hops up, and begins tucking into her breakfast. I finish making the coffees and sit down next to her to eat and drink.

When we finish our breakfast, I take the dishes to the dishwasher. After it's loaded, I reach for Alice's hand. Her fingers link through mine and I guide her to the living room.

"Come sit in the living room. I'll put some Netflix on."

"I really have to go soon. I have to get ready for work tomorrow."

"Yeah, I get that. The boss is a real hard-ass." I glance down at her with my lips turned up and she smiles in response.

"Just sit for ten minutes, and then I'll take you home," I plead.

"Okay."

I pick up the remote and turn the television on. She sits down next to me, and I grab her legs, draping them over the top of mine, and start stroking her soft calves. I feel so at ease with her like this. It seems so natural and far from the relationship I had with Amanda.

It's so much better.

Amanda never liked to sit and watch TV with me. And she definitely didn't like to be touched or held. Which all should've been red flags. But I'd hoped I was wrong about her cheating. Which of course I now know I wasn't.

"Are you ready?" I ask.

"Yeah, let's go."

I drive her home and park in the drive, but before I even have a chance to unbuckle my seat belt, she puts her hand on my chest. "Don't get out. It's fine. You don't need to be a gentleman like that. My roommates are probably waiting up or watching me through the curtains right now."

I chuckle. "Okay, and before you run inside, are you free Saturday night?"

She goes quiet and I'm about to withdraw the invite when she responds. "We work together, remember?"

"It's only a three-month contract. We will still act professional at work, but outside of the hospital we can be together. There is no policy in the hospital against relationships between colleagues, but I respect your choice." I grab her chin and lean in, kissing her lips softly.

She whimpers when I remove my lips from hers. "I want to take you out on a proper date. Just humor me. Please?" I kiss her again before she can respond, but this time, I use my tongue, coaxing her to relax. Alice groans, and I pull away, grinning. Her eyes are closed, and I watch as they slowly flutter open.

She sighs. "You can kiss, Mike. Like, *really* kiss."

"Thank you. You're quite a good kisser too... Now go! I'll talk to you tomorrow.

She shakes her head. "I'll think about it. No guarantees, so stop trying to distract me with your naughty mouth."

"Come here and kiss me once more," I say, wiggling my eyebrows and laughing.

She pecks me on the lips before diving out of the car, giggling to herself as she runs up to the front door, and then she turns around to wave at me. She looks like a goddess, and I am officially screwed.

I pick up a big bouquet of flowers on my way into work, hoping to make Alice feel better. I know sleeping with me is a risk and I want to thank her for an amazing time last night. I need to get to know her outside of the hospital setting. Having a formal date is something I never do. Well, not since Amanda, so it's kind of a big deal... one she doesn't know anything about. I want to tell her why I'm so casual these days, so she can understand me better.

My cell phone rings. I scoop it up from my desk. It's Alex. I accept the call and speak into the receiver. "Hey, what are you doing? This call is earlier than usual. What's up?"

"Hey, bro. Yeah, I'm driving to work. I just got called for an emergency. I just thought I would call and see if you're good for a game of golf this week?"

I double-check the planner Alice organized for me. "I'm actually off tomorrow if that suits you?" I ask.

"Perfect. I have the morning off too. I'll make sure no patients are booked from now until then."

My office door swings opens, and Alice quietly steps in. I instantly smile and recline back in my chair, watching her come toward me. I notice she is blushing and her eyes are glowing.

"I gotta go. I'll see you tomorrow." I don't bother waiting for him to reply before hanging up.

"Good morning." I stand and walk toward her.

"Morning, Doctor Taylor." She smirks.

I chuckle. "You only need to say that when others are around, babe. When it's just you and me, Mike is enough." I stare at her and wish right now I could grab her around her waist and pull her to me and kiss her. But I'm respecting her boundaries—even if it kills me. I smile. "I bought you something."

She frowns, and I chuckle at her expression. "Relax. It's nothing much, just a thank-you for last night."

"Mike, please," she groans. I turn around to grab the flowers, and I bring them to her. I see her eyes widen and become glassy. I slow my steps until I am standing in front of her.

I frown. "What's wrong? Is it too much?"

She shakes her head. "Nothing is wrong. It's just, you're the first man to have ever bought me flowers."

My eyes widen at her confession. "No."

She laughs. "Yes."

"Well, you better get used to being spoiled because when you're with me, this is normal."

Alice takes the bouquet from my hand and leans forward to smell them. She inhales deeply and then glances up with the biggest grin I have ever seen her wear. It's a look I want to see her wear regularly.

"Beautiful," she gushes.

"Just like you."

CHAPTER 13

MIKE

IT'S BEEN A FEW weeks since I have played golf, which is rare. I normally play with Alex every week. It's a slow-paced game that relaxes us and allows us to debrief about work, with the added bonus we are both extremely competitive.

I'm in my golf clothes and waiting alone in the lobby at the local club. I arrived here earlier than usual, but after a few minutes pass, I see Alex's car pull up. I watch him jump out and collect his clubs from the trunk and trek up the path to meet me.

A grin spreads across his face. "Hey, bro, hope you haven't been waiting for me long."

I hug him with my free arm before I answer. "No, it's fine, only been here for a few minutes and I've already checked us in."

He nods. "Sweet, let's go. I have to work this afternoon."

"What time are you starting?" I ask.

"I booked my first patient for three p.m."

"Plenty of time for me to whip your ass," I gloat.

We laugh and wander off to get the cart. Growing up, our parents weren't always around. Being doctors themselves, they gave us what they thought we needed... money. But we didn't want money; we wanted time with them. Growing up meant that Alex, Steph, and I became inseparable. We became each other's cheerleaders, and of course we teased the shit out of each other, but we have always had one another's backs through thick and thin. We try to have dinner as a family one Sunday every month. As our parents have gotten older, we tried to get them to be involved like a normal family... as much as we could get, that is.

I tee off and Alex chimes, "Nice shot."

Alex steps up to tee off now, and he hits it with his driver, slicing it off into the grass.

"Good hit. I hope you don't beat me again. I don't think I'll come out with you again if you obliterate me like you did last time." We laugh and mark our way to the cart to put our clubs away and drive off in the direction of our balls.

"What's the plan this weekend? Are we hitting Luxe?" Alex asks.

"Well, Saturday night I'm taking my new nurse colleague out to dinner."

His mouth hangs open. "Oh really? Who is she?" I can hear the shock in his voice, but I prefer to be honest with Steph and Alex, so I won't lie to him. Besides, he has met her, so I kind of need to tell him.

"Well, you actually danced with and kissed her months ago at Luxe. I was supposed to be hooking up with her after she went to the bathroom, but somehow, she ended up dancing with and kissing you."

"No fucking way. I don't remember that. So, I'm guessing I don't get a shot with her now? You're calling dibs and now I have to back off? Or is she still fair game and just a hook-up?" He parks the cart.

I jump out. "You're not touching her ever again. She is mine. No, she is more than a hook-up. I don't know exactly what we are yet. I'm trying to take it slow so I don't scare her."

Alex slides out of his seat and grabs his next club and I follow suit, pulling my seven iron out to hit my ball first.

"I hope you know I would never be like Liam."

My stomach knots when I hear Liam's name. "Oh, I know, and I'm sure if I had told you that I wanted her that night, you would have backed off." I line up to my ball, swing my club, and hit it, landing the ball directly on the green.

Alex scans the ground to find his ball. "This is the first person you've been serious about since Amanda, right? Over here!" He points to his ball and we both walk over in that direction.

Alex is right. I haven't had anyone get under my skin, not since Amanda over a year ago. No one has even come close to keeping me interested or making me chase. I have enjoyed different women for one or two nights and that's it. I never keep them around out of fear they will get too attached. Some of them hate me even after those two nights, but they get over it soon enough.

He lines up to hit his ball, and I stay quiet as he takes a swing. His ball lands near mine on the green. We walk back to the cart and jump in, continuing up to the green.

"Yeah, no one has caught my eye. However, she thinks I'm a massive player. I understand why, but I don't feel like that about her. She is different. I want to get to know her more, like, see and talk to her all the time. It's been a long time since I have felt this way."

"Have you explained to her what happened with your ex?" he asks.

"Not yet. Amanda came into the office, and it pissed Alice off for some reason. But I want to explain what happened, then she might understand why all the casual sex."

I don't feel bad for what I have done. I'm single and enjoy sex, crave companionship and intimacy. I never take them to dinner or hang out with them. It's purely platonic to fulfill a need, to release the tension, and to know I'm desired. I guess people would see that as me using them, but they are well aware that it's just sex between us, and they are more than happy for just that. On occasion, they want more. They think I'll change for them, but no one has made an impact on me, or made me want to change my mind. Amanda made me distrust women and their loyalty. I realize that it's unfair to other women, but it's hard to change how I feel. I feel broken and hope to find the right person who will make me whole again.

"Bring her to the Sunday family dinner. I'm sure she will love it. It might get you some brownie points from her and Mom." He laughs, wiggling his eyebrows at me.

"You know what? That's a great idea. I'll ask her. It will help her realize how serious I am about her. And Mom will go crazy."

"Would she ever? Anyway, enough shit talk. I need to focus, so I can kick your ass and then you can buy me a beer."

"In your dreams." I say, winking at him then get out of the cart and walk toward my ball. My mind is still thinking about how I called her mine. I wasn't joking. She's literally the woman of my dreams.

CHAPTER 14

ALICE

MIKE HAS BEEN A good surprise. I'm really seeing a different side to him. He is respectful at work, understanding boundaries and keeping it professional. I hope it can stay this way for the entire three months. I have been on the ward for the past week and have only seen him from afar. Smiles are exchanged in passing, but all the women on this floor do it, so I don't stand out.

I need to go shopping for an outfit for Saturday night, so on my way home, I pass by his office. Opening the door, I peer in and see there is no one inside, so I grab a piece of paper and a pen to write down my number for him. I also tell him that I agree to Saturday night, and I ask him to let me know the time I need to be ready by.

I arrive home and I notice a text has come through. Not recognizing the number, I assume it has to be Mike, and a smile plays on my lips as I open the text.

> **Mike:** *Be ready for five thirty p.m. sharp. I look forward to seeing you. Mike.*

I respond to his text, then walk inside to find Maddison and Tahlia folding laundry in the dining room. "Hey, girls." I drop my bag down on a dining chair and help them.

"You go take a shower, Alice. We can do this," Tahlia says.

"It's okay. It will get done faster if I help. Also, I wanted to tell you that Mike asked me on a date." I don't look at any of their faces; instead, I study the pants that I'm busy folding.

"No way!" Maddison whistles.

"Mm-hmm," I mumble back, unable to form words.

"I'm so happy for you," Tahlia says, and I glance up at her after I put the folded pants down. "Would you take me shopping tomorrow? I don't have anything nice to wear," I ask, rolling my lips.

"I would love to. Your car is at the shop getting fixed, so hopefully it will be done soon, Alice," Tahlia says.

"Oh, that's great." I sigh.

"Now, head off and shower as the laundry is sorted," Maddison orders.

The next day Tahlia agrees to help me find the perfect outfit, but Maddison needs to study so she stays home.

While we are driving, she asks, "Where is he taking you tonight?"

"I actually have no idea, which is why I'm struggling with what to wear. It's not like I have a lot of money to waste on an outfit, but I just want to feel good."

"Don't worry about that; we won't spend much. I'm sure we can find a bargain. I'm good at spotting them. If not, I can lend you some cash. I really don't mind."

"No, don't be silly. You're the queen of bargain hunting and I really appreciate you for taking me out to find something with me."

We arrive thirty minutes later at the shopping center and grab a space in the parking garage. Once we are inside, we each grab a coffee and browse around the stores. We have gone into about eight and found nothing so far. Entering the large department store, we notice a sale rack and walk straight for it. There are a few good dresses, so I take them to the changing room to try them on. They are all quite pretty, but one dress stands out. It's a sexy, short, black long-sleeved dress with some white print on it.

Tahlia whistles as I step out from behind the changing room curtain to show her. "Wow, you have to get that dress. He is going to love you in it. It's sexy."

I turn around in the mirror, tugging the dress down. "Don't you think it's too short? I'm worried it's too short, bordering on slutty instead of sexy."

She shakes her head violently. "No way, because of the long sleeves and high neck you can totally get away with it. Trust me. Keep your hair straight. With simple makeup, you can pair it with nude shoes. It will be perfect. It's the one, and it's on sale."

I can't disagree with that. "Yeah, that's true. Okay, done. Let's grab some lunch."

A few hours later a knock comes at the door and my heels click on the tiles as I walk to the front door. I have a shit-eating grin on my face. It's five twenty-five p.m., but to my disappointment, it's not Mike standing there.

"Hello, Miss Winters. My name is Sergio. I'm Mike's driver."

My brows rise. "Oh. Hi, Sergio. I'm Alice."

Sergio looks to be in his sixties, with short gray hair and he's wearing a black suit and tie. "Are you ready to go, Alice?"

"Yes, I am. I'll just run and grab my bag." I spin around and the girls are smiling at me. "Bye, girls." I wave at them.

"Bye," they chime in unison.

I follow Sergio outside and the cool air hitting my legs causes me to shiver. As I close the front door behind me, I notice a black limousine parked in the driveway—not what I was expecting. My mouth is open with my lips twisting up. I have never been in a limousine before, so this will be fun. Sergio opens the door for me to hop in and I take my time getting in, being careful to not flash Sergio or Mike my underwear. When I'm safely inside, I glance up and I feel my heart drop. Mike isn't here.

"Would you like a glass of champagne or wine, Alice?" Sergio's voice cuts through my thoughts.

He is looking at me from the door, waiting while I put my seat belt on. "Oh, yes, please. I'd love a glass of wine." He carefully reaches for a bottle of wine that's sitting in a bucket of ice built into the side of the limousine. He pours me a decent helping and hands it to me with a smile. "Thank you." I take the wineglass and have a large sip. *Mmm, this is very good wine.*

"We will arrive at the destination in approximately thirty to thirty-five minutes, depending on the traffic. In case you need a refill, I'll pop the wine in this ice bucket here." He leans in and puts the bottle back.

"Okay, thank you."

He closes my door, and I ease back into the soft cream leather. The blue lights dim, and as music begins to play, I smile and sing to the lyrics.

CHAPTER 15

ALICE

THE LIMOUSINE STARTS TO slow before the movement completely stops, and leaning forward, I peer out the window, frowning when I see we are parked out in front of the Rialto Building. The door swings wide open and Mike is standing there on the footpath, holding his hand out for me. My breath hitches at the sight of him.

He is wearing a bone-colored suit with a white crisp shirt that is unbuttoned at the top. He has a five-o'clock shadow and his brown hair is styled to perfection. *He is Doctor Dreamy for sure.*

I unbuckle my seat belt with shaky hands and grasp his warm hand in mine and step out of the car. When I straighten up, Mike rakes his eyes over me, checking me out from head to toe before meeting my eyes again. The smoldering flame I see in his eyes sends a shiver that brings me pleasure.

He kisses me briefly before pulling away, smirking when I whimper in protest. "You look breathtaking tonight. Are you ready?"

"I thought we were having dinner first," I say, gazing up at the building.

He chuckles, and it's like he has been reading my thoughts because he has a stupidly handsome, lopsided grin on his face.

"We are, just up there." He gestures to the tower. He takes my hand and leads me inside, and I frown as I follow him in. *Where is he taking me?*

There is an elevator which takes us up to the top floor, and when we step out, I see a sign on the glass door ahead which says, *Vue de Monde*. It sounds fancy, and as we amble in, my jaw drops at the spectacular sight. It's a warmly lit restaurant at the very top of the tower with dark-gray walls, and unique gold art sculptures hung at various intervals, with rich black floors.

When we step inside, we are immediately greeted by a waitress. "Hello, how can I help you this evening?"

"I have a reservation for two, booked under Mike Taylor, for six p.m. tonight," he says smoothly.

The waitress smiles at him with her chest pushed out, and pays no attention to me, as if I'm nothing more than the handbag to some older rich guy. It irks me, but I don't let it show. She doesn't know me, so fuck her and her assumptions; she is clearly jealous.

"Yes, please, come this way. I'll take you to your table, and I'll be your waitress for tonight."

She guides us to the table in the back corner. Glass windows line the walls on one side—we have the best views of the city tonight. "Here's your table. Can I get you both a drink to start off with?"

I pull out Alice's chair and then take a seat opposite her. The waitress places the napkins on our laps and lights the candle in the middle of the table.

"Yes, please. We would like a bottle of your best Riesling," Mike says flatly, while smiling at me and giving her no attention at all. I feel myself blush. He makes me feel like I'm the only person in the world.

"Of course, I'll be right back." She hands each of us a menu, then spins and walks off.

Once we are alone, he smiles at me, and I smile back. He is infectious and charming.

"I have never heard of this place. It's grand. I feel famous or something," I tell him, laughing at the enormity of this place.

"It's the best restaurant in Chicago. I have been here once for work and have always wanted to come here to dine on my own time. I have just never met the right person, until now," he says, staring into my eyes, his words causing me to blush.

"You keep surprising me, Dr. Taylor. First, the flowers and now, dinner. What else is hiding up your sleeve, or will you pull a rabbit out of a hat?" I giggle, lightening the mood, although his eyes stay dark and hazy. If I had to guess, I'd say he is aroused. I pick up the menu to distract myself from just staring at him the whole night.

He laughs. "Definitely no rabbit or hat. Just a fun, enjoyable night, and this is just the beginning."

Would it be rude to just skip dinner and head back to his house right now?

I browse through the menu and there are just so many options, not to mention that half of the dishes have French names, so I have no idea what any of them are.

"Can you help me choose what I should get? It all sounds delicious."

He peers at me from above his menu. "We could share a few dishes and you can get a taste of everything, if that suits you?"

I fold the menu closed and drop it back on the table and nod. "That's a great idea. It saves me from trying to choose."

The waitress comes back with a bottle. "I have Mount Langi Ghiran Riesling." She picks up our glasses, pouring a taster into each, and she waits for our verdict.

Mike swirls it, then smells it before tasting. I take a small sip. "Perfect, yes." *Mmm, it's good. So smooth, not too sweet, not too dry.*

She pours a full glass for each of us and then looks between us. "Are you ready to order, or do you need some more time?"

"No, we are ready," Mike answers.

"Okay, what can I get you?" She smiles and pulls out a small iPad. *Fancy.*

"We would like to order the French onion soup with a cheese and onion brioche bun, the ratatouille, and the confit duck legs with braised lentils. For dessert, we will have the pear tarte tatin and the plateau de fromage. We will be sharing all of these dishes, thank you." He folds his menu and places it on top of mine.

Once the waitress has finished typing the order into the iPad, she grabs our menus from the table. "All great choices. We will bring them one at a time in a smooth transition. If at any stage you want a break, just let me know."

"Okay, thank you."

Once she walks out of earshot, he picks up his wine, and I mimic him when he holds his glass out and says, "I think we should cheers to you finally caving, and coming to the realization I'm not a complete dickhead."

I laugh. "I must have a screw loose. I think I need to get another doctor to check me out."

His brows draw together in a frown. "No other doctor will do such a thing."

"I'm just kidding. Geez, I'm playing with you," I scold, shaking my head at him. I raise my glass to toast. "Anyway, cheers to a great date tonight." Our glasses clink, then I bring the glass to my lips and I take a sip. Setting it down, I sit back, relaxing as I continue staring at him.

He leans in. "I want to know more about you, Alice."

"There isn't too much to tell. I am originally from Bendigo Park, which is where I was born and raised, before moving to the city for college, which you already know because it was on my application letter."

"I did. I knew you were smart from that application. What else?" he ponders aloud, smirking at me from across the table.

"I have a sister, Claire, who is younger than me and is studying teaching at college. Then there is my mom, Angie, who is working as a receptionist in Bendigo Park. We are a small family and remarkably close, so I try to head back to Bendigo Park as often as I can."

Thinking of my mom and sister almost kills me with how much I miss them. I wish they didn't live so far away. I love my roommates, but it's just not the same. My mouth becomes dry, so I reach for my drink and sip some more of the wine. Our first course arrives, and it looks delicious, but I can't help frowning at how small the portions are.

"And what about your dad?" He is looking at me with a blank expression.

I pick up my drink and drain the glass, not caring how classless it is. I need the confidence that the buzz of alcohol can give. I set the empty glass down, taking shallow breaths. Glancing up at Mike, I answer in a quiet voice. "He died."

Sympathy flashes across his face and he leans forward, grabbing my hand and holding it. "I'm so sorry, Alice."

I shrug in response. I gaze down at our joined fingers and rub my thumb over his soft, big hand. "It is what it is, I guess. He died five years ago in his sleep. The doctor said it was from a heart attack."

I keep my gaze down at my rubbing thumb, then take my hand away. "We should eat this before it gets cold."

It's quiet, and I can tell he is thinking about what he wants to say next. The sounds of our cutlery hitting the bowl are the only noise between us. We have just finished the soup and bun when the waitress brings the duck and ratatouille, then tops up our glasses.

"Is that why you wanted to get into nursing?" Mike asks curiously.

I glance up into his curious eyes, picking up my glass and taking a sip, before I nod, adding, "Yes, I was shattered, but beforehand I had no direction or idea of what I wanted to do, and when that happened, I realized I wanted to help others. It was a dream my dad and I had for me when I was young. So, I feel like I'm fulfilling that dream of his."

Remembering how lost I was as a teenager and how rebellious I was, if I had my time again, I would have enjoyed all those precious moments I had with my father, and not spent so much time out, or staying at my friends' houses every weekend. It's probably why I'm such a homebody now.

I bite my lip, then I confess, "I actually really wanted to work on the cardiac ward, but now I feel happy that my direction has changed—the work is incredible, and the staff are so encouraging, helpful, and fun to work with. I can't complain."

His eyes flick all over my face and a satisfied grin forms on his mouth.

My stomach growls, reminding me that the main dish is probably going cold. I take a portion and eat, now talking in between bites. "This is so good. Now I'm going to compare every other restaurant to this when I can't have it again."

"I'll take you whenever you want," he offers.

"Mike, don't be crazy. But in all seriousness, I think my father had something to do with me finding you. I know it sounds silly, but I just feel it." I bite my lip to shut myself up.

His brows shoot up in surprise. "What? I'm not crazy. I'd be happy to bring you here every week, and you're not silly. I wish I could have met him."

His eyes are sincere, and I feel at ease talking to Mike about my dad. *I miss him so much.* He will never get to walk me, or my sister, down the aisle, or meet his grandchildren, or watch us grow up to be women he would have been proud of. It's definitely a hard pill to swallow, and it makes me appreciate my time on this earth even more, because you never know when your time is going to be up.

"You're not taking me here every week. Really, that just solidifies what I thought," I chastise, shaking my head and laughing at him.

We finish the main courses and our bottle of Riesling. I feel light-headed, so I drink water with the desserts, which are mouth wateringly delicious.

I hear him take in a deep breath. "What about your exes? Why did you two break up?"

I twirl my fork in the last bit of the pear tarte tatin and peer up from under my lashes to meet his eyes. "I only had one short high school relationship, but we broke up when my dad died. I wasn't in love with him, so I ended it and focused on my studies instead. I haven't had anything serious since."

I remember how heartbroken Trevor was, but I didn't have time for him. I needed to be with my family. Besides, I think I was just comfortable with him, rather than passionately in love with him, because after we broke up, I never missed him. Looking back now, I realize how wrong that is.

"Nothing since then?" He perks an eyebrow up in question.

I shake my head vigorously. "No. I have had hook-ups here and there, but nothing serious."

We finish our desserts, then the waitress brings the bill.

When I go to grab my purse, Mike covers my hand with his and shakes his head. "Don't. I took you on a date, so I pay the bill. That's how it works."

I nod and sit back. "Okay."

We get up, thanking the waitress, and Mike grabs my hand before opening the door for me. Exiting the restaurant, we wait for the elevator to arrive.

He is standing close to me, still holding my hand, when he breaks the silence. "Thanks for coming. I had a wonderful time. I can't wait for part two. Did you have a nice night, babe?"

I smile. "Yes, Mike, it was a wonderful night, thank you. I have never been on a date like this ever."

The elevator doors open, and we enter, and Mike hits the ground floor button. "Where is part two?" I ask.

"My house." Mike's voice is gravelly, and he squeezes my hand firmly.

My breath starts to quicken, and the anticipation makes me feel as though there are butterflies in my stomach. "So, errr, there is something on my mind that I want to get clear about."

I feel the heat of his stare on my face. "Mmm, ask away."

The elevator reaches the parking lot and when the doors open, I trail beside him to his car. "At Luxe you were talking with a brunette, the same one in your office the other day. Who is she?" I ask.

Mike opens the car door for me, and I climb in, watching him through the windshield as he walks to the other side and slides in. Turning toward me, he sighs. "My ex, Amanda." He turns back around, starting the car. "Let's drive back to my house and finish this conversation there. There's clearly a lot more we need to discuss."

CHAPTER 16

ALICE

WE ARRIVE BACK AT Mike's house and when we are standing in his kitchen, he turns to me. "Would you like a glass of wine?" he asks.

I nod. "Yes, please."

He pours a glass of wine for each of us. I take a seat on a stool at the kitchen counter.

"Your house is spectacular. I have never seen anything this grand in my life. This is a dream house." I scan the modern interior, half expecting to wake up and realize Mike and this entire evening has all been a dream.

Laughing at me, he tells me, "I do love my house. It was designed by me for me. But enough about my house. I have something else planned now, and it will be a great place to finish the conversation we started at dinner. Bring your wine and follow me outside."

"Sure." My hands begin to tremble, so I clutch the glass with both hands to hide it. Sliding off the stool, I walk around to follow him.

He opens the sliding door and closes it behind us. I step out from the paved alfresco area and stop, completely speechless. There in front of my eyes is a grand outdoor projector screen, with fluffy cushions on a rug in front of it, and tables laden with snacks. There are roses and candles everywhere, all lit up, and it's breathtaking. My eyes widen and my lips part in sheer surprise. I pull one of my trembling hands to my neck and start rubbing the back of it, unsure of what to say.

This is even better than the dinner. It's so... me.

Realizing I haven't said a word in several minutes, I quickly clear my throat. "This is stunning."

His beautiful big smile that reaches his eyes is back, and he grabs my hand. "Come on, let's take a seat."

He ushers me over to the rug and my hand tightens in his when a gust of a cool breeze whips my legs and I shiver involuntary.

"Let's grab you some of my clothes so you're more comfortable." He is still holding my hand, but with the other he's gesturing toward my dress. "Even though I love that dress, and how sexy you look in it, I want you to enjoy the movie."

I blush at the way he stares at me with his eyebrow raised, wearing a sexy as sin smirk. I feel my body starting to heat and a throb between my legs. I shuffle side to side to try and rub the ache.

"You are killing me here. I'm trying to go slow." His eyes darken to a deeper shade of blue. "Let's go get you changed."

I follow him up the stairs and into his wardrobe to switch my dress for a cozy pair of fleece gray jogger pants and a hoodie. The hoodie smells of him. His sexy spicy scent is all over it, and I pull the collar of the sweater up and deeply inhale. *Mmm, so good.*

We head back outside and take a seat on the rug. He pats the area in front of him, smiling. "Come here."

I shuffle over until I'm sitting between his legs, leaning my back against his hard body. He wraps his arms around my middle in a tight, warm hug. He pulls a blanket out from next to him, whipping it into the air so it drops over our legs. I twist my head to peer at him. He smiles and leans down and kisses my lips in a too brief kiss.

I slowly blink my eyes open, staring at his heated gaze. "Why me? You could have anyone you want. I'm nothing special."

He moves his head to look away before returning his eyes to mine. "There is a connection I feel toward you. I haven't felt this way with any other woman. It confuses and annoys the hell out of me because you make it so difficult," he teases.

I laugh up at him. "Well, I... How do I say this? Just don't fuck me around. I can't keep denying I have feelings toward you. But I still don't understand why you are single. No marriage or kids, at your age... Should I be worrying why you're not settling down?"

His laugh vibrates against my back. "You make me sound like a dinosaur, or like I'm some antique."

I can't help laughing aloud. He is funny, which surprises me. He keeps surprising me. I keep thinking the bubble will burst any moment. *And I'll be the one left hurt and trying to piece myself back together.*

"I have had one serious girlfriend, which you know about... I thought she was the one, but I was young and dumb and got completely blindsided." He tears his gaze off mine and up to the stars, like remembering all this is hard. I rub his leg to offer comfort and let him know that I'm listening, and I care.

My brows furrow. "Why, what happened?" I ask.

"She fucked me over. She cheated on me with my best friend, Liam. It went on for years behind my back. So, since I ended it just over a year ago, I feel it's easier to not get attached to anyone. That way I don't have to worry about trusting and getting hurt again. It's even hard to trust new friends. I stick to a really small circle of people and my family."

I gasp and cover my mouth with my palm at his confession. "That's awful. I'm sorry. That's so shitty of Amanda and Liam. I'm gathering you aren't friends with him anymore?" I softly question, watching him.

He is still looking away when he draws up one leg and presses his hand against his cheek.

I can feel his deep inhale through my back. "Fuck no. I couldn't be more hurt if he ran me over with his car... but the real kicker here is she screwed around on him too, so karma really is a bitch." He smiles wickedly as he stares down at me and then pecks my lips.

"Why did I see her with you at the nightclub and then again in your office?" I ask.

He sighs loudly, shaking his head. "She wants me back and is always begging me for forgiveness. But I don't want her at all. She doesn't get the hint no matter what I say or do. I just try to ignore her, hoping she will go away."

I nod against him and the tension in his body lets me know he is ready to move the conversation away from his ex. I want to know more, but I don't want to push him right now.

"Moving on from them. What about your family? Tell me about them." I have finished the wine and when he notices, he takes my glass to refill it.

"What movie would you like to watch?"

"I don't know. I'm happy talking for now, but maybe we could listen to some music or something."

"I can put some music on while we talk." Untangling himself from me, he gets up, and when the cool air hits my back, I wrap the blanket more tightly around me.

He puts the music on quietly, and he settles back behind me, wrapping me tight. He kisses my temple, and his breath tickles me when he leans to talk into my ear. "Where were we?" Goosebumps cover my skin at the sensation.

"What about your family? You were going to tell me about them."

He lies back more, settling me down with him. "Right, well, I am the oldest. I have a brother, Alexander, and a sister called Stephanie. Alex is a neurologist and Steph is a dermatologist, and my parents, Margaret and Paul, are both general practitioners at their own clinic."

My eyebrows rise in amazement. "You're kidding,"

"Talking of family, I do a small dinner at my parents' once a month. It's this Sunday. Since we've just established this isn't casual, I would love it if you would come with me."

My back stiffens and my body goes rigid, trying to process what he is asking. It all feels sudden, but I'm the one who said I don't want casual, so he is offering more than that. I'm starting to get a headache from the high and low emotions, and the wine.

"Before you answer, I just have one last bit of information to tell you. I don't know if you're aware of..." I attempt to lift my body up so I can turn around and look at him, but he won't let me. My heart rate picks back up as I wait for him to finish. "You know the guy you kissed at Luxe? That was Alex, my brother."

I jump up too quickly for him to reach out and grab me as I spin around to face him. *Fuck.*

"Mike." I reach out and touch his face. "I'm so sorry. I had no idea. I would never have done that if I'd known. I saw you talking to Amanda, and I was jealous, so I let him dance with me, then kiss me. But I pushed him away." Shaking my head, I continue. "God, I feel awful. What an idiot I was." I drop my chin, avoiding his eyes.

He puts his finger under my chin, lifting my face to his so my gaze is focused on his. "We didn't know each other then. And we weren't a couple. I just wanted to tell you because, obviously, Alex will be there at dinner, and I don't want it to be awkward for any of us. However, I am surprised you haven't seen him at work."

"I was so drunk that night, and I didn't feel anything toward him." I already want to forget this conversation. I rub my forehead, trying to figure out what to do next.

He leans forward and presses the most tender kiss to my lips. He tries to pull back, but I groan and grab his face, holding him in position with both of my hands. My earlier thoughts go out the window when my arousal hits.

I decide to distract us both from the past and climb up onto his lap, straddling him. I feel his dick growing hard with appreciation, which makes my sex achy with desire. I rub myself up and along and then down on him. We both groan at the sensations caused by the friction. I shove my hands through his hair and pull his head back slightly to gain better access to him, and when he opens his mouth with a groan, I take the opportunity to stick my tongue inside, kissing him deeper. His body responds in an instant and he places one hand on my face and the other on my back, guiding me. He takes control from me, and I eagerly follow his direction.

After a minute, he rolls me over and he is on top, kissing me deeply. My head is on the pillow and my body is on the rug. He pulls away from the kiss and I whimper at the loss of his lips. My body is blazing and searching for relief. He pushes the sweater up and laps at my nipple before moving to the other one to show it the same attention.

I am writhing in desire underneath him. "Please," I'm begging now, and I don't care how pathetic I sound. I want him so badly. He has wound me up so tightly.

He hovers over me and kisses my neck. I feel him smile, enjoying the needy pain I'm in. He pecks my lips, whispering, "Soon."

"Unfair." I sulk, and his chest vibrates against me when he chuckles.

He doesn't quicken his pace. If anything, he drags it out even more, which is infuriating.

"You're so fucking beautiful Alice," he grunts as he removes my pants, leaving my panties on, even though they are soaked through.

"You're so ready for me. So, fucking wet. God, do you know how much I want you right now?"

I close my eyes, lying there unable to answer him, and wait for him to remove my panties, when a hard bite on my clit through the material makes me scream. "Ahhh."

"The smell of you is so fucking intoxicating," he says in a low voice that causes me to shudder. I'm so close to coming just from that. My eyes spring open and I look down to see Mike staring up at me. His eyes are so dark and intense it sends a shiver down my spine. "I'm so hard right now. I can't wait to have you."

He moves forward and I watch him, unable to tear my eyes away from him. He leans into my sex, and I feel his nose brush my clit through my panties as he slowly inhales. "Fucking delicious."

I'd normally feel so uncomfortable with that, but Mike makes me feel alive and sexy. He does what he wants, and I watch from under heavily hooded eyes. Goosebumps erupt all over my skin but not from the cold. It's from anticipation as to what Mike will do next.

He moves up to my hips and uses his teeth to tug down my underwear until they're all the way off.

He then leans back and uses his fingers to spread my lips wide and licks. Hearing him groan and moan while licking me sends my body into a state of near pain. Searching for release, I try to grind my sex on his face, but Mike pulls back.

"Not yet baby," he rasps.

I whimper and moan at the loss, but he doesn't leave me waiting long.

The next thing I feel are his fingers entering me and I scream. "Ahhh."

I'm so close to coming now.

I ride his fingers until he stops and pulls back. As I slowly open my eyes, I see him push his pants down and he frees his huge cock. Wrapping his hand around it, he guides it to my opening and enters me in one motion, stilling when he has filled me to the brim. "You feel so good," he says hoarsely.

"Mike," I whimper.

He leaves me feeling full and stretched, and because of his size it's bordering on painful. Even after a few moments when I thought by now, I would have adjusted to his size, it still aches. He waits until my walls relax and then starts to move, his pace torturously slow.

"Mike..." I plead again. "Harder please."

"I'm not going to last if you keep begging like that," he grunts.

I wrap my legs around his waist to push my heels into his back. It doesn't encourage him to move any faster, and instead he continues at this torturous pace. He leans forward to kiss me, and as he speeds up, I feel myself climbing higher. "Yes!" I choke in a ragged breath.

My eyes are shut tight and when the words, "That's it baby. Come now," leave his lips, I instantly unravel and come hard, my body shaking violently, sending him over the edge with me. He collapses next to me, and we both lie there panting heavily and trying to catch our breath.

Once my breathing has returned to normal, I lean up on my elbow and draping my other hand across his stomach, I stare at him. "Thank you, I have always wanted to have sex under the stars."

He lifts his head up and smiling, he pecks my lips. "Are you ready for your movie now?" he asks.

I laugh. "Mmm, yes, please."

He turns off the music and presses play on the movie and comes back to sit with me, positioning himself so he can cuddle me from behind. He doesn't say a word, just holds me throughout the whole movie. Nobody has ever held me like this before.

When the movie is over, I turn in his arms and peer up at him. "I think I should go. It's getting late, Mike."

"Stay here tonight?" he suggests.

"I don't think so, Mike. It's all so much so fast. Even meeting your parents so soon, it's a lot to take in." I sigh.

"We met months ago. It's what I want and how I feel that's important, not the society norm. I don't see my family all that often. It's a casual dinner and I don't want to hide you," he replies.

"I don't know." I bite my lip, the alcohol and tiredness fogging my thoughts.

He smirks down at me and brushes his lips on mine, leaving the softest of kisses on me, in between murmurs. "Is that a 'yes'? Say you will stay and also come tomorrow, please."

"What if they don't like me?" I ask.

His brow lifts. "Is that what you're worried about?"

I nod back without a word.

He stares into my eyes. "They will love you."

His lips recapture mine, way more demanding this time. I pull back and whisper across his lips. "I'll stay...but I can't go to family dinner. It's too soon. Next month, sure."

CHAPTER 17

ALICE

A MONTH LATER

I am getting ready to head to Mike's family dinner and have thrown all my clothes over the bed. I keep holding different outfits up against me in front of the mirror to see if they will work, but I can't decide. I plonk myself on the bed, confused and upset. *What should I wear to impress his parents?*

I have never met a guy's parents before, so I pace my room, scanning all my clothes. *I hate that I can't afford anything nice. I should cancel. I'm going to feel so out of place.* They all have money and are doctors, and then there will be me, dressed in my local discount outfit, and just an intern nurse. I pick up my phone from my bedside table, scroll to find his number, and hit dial.

He answers on the first ring. "Hey, babe, what are you doing?" His voice is sexy and sultry, *and ugh.* I crumble at the sound and just want to go back into his arms.

"I don't know what to wear tonight. Do I really have to go? I don't want to." I know I sound whiny, but I want to make a good impression, and I don't think I can.

"You will look amazing in anything. It's just a casual dinner, so don't dress up. It's nothing exciting."

I huff. "Trust you to say that. You're not the one meeting my family."

He laughs at me. "Babe, just pick something to wear and wear it. You would look hot in a brown paper bag. I can't wait to peel whatever you put on, off you later," he growls, his tone getting deeper.

"Oh, really? Well, how about we just skip the dinner and go straight to that?" I'm already feeling better. He knows just what to say to get my mind to relax.

"Yes, really, now find something to wear and I will pick you up soon. And you're not getting out of it."

"Fine, okay. I'll see you soon," I huff. Hanging up, I toss my phone down on my bed. I look around and decide on a pair of jeans, because I can dress them up with a nice top.

Tahlia pops her head in. "Someone needs a hand. It looks like a bomb went off in here." She gestures at the mess all over the room.

"Yes, please. I have only chosen these jeans, but now I need to decide on shoes and a top."

Tahlia walks into my room and sifts through my things, picking up different tops, and then finally says, "Here, pair this singlet and this blazer with the jeans, and then some wedges. I think you will look classic and have the perfect 'meet the family outfit.'"

"You're a lifesaver."

"I'll be in the kitchen. Come find me when you have it all on." She walks back out of my room.

I get dressed and look in the mirror, assessing my outfit. It looks good, but it's just missing a belt. I pop a belt on and check in the mirror again. I smile at my reflection. *I love it.* I feel sexy and classy, but also casual. I wander out and into the kitchen, and when Tahlia turns around, she smiles widely.

"See? Perfect! In another life, I'll be a stylist."

"You should, you're so good. Now I'll go do my hair and put a little bit of makeup on. I want to appear older. I don't want his mom to know how young I really am."

"You're overthinking it. Age doesn't matter anymore. You can't help who you like or love." She winks knowingly.

Oh God, did she just say that? I haven't said anything to him yet about loving him. *How can she pick it up so easily? Does that mean he knows too? And how does he feel?* I shake my head because I don't have time to think about the answers to these questions. I finish blow-drying my hair, and when I turn off the hair dryer, I know Mike's here because I can hear his smooth, deep voice.

I grab my purse from my bed before heading out to the kitchen. My palms are starting to sweat, and my pulse is rapidly beating inside my chest. I'm giddy seeing him again, but I need to calm down. Taking a deep breath, I walk out to meet him.

I reach the living room where Mike is reclined in the gray L-shaped couch, watching the television. "Hi," I say.

His head snaps up to face me and he rakes his eyes down my body. "I don't know what you were so worried about. You're perfect."

I feel the heat in my chest rise to my cheeks. "You'd say that no matter what I'm wearing." I roll my eyes.

I can see Tahlia smiling in the background. *Great, I have an audience.* I peer down at my toes, embarrassment creeping over me.

"But you are. I'm very lucky." I hear his footsteps as he walks over to me. He lifts my chin up with his finger so his eyes can stare into mine. When he kisses my lips, it lasts a bit longer than a peck but is not long enough to be a proper kiss either. I sigh.

He frowns. "Don't you want to pack a bag?"

"I have work tomorrow, remember?"

His hands drop to my shoulders, and he starts rubbing them. "So?" he questions. "You can stay the night and I will drive us both to work."

"I don't know if that's a great idea. I need to actually sleep before work." I feel warmth spreading over me as I admit this.

"And that's my cue to leave. See you, lovebirds. Have a good night." Tahlia heads off to her room, leaving us alone.

"Pack a bag." The sultry, sexy voice I can't seem to refuse is back. He slides his hands from my shoulders onto my hips.

I sigh. "I'll be right back."

I walk into my room and grab a bag and begin to pack. I zip up my bag and carry it out.

Mike takes the bag from me and asks, "Got everything?" I nod. "Let's go."

He walks me out, his hand firmly on my lower back, sending chills down my spine. *When will the fireworks in my body stop?* They only seem to be getting worse.

On the drive over, I feel tension in the back of my eyes. I have given myself a headache with the overthinking. *I'm hoping they'll like me.* Mike is holding my hand in the car and I stare down at our entwined fingers, lost in thought. Mike is so different from the person I believed he was. He is so thoughtful and caring. There is no sign of the egotistical player that I heard he was and also assumed about him. Yes, he is successful, but he works hard for what he has and that shouldn't be frowned upon. He's allowed to be proud of his accomplishments.

We arrive at the edge of a gated area and wait to be buzzed in. Mike drives through the set of gates, following a long driveway up to his parents' house. It's a white, two-story building, surrounded by a beautiful garden, with stunning flowers everywhere. *Seriously, does anyone in this family have a shit house?* I'm now completely mortified he came to the rental I live in. I'm sure he must have felt like he was visiting a third-world country, not his girlfriend's house. *I just want to curl up and die, right now.*

"You have been quiet for a while, babe. Are you okay?" he questions, leaning over with concern etched on his face.

In my head I count to ten to calm my heart rate down.

"Yeah, I guess. I'm just really nervous. I'm probably very different to the kind of woman they would expect you to be with."

He frowns. "I don't care what they say. It's what I want and feel that matters."

While I appreciate the response, it hasn't eased my thoughts. *Where is the 'they will love you' line? Yep, I'm officially dead.*

"Come on, let's get this show on the road, so I can take you back home and have my way with you." His eyes are shimmering with promise, but my heart rate is peaking, and I have a slight sweat beginning to form on my back.

I laugh, trying to sound like I'm not every bit as nervous as I really feel. "Keep it in your pants, hot Doc."

I start unbuckling my seat belt before opening the door. He races around to help me out of his sports car. Marty is a pain to get in and out of, no matter how expensive or nice he looks.

We walk up to the house holding hands, and though I'm sure he can also feel mine starting to get clammy, he doesn't say anything. I'm one step behind him, trying to use him to shield myself.

Before he can turn the handle, the door flies open and his parents are standing there, beaming at us both. "Good evening, and welcome, Alice."

"Hello, um, thanks for having me." I smile up at them, thankful my voice doesn't wobble.

Mike pulls me into the house, and I shake my hands with his parents, who introduce themselves even though Mike told me their names already.

"My name is Paul, and this is my wife, Margaret. Please come inside. We have heard so much about you."

I squeeze Mike's hand. I hear him chuckle.

Paul and Margaret look to be in their late sixties, slim, and both have short gray hair, but Margaret's is just above her shoulders.

Mike kisses his mom on her cheek and shakes his dad's hand. "Hi, Mom. Hi, Dad."

We follow Paul and Margaret through the entryway and farther into the house. The color scheme and décor are light and breezy, with wooden timber floors, and all their cabinetry is white and has glossy finishes. I glance around, wondering if this is the house Mike and his family grew up in. It seems so cold, and everything looks so new that it doesn't have the usual homey feeling.

We stand in the kitchen and Mike speaks. "Are we the first ones here?"

"Yeah, you are, Steph and Alex should be here any minute, though."

As if right on cue, I hear the door open and then close with a heavy bang. Alex appears, wearing a shit-eating grin. I feel Mike stand a little taller next to me. My breathing starts to quicken, so I once again count to ten to calm down.

"Hey, Mom." Alex walks straight over to give his mom a cuddle and kiss, and then he walks to his dad, shaking his hand before giving him a loving slap on the back.

I smile at their exchange. It reminds me of my own dad and how I would love to have one of his hugs right now.

I can clearly see that Alex has a different relationship with his parents than Mike does. Mike seems to have a wall up and I'm slightly surprised by that because Mike hasn't mentioned he has any issues with his parents. *I'll have to ask him about it later.* Alex wanders over to Mike and me. I stiffen and feel my chest tighten, suddenly feeling awkward.

Alex kisses me on my cheek. "Hey, Alice."

"Hi, Alex," I squeak.

He then shakes Mike's hand, "Hey, bro."

He's acting like nothing happened between us, and I can sense how uncomfortable Mike is. The air around us is thick with tension.

Mike breaks it the moment he answers his brother. "Hi, Alex."

Margaret steps in and asks everyone what they would like to drink.

"A beer would be great," Alex says.

"I'll have the same. Babe, do you want anything?" Mike asks, glancing at me.

I feel like I want to drink a bottle of wine, but I figure that would be inappropriate.

"Just a glass of water for now, please. Do you want a hand, Margaret?" I offer.

She shakes her head. "Oh no, dear, you relax. You're our guest tonight." Smiling at me, she then strolls off to get the boys their beers and a glass of water for me.

I hear the opening and closing of cupboards and then the fridge. She sounds so busy in the kitchen while we are all talking, and I feel bad she won't let me help.

"Okay, come outside and have some nibbles while we wait for Steph and Chris—they shouldn't be too much longer," she orders.

Mike leads me outside by my hand, and as we walk out the door, he leans in toward me. His breath touches my ear, and he whispers softly so no one else can hear, "Are you okay?"

He's so sweet. He can probably tell that I'm still feeling on edge about Alex being here.

Nodding, I squeeze his hand to confirm, and softly whisper, "Yes."

When we step outside there is an outdoor table holding a spectacular platter piled high with a range of deli meats, fruit, sweets, crackers, and dips. They are all elegantly laid out in a seamless pattern.

"Wow, Margaret, did you do all this?" I point to the platter. Stepping over to the table, I grab a plate and start selecting a mixture of different things to eat—it all looks so good and delicious.

"Yes, dear. Now that I'm retired, I have plenty of time to work on things I love, like cooking. I took a semester at college studying cooking." She grabs herself a plate and fills it up.

I move back to stand next to Mike but continue talking to her. "That's impressive. So, how did you meet Paul?" Mike stiffens beside me, and I frown.

"We met in college when we were studying for our MDs." She peeks over at Paul, who smiles and nods at her. "I retired last year, but Paul still works a few days a week."

"Do you miss being a GP, Margaret? Or are you happy you retired?"

I wonder how I would feel about giving up the career I love, and thinking about it, I'm sure it would be so hard to do. I have loved every minute—that might be partly due to Mike—I'm excited to go to work every day, and I love every second I am doing it. The adrenaline, the fast pace, and knowing I'm going to be helping people is such an honor.

"I did. At the start it was extremely hard to go from working to retiring suddenly. It was an extremely hard adjustment. I was moping about it at first, if I'm honest. I was wondering how I was going to fill my days, but then I started joining different classes and clubs. Then my feelings started to change and keeping my brain active and myself busy has worked wonders. I have tried lots of different hobbies, but now I'm in a weekly book club, a golf club, and I'm about to start a course in baking."

My smile grows at her confession. "That's great, and if it makes you happy, then that's wonderful. I don't know how I would feel if I had to give up nursing right now." Talking about it brings a slicing pain through my chest.

A thoughtful smile curves her mouth. "Oh, yes. Mike mentioned you're in your graduate year of nursing at the same hospital. Are you enjoying it?"

I laugh and glance at Mike, who is watching me while he eats some food. *How can he eat that amount of food and still have no body fat under those clothes? It's so unfair.* Facing Margaret, I feel myself flush, embarrassed I was just thinking of her son in that way.

"Yes, I am. It's been exciting. It's a wonderful hospital. Did you know I work with Mike?" I ask.

I can feel his arm snake around my back. He holds me against him by my waist. He really does enjoy talking about this.

Margaret smiles up at Mike and then back at me, her eyes bright with pleasure. "No, I didn't, but I'm surprised Mike agreed to have a nurse to teach."

Mike and I crack up laughing, knowing very well he didn't want me there, but had no choice. We keep that between us.

Behind us, I can hear someone calling, "Hello? Hello, where are you guys?"

Margaret excuses herself and I see a woman with brown hair coming into view with a taller blond male behind her, and I guess this must be Steph. She is greeted by her mom before coming and greeting all of us. She walks out the door, and she is breathtaking, with sky-blue eyes that are framed by big, black lashes. I glance at her stomach to the obvious bump. *Mike didn't mention she was pregnant.*

She heads toward Mike and me, wearing the biggest grin. She wraps her dainty arms around Mike, giving him a hug. "I haven't seen you for weeks, busy boy. I've missed you."

She slips back out of the embrace, her hands cradling the bump, and he smiles brightly back at her. I can see that there's a strong bond between them, causing my own lips to turn up into an easy smile.

"Yes, Steph, it's been a while," he says softly, chuckling at her. I warm at their loving exchange.

She playfully hits his arm. "Too busy to call your sister, I get it." She turns her attention to me. My eyes widen when she leans over to hug me. "And you must be Alice." I reach my hand up and stroke her upper back and she begins to laugh, rubbing her bump as she pulls back. "Sorry about that. I forget it's in the way sometimes."

I grimace and elbow Mike in the ribs. "Mike never mentioned you were expecting. Congratulations. How far along are you?"

He throws his hand over the spot where I elbowed him, wincing. I roll my eyes at his playful dramatics. "Ouch, and I didn't mean to forget, sorry."

I purse my lips at the thought of my own family before responding. "So, you should be."

Steph beams and her eyes watch our exchange with a grin. "I'm twenty-eight weeks along."

The blond guy she arrived with comes up and holds out his hand. "My name is Chris. I'm Steph's husband. It's lovely to meet you."

I smile and put my hand in his for a quick shake and then take it away. "Congratulations, Chris, not long left. I didn't see any other children, so am I right in guessing this one is your first?" I ask.

"Yes, definitely the first, maybe even the last." She rubs her belly, chuckling.

"You will change your mind," Margaret says from behind Steph. "You forget about the bad parts of being pregnant, and then you will have more. The food is ready, so can we all bring our drinks and head inside to the dining room? Steph, I'll grab you a glass of water. You go sit down."

Steph winks at me, then leans into my ear and whispers, "The best part of being pregnant is how your family and husband do everything for you."

I laugh, shaking my head. "Thanks for the tip, I guess?"

I go to step inside, but Mike captures my hand, spins me around to face him, and kisses me. I gasp into his mouth and then melt into his arms as I return the sweet kiss.

He pulls his lips away an inch. My eyes flutter open and I stare straight into his blue eyes. "Are you feeling better now you have met them all? Can I get you a proper drink now?" he asks, smirking.

I chuckle. "Yes, much better, thank you." I smack his chest and I have this urge to kiss him again, so I tug on his top, drawing him closer to me, and close the distance between our lips.

I hear a deep groan from behind me. "Get a room," I hear Alex say, poking fun at us as he heads inside.

Mike removes his lips from mine with a hiss and just shakes his head. "Come on, let's get you some wine and have dinner. The quicker we eat here, the quicker I can eat you for dessert."

My mouth falls open with a gasp, and I playfully punch him in the arm. "Shhh, I'm meeting your family. Don't be dirty here. It's gross," I warn before turning on my heel and moving inside.

"Babe, no one can hear. Settle down." He pinches my bum to get me to hurry inside, and I squeal.

"Stop it and behave!" I scold, but I'm smirking as I say it, because I actually love it when Mike has his hands on me.

Mike raises his hands up in surrender like he didn't do anything wrong.

We get our wine and walk into the dining room to join everyone else. The dining table is long, and Paul is sitting at one end, while Margaret is at the other. Mike guides me to sit down next to Margaret. I frown but take the seat he offers. I have spoken with Margaret a lot and have hardly said more than two words to his dad. It almost seems like he doesn't want to talk to his dad.

Dinner is laid out all down the middle of the large table.

"Alice, dear, Mike didn't say if you are allergic to anything, or if you have any special dietary requirements, so I hope you don't mind what I have cooked for dinner."

"No, no allergies. I definitely don't have a special diet, and I can't wait to taste everything," I reply.

She bows her head and places a palm to her heart. "So different from Amanda," she mumbles under her breath.

CHAPTER 18

MIKE

I GLARE AT MOM from across the table. *Shut up, please.* I'm willing her to glance at me so I can mime for her to zip it because I don't want a discussion about exes at dinner. I want Alice to enjoy herself, not hear about my ex.

But of course, Mom is too busy fussing with the food on the table, so she continues. "She was always on a different diet every time she came for dinner. She wouldn't just eat what I cooked. She was way too high-maintenance." She shakes her head.

I cannot believe it. Everyone is quiet until Alex starts talking to my dad, and I say quietly, "Mom, please, not now." I can't help the stern tone that comes out. I don't like talking to Mom like that, but she needs to drop this topic.

"Sorry." She winces, retaking her seat once she finishes grabbing her food.

Just as I sink into my seat and start eating, Steph decides to drop a bomb. "So, Alice, would you be interested in having children in the next few years? Obviously, you know Mike is thirty-eight, so he needs to settle down soon." *Fuck.* She winks at me, but I glare back, clenching my jaw.

I lean forward and say in a hushed voice, "Enough, Steph. I know you're coming from a kind place, but to be honest, it's none of your business," I snap.

Alice grabs my arm, pulling me back so she can see Steph. "Mike, it's fine, seriously."

She's smiling warmly at me, trying to calm me down, but my heart is racing a million miles a minute. *How can she be okay with answering these questions?* She's only just met them, and they are already asking very forward and personal questions. Hell, *I* haven't even asked her about marriage or kids.

"To answer your question, Steph, I haven't thought much about it. But thinking about it right now, my answer is no. Probably not in the next ten years," Alice responds confidently.

I'd stopped listening until then. I hear cutlery hitting the plate with a clatter. *Excuse me, what did I just hear her say?* I feel like I've been kicked in the stomach. *Ten years.* I must not have heard correctly. How could she not want kids in the next ten years? I know she's a lot younger than I am, but I'll be forty-eight by then. I can provide for her. I have a good job, a car, a house, money, and stability. She would have a comfortable life, and hell, so would our kids. *But it's not fair to her to have her put her dreams aside so maybe she would be better suited to someone her age.*

Fuck, I just want to get out of here and go home. I'm shattered. How did I read her so wrong? I realize it was my cutlery that has been dropped, so I pick them up and continue to eat. I'm not angry, I'm gutted. I know we've not been together for very long, but I thought Alice could possibly be my future. But then again, I once thought the same thing about Amanda.

We finish the dinner and help pack up.

I turn to Alice, waiting for her to finish her conversation with Mom before I ask, "Are you ready to head off, Alice? We have work tomorrow and I'm a little tired."

We say our goodbyes to everyone and walk back to the car. My mind has been trying to figure out how to talk to her about this, and I keep coming up empty.

CHAPTER 19

ALICE

SOMETHING IS OFF WITH Mike.

Walking to the car, hand in hand, I ask, "You seem awfully quiet. Are you okay?"

He opens my door for me to get inside and I stare up into his eyes as he answers, "Yes, I'm good, just a little tired."

I see a different emotion in his eyes, one I haven't seen before. I don't understand it, and my eyebrows furrow in thought. He closes my door, walks around the front of the car, then jumps into the driver's side and drives off.

When we arrive at his house, I follow him as he marches straight upstairs to his room, carrying my overnight bag in his hand. He dumps the bag on the bed and quickly turns to me, grabbing my head roughly between his two hands and bringing me to his lips. Passionately, he tugs my lip, nipping it hard. Something is definitely off with him, but I'm going to turn it around and make him forget whatever is bothering him.

I kiss him back hard, sucking on his tongue and pushing him away slightly so I can remove the shirt he is wearing. *My God, he is magnificent.* I kiss his pecs and run my hands softly over his torso, feeling his soft chest hair beneath my fingers.

Feeling daring, I sink to my knees in front of him and gaze directly into his eyes. I watch as they widen.

"Babe, what are you doing?" he asks.

I grin up at him when I hear my nickname come from his lips. "I want to taste you." I lick my lips, looking directly up at him.

"Fuck," he grunts, closing his eyes. "You're trying to kill me." He thrusts his hand through his hair.

I smirk and return to what I intend to do. I unbutton his pants and tug the zipper down, before removing his pants and briefs altogether, freeing his cock. I can't show my nerves. I want to enjoy this as much as I hope he will, and I'm sure he will make me stop if he finds out I haven't done this before, insisting on me taking small steps. I want him to give me everything.

He steps out of his clothes and kicks them to the side. He strokes my hair and face, while staring at me with such desire that it sends a shiver running all over my body. He is magnificent and far too good for me. I've no idea what he sees in me.

I need to stop thinking.

I grab his cock at the base and lick the head before putting it slightly in my mouth. Sucking the tip gently, I then pull it out and lick him slowly from the head to the base, and back up to the tip. Noticing a bit of precum coating his skin, I lick it off and moan. Glancing up, I see Mike's eyes burning with fire. Wrapping my hair around his fists, he closes his eyes and pushes into my mouth in such a hard thrust I almost choke. I barely manage to catch my breath, but I concentrate on what I'm doing and do my best to ignore the reflex telling me to gag.

He groans, "Fuck, babe." I suck and move him in and out, while sliding my hand up and down in rhythm with my mouth. "You're so good," he chokes out.

This is the encouragement I need to be daring, so I grab his balls and caress them between my fingers. I'm so turned on right now, but I can't think about myself, no matter how aroused I am or how badly I want to put my fingers in my panties and bring myself to climax. I know I'm soaked through.

"I'm going to come in your mouth if you don't stop now," he warns.

I smile around him and move faster until I feel his balls tighten and his hands grip my hair more firmly while he fucks my face until I can taste his salty cum on my tongue and feel it shooting down my throat. When his cock stops pulsing, I gently remove my mouth and look up at him, smirking. *How is he still hard?* His cheeks are flushed, and a light sheen of sweat is covering his body. He removes both of his hands from my hair and helps me up. Welcoming the assistance, I struggle to stand on numb and trembling legs, before I ask nervously, "Was that okay?"

"It was more than okay. Fuck, it was amazing. Now, strip naked and get on all fours on my bed in the next two minutes because I'm going to fuck you so hard."

I giggle and strip as quickly as possible and head over to the bed. My heart is beating faster in my chest and I'm sure I felt my arousal trickle down my thigh. He is insane, and he has no idea how incredible he is. I tremble with anticipation when he stalks over to me.

"Good girl," he growls from behind me.

I feel him at my entrance, and I can't wait, so I edge back. In one thrust, he fills me to the max and I scream. I'm so full, and though there is pain, it quickly turns to pleasure as soon as my walls adjust to his size. Then he starts drawing in and out painfully slow.

"Faster," I moan.

He doesn't change his rhythm, so I try to move with him. This only makes him chuckle, and grabbing hold of my hips, he says, "Trust me to make you feel good."

I nod and try to take slow breaths and just push through the building pleasure. I'm shaking and I can't take much more of this. I don't know if I can hold myself back much longer. The build-up is agonizing, but finally he starts pumping into me faster and harder, and already I'm so close.

"Don't stop, pleeease!" He reaches around to touch my clit and I come so hard I feel dizzy.

"You feel incredible," he grunts behind me.

My body quivers as I come down from my orgasm.

"Fuck. Alice," he rasps out as he reaches his own climax deep inside of me. Afterwards, I want to flop onto the bed but he catches me. Holding me and pulling me flush against him while I regain my energy.

When he catches his breath, he gentle lowers me to the bed and kisses my cheek. "Babe, we better get to bed. We have to be up early in the morning." He steps away from me, and walks off to the bathroom. I hear the water from the shower hitting the tiles and I slowly get up, grabbing my bag to find my pajamas. I walk in only to find him already stepping out.

"Don't want to join me?" I question.

Smirking at me while he dries himself with a towel, he responds, "Next time. Right now, I'm beat and I'm ready to pass out."

"Okay, I won't be long."

I step under the hot spray. *This really is the best shower.* I quickly shower, dry off, and climb into his bed. He is facing away from me... *So strange.* I really don't get it. If he is upset with me, I don't understand why. Shaking off my thoughts, I settle in, and it's so comfortable lying next to him that I drift off in minutes.

In the morning I wake to Mike's arm draped over me, and he's cuddling me from behind. I'm so warm and comfortable that when I hear the alarm go off, I groan. *Not fair.* He stirs and rolls over, turning off the alarm before returning to his previous position.

"Good morning," he says huskily in his sleepy voice. I smile, enjoying the warmth of his body and how cozy I feel.

"We better get moving. Otherwise, we will be late for work." He rolls me so I'm on my back and I'm gazing up at him, and then he kisses me before slipping out of bed and walking to the bathroom. I lie there for another minute before getting up and grabbing my bag to find my work clothes.

Once Mike is done in the bathroom, he makes his way down the stairs, calling out as he goes, "I'll start breakfast!"

"Okay," I yell as I walk into the bathroom.

Once I'm ready, I go downstairs to join him in the kitchen. Walking in, I see him cooking at the stove. *Why is it that every time I see him in a suit, I just want to peel it off him?* He is a handsome sight in his navy suit and light-blue shirt, and I would love nothing more than to strip him and have a repeat of last night, but we have no time for that this morning.

"Can I help you?" I ask.

"No, I'm almost done here, and then I will make us coffee." He continues to stir the eggs on the stove.

"I'm happy to learn how to use the coffee machine if you want to teach me when you're done with the food." I feel a flutter in my stomach, the same sickly feeling I had last night. Something is still off with Mike.

"Sure." He dishes up eggs, bacon, and toast, and it smells and looks amazing. *I can't believe he cooked.*

"You didn't have to go to all this trouble. Really, I would have been happy with cereal or buttered toast," I say slowly.

He quickly pecks my lips. "I don't mind. I told you, I love cooking. Now, let me show you how to work the machine."

He shows me how to make coffee on his huge stainless-steel machine, and then we sit down next to each other on the stools and eat our breakfast. *Mmm, this food is cooked to perfection.* We sit in silence as we eat, which is a bit strange for us, but I try not to overthink it. Once we finish, we pop the dishes in his dishwasher—it feels very domesticated doing chores with him.

"Are you ready to go, Alice?" he questions. He scoops up his car keys and wallet.

"Yes, I'll just grab my bag."

We hold hands in the car, and I momentarily forget Mike's strange mood. Once we arrive, he leans over and kisses me. This kiss is hungry, and it feels almost like he is savoring it, trying to memorize it, and I can't shake this weird feeling I keep getting. *Is it because I slept with him? Now that he has conquered me, will I just be another nurse he fucks and leaves?* I try to shake it off, but it's so hard when he keeps giving me such mixed signals. Once we break apart, I smile at him and he smiles back before giving me another soft peck.

"Let's go," he says, and then he exits the car, making his way around it to open my door. Always, such a gentleman.

We enter the elevator and Mike goes rigid next to me... *Why is he acting so strange?*

CHAPTER 20

MIKE

I HAD ANOTHER AMAZING night with Alice, a blow job for the record book, and sex that was better than the first few times we did it, even though I didn't think that was possible. Then to wake up spooning her—it felt so right. It's a shame we aren't fit for each other. I know I won't get her to change her mind on kids and settling down, and it's not fair to her for me to try. I can't even believe I really want this, but Steph is right. My age has a time limit and I do want to be a father one day, but I can't trap her, so I must let her go... even if it crushes me to watch her move on with another man.

I know I have been quiet last night and this morning, and Alice has noticed my behavior, but I can't help it with the thoughts that are running through my head. *This situation is fucked.*

When I don't think my day can get any worse, Amanda is standing there, staring between Alice and me and smiling knowingly. *Fuck. Why does she have to be here?* The elevator feels like it's moving awfully slow today, but when people exit on the ground floor, I almost run out. I will need another coffee to help me survive the day.

"Hey, Mike. Wait up!" Amanda calls. *Fuuuck!*

I clench my jaw and I turn around to face her. "Yes?" I spit.

Alice is standing outside the elevator, watching me with a confused expression. I nod in the direction of upstairs. She nods her understanding, leaning over to press the button to go up. She doesn't need to see my ex and me talking right now when we already have issues to discuss. I watch the doors close before I drop my gaze to Amanda.

"What do you want?" I ask, and Amanda smirks, which only angers me further.

"Who's that?" She jerks her head in the direction of the elevator.

"None of your business. My life is no longer your concern." I'm fuming; my body is shaking, and my hands are balled into fists.

"I need to talk to you." *Her continued smirking is really pissing me off.*

The muscles in my jaw quiver and I snap. "You know what? Fuck off, Amanda. I don't have time for your shit." I storm off, forgetting about the coffee, and I take the stairs leading to my floor. I want to burn off some frustration. *Women are fucked.* It's so much easier when feelings aren't involved, and I can just sleep around for fun.

I march into my office, and slamming my door behind me, I practically throw myself into my chair, ready to begin work, which will be a welcome distraction. Alice is on the ward today, so when a knock comes, I growl in frustration. *I swear it had better not be Amanda.*

I snap, "What?" I'm sitting at my desk turning my computer on, and when I glance up and notice that it's Kate, I immediately feel guilty. "Sorry, I'm having a really shitty day." I grimace.

Smiling kindly at me, she walks toward me, holding out papers for me. "That's okay, Dr. Taylor. Here, this is the document you need to fill in about Alice."

I take the papers from her outstretched hands. "Thanks."

Her eyebrows rise a fraction. "Do you need anything? Coffee or water? You look awfully pale today."

Kate has been working with me for ten years, so she is able to tell when something is off and throwing me into a mood.

A deep sigh leaves my lips. "No, thanks. I just have a lot on my mind. I should just get started for the day."

"Let me know if you change your mind." She turns on her heel and strides out of my office, closing the door softly behind her.

I log in and take a breath, leaning back in my chair to close my eyes for a second.

What do I want to do with my life in the next few years? Could I give up marriage and kids for Alice? I don't expect it right now, but maybe in a couple of years—a compromise.

My phone rings on my desk. I pick up the receiver to find that I'm being called to an emergency surgery. As I rush to get there, I hesitate. I should probably call Alice to witness the surgery, but I decide I need the space more right now. I know a part of our agreement was to keep work and our relationship separate, but I need some time to think.

Being in the surgery gives me the adrenaline rush of an emergency situation—I love and crave this feeling. I have such a strong sense of purpose and power in doing this, and that gives me a happiness I can't describe. Arriving to my office late, I realize I still have so much work to catch up on, but I am finding that the space is helping calm me down. I send off a text to Alice.

> **Mike:** *Alice, I have been in surgery with an emergency. I still have heaps to do. Do you think you could find a lift home? I don't want you waiting around all day for me to finish.*

> **Alice**: *I'm happy to wait.*

> **Mike:** *No babe. Go home and I'll call you later.*

CHAPTER 21

ALICE

I FINISH MY SHIFT on the ward and grab my bag from my locker. I grab my phone and see a text from Mike. I scrunch my face up. I haven't heard from him today, and I have no idea where he went, so when I open the text and read it, I sigh loudly at the message, but then I quickly get angry. Why didn't he offer to take me with him into the emergency surgery? He knows I'm here to learn and that I have studied well in order to prove myself. Why will he not allow me to follow when I have worked my ass off to get where I am?

I can't think about him right now and why he is doing this. I need to find a way home soon. I pick up my phone and scroll through my contacts until I find Maddison's name. I decide to walk down to the cafeteria and grab a coffee and stand to the side to wait while I text Maddison. I don't want to call in case she is out or studying.

Alice: *Hey, Mads, sorry to do this, but are you busy?*

Maddison: *No, what's up?*

Alice: *I just finished work and I need a lift home. Mike can't take me home today, change of plans.*

Maddison: *Sure, I'll come now.*

Alice: *Thanks, Mads.*

I grab my coffee and move back to stand to the side when a dark shadow appears over my phone. I wince, and when I peek up, I see that it's Mike's ex, Amanda. *What do you want?* I glare up into her eyes and roll them. I have no interest in her or what she has to say. I'm mad at Mike anyway, so I don't need her drama on top of it.

She clears her throat. "Hi there. It's Alice, right?"

I stare blankly at her, and then I shrug. "I guess."

I'm trying to be subtle about how uninterested I am about speaking with you. She doesn't seem to get the memo. Either that, or she doesn't care. I watch her closely as I put my phone in my bag and take a sip of my coffee, never breaking eye contact. I refuse to appear weak.

"I'm Amanda. Mike's ex." Her smile and voice are almost sickly sweet.

I have been staring for a while when I realize I haven't said a word. "Yes, I'm aware of that. How can I help you?" I reply boldly, hoping she doesn't realize how much she has rattled me.

"I just noticed he was with you this morning, looking very cozy together, and I wanted to warn you that he is going to leave you as soon as he gets what he wants—if he hasn't already," she says.

Now that it's just me and her, I'm able to get a good look at her. We are so different, polar opposites. She is so alluring—a real doll—while I'm average. I put on a front to make myself look tougher, wearing it like armor. Her looks make me feel insecure—and I hate it.

"He can't and won't commit to any woman, and no matter what you think you can offer, you're just wasting your time." She is talking to me like she is my friend, by pretending she is offering me some great advice, when all she is doing is showing me how desperate she is.

She can hardly talk. Not when she left him for his best friend. I think it speaks volume of how "nice" a person she is. The half hour I have left to wait for Maddison can't end quickly enough. I desperately want to get the fuck away from her and this hospital. *What a nightmare.*

I feel a soft muscular arm drape over my shoulders and a large hard male body moves to stand flush with my side. One of my arms is crossed into the bend of the other, holding my coffee and protecting myself. I instantly freeze, until I turn and see Alex standing beside me, stony-faced and staring at Amanda. I feel relieved knowing it's him, and I stand taller even as I soften slightly. His expression is hard, and he's vibrating with anger. Clearly Alex is not a fan of her either, but Amanda doesn't seem fazed by him in the slightest. It feels like there is ice in my blood.

"Amanda, what are you doing?" he barks.

"Nothing, Alex. I'm just talking to my friend, Alice, here." She flutters her eyelashes, saying it like we actually *are* friends. *Ugh.*

"Liar. Alice wouldn't be friends with you. You need to stay the fuck away from Mike and Alice. If I find you bothering either of them again, I will hunt you down and make your life hell. Trying to scare Alice won't bring you closer to Mike. He doesn't want you—get it through that thick skull. You fucked his best friend behind his back. *You* did that—not him. So, fuck right off and move on. Mike deserves to be happy, and you are the last person who could give him that."

"He is such a player, Alex! Come on! He will be so bored with Alice. Look at her. What can she offer?" she scoffs.

I bite my lip. I mentally count to ten, trying to calm my speeding heart rate down.

"You're just a nasty, spiteful bitch!" he shouts.

Amanda just throws her head back and laughs, a wicked throaty laugh that sends goosebumps rising all over me, and I decide I can't stand anymore of this.

I clear my throat, and yell, "Mike and I are none of your business!"

Without waiting for a reply, I turn and glance at Alex, who drops his arm from my shoulders. "Thanks, Alex."

He nods and his lip quirks up on one side before hugging me. I'm on the brink of crying so I step back out of the hug and walk off, standing tall with my head held high. I refuse to stay there for another second. I walk outside and suck in fresh cleansing breaths and look around for Maddison's car, sipping my now stone-cold coffee. *Fucking great.*

I throw the coffee in the bin and wait for the shock to wear off and for my body to stop shaking. My brain keeps rehashing her words over and over.

My eyes swell with tears, but I refuse to let them fall, because once I open the dam, I don't think I will be able to stop them. I refuse to do this at work in case anyone I know notices me. I have just had to deal with his crazy ex—once again! Alex was kind and supportive, but he's not the person I wanted or needed.

I needed the comfort of Mike's arms blanketing me, and him telling me I have nothing to worry about. Instead, he has been off and distant toward me without talking to me or telling me what's wrong. I spot Maddison's car and relief instantly floods through me. I take a deep breath, quickly walk up, open the passenger door, and jump in, collapsing into the seat.

"Thanks, Mads. Sorry to spring this on you." It feels like I'm talking with a really dry mouth, making me sound off.

"All good. So, are you going to tell me what happened?" Concern etches itself on her face when she gets a look at me.

"Oh my God, Maddy, where the fuck do I start?" My voice is shaky.

I close my eyes, giving myself a pep talk to not cry over him, telling myself he isn't worth the tears. I hit my head against the headrest, frustrated, before blinking my eyes open.

"It's okay. Just tell me everything right from the start. You know I've got you." She smiles and pulls out into the traffic and heads in the direction of home.

Her words set me off and I feel the hot tears spring to my eyes in a second. Then they fall and continue falling for what feels like a really long time. I cover my face with my hands and just cry into them until I have no tears left. I feel Maddy rubbing my thigh, trying to offer me comfort at the same time as driving.

As I cry, I can hear her soft angelic voice coo, "It's okay, I've got you. Let it all out and then tell me what's going on."

After another few minutes, I slowly stop shaking, and as the tears finally ease, I drop my hands from my face and wipe away the remaining droplets with my hands. I'm sure that my face is a snotty mess.

"Sorry, Mads. I have been holding that in for a while. Now, to fill you in. You know how I went to the family dinner last night?"

Her brows rise. "Yeeeah."

"That wasn't a problem. He has such a wonderful family. I got to meet his parents, his sister, Steph—who is pregnant—her husband, Chris, and his brother, Alex. Dinner was lovely. His mom cooked, and they were all really kind and welcoming—it was sweet, actually. Something weird that I did notice though, was that Mike and his dad seem to have some kind of tension between them." I frown.

"Really? I wonder why?"

"I don't know what's going on there, but they didn't talk to each other much and Mike avoided him as much as possible. It's super weird and I don't know if everyone knew something but me. They all seemed to love me, but near the end of dinner Mike was super quiet." I replay the night in my mind as I tell Maddison the story. "He wasn't rude, just... off. Then when we got to his house, he was quiet and distant. It was like he'd started pulling away from me. This probably sounds weird, but I just feel it."

Her brows crease. "Hmm, that does sound strange, and you can't recall any conversations at dinner that could have caused his mood to shift?" she questions as she tries to help me figure it out.

I think about it, but I really can't recall any odd topics or responses from Mike. The only odd gesture was between Mike and his dad, but that had nothing to do with Mike being off with me.

I shake my head. "No, Mads, it was such a nice dinner." I feel like I'm losing my mind over it. I keep thinking about it over and over in my head.

"And to continue, we get to his house and have the most amazing sex. I then shower and after I get out, I notice he is on his side of the bed, facing away from me."

"What?" Maddison gasps. "No cuddles or kisses? Just... nothing?"

"Uh-huh. I was so tired that I actually passed out pretty quickly, and when I woke up, he was spooning me." I smile at the memory.

"Aww," she coos at me, placing her hand over her heart.

I laugh. "It was nice, yes, but then he got up and was quiet again. Don't get me wrong, he wasn't rude, but he was different. You get me? Or am I totally confusing you now?"

"No, I'm following. Continue," she encourages.

"Today, I got a text from him saying he is staying back at work, something about an emergency surgery and paperwork, and can I grab a lift with someone because he doesn't want me waiting for him. I'm supposed to be going to these surgeries with him, so I don't know why he didn't ask me."

"Okay. The quiet is fine, some guys can be like that, but the fact he has been quiet and distant, and then just sends you a text to get a lift home with someone else. That's just fucking rude. Why didn't he come visit you on your floor or call you?" She is annoyed for me. I can see her jaw ticking. I'm relieved she understands. I don't feel quite so crazy for worrying about this.

"Oh, it gets better." I start laughing and she turns to look at me, raising her eyebrow.

"Oh, God, that doesn't sound good." She winces. "What happened? Come on, hit me with it."

"I decided to grab a coffee and wait in the café for you, when his ex-girlfriend, Amanda decided to come up to me and start warning me about Mike. She was saying some shit about how once he gets what he wants, he is going to leave me if he hasn't already, and that he can't commit to any woman."

"Whoa, no fucking way!" she blurts.

"Yeah, and she was even nice enough to tell me how much of a player he is, and how he will be bored with me 'because what can I offer?'" I wince because that comment cut deep.

Maddy hits the steering wheel. "What do you mean 'what can you offer?' Fuck, you are such a beautiful and intelligent person. He is so lucky to have you! I wish I'd been there to give her a piece of my mind."

"It's okay. Mike's brother, Alex, came up and defended me. He told her to fuck off."

I'm laughing, but in all seriousness, talking about it with Maddison brings the shakes back on. "This is why I didn't want a relationship. They always leave, or they aren't happy with just one woman." I start to get emotional again. My eyes don't have any tears left. Otherwise, I would be crying again.

"Don't give up. They aren't all like that."

Fuck guys. They always let me down and always leave me. And when I love them, they hurt me. The feelings that come over me hurt my heart, and it's a feeling I have had once before, and I never ever wanted to feel it again. I guess I should be happy I never told him I loved him. *I love him.*

Maddison pulls up the drive at home. "Take a shower. It will help you feel better. While you clean up, I will order some takeout and ice cream. We can relax and watch Netflix. Sound good?"

I'm not that hungry, but I don't want to sit alone thinking in bed, so I nod. "Yeah, thanks."

By the time I've showered and dried off, Tahlia is home, and dinner is here.

Maddy hands me a pizza box. "Come, let's sit, eat, and binge-watch *Friends*. By the way, while you were showering, I told T about what happened to save you from retelling it. I hope you don't mind."

I half smile up at her. "Thanks, I definitely don't mind."

Tahlia looks at me with sad eyes and says, "Boys suck."

I chuckle. "That's putting it nicely. Let's just enjoy our night, no more boy talk."

CHAPTER 22

MIKE

THE NEXT DAY, I'M in my office filling in a variety of patient-related paperwork. Alice has the day off, and I'm doing my best to distract myself. I don't want to stop to think about what I saw when I went downstairs to get a coffee yesterday...*Alice and Alex embracing*.

I have to finish all this paperwork that's sitting piled up in front of me and is also scattered all over my desk. Once this is done, I will go home and have a drink.

I really wanted to talk to Alice about each of our future desires, because it's been playing heavily on my mind. I worry we are on two different paths, but after seeing her and Alex yesterday, I won't bother. I'm doubtful that I could ever completely trust her.

I have a few pages left when I hear a knock on my office door. It swings open, and my head snaps up. My breath hitches in my throat. Standing there is Alex, wearing his usual smirk, and I instantly tense in my chair. He clicks the door shut and my jaw is tight as I watch him stroll on in as if nothing is wrong.

He drags the chair out that Alice normally sits in and collapses down, reclining back with a sigh and making himself comfortable.

"Hey, bro, you're still doing paperwork? You slacker." He chuckles.

My jaw ticks, and I glance at him with dark and assessing eyes. His smug smile is pissing me off. I don't answer him. Instead, I lower my gaze and return to my notes from this morning's surgery.

"How's your shift been today? Any interesting cases?"

"Actually, pretty shit," I mumble.

I peer up at him while my brain runs through the memory of this morning's surgery—another emergency, another car accident, and another death. I suck in sharply, thinking over the emotional roller coaster of the last twenty-four hours. Having him here is fucking with my head. I need space to calm down and think.

"What do you want, Alex? I'm busy," I ask impatiently, gesturing to the papers in between us. I just want him to spit it out and leave me alone.

He exhales a breath. "I know things are getting serious with Alice..." He pauses, waiting for me to reply.

"Yes?" My eyebrows crease, and my gaze meets his.

"I just wanted to mention something." I'm staring down my nose at Alex. His face has a conflicted expression which is sending my body temperature rising. *Mmm, I really don't like where this is going.* I cannot believe what I'm hearing.

"I know. I saw it with my own eyes," I snap before he can speak. I'm furious. I rise from my chair, blood surging to my ears, and I have no more words to say. I lean over the side of the desk, gripping the edges of it, adrenaline pumping my veins. I hear his steps, then he touches my shoulder. That sets me off, and without warning, I shove him.

"Jesus, Mike. What the fuck? He stumbles back with a frown.

"I don't trust you haven't done anything more with Alice. You want her. I have seen it with my own eyes!" I yell.

I turn around and swipe my hand hard across the desk, sending all the papers and objects on top of it flying to the floor. "Fuuuck!" I'm so angry, I'm shaking violently. I don't wait for him to say anything or try to stop me. I turn, grab my phone and briefcase, and then take long strides out the door without a second glance, leaving Alex in my office.

All women are cheaters and there is no such thing as "bro code." This is exactly why I didn't want to fall in love again. My heart is disintegrating. I get inside my car, slam the door shut, and sit in the cool interior, trying to calm down. Once my breathing has evened out again and my hands have stopped shaking, I drive home.

When I get through the door, I toss my keys on the counter and kick my shoes off. I then head to the liquor cabinet and pull out a bottle of scotch and a glass, taking both into the living room. I put some football on and drink the rest of the night away. After a few glasses of scotch, I decide to call Alice. She answers straightaway.

"Mike, we need to talk. You have been strange. Why didn't you let me know about the surgery? You should have called—"

I can hear the anger in her tone. I don't bother answering her questions.

"I need a break." I don't wait for her response. I pull the phone away from my ear and hang up. I turn my phone off after that, so I don't have to deal with anyone. I close my eyes and lie down, passing out from the tired, sad, drunk state that I have found myself in.

CHAPTER 23

ALICE

I SLUMP DOWN IN defeat, dropping the phone beside me as I hang my head in my hands, and a stream of tears begins to fall. I try to blink them away, but there is no stopping them. My heart constricts so tight, it feels like it's being ripped out from my chest, leaving a burning hole behind. Maddy mutters under her breath, and I hear her feet patter as she goes to pick up my phone.

"No, please don't. He asked for a break," I choke out.

I really don't want them to go to battle for me. He isn't worth it. *Fuck.* How am I supposed to work with him? I need the money and we both signed the contract. *I have no way out.*

"Fuck. The asshole must have switched his phone off." I frown at hearing Maddison.

"I'm so sorry." I feel Tahlia sit next to me. She hugs me, cooing and stroking my hair.

"Cocksucker," Maddison mumbles.

I laugh at her choice of words. I feel shattered like a glass that's been dropped off a counter and has disintegrated into a million pieces. *That was my heart.* Losing my dad five years ago was tough, and it took forever to let anyone else in, but Mike weaseled his way into my heart, only to suddenly not want me and leave. I feel the urge to be sick and I push Tahlia off me. Getting up, I run from the living room into the bathroom. I cuddle the bowl and empty my insides over and over until all I can do is dry heave.

I can hear the girls in the distance, but all I can make out is a fuzzy noise over my pain. I stay like that for a while until Tahlia and Maddison pull me up and tuck me into bed. I lie down and stare at the picture in the frame that's beside my bed. The picture is of my family—my mom, dad, Claire, and me, all smiling happily. I don't sleep for what feels like hours, but I must have drifted off at some point because my phone buzzing wakes me up the next day. I reach out to my nightstand and look at it.

Three missed calls from my manager, Kate.

Five missed calls from Blake.

Three missed texts from Blake.

I open the text messages first.

> **Blake:** *Where are you? Kate called me. You had me down as an emergency contact. She's asking if I know where you are.*

> **Blake:** *Are you okay, Alice? Did something happen?*

> **Blake:** *If you don't call me back ASAP, I will hunt you down, bitch.*

That message makes me smile, but I'm not ready to deal with anyone right now. I try to swallow but my throat is dry and gross. I get up to grab a bottle of water from the fridge. I walk out into the living room where Maddison and Tahlia are watching television. They quickly sit up when they hear me. They must have been waiting for hours.

"Can I get you something, Alice?" Tahlia says softly as she walks over to the kitchen counter.

I shake my head. I can't talk until I drink something. I open the fridge, grab a bottle of water, and chug it down.

"Are you okay?" Tahlia asks.

When I finish the bottle of water, I pop the empty bottle in the bin and turn to them. "No, thanks, girls." I half smile and wince at the pain in my throat and at how scratchy my voice is. "No, but I guess I will be or should I say, have to be." I glance up sadly at Tahlia.

The girls' eyes hold a mix of sadness and helplessness, which brings tears to my eyes. But I refuse to let them fall. I walk to the kettle and flick it on to make tea, then I grab a cup, turn around, and lift it up to silently ask if they would like one. They both nod, so I grab two extra mugs and grab the tea bags and make us all tea. I clutch the hot cup and carry it to the couch when I remember work and Blake.

"Ugh, girls, could you do me a favor?" *I sound really rough.* "Could you call Blake and tell him what happened? I can't bear to talk or to work, so I know he can do it for me. Tell him I won't be in today."

The girls look at each other before looking back at me. "He called us already and we told him. I'm sure he will tell Kate you're sick, but I will call and make sure he does," Tahlia says, walking off to call Blake.

I expect he'll come around at some point when he is off work, but at least he can tell Kate I'll be off, and then I can just sit and be miserable for the day. I don't want to face the hospital. The thought of working with Mike nearly makes me sick again. I need to get my head and heart sorted before heading back there. I need to get my power back, but that day is not today.

For the rest of the day, we watch back-to-back episodes of *Friends* and drink lots of tea. I haven't got much of an appetite, so I only nibble on some cookies. The girls have taken today off from their studies and work to hang out with me. I appreciate the support even if they aren't going through it themselves. Just having them here makes me feel less alone.

The doorbell rings. *I didn't realize the girls ordered takeout. I wonder what they ordered.* Blake is walking toward me and seeing his face makes me instantly start to cry again.

"Oh, honey, don't cry. Please. I'll start crying and that's no good for anyone. It's not a good look. I have the ugliest cry."

I smile on one side. It's half-assed, but I am trying. I stand up and hug him. The fact that he came here to check on me means so much to me. After a little bit, I feel more settled, and I take a deep breath and step back, giving him a strained smile.

"Thanks for coming here tonight. I appreciate it, but you didn't have to. You must be tired from work."

"Of course, I had to come! For you not to turn up at work and then to ask for a day off, everyone is worried. Plus, what are friends for?" He rubs my back.

Oh God. My mouth opens. *I didn't even think of that.* "What will I tell them?" Frowning, I look at Blake for answers.

"I just told them you were really sick. Kate was really worried. But I said you will be fine for tomorrow. You will be okay by then, won't you?"

"I don't know what to think or feel at the moment. I'm still in shock, and also confused. Why did he end it?" Looking down, I let a breath out. "What did I do?"

"Honey, you did nothing wrong. Don't say that." I didn't realize I said it out loud. I thought it was just in my head. Blake is hugging me now and rubbing his hands up and down my back. I sigh because it feels so nice.

"It's just how I feel. I'm going to shower quickly, and then I need to eat." I push away from Blake. I need to freshen up. I feel disgusting and I want to put on fresh sleepwear.

"We will organize dinner while you shower, and it will be done for when you are out. How does that sound?" Tahlia asks.

"Perfect. Thanks, T."

I leave them to sort out dinner, then go into the bathroom to shower. I just want to be alone for half an hour. Turning it on to hot, I stand under the scalding water and wail. The burn on my back is giving me the feeling that I crave, and I slide down the shower wall and cry into my legs, feeling safe that the water will drown out the sound so I won't have any of them worried and rushing in here.

I sit and cry until the water runs cold, and then I stand up and rinse. Jumping out, I look at myself in the mirror and wince when I see that I look like death. My face is ghostly white, both of my eyes are red and bloodshot, and the skin around them is puffy.

I walk into my room in a bathrobe. I open my wardrobe and see his clothes that I wore home after our first date folded on the shelf, staring back at me. I shiver with vivid recollection and quickly rip open the sleepwear drawer, taking a set out and slamming the door closed, not ready to face anything that reminds me of him yet.

Not feeling hungry now, I walk out and announce, "I'm so tired, guys. I'm going to jump in bed. Thanks for coming over, Blake. You really didn't have to. Thank you." I hug each of them individually.

"Anytime, hon. I'll call you tomorrow. Have a good sleep. I'm sure you will feel better after that."

I smile faintly, then look at Tahlia and Maddison. "Night, girls." I wave at them all and turn to my room.

"Night," they both say back.

I check my phone before sliding under the covers—no new texts or messages. He hasn't bothered to check on me. *Great.*

Chapter 24

Mike

I wake up to the worst migraine. *How much did I drink last night?* My head is thumping so hard it feels like it's about to explode. I try to sit up, but I feel like I want to vomit, so I just roll over and throw my arm over my eyes. My stomach starts to growl, and I strain to remember when I last ate. I don't even remember eating dinner last night. Come to think of it—*I didn't*—I last ate a sandwich for lunch from the café.

I need to get up and find some food or order something greasy to kill this hangover, but I'm still so tired, and I end up falling asleep for another hour.

I push myself up off the couch and enter the walk-in pantry and grab some bread to toast. I use my phone to order some takeaway to be delivered. I'm thinking of a greasy cheesy burger and fries with a large Coke, so I order McDonalds and eat the toast until the fast food arrives. My head still hurts, so I grab some painkillers from the medicine cabinet. I take them and settle onto the couch to watch some football while I dive into my food.

Turning on my phone, I notice missed calls from Alex, my mom, and one from Alice. Not in the mood to deal with anyone today, I put my phone away and spend the remainder of the day watching TV and sleeping.

The next day, I get up and hit the gym to sweat out the disgusting feeling of the shit drink and food I consumed yesterday. My mind is a mess. I keep getting flashes of Amanda, my dad, and then lastly, Alice and Alex. All of this is pissing me right off. Thinking of them while running on the treadmill pushes me to turn up the speed. For ten minutes, I run faster and faster until I'm dripping with sweat.

By the time I finish, I'm heaving and trying to catch my breath. My chest burns as I suck in each stinging breath. I pushed myself to the point of pain, but it's helping soothe my anger. When I finally compose myself, I move over to the weights section and work out for another hour. The frustration has helped me lift a lot more weight than I normally would, and my muscles are throbbing from the exertion.

Even though the blood is pounding in my ears, it doesn't stop my mind from replaying all the moments we've shared together. Including the dinner date. The way her eyes brightened in awe, and the gorgeous smile she wore all night. Fuck!

Why am I thinking of her and our happy times?

I was so sure she was different, but of course I was wrong. I leave the gym, and as I get to my car, my phone lights up. Looking down to see who's calling, I groan. *Alex.* I decline the call and carry on with my day. I'm not in the mood for his shit or his shitty excuses.

I scroll through my contacts and see one of the casual women I used to call and hit dial, but I can't bring myself to go through with it, so I hang up after the first ring. When she calls back, I don't answer it. *I have never been this messed up over a woman before.* I drive home with the plan to get through some more work, to take my mind off everything and get ahead.

CHAPTER 25

ALICE

I'M BACK AT WORK today, and my heart is still crushed. I hate that I'm going to run into and have to work with Mike. Actually, I'm dreading it, because I know I look like a mess. I have hardly eaten because I have had no appetite. My stomach hasn't been feeling right, and I just want to sleep or throw up.

When I arrive at work, I go straight to Kate's office. I knock on the door and wait.

"Come in," she calls.

I open the door and I let out the breath I was holding, relieved to see that Mike isn't in here. I smile at Kate to ease the tension that's clearly written on her face. She stays seated at her desk. I wander into the office, clicking the door shut behind me.

I swallow. "Good morning, Kate. I'm so sorry about yesterday. I was so sick I couldn't get out of bed. I must have eaten something bad," I lie as I drag a chair out and sit down.

She shakes her head. "No, don't be sorry, Alice. I was really worried. It's not like you to not be at work or at least call me. I'm just glad you're okay." Her expression and voice are full of concern.

"I'm better now and I'm sure I'll be back to normal soon." My tone is apologetic as I answer.

"Mike has a conference to attend, so he won't be in this week. Please, can you hang out in there today and organize his paperwork? For some reason, when you're not around it's a disaster."

I smile. I uncurl my fists that I didn't realize I had coiled up so tight.

"Oh, Kate, thank you. Are you sure? I don't want anyone angry or thinking that I'm getting special treatment. I'm sure I'm fine to work on the ward if that would be more helpful."

She frowns. "No, Alice, you need to ease back in and if you feel like you need to leave early, please let me know."

I smile gratefully. "Thanks, I will. I'll be in Mike's office if you need me."

"Call me if you need anything," she says seriously, eyeing me sideways.

I chuckle. "Yes, Kate, I am fine—really."

I stand up and walk out her door, straight into Alex, who is about to knock on Mike's door.

"Morning, Alice." Alex grins as if everything is fine. *Doesn't he know his brother dumped me?*

I squint and look more closely at Alex's face. He has a concerned expression. "Are you okay?" Not letting him get a word in, I continue, "You look rough."

He laughs, but then stops, his tone becoming serious. "I'm fine, and I don't want to discuss it."

I whisper harshly, "Alex. Tell me, *now.*"

He sighs, sensing he won't win this battle. "Mike and I had a little disagreement, but it's fine. It was a misunderstanding." He tries to walk off, but I grab his wrist, stopping him.

"What? Are you serious?" My mouth is slack with shock, and my brows crease in confusion.

"Alice, I'm not having this discussion with you. Is Mike in today?" He nods in the direction of the door.

"No, Kate said he is at a conference for a week."

He sighs. "Well, I'm off then. I'm just trying to catch him."

"What does that mean? Alex, what is going on?" I plead.

"I honestly don't know. That's what I am trying to find out," he huffs.

"I'd better start work." I push open the door, but before I go through, I watch Alex walk off toward the elevator.

What the hell, Mike? What the fuck is going on?

The moment I walk through the office, I get smacked in the face by his scent, and my eyes prick and begin to fill with tears.

I refuse to let him affect my work. I *need* this job. I *need* the money. He will not ruin this for me. I'm strong and I can get through this.

I get to work reorganizing the office and sorting the paperwork. The papers are just skewed all over the desk again. I look over at the bookcase and remember I haven't brought his Tabner's book back, so I make a mental note to be sure I do that.

The week actually goes by pretty quickly, and I'm still so relieved he hasn't been here. I feel the stronger and more powerful Alice slowly returning. Time has gotten away from me, and I should have been out front ages ago. I hurriedly put away a patient's file, then grab my bag and head out. As I scamper toward the elevator, I see Mike ahead of me, and I realize he hasn't noticed me because he is talking to a group of doctors. I quickly dart behind a wall, panting as adrenaline runs through my veins. I watch them until they pass, and as they do, I check Mike out from behind.

Mike is in a stunning designer pale-blue suit and pink shirt. *Who knew pink and pale blue could look so good together?* Obviously, Mike does, because the suit is perfectly tailored to his physique. I notice the group are all engaged in whatever he is saying. They look mesmerized, and I remember feeling the same way, getting lost in his intelligent and charming personality. He has an aura about him that screams power and success. It sucks you in.

Once I realize I'm alone again, I quickly walk to the elevator and press the *Close Doors* button. While keeping an eye on the direction they went in, I watch carefully in case they come back. I'm relieved when they don't and the doors finally shut. Alone in the elevator, I manage to breathe for the first time since seeing him again.

The day was so full on that I'm wrecked when I eventually get home. I had a great day, but now I'm mentally and physically exhausted.

I'm going to grab some fresh clothes to put on after I take a shower when I see his clothes in my wardrobe again. I pick up the sweatshirt and bring it up to my nose and inhale deeply. It still smells like him. Closing my eyes, I remember the night I wore them. It was the best night we had together. Mike was in his most raw and honest state. *Where did we go wrong? Ugh, I miss him so much.*

I put the loungewear and Tabner's book near my bag and write a note for Mike. I will leave these in his office tomorrow when I put the book back. I need to move on.

No matter how much it hurts.

CHAPTER 26

MIKE

CONFERENCES ARE DRAINING AS hell. Although, there was a positive that came out of having one this week—it gave me another day's break from seeing Alice. There was no way I would be ready to deal with her so soon. I needed time to think. The conference consisted of the usual kissing the hospital board's ass, along with giving tours and talking to the funding committee members. In total, I'm forced to spend a twelve-hour day talking, not one of my passions. I say what I have to when asked, but I prefer to be with my patients and save lives. *Isn't that the goal of becoming a surgeon?*

When Kate pulled me aside last week and informed me that Alice was off sick with an unknown illness. I had to hold myself back from asking her too many questions. Her plan is to ease Alice back into work with shorter days, meaning definitely no committee meetings. The hospital board and committee left beaming with pride and offering to donate more money, which is always the goal. Equipment and research are what every hospital needs. The primary need for every hospital is money.

When Kate first told me, I felt a twinge of guilt and then I remembered that she doesn't want the same future and I can't trust her. Considering Alice's passion and drive for nursing, it really surprised me she took a day off.

Walking through the corridors, I feel a rise in adrenaline as I get closer to my office.

I slowly open my office door and sigh in relief. I'm here first. Noticing immediately that everything is back in order, just the way Alice does it. I carefully scan the office and take note of how clean the dark wooden desk looks. Now I can see the polished surface—no more papers strewn everywhere. I love the feeling of having a clean space. I just don't seem to know how to keep it like this.

I'm walking around my desk to sit down in my chair when my phone rings in my pocket. I pull it out and glance down, noticing Mom's name flashing across the phone screen. I can't avoid her forever and it's not her fault one of her sons is a dick. Answering before it goes to voicemail again and before Alice gets here. Running my hand through my hair, I take a deep breath and accept the call.

"Mom."

"Mike, where have you been? I have been trying to reach you all week, and you haven't been answering your phone. I have been really worried about you. I'm too old for this type of stress." She is talking fast, making it hard to follow. I take a seat and turn my computer on while listening to her.

I feel a pang of guilt in my gut. *I hate worrying Mom with my problems.* "Mom, I'm fine. I'm just really busy at work. I didn't mean to worry you. Really, calm down, please."

"Are you sure?"

"Mom, everything is fine. I promise." I sigh.

I hear the door click and look up from my desk to watch as the door opens slowly. I feel my body stiffen, awaiting Alice to enter. I have my phone against my ear and my other hand is gripping my armchair in a death grip. My heart is beating so hard and fast in my chest, I feel like I'm back on the damn treadmill. *Why does she have to have this effect on me?*

My eyes track her as she carefully enters my office, and when I notice she is holding a large bag, I frown. *What's in there?* She strolls to the desk quietly and I watch her place it on the floor, just next to the desk. She then opens the bag. I can hear the rustling of it, and I see her retrieve a book, which I notice is the Tabner's I lent to her. She hasn't looked in my direction yet—or at me at all.

My mom is still talking in my ear, and I make sure to respond with a "Hmm" here and there, so she still thinks I am listening, but my eyes don't leave Alice. She returns the borrowed book to the shelf, sliding it into the gap.

I snap my eyes away before she realizes that I'm checking her out. I go back to the phone call, attempting to concentrate on my mother.

"Well, I'll bring some dinner over when you're finished at work. Is there anything in particular you feel like for dinner?" she asks.

"No, anything will be great. Okay, I'll see you later."

"Okay, son. I love you."

"I love you too," I say and hang up. The corner of my lip lifts as I gaze down at my computer. I have really missed my mom. I hate that I've been ignoring her phone calls, but I've been snapping at everyone lately, and I don't want to do the same to her. She doesn't deserve to be on the receiving end of my asshole behavior.

The clearing of a throat pulls my attention from the computer. I glance up in the direction of the noise and I'm taken aback. Stilled into shock, her face is pale, her beautiful blue eyes are now sunk deep into the sockets and there is a dark shadow under both of her swollen eyes. *What happened to my Alice?* It's like the life has been sucked out of her—or maybe she really was sick. She is still beautiful, but she has lost the sparkle in her eyes. I guess I should be glad she is hurting—but truthfully, I'm not. It's splintering my heart. You can't flick the switch off how you feel, like you would a light switch. Time heals all wounds, even the deepest of cuts.

"You look different."

"Err, thanks, I guess," she mutters under her breath.

I want to ask if she should really be here, but then that would mean more conversation with her, and right now, I'm not interested in it. I can tell she is awaiting direction, so I quickly look at our calendar and emails—bingo—we have an interstate trip planned next week and I don't know if she is aware.

"Next week we have another interstate trip, so we need to prepare for that this week. I'm speaking at the event as a guest speaker, so it's important to be prepared."

"Makes sense. How can I help?"

"I'll type out some notes now, and then can you make a PowerPoint presentation?"

"Yes, I can." Her pleasing attitude is not convincing. I miss the smart-ass Alice. *Where has my feisty woman gone?*

She pulls out the chair in front of my desk and sits down opposite me, then reaches for the mail and starts sorting through it. I look away because I want to say something, but I don't know what. *What's wrong with me? Why my brother? Why can't we want the same things in the future?* But nothing leaves my lips. I pinch them together to prevent anything coming out that isn't work related, and I turn my focus back to the task at hand. Getting the notes done to give her something to do means there's less chance of a conversation happening between us.

I wish in this instance that I had a window, because it's feeling hot and stuffy in here with her and I'm craving fresh air. The more I'm around her, the more I remember our good times. I run my fingers through my hair and type away. Time slips away, and it's not until I hear Alice speak that I stop.

"Thanks for today, Doctor Taylor."

I glance up from my papers and I grunt back, "Thanks." I put my head back down, but I glance up at the bag Alice has placed on my desk.

"This is yours. Thanks for letting me borrow them."

My brows crease, and I stand up and gaze down at her. Alice's eyes are sad, but there is still a lingering heat in them. I see fire and desire—the air turns thick with it, and my chest is desperate for air. But I cannot peel my eyes away. She is everything that I want, but I just can't. I need a little time. Even staring at her and knowing she would love nothing more than for me to spread her on this desk and fuck her hard, can't change how I feel. *Having a heart sucks. I wish I were the tin man.*

Alice walks out, and I open the bag. Peering inside, I see my sweats and a card. I grab the card, open it, and read.

Mike,

I'm returning the clothes I borrowed.

Alice X

Looking at the gray loungewear, I'm reminded of our first date. I get flashbacks of how she came to my house dressed in the tightest and sexiest dress I have ever seen. The memory makes me smile because she thought it was just going to be dinner, but the way her face lit up when she got to see the second part was priceless. That night was the most effort I have ever put into a date, and she is the first woman to ever step foot into my new house. The sex under the stars still features nightly in my dreams—*she wore this loungewear much better than me.*

I scrunch the card in my hand and go home.

After having a quick shower, I get dressed and I'm just about to make my way downstairs when I hear my front door open.

"Hello, Mike," she yells.

"Hey, Mom. Come on in." I walk up to meet her and hug her. Her scent, which makes me think of home, surrounds me with the mix of floral and spice that makes my heart feel light. "Did you want a drink? I was just going to make myself a coffee."

"Yes, love, a coffee would be great. I'll make it. I'm sure you had a busy day."

She tries to walk past me, but I hold out my hand. "Mom, please, I'm a big boy. I can make us one. You're not my slave and you know I appreciate your help with my house, but I'm not incompetent." I smile down at her before turning and stepping to the coffee machine.

My mom is my world. I value the time I get with her now. We missed out on lots of family time, spending more time at our friends' houses and eating with their families, just to get the normal family dinners. Our parents worked long hours—we had chefs and nannies, but it's not the same. I think she feels guilty and keeps trying to make up for it now. But I'm over it. *I get it.* She wants to provide for us in case my dad was ever to leave the family.

"So, love, did you want to talk about the real reason you've been avoiding me and the family?"

I turn around to face her, hurt filling my eyes. "Great, so Alex has gone running to you?"

"No. But he had no choice but to talk to me. You're avoiding everyone. I was worried." Her arms are crossed in front of her, and her eyebrow is raised in question.

"He deserved it," I huff.

"No, Mike, you're wrong. He didn't, and if you would listen to him, you would know that. You're so damn stubborn."

I turn back around and try to concentrate on the task of making coffee, then steady my shaking hands by putting the coffee pods in the machine and some milk into the frother. Anger is rising in my body and it's not her fault, so I don't want to take it out on her. I place a cup of coffee in front of her while meeting her eyes.

"What?" I ask, exhausted.

"He isn't your father." She spits the words out with such venom, they are aimed to sting—it works. I wince.

I take a breath. "He danced with and kissed Alice, Mom. And then I caught them in the cafeteria together."

"Yes, I'm well aware of that, but not when you and Alice were together. He isn't like Liam or your father. Don't treat him like them. That is totally unfair. I don't know about the café, but I know he isn't interested in Alice. He has been talking to someone else."

My eyes widen at her confession. *Who is Alex talking to?* I falter, taking a step back.

She continues without waiting for me to respond. "I'm sorry you had to witness your father cheating on me with his secretary, but it's not a reason not to trust or forgive people. I'm over it and we have worked hard to get where we are. We had you kids to think about, and we worked hard on our relationship together. I am happy."

I swallow hard. I haven't even taken a sip of my coffee yet, but I need to. I need to moisten my tight, constricted throat. I remember that day like it was yesterday. I had come to my parents' clinic to discuss my rotation selections. My parents owned the clinic, so we all had a key. I didn't call. I just turned up and walked in. I walked into the vision of their young redheaded receptionist and my father in a passionate embrace—half-dressed, with her lipstick on his lips. I was so stunned I dropped the keys I was holding when I walked in. I remember looking straight into her eyes, and the shock on her face is etched in my memory. Her emerald eyes were scared and wild as she fumbled, trying to scramble out of his arms. I remember saying the vilest things to them, but I had never been so disgusted.

My dad was fumbling with his clothes when I approached him. With fire burning in my eyes, I snarled, "You will go home and tell Mom your side before she hears mine. I'm out of here. I can't stand the sight of you." I walked off, straight back outside, and got into my car.

I haven't spoken more than a few words to him since that day. My mom wants us to go to therapy, but I just have no desire to spend any energy on him. My time is valuable, and I won't waste a minute of it with him.

I know he told my mom that night because she called me the next day to say they were going to therapy and to not say a word of this to anyone, including Alex and Steph. Honestly, I wouldn't want to tell them because it would be like reliving it again and I have no desire to. I was so hurt for my mom. She worked hard at the clinic and also at home whenever she could, and I will never understand why she stayed with him. Obviously, the receptionist was replaced, and no one has spoken about it until today.

I sip my coffee, deep in thought.

Her voice breaks me from the memory. "I told Alex to come here so we can discuss it over dinner. Please, Mike, listen to him... for me. He has no feelings for Alice. You have it all wrong. You and Alice are so perfect for each other. Everyone can see it. You love her, son."

"Don't be ridiculous, Mom,"

She chuckles. "If you didn't love Alice, this wouldn't matter to you. You wouldn't be heartbroken, moping around, and upset at your brother. You have been with so many women..." I eye her carefully. *How does she know?* I never introduce my casual flings because I don't bring them here. "And no one has come this close to you, not even Amanda. Alice is a sweet soul, kind, and with the biggest heart. I know she loves you too." She winks at me with a smirk on her face.

I shake my head. "I doubt that, Mom. She gave me my stuff back. Plus, I've treated her horribly, so she probably never wants to see me again." I shake my head.

"Not always, son. We women don't like to have reminders lying around and bringing up memories of happier times. You need to talk to her. There's something worth fixing there." She is smiling and drinking her coffee. The doorbell rings and Mom glances up from her cup. "Answer that, it's your brother."

I nod, put the coffee on the counter, and walk toward the door to let him in.

Alex is standing on the doorstep in jeans and a long-sleeve khaki top, a cautious expression on his face. "Hey, bro."

I pull the door open wider to allow him through with a smirk. "Hi, come in."

He chuckles as he walks into my house, and I close the front door behind him.

Following him into the kitchen.

"Thanks, I'm assuming Mom is here and has already spoken to you? That's why you're laughing and not shoving me some more." He has stopped walking to turn around and face me and is now looking at me with a question in his eyes.

"She sure is. The queen of meddling and fixing things is here. I think she is going to cook us up a big dinner. Did you want to come and watch the game with me?"

"Sure."

"Do you want a drink?"

"Yes, please. A beer would be great."

Mom isn't here, so she must be in my laundry room. I grab a beer for Alex, pick up my coffee, and lead him into the living room.

I clear my throat. "I'm sorry for shoving you. I just, ugh, fuck, the Amanda shit has screwed with me, and I don't really trust anyone."

He looks up, nods, and takes a sip from the bottle. "I get that, but I danced with and kissed Alice once at the club. We spoke about that. She isn't interested in me and I'm not into her—she wants you, man." He winks.

I frown. "But I came down to the cafeteria at work and I saw you had your arm around her all cozy. And then you came into my office the very next day and I lost my shit."

"You mean the day Amanda was baiting Alice?"

I sit up. "What, no, what are you talking about? What did she do to Alice?" My lips thin with irritation.

His brows crease. "Didn't you see her standing in front of us?"

"No, I didn't see her there at all! I wouldn't have pushed you if I did. What did she fucking say?"

"Just telling Alice that you will get bored, you will leave her, and you know... just a bunch of shit to make you sound like a player. So, I put my arm around her to say, 'I got you, sister.' Amanda can be intimidating, and you of all people know that. Anyway, I told her to fuck off." His face splits into a shit-eating grin.

I take a deep breath. "She hasn't done anything to deserve any mistrust. My head is just so fucked up."

"You two are meant to be. You will work it out." He smiles.

I nod, leaning back into the couch, and continue to watch the football game in silence. Mom prepares us all dinner, and we sit around my dining table eating and talking together until they leave. *Now, I'm alone again.*

Getting changed upstairs, I find that my mom has put the clothes Alice returned on an empty shelf in my wardrobe. Laughing out loud to no one in particular, I shake my head. She really does behave like I'm still a boy, and when I walk over to the bed, I notice she has opened the note Alice wrote to me, leaving it on my bedside table.

Taking a deep breath, I prepare to relax for the night. I make a mental note to book a therapist appointment and talk to Amanda. Then I can work on getting Alice back, and the best way to start that is by having a good time on our trip.

CHAPTER 27

ALICE

I CAN'T BEAR THE thought of going away with Mike next week when I am struggling being around him as it is. My emotions are all over the place. I am trying to eat more to regain some of the weight I lost, especially after noticing the horror on Mike's face at the sight of me. *Like I haven't looked in the mirror and seen it already.* I know I need to sort myself out, so before I leave today, I need to talk to Rachel and Kate.

Spotting Rachel on the ward, I walk up to her and clear my throat to get her attention. "Excuse me, Rachel, could I talk to you for a moment?"

A frown flashes across her face before the fake smile is quickly plastered on. "Of course. What's up?" She is glancing nervously around to make sure no one can see us having this conversation. *It's like she is embarrassed to be seen with me.* Shoving that thought aside, I say what I need to say.

"Would you take my spot next week to go on a trip with Doctor Taylor? Something came up and I can no longer go," I lie.

"Um, duh, of course. That would be amazing. Thanks!" she squeals.

I internally roll my eyes. "Could you just not mention it to him until you're already at the airport? I'd like to keep it as a surprise. I'm sure he will be thrilled to have you there." I give her the biggest, fakest grin and hand over the documents she'll need. *Take that, Mike.*

I swallow the bile that tries to rise up my throat. I hate lying, but I need to look after myself. *I cannot do this trip, no way!* Him being around all the time would suffocate me. I *need* more time and space.

Instead of going on the interstate trip with Mike, Blake has plans to take me on a fun day outing. I have no idea where he's planning to go, but I look forward to the surprise. If anyone is going to be able to get me out of my funk, it's Blake.

The last stop before heading home for the day is Kate's office. I hand her my request form for a much-needed week off so I can visit Mom and Claire.

CHAPTER 28

MIKE

A WEEK LATER, I dial the number for a psychologist I have found. She is highly recommended and is constantly being raved about, and her waiting list shows how good her reputation is. Lucky for me, someone canceled this week. The next person I plan on destroying is Amanda. *If you fuck with what's mine, you will be burned.*

I've already rang my lawyer and demand that she arrange a restraining order against her for me and Alice. I don't want her near either of us again. She is harming my future. As I finish filling in the papers, there is a knock. *Who could that be?*

I'm not expecting anyone at the moment, but I see a shadow appearing and realize it's Alice. Her brows are creased. "Sorry, Doctor Taylor, I, err, know you're probably not expecting me. I got a weird call and an email this morning about some restraining order against Amanda. I didn't organize that. Did you have something to do with it?"

I huff from my chair, my nostrils flaring with pressure, and I stand up to walk around the desk. "Yes, Amanda is not to be trusted. She is harmful to you and me. I will not tolerate her behavior. I will keep us safe." I feel my eyes narrow in anger at her, remembering my little trip.

"While we are on the topic of crazy people. Alice, why the fuck did you send that moron? You should have been there!" I ask.

She looks at me, puzzled, but I can see the wheels turning in her head. But no words leave her mouth. I watch her lips open and close repeatedly, which just makes me twitch. "Alice. Please. I'm talking to you. Answer me, please!" I bellow with frustration, raking both hands through my hair as I pace in front of her.

"I'm sorry. I can't be around you, Mike. It's just too hard for me." Alice is standing there watching me through her big blue eyes.

With the air crackling between us, you wouldn't be able to hear a pin drop in my office, just both of us breathing in the stuffy air. I'm tired of constantly fighting my feelings. I have tried burying them. *Fuck it.* Crossing my office to stand in front of Alice, I grab her face and drag her to me. Then I kiss her with everything I have. Her lush, pillowy lips follow mine, matching my rhythm. My heart is beating frantically in my chest, and my cock is straining in my pants. *I want her and I fucking need her right now.*

I walk her backward a few steps until she hits my desk. I reach out without breaking our lips and swipe everything onto the floor and lean into her, forcing her to lie on my desk. This has been my fucking dream, having my way on my desk with Alice. *Oh, I have missed her.* I take her top off and she stills. Her eyes pop open and she pushes against my chest, forcing me back.

She shakes her head violently. "No, Mike, I can't do this."

I stumble back, my jaw slack with shock. *Did I do something wrong?* I don't get a word out before she turns and storms out of my office. It's like my brain couldn't register what was happening to get the words out of my mouth.

"Fuck!" I shout to no one as I finish clearing my floor and placing everything back on my desk. Another knock comes and I get up and rush to the door, hoping it's Alice and she has changed her mind. But as the door opens, my smile drops and my back turns to stone. *Amanda.* "Did you not get the message? I can have you arrested just for being here," I spit.

"Please, Mike, why are you doing this? We should be together. I can forgive you for playing around. We both made mistakes. Please, drop the restraining order."

All the hairs on my body are on end and my eyes are blaring my anger directly toward her as I bite out, "You have got to be kidding. Are you fucking high right now?"

"Don't be ridiculous, Mike." She rolls her eyes and puts her hand on her hip.

"You fucked Liam... for *years* behind my back. Don't tell me you forgot that? He was my best friend. I can never forget or forgive either of you. Get the fuck out before I call security!"

My breathing has picked up and I'm so wound up with frustration. *What can't she understand about this?* "I'm leaving, and if you come near Alice or me again, I will call the fucking police."

I open my office door and storm toward the elevator. My back has a layer of sweat coating it from all the tension. The elevator is empty, and I sag against the wall, closing my eyes. *This day can't get any worse.*

CHAPTER 29

MIKE

I HAVEN'T BEEN SLEEPING well for the last few nights. Just thinking about opening up to a complete stranger about my life, to my fears and thoughts—it scares the fuck out of me. I'm always on the go and I never think about looking after myself, especially my mental health. But losing Alice has definitely changed my mind, and I know I need to sort my head out if I want to win her back and have a healthy relationship. I'm done being angry with life. *I can do it—I can talk to a stranger about my feelings. The quicker you get there, the quicker it's done.*

Standing outside the building, my hands start to sweat but I tuck them into my suit pants to keep myself from fidgeting. I walk up to the receptionist and peer around, wondering why it's unusually quiet in here.

I clear my throat and speak softly. "Hi, um, I'm Mike Taylor and I have a five-p.m. appointment with Dr. Keating." I'm leaning over toward her side of the desk so only she can hear me speak, because there are other people waiting in the room and I don't want them hearing my name. I keep turning around and checking to make sure no one I know is here. *Is it too late to run?*

The receptionist glances up from her computer and talks so loudly I inwardly grimace at the volume. "Good evening, Mike. Do you have an insurance card and a referral letter from your local doctor?"

I frown at her, puzzled, and the sweat is now moving toward my forehead. *What is she talking about?* I lean forward again. "No, when I booked the appointment, they never mentioned anything about bringing a referral, but I do have my insurance card." I grab my wallet out of my pocket and hand the card over to her.

She stops typing and takes the card from me, bringing it toward her computer and filling my details in. "No, not everyone does, but just so you know, if you get a doctor referral, you can get a small discount."

I lean back, understanding now. She isn't going to know that money isn't an issue for me. She finishes typing in my details, hands back my card, and I pop it back into my wallet. "Okay, Mike, please take a seat in our waiting room. The doctor shouldn't be long." She points toward the seats where other patients are seated and waiting. *How late is the doctor running?*

"Thank you." I smile and then turn around, scanning the room for a spot to sit. I locate an empty chair in the corner and take a seat. Keeping my head down, I take my phone out and start scrolling through my emails. My leg is bouncing up and down nervously. *How much longer?*

From my left I hear a soft, older woman's voice call out, "Mike Taylor?"

I glance up and notice she is looking around at the few people who are sitting, so I stand and put my hand up to let her know I'm here instead of answering.

As I walk toward her, she notices me approaching and says warmly, "Follow me this way."

We make our way around the receptionist desk. I feel my heart beating fast in my chest, and my palms are starting to sweat again. I feel like I am running a marathon. *What am I doing?* I try to take slow, deep breaths to calm myself down while I follow her into what must be her office. *You can do this. Think of Alice.*

We enter a softly lit room, with a large brown desk that has a chair behind it. In the middle of the room is a cream sofa with a recliner chair beside it. It surprises me that it's not sterile and cold like I had envisioned.

Ushering me to the couch, I let her direct me. "Sorry to keep you waiting. My name is Doctor Anne Keating. Please, take a seat and we will get started."

The couch is soft and comfortable to sit on and I sink into it. I glance up and notice she has walked to her desk to grab a pen and paper. She then steps over to the recliner across from me. Anne looks to be in her mid-fifties, with short, wavy gray hair. She's wearing tortoise shell-patterned glasses and an emerald-green blouse. I feel my back straighten and my body tighten at the sight of the pen and paper in her hand.

She smiles. "Don't worry, Mike. The pen and paper are only for certain notes, like names. Until I get to know the people in your life, I'll need a reference." I drop my shoulders again and relax a little. *Makes sense.* "What brings you here today?"

Looking directly into her eyes, I laugh awkwardly. "Where do I start?" *Help me.*

Anne offers me a kind smile. "How about this—have you seen someone before?"

Shaking my head, I answer, "No, never."

"Well, if there is nothing urgent that needs addressing, then I would love to start with your childhood." She gets her pen and paper ready, and I take a deep breath, then lean back into the couch. *Where do I start?*

I gaze out her window instead of at her and begin speaking. "My family consists of my mom, Margaret, and my dad, Paul. I also have a younger brother and sister, Alex and Steph."

"You are the oldest?" she asks.

"Yes, that's correct."

"Hmm." She writes this down. "How was your relationship with each of your parents?"

"My family are all doctors, including me." I feel embarrassed to say it, but she will understand when I continue, and I know I need to be open to work on myself.

She pops a brow. "Everyone?"

"Yes, my parents are local doctors, and they have their own clinic, although my mom is now retired. My brother is a neurosurgeon, and then my sister is a dermatologist."

"And what are you?"

I laugh. "Oh yeah, I'm an orthopedic surgeon." I'm glad she doesn't seem to have recognized my name. Either that or she is pretending not to know. Regardless, I'm happy she is being quiet about it. She is sitting silently, waiting for me to continue. *Where was I?* "When we were growing up, my parents were always working. My mom was attentive when she was home, but it wasn't the same as having traditional parents."

She is taking notes, but she pauses to ask, "And your dad?"

I take an audible breath and gaze down at my clasped hands before meeting her eyes again. "We were close. He was someone I admired growing up. Yes, he worked a lot of hours, but he would play with us kids when he could."

"What did you mean by traditional parents?"

"We had nannies growing up because my parents weren't always there, and my friends didn't have that. They had parents who took them to school, did homework with them, and had dinner together. Not us. We only had our parents for an hour before bed."

"And how did that make you feel?"

Gazing out the window, I'm unable to face her and I don't answer straightaway, thinking back to how I felt. "I remember at the time being sad and jealous of my friends." I shrug.

"Have you ever told your parents you felt that way?"

I don't ever recall telling my parents anything. I've always been too afraid to upset them. "No."

"How was your relationship with Alex and Steph?"

I grin because I have great memories of times we spent together. "Wonderful."

"Talking about them makes you happy. I can tell by your smile. Your face lit up."

I feel a warm flush spread across my cheeks. "We were so close growing up. We used to play pranks on the poor nannies, and we actually chased a few away over the years." I laugh.

"If you could make any positive changes in your life, what would you make happen?"

This stumps me for a minute, and I frown. *I need to think of the best way to word this.* "I want to be able to trust people in my life wholeheartedly, and improve my relationship with my father." Saying it out loud feels surprisingly good.

"I can help you with both of those, but just so you know, the rebuilding of trust takes time, patience, and work, just as it does to establish it in the first place. What do you feel is the issue with your father?"

"I caught him cheating on my mom. I still feel very angry toward him and also confused as to how and why he would do that to her, and us."

"Have you ever asked him why he did it?"

"No, I can't." *There is no excuse.*

"It is important to talk to him. I know you might feel uncomfortable, but if you find out the reason why and get your feelings out to him, you can then work on your relationship. But you both require dignity and respect in order to rebuild trust. I want you to start working on a few things before our next session. One of those being that you need to start saying what you mean and meaning what you say. You need to stop saying things that you won't follow through on—even the minor things—and give him the benefit of the doubt even just a little bit. This will be hard and you will want to put up walls, which you can at the start, but here and there you should try to let them down."

"But how do I have a conversation without shouting or attacking him? I go from zero to one hundred in a second with him in front of me."

"This entails maturity, to be perfectly frank. You need to give him the opportunity to talk, and you need to work on methods which will allow you to talk about difficult feelings in a way that is helpful and respectful. I want you to let yourself be vulnerable, starting small."

My mouth tightens into a thin line. *How do I do that with someone I can't stand? This is going to be hard and will push me beyond my comfort zone—but maybe that's her goal.*

Anne smiles and leans forward in her chair. "I can see you are shocked, but please listen closely. Trust is built when the other person has the opportunity to let us down or hurt us, but they do not allow it to happen. Take small, gradual steps to rebuild the trust between you. How about going to a sports game or play tennis? Maybe find something you can do that is outside, but will also give you the time to talk. Can you think of anything that you two could do together?"

It doesn't take me long to respond because we both like to do it, but it's currently at different times. *I've been avoiding going when I know he'll be there.* "I guess we could play a game of golf."

"Great idea, and that's all the time we have today. I am sure you have a lot to think about. Thank you for coming. I sincerely hope I didn't scare you off and that you come back." I smile and stand. She follows suit, and once she has put the pen and paper on her desk, I hold my hand out to shake hers. She steps over and puts her soft hand into mine.

"Thank you, Dr. Keating, for your time. I will work on having a conversation with my father and hearing him out. Thank you again. I will be back soon."

I have a splitting headache from all the information I have processed. On the way to my car, I take out my phone, and before I can lose my nerve, I take a deep breath and I quickly type out a message.

> **Mike:** *Can you meet me for a 9-hole game of golf tomorrow at eleven a.m.? I'm ready to talk. Mike*

I press send before I change my mind and decide to delete it. The dots start bouncing around straightaway as he types a response. *I can't believe I'm really doing this. Can I forgive him?*

> **Dad:** *Yes, that would be lovely. Thank you, Mike. I'll see you tomorrow. Love, Dad*

Throwing my phone into the console of the car, I turn on my music and pull out onto the street.

Chapter 30

Mike

Waking up early the next morning, I feel slightly nervous about the day ahead, so I get up and make my way down to the hospital to check on a patient whose health has been declining since their surgery on Thursday. I have been receiving phone calls about the patient all night regarding their low blood pressure and high heart rate. Before meeting Dad, I need to visit the patient, so I won't get phone calls during our time together.

I put my active wear on in case I have time to head to the gym for a quick workout, too. I need to burn some of these nerves off with activity. I don't want to be frustrated when talking to him. I need this to work, to then help me with Alice.

I pull into my parking spot and ride the elevator up to the ward. I chat with the charge nurse to discuss their concerns. After reviewing the patient's chart and assessing their condition, I decide not to take the patient back to the OR but watch and review instead, as well as creating an appropriate treatment plan.

The nurses are happy, so I take off in order to grab a coffee from the cafeteria before meeting Dad. I come out of the main elevator and glance up, spotting Alice who is ordering something from the barista. I warm at the mere sight of her, my lips twitching with the words I want to say. *What do I say first*? My legs refuse to move, but I force myself to snap out of it and go join the queue.

There are only a few people between Alice and me, and she hasn't noticed me yet, so I use the opportunity to stare and take her in. She has her work uniform on, and I get flashes of memories of her perfectly tight body—she had the softest skin I have ever touched beneath my fingertips. I still crave her.

Looking at her now, all I want to do is walk over and kiss the shit out of her. *Would she let me?* Her hair is tied up in an untidy ponytail and her bangs are all messy over her face. She has no makeup on, but her lips are still pink and pouty, which makes my dick tingle at the thought of wrapping her hair in my hands and yanking it hard while kissing her. She hasn't looked up, but I know behind her bangs is a magnificent pair of vibrant blue eyes. I want to take her back to my office and finish what I started with her on my desk the other day. I shiver with hopeful anticipation.

The barista looks up and winks when he catches my eye. I know all the employees well. I order daily and pay my bill in advance. It makes my life so easy—I added Alice to my bill when we started dating. Even though she knows I pay for her, she hasn't taken advantage of or gone crazy with it, and this is why she is different. I was expecting her to message me about it, but she didn't. I haven't heard from her at all.

After she orders, she moves to stand in the waiting area for her coffee, and my eyes follow her every move. As she walks past where I'm standing and I catch a whiff of her vanilla scent, it causes my pulse rate to rapidly increase.

I hear the barista calling out in the distance, which breaks me from my trance. I glance over, catching him smirking and shaking his head side to side. *Busted*.

I quickly walk up to the counter and sheepishly place my order. "The usual, please."

He nods and I take off in the direction Alice went. She is on her phone, gazing down at it with a blank expression on her face.

I stand directly in front of her, comb my hair back with my hand, then put it in my pocket before I whisper, "Alice."

She jerks her head up. Her beautiful eyes immediately meet mine and widen with shock and recognition. She doesn't say anything as she takes a small step back, which makes my casual smile transform into a big shit-eating grin.

"I miss you, babe. I made a mistake and I want you back."

CHAPTER 31

ALICE

I WAS ROSTERED FOR an early morning shift, and it's a Saturday, so I'm already dead tired. I have been here since six thirty a.m. and I decided to grab a coffee on my break and take a walk to perk me up. I'm still waiting for my order and am passing the time by scrolling aimlessly through Facebook and Instagram. When I hear *his* voice just in front of me, my body goes rigid, and I slip into a state of shock.

I glance up to see a familiar set of dreamy ocean-blue eyes. I am so shocked that no words can form in my brain, and I have to take a small step back while I try to steady myself. The man is overwhelming me all over again. Every one of my senses is heightened in his proximity.

I was not expecting to see him here on a Saturday. Raking my eyes over his body from head to toe, I note that he is wearing workout clothes, sneakers, and a shit-eating grin. *Fuck.* He is sexy, which he knows damn well.

I snap back to reality when the words he's saying register. "I miss you, babe. I made a mistake and I want you back."

That frustrates me so I snap, "I'm not your 'babe.' Do *not* call me that and especially not while you are here. Also, why have you been paying for my bills at the cafeteria? You do realize I can afford it myself, right? Besides, you are the one who broke up with me, so you shouldn't even be doing this!" I'm glaring at him and I stand a little taller. *I'm not taking your shit, you beautiful bastard.*

His smile widens an inch, which annoys me further.

"Yes, I understand. But I want to look after you." He is standing there all cool, calm, and collected, while my body temperature is rising and I'm trying to not explode in public. I take some breaths to help me stay in control.

"Why? I'm not yours to look after, not anymore," I snap, giving him a pleading look. *Why is he is doing this?* "I don't need your help. I earn my own money from having my own career." *I don't need your money.*

Being this close to him means I can smell his scent—so spicy and masculine. Meeting him all those months ago to now working so closely alongside him has given him the power to destroy me and literally bring me to my knees.

"I'll repeat, I miss you, and I care," he whispers, barely loud enough for me to hear. His expression and tone are firm. It's as if he's annoyed at me for not knowing this.

My head is spinning because he is repeating the exact same sweet things he spoke not too long ago. *I can't bear this. I need space.* The barista calls out my order, and relief immediately floods me. *Space, finally! I need air.* I turn my head to see where the barista has put my drink, and I storm off to get it. Unfortunately for me, it's not only my order that's ready, because as I pick up my cup, the barista is putting more orders down.

I can feel Mike right beside me, his body and his size overwhelming me. His hand softly brushes the back of mine, which makes the hairs on my body stand up. I snatch my cup up—too quickly—and spill my coffee on the counter. Sighing, I grab a handful of napkins to clean up the mess.

"Are you okay?" Mike questions.

I turn to see Mike waiting for me, holding his coffee. *Why are you still here?* "Yes, I'm fine. I need to get upstairs; my break is over," I bark and walk off in the direction of the main elevator.

"Alice! Wait! You only just ordered." His stern tone makes me stop in my tracks. *What now?* I fight the urge to turn around. *I hate how he has the power over me with his voice, but I can't seem to ignore it.* His hard and serious expression makes me soften slightly. I sip what's left of my drink and wait for him to start talking. "I need to explain to you why I broke things off. I have my reasons and I want the opportunity to tell you. Please?" The vulnerability in his tone breaks my resolve, shattering something deep in my core. I'm so unsure of what the right thing to do is, but right now, I don't want to hear it.

"I can't, Mike." Before I decide to give him the opportunity to say anything more, I walk off toward the elevator, quickly calling out over my shoulder, "Bye, Mike."

CHAPTER 32

MIKE

HOW AM I GOING to get her to listen to me? She took off so fast and I don't have the time to chase her right now. I have to meet up with Dad soon. I walk off with my coffee toward the elevator and drink it on my way down to my car.

Driving to the gym, I feel pumped, and the energy starts kicking into action in my veins. I get the best sprints in, and by the time I'm done, I have a sheen of sweat dusting over my skin and trickling down the middle of my chest, making my shirt cling to me. I hit the showers at the gym, get my golf clothes on, then jump in my car and roar down the freeway to the golf resort.

I haven't been to the golf resort with my father in years and I don't know how good he is now. Growing up, he was the one to teach Alex and me how to play and how to do it well. We even competed in a few local competitions, but we didn't want to make careers out of it, although we do enjoy playing for fun and beating each other. Now that I'm here with Dad, it brings back memories of how patient he was when he taught us, and how we did have some good times together.

I spot his four-wheel drive in the parking lot, and I roll up next to it. He isn't in it, so I get out and peer around to see if anyone else I know is here. It's all clear, so I retrieve my clubs out of the trunk. My car isn't the most practical for putting clubs in, but I'm not getting a shit car just to put clubs in. My Aston is my pride and joy and I worked fucking hard for it. It's sexy, powerful, and fast, just like me. If I were a car, this would be it. *Except for Alice nicknaming it Marty... That's not a sexy name.* But I warm at the thought of her, reminding me why I'm here.

I press the lock and drag my all-black Vessel golf bag behind me. Just like my car, my golf bag and clubs are top of the line. I always get questions from fellow golfers admiring my bag while I'm playing.

I reach the entrance to the golf club. Now my palm is sweating, making it hard to keep a good grip on my bag as I slowly walk up to the desk and check in. On my way over, I spot my dad and instantly stiffen. I begin grinding my teeth. *No going back now.* Dad beams and waves like an idiot. I roll my eyes and a dark laugh leaves my lips.

Dad walks over, quickly dragging his bag behind him, and pausing in front of me, he holds his hand out for me to shake. "Hi, son."

I glance down at his hand. *It's now or never.* I take a deep breath and raise my hand slowly, then shake his outstretched hand. He yanks on my hand, tugging me forward, giving me no chance to escape as he pulls me in for a hug and slaps my back.

"Thank you for today," he says into my ear. I jerk back, trying to put distance between us. He releases me and lets me stand back. "You won't regret this."

"I hope not," I murmur under my breath, so he can't hear my negativity.

"Have you checked in yet?" I ask, staring directly into his eyes. They are the exact same color as mine. There is no mistaking him for anyone other than my father.

Shaking his head, he replies sheepishly, "No, I thought I'd make sure you turned up first. I didn't want to pay only to be stood up."

"Trust me, I thought about it," I say coldly.

I have to keep my guard up. I need to hear his reasons before we even think about going back to being father and son.

"Let's check in." I tilt my head in the direction of the clerk.

We walk side by side over to the large white desk that has wood paneling on the walls behind it. I smile at the woman who is professionally dressed in her navy suit.

"Good morning, I have a booking for two at nine a.m. under Taylor."

"Good morning, gentlemen. I'll sign you both in. Is there anything you need for your game today?"

"Just a set of cart keys, please."

"Of course." She walks to grab a set of keys and two bottles of water, smiling warmly at me as she hands them over. "Here you go. Hope you two have a nice game. Let us know if we can get you anything else."

"Okay, thank you."

The golf resort was designed by skilled architects to be luxurious, with a modern twist. The building features interior walls of exposed brick, glass views in every direction, and a white render complete with a white peak, indoor and outdoor dining, and they have rooms for overnight stays. This is *not* your basic golf course.

We step out through a double set of glass doors and silently walk over to our assigned cart and put our bags in the back. My heart is beating fast; my nerves are kicking in, and I'm waiting for the serious part of the day to finally arrive. It is pure torture waiting for him to bring up a conversation. To give my brain something to do, I jump into the driver's side. *Take control.* We park near the first green, head around to our bags to get our clubs and balls and get ready to tee off.

Pulling out my driver and golf ball, my dad follows suit, and I wander over to the green with him on trembling knees.

My dad whistles appreciatively. "Nice clubs, Mike. Are they Tay-lorMade?" he asks, trying to get a better look. I freeze when he is standing close again.

"Yeah, M5, 9 degrees. It's so smooth and light."

He is trying to make conversation, which I appreciate. It's melting one of the icicles that I have built around my heart. I'm overthinking how to bring up the conversation we need to have, and I'm waiting for the right moment. After we hit our first balls, I'm going to bite the bullet, or I will end up playing the worst round of golf in my whole life. I need to get my nerves under control. I hit the ball, and it sails perfectly into the spot I wanted it to go. *Thank God.*

Dad's turn is next, and he also has a good first hit. As we wander slowly back to the cart, my feet feel so heavy that it's like I'm walking in concrete, and my forehead is starting to perspire. Clearing my throat, I prepare to speak.

"I want to talk to you about the past. That's why I asked you to come meet me today."

"I figured."

I gaze out onto the course and not at him, but I feel the weight of his stare as we come to a stop beside the cart. I have to give him credit because he isn't bowing out; he is looking directly at me and talking.

"Why?" Three letters, but so powerful... and it's the one word I have wanted to utter but been too scared to actually hear the answers to in case the pain splits me in half. I turn to face him because I want to watch him as he answers.

He inhales deeply through his nose; his nostrils suck in before flaring out with his exhale. "To put it simply, we were both emotionally withdrawn from our relationship." *What?*

"What do you mean?" My brows crease. I fold my arms across my chest.

"I was feeling neglected, and she fell out of love with me." His eyes look pained, and his head droops. My eyes widen in horror. *What the fuck?* Before I have a chance to process the statement, he continues. "It's not an excuse. I feel awful, and it never should have happened. It was just once."

Rolling my eyes, I scoff aloud. "Yeah, they all say that."

"I'll admit, son, we flirted a lot to begin with. It started out just nice, but then she began paying me even more attention and I fell for it. It's not an excuse, but I am just telling you what happened."

Not having the words to say to that, I drop my arms and I turn around. Heading to the cart, I jump in as he slowly follows. *I need some space for a second.* I sit there holding the steering wheel, gripping it like a vise. My head is thumping out the start of a headache. He hops in next to me quietly, waiting for a reaction, no doubt fearing I'll fly off the handle or not talk anymore. But I need to get Alice back and begin trusting her. I can't keep going around in circles and the therapist strongly suggested that talking to him will help. I need to figure this out. *I can do this.*

"I still don't get why you would do it when you have us kids." I close my eyes, hoping that when I snap them open again, I'll understand his logic.

"I didn't plan it. I love you kids and your mother. Over time, we'd both worked too hard and neglected each other. She fell out of love with me, and then I cheated on her. We both hurt each other, just differently."

"Why did she forgive you? How could she?" I open my eyes and turn to face him.

"When it happened, we fought a lot. I hurt your mother and I hurt my kids, mainly you. For that I am truly, deeply sorry. I can never erase that. After a few weeks, we were talking things over and realized we had both made mistakes in the relationship and we needed outside help. We couldn't keep fighting and we deserved to try to make it work for our marriage and you kids." I nod, so he knows I'm listening. My lips are rammed shut like a vise. No words can come out of me, so nodding is all I can offer.

"One night we decided marriage counseling was the best thing to try. We went regularly for years and to this day we still go at least once a year."

"What? Really?" I splutter, my eyes widening as my mouth slackens. *When?*

"Anne helps your mother and I work through our life changes and helps keep our marriage happy. If needed, we visit her individually if she feels we need to work on something alone."

My breath quickens. "Sorry, who did you just say?" *No, it can't be, can it?*

Laughing softly, he apologizes. "Sorry, we call her by her first name. We have known her a while, but her name is Doctor Anne Keating." *No fucking way!*

I'm speechless, staring at him and waiting for an "I'm joking" speech. But it never comes. Of all the people I could go to see, I made an appointment with the exact same doctor my parents use. *No wonder she wanted me to talk to him. This makes sense now.*

My headache is getting worse with every minute that passes, and I want to finish this conversation for the day. "Let's finish the game. I need to get out of here."

Two hours later, I win by the skin of my teeth. I'm so lucky to scrape that win, because my dad is actually *very* good at golf. I had a lot of fun, surprisingly.

On our walk back to hand the keys to reception, I say, "Thanks for today. I have a lot to think about. I just need time to process."

I should say more, but I just don't know exactly what I want to say to him or how. I have some answers and it has me thinking. I just need to work out how to move forward with him.

"I understand, son." He gently slaps my back and squeezes my shoulder.

At first it feels awkward, and I tense up. This whole touching thing is new, and I'm not sure I feel comfortable enough with him yet. He drops his hand and I instantly relax. I head to the car, wheeling my bag, lost in my thoughts.

He shouts and waves before jumping in his own car. "Bye, and thanks again for a great day."

I wave and hop into my car without saying a word.

I wish I could pick up the phone and call Alice to ask her what she thinks. She would know the right things to say. But now that I have worked on rebuilding trust with my father, it's time to turn my attention to Alice. I climb into my car and drive straight over to Alice's house. I need to talk to her, to try again. *I'm not waiting another minute. I want her back.*

I park out front and notice her car isn't there, but I walk up her driveway to the house anyway. I know she'll have finished work for the day, and I can always wait for her to come back if she is out at the shops. Taking the steps to the front door, I knock... I hear nothing. I frown and look through the windows, but I can't see anything because the curtains are all closed. I know the girls are home because Maddison's and Tahlia's cars are in the driveway, so I knock again. Five minutes later, I'm beginning to get impatient, so I hit the window this time. *It's afternoon; why are they still asleep?*

After a minute, I hear footsteps and movement coming from inside. I take a step back, run my fingers through my hair, and then put my hands back in my pockets. The door creaks open a smidge and Tahlia peeks around the door. She looks rough. I tense. *Have they all been out clubbing?*

"Good afternoon, Tahlia. Did I wake you?" I ask.

"Hi... ugh, yes." Tahlia's voice is raspy, like she has been smoking all night. She grimaces when she tries to swallow.

"Sorry, but I want to see Alice." I pull my hands out of my pockets and cross my arms over my chest.

Tahlia grabs her head, groaning. "Shhh, my head hurts. Don't yell. She isn't here."

I am not speaking very loud. I chuckle. "Nice hangover. Where is she then? Or when will she be back?" I question.

"Ugh, well, she went to her mom's house for a week."

"What? Why?" I ask softly, dropping my arms instantly as I take a step forward.

"Umm, well…"

"Spit it out," I say firmly, frustrated and annoyed. I like Tahlia. She's a great friend to Alice, but I need her to tell me where Alice is and why she left.

"She needed space, so she booked leave from work. Didn't you know?" Her brows crease at me.

Why didn't Kate tell me? Fuck! "I need the address, Tahlia."

She opens the door wider, surrendering. "Come in. I'll find the address and write it down. I shouldn't be doing this. She will kill me when she next sees me, but I know you two need to talk. She is miserable without you."

I step into the house, closing the door behind me. I follow Tahlia down the hall and into the kitchen, where she pulls open a drawer and looks through the handful of papers. I stand, leaning my hip against the counter, tugging my hair nervously. *I hope she finds it.* The thought of Alice being miserable pulls at my own aching heart. *I need to fix the mess I've created.*

"Ahh, here it is." She pulls out a little address book, puts it on the counter, and begins flipping through it. Waiting for her to find it feels like it's taking hours, but after a few minutes she finds it and looks around.

"I'll type it in Google Maps. Don't worry about writing it down."

She nods, her shoulders relax, then she shows me the address so I can type it in.

After I type it in my phone and put it in my pocket, I glance up at Tahlia. "She drove alone, in Lady?" I question.

Rolling her eyes, she giggles. "Yeah, she drives those roads all the time. Calm down, caveman."

"Her car is a bucket of shit."

"Agreed, and I have tried to tell her that many times."

"I need to find her."

I walk back to the door and once I reach for the handle, I turn to Tahlia, who is following closely behind me, and I say sheepishly, "Thanks, Tahlia. I know you didn't have to help me… but I do appreciate it."

"Anytime. I hope you two can figure it out." She offers me a half smile.

I turn around, open the door, and head back to my car. I pause at my driver's side door and glance up at the house, where Tahlia waves before going back inside. I set up Google Maps and start the journey to Alice's mom's house. The entire way there, I think about what I am going to say to Alice to win her back.

CHAPTER 33

ALICE

I FINALLY ARRIVE AT Mom's and Claire's. They are already waiting for me on the front step. I can see them waving with matching big grins on their faces. *My family is my life.* I texted them when I left home, so they knew when to expect me.

I hop out of the car and walk straight up into my mom's warm arms. I sigh, relieved and happy. *It's so good to be home. I have missed them so much.* "It's been too long," I say into Mom's shoulder.

She rubs my back while we hug, which sends warm shivers over my body. My family are cuddlers. I remember when growing up, we'd watch movies on the couch, and Mom or Dad would lightly tickle my back, making me fall asleep. *It was so warm and relaxing.* Watching movies in the living room were our treasured family moments. Since Dad died, I've tried to keep them going when I'm here, so we remember the good times. Even if it's hard and sad, we all manage to smile and enjoy the time together. At least with us all being girls, we can watch romance movies with no moaning and groaning.

Pulling back from our warm embrace, I'm wearing the biggest smile on my face. *My heart feels full and content.* "Hi, Mom."

"Hi, sweetheart." She pats my hair.

"Let me grab my bag. Then we can go inside and catch up."

Claire has beaten me to it. She has my bag in her hand before I've even turned around. "I got it." She winks, and I move over to hug her.

"Hey, Claire-bear."

"Hey, Ally."

Claire is a spitting image of our dad. She is younger than me with hourglass curves, our dad's olive skin, rich black hair which flows down her back, and our vibrant blue eyes. She is stunning, and I used to be so envious, but as I have gotten older, I became proud. She isn't just a beauty; she is smart too. She is studying teaching at the college in Bendigo Park because she doesn't want to leave Mom alone. And I'm so grateful to her for that. I can't bear the thought of Mom being alone, but I can't move until I have a few good years of experience in the busy city and spent time exploring the different types of nursing and patients.

Mom's little cottage house is a classically designed house, and I love it. It has a white picket fence. In the garden there is beautiful, thick green grass, and lining the house are white roses and hedges. It's not the biggest house, but it is a large block of land compared to some of the city homes.

I follow Mom and Claire inside, and Claire pops my bag into my old room. It hasn't been touched since I left except to clean. Mom lets us change what we want when it suits us—she wants us to feel at home when we come back, which I'm always grateful for. She keeps the house modern without losing the cottage feel, with its stunning hardwood floors and white country-style kitchen. I walk to my room to put the rest of my stuff down and head back out to the kitchen.

"Tea, dear?" Mom asks, flicking the kettle on.

"Mmm, yes, please." I need tea and something to eat after being on the road. I open the pantry to help Mom get the tea bags and make the tea.

Claire is busy clearing the table. "I'm so happy you're back, Ally. I have missed you. I'm sure you have so much to fill us in about. It's been ages."

I laugh, beaming at how enthusiastic she is. "Yes, don't worry, I will." I put the cups on the table and Mom brings out a plate of food that she has prepared. My stomach grumbles, reminding me I have hardly eaten today. "This looks great, Mom, thank you. You didn't have to go to all this trouble."

"It's nothing much. Take a seat."

We take our spots at the table. None of us ever sit in Dad's seat. It is always left empty. If anyone comes over, they sit in it. But we as a family always leave it empty for him. It feels like he is with us.

"Okay, okay. Hmm, where to start? So, as you two know, I got the position on the fracture and emergency ward, which has been amazing. Seriously, it's so fascinating and I'm learning so much. I'm still finding my feet, but it's been great."

They coo and drink their tea. I grab some cookies to eat because I'm feeling sick from not eating.

"Any boys?" I sip my tea at the wrong moment because as soon as Mom says it, I cough and spit tea everywhere. She grabs a napkin and starts cleaning it up. "Are you okay, Alice?" she asks, rubbing my back while I try to calm my burning chest.

After a few coughs and trying to clear my throat, I nod, unwilling to talk yet, and take a nice sip of my tea. "Yeah, sorry, it just went down the wrong way."

I don't dare tell her about the Mike situation because I'm not interested in hearing any more opinions. I hear my phone beep in my bag, but I don't get up to check it. The most important people know where I am, and I am here with the others. Whoever is texting can wait. *I need to change this subject.*

"The team on my ward is amazing, and Kate is just the nicest boss I have ever had. She is so caring and approachable. I love going to work. Oh, but there is also this bitch at work. She is a total nightmare."

"Isn't that where the famous doctor... what's his name? Oh, I can't think right now... it will come to me. Just give me a minute." Claire starts tapping the table with her fingernail, bouncing in her seat, willing the name to come to her. *Don't remember his name, please.*

"Oh! That's it! Doctor Mike Taylor!" she shouts, happy that she finally remembered.

My eyes bug out of their sockets. *Shit. How does she know?* "Never heard of him. Are you sure he is from my hospital?"

"No, I'm sure. He is insanely hot, Alice. How have you not seen him around?" *Great, it keeps getting better and better.*

"Err, maybe I have seen him, and he is alright I guess." I shrug.

"Are you kidding?" She drops her head back, exacerbated.

"He isn't famous. He isn't a celebrity." I roll my eyes at her.

"Ohhh, yes, he is! Let me show you."

"You girls." Mom giggles and gets up from the table. "I'll grab us some water."

Claire pulls her phone out of her pocket and is scrolling through it with a look of extreme concentration on her face. *I can't seem to run away from him. He is everywhere.* I thought by coming here I'd be safe from hearing about him.

"Here it is. I knew it was him." She stands up and strolls over to me, putting her phone in front of my face.

I stare directly at the photo of Mike, who is staring motionlessly back at me in a delicious navy suit. *Damn it, why is he fucking hot? If only Claire knew how well I know him, and how much hotter he is beneath the suit.*

"He is hot, isn't he? But look at his work. He has so many awards. He was voted the best in the world for orthopedic surgeons."

"Can I read it?" I take the phone out of her hands to read the article. Claire is standing directly behind me as Mom places glasses of water on the table. "Thanks, Mom." I take a big sip, hoping the icy water will cool my now burning-hot body down, as Claire heads back to her chair.

"Of course... I can't believe you didn't already know this." She digs into the food Mom prepared as I read the article in front of me. I'm already halfway through and I'm floored. *He is amazing, like seriously fucking ridiculously smart. I never knew this scale of intelligence. But this is more than smart, this is Einstein level smart. Holy shit.*

"Wow," I mutter under my breath, still reading.

The doorbell rings, breaking me from the spell. Mom looks puzzled. "Who is that?" She checks her watch and heads to the door, clearly not expecting anything or anyone.

I take another mouthful of water.

"Good afternoon, are you Ms. Winters?"

I know that voice. His tone is so seductive, and it's running through my body. Even from afar, it has such a strong effect on me. *What in the world is he doing here and how did he get this address?*

"Hello, yes, that is me. How may I help you?" I can hear the smile in my mom's voice. *He is a charming son of a bitch. Great.*

"I'm a friend of your daughter, Alice, and I was told that she is here. Also, these are for you." Smooth talk to persuade Mom to let him in. *Please don't invite him in. Please.*

"Oh, my favorite flowers, thank you. Alice is here, so why don't you come in? We just sat down for a late bite to eat. Come join us."

My entire body tenses, waiting... I can hear his footsteps coming inside, the front door closing, and then Mom's steps following Mike's.

It feels like everything is moving in slow motion when really, it's been only a minute. I quickly close the browser on Claire's phone because I don't need him thinking I'm some kind of stalker.

I know he is standing behind me because I can feel the heat and energy coming from him, and my body is buzzing from him being so close. *Damn traitorous body, get a grip.* I'm looking at Claire, who glances up.

"Whoa, no way." She is laughing and smiling as she darts her eyes between Mike and me until she finally stops on mine and her eyes widen. She points at her phone. "Liar! You do know him," she accuses in a mocking tone. *Fuck my life.*

I can feel my cheeks heating, and right this second, I want the ground to swallow me up.

"Did I miss something?" Mike questions, and Claire drags her eyes up to meet his. I can see her eyes shimmering at him in delight.

"I was showing my sister the news article about your awards that she clearly does know about." She looks back down at me with an arch in her brow.

"I know him, and I didn't know about that." I push out the phone toward her.

Mike chuckles. It's the sexiest sound and I feel it right down in my bones. "The awards were only recent. Anyway, I'm Mike. It's nice to meet you." His hand and arm shoot past my left shoulder and Claire sticks out her hand to grip his.

"I'm Claire, Alice's younger sister, and yes, I know who you are," she says, grinning wider.

Mom speaks up then. "Come, Mike. Please take a seat. Did you want a tea or coffee?"

"Please, Ms. Winters, I would love a black coffee." He makes his way over to Dad's chair and pops himself in it.

I glance over at Mom whose cheeks are now slightly pink. *Oh God, it's getting worse the longer he stays.*

"Please call me Angie," she says, shaking her head before turning toward me. "Don't be so rude, Alice," she accuses, while grabbing a vase to put the flowers in.

"I haven't done anything, and I haven't said a word," I huff back.

"It's okay. I should have warned you I was coming." He is sitting directly across from me at the round table. He is beaming at me cheekily, and then he winks. A shiver runs through me.

I need to talk to him alone, but at that moment, Mom brings his coffee over. "Thank you, Angie."

She smiles at him in return. *Mom loves him already... great.* I bet she wouldn't if she knew how much of a player he was or how much he hurt me.

While he sips his coffee, I take him in. He has on a white V-neck t-shirt that is perfectly fitted to his toned body. His arms are tanned, defined, and his long fingers wrap around the coffee cup. *I want him to hold me and wrap his fingers around me.* His hair is roughly styled which makes me think he has probably been running his hands through it all the way here. When I bring my eyes down to his lips, I can almost feel it in my sex as his tongue darts out to swipe along the bottom one. I dart my eyes to his, which are mocking me with a devious twinkle. *Gosh, why does he have to look so hot?*

I stand up quickly. I feel uncomfortable, and I need a minute to regroup. "I'm going to grab my shoes, so when you're done with that coffee, can we go out back and talk?" I walk off toward my bedroom without waiting for him to respond.

I get into my room and grab my handbag so I can get my phone and text the girls. I notice a few missed calls from Tahlia and also a text.

> **Tahlia:** *Mike came looking for you this morning. I told him your mom's address. I am so sorry. Please talk to him. You guys need to work things out. Tahlia*

Fuck. I am going to kill her when I next speak to her. I don't have time to call her, and I don't need anybody overhearing it, especially not Mike. I throw my phone back in my bag, grab my shoes, and put them on before making my way back to the kitchen. Mike has finished his coffee and is helping Mom and Claire pack up as they ask him work questions. He notices me enter straightaway and smiles darkly at me. The pull we have when we are in the same room is strong, and I can't help but smirk back.

He looks perfect in my mom's house.

"Are you ready?"

"Yes." He puts the towel down to follow me.

"Mom, we are going out back to talk."

"Okay, dear."

I move to the sliding doors, opening it for us. I step out and hold the door open, and once he steps into the garden after me, I shut the door behind him. I saunter past him and guide him up to the old swinging chair that was my father's favorite place in the garden. He used to tell me made-up stories whenever we sat here alone. I climb up onto the metal frame, and Mike sits next to me. With our thighs touching, heat surges between us, flowing through my body, and a throb begins in my sex.

Chapter 34

Mike

I FOLLOW HER OUTSIDE toward a seated metal swing, which looks very old. It overlooks a manicured family garden, which has a mixture of vegetables and flowers—it's magnificent.

Walking behind Alice means I get to check her ass out in her jeans. *Better than the navy uniform she wears at work.* Her hips swing side to side and I just want to squeeze and spank her ass, but it's not appropriate right now. She takes a seat on the swing, and I sit intentionally right beside her, so our bodies are touching. I have this *need* to be as close to her as possible... always. This connection is new and unexpected.

I thrust my hand through my hair and turn my head to gaze at her while I speak. "Alice, I'm here to try to talk to you. I realize you don't want to talk at work, and I completely understand. It's inappropriate and it also won't be a quick conversation... I went to your house to have this conversation with you, but you weren't there. Tahlia told me you were here—well, I should say I forced her to tell me where you were." I smirk.

She laughs and mumbles under her breath, "I bet."

Her laugh sends a spark of joy through my heart, but I pretend not to hear her words, and I continue to talk. I need to get everything out in the open if I'm going to win her back. "Firstly, I want to apologize to you. I'm sorry I pushed you away and asked for a break without talking to you. I regret that so much." I touch her thigh with my fingers and her eyes dart to mine, darkening with desire. "I think if you were to give me a second chance, to be able to trust me, and hopefully date me again, then I need to be more honest about everything."

We are swinging slowly, and I'm staring at Alice, trying to gauge her emotions, but she has turned her face away and is looking out at the garden. I follow her gaze and take a big deep breath in. "My dad cheated on my mom, and then Amanda cheated on me. I decided to see a counselor and get help working through my trust issues."

Under my palm, I feel her thigh twitch. *What's that about?* I gently stroke her thigh with my thumb in a soothing rhythm. "Let me get it all out and get everything off my chest. Otherwise, I won't be able to tell you everything I really want and need you to know."

I swallow. "I argued with Alex for having his arm around you in the cafeteria. He told me later that you guys were talking to Amanda, but I didn't see her there. I only saw you and Alex. After him dancing and trying to kiss you in the nightclub and then that—I naturally thought you two were playing around behind my back. It was like Amanda and Liam all over again."

Alice gasps, but she doesn't move or say a word, and I continue to stroke her thigh, even though I can feel her tense muscles under my palm.

"I was so hurt and angry that my brother could do that to me, but I didn't hear him out when he came to my office to talk to me about what Amanda had said to you. I heard Alex, and saw his arm and body draped over you from afar and lost my shit. Mom came over and talked some sense into me about how I'm wrong about Alex. She even invited him over so we could talk," I pause to catch a breath looking up at the blue sky before I continue. "Obviously, I'm now well aware of the truth. You and he danced and kissed before we were officially even together, and the arm was to protect you from Amanda and her disgusting accusations—hence the restraining order. I get that now. I'm sorry that I doubted you. After talking to Mom, I realized I needed help. I can't do it alone and it's not fair to you to be with someone who won't trust you due to their own issues. I want to trust you, but I just needed to talk to a professional to see how I can begin to do that." Birds begin chirping loudly around us and I wait until they quieten to finish.

"So, I booked an appointment with the doctor and when I went there, she told me I really needed to hear my dad out to move forward. I needed to talk to him first and then work on our relationship. The therapist was great. I found her helpful. I obviously need more than one session, but it's a start. I met with my dad this morning to play a game of golf, and I got to ask him the biggest question I have been holding on to—why, and how could he do that to Mom and us? I heard him out and discovered that Mom had emotionally checked out of the relationship, so it wasn't just black and white. I can see that now. Now, get this, I also found out the doctor I went and had the session with... is also my parents' therapist."

"No way!" Alice gasps, turning her shocked face toward me. I'm sure I looked like she does now when I found out.

"Weird, right? Considering I never told a soul, I just looked her up and booked in. She was great, very professional and warm. I definitely need to book more sessions, because I haven't touched on the subject of Amanda and Liam. I want to be able to move on from the hurt, not carry the baggage around any longer. The last part that was playing on my mind was the fact you said you didn't want kids in the next ten years. I didn't want to hold you back. I know you want to have your career. And your passion is one of the things I am attracted to. I just realized in that moment that I want children with you... But I will just have to compromise because I would rather have you in my life than out of it. My life is so much better with you in it. You are so light, warm, and kind. You bring the best out of me." I don't speak for a while. I just listen to her steady breaths.

Alice speaks in a broken voice. "That's a lot to take in, Mike."

I slightly turn my body toward her, and I grab her hands in mine—they are so large in comparison; hers are so small and pale. I'm gazing down at them as I speak. "Alice, I'm sorry. I should have trusted you, talked to you, and let you explain. Instead, I broke things off and went cold without a conversation. I just shut down and don't let anybody in past my walls." Shaking my head, I think frantically, *I hope I don't screw this up.* "Fuck, I screwed up the best thing that's ever happened to me. I'm sorry." I glance up and Alice turns her blue eyes to me. They are rimmed with unshed tears. "I love you so much." I say every word slowly and clearly, meaning every damn one of them and hoping it will be enough. I see a tear leak out onto her cheek and slide into the corner of her mouth. I take one hand out of our joined ones and use my thumb to wipe it away. "Please don't cry, babe; it kills me that I've hurt you this deeply." I pull her into my arms and hug her soft frame, inhaling that rich, sweet vanilla scent that I love, and relief hits me. I sag when I feel her hands rise up and she hugs me back.

After a while, she pulls out of our warm embrace. I want to give her space, so she can come to me when she is ready. Wiping her cheeks free of tears with my thumbs, she glances back at me with her dazzling eyes.

"Thank you for the apology. I appreciate it. You hurt me when you left me without any explanation. I have missed you so much, but I can't just go back to where we were." The confliction on her face kills me.

I nod. "I understand. I just want another chance to maybe start over. That's if you want to?"

She glances away back into the garden. I can tell she is thinking, but I wish I knew what to do to help her change her mind.

CHAPTER 35

ALICE

HE HAS TOLD ME so much that I don't know how to begin processing any of it. Being here with him makes me miss him more, even in his space. *I need to use my head, not just my heart.* Looking at my dad's garden and swinging in his beloved swing, I wish I had a sign to help me—but then again, *Mike chasing me, being here in my dad's space, apologizing... That is saying something, isn't it?* Apologizing and truly meaning it from the heart, takes a lot. I stare out into the garden, then down at our joined hands for an answer.

"I need some more time," I whisper. My heart squeezes inside my chest and I feel fresh warm tears slide along my cheeks. "I'm sorry."

"Don't be sorry. I'm the one who fucked up." I hear a sigh leave his mouth. It would be so easy for me to forgive him, but I just need to make sure I make the right decision.

"What time do you need to drive back?" I ask, trying to break the tension.

"I'm off this weekend, but I best get back. I'm watching the football game tomorrow with my friends."

A twist of guilt hits my stomach that he drove all this way and has to drive back home again. "Oh, sounds fun."

I stand up from the swing and he does too. I lead him back into the house where Mom is messing around in the kitchen, clearly pretending to clean, but obviously watching us.

Claire is on the couch watching television.

"Hey, Claire, do you mind pausing that and coming to the table for a second, please? Mike is leaving."

Claire pauses the show, and turning to face us, the biggest and cheesiest grin immediately lights up her whole face, but when she sees my face, she frowns. I glance over my shoulder, noticing that Mom is already standing at the table, but her face is a little more reserved, clearly wondering what is going on. *I know this is the right decision. I need a little bit of time to think away from him.*

"Thanks for inviting me in. It was lovely to meet you both." He hugs my mom and Claire and kisses them both on the cheek.

I lead him down the hall and out the front door, then I walk with him to the car without saying a word.

As we arrive at his car, he turns to face me. "You have a wonderful, supportive family, and I wish I could have met your dad."

"Me too. You would have loved him and got along so well."

"I bet."

"Text me when you get home," I say, gazing into his sad eyes. I feel his hand press into my hair and arch my face up. My heart accelerates. Our lips inches apart, I can feel his breath tickle my lips, and I blink and slam my lips shut to prevent words escaping.

I reluctantly pull out of his grip and take a step back. Our eyes locked, his hand drops, and he rips open his car door. I watch his frame climb into the car and reverse out of the drive and drive away. I stand there alone, taking a few deep breaths before I enter Mom's house. When I get inside, they are sitting at the table, all eyes on me. I sit back down in my chair. I feel myself flush red from the chest up. I hate awkward conversations or conversations involving me.

I clear my throat. "So…" I keep my eyes on Mom when I talk, and she watches me back with curiosity etched on her face. "Err, so, obviously, I need to tell you about Mike."

They wait patiently for me to begin.

"I met Mike at work, and we have kind of been dating." I wince and glance across at Mom, whose mouth is turned up in the corner.

"That's wonderful news. I'm happy for you. He seems like a gentleman. The way he looks at you, you're clearly special to him."

If only she knew.

Before I can say anything, a slap comes from beside me. "Ouch! Claire, what was that for?" I yell.

"I knew it! Why didn't you say something sooner?" she demands, raising her eyebrows at me.

"I didn't want to say anything until I was sure it was serious."

"Yes, I understand. Well, hopefully next time he can stay longer." Her statement is really a question, but I don't want to talk about this any longer.

My stomach grumbles. "I'll order us some pizzas for dinner and let's watch a movie." I get up from the table and grab the takeout menus.

Claire chooses a movie, then the pizzas arrive and we eat while watching without another word. I hear my phone chime. I check it. It's a text from Mike.

> **Mike:** *I just arrived home. I miss you. Again, I am sorry.*

I don't answer. I just enjoy hanging out with my family. Once the movie is over, we get up, and Mom kisses my cheek, then turns to Claire and kisses her too. "Goodnight, everyone."

Claire strolls off to her room too, waving. "I'm stuffed too. Good night."

"Good night, Claire," I say before crawling into my bed after an emotional day. As soon as I get into bed and lay down, I think about Mike's words. He told me he loved me and discussed openly about having kids. We've fought so hard that I need to take a moment to let all his words settle. Since we've met it's been such a rush. There's no doubt I love him I think I started falling the moment we met.

On Monday, I wake to the smell of bacon and coffee, and opening my eyes, I smile when I remember where I am. I get up, feeling tired, but I'm happy because I am back home. I grab my t-shirt and jeans and move to the bathroom to clean up. I wander into the kitchen where Mom is at the stove turning bacon, and I peek around but cannot see Claire.

"Good morning." My voice is croaky from the lack of sleep.

"Good morning, love. I'm just cooking breakfast. Claire is still sleeping, but at least that gives me alone time with you to talk."

I swallow. My happy feeling disappears, now replaced with butter-flies.

"Where can I help?" I ask nervously. *What does she want to talk to me about?*

"How about you grab the eggs out of the fridge and make yourself a coffee? I already have mine, and the kettle has just boiled."

I walk to the fridge, then hand her the eggs.

"Thank you."

I finish making coffee, and standing beside her, I help cook.

"Now, I don't want to be rude, but I just need to ask you, how old is Mike?"

Shit! I knew this would come up. "He is thirty-eight."

She nods thoughtfully, then turns to look at me. "You're only twenty-three, Alice. Aren't you in different phases of your life? He must want to settle down soon, and you have only just started your career."

I have thought about this before and when Mike brought it up yes-terday, I knew my answer. But I think for a moment before replying, because this is Mom, and she is an important person to me, so her opinion matters more than most.

"Yes, I must admit I wish we were closer in age, but to be honest, I can't walk away. I love him." The feeling of warmth fills my body as I say that out loud to Mom.

"Hmm," she hums.

"Now, don't get me wrong. He is smart, handsome, and clearly makes you happy. I just don't want you hurt due to different life expectations. I will respect your decision and I won't stand in your way if you choose a life with Mike."

I smile back at her.

"I'll set the table and pop some toast on, and then I'll go wake up Claire."

"Good idea, love. Breakfast is almost ready." She finishes flipping the last two eggs, which has my stomach growling in hunger.

I walk to Claire's room and bang on the door before I slowly open it.

I peek around the door and see she is moving. "Claire, breakfast is ready! Come join us. I'll make you some tea."

She mumbles and grumbles and I have no idea what she is saying, but at least I know she is awake, so I walk out, closing the door behind me, and begin making my way back to the kitchen to prepare us tea. We sit around the table and silently enjoy our breakfast.

I hear my phone ring, and I rush to my room to retrieve it. I see my boss' name, Kate, flash across the screen.

"Hello, Kate?" I answer.

"Hi, Alice. How are you? Hope I am not interrupting you."

I sit down on the bed, clutching the phone. "Um, no, you're not interrupting. Is everything okay?"

For a split second, my mind jumps to Mike. *Shit, something has happened.*

She laughs. "Yes, everything is good. Great, actually."

My brows furrow. "Okay?"

"I just wanted to offer you a scholarship for a pre-med course. Doctor Taylor recommended you to the board, and I received the formal offer."

I suck in a sharp breath.

My eyes instantly fill with tears. My throat is dry and constricts. I cannot speak.

He put my name down for a scholarship to study to become a doctor. Prior to our rotation, I would never have thought I wanted to become one, but working with Mike, I have loved every second. But in the back of my mind, I knew I couldn't afford the course. But this would mean I don't pay.

"I can tell you're in shock, but we have seen in the short amount of time the potential. Obviously, it's your decision, and you can say no. It's a long time to study, but you have the best teacher." I hear the lightness in her tone.

It makes me smile, and my mind is racing. I need to speak. I clear my throat as the tears threaten to leak. "Wow, I am shocked. I had no idea. I would love to take the scholarship. Thank you."

"I can't take the credit, Miss Winters. It was Doctor Taylor's idea. But you're very welcome. I will see you when you return to work."

My heart skips at hearing that, and I close my eyes for a second. *He truly is something.*

"Thank you, Kate. I will see you back at work."

"See you then. Bye."

"Bye." I hang up and just sit unmoving.

I need to call Mike. My heart and mind are racing. I have adrenaline coursing through me, and my head is spinning. *I have missed him.*

I want him.

I can hear mumbling in the kitchen, so I toss my phone down and walk to the kitchen. "I just got offered a scholarship for a pre-med course. Mike recommended me," I say.

Mom's eyes instantly fill with tears, and she covers her mouth with her hand.

"Oh, Mom." I stand and move to her, embracing her.

"I'm so proud of you," she mumbles into my shoulder.

"Ally, that's awesome. I'm so happy for you."

"Thanks, I don't have any more information just yet. It's just so unexpected."

"Did you want to head up to the main street, check out some local spots, have a drink to celebrate?" Claire offers.

"I would love that." She smiles.

"We should shower and get ready, so we have plenty of time to walk around." I stand and stack the dishes up before taking them to the dishwasher and lining the shelves. "I'll have my shower first. I take longer than you," I say.

Claire nods.

"Mom, did you want to come?"

She shakes her head vigorously. "No, dear. You two spend some time together."

I take off to get ready and once I am done, I come out of the bathroom, only to find Claire, who is still in her sleepwear with a blanket draped over her knees and a cup of tea in her hand.

"Are you ready?" she calls.

"Yep, your turn." She gets off the couch and heads off down the hall to shower.

Mom joins me on the couch, watching the TV until Claire walks out. "Are you ready?"

"Yep," I say. Jumping up from the couch, I step over to kiss Mom on the cheek. "We will be back soon. We will bring lunch!" I call out.

"Have fun, you two," Mom shouts back.

We climb into my car and I feel Claire staring at me intently. "What?" I snap.

"How is he real? Tell me all the gossip. Right now!"

I crack up, laughing a full belly laugh, and smack her arm with my hand. "Shhh, I haven't left the drive yet."

I begin reversing and driving through the streets.

"I'm waiting, Ally," she huffs.

After shaking my head at her persistence, I answer, "He is amazing, and yes, his body is incredible, but he's even more than that, Claire. He is kind, caring, and fun." I sigh. *The dream boyfriend.* "Don't say anything to Mom, but we are on a small break. But I am so unhappy without him. I miss him so much. I just needed time to think about what I want, whether it was love or infatuation. But I feel miserable without him. I'm so in love with him. I know I don't have much to compare to as I haven't had a lot of boyfriends, but something just clicks with us. He is different." She is sitting up, listening to me.

"I can tell you two were made for one another; the electricity in the room when you're both in it is hot. Like, take-off-my-clothes-I-need-a-cold-shower hot." She fans her face with one hand for effect. *Oh, my God.*

I laugh and feel my face blush red. "How embarrassing."

"Oh, don't be embarrassed. It's just not fair. I need an older, hot, and sexy-as-hell, successful man. Help a sister out, will you?" she begs, and we both fall into hysterical laughter.

We arrive in town and prowl the streets, arms linked. The time off is exactly what I needed.

After a few hours of tasting a variety of food, smelling candles and looking at all the handmade crafts, we pull up in Mom's driveway.

Inside we all eat lunch, and then, I excuse myself and walk to my room to call Mike. I scroll and find his name and decide that I need to give myself another few days. *It's still too early. Give yourself a few more days.* Resisting temptation, I turn my phone off and walk back out.

CHAPTER 36

ALICE

A FEW DAYS LATER

Mom and Claire have gone to get some food for dinner. I take the opportunity to phone Mike without being caught.

I hear the ringing in my ear and after only two rings, he answers.

"Alice?"

"Hi, Mike." I hear noise in the background before a door opens and closes.

"Is this a bad time to call?" I ask.

"No, no, no. I just got back to my office after surgery. Are you okay?" His voice is strained.

I feel my heart drop, wishing I was at work, working with him. "Okay, well, I won't take too much of your time. I just wanted to thank you for putting my name in for the scholarship."

"You can never bother me. Call me anytime... You're more than welcome. You deserve it. You would make a wonderful doctor." His words warm my heart, spreading through my body and wrapping me with love.

It's silent for a moment. I can hear his breath through the phone. He is waiting for me. He hasn't bothered me after he left, only sending the one text saying he got home. I appreciate how he listened to me, gave me the space I craved. But I made a decision.

"I'm willing to try, but really slowly though."

I hear a hitch in his voice. "Thank you, Alice. I will take anything. I miss you—so very much."

My stomach is fluttering. "I miss you too."

I hear the door open and know they are back from the shops. "I have to go help my family. Text me when you get home?"

"Sure. Speak to you soon, babe."

I smile and hang up.

A few hours later, I get a text. A warm tingle rises in my body as I open it.

> **Mike:** *I just arrived home. Wish you were with me. I am awfully lonely.*▢

> **Alice:** *I wish I was too. It's only a few more days. I'm sure work will keep you busy.*

> **Mike:** *I'd prefer to be busy with you.*

> **Alice:** *Oh really? How?*

> **Mike:** *Yes, very much, and naked, to be specific.*

> **Alice:** *I figured, you crazy man.*

Mike: *Send me a pic.*

Alice: *No way. I am on the couch with my sister and Mom. That's not very sexy.*

Mike: *You are sexy in anything.*

I take a picture of myself smiling and send it to him.

Mike: *You're so beautiful, and I'm so lucky.*

Alice: *Aww, thanks. I feel lucky too.*

Mike: *Well, I need to head out to the gym and get some food for the week. I'll text you when I get back.*

Alice: *Where is my pic?*

Mike: *Soon.*

Alice: ☺

A few hours pass and I'm just getting ready for dinner when my phone chimes. I check it and see it's another message from Mike, so I open it. *Whoa!* It's a picture of him—his gym shorts hang low; his top half is naked; his torso is dripping with sweat, and his wet, dark hair is sticking to his forehead. *How I want to run my hands through his hair.*

I'm rendered speechless for five minutes, staring at this impeccable picture. It's like I just got porn. I am so edgy and hot down in my sex right now. It's begging for attention. *Thanks, Mike, you royally fucked with my head and my pussy with one photo.* I excuse myself and go into my room to text Mike.

Alice: *How are you real?*

Mike: *Is that even a question? Do I need to remind you?*

Alice: *I'm pretty sure I almost died on the spot when you sent that picture. Now, I'm horny and you're not here to help me.*

Mike: *Well... I can help you now.*

Alice: *How?*

Mike: *Dirty texting and pictures, Alice.*

Alice: *Oh.*

Mike: *Yes, oh.*

Mike: *I will help you and you help me. We can get off together.*

Alice: *I haven't done this before.*

Mike: *It's fine. You'll be perfect. Don't worry.*

Alice: *Okay, lead the way.*

Mike: *Send me a picture right now. Don't overthink it. Just send a picture of you.*

I take a picture of me lying on my bed. I have a t-shirt on, and my hair is down and messy, fanning around my pillow. I hit send. Waiting for a reply feels like forever; my heart is beating fast in my chest, but I see the bubbles move within seconds.

Mike: *So beautiful. Now, take off your top.*

I quickly type back.

Alice: *Where is my picture?*

Mike: *It's coming. Give me a minute to take it. For every picture I send, I'm going to ask for one of you. I will send you one back, I promise.*

That makes me feel instantly better. I relax, taking slow deep breaths while I wait.

Mike: *Picture*

Mike is lying on his bed, pillows all around him. He is propped up on a few of them and has his arm behind his head. He is topless and his tanned body, with the light misting of dark hair on his chest, reminds me of how much of a man he really is. His lips are tilted to one side in a smirk. His eyes are a darker blue from desire, and, as usual, his hair looks like he has been running his fingers through it.

I feel hot. My skin has little goosebumps all over it, and my body temperature is rising by the second.

Alice: *You are so sexy. I want to kiss you so badly right now.*

Mike: *What else? Talk to me. Tell me... What else do you want to do to me? Don't hold back.*

> **Alice:** *I would touch your shoulders, smoothing my hands all over them. I'd trace them down your chest, lean forward and take your nipple into my mouth and suck, pulling on it with my teeth. Then I would go back to feeling my way down your abs, enjoying the rock-hard muscles under my palms. Then I'd help take your pants and boxer briefs off. I want you naked ASAP.*

While I wait, I remember he asked to take my top off—so I remove it and throw it on the floor. Do I take my bra off yet? No, I leave it on. He didn't ask for it to come off. I wish I had a sexier bra on, not just a basic white cotton. I need to go shopping for some sexy bras and panties.

> **Mike:** *You are so good at this, and you are making me so hard. I want you here touching me everywhere, taking my clothes off, and I would make you touch my cock. It's so hard and needy. Send me another pic.*

I quickly snap a picture and send it to him. I'm in the same position but without my shirt.

> **Mike:** *Beautiful. I wish I could squeeze your plump breasts in my hands and hear you moan. Then I would take your bra off and suck on your nipples, biting them, tugging on them with my teeth. You have the most perfect tits. Send me another picture of you. Topless this time.*

I receive another picture from Mike straightaway. My eyes nearly bug out of my head. His words are hot, but seeing him nude? He is covering his dick with his blankets—which is unfair—but I can see his snail trail of dark hair that leads to the treasure, and his *V* is delicious. I want to touch him. It's like a perfect arrow pointing straight down to his cock.

I take off my bra in a hurry and lie back down, sending him a topless pic, but to make it better, I'm touching my nipple with my finger. I decide that instead of a picture, I'm going to send a short video of me squeezing my tit and playing with my nipple. *This will make him crazy.* I can see that he has watched the video, then he responds.

> **Mike:** *Fuck me. You are a natural, dirty fucking girl. It makes me want to jump in my car and fuck you so hard on your bed we will wake your mom and sister up with all the noise. Take off the rest of your clothes because I need to see you naked. Now.*

> **Alice:** *Take off the sheet. It's only fair. I want to see all of you.*

He decides to send me a little video, and it's him removing the sheet slowly off his cock and once it's removed... It ends.

> **Alice:** *Unfair!!!! Send more. Touch yourself. I want to watch.*

> **Mike:** *Send me a pic of you nude.*

I rush to take all my clothes off and grab my little pink clit stimulator out of my bag and snap a picture of my clit up close. I have the toy strategically lying next to my waist.

> **Mike:** *Is that what I think it is? Fuck, you're killing me, babe. I fucking love it. I love you. You're so fucking dirty.*

He sends me a video of him slowly pulling on himself. I see precum on the tip and he takes his thumb and smears it. It's so damn erotic watching him pull on himself.

> **Alice:** *I wish I could taste you, and it be my hands on you. Pretend it's me sending you over the edge.*

That is all I send because I need to touch myself. I decide to video me using my hands to touch my body, and then I grab my clit stimulator and rub it against me. After a minute, I drop it, put two fingers inside, and pump until I'm at the edge. I hit send and continue, because the build-up is climbing. I can feel I'm close. My eyes are shut and I'm leaning back on my bed, envisioning Mike, when my phone chimes.

I open to see a video of him pulling and he comes all over his stomach. His hot sticky white cum covers his abs. The sight has me climbing even higher, and I push harder and faster, dropping my phone as I shiver when I come apart. I haven't come by myself like that—ever, and it takes me a few minutes to recover before I am reaching for my buzzing phone. He's calling me.

"Mike?" I answer.

"I needed to hear your voice. Baby, I miss you so much."

CHAPTER 37

ALICE

A FEW DAYS LATER

"What time are you leaving today?" Mom asks.

I glance at the clock hanging on the kitchen wall. "I will probably leave after lunch. I don't want to be too tired for my early shifts this week."

I finish my breakfast and help clean up.

I have been up at Mom's for the whole week now, and it's time to get back home. I want a day to catch up with the girls, get some groceries, and get myself organized for the next week when I'm back at work. I also want to see Mike. We text every day, all day, but it isn't the same. I want to kiss him and hug him and just be with him. The break has been perfect, but I am eager to get back to my life and routine now.

"Please come back sooner next time. I enjoyed hanging out with you again, Ally," Claire pleads.

"Yes, I know. That's my fault. I should have asked for time off way before now. I had so much fun. I miss being home." I sigh.

I say goodbye to Mom and Claire, then I hit the road, listening to music. I sent a text to the girls before I left, letting them know to expect me in a few hours.

When I arrive home, I notice a brand-new sporty black Range Rover parked out front. Wondering who is over visiting the girls in such a nice car, I run up the steps and open the door. I hear the television going as I head inside. Walking into the dining room, I see Tahlia is dusting and Maddison has all her books open in front of her and is writing, so I know she is studying.

"Hey, girls!" I shout to be heard over the TV. I quickly go to my room and throw my bag inside before heading to the dining table and sitting next to Maddison.

"Hey, how was it?" Tahlia wanders over, still holding the duster.

"So good. I'm mad I didn't head back sooner. I miss them."

"I bet. Don't leave it so long next time, and how was lover boy?" Maddison is wiggling her eyebrows at me.

I close my eyes, laughing at her comment. "Amazing, of course, and my family loves him." I roll my eyes.

"And that annoys you, doesn't it?" Tahlia mocks.

I laugh. "Yes. You should have seen Claire! She had a bio on the guy, and when he turned up, he had a bunch of Mom's favorite flowers. Both of them were drooling over him. It was so embarrassing."

"So, they all got along. See? It wasn't so bad, me telling him where you were."

"No, no, no, you're still in big trouble, T! How are you girls? Do anything exciting?"

Maddison points to where her books and papers are sprawled out. "This was my life. I have to hand in an assignment tomorrow."

I noticed Tahlia doesn't say anything. "What about you, T?" I question.

Her cheeks change to a shade of pink. "Err, nothing much, really."

Maddy's head spins quickly up at Tahlia and says, "Tell her."

I frown. "Tell me what?"

"I just went out for dinner. Nothing much. Did you see the car out front?" I know she is changing subjects to divert my questioning off her, but I don't want to push. Tahlia will tell me when she is ready.

"Yeah, but whose is it? No one is visiting us, so which neighbors' visitor parked out front this time?" I ask.

They both look at each other, smile, and stare at me while laughing. My stomach drops. *I don't like the sound of this.*

"What?" I snap. "Tell me what's going on." I lean back in the chair, bouncing my eyes between them.

"Did you look in your room properly?" Tahlia says coyly.

"No, I threw my bag in and came out here. What's in there?" I huff.

I'm suspicious. These girls are hiding shit from me and it's pissing me off.

"Calm down. Just go in there and look around," Maddison says before returning to her studies, dismissing me, and when I glance at Tahlia, she smiles and gets back to dusting. *Bitches.*

I wander back to my room and that's when I see the massive bunch of roses, and as I move over to take a look, they are such a strong smell. It hits me and I instantly know who they are from. I smile and shake my head. It doesn't answer the car question, but it makes me flush that he brought me these. I have missed him this week. I trail over to my bedside table to where vase is, and I notice the card... and an envelope. I open the card.

Alice,

Words cannot describe how much I have missed you, how far I have fallen for you in ways I never thought possible. Time really does make the heart grow fonder.

You are my world. You have changed me in the best possible way. Nothing will ever be enough to show you how grateful I am.

Please take my gift as a small thank you.

Love you so much,

Mike X

I grip the card tightly and bring it to my chest. My eyes well up with tears that are threatening to leak out, but I shake myself. He is sweet. One of the few times we managed to speak, he told me he has been back to his therapist this week, and he has said how much she has helped him open up. This card is definitely proof of that. There are no "player" remarks, it's just his heart. This is what I want, his heart to be open to me. I'm in love with him, and these words tell me he feels the same. I put the card back down next to the roses and open up the envelope. This has a set of keys and a note.

Alice,

The thought of you driving that death trap around, especially to your mom's and back scares me. I hope you like the car. It's my gift to you.

I will not take it back, so don't even bother asking. You know I can afford this and keeping you safe is my number one priority.

Someone is due to pick up Lady this afternoon. You cannot return the Range Rover, but it is registered in your name.

Mike X

P.S. It just needs a name.

I stare at the note and then at the keys. *What the? He is crazy.* I know my car is becoming dangerous to drive, but I have been saving up for a new second-hand car. I put the note down but keep hold of the keys as I pick up my bag and look around for my phone. Retrieving it, I dial him. I know he is at work, but I need to talk to him. He doesn't answer, so I send him a text.

Alice: *Call me when you can.*

I put the phone in my pocket and walk out of my room. The girls look up at me, waiting for my reaction.

"He is crazy if he thinks I am accepting that," I tell them, pointing in the direction of the front door.

"I don't think you have much choice," Tahlia mocks with a smirk on her face.

"I'll take it if you don't want it, but I'm sure Mike won't allow that." Maddison laughs.

"Let's just have a look at it, and then you can make your decision." Tahlia smiles.

"Okay, come on then. I can see you have been bursting to check it out." I roll my eyes at them.

"Have we ever?" Maddison is bouncing on her heels.

I look at the keys. There is an unlock button, so I press it. The car lights up. We walk toward it and I go to the driver's side. Maddison goes for the passenger side, and Tahlia opens the rear door. *Wow, it's stunning.* It has a cream leather interior, sunroof, and a hi-tech dash. I jump in and sit, and it's so soft. Scanning around, I grudgingly admit to myself that this is so nice. This is a dream car, and I feel like I am living a dream life that will disappear when I wake up tomorrow.

My phone rings in my pocket. I see his name flash. I answer it.

"Hey, babe, I assume this call is about the car?"

"Mike, this is ridiculous. It's way too much. This must have cost you a fortune. It has cream leather seats and a sunroof!"

"You're inside it, so you like it then. I made a good choice." I can hear the smile in his voice.

"Did you not listen to a word I just said? I cannot accept it," I huff.

"You are not driving around in a shitty car when I can easily afford a better and safer car for you. I would feel much happier knowing you are taken care of. Please accept this from me. It would mean a lot to me." The pleading in his tone has me sighing. *How can I refuse? Fuck him and his sweet mouth.*

"Fine, but I don't want you to think you have to buy me expensive things. I love you and that's all I need."

"Okay, I understand, and babe?" He pauses, waiting for me to respond.

"Yes?"

"Thank you, I love you. I do have to get back to work, but I will call you when I leave here. I can't wait to see you. I have missed you," he purrs in my ear.

I flush, knowing I will be driving to his house soon. And if the texts are anything to go by, I will be thoroughly fucked.

"Okay, I love you too. Talk soon."

I hang up and the girls start squealing, but I just laugh and shake my head. "Calm down, it's just a car."

"Take us for a spin! "Maddison squeals.

"I thought you had to study?"

"A quick car drive will be fine." *Of course, it will.*

"Okay, let me run in and grab my purse and lock up."

As I pull up at Mike's house, my palms begin to sweat and my heart skips a beat when he opens the door. I exit the car in a hurry and walk up to him.

"I have missed you," I say.

Mike's eyes turn dark. *He liked that answer.*

He leans toward me, closing his eyes, and I meet him halfway. When our lips join, it's the softest and sweetest kiss. His spicy scent fills my nose, and my stomach is fluttering. My sex is hot, causing the throb to become really uncomfortable. I pull away, glancing down again at our entwined hands. He helps me inside and peers down at me and kisses me again before he pulls away, biting and dragging my lip between his teeth. *Oh shit.*

I feel it in my lower belly, and my sex begins to pulse again.

"Bed," he grunts.

I can tell he is barely holding on too.

CHAPTER 38

MIKE

WHEN WE GET TO our room, I follow her inside and close the door quietly. Standing in front of the door, with my face near hers, I reach out and grab the back of her neck, bringing her close to me until her lips hit mine.

She moans, "Ohhh."

That sound is killing my restraint. I just want to strip her down and fuck her so hard right now, and then again, right after. We still need to make up for all the lost time, but we can't while we're here, so for now I kiss the fuck out of her mouth, forcing my tongue inside and stroking hers. She moans and I smile against her lips.

I kiss her for another minute before pulling away. Her lips are plump and red from the kiss, with my saliva covering them. I gently wipe them with my thumb.

I lean into her ear, and putting my mouth onto her lobe, I bite and tug it hard. When she whimpers, I speak into her ear in a grunt, barely hanging on. "I want you so bad. I want to fuck you right now."

Her eyes are half shut. Looking down at her face with my hooded eyes, I can tell she is falling and wanting to release the built-up sexual tension that I'm sure is rising between her legs. I can smell her scent and it's so delicious. *I want to taste her again.* It's been ages since I tasted her. Her hands are holding on to my waist, and she opens her eyes, bringing her gaze up to meet mine.

"Please..." she begs, and it's turning me on further.

My dick is getting painfully hard, straining in my jeans. I'm too wound up. *Fuck it.* Pushing her away gently so she takes a step back, she opens her eyes and drops her hands.

"Take off your clothes," I whisper. She smiles, a devilish grin as she quickly rips her t-shirt off over her head, which has me quietly snapping at her, "Slowly."

I want to enjoy this. I won't last long, so I want to savor these moments. She stares at me, but doesn't say a word, just begins to remove her jeans slowly until she is standing in front of me wearing only her black cotton bra and pink panties. The vision makes me smile. I love how she goes for comfort, but I still plan to buy her some lacy sets with suspenders and stockings for a touch of variety.

Her body is incredible, and I can't help but wonder if she was made just for me. I take her in, looking her up and down so slowly. Goosebumps cover her skin and I know she isn't cold. She's turned on.

"Take your bra and panties off. I want to see all of you."

She brings her arm around her back and unclasps the bra and pushes the straps off her shoulders, which makes the bra drop to the floor. My cock pulses. Her perfect size breasts and perky, pink nipples are waiting for attention. *Soon*, I think to myself, *I will devour them.* She breaks me from my spell by dragging her pink panties down her legs and stepping out of them.

She is completely bare, and her body is on display just for me.

I take a deep breath, curling my finger toward her. "Come here and strip me now." Her eyes gleam at that and she rushes over, immediately sliding her hands up the sides of my waist. Dragging my t-shirt up, she pulls it over my head and rubs her delicate hands all over my shoulders, pecs, and abs. I glance down at her hands, which are now grabbing at the button and zipper on my jeans.

She tugs them down over my ass, and I have my Calvin Klein briefs on. I chuckle when I hear her whisper under her breath, "Jesus."

My cock springs free when she pushes my briefs down, and without any warning, she grabs my dick with her hand and starts rubbing my precum over the tip with her thumb. I need to pleasure her first because I will not last at this rate.

I pick her up by her thighs and wrap them around my waist. Alice loops her arms around my neck while I walk her over to her bed and lie her down, hovering close and covering her body with mine. I'm breathing hard and heavy, trying to calm myself. My pulse is running a rapid marathon in my chest.

Alice's cheeks are flushed pink, and her eyes are dark, sparkling with arousal. *Fuck.* My dick pulsates. I drop to my knees and open her legs wide with my palms and see that she's glistening with heavy desire. I drag my finger through her wet, slick sex. I spread the arousal up to her clit and rub it in circles. Her eyes close, and she moans. "Mike."

She bites her pillow to prevent sounds from leaving her mouth while I get back to my treasure and start gliding a finger through her slickness. I slide it inside her, which gets me a mumble from under the pillow. I dip my head down and kiss the top of her lower abdomen, bringing my gentle fluttery kisses lower, until I hit her clit and stroke it with my tongue at the same time as I insert another finger in.

Then I pump her harder, pressing my fingers down on her tight wall. She is writhing around so I use my spare arm to lock her hips down so she can't move, which, seconds later, has her coming violently. Once I know she is finished and I've enjoyed every last drop, I stand up and look at her, noticing her closed eyes and very flushed face. When she finally reopens them, her eyes are crystal clear. *Stunning.*

She smiles up at me, then grabs my head and forces it down toward hers so she can kiss me passionately. I'm so hard, and I know she can feel it against her stomach because she is trying to guide me to her wet entrance. I welcome the way her hand wraps around me and guides me inside her. Our lips disconnect when I slide deep inside of her. "This feels so fucking good." I grunt and begin to fuck her hard.

There's no time for gentle.

I thrust repeatedly in the angle that allows me to hit the right spot for her. She whimpers. I continue to pump as hard and as deep as I can. Her fingernails claw at my shoulder as she chases her orgasm.

"Alice, I'm going to fill your tight pussy with my cum," I growl, knowing I won't be able to hold on much longer.

Her lips part and she tips her head back as her body shudders with another orgasm.

"Yes. Mike," she cries out.

I keep moving in and out furiously until I climax.

Laying down beside her, I wrap my arm around her waist and hold her. I smile at her sleepy face, cherishing every second before laying a kiss on her lips. "Sleep well, my love. I love you."

Her eyes spring open and she stares at me with a smirk on her face. "I love you too." My heart constricts in my chest. *She can own me with just one look.*

Now that she is back here, I will never let her go again.

EPILOGUE

Alice

A MONTH LATER

Ever since I got back from Mom's I have been wrapped in Mike's bubble and haven't caught up with Blake and the girls much.

I decide to call Blake on my way in.

"Oh, hello stranger!"

"Good morning. I didn't know if you were on the morning shift, so I thought I would take my chance."

"Yeah, another day, another morning." He sighs.

"Is everything okay?" I ask.

"Yeah, I am just over my ward. I think I need to find something else."

"I know our ward is looking for more nurses. I could check with Kate for you."

"Listen, I wouldn't say no."

I chuckle. "I just parked, but would you be free to meet for lunch so we can chat more? I have missed you." I climb out and walk toward the elevator.

"Sounds perfect."

"I'll catch you at your hospital cafeteria for lunch. Let's say noon, and if you need to change it, let me know. Just send me a text."

"Will do."

I hang up and wander to the ward.

Lunchtime arrives and I have no messages on my phone, so it looks like noon is still on. I see Blake sitting at the table with his head down and buried in his phone. I walk over to the table.

"Hey, what's for lunch today? My treat."

He hits his phone, pops it down, and glances up, beaming. "Hi. No idea. Let's go for a stroll and see what we can find." He joins me in standing and we go over to the buffet, walking along the table.

"This place has way too many choices. I'll stick to what I know."

"Pasta?" I ask.

He nods. "Exactly. At least I know it's good."

"I'm going to grab a sandwich. Meet you at the table?"

"Okay, see you soon." I walk off toward the sandwich station and he heads toward the pasta.

I order my usual chicken sandwich, and once we are seated, we dig into our food.

"Kate said to drop her off a resume. Are you working tomorrow?" I ask between bites of my sandwich.

"Awesome, thanks for asking. I am. There is so much overtime. We are shorthanded every day. Hence why I am tired and over it."

"That's rough." I sigh.

I gaze down and though I haven't eaten much, I feel like I want to throw up. "This chicken must not be cooked properly." I peel back the bread, inspecting the chicken.

"Hmm, why is that?"

"I feel like I want to vomit." Blake eyes me weirdly. "Alice, you have barely eaten anything, and you can't get symptoms of food poisoning that quickly. Have you been feeling off for a bit, like getting sick other days?"

Thinking about it, I nod. "Come to think about it, yes."

His eyebrows rise. "When's your period due?"

"No idea, it's irregular. I think soon, though, like any day now."

"You're pr—"

I cut him off. "No way, no chance." I wave my arms around.

"Only one way to find out for sure," he says with a shrug.

I gaze around and spot a pregnant woman, hand on her stomach, walking hand in hand with her partner through the cafeteria. I have never thought about it before but seeing her, smiling and happy, I let myself think about it for a second and I decide I want that with Mike.

I wander back to work thinking about it, and the longer I think, I slowly realize that the last week I have been extra emotional, had a heightened sense of smell... *Could I be?*

Getting home was like a blur. I hardly remember how I got here. I stopped off at the pharmacy on my way to pick up a test. I feel sick, like I really, really want to be sick. I pull into the driveway at home. Jumping out, I lock the car and run up the path and into the house, bolting to the bathroom as fast as my legs will take me.

I vomit violently into the toilet. My entire body is shaking involuntarily. I pull myself back to sit on my heels and lean against the toilet bowl. I try to calm myself down, taking slow deep breaths, trying to slow down my rapid pulse. I can feel my nerves kicking up. My chest is tight, and panic is flowing through my mind. I count. Ten, nine, eight... but after a few really good deep breaths, I'm slowly calming down. A knock at the door startles me.

"Alice, are you okay?" I hear Mike's concerned voice coming through the door.

"Yeah, I must have eaten bad chicken at lunch today," I mumble back. I hate lying, but until I know for sure, I can't say a word. I don't want to get his hopes up.

"Are you sure? You sound awful. I'll be out here if you need anything. Just call out."

"I'm fine. I'll call you if I need anything," I yell out.

"Okay." I hear his heavy footsteps lead away from the door.

I sigh. I pull open the pregnancy kit box out of my handbag and sit looking at the box. *I don't want to do it. Surely, I can't be pregnant. Surely.* My heart is beating erratically inside my chest. Before I can overthink it, I tear open the box and read the instructions. I know I have to wait three minutes, but I can't sit in here for that long. I rip open the film covering the test strip and once I've done the test, I cover the stick with the lid and lay it flat. I finish tidying myself up and head straight toward the shower.

"Just having a quick shower. I won't be long!" I call out to Mike.

In the bathroom, I put the stick on the counter and turn the shower on. I strip and get under the water. Being in here, I feel so relaxed with the hot water spraying on my back and helping settle my stomach. What will Mike think if I *am* pregnant?

I wash and condition my hair, shave my legs, and with nothing else left to do in the shower, I turn it off. Drying myself off, I know I'm drawing it out because I know I'm close to looking at the test, which has my nerves picking up the speed in my chest again. When I'm dry, I know I can't avoid it any longer, so I wrap the towel tightly around me and step over to the counter.

Those steps feel heavy and long when I finally reach it. I lean forward and look at the little window. *Pregnant.* Instantly, tears fill my eyes and start to stream down my face. Surprisingly, I'm happy and not completely miserable about the prospect of having a baby. I wanted this to go slow, but I'm pregnant now and I want this. I stand up, brush my teeth and finish getting dressed.

I wander out to the kitchen, where I spot Mike sprawled out on the couch, watching football. I walk over to him. Every step I take I swallow back bile. I have never been this nervous in my whole life.

His head spins and his face falls. Quickly sitting up in a panic, he says, "Babe, what's wrong?"

Warm tears stream down my face. I hiccup and hand him the stick I have been clutching in my fingers. With a shaky hand, I pass it over. His head tilts and his eyes widen. He stares down at the positive stick. I cover my face with my hands and sob.

"Babe, you serious? You're pregnant?" he says, his voice breaking. His heavy steps coming around to me. I feel his strong arms envelop me and I hug him back.

I nod into his chest.

"*Wow.*"

A soft chuckle leaves my lips. "You're happy, yeah?" I lean back to look at his face.

"Fuck yeah, babe." He leans down and pecks me.

I tangle my fingers and pull on his hair, pushing my body up against his. I kiss him and when I eventually pull back, his eyes are closed, and we are both breathing hard and fast.

He opens them, and they are a dark, shimmering blue. "Fuck me, Mama, are you horny?" I don't bother answering him with words.

Instead, I grab his top and rip it from his body. "Fuck, this is going to be the best nine months of my life if this is what your pregnancy hormones do."

I smirk up at him, and then my hands are roaming his body, and he is moaning. *I love torturing him.* I drop to my knees and the moment I undo his button, I hear the word, "Fuck" leave his lips. I lick my own and unzip his jeans, pushing them down along with his white briefs. His cock is hard and right in front of my face, so I grab it and lick it. His hands drop to my head and curl in my hair when I take him in my mouth. He is pulling on my hair, but I love that I'm the one taking the power tonight.

"Babe, I can't hold on much longer, so you need to stop, or I'll be shooting down your throat." His voice is gravelly with desire. I smile around his cock and pull him at the base even harder. "I'm coming." I feel the hot liquid hit the back of my throat seconds after his shout.

When he's done, I pull back and look up at him. His eyes are closed, and one of his hands is on his head. His chin is lifted up, and his breathing is fast and uneven. This makes me happy. He is a vision standing there naked while I'm still fully dressed. I slowly stand, which snaps him out of his daze.

His eyes open and he smirks at me, but when I strip my top and bra off, I smirk back, shaking my head. "My rules tonight."

His eyebrows rise. "Is that how it is?" His eyes are focused on me as he watches me remove my clothes and I slowly walk back to the bed.

"Yes." I take my pants and briefs off. He has followed me over while keeping his distance—respecting my rules tonight.

"How am I so lucky?"

"I want you to fuck me hard tonight. I want to scream your name as I orgasm."

That has him grinning wickedly, and he stalks over until he is standing in front of me. "You got it, babe."

He bends down, grabbing my legs and lifting me up so I can wrap my legs around his middle and moves me to the center of the bed. He hovers over me and kisses me, before pulling back and kissing along my neck, working his way down to my nipples, which he licks, sucks, and tugs each one between his lips and teeth. The sensations have me moaning and groaning for more. My hips are bucking up to find release and relief for the pressure building between my legs.

He slowly kisses and licks down my stomach, skipping my sex. I groan, frustrated at his teasing as he lightly kisses up both my inner thighs, one leg at a time and until he finally reaches my sex. He doesn't move, so I push my hands on his head, trying to get him to do something. He chuckles and blows air onto my dripping sex. *This is pure torture; I need release.* He blows one more time and my hips buck again, so he grabs my thighs, holding them down and apart.

He licks and sucks my sex until I can feel myself climbing, and I'm so close to orgasm. *He knows my body so well.* When I'm almost there, he pushes two fingers inside and rubs my clit at the same time as his tongue. I come hard on his fingers. He laps it up even while his hand is still fucking me and stimulating my clit. I knew his hands had won awards for his work as a doctor, but he's even better as a lover.

These hands are perfect. Once he finishes licking up every drop, he moves up to hover over me again and kisses me.

He lines himself up, and he thrusts in hard, exactly the way I asked. I'm building up quickly again. I have never come more than once with anyone else; I didn't think it was possible. But Mike knows how to turn me on and quickly bring me over the edge. He is thrusting into me, but I can tell he wants to go deeper, so he rolls me over until I'm on all fours, then he pushes my shoulders down and re-enters me. This new position hits the spot. One of his hands is playing with my breast and nipple and the other is rubbing my clit.

I feel overwhelmed. The pressure inside me is building up, but I'm not quite there. "Harder." His thrusts become more intense, and he begins to rub my clit, adding even more pressure. "I'm coming!"

"Me too," he groans gruffly.

I come as a powerful orgasm takes over me and I feel his cock empty inside of my body. When he is finished, he pulls out and gently lies me down on my side, cleans up, and then returns to spoon me until we both fall asleep.

EXTENDED EPILOGUE

Mike

MONTHS LATER

I have known since I met Alice that she was 'the one,' but I didn't think I would be lucky enough to be getting to have a baby with her so soon. I still want to make it clear that we are a family and I want to marry her. I want her to have my name. She already agreed that the baby will have my last name, but I want her to have it as well.

Standing in the jewelry store, I'm staring at this sparkling emerald cut ring that I have in the palm of my hand. All I see is Alice, with the unique shape and the sparkle that perfectly matches how I view her. She is going to kill me if she ever finds out how much this ring cost me, but hopefully, she never will. She deserves the best, and this is the best right here.

I glance up at the store manager. "I'll take it."

I hand over the ring and he smiles. "Good choice, sir. She will love it."

He seems kind, but I'm sure he uses that sales pitch on everyone. I don't care, though, because this is Alice's ring. The baby is due tomorrow and even if he or she doesn't arrive, then I'm going to propose. I have waited long enough. I didn't want to overwhelm Alice. The last few months have been hectic: with her moving in, all the renovations, her finishing up at work. She hasn't stopped, but I want this. My heart is telling me that this is the right time to do it.

I pay for the ring and leave the jewelry store. I pick up Alice's favorite smoothie before heading to my car. Her cravings have been the weirdest mix, and I have gone out for food at the most random of hours. But I would do anything for her. I haven't missed a single appointment or scan. I have been there every step of the way. This is my miracle family.

The sex is still crazy. She is hornier than ever, and I hope this lasts even after the baby is born. When I get home, she is asleep on the sofa. I pick her up and carry her to our bed, and set the smoothie down on the bedside table. As I step back downstairs, an idea pops into my head for how I'll propose tomorrow.

I call up Blake, Tahlia, Maddison, Angie, Claire, and my family. I set them all assigned tasks. Everyone is excited and in on the surprise.

I wake in the morning after only a few hours of sleep. I tossed and turned all night, my heart and mind both racing with nerves about today. I'm slightly sweaty, thinking about asking her, but I know she won't say no. *Well, I hope not.* Rolling over, I see she is still deeply asleep, hugging her pregnancy pillow. *That is one thing I won't miss when the baby comes.* I miss us being wrapped around each other, but at the moment, all she wants is to cuddle that massive pillow. I'm glad it's only nine months. Otherwise, I'd need a new bed. I climb out, careful not to wake her, and go get organized.

She still hasn't moved by the time I'm ready to head downstairs. I leave her a note to get ready before coming down. I immediately get started with setting up a special breakfast. I could have taken her to the best restaurant or done something grand, but I know Alice, and she will want all her closest people with her on her special day. Nothing fancy, just love, friends, and family.

The first to arrive is Blake, with Tahlia and Maddison, and a few minutes later, Alex walks into my house. Something is up with my brother; he has been different lately, but I can't put my finger on it. I've no time to dwell on it now. They help me set the table and get the decorations set up. I have already organized everything outside, and once we are finished inside, I tell them to wait out there in case Alice comes down. The rest of our families arrive not too long after, and I'm just in the kitchen making coffee when I hear Alice walking down the stairs. I grab my phone and text Alex.

Mike: *She is on her way down now. Get everyone ready. ASAP.*

When she arrives in the kitchen, I feel so happy when I see her and the bump which holds our baby. She is the most beautiful pregnant woman I have ever seen.

"Good morning, babe."

She frowns. "Hi. What's going on? Why did you ask me to get ready?" She is eyeing me and then looks at the table. Her eyes widen at the setup, and she stares, taking it all in.

"I thought I'd invite our family and your friends over for the baby brunch. They should be here soon."

Her eyes are suspicious, but she shrugs it off. "Ohhh, it will be so nice to see them. Being this pregnant, I can't move much now."

I walk over to her and kiss her. "Not long now." I beam at her.

She nods. "No, any day now."

"Well, do you mind heading outside with me? I want to show you something before they all arrive."

Her brows furrow. "Yeah, what is it?"

"Just come with me. We won't be long," I plead.

I grab her hand, holding it while we walk out the door.

She gasps and tears immediately run down her face. "Oh, my God!"

I've set everything up exactly how it was for our first date, with the projector and cushions. Everything is the same.

"Come here for a moment."

She follows me over to the rug, and grabbing both her hands, I stare directly into her eyes. *This is it.* I take a big breath in and slowly kneel in front of her. She lets go of one of my hands to cover her mouth in shock. Tears are streaming down her face. I have to do this quickly, so I can comfort her.

"Alice, from the moment we met at Luxe to now, you have been nothing but perfect. You are the most beautiful, kind, and generous woman I have ever met. I'm honored to be having a baby with you and I would love it if you would honor me again by agreeing to be my wife. Alice Winters, will you marry me?"

She is nodding and spluttering through her tears, "Yes, yes, yes!"

I pull the ring out of the box and slide it on her finger. She lifts her hand to cover her mouth again and sobs. I stand up and hug her.

Everyone then jumps out, yelling, screaming, and crying out, "Congratulations!" Alice sobs again, and when she notices her mom, she wobbles over and embraces her. Everyone does a round of congratulating us both, and when Alice comes back to stand with me, she wraps her arm around my waist.

For the rest of the day, everyone eats and drinks before leaving.

When there is only Alice and I left, I ask her, "Are you ready to watch the movie now?"

"Yes, please, Mike. Thank you for a wonderful day. It was perfect, just like you."

A few days later, at three a.m., Alice's water breaks in bed. She wakes me up, and I have never been more scared in my life. I forget all things medical and start to freak out like a madman. Poor Alice has to comfort me and calm me down between the start of her contractions.

"Calm down, Mike. Grab my bag and call the obstetrician."

I nod, then walk off and do exactly that.

The obstetrician asks us to come to the hospital so Alice can get the baby monitored and delivered by her doctor and midwife. Half an hour later, we have the car packed and are on our way. I bought myself a "Dad car." Alice thinks it's ridiculous, but I don't. I love it.

Eight hours later, I meet and hold my son, Ethan. I have never cried so much in my life. Alice handled labor like a champion. She is my queen, giving me the most precious gift of all. He is the spitting image of her and that only makes me cry harder. My chest feels like it will combust with love when I finally get to cuddle my two miracles.

BONUS SCENE

Mikes POV on the night at Luxe

MIKE

The boys want to go back to Luxe tonight. It's only been open for a few weeks, but we all bought memberships and came to the opening party. I'm here tonight with my brother, Alex, and our friends, Ryan and Jackson.

I love the atmosphere of this club. It's sexy, warm, and the crowd is full of like-minded people. It's the perfect place to pick up classy women, and the bonus is that the ratio of women to men is even, leaving plenty of both to go around. It's a great place to come and unwind after a long workweek.

We've only just arrived, and Jackson has already snagged a couch near the back of the club. It's wonderful to be able to sit down, talk, and enjoy our drinks. When it's my turn to buy a round of drinks, Ryan comes with me to help carry them back to the guys. On our way over, I notice this little knockout leaning over the bar, with her dress barely covering her ass. If she leans over any farther, I'm sure I'll come in my pants like a twelve-year-old boy. My walk falters and I'm unable to remove my eyes from her. She is in the smallest, tightest dress I have ever seen, but that's not what has snagged my attention. What I can't tear my eyes away from is her smile. It's captivating and real; she is smiling and laughing so wide it reaches her eyes.

"What's up, Mike?"

I nod in the direction of her with my chin and run my fingers through my hair. Following my line of sight, he scans around until he spots her and smiles in appreciation. "Nice."

I notice she is with a guy who's wearing really tight pants with a peach shirt. *Very strange outfit for this type of crowd.* I watch them interact for a second, noting how he is gazing around at everyone, checking them out from head to toe, but only concentrating on the men around him. I'm pretty certain they are just friends because if he is her boyfriend, then that's pretty fucked up. Ryan and I walk to the bar, joining the queue. Ryan stands beside me, and when it's my turn to order, I lean over the bar to whisper to the bartender.

"I need four scotch on the rocks, please, and do you see the girl there in the black dress and ponytail?" I tilt my head in her direction.

He looks over his shoulder until he spots her and then spins his head back to me. His brows furrow.

"Add all her bills for the night to my tab, but do not tell her it was from me."

I hand over a few hundred-dollar bills, and he takes them, stuffing them in his pocket before smiling back at me. "Deal."

While he sets off to make our scotches, I continue sneaking glances her way. I can't afford to be staring now or she will know the drinks were from me, or her friend will notice and tell her.

The bartender comes back and serves us our drinks. I scoop two glasses up and Ryan picks up the other two. "Let's head back," I mumble to Ryan. He eyes me suspiciously, and I frown back at him. "I'll be able to see her better from where we are."

Ryan nods. "Lead the way."

We walk back to our couch, carrying two drinks each. I stand next to the couch instead of sitting down so I can watch her from afar. I can see her and the guy looking around, no doubt trying to figure out who bought their drinks. Smirking, I raise my glass and take a sip.

The friend leaves her side and moves over to watch the people on the dance floor and finish his drink. She pushes off the bar and follows slowly behind. Watching her saunter toward the dance floor opposite to where I'm standing, I lick my lips, tasting the residue of scotch on my skin. She joins him on the dance floor, still holding their drinks and looking around.

A zap runs down my spine when her gaze finds mine. In that moment, I take a pull of my scotch, letting the burn of the alcohol warm my throat. I continue to stare back, never breaking our intense eye contact. She drops her glass, and it smashes to the ground, sending shards flying everywhere. I watch her squat in her tiny dress and attempt to clean it up. *A born helper.* When her friend stops her by reaching for her arm, she then leaves him while he waits for someone to clean up, and I take this opportunity to go talk to her.

I walk a little too quickly to catch up with her and purposefully crash into her. She steps backward and I reach out to grab on to her arms. "Shit, I'm so sorry."

Her eyes widen under my stare and her cheeks turn a sweet shade of pink. *Adorable.* Her sweet vanilla scent wafts through my nose, causing my pulse to beat erratically in my chest. She nods and I use this chance to take in her beauty. Standing so close, she is even more delectable. I watch as her tongue pokes out and skims her bottom lip, causing my dick to harden inside my pants.

Touching her and standing so close is elevating my body temperature to an uncomfortable level. My mouth is dry, and I need refreshment, but I don't want to leave her.

"Can I buy you a drink?" I blurt.

I stare down at her, watching her pretty pink lips part. Her eyes flutter closed, and she moves her head toward me. I don't hesitate. I bring my lips down to capture hers. I enjoy the passionate kiss, savoring her sweet taste. I am just getting started when she pulls away panting.

She clears her throat, pretending to not be affected. But her body betrays her, and before I can get another word in, she speaks. "I have to go to the bathroom. I'll catch up with you later."

I step back, dropping my hands, and watch as she saunters off into the direction of the bathroom.

What the fuck just happened? Fuck. I take off to the bar and grab another drink before rejoining the boys at the couch. I'm holding another glass of scotch when she spots me again, and I raise the glass to my lips, not breaking eye contact the whole time. The buzz between us is electric. I watch as her friend drags her to the dance floor and breaks our gaze again, so when I finish my glass, I walk around and order another one. *These are going down smoothly tonight.* It's been a long week and going home to an empty house isn't appealing. After I order, I return to the dance floor and scan it for her, still sipping my drink.

"Hello, Mike. Are you here alone?"

I look down my nose and see my ex-girlfriend, Amanda. The music is so loud I have to lean forward so she can hear me. "No, I'm here with my friends." It's simple and blunt, but I'm still trying to spot the one person I do want to talk to tonight.

Amanda continues trying to talk to me, but I only respond with one-word answers. I spot Alex in the crowd, grinding with a woman to the beat of the music, and then he spins *her*, and I freeze. Amanda is still trying to get me to pay attention to her, but I can't hear anything anymore. I shot my drink, the scotch burning my throat with its intense warmth that makes me cough as it burns down to my chest.

A server passes by, and I slam the glass on the tray and shove my hands in my pockets. I'm too engrossed with what's unfolding in front of my eyes to listen to Amanda. I gasp and grit my teeth as Alex leans down, and I'm forced to watch their lips join. Everything around me seems to fall silent, and I can no longer hear or see the girl in front of me at all.

I watch her with Alex until I'm sure she must feel my eyes burning through her. She glances over and our eyes connect again. Her eyes widen, and she drops her hands from Alex. My hands are firmly stuffed inside my pockets, and I ball them into fists.

Neither of us attempts to look away until her friend breaks our connection, and I watch as she stalks off without a second glance in my direction. A heavy sigh leaves my lips. No longer wanting to talk to anyone else tonight, I storm off and grab a taxi home, alone. *I'm always alone.*

The End.

DOCTOR I DO

SHARON WOODS

Chapter 1

Alex

"Come back to bed," my one-night stand rasps out.

My head turns, following her voice. I smile when I spot the sultry redhead leaning up on her elbow, staring sleepily up at me. Her brown eyes are trying to pull me in. When my eyes drop to the blanket that's barely covering her breasts, I resist the temptation to lean over and pull it all the way down to expose her. Memories of the sex and fun we shared last night are enough, though.

"I gotta get to work," I say, shaking my head.

As soon as she leaves, I'll never call or see her again. It's just what I do. Even at the ripe age of thirty-two, I haven't been able to settle down. Nobody seems to hold my interest or has made me fall in love. On top of never growing attached to a woman, I'm too busy with work. Most women I meet at my age want to settle down and get married and have kids. And I'm not where I want to be in my career for that...well, not yet.

I spent so long in school to become a doctor that I've only been out a couple of years as a neurologist. I want to spend a couple more years developing my skills and traveling for conferences and courses. If I was married with kids, I'd feel guilty for leaving them. Being carefree and just having fun with no strings attached suits me.

"Work is so overrated," she mumbles cutely.

I chuckle. "Looks like you haven't found your dream job."

"But I found my dream man," she purrs and flutters her lashes, trying to tempt me to crawl back into bed.

I shake my head. "I'm not him, trust me." And I don't give her a chance to argue because it would be pointless. Instead, I walk to my bathroom to shower and get ready for work.

Afterwards, I step back into the bedroom to find her sitting on the edge of my unmade bed, bent over and putting on her shoes. I know I should feel guilty, because I'm practically kicking her out, but I don't...I feel numb.

"I wish I didn't have to leave," she whispers on my doorstep.

I peer down, wishing my heart or body would react, but the same empty feeling stays. I don't answer.

"Call me later," she says, waving as she walks off.

I remain silent, knowing I won't. I don't want to lead her on.

As she climbs into her car, I wonder if I'm broken. Will my future only consist of unfulfilling hook-ups? I thought there was meant to be a person for everyone.

I'm thinking that's not in the cards for me.

Flashing the light between the patient's eyes, I watch her pupils dilate under the brightness. I nod when I see everything's as it should be, turning off the light and putting it away. Once I leave the bedside, I order a range of tests and write up her notes and a new treatment plan.

As I sit at the nurse's desk, my phone rings. When I see my brother Mike's name, I answer immediately, as I've been waiting for the call that he and his wife had their baby. "Bro."

"Hey, Alex. Ah." He sounds out of breath, and it causes me to frown and sit up, closing the file.

"Yeah," I push.

"Alice and I had the baby," he says in a monotone voice.

"Congrats!" I bellow with a grin. But why the fuck does my brother not sound excited? A wave of worry hits me. "Are you okay?"

"I...uh...don't know. It was hectic."

"Is Alice, okay?" I ask.

"Yes. But me? Not so much. I'm traumatized."

I chuckle. My older brother has always been a drama queen. "I'm assuming birth was more intense than you thought."

"Yeah, watching your wife in pain fucking sucks," he chokes out.

I swallow hard, because I can't imagine having someone you feel so strongly about that you choke on your words. Staring down at the closed file, I say, "Let me finish up here, and I'll come right up. Did you need anything?"

He breathes heavily down the line. "Nah. I'm okay."

Doesn't sound like it, but I don't say that. "All right, see you soon. And, by the way, bro, I'm pumped for you. You're going to be an amazing dad."

"Thanks. Catch ya soon."

I hang up, but my phone buzzes again. Mom's name flashes on the screen. A small laugh escapes my lips as I answer. "Yes, Mom."

"Your brother and—"

"I know. I know." I chuckle, cutting her off. "I'm trying to finish work so I can head up."

Hearing the noises in the background, I can tell she's already upstairs.

"Okay, well, don't be too long," she says kindly. Mom is a retired doctor, so she knows how much we work. But she has been pushing for more of a work-life balance...well, more on me, because of my lack of a committed relationship. I can only hope she'll leave me alone now, being too busy in the new grandma role to worry about me.

"I gotta go. I'll finish some notes and talk to the patient, and then I'll be up, okay?"

"Okay, love, see you soon," she sings-songs.

I hang up and re-open the file. I scan the observations and other notes before picking up the file and heading into the patient's room to deliver the news. As I leave their room, it's with a heavy heart, knowing the prognosis doesn't seem bright, but being a neurologist, I barely get to deliver the good news. Maybe it's because of this job I've learned to switch off my feelings.

Yeah, that could be it.

I've had to toughen up.

I'm reading emails as I enter the hospital elevator, my stomach growling, reminding me I've only had coffee today. As I'm heading downstairs to grab something to eat along the way, the doors open, and a friendly face is revealed.

"Hi, Tahlia," I say with a lopsided grin.

Tahlia is Alice's best friend. As I take her in. I remember the last time I saw her. She was dressed up for Mike and Alice's wedding. Unlike today where she's dressed for comfort. Her blonde hair is tied up in a high ponytail. A few tendrils have fallen out. They now hang loose around the sides of her heart shaped face. She's staring back at me, with big glossy green eyes framed by dark lashes. She has the cutest button nose and pouty lips that are currently parting.

"Ale—" she tries to say, but the box of cupcakes she's holding fall from her grip.

I'm moving before I register what's happening, dropping to my knees to help with the mess.

"Great," Tahlia mumbles under her breath. She squats in her dark blue skinny jeans, that I see now have pale blue icing down the side, trying to pick up the cupcakes that have dropped on the floor. From this angle, I get an up-close view of her slim neck that leads down to her low cut shirt. Ample cleavage I have no right staring at but can't help wondering how good they'd feel in my hands. I force my gaze up with a smile.

"At least you look good in blue." I try to lighten her up, and that has her eyes meeting mine. On our knees, we're closer than I thought, and I suddenly feel like I'm in the desert, desperate for a trace of water. Am I in need of some sleep, or are sparks flying?

This is new.

She peers back down, her cheeks flushed, and I finish helping her pick up the scattered cupcake destruction, pushing any wayward thoughts aside. But the icing is stuck to the floor, making it a bit slippery, so I stand and say, "I'll grab some napkins. Hang on a sec."

I stride to the cafe and grab the napkins, and when I walk back she reaches out for them, but I shake my head. "Let me."

"I would fight you on it, but I'm certain my hands aren't working properly right now." She gives me a half smile before nibbling at her lip.

I wonder if she is nervous about her best friend who just had a baby, or if it's something else.

Me?

Do I make her nervous?

Don't be ridiculous...

After I wipe the floor clean and throw the napkins in the garbage, Tahlia looks up at me curiously. "Are you working today?"

"Yeah. Do my clothes give it away?"

She drops her gaze over me. When she finishes checking me out, her green eyes land on mine again. Her tongue slides across her bottom lip as she says back with a mischievous gleam in her eye. "Navy suits you."

My heart hammers. I'm glad she likes what she see's. I can't stop the smirk spreading on my lips, knowing I feel the same way. I like what I see. "Did you work today?"

She sighs, tucking a strand of hair behind her ear. "Yeah. Even though I think my parents were right. I should've stayed in college."

Her answer surprises me. "You could always go back. It's never too late."

"I could..."

"You don't want to?"

"No. Ah...Have you seen the baby yet?" she asks, changing the subject.

I shake my head. "No, I was going to grab something to eat and head up."

"I might need to get new cupcakes." She giggles, and it's the cutest, lightest laugh. I've heard it once before at Mike and Alice's wedding, but I've forgotten just how much I love it. Hearing it again makes me feel a way I'm not used to.

I peek down and see only one cupcake could be saved. And I don't dare tell her I didn't know it was a boy, since the blue icing gave it away.

"Did you get them from here?" I wouldn't object to one right now.

"No, I picked them up at a bakery by the coffee house where I work." Her eyes flick to me, and I swear she almost seems embarrassed.

"Let's grab something for you to take up there, but first, have you had a coffee or something to eat?" I ask.

"Maybe I shouldn't have a coffee. I'm already jumpy." I swallow the disappointment swirling in my gut. I want to spend more time with just her.

"But I might go for tea and something to eat. I've worked all day and have barely eaten anything," she adds, and I spring to life at the knowledge she'll sit down with me.

"Same. I'm living on coffee."

I don't miss the way her eyes flick to my body before moving away to the food counter, clutching her cupcake box to her chest. "I'll find something to take up after."

"Good idea, but maybe pop them in the garbage before you wear any more of them."

Her head turns quickly, and she pulls the box out, to see her white long-sleeve has a smear of blue across the middle.

"Oh, God. I'm getting worse by the second."

I smile. "Let me take the box and put it in the garbage so you can go to the bathroom and clean up. I'll grab you a drink and something to eat."

She sighs with relief. "Are you sure?"

"It would be my pleasure," I say with an honest smile, trying to tell her with my face that I'm here to help her.

I take the box from her, and try to ignore how my hands graze her soft ones. I've never been so distracted by a simple touch. Clearing my throat, I get my thoughts back on track.

"Order?"

"Oh, yeah. A hot chocolate and a cookie, please."

"As a doctor, that is the worst choice, but as a friend, I'll say I'll meet you over at one of those tables." I point toward the empty tables and chairs.

"Don't doctor me around. I just need to eat my feelings right now." She smirks, and a stupid grin settles on my face as I look at her. Spinning on her heel, she walks off, but in the opposite direction of the bathroom.

"T," I call out and she turns around, brow furrowed.

I lift a hand and point in the direction of where she needs to go. "That way."

A pained expression hits her face, and I read her lips. *What is wrong with me today?*

Her face is crimson, and she keeps it down and walks fast in the right direction. I turn and dump the box in the nearest bin and set out to get us drinks and food.

As I go to order her a cookie, I scan the different flavors, wondering which one she likes.

I peer over my shoulder catching sight of her. As if feeling my eyes on her she glances back. Our eyes hold momentarily before she turns and disappears into the bathroom. I stare dumbfounded at the door she just entered. My body is excited by her. And I've never been exhilarated by a woman. That revelation leaves me pondering. Who is Tahlia Adams other than beautiful?

CHAPTER 2

TAHLIA

I'M SO DAMN EMBARRASSED, and I can't shake it. As I scrub my soiled top with hand soap and water, trying to get the blue icing out, I mutter to myself about how ditzy I seemed in front of Alex. When I saw him come out of the elevator, I was so shocked at the sight of him.

In my defense, it's the first time I've seen him in scrubs. He looked so sexy with the navy material hugging his broad chest that I fumbled and tipped the box.

He seems to unravel me unintentionally, but I need to remember he's eight years older, a playboy, and my friend's brother-in-law.

My mind goes back to the first time I met Alex, over a year and a half ago. I was on a night out with my friends at a club called Luxe, and he was dancing with Alice when I interrupted to tell her I wanted to leave. But as my eyes held Alex's bright blues, something inside of my chest jolted. And it happened again today.

That has to be why I'm clumsy and flustered today. It can't be the way his tall frame looked stupidly handsome.

His eyes framed beneath dark brows, brown hair tousled to perfection, his sharp jawline dusted with scruff, and when I dragged my gaze up to his throat. I froze. Even that part of him is sexy. How weird is that for me to think? But it is. When he swallowed, his Adam's apple bobbed, and I imagine for a second me leaning over to lick it...yeah, like I said, I'm losing my mind.

I don't like him, not like that, and I definitely couldn't fall for him.

I huff, annoyed that I can't stop thinking about him. I've already spent too long in here, so I give up when there's only a tiny bit of blue left and move to the hand dryer. Quickly, I dry it as much as I can, so I don't go out in a see-through top. I think I've managed to make a fool out of myself enough in front of Alex.

After I take a deep breath to calm the swarm of nerves in my belly, I head back out to find Alex.

I tell myself not to change subjects if he wants to discuss my job or college this time. I can talk about it. I chose this path. So, I shouldn't be embarrassed that I had no idea what I wanted to do when I finished school. Therefore, I studied what my parents wanted me to. But it didn't last long. I quit college after 2 years. I wanted to choose my future. Not have them tell me what to do. That's how I found myself working in a coffee house.

Recently, my grandfather passed, leaving me, a stake in the family business. But the condition to receive the inheritance isn't conceivable.

It isn't long before I spot him in the crowd of tables and walk up to him with a smile. I can't help but chuckle at the piles littered all over the table. Staring down at all the bags and bags of cookies, I tease him. "Are you hungry? I thought doctors ate healthily."

His face morphs with amusement, and he gives me one of his signature smirks that makes every woman drool. And I can't lie. I'm one of them, but I quickly push it away.

"I do. But, ah, I didn't know what flavor you liked, so I, um, ordered them all." His gaze drops and he looks around, as if embarrassed. It's such an odd look for such a confident man.

My mouth slacks and my heart thumps harder. He ordered me every flavor because he didn't know what I'd like.

Who does that?

He does, apparently.

My mouth opens, then closes, and I finally find my voice. "Wow, thanks. That's so kind of you," I say quietly and drag out a chair to sit. I'm in a state of shock. I can't remember the last time a man was nice to me. Especially one as hot as Alex.

"So, what is it?" he asks.

I glance up at him, still in la-la land, thinking about his sweet gesture.

"What's your favorite flavor?"

Ah, what type of cookie I like.

I answer with ease. "Chocolate chip."

He snaps his fingers and leans back into the chair. "I was gonna guess that."

I smile at his enthusiasm. I'm enjoying being around him like this. We've never had one-on-one time together; it's always been with our shared friends around.

He pushes one bag closer to me. "Here."

My gaze flicks to his, and he stares back with warm eyes. "This one is yours."

I smirk back and pick it up to peer inside. When I see the big chocolate chunks, my stomach growls. I pull it out without hesitation and take a big bite, instantly closing my eyes and moaning loudly, savoring the sugary taste on my tongue. When I open my eyes to grab my drink, I'm met with a fixed, heated gaze, thin lips and something swirling between us that feels a lot like sexual tension.

A piece of the cookie becomes lodged in my throat right at the moment he licks his lips, and I concentrate on swallowing it down, but my mouth is too dry. I grab my hot chocolate, and he reaches out, lips parting to speak, but it's too late. I've already taken a big sip, and it burns all the way down. I gasp, and wince screwing up my face as I hold back a swear but fail. "Fuck, that's hot."

"Sorry, I tried to warn you. They were hot to the touch when I carried them over," he says quietly.

I try to lighten the mood by joking. "Hence why you haven't had a sip of your coffee."

His face softens and a small lift in the corner of his lips lets me know it worked, and I watch as he opens one of the bags and takes out a cookie. Watching him chew is too mesmerizing, but I catch myself before my attraction takes over my face. I hope...

I look away to take a breath and focus on something else before I return to eating the rest of my cookie. This time, with no moaning.

"It's a decent cookie," he says, causing me to look back up at him as he wipes his mouth with a napkin.

"Yeah? When was the last time you ate a cookie?" I keep my gaze on his eyes and don't let them wander. No, my mind needs to stay away from the gutter. But I'm only human, and I can't help but sneak a glance over his body—just for a second.

A very long second...

"I can't remember, but it's a damn shame."

I scrunch up my now empty cookie bag, and then hold up my hot chocolate and ask, "Should we take these upstairs?"

"What's the rush? They aren't leaving today. Are you trying to run away from me, T?" His playful tone makes a laugh slip out of me.

I shake my head. "No rush. I just want to meet the baby and see how Alice is." It's half the truth, because I really do want to see them, but I also need to get away from Alex and his effortless sex appeal.

He stands. "Fair enough. These are too hot to drink anyway, so we can carry them up."

I raise a brow at him, surprised he is giving in to me so easily. Before I can say anything else, he continues.

"Well, maybe I should carry both, in case another accident arises." He winks at me, causing me to laugh loudly.

"No, I'm good. There'll be no more accidents for me." I pick up my drink and add, "Oh, but I need to grab some new cupcakes before we go."

"Nah, I got them already." He reaches down beside him and lifts a box to the table. I look at the box, and then back at him, at a total loss for words. He's a lot more thoughtful than I assumed he would be. I imagined him as a selfish and hard to talk to type of guy, but so far, he's been the complete opposite.

"How?" I ask, confused.

"Ordered and delivered them from a bakery nearby."

I must've been in the bathroom longer than I thought...

"Thanks."

He rubs his chin like he's pondering over something. "They're not the same cupcakes you had."

I shrug. Knowing I'm grateful for anything other than empty hands. 'That's okay. What do I owe you?" I grab my purse to pay for them.

"Don't be silly. They're my family too." He shakes it off like he's offended.

"But it's my gift."

"I won't tell them if you don't."

I blink, totally taken off guard by his kindness. "After my day so far, I don't have it in me to fight you."

He leans down, his breath hitting the side of my face and causing the hair on my neck to prickle at the closeness. "You wouldn't win anyway."

∾

The walk to the elevator is almost painful. I'm taking steps with care in an attempt to not make a fool out of myself in front of him. Again.

There's a hint of sexual desire—totally coming from me—that's circling around us, one I'm finding very hard to ignore.

Once we arrive at the elevator, he presses the button, and we remain silent. His deep woodsy and caramel scent are so strong, I can almost taste it. It causes the tingle to spread between my thighs. Maybe the fact he showed me his tender side is making me sensitive. It's tricking my body into thinking what if he was naked and all I could inhale with every breath was him?

Yeah, no, dumb idea. I'll never give in to the temptation with him.

We step into the elevator, and I sag against the wall, grateful for the people inside, even though I stay standing beside him. It feels better knowing the people are barriers for my dirty mind today.

My mouth parts into an easy smile when I realize I'm about to see my friend. I push the tingling feeling for Alex away and replace it with pure happiness. "I can't want to see if he'll look like Alice or Mike."

"I bet he looks like Mike. It's a boy, after all, Tahlia." The way he says the word "boy," my heart drops, and I gasp, lifting my gaze to his humorous one.

"You didn't know, did you?" I ask with wide eyes.

He shakes his head, but the playful smile keeps me from feeling any worse than I do. And right now, I want to kick myself for being so stupid.

I drop my chin to look at the floor.

"Hey. I don't mind. I'm the shit brother who never asked when Mike called."

My head lifts, and my eyes hold his as he continues. "Don't beat yourself up, but maybe don't tell me his name." He winks, and I can't help but laugh.

The elevator doors open, and we exit, walking through the short corridor and straight up to the nurses' desk.

"Hi, Doctor Taylor." I watch as the nurse looks up at Alex with hearts in her eyes and a flush across her cheeks. Suddenly, I'm a little jealous.

"Hey. Can you tell us which room Mike's in?" he says without even a flicker of flirting to be deciphered, which I didn't expect. I've seen him flirt. Maybe because he's at work? Yeah, that's probably it. But secretly, I wouldn't mind if it was because of me.

"Sure." Ignoring me completely, she glances at a piece of paper, then up at Alex. "Room twelve," she answers sweetly.

"Thanks," he replies with a charming smile before pushing off.

He really could charm anyone.

I walk off in the direction of their room and knock on the door. Alex's shoes sound behind me, but I don't wait. I want to see my best friend and her baby.

"Come in," Mike's voice bellows from behind the door.

I hurry inside and beam as I see Alice holding her baby. Tears prickle behind my eyes as she smiles through puffy, tired eyes up at me.

I step straight over to her and hug her, whispering into her ear, "Congratulations," before sitting down in the nearby chair. "Tell me everything." I shuffle my butt to the edge of the chair to get even closer.

"I'm not going to scare you, but it was intense. The ring of fire is something I don't want to feel again anytime soon." She shudders, as if remembering it vividly.

I scrunch up my face, telling myself to not Google it, because it will probably turn me off from having kids in the future. And one day, I want a family of my own.

"I'll take your word for it," I say.

Her eyes drift to Alex and then back to me, and her brow raises.

"What?" My voice stays hushed so the guys can't hear.

Her eyes flick to Alex again before answering in a soft tone. "What's going on there?"

Swallowing, I reply flatly, trying to seem unaffected. "Nothing."

"Are you sure? He keeps looking over at you."

He does?

I can't help but peek over from the corner of my eye, and she's right. He stands in the back of the room with Mike, his hands inside his pockets and those blue eyes set straight on me.

He's not interested. They're probably just talking about the baby or my cupcake incident downstairs, not about me, specifically.

"I dropped the cupcakes for you downstairs and wore half of them. He's probably retelling Mike how much of a clumsy mess I am."

"No, you didn't," she says with a chuckle that causes the baby to cry.

"I did."

She cuddles him closer, cooing to soothe him, and I use the opportunity to get off the topic of Alex fast.

"How long was labor?" I ask, but instantly regret it. I don't really want to know how long my best friend was in pain.

"Twelve hours."

Yeah, that sounds awful.

"That's a really long time," I say with a wince.

She shrugs, and then asks me, "Did you want to hold Ethan?"

My mouth opens with a wide smile. "Do I? Of course, and by the way, I love his name."

"It's sweet, just like him," she says as she looks at Mike longingly, and I wonder what that would feel like. To be utterly consumed with a man who you can trust and love wholeheartedly.

She gently places Ethan into my arms and giggles.

I look up at her and frown. "What?" I ask in a rush, thinking I'm doing something wrong and hurting him somehow. I haven't got experience with babies.

"You won't hurt him, relax. You're so uptight."

It does feel uncomfortable to be sitting so straight, so I take a big breath and ease back into the chair, staring down at Ethan. Smiling, I think of what Alex said to me earlier, and I look over at him. I'm taken aback, as his tight expression is firmly focused on me. It's so intimate and unexpected, it causes my throat to tighten. I swallow so I can speak. "You're right, he looks like Mike."

Alex doesn't move or say anything, he just stands all hot and broody across the room, watching me. I feel like I'm on fire again.

"Told you," Mike says, and I tear my eyes to Mike and his bemused face looks directly at Alice.

I drag my eyes back to Ethan, but I still have Alex's gaze burning a hole through the side of my face.

Chapter 3

Alex

I'VE GONE FROM WANTING to know what color panties and bra set she's wearing to watching her hold a baby. I've never been a family man, but there is something holding me tightly by the throat at watching her with Ethan. There is this new glow on her face, and when she locked eyes with me, there was a wave of peace shining in her eyes. Ethan stayed asleep, and once she eased back in the chair, I thought straight away she was a natural at this.

"How's the dad mobile?" I ask, but I'm unable to tear my gaze from Tahlia.

He grumbles and mutters, "It's okay, I guess..."

"You still sour because you had to give up Marty?" This time, I turn to him with a shit-eating grin. Alice nicknamed his Aston Martin "Marty," and he will never live it down. It's the fun side of Alice. She is so innocently sweet, ignoring anyone who laughed at her habit of naming cars. It's her thing and I kind of love it about her.

My gaze wanders back to the woman in the chair. After today, I probably won't see her again until Ethan's first birthday, and what a damn shame that is. I run my gaze over her and memorize every dip and curve in her delectable body.

"You should have seen how much I cried after Ethan was born."

My lips part. "Wh-what?" I stutter, shock transforming my expression.

His eyes focus on Alice, who stares back at him warmly. "She handled labor so well. Like, it's fucking traumatizing. And then, the next minute, they lifted a little piece of me and her onto her chest, and I bawled like a fucking baby. The feelings were so overwhelming."

"How come you felt like that?" I didn't mean for that question to leave my lips, but I'm curious about what made my hard-ass brother break down. It's not like him.

"I remember it all too well; it's so fresh in my mind. My chest was going to combust with pride. She's a warrior."

While he's all soft and sleep deprived and won't think anything about my questions, I ask what I'm dying to know. "How did you know she was the one?" I say it quietly, not wanting the girls to overhear.

His face breaks into a bright beam of glee. "She feels like home. Keeping me safe, warm, and loved."

Home?

What does that mean?

I don't ask, because I figure if I have to ask, then I've never felt it.

I remember last night, when I was with another meaningless hook-up, how numb and hollow I felt...definitely not a feeling of home.

I was cold, not warm.

There was no care or desire to hold on to them because I love her with every piece of me.

Yeah, no, that's not where I'm at. My life is to focus on my career, and when it's my time, I'm sure I'll know.

"Yeah, that makes sense."

The girls have stopped talking, and the room is now quiet. I'm still leaning back, watching Tahlia hold Ethan with fascination. "Why'd you ask? Are you seeing someone?" Mike asks.

Tahlia's head turns to us curiously, so I say loud enough for her to hear, so she knows, I can see her listening in.

"No, I'm just curious, that's all." I shrug, and he nods, and luckily doesn't push any further.

A knock sounds at the door, and it swings open.

"Where is this little man?"

I peer over and see Tahlia's roommate Maddison, and her friend Blake. Everyone says hi, including me, but I know it's my cue to leave. There are too many people in this room.

I turn to Mike, whose puzzled expression stares back at me. "I'll let you all catch up, and then I'll come back later for a hug."

Blake and Maddison take a seat directly next to Tahlia, and she stands immediately, handing over Ethan into Maddison's arms.

Mike rolls his lips, as if deliberating something. "You know what, I might grab a coffee from downstairs and let them be alone for a minute," he says.

I nod and wait as he crosses to the other side of Alice. She smiles lovingly as he whispers something and presses a soft kiss to her lips before rejoining me.

"Ready?" he asks.

I walk over to the group, Mike behind me.

Tahlia looks up, curiosity etched into her face.

"I'm going to leave you all to meet Ethan. Nice seeing you again T, Blake, and Maddy. I hope to see you again soon."

Blake winks. "I'll probably see you at Luxe this weekend."

"Maybe." I shrug, not knowing what I'll be doing. I have a membership that costs me a small fortune, and it's a good place to drink and unwind after work, so I might just be.

I give them a genuine smile, then look over at Alice. "I'll see you soon. Rest up and kick them out if they're annoying you." I wink.

As the group gasp, Maddison fires back, "Shut up, you."

I chuckle and take one last glance at Tahlia before giving her a smile, to which she gives me a wide one back. I dip my chin, and, for some reason, my chest feels heavy as I exit the room.

I swing my driver and hit the ball, watching as it sails into the air.

"Nice shot, son," my dad says proudly.

My lips part into a smug grin before watching it land on the green perfectly. Fuck yeah.

"Think you'll be going down, old man," I say as we walk back to the golf cart. I take my seat on the driver's side as he slips in beside me, holding on to the bar when I take off.

"I think I might be buying you beers today."

"You may have had a better chance if Mike was here," I tell him, taking a quick glance at his profile.

"Ha. You mean come in second instead of last?" He meets my stare.

"Exactly." Still grinning, I look ahead of me and put my foot down to go a little faster until we arrive at our golf balls. I park.

"Are you on call this weekend?" Dad asks, as we both step out of the cart.

He walks around to pull a driver out of his bag and walk up to his ball.

I stay silent as he makes his hit, and then I answer, "No, I'm off, so I'll catch up on a little paperwork, maybe watch the game, or go to Luxe, but really, nothing much."

He walks over to me, fit as the sixty-six-year-old he is, and comes to stand beside me. I keep my arms over my chest as his ball lands closer to the hole.

"Nice," I mutter.

"Is there someone you're meeting up with at Luxe?"

I tilt my head in the cart direction in silence, offering to get in the cart.

"Do you mean a woman?" I pull on the brim of my green hat, shielding the sun from my eyes. I'm pissed I forgot my sunglasses at home.

"Of course, I mean a woman."

I chuckle. "I'm just checking. But to answer your question, no, I'm just catching up with my friends, Ryan and Jackson."

"You know your mom kills my eardrums over you not settling down or bringing anyone to Sunday dinner."

I roll my eyes, picturing her talking my dad's ear off about my single life and how I need to settle down, as Mike and my sister Stephanie did.

"I can imagine her following you around the house, lecturing you. How I'm the last one and how disappointed she is."

I pinch my lips closed at the last part, hoping he didn't hear it, but it slipped out. It was supposed to stay in my head. But of course, I'm not lucky and the old bugger has the best hearing.

"She isn't disappointed; she just doesn't want you lonely or to never experience love."

Sitting in the parked cart, I don't make any moves to get out. I sit still, holding the wheel in my hands, and stare out at the lake the course backs onto. The trees, shrubs, and peacefulness are hard to beat out here. It's the best course to play at. I try to do this once a week with him now that he's semi-retired, but I've been so snowed under with work that I've missed a few weeks. I continue watching the lake, not wanting to face him when I talk about how I feel. It's not that easy to confess the hollowness, the empty sex, and the lack of connections I fill my life with.

"I don't believe I'll be lonely...but I don't know about love. I don't have much faith that it's out there for me."

"I think you will find the right person at the right time. Well, that's what I tell your mom anyway." He grabs my shoulder with his hand and squeezes. Not a tight one, just a dad offering his soft, reassuring squeeze.

I'm hoping he's right.

Chapter 4

Tahlia

"How was work?" Blake asks, watching me grab some Doritos from the cupboard for us to graze on while we chat in my kitchen.

"Crap. I seriously hate my life right now," I mumble as I tear open the bag and pop one in my mouth. I'm hangry. I didn't get time for a break today.

"I get that. But quit." He grabs the bag off me to eat a chip, chewing it loudly.

"I can't. I don't wanna sit around all day. I need to keep busy. But this wasn't the life I thought I'd live."

"Why's that?" he asks with a slight frown.

I grab another chip and shake my head as I eat it before speaking.

"I rent, I'm single, and I hate my job, but I can't quit because I don't even know what to do instead. There's nothing I like other than styling clothes, and college isn't for me."

He turns to the fridge, grabbing the wine out to refill our glasses.

"You're only twenty-four. Calm the fuck down. Things will pan out the way they're meant to."

"I hope you're right," I mumble.

"I'm always right. Oh, and before I forget, your mom called, looking for you."

I roll my eyes. "I'll call her back."

"When?" he asks with a raised brow.

I sigh, knowing I'm not calling my parents back tonight. "Soon. I just need a second before dealing with people who have my life mapped out for me."

"Fair enough, babe. It's your life. I'm just the messenger," he says as he fills the glasses.

"Not too much, Blake." I hold my hand out. We've already had one glass of wine, and it doesn't take much alcohol for me to feel a buzz running through my body. Especially with the lack of food today.

"All right. All right. Keep your panties on," Blake replies with an eye roll.

I take the glass he offers me with a smile, and he lifts his to cheers with me. "To a good night."

"To a good night," Blake says.

We almost clink our glasses when we hear a screech. I jump from the surprise.

"Wait! I'm coming," Maddison adds, her heels clicking fast on the tile behind me. I spin and watch her approach. Gripping the counter with one hand, she grabs her glass with the other and holds it between us. "Cheers."

I flick my gaze from hers to Blake's, and we all say "Cheers," clinking our glasses together before taking a generous sip.

My phone rings. I put my glass down and run to my bedroom and pull it off the charger, seeing Alice's name on the screen. Answering the video call, I hold the phone out, smiling.

"Hi," I whisper, seeing Ethan in her arms. I head back to Maddison and Blake, turning around so we can all huddle together to talk to Alice.

"Where's that hottie of a husband of yours?" Blake asks.

Alice's eyes light up and it's like she just got married, not just had a baby. I've heard there's a new love for your husband when you have a child, seeing the way they dote on you and the baby and how you look at them with a newfound love. And she's definitely glowing, her cheeks flushing at the mention of Mike.

"He's gone home to shower and eat."

"I was going to say, I'm surprised he left your side," I tease.

"It wasn't easy. He took a lot of convincing," she says.

"You mean you offered him a blow job," Blake counters.

I suck in a breath and turn to Blake to narrow my eyes. "Little ears."

"Come on, T, lighten up; he's a baby."

"Not the point," I grumble, leaning back and grab my wine to take a sip.

"Wine? Where are you all off to?"

"Good old Luxe," Blake answers with enthusiasm. He's always the most excited to go compared to the rest of us. Don't get me wrong, it's the best place in town, and it doesn't have sleezy drunk men everywhere. It's filled with the most successful men and women around, so out of all the clubs, it's the place to be.

Alice's face pinches. I know there is a mix of happy and painful memories from Luxe. And I wonder if I'd rather be going out or be her, married with kids.

If I were Alice, I'd be right where she is, but I'm still trying to figure out my life and career, whereas she was a nurse and following her dreams. Me...well, I have no idea who Tahlia Adams is. That chapter is still to come.

"Well, come on, if I can't be there, show me what you're all wearing."

I show Maddison's and Blake's outfits off before facing it to me. As I tilt the phone, Alice grins at my tight white dress. White is risky, but it is one of my favorite colors to wear. I just don't know how much dancing I'll be doing in it.

"Of course, T outdoes us all by rocking something unusual and stylish. Bordering between slutty and sexy," Blake cuts in.

An easy smile plays on my lips. I do have style. Maddison requested I help her find an outfit tonight, so I loaned her my new black dress that has rhinestones on it, outlining her curves. I paired it with her own black peep-toe stilettos and a matching black bag. Blake chose his own colorful tropical shirt. I'd love to style him, but he flat-out refuses. He likes his unique look. And to me, that's what styling is about. A look you love and feel your best in.

"You all look amazing. T, you've heard me say this before, but you should be a stylist," she coos, before adding, "I'm not jealous, other than wanting wine, but I can't while I'm feeding. But soon, wine nights at my house."

"Oh, look at you, Momma. Already needing the booze," Blake teases.

"No, but I'm still young and want to be around my friends. I have zero desire to go to Luxe, but wine...yes, please."

"Why are you talking about wine?" Mike's voice can be heard in the background.

"Nothing, calm down." Alice rolls her eyes at us, but the lift in the corner of her lips lets us know she loves the bossy attitude Mike exudes. "I've gotta go feed Ethan."

"Okay. We should go call a taxi, so you guys have a good night. Thanks for calling. Miss you," I say, waving my hand at the camera.

"See you all soon."

We all say bye, and then I hang up and put the phone down on the counter.

"I ordered the cab," Maddison says.

"Thanks," I say picking up my drink, I take another sip.

"I can't believe she has a baby," Blake says.

"I know! She is a baby herself," Maddison replies.

"She's not a baby," I argue.

"No, I know, but she's still young. Are you saying you'd be down for a baby at this age?" Blake asks.

My face drops in horror, and I shake my head vigorously. "No way. I can't care for a child. I haven't got a house, or a stable career, or—"

"A man," Blake interjects.

"Exactly! No. I'm not ready. You two have more of a chance of settling down than me," I say.

They both turn toward each other and burst out laughing. And I can't help but join them.

Blake composes himself quickly to throw back his drink in one go before demanding, "Chug, girls."

My brows pull together, not understanding what's the rush.

"The cab's here," he says, answering my silent question.

I hold the glass up and see it's still half full. Bringing it to my lips, I drink it quickly. I should't be drinking anymore tonight, I have work again tomorrow. I don't want to be hungover while dealing with my arrogant asshole of a boss. He is bad enough sober.

Putting the glass down, we grab our bags. We don't bother with coats, knowing it's always warm inside the club. We will only be cold for the few minutes lining up.

The drive isn't long, and when we arrive at Luxe, we join the line to get in.

Once we're inside, Maddison and Blake go straight for the bar.

"Wait. Not for me," I call out, grabbing Blakes arm to stop him.

"Come on," Blake pleads, clasping his hands together and fluttering his lashes.

I playfully hit his shoulder. "No, I'm pacing myself. I'll have one soon. I'm already warm from the first two drinks."

"Lightweight." Maddison laughs, and I nod.

They turn to the bar while I go looking for a free area for us to sit down. Spotting one in one of the very back corners, I turn and yell, "Blake."

He turns, and I point in the direction I'm going in. "Chairs."

I ease myself between all the hot suits and sleek dresses, and as I'm about to sit, I see a man sitting too. He's on a call. I'm about to speak when I realize who it is. At the sight of Alex, I'm gulping down air like I need the breath to speak.

He hangs up and tucks the phone into his pocket.

"What a nice surprise," his velvety voice says, pulling my gaze up to his amused face. He must've caught me checking him out. It's not my fault he wears a suit so well.

"Hi, Alex," I say, my head tilting to the side. If I was a smart woman, I'd think of a way to get up and leave and not see him for the rest of the night. But I'm not smart when it comes to Alex.

"I haven't seen you here for a while," he replies, his eyes dropping to my mouth.

"Yeah, I don't come as often as you, clearly," I tease, licking my glossy lips.

His smile broadens before his eyes meet mine and hold them. "Are you jealous?"

"What? No!" I scoff, pretending to be offended.

I'm not...right?

Even if there was a slight green-eyed monster, I would never let him know. His ego is as big as this room.

"You seem defensive."

"And you're being an ass," I say without thinking. My hand flies up to my mouth, unable to comprehend the fact I just said that to him.

He doesn't seem bothered at all. Instead, as I stare back, I see humor and a twinkle in his eye. He leans in. "I knew you'd be like this."

I want to ask what he means by that. Knew I'd be like what?

But as Blake and Maddison take their seat, there is no way I'm asking now. I pick up my drink and take a big sip, my dry mouth thankful for the cold liquid.

"What were you two talking about?" Maddison probes. Her eyes dance between me and Alex.

He eases back in his chair and my hand trembles, so I lower the glass, scared I'll break it with my nervous energy.

I glare at Alex and silently beg for him not to tell them, but of course, he doesn't listen.

"Tahlia called me an ass."

"I said you're *being* an ass," I fire back, clutching my hand into a fist and biting down on my finger. Dammit!

Blake and Maddison let out a roar of a laugh and I roll my eyes at their reaction.

"You're two are being ridiculous," I say, crossing my arms over my chest. But secretly, I'm pinching my lips together to prevent a smile from leaking through. Alex is watching me with a dark expression the whole time. I desperately want to ask what he's thinking.

Alex sits talking to Blake and Maddison, but I can't seem to find my voice right now.

My body is quivering with desire. I can't concentrate long enough to think. The way he keeps looking at me makes me worry about how much restraint I have to keep my hands to myself tonight.

"I better get back to my friends," he says. His smooth voice feels like a caress over my skin, and I bite down on my lip to stop from asking him to stay a bit longer.

Maybe it's better for me if there's distance between us. He doesn't remove his gaze from me, and for a minute, I think he won't go, but then he dips his chin and moves to join his two friends. Ryan and Jackson. They stand by the dancefloor clutching glasses filled with amber liquid as they talk. I didn't even notice them when he was here. Maybe because he clouds my thoughts.

I haven't been able to take my eyes off him since he walked off. My eyes linger over his tall, suited frame and admire how he holds himself with others.

He exumes sex and power.

All eyes are on him.

Including mine.

Annoyed at myself, I drag my gaze back to my friends, who wear curious expressions. Taking a deep breath, I sit back, expecting a lashing. But they look away. I don't miss the way Blake shakes his head before sipping his drink.

I turn to avoid Alex, so I swivel to watch the crowd on the dancefloor under the strobe lights. The club music is much louder than when we arrived, trying to get everyone on the dancefloor and away from the outer edges. I know soon we will be down there until our feet ache, and we want to collapse from exhaustion.

"Did you want another round of drinks?" I yell, cutting through their conversation.

"Yeah! Then let's dance!" Maddison shrieks, as if her voice wasn't loud enough. I can't help but giggle and nod. Rising to my feet, I speak when my bladder twinges.

"I need the bathroom before our next round," I confess.

"Same," Blake says loudly.

We all stand, and before I move a step, I peek over my shoulder at Alex and his friends. His back is to me, but I notice a few women are now talking to them, and a sigh slips from my lips. Just as I turn back around, he catches my eyes and holds my gaze. He scans me openly. As if he's undressing me with his eyes. My heart thumps louder in my ear at the attention. I give him a small smile before walking off. I need a moment alone to cool down. The sexual chemistry between us tonight is palpable.

Making my way through the crowd to the bathroom is a mission, but getting to the front of the bar afterward is almost impossible. I slide against bodies to get to the front, and once I order a round, we stand together, swaying to the new song.

As soon as Maddison finishes her drink, she shouts, "Let's go."

"Hang on, I'm not done." But as the words leave me, Blake tips his head back and drains his glass.

Dammit. Now I have to hurry.

I take a big sip, but wince from the taste of alcohol. This vodka cranberry is so strong, my stomach dry retches. I can't drink the rest, so I lower the glass and follow them out onto the dance floor.

It isn't long before I'm moving my hips to the beat, getting lost, and sweat beads trickle from my neck down my back. I grab my hair and bring it to one side, trying to cool off. The dance floor is crowded, and my feet keep getting stepped on every two minutes, but I'm lucky they're aching from dancing, so I can't feel them anyway.

The next song comes on, and it's slower, so I slow my hips to a rocking motion. A moment later, I hear a tear and a cool draft hits my legs, I know it's the back of my dress. Internally, I curse and squeeze my eyes closed. Why is my luck so bad lately? Who have I pissed off?

I reach down quickly and touch it, happy to find only a small tear. But I don't have long to dwell on it, because I'm met with surprise when I back into someone. I jolt, and I'm about to spin, but a warm hand snakes around my waist. It's causing my throat to constrict with the panic rising, and I'm about to tell him to remove it.

But then there's a warm breath against my neck as someone whispers in my ear, the panic transforming to a hum when I recognize the deep, velvety voice.

"It's me. I've got you, T. Dance with me." Alex's words tickle my neck, and his scent is even stronger and more intoxicating this close. Suddenly, I feel lightheaded, and it's not from the alcohol.

Did he know my dress ripped, and he's helping me cover myself?

The song changes to more of a R&B rhythm, and I feel the bass in my chest. His body slides behind me, closing the distance between us, so we are flush together. The movement causes all the air to leave my lungs.

"Grab onto me," he whispers against my neck, and I follow his direction without a second thought. I want to dance with him.

As soon as my hands grasp his forearms, I notice how thick and muscular they are, and then his soft hair adds some texture. I move my hands lower to intertwine with his. He accepts and then tightens his grip. A spark of electricity thrums through me. I rest my head against his powerful chest and brush my ass against his groin. Our hips move in a sensual rhythm, making my body tremble. There's a need between my thighs I've never felt before. Feeling his obvious erection against my lower back sends a dull throb into my sex, and I want more than anything for his hand to slide under my dress and inside my panties.

"What are you doing?" I ask as loudly as I can through my dry throat.

He steps back and spins me, and I stare up into his eyes as I'm pulled against his chest. They are heavy with lust, and it makes me feel desired, wanted...sexier than ever. His hands hold my hips, and he continues to dance, bringing me closer, our eyes locked on one another's. Both of us are breathing heavily, his breaths coasting over my face. When he moves his lips closer, I wonder if he's about to kiss me. I want him to. I even lick my lips in preparation.

"Dancing with you," he answers simply. His words pull me from my lust-filled haze, and my gaze moves from his perfectly shaped lips over his sloped nose and up to his dark, heated blues.

I stare back, at a loss.

He moves his face into my hair, his hot breath tickling my ear. "Does this feel good?"

I'm too transfixed with his face being so close to mine that I need to concentrate on breathing.

Yes, this feels good...a little too good.

CHAPTER 5

ALEX

"T, HONEY, ANSWER ME." My voice is husky from the desire coursing through my veins. Our faces are dangerously close, I can hear her pant.

I'm so hard from Tahlia's sexy ass grinding against me. There's no way she didn't feel it.

I need a second to pull myself together. It seems she does too. Her mouth opens and closes. She's still trying to catch her breath.

The alcohol I consumed evaporated the moment I had her in my arms; the soft curves of her body fit perfectly against my hard ridges. I enjoy holding her, but spinning her and seeing those heavy, lust-filled eyes sent a thrill up my spine. I noticed the tear in her fitted white dress, and I know she wanted to leave, but I saw it as my opportunity to sweep in and cover her up. But the moment I held her, I wanted to dance with her. Enjoy the moment.

A smile erupts on her face, telling me this is a really good idea. Most of her blonde hair is to one side, but some pieces are cascading down her back. Dropping my gaze lower, the white fabric clings to her and enhances her lush, full ass that looks like a good handful. I'd love to get my hands on her curves and lift her up into my arms, but I don't want to scare her away, or worse, tear her dress further and expose her to other guys here. The thought makes my teeth clench, not wanting anyone to see her body, so instead, I keep my hands around her hips.

"Mm-hmm," is all she says.

Leaning toward her ear, so she can hear me, I'm hit with her strawberries and white chocolate scent, and it makes me swallow a groan from how perfect it is. It's everything her—sexy, sweet, warm, and Jesus, I want a taste.

"Where's your voice tonight? Are you enjoying this?" I ask again.

"No. I just...like this music," she says, highly amused.

"If you say so," I reply playfully.

I swallow at how close her face is to mine. She's so close I can almost taste her breath, and I wonder what those lips would be like to kiss. She's staring at me with come-fuck-me eyes, and even if it kills me, I don't give in.

"Of course, I'm enjoying this. I'm sure you can tell. But I'm surprised you can dance," she says with a teasing tone.

I cock a brow. "Really? Did you think I was that uncoordinated?"

She peeks up at me, blinking, her thick black lashes standing out against her bright green eyes. They are drawing me in. "Yes, I didn't picture you to be good at dancing. I thought grinding would be the best hip action you could do." Her lips pinch together to prevent a smile, and she turns her head to stare out at the crowd.

"Why?" I tilt my head, only getting a view of her profile, as she refuses to look at me.

Her lips part and she mutters, "Because having a woman in front of you, directing you, is easy."

She has no idea how much restraint I have right now not to come inside my pants from the way her ass moves against me.

Taking a deep breath, I speak directly into her ear.

"I would love a woman to direct me and show me what she wants me to do with these hips." And I don't have to wonder if she gets my double meaning, because her eyes roll. I bet underneath her sweetness is a bold and sassy woman, yearning to be set free. She seems very close-lipped with me, and I can't help but be excited by that.

Maybe I'm different for her?

"Always a hook-up with you," she says in a clipped tone like the word "hook-up" is disgusting to her.

I'm about to argue, when Blake cuts in, yelling, "Look at you two, the picture-perfect couple."

As soon as those words leave his lips, Tahlia's warm body and presence slip away, and my body mourns the loss with a shudder. I don't turn to Blake or respond, as I'm too busy stopping myself from begging her to come back and dance with me. The way her arms are crossing under her chest, it pushes her breasts up and out of her dress, and my brain isn't working properly, too busy lost in dirty sex positions with my dick and her tits.

"No way," she yells back, but it lacks conviction.

And I can't be irritated, even though I know we shouldn't hook up for the sake of her heart. I'm sure I'd break it, and then Mike would lose his shit at me over it, because Alice would be upset, and no one upsets his wife.

"Imagine the hot babies," Blake says.

Yeah, no, that's drawing a line, even for me. "Sorry, bud. Not happening."

Maddison comes over with a fresh round of drinks. I look over at Tahlia, and she's wearing a hurt expression. Surely, not over the kid comment, or because I won't kiss her? No way, it must be something else. But before I can ask if she's okay, she turns away, telling Maddison she isn't drinking anymore tonight. When she faces me again, the hurt has gone, and her smile is back.

We dance for a little longer, and this time, I hate it. I'm not touching her at all, not even our fingers lacing together. I keep my gaze locked on her hips, watching them sway from side to side and moving to the beat of the music. We're all pushed closer together, and with each song, the crowd gets drunker. I take the opportunity to speak to her while everyone's distracted.

"Are my dance moves getting any better?"

Her eyes glow under the strobe lights and the little tilt of her head makes me grin.

"You're not bad. I'll give you that, Doctor."

My brow rises and my lips quirk. "Doctor?" I ask with mischief.

"Well, you are one, right?"

"Oh, the sass on you, T," Maddison says.

I flick my gaze to Maddison, wishing she didn't hear our chat, because Tahlia curls back away from me. All the humor gone. She's back to the quiet Tahlia I've seen when I've been around her with Mike and Alice. But at the hospital and tonight, she's flirted with me, and I have to admit, I like her relaxed and flirty.

"What? He's a doctor, that's all," she replies to Maddison's and Blake's shocked expressions. They don't seem so sure about it, and I'm not saying a word.

"I am a pretty good one too," I say, giving Tahlia a lopsided grin.

She rolls her eyes and smirks back. "I would hope so."

Maddison and Blake finish their drinks, and as soon as Tahlia notices, she says, "You guys ready to go? I've gotta work tomorrow."

And I wonder if she's speaking the truth, or if she's trying to run away from me.

"Yeah, good idea. I'm done," Blake confesses, running a hand through his sweaty hair.

"I guess I'll see you next time," I say, waving at Blake and Maddison.

I turn to Tahlia, and I can't help the way my hand reaches out to touch her waist. "Nice seeing you again."

Her gaze drops before looking up. I take in her flushed nose where her makeup has worn off. It's adorable. "Same. Bye, Alex."

"Night." I don't remove my hand, and she doesn't twist out of my grip until they all turn to walk away. And I can't help but watch her walk out the door, stopping myself from offering to make sure she gets home safe. Even though I know it's ridiculous, because she lives with Maddison.

What on earth is wrong with me?

Must've been the alcohol tonight…maybe it was stronger than usual.

Yeah, that's it.

"Where did you go?" Ryan asks sliding his arm around a woman he was kissing passionately only moments ago. He's wearing a smug grin, probably thinking I've been hooking up with someone.

I wish I had another drink in hand. "Dancing."

I take my seat back on the sofa and, suddenly, I want to leave too. Being here is no longer appealing without Tahlia.

"I saw you talking to Alice's friend. What's her name?" He clicks his finger.

"Tahlia," I answer, but immediately wish I didn't.

"You going to tap that?"

I scoff. "No way. Mike and Alice would cut off my balls."

Ryan snorts. "That's true. But she's hot, even if she's a tad quiet—"

"But it's always the quiet ones," Jackson cuts him off and bumps his shoulder, winking.

I stay silent, looking down, knowing they might be right. However, it's not going to happen, no matter what I think or want.

Since I've been dancing with Tahlia, the guys have acquired a group of women hanging around us. Usually, I'd be chatting one up, with plans of taking one home for the night, but it's doing the opposite. My stomach rolls as I think about it, and bile rises when one sits down beside me, purring into my ear and asking if I want to dance with her.

No, I don't. As a matter of fact, I want the petite blonde to get her sweet ass back here so I can dance with her instead. The woman lays her hand on my thigh and squeezes, and I immediately rise to my feet, hating her touch on me.

Peering down at her, and then over to Ryan and Jackson, I clear my throat. "I'm out of here. You two comin'?"

"You want to leave already?" Jackson bellows with a frown, clearly upset I'm even asking.

"Yeah, a big week at work," I lie, not wanting to tell them I had a feel of Tahlia, and the idea of another woman touching me irks me. That isn't something I want to confess to my buddies right now, if ever.

"Can we stay a little longer?" Ryan asks.

I don't want them to leave because I'm being a grumpy dick. "You two stay. I'll call my driver."

"You sure?" Jackson asks.

"Yep. I'll talk to you tomorrow," I say, pulling out my phone and texting my driver to meet me out the front.

I stop by the bar, grab a shot, and walk through the crowd, and straight out to grab my ride. Sitting in the back of the car, I slump, staring at my phone with deliberation. I want to text her and see if she got home okay, but I don't. Instead, I stare out the window, replaying the night in my head. From how she looked in that sexy dress, to the way her warm skin felt, and her sweet scent causing my brain to misfire. It was a good thing she left, because if we were to hook up, I know how it works the next day. I know how I am, and she wouldn't be any different. Would she?

CHAPTER 6

TAHLIA

SURELY, THERE IS MORE to life than making coffee?

Yeah, that's the same question I keep asking myself as the manager's son, berates me for burning a customer's coffee.

When your head is thumping and your eyes feel like they are going to come out of their sockets from sleep deprivation, the last thing you care about is coffee. I want to go home and sit on my sofa with Maddison and eat cheesy pizza and chug soda while watching trashy movies until I fall asleep. But I'm here, getting my ass handed to me for making a mistake. Does he think he's perfect? Has he never used the wrong temperature water?

That's right, he doesn't know how to make one. The way he struts around, belittling everyone. Acting like we are nothing more than a piece of gum on his shoe. He's such a jerk.

"How long have you worked here Ta-le-a?" He tsks.

I bite down on the inside of my cheek. He says my name incorrectly, but I'm the sweet girl, not the one who loses their cool at the workplace. Instead, I stand here, looking glum and nodding, keeping my focus on him, flinching with every spit word that comes toward me through his teeth. His hands are on his hips and he's tapping a foot, waiting for my answer.

I want to say, "too long," but he's not worth it.

"Four years," I reply.

"Exactly. And you still can't make coffee," he says, screwing up his face and shaking his head.

I don't want to apologize, but I'm wondering how else to salvage this situation.

I stay silent, waiting for him to get everything off his chest before I can finish my shift.

"Do you think you can make another one without destroying it?"

"Yes."

He huffs. "Well, get back there and make a fresh cup, and I'll go calm the customers down and apologize for you."

"I can do it," I reply, not wanting him to do it for me. I'm capable of doing it myself.

He narrows his eyes at me, but I don't shrink inside myself. I stare back at him, taking his insult on the chin. "I think you've done enough today. Just get back there and make a fresh cup of coffee."

I don't want this job anymore. I'm so done with it. I officially can't take another second.

Removing my apron, I toss it on the counter with a deep breath. Then I straighten my spine. "You know what? I'm done!"

He crosses his arms over his chest. His bushy brows rise and pull further together. "Don't be ridiculous, Tahlia. Put your apron on and get to work."

I shake my head. "No. I quit."

"Who is going to make the customer his new coffee?"

I shrug, uninterested. "You."

"Fine. You were useless anyway!" he spits.

"Well then, it looks like I'm doing you a favor."

His jaw ticks, but I spin on my heel, feeling the lightest I have in a very long time.

The buzz in my bag frightens me as I exit work, jobless. I rummage through my bag, but I can't find my phone with the mountain of rubbish inside of it. I drop to the ground and follow the vibrations, my eyes widening as I see the name.

I accidentally hit the answer button. Bringing it up to my ear, I speak. "Mom. Hi."

"Tahlia, darling, where have you been?"

A soft sigh slips out because I know the words that will spill from her mouth next. I mime them as she says them.

"When are you coming to visit? It's been too long," she whines, and I can't help but smile to myself getting almost all the words correct.

"Soon, Mom."

I don't know how soon, but I figure it's an answer that I can get out of. After today, I need to go home and search through jobs until I find something fulfilling.

I stand up and reposition the bag on my shoulder as I walk to a vacant bench. She will want to talk for a while, so I take a seat, scanning to check no one can hear our conversation.

"Where are you?"

"Sitting outside. I quit Frank's." I turn around, looking back at the glass door leading into the coffeehouse, relieved I'm never going back.

"Finally. Well, remember, your father and I have told you that when you turn twenty-five, if you aren't married, you won't get your inheritance from your grandfather. Your stake stays with us to sell to another investor. That would be unfortunate. You know Emerald Designs is a good job. Well paying. You become the majority stake owner. Be your own boss…"

How could I forget? The Adam's family fashion business; Emerald Design's.

My parents took over the business from my Grandfather, who passed away recently.

"Mom, women don't need to be married off at twenty-five. They can run businesses and be happily single," I argue.

"Your grandfather made the clause. I have no power to change it."

Blowing out a breath, I run my hand through my hair and scratch the base of my neck. I'm not even dating, let alone engaged to be married.

His death was unexpected. So, to think about owning a majority of stake in a business I knew nothing about, in a short amount of time, was too much pressure. It's like there's a countdown hovering over my head.

But now, I know, I want to learn about the business. My inheritance. A fulfilling future. There's just one major problem. I don't want a husband.

I pause for a moment too long, because she adds, "You know we have a handsome young man who comes from a great family. You've met Ma—"

"I'm dating a guy named Alex," I blurt without thinking.

I'm lying to my mother.

I'm so going to hell for this.

Why do I need to be married, or settle down? Yes, I live with friends and go out clubbing to Luxe. I know they disapprove of it all, but I want to live like a normal twenty-four-year-old, not the old-fashioned way they want me to. I've never given them a reason not to trust me, but they continually want to control my future.

"And you won't marry him?"

Date him is one thing, but to marry him.

"I don't know what he's thinking," I lie again, because I don't know what else to say now that I've started this.

I stare out at the people walking around, couples holding hands, kissing, all the things a couple would do. Could I hold his hand, cuddle him, or worse, kiss him like we're dating?

Yes. It's not like I'll get attached.

I just need to do this until I get my part of the business transferred to me.

Could I get him to go along with it?

I hope so. I probably should have thought of that important bit before.

"So, how is it going between you? This is the first time you've mentioned him," she presses, pulling me from my wandering thoughts.

I close my eyes and squeeze my neck before throwing my hand in the air. Why did I think it was a good idea to lie?!

"We're good, Mom. I was going to tell you and Dad next time I saw you."

"When do we get to meet him?"

And by *we*, I know she means her and my father.

I chuckle, but it's not a light, funny one, it's an awkward, strained one.

"Soon."

She gasps excitedly, and I almost feel bad, but I need to take this chance at a career change and a way to make something of myself. Make myself proud. I'm desperate for this chance, and I'm willing to sacrifice a little to make this happen. I'm going to blame the movie Maddison and I watched the other night with this 'fake dating' premise.

I just hope Alex won't mind. I don't think he would. But then again, he's a player and will have to agree to not see anyone or sleep with anyone else while being with me. Could he do that? I won't be giving him sex in any form, that's for sure. A kiss, well, I could do that, but anything further is out of the question.

"Send me a picture."

Panic clutches at my throat. I don't have a picture of us.

Think, Tahlia! Think!

"I'll show you in real life. Pictures don't do him justice."

"Okay, well, tomorrow night, you come here for dinner and bring your boyfriend, Alex. Your father and I can't wait to meet him." She sounds happy, and I can't believe she bought it. I just need to get Alex to agree and somehow act like a real couple in front of them.

This is so bad. I have dug myself the biggest hole and I don't know how I'll get out of it. If they were to figure out the truth, I can only imagine the disappointment I would be to them.

"I don't kn—"

"Tahlia, I'll see you and Alex at six p.m. sharp. Don't be late."

I slouch down on the hard wooden bench and give in to her request. "Okay, Mom."

We hang up, and I sit staring at the phone.

How am I going to ask Alex?

I picture it. Me nervously trying to explain that I need his help to be my fake boyfriend so I can get my inheritance. Then I say, "Oh, but we need to get married." I can imagine the horror on his face. Yep, I'm so screwed.

But if I at least get him to agree to fake date me, I might be able to figure out a way to convince him.

Do I turn up at his work, home, or call him?

I don't have his address, so that rules out the home option. He could be in surgery or on the ward or not even be at work…Calling is my only option at this point.

I suck in a big, deep breath and scroll through my contacts. Thankful we swapped numbers for Mike and Alice's wedding present.

It isn't long before my thumb hovers over his name.

I can do it…

Shit, I'm doing it.

It's ringing.

Butterflies hit my stomach, and I don't know if I'm going to be sick. But it's too late because he answers.

"Hello?" he says, clearly without recognizing my number. I'm a little bummed, if I'm honest.

"Ouch, you don't even have my number saved."

A deep chuckle sounds down the line, and it makes me smile. "Ahhh, T. I better get to saving, then. Can't have my favorite girl upset."

His flirty words cause my stomach to flip, but I laugh it off and mutter, "I bet you say that to all the ladies."

"Nope," he says, and then whispers, "Only you."

My heart picks up speed, and I'm trying not to overthink this and let it derail me.

"I don't know how much you're going to like me soon."

He clears his throat, and I tilt my head and close my eyes as I let the sun hit my face.

Just say it.

"Wha—" he asks curiously.

My nerves are bubbling, and I can't help but cut him off, trying to hurry the words out.

"Would you be my pretend boyfriend?"

"What? Why would you need a pretend boyfriend?" he chokes out. I've definitely surprised him.

"I need my parents to take me seriously."

He coughs and splutters before composing himself. "What the hell for? That's a big favor without giving me all the details."

I sigh loudly and drop my chin back down. My nerves hit my chest as I talk. "My grandfather left a will. He owned a fashion business called Emerald Designs. He left my parents with 40% stake, and me the rest. But there's a clause. I can't inherit my stake unless I'm married by my twenty-fifth birthday. Otherwise, my parents can sell my 60% stake to another investor. When I quit Frank's today, I realized I want my stake in the family business."

I figure I can't hold anything back if he is to play the part for real. He needs to know all the lies I spilled to my mom.

"Shit! You really want this, don't you? I wasn't expecting this call today."

I can't help but smile at his rambling. It eases my nerves a little.

"I know, and I'm sorry. I'm just sick and tired of my life. I'm going through the motions without enjoying it. Quitting Frank's is one way of taking back my happiness. And getting my stake in the family's business would be another."

"How did Frank. I'm guessing that's his name, take it?"

"He told me I was useless anyway."

"Do you want me to come down after surgery today and yell at the dumbass?"

I giggle, but it turns into a snort, loving this protective side to him. "Nah, I'm good. It's nothing I can't handle."

"You shouldn't have to handle that." His voice is serious.

"Well, hopefully, I'll have a business to run, and he won't matter anymore..." I trail off, hoping he agrees to my offer.

"Oh, yeah. That's where I come in, right? Boyfriend. But let me get this straight; I have to do this until your birthday, which is in December, right?"

Him saying he has to do this gets me excited. He may actually say yes.

"Yeah. Does this mean you'll agree?" I ask with the sweetest, pleasing tone.

"Are you going to beg me?"

I grumble, and he chuckles again.

"I'm kidding...sorta," he teases.

"Fine. If I have to beg, I will."

He sucks in an audible breath. "For anyone else, I'd say hell no, but for you, T, I'll do it."

My breathing shallows, and my heart thumps loudly in my chest. I'm lost in the thought of being special to him. I'm somehow different. But why?

I don't dare ask that. I need to stick to the point of the phone call.

"But there are conditions," I say to stop my racing mind.

"Like what?" he asks.

Do I say it now, or wait to see him face-to-face? Nope, that would be worse. Rip the Band-Aid off.

"It would mean you're exclusive to me. No one else," I say, much too quietly. I'm surprised he even heard it, but when he answers, I know he did.

"Right," he mumbles. I can imagine him thinking it over, but then he asks, "What will we do?"

My throat is dry, constricting. I'm suddenly feeling warm all over.

Gripping the phone, I try to act like this is a totally normal conversation. "Hold hands, cuddle, and um, kiss, probably, just for show."

It's silent for a beat, and I hold my breath, waiting for him to say something. All I can hear is him breathing heavily down the line.

"Okay," he finally answers, after what feels like ten minutes.

"Okay?" I clarify, my heart thundering in my chest.

"Okay. But I have my own condition."

"Anything," I reply immediately.

"I can tell getting the business is important to you. So, if it requires you to get married, let's be engaged and get married," he suggests, as if it's not a big deal.

I gasp. *Wow*. I wasn't expecting that.

My brain falters a little in shock. When I let his offer sink in, I clear my throat, not hating the idea. "You'd do that?"

"Yeah, why not? It'll be fun, and you get something that means a lot to you." He states it so easily. Yet I'm trembling with the trouble I'm getting myself into.

"What time tomorrow?" His voice pulls me from my distracting thoughts once again.

"Dinner is at six."

"All right. We need to meet before dinner to talk things over, and then we can leave together."

"I can drive to Bar 9 at five. It's on the way to my parents," I say, as I could do with the wine.

"Are you telling anyone?" he asks.

"Not yet."

"Why? Are you embarrassed?" he gruffs, sounding hurt.

"No, no, no," I rush out, sitting taller. "I hung up from my mother after blurting you're my new boyfriend and called you immediately. I haven't had time to get my thoughts together yet."

"Your mom believed you telling her that you have a random boyfriend?"

I sigh. "Seems so. She was trying to set me up with someone. And I'm not being fixed up with her choice."

"Should I be worried about you being able to lie that well?" He isn't serious; he's teasing me, and it makes me giggle.

"No, I detest lying. But the will my grandfather left, leaves me no option. I had to tell them a small white lie to get my stake."

"Whatever you need to tell yourself to sleep at night," he jokes.

We laugh together and I have to pinch myself with how easy it is to talk and laugh with him. Maybe a little too easy...

CHAPTER 7

TAHLIA

AT FIVE O'CLOCK, I walk into Bar 9 and scan the room. The dim lighting makes it hard to see faces clearly. As I make my way through the crowd hovering around the bar, then over by the tables, I see Alex waving me in. His face lights up as I walk closer, and I don't miss the way his gaze drops over my outfit.

I dip my head and run my hand over my black leather skirt, and then re-adjust my off-the-shoulder sweater. It's a mix of sexy and comfortable.

When I approach, I begin internally panicking. How do I greet him? Kiss on the cheek? Shake his hand?

He pulls out my chair, answering my overworking brain.

"Thanks," I say as I sit down.

I feel the heat tickle my cheeks, and I'm glad I put foundation and blush on. Hopefully, it's hiding the embarrassment written on my face.

"You look stunning," he says as he walks around to take his seat opposite me, but not before I run my own eyes over his outfit. My blush deepens. He's hot. His dark jeans cling to his thick thighs, and his brown sweater and denim jacket complement his five-o'clock shadow and blue eyes. His styled hair and smirk are the real killer, though. And before I know what's happening, I'm blurting out, "You look good, too."

His smile broadens, and his eyes crinkle, which adds to his appeal. Now my butterflies have turned into a full flutter.

A server comes over and we order drinks. I get a white wine and he gets a beer.

He leans to the side of his chair, rubbing his jaw roughly. The wheels are turning in his head. I'm about to ask what he's thinking about when he says, "You're not what I envisioned."

My eyes widen at his confession.

He straightens in his chair, shaking his head. "No. Better."

I let go of the air I was holding and giggle. "I was hoping it was a good thing."

"Oh, it is."

My interest is piqued. "Why?" I ask.

His brows pinch together in confusion.

I clear my throat. "Why am I better than what you envisioned?"

A chuckle rumbles from his chest. "Ah. Well. You're kind, obviously. But there's this adventurous spark with a hint of boldness about you. I can see it in your eyes."

His gaze holds mine a moment too long, and I find myself needing a sip of water. With Alex, I don't have to wonder how daring I could be. It would be a given. He knows how to pleasure a woman, and I'd have fun being on the receiving end. But here I am jumping right to steamy thoughts again...

I wiggle my brows to lighten the mood, which causes us both to laugh.

"Am I what you were expecting?" he asks, and I think of how he hasn't made me feel icky or dirty. Instead, comfortable and sexy.

"You actually want me to answer that?" I tease, lowering my glass.

He leans forward, wiggling his dark brows. "Yes. Hit me."

I shrink a little knowing I judged him harshly. "I expected you to be obnoxious and full of yourself."

"Ouch," he says, rubbing the back of his head, careful not to mess up his hair.

I shake my head. "But you're not."

A playful yet dazzling smile erupts on his face. He liked my answer.

"You're thoughtful, caring, and surprisingly sweet."

"Sounds like I need to grow a set of balls."

My mouth opens and closes.

"Don't. They're great qualities. More men should be that way," I add with a soft smile.

"Sounds like you're ready to marry me, T," he replies with a dark stare.

"I wouldn't say that..." I trail off.

My hands are on my lap, gripped together, as I eagerly wait on my wine. I need it to take the edge off.

"You're clearly shitting yourself about this engagement." He smirks, as if it's funny. There's not a trace of nerves coming off him. I didn't need to worry about him charming my parents. He has charm in spades. It's me who might give us away.

"What are the details of this deal?" I ask, opening my bag and hoping I can find a pen.

"Don't tell me you're going to write it down?"

I pause my search and close the bag, dropping it back down beside me. "Fine. Let's talk."

He smiles smugly. "Rule one. Have fun."

I roll my eyes and shake my head. "Of course, you'd say that."

"No, I mean it. Everything we do, it's got to be fun. The venue, the cake, suits and dress shopping, bachelor/bachelorette party. It all has to be fun."

I rub my finger over my lip, thinking. It sounds less stressful and like something I could get on board with. He'd make it easy, I know that. "Yeah. I like that rule."

He leans back, asking casually, "What's one of your rules?"

Dropping my finger away from my lip, an easy thought comes to me. "No lying or hurting the other person."

"Respecting each other."

I nod. "Exactly."

"Can we tell people about what we're doing?" I ask, knowing I'll need to confess to my best friends. There's no way I could hold something like this to myself. Blake, Maddison, and Alice are practically my family.

He shrugs. "Just not the parents. Friends, sure. Why not? Oh, I'll probably tell Mike, but not my sister. She can't keep a secret to save herself. And the fewer people who know, the less chance someone will slip."

I smile at the tidbit of information about his sister. "Yeah, I'd tell Alice, so it would be good if they both knew."

I know they'd all be supportive of us. Everyone would think this was crazy, but they'd understand and help in any way they could. "I'll only tell them on an as-needed basis. I'm not hosting a party to tell them or anything," I admit, huffing a laugh.

"How did you want to break up?" he asks.

"Just say we weren't the right fit. And apply for a divorce," I reply.

He dips his head. "We'd need to wait for you to get complete control of your stake first."

"Yeah, good idea."

We gaze at each other in silence. I consider other rules but he's distracting. I shrug it off. I'm sure more will pop up at another stage.

"I have one more," he adds, looking me seriously in the eyes. "No falling in love with me, Tahlia. I don't catch feelings, so it's better this is out in the open, and there are no expectations that I'm some Prince Charming."

I scoff, which turns to a giggle, thinking he's joking. When I recover, I lean in so the whole restaurant doesn't hear. "You wish. You know it's not like that." I wave my finger between us. "This is a business deal, and that's it. By the way, these rules aren't helping. I'm currently still freaking out about it," I whisper through my teeth.

His eyes light up at my confession. "Don't be nervous. We need to know more about each other, though, so give me some basic information about you before I get to your parents."

"Good idea." I shuffle through the basics. "I'm twenty-four and my birth date is December 8. My favorite color is blue, and I'm an only child."

"Favorite food and drink?"

"Oh, yes. Italian food, and my drink of choice is white wine," I say. He nods.

Our drinks arrive, and when she leaves, I'm quick to pick up my wine, holding it up. "Thank you, Alex, for helping me with this. I hope you understand how much I appreciate it, and you."

We clink glasses. And as our eyes meet, his dilate. It's quiet for a moment as we both take a good, long sip of our drinks.

Lowering his beer to the table, where he cradles it in his palms, he gazes at me, asking, "Do you have allergies? Or things you dislike?"

I hold my wine in my hand, enjoying the cold glass on my sweaty palm. "No, and ah, I don't think so."

His brows lift high into his hair line.

I tap the glass with my nail, mulling over the question. I wasn't expecting it.

"Rude people, liars, cheaters, and onions," I say on a breath. Thank God my brain decided to work again.

He chuckles, picking his beer up, but before he drinks, there's a soft shake of his head.

"What?" I ask.

"Just after that list, I wasn't expecting onions."

I take a sip of my wine.

"Oh, and Mom's name is Sonya, and my dad's is Hector. But what about you? I need to know your birthday, favorite color, and family."

"My birthday is March 1st. I don't really have a favorite color, but I have Mike and a sister Steph. My parents are both doctors, and their names are Margaret and Paul. Steph is a Dermatologist. Oh, and I like to play golf and watch football."

"I could've guessed that," I tease with a smile.

"But did you know I'm a better golfer than Mike?"

I roll my eyes playfully. "I bet you and Mike have always been competitive."

"Yeah, definitely about golf. But my dad kicks both of our asses," he says with fondness before picking up his drink and gulping some down.

"I think my dad will like that piece of information."

He drains his beer. "He plays golf?"

"Sometimes." I smile.

"I'll have to get him to play so I can win him over." He winks.

"I think you'll do it without that," I mumble before I drain my glass, too.

He stares at me with amusement, and I expect him to call me out on it, but he doesn't.

"I know you go to Luxe, and you used to work at Frank's, and you went to college for a bit for business but quit. What hobbies do you have?"

"I work out and watch a lot of movies and TV."

He nods and leans back in his chair, digging in his pocket for something. I take the opportunity to get a better look around the cozy bar. It's beginning to fill with more people. Groups of friends and couples. Tonight has been relaxing and I'm surprisingly having a nice time with him.

"T." His voice pulls my gaze back to him.

He's holding a velvet box open with an engagement ring. The solitaire diamond sits on a classic gold band. It looks to be at least two carats. This snaps me back to the reality of what we're doing.

My mouth falls open, and I stare at it as if it's going to disappear.

"Alex, it's beautiful," I breathe.

He clears his throat. "I was scared it was too simple."

I blink over and over, trying to make sure it's real.

"Do you want this back?" I blurt out.

He frowns. "What are you talking about?"

I whisper. "When this is over, what am I meant to do with this?" I point at the ring.

"Keep it."

"You bought this beautiful ring for me to keep? You realize that we're not staying married," I say, feeling like I need to remind him.

"I know. After you get your inheritance, and we break up, you could take it back to the Jeweller. It's up to you."

I push the hair away from my face and gaze back at him. I'm still in shock at the ring's beauty.

"This wouldn't have been cheap," I mumble, flicking my gaze back down to the box. It's hard not to stare at it the whole time.

"Your parents will find out I'm a doctor. If they're to believe the engagement is real, I needed you to have a ring. And I don't want you getting something cheap and fake. You deserve a nice ring."

I wish I had more wine right now. "Alex. This is a lot," I whisper.

"At least you like it. I was at the shop stressing."

I giggle, trying to picture the scene. "You in a jewelry store. Now that would've been funny to see. I wish I could've been there."

"I surprisingly didn't hate it. They just had too many options." He inches forward with the box, a silent urge to get me to take the ring.

I pluck it from the box, moving the diamond around between my fingers. The sparkle is captivating. "What made you choose this one?"

"I wanted a classic but elegant ring. When I saw this one, I knew it was the one."

I peer up from the diamond to stare into his eyes. His blue eyes gleam under the bar's lights. I'm speechless. How did he know this would be my choice? I shake my head at the silly thought. He didn't. It was a fluke.

The server comes back, asking if we want more drinks, but as we look at the time, his eyes hold mine. "Are you ready to go?" he asks, handing over cash to the server and rising.

I take a deep breath, slip the ring on my finger, and stand. "I think so."

"I got you," he says, trying to reassure me.

I offer a weak smile. I can't shake the fear that this will all crumble, and my only hope of a future will fail. Then all this will be for nothing.

CHAPTER 8

ALEX

SHE'S BEEN QUIET SINCE we left the bar. The pinch between her brows sits embedded, and I hate to see the stress having an effect on her.

We're on our way to her parents' house in my car. I prefer to drive, and it will look better for me to be driving us anyway.

Tonight, was unexpectedly enjoyable. The banter, chit-chat, and overall mood was fun and easy between us. At no time did anything feel awkward or forced, just smooth and comfortable. It's nice to see the outgoing T, not the one who reverts back into her shell.

The music plays in the background, but still, it will be a long ass drive if we don't speak. Especially now, since her knee is bouncing up and down. I'm a tad nervous about slipping up, but I'll do everything I can to help her.

"So, is the business successful?" I ask, catching a brief look at her before focusing on the road.

Her frame taunted me when she entered the bar in that sexy-as-hell outfit. The way the skirt rests on her waist complements her hourglass frame. I had to hold myself back from walking to her and laying a kiss on her exposed shoulder and dragging my lips up her neck.

I don't know what it is about her, but she has a way of getting me to not think straight.

"Yeah, very," she says too quietly. I could barely hear her.

"That will help when you take majority of it over."

She grumbles, "I don't know about that. I could screw it up."

"Is that what you're worried about?"

She stares out her window. I wonder what's running through her head.

"I've never run a business before. I didn't finish the business course at college. I haven't learned how to run a successful business or studied fashion...I'm not prepared for this at all. I just know I want it."

"Most people I know who are successful will say you don't need to go to college or have experience. The work itself will give you all the experience you need. You'll figure it out."

"I beg to differ."

"Why are you so hard on yourself? You have time to learn the ropes from your parents and ask questions as you go. You're freaking out because you're looking too far ahead. One day at a time, T."

It's silent for a beat, and I think that's all she'll say, but then she surprises me. "I feel like a failure to my parents. My friends all have their shit together, and I don't. I have money and the smarts, yet I couldn't figure out what I wanted to do before now. I'm already in my mid-twenties with no achievements under my belt."

I'm stunned by her confession. I'm also sad for her.

"You shouldn't compare yourself to them, because there isn't anything wrong with you. I'm glad you've figured out what you really want. Even if I'm on this crazy fake journey with you."

"Yeah, it's going to be a ride."

I look over at her again and see her slumped body is more comfortable. My gaze doesn't miss the way her skirt has ridden up above her knee, showing more of her leg to me. I bite back a growl.

"You know, my friends and I have joked about how I should be a stylist."

"Really? Then why didn't you work in the family business after school?"

"I wasn't ready, and seeing how much they worked, it was a turnoff. No life other than work. I wanted a bit of freedom."

"Being an established business, it shouldn't require as much work, right?" I ask.

I take a quick peek over at her, and she's staring my way. Her eyes have a way of pulling me in. I refocus on driving, wanting us to get there in one piece.

"They have a lot of staff in all different areas, so no it shouldn't be. But I guess I'll find out soon enough."

"You sure will. And remember, you can always discuss with them about changing the direction of the business. It's majority yours to do what you want with, right?"

She makes a humming sound. I'm surprised by how nice it is to talk to a woman instead of chatting them up with a purpose to fuck them. I've never spoken to them about life problems, or in this case, work issues.

I like the mental connection it brings. Physical isn't an issue whenever Tahlia is around. She's hot, but her vulnerability is killing me more than my attraction to her, and I want to make her better.

My phone rings through the car, and Nancy's number pops up. I cringe.

I plan to just let it ring, but Tahlia asks, "Are you going to answer that?"

"No."

"You can, I don't mind." She shrugs nonchalantly.

I clear my throat, wondering how I explain that Nancy will only be asking when she can fuck me, because I don't share my personal life with anyone.

"No, I'm good." I press the hang-up button. But of course, Nancy calls back. I hit the decline button again, and the temperature in the car turns up. I feel suffocated with having to explain, but knowing it's not something she'll want to know about me. Fuck, I don't even like myself.

Once the ringing stops, I get a message pop through, but neither of us speaks.

Before I get the chance to apologize to Tahlia, she cuts in.

"Just here." I follow her pointed finger through the trees.

I sigh. Ready or not, here we go.

I pull up to the double brick brown home and park in the drive. I take it all in. There's a manicured garden surrounding steps that lead to a pair of dark brown double wooden doors. We sit in the car a moment. I'm staring at her family's porch when her voice pulls me away.

"You ready?" she asks, biting on her nails.

I touch her hand, and she stops, allowing me to drop her hand away from her mouth. Her gaze flicks to me and the beginning of a smile tips the corners of her lips. I can't promise her this will go smoothly, or that they will believe us, but the look on her face makes me want to try harder.

"Ready? Let's go, soon-to-be Mrs. Tahlia Taylor." After the words leave my mouth, I'm surprised by how good it sounds. No feelings of dread take over.

"Let's go, Mr. Taylor."

"Dr. Taylor, but I'll let it slide for you." I wink, and a big open grin forms on my face.

I know the playful side of us ends now, though. It's time to be serious.

She opens the car door, and it makes me dart out like my ass is on fire, running around to finish opening the door for her.

She smiles when I hold out my hand and close the door for her. Her grip loosens, as if she's about to disconnect our hands, but I interlock them and tug on it to bring her eyes to my face.

When she holds my gaze, I lean into her ear, inhaling her sweet perfume, and whisper, "We've got this."

She blows out her cheeks and nods, as if trying to convince herself.

We take the steps. But before we hit the doorbell, the doors open to reveal an older couple, both smiling warmly at us. Her dad doesn't look like he wants to kill me, but I'm sure he will when we're alone and he berates me for not asking for her hand in marriage. If I were him, I'd cut my son-in-law's balls off for not asking me.

"Hello and welcome," her mom, Sonya, says as she flicks her gaze between us.

"Thank you for having us," I reply.

Tahlia drops her fingers from mine, and I mourn the loss.

She hugs her dad and mother, giving them double cheek kisses, and I wonder if I have to follow suit.

"Alex," I say, and extend my hand to shake her dad's. His handshake is firm, and his face wears a curious expression as he introduces himself. But before he can read my face, I move to her mother and kiss her cheeks like I saw Tahlia do a moment ago. Then I take a step behind and slip my hand on Tahlia's lower back, feeling her shiver.

We step inside the house, then follow her mom and dad farther into the house, we're led to the living room.

"Can I grab you a drink?" Sonya asks.

"A soda would be great?" I reply.

"You don't want a beer or whiskey?" Hector asks me, frowning.

"No, I'm starting early tomorrow," I reply, not wanting to drink in front of them. I need to be on my best behavior for Tahlia.

Sonya walks toward the kitchen for the drinks.

"What is it that you do?" Hector asks.

"I'm a neurologist," I say proudly.

Hector's face softens, and he nods. "Good job."

"It's very rewarding," I reply, knowing there's more to being a doctor than the money.

Sonya hands us our drinks and I thank her. I watch her grab Tahlia and pull her over to the sofa on the other side of the room. I stay standing with Hector. Who starts firing questions at me.

"Will my daughter be left alone a lot? I know doctors' schedules are very busy."

I hope not.

His question is fair, and I think for a moment how to speak the truth but also keep up with our lie.

I glance over to where Tahlia sits talking with her mother. She must feel my eyes on her because she turns and the lift of those lips in a secret smile causes my breath to catch.

Turning back to face her father, I can only be honest. "I will do my best to always be there for her in all ways. I can't promise to give her a nine-to-five job, but I promise when I'm home, she will be all I focus on every minute of the day or night."

He dips his head and sips his amber liquid, and I sip the refreshing soda and wait for the next question. Because it's her dad, after all, so I'd be stupid to think he would only ask one.

"You're engaged?" her mom shrieks.

My head whips back around, and I watch her mom pull out of a hug and grab Tahlia's hand.

Tahlia's face has a dusting of pink as her mom moves her head this way and that to get a good look.

"Hector, come look at the size of this ring," her mom gushes, smiling brightly, pushing Tahlia's hand out in our direction.

"In a minute, Sonya."

I turn around again, knowing this means he hasn't finished drilling me.

"Why didn't you ask me?" he asks in a deep, yet quiet, voice.

Oh, fuck. Here we go.

When I don't respond right away he asks again. "Why didn't you ask me for my daughter's hand in marriage?"

I swallow hard. I need to be convincing.

"Well, I…" Clearing my throat, I take a breath. "I hadn't met you yet and didn't think telling you over the phone was appropriate." I'm rattling off bullshit, and I just hope it saves me.

He stays silent, his eyes trained on Tahlia. I decide to turn the conversation around. Get it off Tahlia and our fake engagement. "How long have you been married?"

He twists his face to me, bringing his tumbler to his mouth and taking a sip before answering. "Thirty wonderful years."

I want to ask him how he knew she was the one, but considering I'm marrying his daughter, I should know that already. Only he doesn't understand that I'm broken inside, and this engagement is fake.

I'm totally fucked. I run my hand through my hair.

A woman wearing an apron comes into the room and informs us that dinner is ready. Taking my soda, I go toward Tahlia and walk with her to the dining room where a large rectangle table is. I'm careful to keep close to her. As I remember all the things Mike and Alice do, so tonight goes seamlessly.

However, I just realized that we have to keep this up until her birthday, so how many times will I see her parents?

I hope not many.

A couple of times I can handle. More than that, I can't promise not to slip up.

The table is already set for dinner. There's silverware, dinner plates, water glasses, bread, and butter.

Tahlia takes a seat, her face pinched. I lean down to whisper in her ear, "Are you okay?"

Her chest heaves, and I swallow a groan. Her breasts move up and down in her sweater, and the way the skin is teasing me, I have to take a seat to hide the tent that's forming in my pants.

I haven't even fucking touched her. Or even tasted her. Yet I'm rock hard and desperate to sink myself inside her.

That part of the marriage I could be good at.

Sex is easy.

A relationship, I'm doomed.

Everyone calls me the playboy, and that's all I am.

At least, I think so...

The steak, vegetables, and potatoes look delicious, and even though my thighs are spread while I wait for the uncomfortable erection to calm down, I focus on the food, which helps the deflation.

Sonya speaks once we've all taken our first bite. "How many children will you have?"

"Mom," Tahlia shrieks, her mortified expression making me cough. Was she expecting kids? Because I really didn't sign up for that.

"What it's a legitimate question. He's..."

And I know she's asking me how old I am.

I swallow my mouthful of food and answer. "Thirty-two."

"See, in the next few years, he'll be thinking of children, Tahlia."

I lower my fork and knife, suddenly not as hungry. "We want to travel a bit before we have children. Right, honey?" I turn to Tahlia, trying to act calm, even though my body temperature is rising. As I tuck a loose strand of hair behind her ear, she melts into my hand with a soft smile. Her eyes have a sheen of relief, as if she's glad I got us out of an awkward conversation.

I finally drop my hand, skimming her exposed shoulder so I can touch her teasingly warm skin. It's tempting to keep my fingers there and seek more, but we are at dinner with her parents. So I curl my fingers and return them to my lap.

My gaze catches her father's, and it flicks to Tahlia and then me, a frown pinched between his brows. Suddenly, a slight worry runs through me. I try to think if I've not acted attentive or like a fiancé, but I'm coming up empty.

Maybe he just doesn't like the idea of me touching his daughter. Unfortunately for him, I seem to like it, and so does she.

"How long have you two been dating?" Hector asks, his finger rubbing along his bottom lip.

I tug at the collar of my shirt. It's a little hot in here.

"About six months," Tahlia answers.

"How did you meet? Seems like a rushed engagement. You're not pregnant, are you?"

My eyes widen. *Immaculate conception*, I want to say, but I keep my mouth shut.

"I'm not pregnant. And Alice's husband is Alex's brother," Tahlia explains. She speaks so easily. She's a damn good actor.

I wash down my food with more soda, welcoming the cold beverage.

"That makes sense," Sonya mumbles.

"It doesn't to me," Hector grunts, lifting his glass to his mouth to take a drink. He watches me over the glass.

This is not fucking good.

Sonya's clearly convinced by our relationship. But Hector isn't.

The way he's staring at me, I could bet on my life that he's not buying our relationship or that I love Tahlia.

"Where do you live Alex?" Sonya asks, lowering her silverware.

I'm grateful for the question. It pulls me away from her husbands death stare.

"In the Park area," I answer.

Hector lowers his glass back to the table, then sits back in his chair, arms crossed, and keeps his eyes trained on me. I'm really feeling the heat of meeting the parents. No wonder everyone always dreads it.

"It's a nice brick home." Tahlia says, but her voice wavers.

We never discussed this question. But we need to up the stakes and get him to buy our love.

"Yeah. A tudor home. She actually just moved in," I blurt, like the dumbass I am. I seem to have foot-in-mouth disease.

I hear a small gasp leave Tahlia's mouth. But I try to stay calm. I need to play the part. As if it is true.

"Everything seems new," Hector mumbles, taking another a large sip of his drink.

Sonya widens her eyes at him. "Hector," she says through clenched teeth. "Be nice."

"I am. I'm just asking questions," he gruffs back.

"You're not. Stop being a grumpy old man and be happy for your daughter and future son-in-law."

"We'll have to drop in sometime," Hector adds, not responding to his wife's grumpy comment.

Tahlia and I remain quiet, giving them the time to squabble.

I reach over and grab her knee. I want her to look at me.

This wasn't part of the plan. Is she okay with me saying that? Her head flicks to me as soon as I squeeze.

I offer an *are you okay?* smile.

To my relief, she gives me an easy one back.

It still doesn't solve the huge shit I've put us in, but it can't be worse than what we were already doing.

I guess this playboy is getting a roommate...a hot one at that.

CHAPTER 9

TAHLIA

"THAT WASN'T AS BAD as I thought," Alex says as my parents' house disappears from view.

"Are you kidding?" I gape, turning the music down to talk.

"All right, your dad fucking hates me," he says, gripping the steering wheel.

I laugh at his words. "He doesn't hate you." I stare out the car window, watching all the stars light up the night sky.

"He strongly dislikes me?" he suggests in his teasing tone.

I recline into the soft leather seat and turn my head to face his profile. "Yeah, that's better."

"Not really. There's no chance you'll get your inheritance if he doesn't believe us."

I know my dad is a hard-ass, but I'm the only child he has. Therefore, it gives him a strong urge to protect me at all costs.

"Because I got Mom on board, Dad will automatically follow."

He tilts his head. "I'm not sold."

"Hey, you totally threw us under the bus in the end!"

"I did, didn't I?" He rubs at his five o'clock shadow. "I don't know what happened. It just slipped out."

My hands twitch, wanting to know what his stubble would feel like against my palm...or between my thighs.

"We need to talk out the details of the move."

"How about a drink at my house? I think I need one after tonight. Your dad drilled me hard."

I giggle. I've had a surprisingly good time tonight, and it would be a shame for it to end already.

"Yeah, I wouldn't say no to another glass. If we hash out some more details. I thought our meet-up was good and that we covered enough."

"Clearly it wasn't enough," he jokes.

I face the window watching houses pass by. I'm still unable to believe we made it through four hours with my family and now we're on our way to his place for a drink.

"T?"

Pulling my gaze from outside to him, I hadn't realized I'd zoned out. "Y-yeah."

"Are you okay?" His tone is soft, yet commanding, and I don't want to admit that guilt is hitting me. Lying isn't something I do. Yet I did it. And now we're adding another layer to it, so I'm still trying to process how that makes me feel.

"Yeah, I'm okay. Just a little stunned. That's all."

He reaches over and touches my hand, startling me. His large one covers mine and an unexpected warmth surges through me.

These tender moments he shares with me leave me astonished. I can't tear my hand away, even though my brain is yelling at me, telling me my parents aren't here, so we don't have to act anymore. He doesn't have to do this. For a brief moment, I wonder if he wants to, though. The throb in my temples from stress has me reclining the car seat, all the way back. "I'm going to close my eyes for the rest of the drive. I have a headache starting."

"Yeah, of course. Let me know if you need me to pull over or something. Are you comfortable?"

His soft leather seats and his warm hand in mine have me feeling just that. I smile softly. "Yes, very."

"Good."

My eyes are already closed, and the heaviness takes over.

It isn't until strong arms are lifting me that I feel like I'm floating. It's a nice dream. The cold night air gushes around me, and I snuggle into a neck.

A neck?

I take a sharp intake of breath and jerk. My body is currently flushed to a solid bit of muscle. Firm hands grip me harder as my eyes fly open.

"Shhh, I'll take you inside."

I blink rapidly. I fell asleep in his car?

I thought I would just close my eyes. I never thought in a million years, I'd fall asleep.

This thoughtful moment makes my brain turn to mush, and I just merely stare at him, blank yet amazed. With no fight in me, I simply nod, succumbing to his care.

At his front door, he struggles to open the door.

"I'm awake. Put me down, and I'll walk in," I suggest with a light tone.

"It's okay, I can do it, and hey, think of it as practice for our wedding day."

I shake my head, trying to ignore his heavenly scent. Being this close makes it stronger.

I wiggle out of his arms, giving him no choice but to lower me. Once my feet are safely cemented on the ground, I expect him to open the door. Yet, his hands stay touching my waist and mine on his shoulders. As if we are both enjoying the touch of each other too much for either of us to stop. It's as if this is natural.

He's staring down intently at me before he slowly and seductively gazes over my body. When he meets my eyes again, my blood is pounding in my ears. He leans in, and the emotions around us are melting my resolve.

"Are we going to practice kissing?" he asks in a hoarse voice, licking his lips.

"Do we need to?" My eyes bounce between his. I want him to kiss me. Badly.

"I think it would be good if we do it without an audience, just in case we suck." His breath dusts my lips, causing a shiver to run up my spine.

I laugh, but then I'm straight back into a lustful state. My brain tells me this is a bad idea and to take a step back and go home, but then the other side of me is saying I need to stop overthinking and just try to enjoy the moment.

It's just a simple kiss. After that, we can go back to playing pretend. I haven't kissed a man in a really long time. And I've never kissed a man this hot or oozing this much sexual energy.

I don't answer with words, because my stomach is in a wild swirl of anticipation. When our lips touch, my eyes flutter closed, and I sink deep into it. His strong hand is on the back of my head while the other roams over my back and rests on the crease of my lower back just above my ass. The trail of heat from where his hands are makes me inch closer, closing any distance between us. My hands move from his broad shoulders up his thick neck, and I run my fingers through his hair before curling my grip.

I'd like to think this kiss confirms there is nothing between us, but I feel everything. Our closeness is like a drug, only bringing me closer to euphoria. It's unhinged and feral and unexpected.

His tongue runs over my bottom lip, seeking entry. I groan from the feeling of his tongue inside my mouth. Sweet and warm and captivating. I want more.

I need more.

The erratic beating of my heart feels like it's about to come out of my chest. Everything around us drowns out and my earlier sleepy state is now the opposite. I'm wired with desire.

And it's safe to say he's feeling the same. The way his hand grips my ass and brings me flush against his hard erection, there is no mistaking the sparks. I grind myself against him, causing him to growl.

Our tongues move in fluid strokes. I lap up his taste, and a whimper leaves my chest. No time to be embarrassed or silent. I can't hold myself back even if I wanted to.

Every sweep of his tongue I match it with my own in perfect rhythm. He's a good kisser; it's borderline going to make me second-guess the fake part.

When we pull apart gasping for oxygen, I bring my eyes to his and hold them, seeing the same struggle and conflict I feel. And I wonder what he's thinking, but before I get a chance to ask, he pecks my lips with soft slow kisses. Not once, no, not twice, no, three times before he moves his lips to my hair, whispering, "Let's go inside and have a drink."

Once we get inside his house, it's too dark to take everything in other than his large sofa. I walk directly over to it. Sitting down, I sink into the fabric, feeling almost lightheaded from what we just shared.

"I'll use the bathroom and then fix you a wine or tea?"

Twisting my head, I look over the sofa to meet his gaze with a smile. I ignore how my body still hums with a strong need to kiss him again and focus on the gentleness that's written across his face. It reminds me why he's a doctor. How he likes to care for people. Even now with me, in his home. I've not had someone. Specifically, a man that I'm attracted to want to do that for me. And right now, I admit, after the hot kiss we shared, it feels nice.

Deciding I need the alcohol to calm me. "Wine sounds good." I reply, sounding breathless.

His lips twitch. "All right, won't be long."

The next morning, I open my eyes and realize I'm in a bed that's not my own. I last remember being on Alex's sofa, drinking wine. A lot of it. I must've passed out. Looking around, the other side isn't touched, so I must be in the guest room. It's light from the sun beaming through the curtains. I glance around at the wooden furniture, large TV, cream and beige bedding.

It's not the bachelor pad I expected. No, this is lovely.

Getting up, I leave the room and head down the light wooden stairs. I find myself near the living room which has the same white walls, beige, and leather furnishings. As I make my way to his kitchen and living area, his voice booms from behind me. "I got you breakfast and a coffee."

I jerk around to find him holding two coffees and two brown bags.

"Thanks," I say, taking in his soaked white training top, showing off his toned chest and every ripple of his abs. The dusting of dark hair between his pecs reminds me he's all man. I know I should stop staring, but I continue my inspection. His black training shorts cling to his thighs, and when I make my way back to his face, beads of sweat drip along his temples, causing some of his dark hair to stick to his forehead. My hand twitches to push it back off his face.

His lop-sided smirk has me thinking he knows exactly how much I appreciate his looks.

My throat runs dry, so I take a step and accept the coffee from his grip, ignoring the spark from grazing his hand with mine. I sit at the breakfast bar and sip the caffeine like it's water. It's definitely not going to calm my rapid pulse, but at least the warm, familiar latte comforts me.

"What's in there?" I ask, nudging my nose toward the brown paper bag.

He slides it across to me. "Croissants."

I open the bag and my stomach grumbles on cue.

"I didn't know if you wanted it plain or something else. So, I got one plain and one with ham and cheese."

Of course, he did, because he can't stop being nice. I peek up at him from the bags as he walks around the counter.

"You can choose, and I'll have whatever one you don't want." He takes a seat on the stool next to me.

"That doesn't seem fair."

He shrugs. "Why? I'm a guy. I eat anything."

"Always hungry."

"Always." His voice is gravelly, and we've fallen back into the flirty behavior of last night.

I tear open the bag to occupy my thoughts and eat the plain croissant, enjoying the buttery flavor on my tongue. I didn't realize I was hungry until I started eating.

As I chew, his phone chimes. He glances down with a frown at his phone before looking back at me.

"I just got paged for an emergency surgery. I don't know how long I'll be, but my guess is at least a couple of hours. You're welcome to stay longer. Your car is in the drive."

"How?" I ask, popping the last mouthful of my croissant in my mouth.

"I had it moved last night. When you fell asleep on the sofa," he says it like it's no big deal. But to me, it is.

"You didn't have to. But thanks," I say, grateful for his generosity.

"On the topic of moving. You're going to need to start moving your stuff here today," he announces. He doesn't bat an eyelid. He doesn't seem bothered I'm about to move in here. Unlike me, because I'm wondering how I'll be able to leave with the tension after last night. Will we kiss again?

"Is that right?" I ask in a light voice, challenging him.

He smirks back, knowing I'm playing with him. "Yes. I can help you after work, or I can swing by on my way home and grab everything from your old house and do it for you."

I shake my head. "No. I want to do it. I'm sure it won't take me long and I need to do something today."

I don't need him going into my room and bringing everything here. If I go, I'll know exactly what I need to bring and what I can leave there for when I move back.

"All right, but if you change your mind, call me." He dips his chin and takes my now empty bag, rolling it into a ball and tossing it into the bin. Then he grabs his keys. "I'll see you when I get home." He winks and walks out, leaving me alone in his house.

Soon to be *our house*.

Why does it feel comfortable between us already? It scares me a little. I could easily fall for him, and that's a huge problem when he's not the type of guy to settle down.

CHAPTER 10

TAHLIA

ALL MY CLOTHES ARE laid out in my room. It's daunting seeing the amount of clothes I've acquired over the years of living here. I need to cull some. But today isn't the day to do that. No, today is about moving. I'm still trying to wrap my head around how fast everything is happening and all the big changes going on in my life. One after another.

I never thought I'd be moving out of this house with a guy for a fake engagement. I always thought it would be for love. This isn't love, though. I run my hand through my hair, wondering how it feels for him to have me move into his space. If this is a lot for me, how does it feel for him? And after last night, there's a new dynamic. A playful shift between us. If it was flowing easily before, it's thickening with some heat now. Well, it is for me. Soon, we'll be under one roof, with a kiss between us and a whole heap of sexual tension.

I shake my head to clear it. I need to be a big girl and focus on packing. If my parents decide to visit, I need to be at Alex's.

I open my suitcase, but after a few hours, I need a break. Since getting back home, I haven't stopped. I make my way into the kitchen to make some tea.

The front door opens as I pour the boiling water into my cup, and Maddison enters the room, wearing an exhausted expression.

She gives me a half smile.

"Would you like me to make you some tea?" I ask her.

She lets out a loud sigh. "Please." She tosses her bag on the table.

"Bad day?" I grab a cup and make her one.

"Just long, and I'm tired."

Once it's finished brewing, I hand it over.

"Thanks," she mumbles, taking a large sip.

"I have to tell you something," I start.

She frowns. "Yeah, what is it?"

"I need to move out for a bit," I say, taking another sip of my warm tea.

Her forehead creases. "Why?"

"You know how I quit Frank's?"

"Mm-hmm," she mumbles, staring at me, perplexed.

"Mom called right after and reminded me I won't get Emerald Designs if I don't get married, and I realized I do want it. So I blurted out I was dating."

She folds over laughing. "To fucking who?"

It makes me laugh too. Because it's the only way to survive this whole ridiculous idea.

"Alex."

"Alex wh—" Her eyes grow wide as she figures out who it is.

"You told your parents your boyfriend is Alex Taylor?"

I nod. "Yep. And that we're engaged and living together."

I lift my left hand, showing her my engagement ring, letting the sparkle of the diamond catch the light.

"Get fucked," she scoffs. "Did he buy this?"

Her eyes meet mine. I can see the wheels turning at all this new information.

"Yeah. Crazy, isn't it?"

"You think?" She shakes her head.

"I'll still pay my half of the rent, and I'll be back before you know it."

"As long as this is what you want to do." I can hear the worry in her tone.

"It is. I have this new fire in my belly at the thought of getting a stake in the business. I really want it. So, yeah. I need to be at his house in case my parents call and want to drop in." I take a big sip to wet my parched throat.

She wears a knowing smirk. "You're screwed...literally. He'll try to get in your pants the first night you stay over."

"I accidentally passed out on his sofa last night."

"Jesus, this gets worse by the second. Did you sleep with him?"

I shake my head. "No. I must've been exhausted from the big day and the alcohol I drank." I'm not opposed to the idea of sleeping with him like I was before we started this arrangement.

"Sounds like you need wine, not tea. Do you want help packing?"

"Please," I say excitedly. I begin to walk to my room. She follows.

She looks around at my clutter. "Where do you want me to start?"

My mouth curves into the biggest, warmest smile. I'm so grateful for our friendship.

"Can you pack my bathroom stuff?"

"Into what? I don't see any spare cases."

I groan and scan the room. Finding a shopping bag, I shake it out and hand it out to her. "This will do."

She turns and walks off, calling over her shoulder, "You owe me, bitch."

I chuckle and refocus on packing more clothes into the case.

After an hour, I have a big case, and another smaller bag overflowing with my belongings. If I need anything else, I'll get it when I come by and visit Maddison.

"I'm kinda pissed you're leaving me alone, but then on the flip side, I get this place to myself. I can have a guy over and you wouldn't know."

My mouth parts in surprise. "You wouldn't," I say, clutching my chest.

"As if I could. I have the biggest mouth, and if I had gossip, you'd be the first to know."

I exhale. "Good."

"But that works both ways, T," she drawls out my name, and I know what she means.

I can be quiet compared to her and keep things to myself, but there isn't anything to share about Alex and me. We're friends with a mutual attraction to each other. Nothing more.

"Nothing will happen between Alex and me, I can assure you."

Her face brightens at the suggestion. "I didn't say anything about Alex."

The corner of my lip lifts into a small smile. "As if you didn't insinuate if something happens with Alex."

"Well, if something does..."

I don't bother replying, because I'm not going to win. And if something were to happen, I'd want to share it with my best friends.

I put my hands on my hips, looking at the two bags, and then back at Maddison.

"All right, that's it. I better get over to his house," I breathe out.

"Good luck." And as she happily waves me goodbye, she sends me a wink. Maybe I am screwed.

CHAPTER 11

ALEX

WORK ENDED UP TAKING longer than planned, but that's what happens when you're on call. You never know what you're walking into. Pulling into my driveway, I see her parked car and wonder what she did today. Did she leave my house at all, or did she stay in and relax?

The kiss we shared last night was more passionate than I would have ever expected. Our spark intensified as our mouths joined together. I never wanted it to end. I'd kiss her again, but I can't have more with her. I don't ever want to hurt her, and I know I will. I always end up hurting women.

I shake off any more longing thoughts and take a breath. I have food I picked up from the store.

Inside the house, noises clatter upstairs. I lower the food to the counter and dump my keys and phone before heading to find her. I've never come home to a woman, so this is something new. And surprisingly, I don't hate it.

I pause at the guest room door, but I can't see her. Moving closer, I find her sitting in the walk-in closet, finishing up unpacking her clothes. Her hair is in a messy bun, high up on her head, with tendrils falling down around her face. She looks like she's had a busy day.

"Hey. You went home and grabbed your stuff?"

Her head whips to me, and I get a good look at her flushed face.

"Yeah, it's a workout," she puffs out breathlessly. "This is a closet of dreams, though."

"I wanted my guests to have the same luxury as me." I step forward, pushing the strand of hair behind her ear. "You want a hand?"

"Alex," she murmurs, my name falling from her lips in a whisper.

I'm surrounded by her sexy body and those pink pouty lips, and as I stare at her, all I can think about is tasting her again.

She picks up a pile of pants, popping them into a drawer. Her case is now empty. I grab the case and zip it, standing it up for her.

I must stare too long, and with no words being spoken, she clears her throat and drops her gaze to my lips. "What are you doing, Alex?"

I'd like to know too. I'm confused by my reaction to her.

"Seeing if you want a hand," I repeat, leaning in.

Our faces are now so close that I can almost taste her strawberries and white chocolate scent. She doesn't pull away, instead her breath hitches from my advance. I look down to where her tongue runs along her bottom lip. It's a secret challenge. She wants me to kiss her.

"No, I'm done now. But I never got a chance to look around. I left not long after you to head home. I only got here, I don't know, maybe an hour ago."

My eyes meet hers again, and a smile pulls on her lips. She's so effortlessly seductive, and I'm feeling a pull toward her. "Do you want a tour before dinner, then?" I offer, needing to move and clear my head.

I offer her a hand, which she takes. My hand closes gently over hers, and I help her up. "Thanks."

Her soft, warm hand fits easily in mine. But she trips over the suitcases, causing her to land into my chest. I catch her. One hand settles on her lower back, the other on her shoulder. She gasps. Her hand lands on my heart, and I expect her to pull away, but she doesn't. Instead, she looks up at me with interest.

My eyes bore into hers. "Are you all right?" I ask.

My words seem to snap her out of her fixed stare. She gently swats my arm and takes a breath. "Don't think you're getting another practice kiss right now," she says, but it lacks conviction. I can read her easily. She wants to kiss me.

She steps back, and a deep chuckle leaves my chest. "Never."

"Good. Don't get any ideas now that I live here." She laughs warmly.

Looking into her green eyes, I can help but know there's something about Tahlia that's seeping deep inside of my chest. "Never. Now come on. I'll give you a proper tour of your new home."

I love this house. It's bright, with white walls and timber accents. Splashes of dark brown and leather to keep it manly. It was important that the designer make it suit me.

"Let's start downstairs. I need to pop some stuff in the fridge. I grabbed a few things, but until I know what you like, I didn't want to go overboard," I say, walking downstairs and into the kitchen. She follows behind me.

I open the shopping bag and pull items out.

"Thanks. I can pick up some food, though," she replies, nibbling on her bottom lip.

"I have a housekeeper who normally does it for me," I say as I put the milk, fruits, and veggies in the fridge.

"Does she cook for you too?" she asks jokingly.

My jaw twitches at being called out.

"She does."

She laughs. And my mouth forms a grin at hearing her laugh again.

"But in my defense, I don't have time. Work hours can be intense, and the call-in hours are rough. The last thing I want to do is cook most days."

"Yeah, I don't know how you can be a doctor. It's tough." Her tone drops, and I don't want her to feel bad.

"It is, but it's also rewarding. Enough work talk, let's continue the tour. I'm done packing food away." We walk through the lower section of the house. "There's a bathroom down here. And these doors open to the pool and barbecue area."

She stares out at the vibrant blue pool with lounge chairs around it. "It's okay. I won't need the barbecue I won't be hosting a party, but I might use the pool."

"Please. It deserves to be used more," I say, looking out to the pool and the garden before adding, "Let's head back upstairs."

I turn and wander upstairs, with her following behind.

"I'm surprised by how homey it feels, even though it's also very modern."

We stop at my large bedroom. I stand inside it, and her at the doorway.

"Here is the most important room."

Her eyes hold mine, and I wink.

She rolls her eyes, but they move lazily over my bed in approval, as if taking it in. "I'm not sleeping in your bed."

"Dammit." I shrug and enter my room. "It was worth a try."

She laughs. "It's okay. I don't need a tour of your space," she says, stopping me from walking farther inside.

I turn around, catching something intense flaring through her entrancement. "Well, I'm here if you need me, roomie. Or should I say, fiancée?"

"Are you going to make me regret getting married to you?" she says with a trace of laughter in her voice.

"Not at all. I'm just getting into the role."

She walks away, her hips swaying, calling over her shoulder, "Well, fiancé, I'm going downstairs to eat before I pass out."

I walk out of my room and follow her. Something I wouldn't normally do, but when it comes to her, I'll gladly follow her anywhere.

CHAPTER 12

TAHLIA

MY HEAD IS THUMPING from a full day at Emerald Designs. I shadowed the design department and finance. I'm trying to wrap my head around these numbers when footsteps pad down the stairs. I nibble on the end of a pen and keep reading.

Until Alex enters the kitchen in navy suit pants...and nothing else. My eyes widen at his muscular chest.

In the past few days, I've encountered him bare-chested numerous times. The other night, he came down after a shower with only a towel wrapped around his hips. His dark hair was damp and his chest still glistening with water. It was as if he didn't bother checking he was completely dry before padding downstairs for something to eat. He couldn't put clothes on for that? I know this is his house, and it's probably what he did before I moved in, but he's making me hot and bothered.

He pauses close to me, resting a hand on the counter, looking at my books and notes. The movement of his hand causes his chest muscles to twitch, and I remember when my hand landed on his chest on the dance floor at Luxe. How those same chest muscles contracted under my touch. My gaze drops to the dusting of dark hair between his pecs. My hands twitch to know what it would feel like to run my fingers through it and over every hard bit of muscle on him.

I drop my gaze lower, taking in the hard ridges of his abs. His half-naked body makes my face flush. The longer I live here, the more my attraction grows. Will it ever fade?

I should read my finance book instead of studying his body.

He's a tease.

Yet, he doesn't give a fuck that he's distracting me by only wearing pants.

I suspected he was solid muscle, but all the times I've seen him half-naked confirmed it. And it's the right amount of muscle, not too big to imply he lives at a gym, but the type that says he takes care of himself. The perfect shape.

Living with a man I want to kiss again is dangerous. What's even worse is moments like this. He tests my resilience.

He moves from the counter and saunters into the laundry, and I continue to chew on the end of my pen as I enjoy the image of his broad back disappearing into the room. His tapered waist and his tight ass in those pants make me twitch.

Once he is safely out of my sight, I return to the page I was on and get back to writing notes.

A crash sounds and I jump. My body is still worked up and on edge from seeing the hard lines trailing down into his pants. Is he doing this on purpose?

Unable to concentrate while he's near, I stare at the open door of the laundry room.

"Where are you going? I ask.

"Work," he calls out.

I shake my head for asking the obvious. Where else would he be going dressed in suit pants?

I'm going to blame his sexiness for making me dumb right now. Yeah, that's it.

Another bang sounds in the laundry. What the heck is he doing in there? I get up and take a deep, steadying breath. Then I cross to the laundry room, trying to prepare myself for the sight of him shirtless. If that's even possible.

"What are you doing in here? Murdering the washing machine?" I try to hold back a laugh from my own lame joke, but a small one slips past my lips.

He turns toward me with amusement on his face. His hand gestures to the dryer. "I think this is broken."

"Why?" I stare at the white shirt he's holding. It looks dry to me.

He peers down at the fabric and then back at me. "The creases are still there."

I roll my lips to stop the laugh that's bubbling inside my chest.

"What?" He gruffs with a frown.

"You need an iron to get creases out."

His brows pinch tighter together. "Right. Where is one?"

I pull on all the cabinet doors to look inside. So far, coming up empty.

I peer over my shoulder to find him staring at me with fascination. The heat returns to my face. "Who normally irons your shirts?" I ask, still trying to locate the iron.

"My housekeeper, but she was busy this week."

"And you thought you could do it yourself?" I tease.

I finally find the white iron in the cabinet to the far left and pull it out.

"This is an iron." I hold it up to show him.

"Okay, let's plug it in."

I shake my head. "You need to make sure it has water in it first."

He scratches his head, but watches me check the water-fill line. He's so close, it makes my pulse race, so I step away from his magnetism.

"It's good," I say, sounding a little breathy as I open the large cupboard and find the ironing board. I pull it out and bring it to the middle of the room. He doesn't move, and it causes my ass to brush against him. Memories of us dancing hit me, making it hard to breathe. The air feels thick, as if I'm in a sauna.

I force myself to keep my eyes off his chest and open the board, concentrating on the task at hand and not on him. His eyes don't stray from me and my body is so hot, I could probably use it to iron his shirt.

"Thanks for helping me," he says.

"No problem," I say, laying the shirt on the board.

"I can take it from here," he says, but I shake my head at him.

"Maybe you should watch me first."

He smirks. "That, I can do."

And he does. He moves closer, too close, and watches me with his hands settled on his hips.

Thankfully, I don't burn any holes in his shirt with my shaky hands. Once I'm done, I unplug the iron, and he shrugs his shirt on. As I watch him dress, my feet automatically step toward him. I help him with his buttons. My knuckles brush the ripples of his abs underneath, confirming they are, in fact, hard as steel.

"I'll do the ironing for you," I offer, keeping my eyes on my shaky fingers.

"You would?" he asks. "Why?"

"I live here, and I enjoy ironing. It's relaxing." I finish the last button at the collar and he swallows hard. The same desire to lick his neck slams into me. I fight the urge, though. But his neck veins and Adam's apple are captivating me.

He points to where I was ironing, breaking my dirty fantasy. "That is what you find relaxing?"

I shrug. "Yeah, so?"

He shakes his head. "You're quite unusual." His lips twist in a slow, amused smile.

"Thanks. Now I can go back to studying." I say, tipping my head back to find his fixed glare. I turn before he can stop me and wander back out to where there can be more space between us. A whole kitchen counter, in fact.

"What are you reading?" he asks, following me.

"Finance," I answer.

We stare at each other a beat and then he says, "I won't distract you any longer." He gives me a crooked, knowing smile and leaves to head back upstairs.

He knows exactly what he did to me. But the prickles on my skin were hidden underneath my clothes and the ache between my thighs wasn't visible. So how did he know?

He didn't. I'm clearly becoming delusional living here.

A few minutes later, he leaves for work and I go back to reading and making notes. After a while, I take a break and call Alice to check in.

"Hello," she answers after a couple of rings.

"Hi. Is it a bad time to talk?" I ask. Not having kids myself means I don't know when the best time to call is. I'll call to check in when I can and she can always tell me to call back another time.

"No. Great, actually. I popped Ethan down for a nap."

"How are you feeling?"

"I'm tired and my nipples are sore from feeding, but other than that, I'm good."

"Alice, that sounds awful and not something to feel good about. Maybe check in with your doctor." I laugh as the words leave my lips and so does she.

"Oh, don't worry. Mike is loving being a doctor for me."

I want to say much information, but I'm too busy laughing.

"Enough about me. How are you going? Living with Alex?"

I told Alice and Blake about the arrangement after I spoke to Maddison. They were very understanding and totally supportive. I did, however, have to beg Alice not to tell Mike, and let Alex tell his brother. She reluctantly agreed.

To answer Alice's question three words come to me.

Hard. Good. Hot.

I don't say that. Instead, I end up saying what's been on my mind for the last half an hour. "Alice, I don't think the guy knows how to wear a shirt."

A giggle sounds down the line. "Why?"

"He's constantly without one," I mumble.

"And? He's at home. Is it a nice body?"

I screw up my face. "Alice, he's your brother-in-law."

"I'm not asking for me..."

The image of him earlier plays in front of me. It's more than a nice body. It's one I want to get lost in.

I won't admit that. Instead, I swallow hard and say, "I'm not going there with Alex."

"I didn't ask that question. I asked if his body is nice. So, is it?"

I smile at her words, and I can't help but answer. "Yes. It's very nice."

"I say enjoy the show. But maybe you could tease him back."

"I'm not walking around shirtless, Alice," I say deadpan, ignoring the way my nipples stiffen at the thought of teasing him.

She chuckles, and it turns to a snort. "You idiot. I don't mean naked but tease him a little. Give him a little taste of his own medicine. It'll drive him wild."

It would be nice to have him on edge like I've been for him. "Not before he drives me crazy."

"You're in deep shit."

"I'm not," I say, trying to sound convincing. "I have control."

I think...

CHAPTER 13

TAHLIA

The next day we've just finished dinner in the dining room. I noticed he picked Italian takeout, knowing it's my favorite food. He even asked what specific items I normally order, so that next time, he can order that. He's being a lot more attentive than I thought he'd be. With my belly full, another big work day is finally catching up to me. I'm exhausted. And so ready to shower and fall asleep.

"I'm going to go shower and crawl into bed. Goodnight and thanks for dinner."

"Wait up," he says, walking over. A second later, he swoops me off my feet, and I squeal. I'm alert now.

"What the hell are you doing?"

"Practicing carrying you for our wedding night," he replies nonchalantly.

Like a husband carries his wife on their wedding night. Only, we aren't a real couple, and we are going to separate beds. Why does that sudden realization leave me on chokehold?

I'm silent. I'm too tired to argue. He climbs the stairs, and I relax completely, enjoying being in his arms again. But smelling his woodsy aftershave is playing tricks on me, causing me to desire things with Alex.

He takes the steps to my room and pauses inside, slowly lowering me down. My feet find the plush carpet, and I wobble, but he holds my arms until I find my working feet. Tipping my head back, I stare into his blue eyes and his handsome face hits me full force. I need to move back, put some distance between us. Being close to him and having his arms hold me tenderly is messing with every thought I had of him. He's Mike's brother, for God's sake. He doesn't want me.

I force my feet to step back, and I offer him a genuine smile. "Thanks for helping me upstairs."

Once he is out of reach, I tuck my hands under my arms, suddenly cold without him holding me.

"Let me run you a bath; it will help you wind down before you slip into bed."

I'm too surprised to do more than nod. And the sound of a bath sounds exquisite.

He swiftly turns and enters my bathroom. The water tap sounds, and cupboard doors open, and I wonder what he's doing. Walking into my closet, I grab my sleepwear for tonight, then step into the bathroom. I find him whisking the soft pink water caused by a bath bomb.

"You didn't have to," I whisper, biting my lip.

His eyes flick to mine, and the way they look from the light in here makes the butterflies return.

"I want to," he breathes.

My mouth drops open, and I'm too stunned to speak, so I step closer to take a look at the flecks of gold floating in the bath water. I won't lie, it looks amazing, and when I'm chin deep in it, my muscles will appreciate him.

"Is it warm enough?" he asks.

I reach out and touch it. "Yes, it's perfect." I let my gaze trail over his strong body until I meet his blazing eyes, the twinge between my thighs returning.

I need him to go, but I want him to stay.

"Well, I think that's enough water. I better go." His deep voice causes my skin to prickle with goosebumps.

I hear the struggle he's having in his voice. I'm glad it's not just me feeling something between us. The way my body is reacting to him is unlike anything I've ever felt.

"Thanks for running the bath. I'm going to enjoy this."

"Good," is all he says back as he slips out of the room, leaving me alone.

I let out a sigh and undress, piling the clothes on the floor, and then step into the bath. A soft moan slips from the warmth hitting my skin, and as I sit lower and relax my head back, the water comes up to my neck. Minutes pass, and then...a knock sounds on the door.

"Come in," I call out

"You look relaxed," Alex murmurs, entering the bathroom again.

I inhale a sharp breath and stare at him. He's holding a glass of wine. This sexy man is taking care of me again. I wish it was in other ways.

He pops a brow at me, as if reading my thoughts. His eyes darken with a wash of hunger.

The air crackles around us. "Is that for me?"

My question has his face softening. He looks at the glass and then meets my gaze.

"Yes. I thought you might enjoy a glass of wine in here."

"Thank you," I say, needing to calm the butterflies in my stomach.

"How's the bath?"

I know this is my chance to be daring. Try to seduce him. I need to get him out of my system.

"Relaxing but I have these knots in my shoulders," I say, rolling my shoulders.

He steps forward, taking a seat on the edge of the bath. I reach my arm out, totally forgetting that I'm naked beneath the water, until his gaze dips down, and he swallows hard. Following his line of sight, my nipples perk into the tightest buds. I'm wearing my desire for him, pretty much saying I'm turned on for him and come fuck me.

He clears his throat and rolls his shirt sleeves up as I hold the wine and take a decent sip. Cradling the glass, I lower it to the ledge on the side of the bathtub, then sink back down.

When he speaks from behind me, my chest heaves.

"Close your eyes."

The way his gravelly tone coats my skin, I don't bother fighting. I ease back, and as soon as his fingers touch my shoulders, I moan.

"You have knots."

"All the stress," I mumble.

The way his fingers and thumbs work to rid my knots in perfect rhythm, it's like he's a masseuse.

"Let's eliminate them so you can enjoy your bath and sleep well."

I'm unable to speak at his touch. This is intimate yet respectful, and it's playing with my head.

His touch slides slowly to the sides of my arms, making their way across my decolletage. I stop breathing for a moment, but his soft touch runs slowly up to my neck, and then down to the tops of my breasts. I bite my lips together to stop myself from begging him to dip his hands under the water and touch my full, heavy breasts.

I don't know how long he's been sitting massaging as I've lost track of time, but when he stands, I groan from the loss of touch. I try to clamp my mouth shut, but he definitely heard it, because he chuckles.

My eyes blink open. I find him standing at the sink with his back is to me. He's drying his hands. I take the opportunity to admire his broad back, then trail my eyes slowly down to his tight ass. I'm practically panting when he turns his head to stare at me over his shoulder. Amusement is written on his face. I'm busted.

"You feel better?"

I nod sheepishly. "Much."

"Good."

I pick up my glass, and I watch him under hooded eyes as he steps closer to me. My breath hitches when he leans forward. He presses his lips to my cheek in a lingering kiss. His lips are soft, but his scruff feels good against my skin. I want him to kiss me on my lips again. Only this time, it wouldn't be for practice. I tilt my face, but he moves his mouth to my ear, and I hear his breaths before he whispers, "I should get to bed. You stay here and relax. Goodnight."

My skin scatters with goosebumps, and my eyes flutter, struggling to stay open. I manage to find my voice to say, "Goodnight." It's coated with confusion, hurt, and mostly desire. I know he wants me, and the way the corner of his mouth forms a sly smirk makes me want to cry from desperation.

I know he fucks every woman he wants, so he must not want me...this really is all for show.

CHAPTER 14

ALEX

WHEN I WALKED INTO my house, I never expected to find Tahlia skinny dipping in the pool at lunchtime. Her black bikini is scattered on the sun lounger. Two days in a row, I've found her wet and naked in my house. Taunting and teasing me.

She's fucking with me. Yet I can't help the way my legs move closer. I sit in another lounger and don't speak. I just watch her. She hasn't noticed me sitting here staring. Her plump breasts are hidden, and the memory of last night and the way they perched out of the water, showing me her rosy nipples comes to my mind. The tight pebbles straining, telling me just how aroused she was, had me leaving before my growing erection scared her.

I could get used to coming home to this...to her. Except the only difference is I'd be naked in the pool and fucking her.

I watch her gracefully swim, her head occasionally going underwater. The sun beams down on me, causing me to sweat, and I want to cool off too. Standing, I tug off my shirt, dropping it to the lounger.

"Hey," her soft voice calls out.

I give her a crooked smile.

"You're coming in knowing I'm naked? I thought you'd bolt again," she taunts, swimming closer to me. She isn't hiding her body and her face is relaxed. Not a pinch of fear in sight.

Fuck...

"I didn't bolt last night, and I'm very aware of your nakedness," I say hoarsely.

I unbutton my pants and push them down. I stay in my briefs as I move to the edge and slip under, welcoming the cool water on my skin.

"If that's what you wanna tell yourself," she murmurs.

"What?" My brows pinch together at her boldness.

"You heard me, honey," she mocks, sliding her hands up to her hair and gathering her long blond locks in her hands. I shouldn't look, knowing it's a bad idea, but my favorite part of her exposed neck is on full display right now. My fingers move under the water, remembering how her skin felt under the pads of my fingers. Soft, delicate, sexy. Tahlia is a deadly combination.

"Don't be a brat."

"Why am I frustrating you?" she asks with a devilish smirk, totally challenging me.

Yep, this woman is taunting me for leaving the bathroom last night. I float closer to her, forgetting this is a bad idea. I want this just as much as she seems to.

"Not at all," I lie. If she were any other woman, I'd have fucked her so many times by now. But she's not just anyone. She's someone I care deeply about and someone I really like. The more I've gotten to know her, the more I like her. And fuck, I don't want to hurt her. And that's how this always goes the moment I have sex.

"Liar," she argues with a knowing smile. Her cheeks are flushed from the heat of the sun. She looks incredibly sultry, and I'm struggling to hold back and not approach her.

"I have good control, unlike some," I taunt her.

"You wish." She bites back a grin and splashes me. Laughing hysterically, she swims away.

My dick twitches at how much I'd love to catch her and fuck her against the pool edge. Make her come so hard she'll beg me to do it again and again.

And then I dive for her. She squeals and peers over her shoulder to see how close I am before a screech leaves her as she realizes I'm going to catch her.

As soon as I'm within reach, I grab her arm and she spins to back herself into the side of the pool. She's breathing hard and fast. I remind myself she doesn't deserve a quick fuck by the pool with an emotionless bastard.

But I still want to be near her. So, I close the distance between us, leaving only a few inches.

"You wanted me to chase you, didn't you?" I ask, unable to tear my gaze away.

Her teeth catch her lip as she nods. "Of course. And you did," she admits.

Her eyes don't shift from mine. Holding strong.

"You thought I wouldn't catch you?" I whisper darkly.

A wicked laugh slips from her lips before she breathes, "I don't know what I was thinking, honestly."

"I do," I rasp, inching closer again, until my erection hits her stomach. She whimpers.

"No, you don't," she argues. "You wish."

My head dips to whisper into her ear through clenched teeth. "I don't need to wish. I know."

I tilt my hips up, and she gasps, her head rolling back. I move my lips to her neck, breathing heavily. She rocks her body, so she slips over my erection. Growling, my hands fly to her hips, and I hold her still. I grind my hard cock over her naked pussy, and she cries out in pleasure.

I'm about to reach out to grab her face and bring her lips to mine when my pager goes off. Emergency call-in again.

Seriously?

"Fuck," I grunt, dropping my hand back into the water. I get an idea as I pull away. With a playful smile on my lips, I splash her this time.

She squeals, "Alex."

I swim away fast.

Her undiluted laughter fills the air as I go.

Chapter 15

Alex

The next morning, I'm standing under the hot water of my shower, welcoming the hard hot sprays on my back. Trying to wake up after the worst night's sleep.

Have you ever walked away from someone and felt tormented? Well, that's me, but I push away the heavy feeling in my gut.

Stepping out of the shower, I get dressed, then pad down the hall and stairs quietly, not wanting to wake Tahlia. But when I pass her bedroom, I notice her door is open. I hesitate, knowing this is a little creepy, but I can't help myself and think it'll just be a quick look. Once inside, I peer around, but she isn't lying in the bed. Other than getting hit by her scent like a bus, I see she made her bed, and there're no clothes on the floor. Her room looks like new, so I push on and walk down the stairs. I hope she hasn't left.

It's a strange feeling to not want a woman to leave, but I don't think anything of it. We've been friends for a bit now, so I'm sure it must be the company. We haven't even slept together; it's just a natural reaction to having a roommate.

And I'm sure if she left, I'd have heard her. In my restlessness, I was wide awake. I take the final step and round the corner and see her stirring cups. I can finally breathe.

Realization hits me. She has made me a cup of coffee, and fuck if it doesn't make me smile.

But what's even better is her wearing this tiny pale blue night dress thing. I see the outline of her nipples, confirming she's not wearing a bra. I know I shouldn't be looking, as it will only make things harder on me, but I can't help myself. My eyes rake down over her body to her hips, trying to look for an outline of panties. I'm hoping she sleeps with no panties either.

"Good morning," I say as I walk toward her.

Her face lifts at the sound of my voice, but I don't miss the cute bags under her eyes. Glad I'm not the only one who struggled with sleeping last night.

"Morning," she says cheerily.

The metal spoon hit the sides of the cup with a final mix.

"You're all happy this morning. Did you sleep well?" I ask. I'm stirring the pot because I can almost guarantee she thought of me all night. With that knowledge, I can't help but get off on it.

"Not really," she says, choking on the most adorable laugh. Picking up both cups, she ambles over to me. I carefully take one.

"You figured out the machine?" I'm happy she's making herself at home here, and when I peer over toward the expresso machine, I wince. It looks like a bomb went off.

Ignoring it, I take a sip of my coffee, but it's steaming and burns my tongue.

Fuck, that's hot.

She definitely needs to practice making coffee here.

"Not so much. I'll need more practice."

I pinch my lips together, because it's exactly what I was thinking. And with the way she peeks down when a blush creeps on her face, I'm totally unfazed by the mess.

"Didn't you make coffee using machines at Frank's?" I tease.

Her head whips up, her eyes glaring at me. "Hey!"

"Am I wrong?" I blow the steam off my coffee as I wait for her to reply.

"No. But every machine's different," she clarifies.

I nod, set my cup down, and move to make breakfast.

"Did you want some toast? Eggs? Cereal?" I ask, ready to whip us up a hearty meal before I head into work.

I don't miss the way her eyes flick over to the oven.

"I made us breakfast," she says between sips of her coffee.

"You made me breakfast?"

She shrugs. "Yeah. I was hungry, and I figured you'd be too."

"Well, yeah," I mumble. My mind is in overdrive as I watch her move to the oven and pull out a baking tray.

A fucking tray, not a plate of food.

"T, this is so not expected. But I can't lie. This looks downright delicious." My stomach is grumbling with the need to taste the food she's cooked. The other part of me is laughing with wonder.

Will it be as bad as the coffee?

This morning is so different from any other I've experienced with a woman. She made me coffee and breakfast. No one has ever attempted. They always expect to be waited on.

"You're not doing all this because you want me to sleep with you?" I wiggle my brows at her with an amused look.

Horrified, she blinks rapidly, her eyes wide and completely bewildered. "Of course not. I—"

I wave and put her out of her misery. "It's fine. Just checking you're not doing anything you don't want to."

"It's only breakfast. I need to eat too," she argues, pursuing her pouty bow lips. I love it when she bites back.

I pick up my coffee, needing to distract myself from her mouth, otherwise my morning wood will be back with full force. And I don't have time for a quick hand job before getting to work. The lack of sleep last night made me hit snooze a few times more than I usually would.

"I know. I'm just saying, you don't need to do this for me as some thank you for the fake fiancé shit."

Her lips thin into a straight line, and I expect her to argue again, but she turns and grabs plates and silverware and sets everything on the counter. Then she takes her seat on a stool.

"If you don't sit and eat, I'll eat it all," she says. "I need to get ready."

Her words snap me out of my daze. I move to the stool beside her and sit, taking in the toast, eggs, muffins, turkey bacon, and potatoes and filling my plate.

"What do you have planned today?" I ask curiously.

She's already eating, so she doesn't answer straight away. She covers her mouth with her hand and mumbles, "I want to head into work at 9:30, but it will take time with traffic. Plus, I want to go for a walk and shower."

Thinking of her all sweaty from a workout or even just watching her workout has my dick twitching. The damn traitor keeps ignoring my brain.

I widen my legs on the stool and ask, "Will you use the gym here?" I take a bite of toast.

I'm hoping she says yes, because I don't know how I would take knowing she would be in a commercial gym. I imagine all the guys perving on her. My body turns ridged, and I know my answer. Yet I perve on her too. Go figure.

"Yeah, if that's all right? I don't have a gym membership, but your setup here looks fun."

I chuckle at how adorable she is. "Definitely not fun if you do it correctly. If you need a hand..." I smirk at her, and she rolls her eyes playfully back.

"No. I'm good," she retorts.

I laugh loudly at how fast she turned me down. Being her personal trainer in my house spells disaster. I don't know if I'd be strong enough if I had to watch her cute nose scrunch up, or blow out breaths, or worse, sweat coating her delectable body. Suddenly, my mouth is bone dry, and I take a sip of the shit coffee, just to add enough moisture to speak.

"Offers always there," I say, before we eat in silence for a bit.

"So, you're going into work again after a long day and night on call? Have you always wanted to work as a doctor?"

"Hitting me with the deep questions before 8 a.m." I raise my brows and give her a smirk before answering. "Surprisingly, I found the brain and spinal cord fascinating, plus the surgery component sounded fun."

Satisfaction purses her mouth as she nods.

"Hey, how come I don't get to ask you the hard-hitting questions?" I ask.

She pauses, bringing her cup to her lips. "You know everything about me, Alex," she mutters before sipping.

The way her face sags, and she bows her head, has me drawing in closer to her. I reach out, and she intakes a quick breath as I lightly finger a loose strand of hair that's fallen on her cheek. Her eyes hold mine and I could easily lean in and devour her lips in a hot kiss.

"I don't know everything." I'm dying to know when the last time she truly enjoyed herself with a man was.

"Ask me. I'm an open book." She raises her brow in a challenge.

"What are you most scared of?"

Her gaze looks turbulent. "I don't know if I can run the business." It's only a breath, but I catch it.

I reach out and stroke her cheek softly. "Hey. You can. I'm not a guy who runs his own company, but I can try to help you."

Her mouth quirks, and I swear I see amusement, but I didn't say anything funny. "What? Why are you looking at me like that?"

I see an amazing opportunity to take over this company and do whatever the hell she wants with it. She just needs to see beyond her parents' company, because soon it will be majority hers. And the Tahlia I saw in the pool yesterday is powerful.

"You seem way too invested, considering you have to be in a fake engagement with me."

"With you, it's not that hard."

I didn't mean for that to slip, but now that it hangs in the air between us, I own it. If I was ever going to do something crazy, it's for Tahlia. The only woman I've fantasized about before. Being around her in any shape or form is better than not having her at all.

But I will hold myself back from hurting her by not crossing that line, even if it kills me.

CHAPTER 16

ALEX

I'm finally home from an afternoon shift, dumping my keys and case down in the kitchen. I rush upstairs, calling out Tahlia's name loudly, but I don't get a response back.

The pool was empty, and there is no evidence or noises she's here. I bet she's working.

Lately she's been working late into the night, trying to learn the new business. Which means I'll have time to jerk off before she tempts me with her presence all night.

Entering my room, I kick off my shoes. I need some alone time to deal with my erection that I've been fighting all day. Because of her and all the little things she does. She's literally driving me insane.

I don't even shower before lying on my bed, propped up by pillows. The sinking way my body relaxes into the mattress helps the tension ease.

I drag a hand over my face and new stubble. I can't believe I am about to jerk off when all I want is to sink my dick into Tahlia's mouth or deep inside of her pussy.

That's not an option, though, so I unfasten my pants and push my briefs and pants down past my hips.

My balls sit tight and heavy between my legs, and my cock is straining with excitement. I'm about to give it a release, finally.

I grip my hand around the base and pull in languid strokes. My breath catches in my lungs before I blow it out.

After a few hard pulls, I slide my hand over my balls and touch them. Giving them a squeeze as a groan leaves me. I glide my hand back up and return to stroking my cock. My body is feverish as my hand works me harder. I close my eyes and tip my head back, enjoying the images of Tahlia's face and how her kiss and body felt to touch and taste. Pre-cum leaks, I widen my legs and rub the head of my thick cock. Working it as if it was Tahlia's hand or mouth instead of mine. I pull harder and faster, chasing the release, unable to slow myself down now that I'm this close to the edge.

Suddenly, the heat in this room has turned up by a thousand degrees. I stop to tear my shirt off. As I lower back down, I glance over to the doorway. Tahlia stands there, her dazzling green eyes staring back at me with so much longing.

There's no shy smile on her face. No, she's fearless. It's like she can't tear herself away and I don't want her to walk away either.

I welcome her eyes on me. I can't believe I didn't hear her come in. No footsteps, no words, but this is a nice surprise.

A real fucking nice surprise.

And there's no need to keep my memories when all I have to do is turn my head and stare back into those big doe eyes in all their glory.

I wrap my fist tighter around me and return to pulling with rapid strokes. I watch her mouth part wider, and she inhales a quick breath. The rise and fall of her chest urges me on. I grunt as I feel my orgasm building. Her eyes flick from my dick to my eyes, and then back to my hand. This is hot, her watching me. If only she knew it was because of her. Maybe she does know. And that's why she is shuffling her feet and gripping the door. She's probably achy and throbbing, and I wonder if she will want to self-pleasure after this show. Would she let me watch?

Fuck, if I heard it, you wouldn't be able to stop me. I'd be like a beast wanting to ravage. I'd offer my hand, my mouth, anything. That thought alone has my balls tightening up to my body. I grunt louder as I stroke myself. Her teeth sink into her full bottom lip as her eyes hold mine. Her eyes are heavy with lust and desire. I get lost in the forest color until I can't hold back anymore.

Her eyes drop to my hand again, and I want to beg her to hold my gaze while I come. But I also know if I were in her position, I would find it difficult. And it's as if she can mind read, because as soon as her gaze hits mine, I come with her name on my lips. My hot slick cum spills all over my stomach as I groan, not even sounding like myself. I swear I hear her moan, and if I didn't just come as hard as I did, I may have been able to back it up for another round.

But she takes the choice away from me. Pushing off the door, she smirks, but I don't miss the twinkle in her eye or the way her cheeks are flushed a cute shade of pink.

"T." Her name leaves my lips in a silent plea.

But she shakes her head and walks away.

CHAPTER 17

TAHLIA

THE NEXT MORNING, I make my way down to the kitchen ready to tease Alex about last night, about how he called out my name as he came. But a disappointing sigh leaves me when my feet hit the bottom wooden step, and I realize Alex isn't here. He must be at work already. Approaching the kitchen counter, I see a note propped up.

Picking it up, I read.

To my darling fiancée.

I stupidly smile at his words.

He's being cute and funny in the only way Alex knows. But I'm enjoying the snippets of the genuine Alex seeping through. The playboy one only creeps back in here and there.

I open the note.

T,

I'm taking you out for dinner tonight. Be ready by 5.

Alex

I set the note down and carry on with my morning, only now I'm excited at what tonight brings. At least I have Emerald Designs to keep me busy today. Otherwise, I'm sure I'd be watching the clock until it was time to come home and get ready.

We need to hang out like a couple, because we need to play the part. We need to test the waters to see how we are out in public doing couple-y things.

The rest of the day flies, and I'm home at four. I jog up the stairs and begin date night prepping.

I lay out a knee-length, tight black dress with a slit on one side, showing off one of my legs. This dress is sexy, and with the matching black stilettos, I know I'm going to make it a challenge to keep his mind off the tension between us.

I head into the bathroom, and I go to pull out my makeup and cleansers, but when I open the cabinet under the sink, I suck in a sharp breath. My perfume stares back at me. You know the signature perfume you're known for? Yeah, well, a brand new one is staring back at me, along with a range of shampoos, conditioners, body washes, and luxurious body creams. Even some more pink bath bombs. After the last bath I had, when he brought me wine, I'm definitely making use of that again.

But the perfume still mocks me...Did he buy this?

He must have noticed the other bottle running low. I was going to buy more. I just haven't had time to run to the shops.

I'm reading way too far into this, and I don't have time. It's a kind gesture, so I leave it at that.

After a shower full of shaving, scrubbing, and conditioning, I'm primed for a date.

I spray myself with the perfume, before running my hands through my freshly curled hair, detangling them to give it more of a wavy look. And then I keep my makeup simple. I suck in a deep breath, knowing it's almost time. I'm about to see him. See what he's wearing. He'll be looking handsome, that I know for sure. I can't seem to keep the swarm of butterflies away at the thought of what Alex will think of me. I hope he likes what he sees.

With no more time to think, I pull my door open. Let's do this.

I take the stairs slowly, so I don't trip. When I near the bottom, I see the back of his head. He's leaned back on the sofa, but as I hit the floor, my heels click and grab his attention. His head turns, and those blue eyes drink me in. I internally shudder at how sexual he is. He's definitely playing his role really well, and I need to remember that this is all just temporary.

But when he looks at me like he's starving, I'm worried if I have the restraint in me to hold back.

He stands eagerly and rounds the cream sofa, fastening his cuff while whistling at me.

"You look incredible," he rasps. His hungry eyes drop slowly over my body.

I smile proudly at his words. But I can't stop the blush that's creeping up my neck and hitting my cheeks.

My gaze runs lazily over him, and I can't help the shiver of a thrill that runs through me. The black suit with no tie and a crisp white designer shirt. His beard is trimmed and his dark hair is in that finger-swept wave I love.

"Well, don't you look handsome," I breathe.

He rubs his hands together, and a grin forms on his face. He likes compliments. Scratch that. He loves compliments.

"Thanks, but not only do you look beautiful, you smell tantalizing."

"I probably sprayed a little too much."

"It's never enough. It's so perfectly you."

My heart catches in my throat.

"How did you know what my favorite perfume was?" I whisper.

"I went to the department store and described it to the assistant and smelt a bunch until I found it."

"You went to the store?"

"For the perfume. Yeah, so?"

How doesn't he see how sweet that is?

How non-playboy an act like that is?

My mind is spinning.

"Are you ready?" He moves to me and holds out his elbow.

I nod, taking his arm.

As he drives us to the restaurant, he tells me it's a local Greek place that is always booked, but he's friends with the owner. His excitement about how good the food is makes my mouth water. The butterflies in my stomach today made me too nervous to eat.

He opens my car door, and I again loop my arm through his elbow. Inside, we are ushered to our seats.

The city views are beautiful from here. It's the perfect backdrop for dinner.

He shrugs out of his jacket, and I try not to let my eyes linger too much over how good he looks. The waiter takes it, and we sit.

"Did you want to share a bottle of wine?" Alex asks. "Or would you prefer something else?"

"Sharing a bottle sounds nice."

He nods and orders the wine.

"Doc, I'm so glad you finally took my offer."

My eyes flick to the male voice. This must be the owner and Alex's friend.

"Hey, Gary." Alex stands and shakes his hand. "I wanted to take my fiancée Tahlia out."

I smile when he says it, and Gary's face lights up. It's weird hearing Alex refer to me as his fiancée. Not in a bad way. More of a surprise still. I don't have long to think about it, because Alex faces me, and I know I'm about to be formally introduced.

"Hi, I'm Gary. It's so nice to meet you. I've been telling your man to come here for months as repayment."

"Hi. It's lovely to meet you," I reply with a grin.

"You don't owe me anything," Alex says, shaking his head.

"Garbage. I owe you my life."

The way Gary says it stuns me silent. I want to know the story.

Gary clears his throat and hands the food menu over. "Here is the menu. The way I'd order is one from each section and share. I made them to share."

Sounds good. I like to have a little bit of everything.

Gary gazes at Alex and me. "I'll be back to take your order soon."

"Thank you," I say.

Gary walks off and we read the menu. I'm thinking it will be better if Alex takes charge here. Everything sounds delicious; I'm having a hard time choosing.

"How do you know him?" I ask curiously.

He lowers his menu to the table and leans in, clearly not wanting to shout it out. I mimic him, understanding he'll be whispering. "I operated on him."

My brows rise to my forehead, and I lean back with an O-shaped mouth. "Ah. Right. That makes sense. So, you dine here often?"

"To be honest, I don't dine in at restaurants," he replies.

"Anywhere?"

"Anywhere," he deadpans.

"But why?" I ask, totally confused.

"I work a lot."

"That's a shame, and that's part of the reason having majority of the business that scares me. No life."

He shakes his head. "You can do whatever you want soon. You'll be one of the bosses. That's why you need to figure out where the business is right now and work out how you want to run it. You can hire people to work. You don't have to work twenty-four-seven."

"Yeah. I need to think more about the way I want to run it. At the moment, I'm listening to the way my parents run everything, just to understand things first."

I relax, realizing I'm taking this business as my own. And I'm really loving the work so far, even if I'm just standing back and watching for the moment.

"Definitely take this time to sit back and observe. Then after some time, if you see an area needing improvement, step in and change it," he says, offering advice.

"Good idea. Not just a handsome face, are you?" I wink playfully at him.

"If only I was handsome on the inside," he mutters.

My face drops at his words. "What makes you say that?"

"I'm ugly on the inside." Alex's words are ice cold. "But at least you find me hot," he adds in his familiar light tone and wiggling his brows.

I stare into his detached eyes with a gut feeling he's internally struggling with something.

If I'm right, I need to tread carefully. I don't want to push him and have him shut down. Instead, I want him to know if he's ready to share I'll be here.

"No one is perfect. We all have blemishes. Including me."

He puts his hand over mine on the table. His thumb swipes back and forth over my skin. It's hypnotizing.

"You're beautiful Tahlia," he whispers. "So, fucking beautiful."

CHAPTER 18

TAHLIA

AN INDISTINCT, SENSUOUS LIGHT passes between Alex and me.

Is it because he shows he cares about me, that he brings up this hidden, unnerving desire? He speaks directly to my heart in the most unique way.

I pick up my drink, taking a sip and swallowing, but keep my eyes trained on him. He unbuttons another button on his white shirt, showing more of his exposed chest, up to his thick neck. I know I shouldn't watch, but I can't help it. The sexual magnetism makes me self-confident and has me throwing my worries away. His hungry eyes leave no room for not knowing he wants me, and I can't hide my attraction for him either. I admire the way his massive shoulders fill the white shirt he wears. My fingers tingle with a desperate need to touch him.

The food comes out, and I wince.

He must read my face because he's quick to ask, "What's wrong?" His voice is full of worry.

"Ah, I forgot to mention to the waiter that I have an intolerance to onions. It'll be fine."

He shakes his head, then he waves down a waiter, and I want to hide right now. Why didn't I keep my big mouth shut?

He sits back down and says, "It won't be long, and they will have one Pastitsio with no onion in the sauce."

"You didn't have to," I say, still mortified he wants the food replaced.

"And you shouldn't have to eat food you're intolerant too."

Fair point.

"You could have kept yours."

"No, I'll eat when you do."

I dip my chin and wonder how he can be this considerate.

"I'm sorry about the dishes, guys. Here's some flatbread to tie you over." Gary lowers a plate between us, and it looks puffed.

Alex chuckles and nudges his nose to me encourage me. "Poke it with your knife."

I don't argue; I'm way too intrigued.

I poke the bread and it loses the air, and I smile with utter fascination, mumbling under my breath. "That's cool."

"I'll let you eat the bread, and the pastitsio will be out with no onion soon."

"No rush," Alex says as Gary wanders off.

The warm bread aroma hits my nose, and I suck in a deep breath, my mouth watering. I'm so hungry, so I tear off a piece and chew. Alex copies and we stay silent as we eat.

"This is so good," I say when I finish my share, dusting my hands on my napkin. Leaning back, I add, "We need to come back here."

I can't believe how easy that was to say. *We.*

"I agree. It might be a weekly thing until we get married."

And I don't know why a wash of disappointment and a twang of pain hits me but hearing him admit this will be over makes me feel anything but relief.

"I don't know about weekly, but at least monthly."

"Deal. Before I leave, I'll let Gary know. It might be on different nights because of work, but I'll try not to work too much."

"You don't have to. That wasn't part of the agreement."

"I know, but the thought of you alone in my house doesn't sit well with me."

I don't answer. I don't know what to say.

Is he meant to care about me this much?

No. Not at all, because this wasn't part of our agreement.

But do I like that he cares about me? It blurs a line that was disintegrating anyway, and I know it will be dangerous since more time with him is tempting...

"Aw, look at you two. The perfect pair."

I jerk, turning to my mother's voice. My heart races. Do we look like we're on a date?

Reading her face, I can tell she's delighted. Her pouty lips are coated in her favorite plum lipstick, and she's in a navy Chanel dress and matching navy heels. She steps back to stand beside my dad, who finishes shaking Alex's hand. My eyes move to Alex, and he doesn't seem fazed they interrupted.

Waving her polished, delicate hand in the air, it's her way of getting him to say hello to her. Not subtle at all. I smile and watch the exchange.

Alex's attention on my parents is comforting. Even if it's all going to end soon, and he'll be back to his playboy ways. I'll treasure moments like these.

"Hi, Mrs. Adams."

He rises to give her a kiss on the cheek, and I shake my head at how charming he is. I don't miss the way my mom's face lights up. He makes everyone fall for him. Meeting my eyes, he winks. I peer over at Dad, and I'm surprised to find a relaxed face.

Maybe finding us out on a date was a great thing. Cementing to them it's in fact real.

We're real.

However, breaking up this fake relationship will be hard if my parents grow attached.

This is becoming more of a mess.

I grab some water. And then I rise to Mom.

"He's better than any pick I had for you," she gushes.

My lips twitch at her confession. She's happy with a choice I've made. Finally.

"He's a good man." My eyes move to him talking to my dad.

I wonder what they're discussing since I've been talking to mom.

I'm going to guess, work, golf, or me. No matter what it is, I'm humbled that he's trying with my dad.

They end up joining us for a while. I step closer. My dad is discussing their business.

Error.

Soon-to-be majority my business.

"She'll make the best CEO. I have no doubt—"

Alex's compliment, and the earnest way he says it, makes me shy...yet also giddy.

"All right, you two, stop talking about me and let me get back to my date."

Alex puts his arm around me and pulls me close to him. He peers down with fire in his eyes. Yeah, the tension between us keeps building, making all these moments more intense.

Both men look at me with warm smiles, and my heart swells with pure happiness. My parents joining us surprised me because I didn't hate it.

Is it possible that Alex could help improve my relationship with them?

I never used to see them this much. Because I felt like the biggest letdown. Their child with no finished college degree or aspirations. Worse, no partner in sight. My family looks at me differently now.

It's all thanks to him.

My parents say goodbye and turn to their table, but not before Mom mentions she's organized a wedding planner for us at their house tomorrow. There's no rebutting. It was an order.

I turn and Alex slips his hand over my shoulders and massages my tightening knots. A moan slips from my lips at how good it feels.

He's standing behind me, and he whispers into my hair so only I can hear. "I'm going to have to finish this when we get home," he warns, and heat floods my body.

Him and me alone, with his skilled hands on me.

Yeah, not a good idea.

But I don't think I have any resolve left to fight.

"Here's the pastitsio," Gary interrupts, and we smile back, giving him our thanks as we take our seats again.

"This looks incredible," I say.

Alex agrees, and we dig in.

Afterward, I'm stuffed and ready to curl up on the sofa and watch my trash TV shows.

"Dessert?" he asks.

"I'm full..." But my voice is unconvincing.

"How about we share?" he suggests with a sparkle in his eye.

I shrug. "Sure."

Scanning the menu, we decide on a chocolate mousse.

I look over at where my parents sit, but a touch on my thigh has me jumping in my seat. I turn my face, and I'm met with his mesmerizing eyes.

"Are you okay?" he asks quietly.

I welcome his hands on me, but at the same time, it awakens the burning desire I keep trying to bury.

It's been bubbling underneath the surface, and at times like these, it hits in full force. All I want to do right now is move his hands up my thigh to my pussy. I've never done anything in public but with him? Right now? I would. I'm desperate to ease the ache, but our dessert arrives, interrupting my thoughts.

I eat in silence. When we finish, he walks behind my chair. I peer up to find his blue eyes full of longing, and I know mine mirror his.

He leans in, his thumb wiping across my lips. My heart is racing watching him bring it to his own lips and suck mousse remnants off. I know I should be embarrassed I had mousse on my mouth, but if it got him to do that, I'd do it again happily.

He gives me an all-consuming grin, then dips his head and kisses my open lips before whispering, "You ready?"

The air from his breath on my lips sends a small shudder down my spine.

I nod. "Yeah."

He kisses my temple, his warm lips on my skin teasing me again before he stands and holds out his hand for me. I take it, knowing it feels so right when I do.

Chapter 19

Tahlia

I look down at my hand and twirl the ring, admiring the way the light catches it. It really is something else. But I'm pulled quickly from my runaway thoughts by my mom's voice.

"I'd like you all to meet Yolanda. She's a wedding planner, and I asked her here today to run through a couple of things. Because we're having coffee, how great would it be to do the cake testing?"

I'm surprised she isn't clapping with the way she is grinning excitedly at us all. I'm speechless at her audacity. No discussion. No warning. Just here, we're doing cake today.

I know she's excited, but this adds to my ever-growing guilt. Maybe I should confess? That this isn't real. It's all a setup and I'm doing this for my part of the business. Admit to her that Alex and I don't actually love each other.

I suddenly need wine. I get up, grab a bottle of champagne from their wine fridge, and then some glasses for everyone, and return to the table.

I open it and pour everyone a glass. Mom beams back, and I know it's because she thinks by me grabbing champagne, I'm loving the fact she's organized this. However, my stomach is hard from the number of knots inside it. This is serious. I was hoping not to do any actual wedding planning before my birthday.

Today is the start. Meeting the wedding planner and cake tasting. Soon she'll be asking to take me venue and dress shopping.

There's a piece of cake pushed in front of me, and I wish it had the answers. I didn't think this fake husband thing through. Stabbing a big piece of the white chocolate and raspberry cake, I welcome the sweet taste when it hits my tongue. It's delicious, but it can't replace the mess I'm currently in. However, at least, I can eat my bodyweight in cake. I'm excited to leave here with a full belly and go home to lie on the sofa, watching my shows with Alex.

My brows pinch when the doorbell rings.

"I have a little surprise for you both," Mom says, and a wave of worry hits me.

What has she organized now?

She doesn't stop to explain, instead she takes off to the door, and I turn to my dad for an explanation.

He's already shaking his head. "Don't ask me. You know your mother."

That's exactly the problem.

Next up, I'm saying hello to the celebrant.

I arrive back to Alex's house and make a beeline for his cream plush sofa. I need to sit in this food coma a little longer.

The sofa feels divine as I sink deeply and turn on a home renovation show and snuggle up.

"You don't happen to have a blanket?" I ask as Alex fusses in the kitchen, doing God knows what.

"Yes. In the drawer under the TV."

I grab a cozy fluffy cream blanket and amble back to the sofa. Tucking my legs under me, I cover myself in the warm blanket and get comfortable.

"Did you want a cup of tea?" he asks.

"Mmm. Yes, please."

My mind is a little lost in what he's doing right now. Surely, this little play will end soon.

"Herbal?" he asks.

"Peppermint, if you have any," I call back.

"Sure."

"Tea bag left, please," I call out.

"Demanding, aren't you, honey?" he teases quietly.

I chuckle softly to myself.

But a couple of minutes later, he brings over snacks and my tea. I grab the cup from his outstretched hand, and I'm careful not to touch him, but, of course, it's impossible when the cup is a lot smaller than our two hands.

I ignore the sparks and say, "Thanks."

He offers me cookies, but there's no way I could eat another thing. I decline. But when he sits beside me and munches on one, my mouth hangs open, and I sneer. "Unfair."

He looks at me, waiting for an explanation.

"You can eat desserts and cookies and still—" I purse my lips and hold what I was going to say, because he will know I've noticed how fit he is.

"Still what?"

He pushes with humorous eyes. I can't help but roll my eyes and wave my hand over his body. "You still look great." I sound annoyed, even to my own ears.

"Noticing me, are you, fiancée?"

"No, I just need your metabolism."

He eases back into the sofa to get comfortable, and he taps my feet, so I go to move my legs off. "No. Leave them."

I pause and look at him, puzzled.

He has no tea, whereas I'm clutching my hot one so I can't fight off his hands that are grabbing my feet and laying them in his lap.

My pulse picks up, and when he begins to massage the arch of my feet, I can't help the moan that slips.

I'm appalled and embarrassed, which I never thought possible. But with Alex, everything is possible.

"Just lie back and sip your tea. Let me ease some tension."

I follow his command. I can't argue with him when the strokes on my feet feel incredibly good.

I sip my tea and watch my show.

"What shit are you watching?" he teases.

"I don't know, some renovation show," I mumble between sips.

"More like reality."

I can't argue there, but it's more like a mash-up, and I explain that to him. He just nods, and we fall into a comfortable silence. Him massaging both my feet, and me sipping my tea and watching TV. As soon as I finish my drink, I put the cup down and rest my head on the arm of the sofa.

Somewhere along the line, my eyes grew heavy, and I must have dosed off. I'm being lifted from the sofa, and when my eyes fling open, I'm back up next to his face as he walks.

"I'm awake. Put me down, and I'll walk."

"It's okay, I can do it, and hey, think of it as more practice."

I slump down, too exhausted to care.

His scent this close is so heavenly, I just soak it in. Up the stairs, I know we are in my room, and he lowers me down.

His hands stay touching my waist and mine on his shoulders. The erratic beating of my heart feels like it's about to come out of my chest. Everything around us drowns out, and my earlier sleepy state is now the opposite.

He's staring down at me intently, before he slowly and seductively gazes over my body. When he meets my eyes again, my blood is pounding in my ears. Then he leans in, and the emotions around us are melting my resolve.

I wonder what he's thinking, but before I get a chance to ask, he pecks my lips with soft, slow kisses. Not once, no, not twice, no, three times before he moves his lips to my hair, whispering, "Goodnight."

CHAPTER 20

TAHLIA

I'M SO FRUSTRATED, I could cry. Why didn't he kiss me passionately last night? I was practically begging him. I even leaned in, but he just...pecked me on the damn lips!

He spun around and strolled into his room as if nothing happened. Leaving me shocked and breathless. When I finally got my legs to work, they were shaky. I barely slept last night, because I couldn't stop dreaming about him. The way his strong hands massaged my shoulders. Or the way his breath touched my ear when he whispered into it.

I know I shouldn't want him, but I can't rein it back in now. And if he didn't already turn me down, I would have crawled into his bed and begged him to touch me. But I've had enough humiliation.

I open my bedroom door, ready to stomp down the stairs, a mix of exhaustion and anger overwhelming me. I didn't bother changing into the sweats to cover myself. I'm back in my slinky nightie, wearing it proudly to fuck with him. I'm not covering myself up; I want him to walk around with the same amount of ache that I have. A wicked smirk parts my lips as I imagine him hard as a rock, walking around at work in scrubs for me. Yeah...I can't deny the thrill that thought hits me with.

Of course, he stands outside my bedroom with his hand up like he was ready to knock on my door. "Morning," he says in his gravelly morning voice.

I catch his eyes roaming up over my naked legs. Instinctively, I cross one foot over the other to squeeze the throb between my thighs. His eyes widen at the movement. I love the way he looks at me. It makes me feel adored...wanted. Yet his actions do the other.

He's so damn confusing. It hurts my brain to think.

The only sign he gives me, or at least I think I'm seeing, is a deep hunger in his glare. Then there're his heavy breaths and his Adam's apple as he tries to swallow when he finishes his inspection.

"Did you sleep well?" he asks through a thick voice.

I want to tell him I'm achy, aroused, and borderline close to begging him to fuck me here in my room. Even taking in his sweats, it's hard for me to focus.

"Yeah, all right." It's the best I can come up with. I try not to show him how affected I am by his looks.

The way his lips twitch and brow lifts, I expect him to call me out. But instead, he watches me closely.

Needing to break the tension, I cross my arms over my chest. I'm trying to calm the noise in my head that's telling me to step forward and capture his mouth with mine. My body is on fire, and I know he's watching me.

His hand reaches out to run a finger along my temple and over my lips. They part, desperate for him, just like the rest of me.

His touch on my lips is so delicate, it's like he's deliberating.

Do it, my head screams. Kiss me...

"Yes..." I breathe, my voice cracking.

His fingers trail down my neck, over my rapid pulse, before he moves to my shoulder. I watch him, and his brows pull down as his tongue pokes out of his mouth. My breath catches. His hand has moved to the divot in my chest, and his finger trails delicately down the center between my heavy breasts, my nipples tight and ready for his touch. His fingers linger over my wildly beating heart.

"I shouldn't..." His voice is low and strangled, mirroring my own struggle. But he has some kind of internal fight that he isn't voicing. His dark eyes stay trained on his finger that's headed back to the base of my throat, setting my body to shivering.

"Why not?" I push, ignoring my own dark thoughts coming up about how much of a playboy he is, and that he will only break my heart. I'll be the one left disappointed.

"I don't do this."

I frown, not understanding. I try not to focus on his finger caressing up my arm again and how he could see my nipples tight through my nightie. Instead, I force myself to focus on his words.

"Don't do what?" I whisper softly, trying to get him to let his walls down and allow me in.

He stays silent as he skims his finger over the strap sitting on my shoulder, moving it effortlessly. I close my eyes; my body frozen, hoping he will slide the strap off.

"Alex..." I say, a gentle plea, willing him to take this further.

His finger moves across to the other arm, repeating the same torturous motion. A deep, heavy sigh slips through my lips.

His eyes momentarily flick to mine, blazing with so much heat. A breath catches in my lungs at the sight. And I have to focus on exhaling to calm my erratic body down.

"This. T. I don't. I can't do this to you." His finger stops on my wrist, over my pulse. It's spilling my secrets without me having to utter a word. I'm desperate for him. I don't want him to stop. I feel like I could break from the overwhelming need to have him.

But, of course, he fucking stops. My eyes sting, so I squeeze them shut and then re-open them. Steadying myself, I try to get a read of his face. His lips are thin and his face tight. I see the pain, but I don't get why. I'm offering myself on a silver platter, and he's denying us...why?

"What. Why?" I ask. Attempting to get him to talk without the distraction of our skin touching. Knowing how it short-circuits my brain.

He shakes his head as he runs his hand through his gelled hair, messing it up. Like he can't quite believe he just did that. "I've gotta go." His voice is low and defeated.

He turns around and walks to his room. When I hear his door slam shut, I sigh. I sit lightheaded and dizzy in lust...And a lot confused.

"Tea or coffee?" Maddison calls out from the kitchen. I'm sunk into the sofa with a blanket. The comfort of being in my own home settles in, where I'm not confused or sexually frustrated. What is going on in Alex's brain; I'd love to know.

Maddison is an open book, not hiding how she feels or what she's thinking. I welcome the familiarity, just like all the times I've been on this sofa with her and Alice.

Talking boys, food, or the latest episode of a recent TV show we're bingeing.

"Wine?" I ask.

"Sure." she says.

"Wanna hand?"

"Nope, I'll be a second."

A couple of minutes later, she walks in carrying our glasses, handing me one. "Thanks."

As she settles into the sofa, she speaks. "Wine for lunch. This is new."

I turn my gaze away from her wiggling brows. I take a big sip, welcoming the sweet taste on my tongue.

"Come on. Clearly, something is going on. You haven't been here since you left."

"I h—" My voice dies when I realize I haven't been back. And now I'm expecting to come here and hang out? We've been friends for years. Maddison speaks her mind. Her no bullshit approach is probably what I need to hear. But then I'd have to hear my own desperate attempts of trying to come on to Alex when he clearly doesn't want me.

"See. So, spill it."

I sigh. "Fine."

She chuckles, and I side glance at her with a sneer that turns into a giggle.

"One guess."

She gives me a knowing look. "Hot doc."

My lips twist, and I try to pinch them together to stop the grin that's forming on my face.

I've never been one to hide my feelings.

"Yeah, him."

She claps. "No denying he's hot. That's a start."

"We haven't hooked up, so slow down."

No, he prefers to mess with me instead...

I twist to face her. And she mirrors me, clutching the glass. I tell her what's eating me up. Hopefully when I leave her, I'm less of a mess.

"There is something going on between us. I swear, we've come close." I sigh, staring into the yellow liquid.

"Like how close?" she asks, sipping her drink.

My stomach is too filled with nerves to drink any more right now.

"He was touching my neck, shoulders, arms, and chest." I rub my finger along the same lines he traced this morning. It doesn't feel as good as his touch, but it still shudders me with the memory as if it was him.

She nods. "And you didn't kiss?"

I shake my head. "He said he needed to go and practically ran to his room."

Her eyes widen at my answer. I giggle at her reaction.

"Yeah. I'm hoping I'm not that repulsive..."

"T. He's into you. Maybe..." She doesn't finish her sentence, making me antsy.

I sit up, waiting for her, but she just bites her lip.

"Maybe what?" I ask.

She lets out a deep, loud breath. Her face is scrunched up. "You don't think there's...someone else?"

The words I kept deep down, hidden with fear that's what he's hiding.

But I need to trust him, so I shake my head. "We had a deal that while we're in this fake marriage, neither of us would see anyone."

"He agreed?" she asks in shock, draining her glass and lowering it to the floor.

"Yeah, he was believable."

She flips her hair to one side and leans on her elbow on the back of the sofa. "Maybe he isn't seeing anyone else."

"Then why not go there?" My stomach is less bubbly, so I sip more of my drink. "Why not kiss me?"

My stomach grumbles loudly, letting me know it needs food, so I decide to order us some takeout. It's the least I can do for coming here and talking her ear off with my problems.

"My other guess would be Mike and Alice."

My brows pull together and crease. "It is awkward, I guess...but I didn't think it would be a problem."

I didn't think they would mind. Alice and Mike seem so happy in love that they want everyone to find what they have. Why would they care about me and Alex?

She taps her lip and then holds the finger up. "Wait. What if Mike told him he'd kill him if he touches you?"

That's more of what could be happening, because Alice would talk to me, and she hasn't.

"Possibly," I mumble. Not knowing if it is that...what do I do? Talking to Mike isn't an option. And Alice is recovering from having Ethan. I don't need to burden her again with my little crush. But I can't keep living there with feelings bubbling to the surface every time I see him. It's becoming worse with every minute we spend time together. I'm a band ready to snap.

"What's it like living together?" she asks curiously.

That part is easy. I smile as I think of our usual mornings. Well, except for today.

"Surprisingly nice." I smile and continue. "He makes me breakfast and coffee. We hang out and he watches TV with me. I even got a massage."

She giggles hard.

"What?" I clip, a little salty at her laughing at me. I'm lost. Not understanding what I said that's funny.

"You got a *massage*, huh?" She looks at me with a smart-ass grin.

I roll my eyes and softly shake my head. I kinda wish it was that type of massage. But it definitely wasn't. No, this was a PG-rated massage. I'd have happily taken an R.

"It was strictly on my feet."

She scoffs. "Boring."

"I kind of have to agree." I smile into my glass, draining it.

"Have you spoken to him about why he's not wanting to go there with you?"

"No. Not yet."

Which is why I'm so confused by what we are. It feels more than friendship. Like we're towing the line of more. It's too easy to be with him. And the way I feel about him is not the same I feel about the other male friendships I have. With Alex, it's different. There's sexual chemistry, but more than that, there's a deeper connection. I could sit with him for hours in silence and not get sick of him. A touch here or a hold there. Some feelings are happening between us. I just don't know what exactly it is.

"I mean, you need to straight-up ask."

I laugh. "I will. Give me sometime."

"Okay. Okay. Just checking. Sometimes you're not as forthcoming."

"Not everyone is an open book, Maddy," I argue.

"I'm not that bad. Come on. I just like to talk."

I smile, reaching across to grab her hand in mine. "And I love you for it. Thanks for listening to me bitch and moan."

She reaches forward, squeezing my hand. "Anytime. I wish I had an exciting story."

"You don't wish this."

My head hurts from thinking too hard. Or is it the wine? I don't know, but either way, I'm grateful when the bell rings. Jumping up, I grab her glass from the ground and make my way to the door. Knowing the conversation about Alex and me is over, and I've got no new ideas. I am where I was when I walked in. I'll just have to go home and go back to the awkward dancing around our attraction again.

CHAPTER 21

ALEX

"I'M ENGAGED TO TAHLIA," I blurt out as my brother swings his driver.

He hits the worst shot, and I burst out laughing.

Perfect.

He's beating me, and I can't have that. I need to win today. Take back some control. I haven't been feeling like I'm in control when it comes to Tahlia. She's consuming me without even knowing. Yes, when we're together, we're fiery and the passion is there, but what's worse are the moments we aren't together.

The unhealthy amount of time my mind drifts to her...I wonder what she's learning from her parents at work today. If she's thinking of me. If she's going to be swimming naked in my pool when I get home.

Mike spins, leaning on his driver for support. "What the fuck did you just say?"

"Nice hit," I taunt.

"Fuck you." He smirks. "Now tell me you're joking?"

"Nope. But it's not real," I admit.

Mike waves his free hand in the air before scratching his temple, utterly confused.

"I think I need a drink."

"You want to stop playing and have a beer?" I ask, hopeful. It means I win if we stop now. Yes, it's by default, but a win's a win.

"Yeah, I'm not going to be able to concentrate until I know everything."

"Okay, sweet. Let's get rid of our clubs and get drinks. You're a loser."

"You're an asshole," Mike grumbles.

"A winning asshole," I reply, laughing.

We get back to the bar, where we hold beers. Mike already finished half of it.

Mike's focus is on me. He wants me to spill everything.

There's a worried expression, and I can take a stab that it'll be for Alice. Alice and Tahlia are best friends, so if his wife's upset, so is he.

I'm trying not to hurt Tahlia, but it seems I keep doing it. When really, I'm trying to protect her.

"When did you get engaged? I never knew you two were a thing."

"We weren't."

"What the fuck, Alex. Spit it out. Stop messing around."

"She asked me to be a fake boyfriend to her parents—"

Mike interrupts, "Why?"

"She quit Frank's and wanted her inheritance. But to do that, she needs to get married."

"Christ," Mike splutters before taking a decent pull of his beer.

"I told her, let's get engaged so she can get her part of the business. I'm glad I did. You should see her slowly changing. The way she wants to learn everything possible about the business is so fucking alluring."

"So, hang on. Let me get this straight. You're definitely getting married."

"Yeah, we've been doing all the wedding prep, so I need to ask you something."

"Yeah, what?" Mike asks.

"Will you be my best man?"

He stares for a second before laughing. "Yeah, why not? I'll happily play the fake best man."

"This means I get to organize a bachelor party." Mike smirks, rubbing his hands together.

"Nothing that can get me in trouble."

"You sound like you've caught the feels."

I roll my eyes. "Yeah, so what? That doesn't mean I've acted on it."

"Why?"

"She deserves better than me. I don't want to hurt her."

"You won't."

The next day after I've finished work, I pull into the driveway, and notice her car is missing. I don't recall her saying she had work today, but this morning I wasn't thinking clearly. I park and wander up the stairs, admitting her not being home right now is probably for the best. This morning was intense. I had a hard time concentrating today, because of my wandering thoughts about Tahlia. Every gasp, shiver, and moan fixed into my brain. I'm annoyed at myself that I can't switch off these feelings.

When I step inside, I walk around through the quiet house. I hate her not being home. I miss the TV being obnoxiously loud and her mess in the kitchen. Or her warm, sweet chocolate scent that hits me as I walk up the stairs and past her room to go into mine. Even making her breakfast and coffee in the morning is a highlight, and I never thought living with a woman could be so easy. But Tahlia's presence has grown on me.

And now I've probably upset her by turning down her advances. She's given me every indication she's interested. The only thing she hasn't done is kiss me. I know I've been teasing her, but not completely giving in. Just dangling her along with a carrot.

I'm such an asshole.

The player I'm known for.

I wish I could hold back from going near her, but I can't control myself. My mind and cock are at war with themselves.

So, can I blame her for being mad? I practically ran out of the house this morning like a child. Instead of opening my mouth and telling her why I don't think it's a good idea, we cross the boundary.

But whenever she is near, I choke up on the words and say nothing.

After changing into activewear I leave my room to hit the home gym.

I begin lifting weights, but after a few heavy sets, I rip my shirt off. I must be engrossed, not even hearing the door, because when I turn, I freeze. She's standing there with flushed cheeks and her bottom lip between her teeth as her gaze hits me. I like her in my house. A lot more than I thought was possible.

Peering down, I mumble a curse under my breath. The way her eyes are eating me up, is not making this easy on me.

"Hey." My voice is a little shaky, but I manage to hide it well.

"Hi."

I need to stop looking at those green eyes. "You want to work out with me?"

"I'm going out tonight."

The pit of my stomach hardens. A wave of jealousy hits me. She wouldn't go on a date right? Shaking my ridiculous thoughts off, I clear my throat to make sure I don't sound rude.

"Yeah. Cool. Where you off too?"

I turn to finish my set, watching her in the mirror. Her gaze shoots down as soon as I turn, and the flush across her cheeks tells me she likes what she sees.

"Just Luxe with Maddy and Blake."

A sudden wave of worry hits me. "You don't need me to come?"

I take in her heart-shaped face and prominent cheekbones. She's really beautiful in this light. And I don't like the thought of other men looking at her. Even talking to her.

Her face softens with slight amusement. "No. We've gone there plenty of times without you."

But now it's different. Now you're my fiancée. Now you live with me...

It's not my place to say any of that, so I hold that back.

"True. And you'll behave, right?"

Her eyes narrow at me. "Yes, Dad."

"Don't call me that," I say as nausea rolls in my gut.

She chuckles at my hard expression, clearly reading my unimpressed face.

"Makes me feel gross. I don't look at you that way."

She snorts. "I hope not."

Blinking at her, a new thought occurs to me. "You'll wear your ring?" My back is still facing her, because I don't want her to see my worried expression.

I trust her. I'm just...falling.

The thought makes my heart race and my throat dry. I've been falling for her all this time. Every moment we've shared together had a part of me becoming infatuated.

"Yes. We have a deal, right? Neither of us is seeing anyone else while we are in this agreement."

My shoulders sag with relief. Blowing out a breath, I turn to face her.

"I'll wear your ring." She holds up her hand, where my ring sits, and she waves, so it catches the light.

Her cute smile on her face is totally calling me out on my protectiveness, but I like that she isn't fighting me. Instead, she's reassuring me. I just need to relax and let her be without me for a night.

BANG! I must've fallen asleep on the sofa, because it isn't until I hear banging and crashing outside that I'm wide awake. Standing up in a rush, I go to the door, hearing Tahlia giggle.

I open the door and the air leaves my lungs. She's in her sexy black dress, on her hands and knees. Her green eyes lock onto mine, and a hand covers her mouth. "I'm sorry. Did I wake you?"

"Not really. But what are you doing down there?"

Her face scrunches up, her eyes glassy from alcohol. "What do you mean, not really?"

"As in, I just fell asleep on the sofa." I huff, slightly annoyed, but also struggling with the sight of her on her hands and knees.

I hold out my hand. "Come on, let's get you inside."

She drops her head and feels around on the ground. "I can't, I'm looking for my keys. I was trying to open the door when they dropped. Probably all those shots."

I chuckle, knowing how shots get you from zero to one hundred in a matter of hours.

I drop to my hands and knees and help her look.

"What are you doing?" she asks. Her words are slurry.

I peer around for her keys. I pad the area with my hands, trying to locate them.

"Helping you find the keys."

"Oh."

I smile, spotting them near her. "There they are. Just reach over to your left."

When she swipes them up, we stand, but she drops them again. Both of us squat down to pick them up. Our faces are inches apart and her eyes bore into mine. The alcohol brightens up her irises, which I didn't think was possible. Her gaze roams over me leisurely, and she doesn't look away embarrassed. Drunk Tahlia is bolder.

She inches closer, her breath tickling my lips. Her lips are already parted and her eyes heavy, gaze flicking between my eyes and mouth. I'm frozen. I should stand.

"Here are your keys." I look down and watch as she opens her hand and I lay them in her palm. She closes her fingers over them. I run my eyes over the skin on her shoulder and up over her shiny blonde curls, and then over her pouty parted lips and cute dainty nose.

"Kiss me," she breathes.

The beg in her voice kills my restraint, and I can't deny I want it. I run my hand along the side of her face, brushing the hair away. Bringing my lips close to hers, our breaths mingle. Her warm, short pants hit my lips, and when she licks them, I pull back before I cave.

"Ahhh. What are you doing?"

"Going inside, it's freezing out here," I say.

"No. Stay here and tell me what—"

"Come on. Let's get you a drink of water and then let you sleep."

She mumbles, "Sleep sounds good."

I help her stand by grabbing her around her waist, but she sags against me. She's drunk so I pick her up and carry her instead. She doesn't fight me. Instead, she lets out a loud sigh. When I hold her like this, I enjoy the feeling of her luscious curves under my hand. She grabs around my neck and lays her head against my shoulder. I stop to grab a bottle of water from the fridge. Then I walk her upstairs and into her bedroom. Moving beside her bed, I pull back the covers, and lay her down gently. She immediately settles her head into the pillow and curls up on her side. Her eyes close, but as I go to move a step back, I hear her mumble, "Stay."

I shake my head. Telling myself to not even think about it. I lean forward, hovering over her, then kiss her temple and watch her drift into a deep sleep. "I wish," I whisper. After I pull the covers up over her, I walk out, returning to the safety of my bedroom.

CHAPTER 22

TAHLIA

MOVING AROUND MY BEDROOM, I'm quick to realize what a mistake it was drinking so much at the club last night. I'll blame Maddison for buying the drinks, but I only have myself to blame for the consumption.

The room seems to move when I feel the hard walls against my fingertips as I enter the bathroom. My stomach twists and my mouth makes excess saliva, letting me know I'm going to be sick.

I can't even run to make it, but I'm grateful I needed to pee, so I'm already here, and in two steps, I've thrown up my night.

And I repeat the sickness a few more rounds. I didn't think I could feel any worse until a gentle touch to my shoulder makes me want to hide somewhere. But unfortunately for me, this is Alex's house and there's nowhere to hide when my stomach empties again.

"Can I get you anything?"

I wipe my mouth, but keep my head down to the bowl, embarrassed to face him. "No. I'm okay. I deserve this." I laugh, keeping my chin down. Sitting back on my heels, my hands hold on to the rim.

His hand continues to rub slow circles on my back. "I would say no, but you did say you had shots."

The flashbacks of the night hit me...there wasn't just one round of shots.

I groan. "Yeah, shots. I can't believe I drank them. I know they are lethal, yet I did it anyway."

"You're allowed to have fun. Relax, you'll feel better in a couple of hours."

I wish. I launch myself forward, expelling whatever is left in my stomach. It actually hurts my stomach now.

His hands hold my hair before draping it over my shoulder and down my back in one soft stroke. "I'll get you some Hydralyte and Tylenol."

I nod. His heavy steps leave my room and move down the stairs, and I drop my head on my arm to close my eyes.

A few minutes later, he's back and lifting me in his arms. His hard chest, warm body, and calming scent surround me.

"What are you doing?" I murmur, half asleep.

"Taking you to bed," he whispers.

He eases me down onto the bed, and I blink, trying to focus on his face.

His hand reaches out to shift a strand of hair away from my eyes. "Hey." He smiles, and it's a boyish one.

If I had the energy, I would grumble, but I just muster up a smile back.

"Sit up for a second and take these, then let yourself sleep."

I nod as he turns and grabs the pills, helping me take them, and then I shuffle back down as he hovers over me to tuck me in.

When I next wake, I blink and stretch. "You're awake."

His deep voice has me tilting my head back, and I see him sitting in a chair.

"What are you doing there?"

The way he's easing back, scrolling on his phone with a leg crossed over the other knee, he's totally relaxed. It's as if sitting in the corner of my room watching me sleep isn't weird or abnormal.

I stare at his profile. I'm mad at how perfect his jawline is and the dark beard that's forming as the day draws on. The lines around his eyes give him a sexy older vibe, and his dark brows frame those damn captivating blue eyes.

His hair has managed to stay perfectly styled on top of his head, and I curl my hands to prevent myself from walking over and running my fingers through it. Messing it up. I liked the messy hair I saw the night I caught him jerking off.

I like the relaxed version. The charming version is nice, but I want the Alex who's reserved for just me.

Yeah, I want more of that. Except I shouldn't after he's turned me down.

His velvety voice takes me away from my lost thoughts. "Just making sure you're okay." He shrugs and uncrosses his leg as he tucks his phone away.

"Oh," I mumble, not knowing what else to say.

My mouth feels dry, and there is an awful taste, so I sit up and I expect to feel dizzy and sick, but I'm grateful that I only feel hungry and off. Not something I can pinpoint.

"Woah. Where are you going?" He moves fast to stand in front of me. It's like since our near kiss he is more attentive, and I don't know if I can handle it. I'm more confused than ever.

"Um. To get some food."

"You feel well enough to leave the room, or did you want me to cook you something and bring it here?"

This is definitely too much caring for me.

"I'm okay. I need to get out of this room."

"Need a change of scenery?"

"Something like that," I mumble.

I stand and move toward the bathroom. And he's right beside me.

"Thanks for helping, but I need to pee, and it would be weird for you to watch."

"You want me to meet you out here?" he asks, raising a brow at me.

I shake my head. "Downstairs," I say, knowing I need a minute without him clouding my head. He's too tempting when he's being all attentive, and I'm a hot mess from being this hungover.

He nods, and I go into the bathroom and close the door. A deep breath expels, and I decide to take a quick shower, brush my teeth, put some fresh sweats on, and throw my hair up into a bun. I know that will make me feel brand new.

Half an hour later, I'm making my way downstairs. The back of his head rests on the sofa as he watches football. I move to the kitchen to make plain toast with butter. His heavy steps come over, and my lips quirk as I look for the butter in the fridge.

"I hope you're not over here offering to help, Doc."

I find it, then turn to face him.

"Wouldn't dare to." He treks back to the sofa.

I turn to grab the bread before a big smile erupts on my face.

I can't help the silly flutters that my stomach makes for knowing he continually wants to check on me.

I bring my food and more Hydralyte over to the sofa and eat. When I'm finished Alex puts a pillow in his lap.

"Here," Alex says, patting it for me to lay down. It'll be the only thing between me and his dick. Thankfully. But I don't move. Sensing my hesitation, he rolls his eyes and smirks. "Come on I'm only offering you a place to lie down and relax."

I lower down. I don't have any energy to resist.

As soon as I relax, he flicks it back over to my reality TV show.

"I'm training you well," I joke.

"Hey, you. None of that."

A giggle rumbles out of me.

And he digs his hand into my ribs, tickling me. I wriggle around, trying to remove his hand to stop him. I'm laughing so loud, and his face wears the happiest grin. "You're very ticklish."

He stops, and I take short, sharp breaths, trying to recover before I ease back down. "Yeah, and now you know my weak spots."

A deep chuckle leaves his chest. "That I do."

We fall into a comfortable silence and watch the TV show. I'm surprised when his hand tugs gently on my hair tie. When he frees my strands, I moan at his touch. He rubs his hand along my scalp with a massage, easing the stupid headache throbbing in my temples.

I struggle to keep my eyes open with how good it feels. The simple atmosphere of us being here feels natural, and it should scare me. The fact it could ruin my journey to find a stable career for myself.

But it's not.

I stand behind Alex as he opens the door to welcome Mike and Alice inside for coffee. Alex doesn't seem the least bit uneasy. I'm not uncomfortable, but this does feel a tad strange between us—almost domesticated.

"Hi, T," Alice greets me with a smug smile and a twinkle in her eye. What is that about?

I don't get any time to think about it, though, because Mike is coming over to say hi.

Once inside, I head back to the kitchen to prepare snacks and Alice is quick to add that she'll join me. Adding to my curiosity if she's doing okay.

The boys go to the living room with the baby, leaving me and Alice alone.

I'm elated to have a friend over and just not think about Alex and the whiplash I'm getting. The moments of him stroking my back or running his hands through my hair. I wonder what he would be like in the bedroom. Would he be gentle or rough? The latter causes my sex to tingle. I really don't need more sexual frustration, as I'm borderline close to crying, or worse, begging for him to touch me just once.

And that would be utterly mortifying. I have never begged for sex from a guy, but with Alex, I'm contemplating it.

Why?

What's so different about him?

All I know is he's a player, but other than his words, his actions around me have been anything but. I don't know if it's just him pushing me away, or if he really is a commitment-phobe.

I may not have my shit together, but it doesn't mean I haven't wanted the perfect husband and children. And playing fiancée in this house is all too sweet.

Maybe if we had sex, I'd get over the fantasy. And the flutters will disappear.

But what if they don't...

I shake my head. I can't think about any of this anymore. I need to remember he isn't interested in a relationship. I can just push the silly feelings aside, and they will go away as soon as this deal is done and we are back to our old lives.

I shudder.

Old life...

I don't miss that.

Maybe instead of coffee, I should have something stronger. But then bile leaves my stomach at the thought of my head in the toilet.

Yeah. No.

There will be no alcohol today.

"It's so good to see you. How's life with Ethan?" I ask Alice with a warm smile.

"Wonderful, for the most part. But I can't pretend it's always great, because when I'm awake every two hours, I wonder why I did this to myself."

She laughs, and I'm unable to hold back my own laugh at her honesty. "I guess it's better than my life. Faking a relationship to get my inheritance."

She reaches out to touch my shoulder, gently squeezing it. "Don't be like that. You've needed to find yourself."

"I know." I grimace. "Even in this gorgeous place, it doesn't change the fact I need to figure out my life. Changing the house doesn't change my situation."

It's quiet for a moment before she nods. "And how's everything going since we last spoke?" Alice asks in a low voice.

My gaze flicks to Alex and Mike, and then back to Alice. The twinkles back in her eye, and I swear I see hope. Does she hope we are more too?

A heavy sigh slips, and I lean forward on the counter, ceasing any further preparations on coffee and snacks. Alex has given me a few lessons on how to work the machine now.

"Honestly?" I whisper. A swirl of nerves rolls down my stomach at opening up about my struggles with Alex and me.

"Tell me, T," she begs. "I know you like to keep things to yourself, but it's not healthy. Is he being awful to you?"

I shake my head. "I wish." I laugh, but it's strained.

Straightening up, I return to the plate of cookies, fruit, and cakes, arranging them in a nice order.

"What is it then?"

My eyes flick over to see Mike hand baby Ethan to Alex, and I bite down on my lip. The way my ovaries are dancing at the sight has me blurting, "This strange attraction I have for him."

"Oh." Her face opens up with surprise.

I turn back to him, unable to turn away for too long. The way he's rocking and peering down at Ethan is too sweet. I can see mouth movements but can't hear them. I'm guessing it's cooing to calm Ethan. And God, this makes me want to fall into a puddle on his kitchen floor. Dammit. Why does a hot guy holding a baby make my knees go weak?

"Have you acted on it?"

Her question has me taking in his biceps, which are on show at this angle.

He's hot, and holding a baby, it's like Kryptonite.

"We've come close," I admit.

"But you don't want it?"

I bite my lip, willing my blush to stay away. But it fails, and I feel the heat hit my cheeks. I drag my gaze to the food, picking up a cookie and taking a bite. "Just the opposite."

"Oh, T, don't be embarrassed."

"Why not? I've made it obvious on more than one occasion, and both times, he has turned me away."

Her head turns, and I follow her gaze, looking at Alex and Mike sitting on the sofa. Ethan is quiet and content, not making a sound. He's like a baby whisperer on top of a doctor. Maybe he should have worked with children instead. He seems to be good at it. But he also seems to be good at everything.

"I see something in him. He's a really good guy. From the moment I met him, I thought he was special, and hey, he agreed to be your fake husband. Let's remember that he did that for you."

I let her words sink in. But they make me a little irritated. Not at him, but at me. Why does he have to be so kind to pretend when there's nothing in it for him? I was sure he did it for me, but avoiding any advances and turning me down doesn't ease the turmoil running through me. "Then why avoid kissing me or taking things further?" I ask the burning question. I know she doesn't have the answer—only he does. But I want to hear her answer. I need to hear other people's thoughts and opinions, other than my own conclusions.

"Maybe because he doesn't want to ruin what you two have."

I've thought that too.

"Maybe," I say, but not really believing her.

"You could ask him."

"That's a bit awkward. Can you imagine me saying, 'Hey, Alex, how come you turn me down?'" I wince at how bad that sounds.

No chance.

I can't ask him.

I'm hanging on to whatever dignity I can.

She smiles kindly at me. "It's not mortifying, just ask him. You might be surprised by the answer."

I doubt it.

"I think I'm not his type, because he likes casual hook-ups."

"I think you need to talk to him."

"Maybe..." I ponder as I watch Alex lay a soft kiss on Ethan's head.

I worry the crack in my chest knows the real answer. Will I be able to do casual?

CHAPTER 23

TAHLIA

MIKE AND ALICE HAVE gone home, leaving us alone again. When I decided to work out, it didn't occur to me that he would join.

Now I'm in my room, overthinking about what outfit I'm going to wear. Down to the color and fabric of my panties. I must be going insane to be caught up on which active crop top will show off my curves the best. Blowing out a breath, I sift through the items one by one. Making a pros and cons list.

I've officially lost it.

I try to tell myself to not think about the panties, because he won't see them anyway. Therefore, I choose my favorite baby blue activewear set and basic cotton panties.

Dressing for me, not for Alex.

That's what I tell myself anyway.

I can't help the way my heart thumps at how nervous I am. I'm not great at exercising to begin with, so this session will be interesting.

Entering the home gym, I look around. My shoulders drop with relief, as I've beaten him here. Intimidated by all the unfamiliar equipment, I move to the treadmill. I warm up and peer around at his equipment, wondering what exercises I can do.

When I catch his bright eyes in the mirror, my breath hitches, and I stumble on the treadmill. I wince. How do I stumble walking?

Why is this happening to me?

His mouth twists into a smug grin.

"Are you laughing at me?"

"No, honey, I'd never."

The endearment washes over me like a cozy blanket. Makes me feel warm and fuzzy. I hold on to the sides of the treadmill and watch as he steps forward in his gray Nike outfit. The shirt he wears shows off his toned arms and broad shoulders, while his shorts give me a glimpse of his muscled legs. He heads straight over to the weights and curiosity gets the better of me.

"Why don't you warm up?" I call out.

He shrugs as he picks up weights. "I don't like cardio."

I frown. "But why do you have all the cardio pieces here?"

"For guests."

Like me.

I swallow the lump sitting in my throat, not understanding my body's reaction to his statement. It's not like I didn't know what this was. So why does the thought unease me?

I guess when it's said out loud, it hits me harder. I need to sweat out some of my sexual frustration.

I continue to walk slowly on the treadmill and openly watch him. He begins grunting, and I catch my shoe on the walking pad again, luckily saving myself this time. I'm curiously following his movements as he picks up a heavier pair of dumbbells and sits on a bench. Sitting up, he pushes the weights above his shoulders. With every flex of his muscles, my heart hammers inside my chest.

Looking at myself in the mirror, my cheeks are flushed, and I think it has more to do with him than from me working out, but I don't want to faint right now, so I stop the walk. Getting off, I move to stand in front of the weight rack. Feeling like I'm being watched, I look up to find his eyes on me. He's raising the weights to the sides of his body.

I look back down at the neatly racked weights. Picking up a pair, I lift them, but then realize they are too heavy and put them back.

"Do you want a hand?" he asks in an amused tone.

I giggle. "I clearly need it. I'm that obvious, aren't I?"

His sharp eyes drop over my outfit. "Not at all."

"Can you show me some basic exercises?" I ask, figuring if he's going to watch me, he may as well help.

He drops his weights to the floor and grabs a small pair of dumbbells.

I raise a brow. "Are you joking? These seem too light."

"Correct form is better than lifting heavy for ego."

My words are lost when I follow a bead of sweat that trickles down from his dark hair over his temple onto his perspiring chest. Being this close means I can smell his masculine soap mixed with sweat, and the way he looks is just making my flushed cheeks warmer.

I blink rapidly and try to refocus on what he's saying instead of what he looks like.

"Okay. What's the first exercise?"

"You can do the same exercises as me."

"You mean train together?" I clarify.

He shrugs. "Something like that."

"That could be dangerous," I mumble under my breath. It will be hard enough to get through tonight. Now to work out closely with him, this could really test my restraint.

He moves to stand behind me, watching me as I mimic what he did earlier. I stare at myself in the mirror, studying my form. I'm not great, but I'm not exactly bad either. With more of his help, I think I can improve.

After I finish those exercises, I move to the side raises before he shows me two more exercises to finish.

"That's it for tonight," he says, packing away the weights.

I help him, putting away my own weights. "That wasn't so bad." Even though I'm still catching my breath, it was surprisingly fun, and I feel better.

"Want to have a protein shake with me?"

I scrunch up my nose, totally confused. "Share a shake?"

He chuckles and pokes my ribs. "I mean, we both make our own."

I fold forward, laughing at the tickle. "Yes. I'll try one."

"You've never had that either?"

"Nope." I smile shyly.

"I'm teaching you so many things."

Things he has no idea about.

Approaching the kitchen, he gestures for me to sit. I shake my head. "Can you teach me?"

His eyes meet mine. "Of course. Come."

We stand side by side, and we add the ingredients in before using the Bullet to mix it.

Tasting the chocolate drink, I can't help but moan. "Yum."

"Good, right?"

I lower the cup and face him, noticing his blue eyes are now a shade darker. "This is really good."

His hand reaches out and his thumb dusts beside my mouth, grazing my bottom lip. I freeze from the warm touch.

He clears his throat to explain. "You had some on your face." Removing his hand, he picks up his cup and drinks.

"Oh. Right. Okay. Thanks."

I roll my lips and pick up my own drink. Neither of us say another word.

Later that night, I'm lying in bed, wearing my nightie. My back is to the door. I hear my door open and the bed dips beside me. A tingle runs over my body at him coming into my room like this. I don't want to turn over because of the nerves freezing me.

One of his arms comes around my middle. He's holding me. I don't know what to think about this.

"What are you doing?" I whisper.

"Truthfully. I don't know. But I couldn't stop myself."

With his honesty, I can't help but blurt out, "I want you."

He exhales deeply, and I expect him to pull away. So I'm surprised when he pulls me closer and his hand moves to touch the outside of my leg. His hot fingers skim my thigh, causing goosebumps to pop along my flesh. My body is coming alive from a single touch. On the next stroke, he moves to the inner thigh, almost touching my core. His fingers run along the edge of my panties, and I shiver with need.

"Fuck. You feel so good," he growls into the back of my neck, where his hot breath tickles my ear. His hand still caresses my inner thigh in a tease that makes me wriggle with a crazy need. I expect him to glide his hand inside to find me hot, achy, and ready. But he only runs along the edge, slipping in the smallest amount and bringing me to the edge of desperation.

I suck in a sharp breath and reach around to touch him. I want to encourage him by making him join me on the edge of desperation. My hand meets his hot skin, and he lets out a feral hiss. I'm thinking he's giving me the green light.

He sighs and grabs my hand, bringing it in front of me as he squeezes my middle, then mutters against my neck. "I'm sorry. I want you. I really do. But we can't."

The nearness of his face annoys me. "We can. You're choosing to say no." I turn angrily to face him.

"Fuck." He wipes his face with his hand roughly. "It's not that. I just. Fuck, I can't."

"Why?" I ask.

"Because there's something wrong with me. Can we just drop it?"

He leaves me gasping for air and wondering why. I'm still clueless what's wrong with him. I should tell him to get the hell out of my room, but the words won't leave my throat.

He kisses the back of my head before reaching out to touch my hair as he whispers, "I want you. But you're too fucking good for me."

Of course, with him here caressing my hair in soft, soothing strokes, I reluctantly find myself relaxing into him. His hand then wraps around my waist and holds me tight. I squeeze my eyes shut. I want to argue. But the words won't come out. Knowing I can't change his mind, I soak in this moment of comfort he gives because, truthfully, I want this. I want whatever this growing thing between us is.

He nuzzles his nose into my hair, and our bodies press together so tightly we're almost fused together. And I know in this moment, I'll sleep better with him here.

CHAPTER 24

TAHLIA

"I CAN'T WAIT." MOM turns in her seat to give me a side glance and a full smile.

We have both finished work. Today I learned all about spec sheets. How to fill the technical document in and how to measure each product with its functions and specific features. It's been my favorite thing to learn so far.

Now I'm in the car with her and the wedding planner, on our way to the florist. When she told me this morning, it wasn't like I could turn her down. I'm getting married in two weeks, so things like this need to be chosen and booked. I'm grateful she didn't insist Alex come. Right now, I need some space. He's consuming my every thought. I've never been this worked up over hooking up with a guy.

"Me too," I muse, but my voice lacks conviction, because in the next couple of days, I'm due to try dresses on. The thought makes my stomach flip with nerves. I've never tried a wedding dress on. Heck, I haven't even looked at one in person. But lately, I've scrolled online and envisioned the style of dress I'd like. Never in my wildest dreams would I have believed it would be happening so soon. But here we are, having a wedding, all for me to have a career.

"What colors do you like?"

Staring outside the car window, I look at the trees and flowers as we pass. I let myself answer freely. "Elegant and classic."

"White roses, peonies, and hydrangeas?" the wedding planner asks, her notepad opened waiting for my answer.

I smile, seeing them as my bouquet. "Yes."

She hums her approval. "For all the flowers, including the ones on the tables and along the roof?"

I jerk. My head turns to face the planner. "The roof?"

"When your mom and I went to the Greek restaurant you requested the reception to be at, we wanted to make it more elegant. Here, look at these photos." The planner hands over her phone. "Scroll them."

Holding her phone, I stare down at the most breathtaking arrangement of flowers dripping from the roof. My hand comes to touch my lips. It almost feels like such a waste for a fake marriage.

"What do you think?" Mom asks.

"It's beautiful," I breathe.

"Which one, in particular, do you like?" the planner asks.

I hand back her phone and say, "The white one, where the candles run along the table. It's so..."

"Romantic."

"Yes," I say quietly. Romantic for two people who aren't in a romantic relationship. It's comical, only it's not. But if I can get my dream wedding, even if it's fake, I'm going to do it right. Get what I like, because God knows when I'll actually get married for real.

I swallow the bile rising from the lies I've had to tell my parents to get here. It's so against anything I'd ever do, but it's a necessary evil. Working at the company I can soon run gives me a thrill I haven't felt before. I just need to keep that in the forefront of my mind.

Not Alex...

Ten minutes later, we're at the florist. Thankfully, we don't have to spend too much time in here, because I've already made a couple of decisions. We also asked for some flowers to be on the cake to tie it all together.

Afterward, Mom drops me off at my car that's still parked at work. Sitting in the car, I can't bring myself to drive to Alex's house. Alex is on a afternoon shift today, which means I'll be going home alone. Which gives me an idea. A sexy and out-of-character idea...

Grabbing my phone with a new determination. Maddison answers on the second ring.

"Hi, where are you?" I rush out.

"At home, why?" Maddison answers curiously.

"I'm picking you up. I'm doing something embarrassing, and I can't do it alone. I need moral support."

She laughs. "What is it?"

Laying my head back on the headrest, I swallow past the shame. "We're going to buy me a vibrator or dildo. I don't know which one, just something to take the edge off."

The line is dead silent for a moment before she breathes. "You're serious?"

I sit up with a half-smile, knowing this wouldn't be something she expected from me. "Very," I say. "See you soon. Be ready."

I hang up and drive to the house I lived in with Maddison before I asked Alex to help me. Walking up the stairs and into the house now feels odd, and I don't miss it as much as I should. Living with Alex has become easy. But in five months, my life will return to the way it was. And I'll have to forget about our morning coffees together, his crooked smiles, our chats on the sofa, and, recently, him lying next to me in bed. I think this fake marriage has shifted my feelings for Alex. And it's dangerous. Liking a known bachelor is only going to end in heartbreak, but for some silly reason, I can't tell my heart to stop.

Hopefully, releasing some of this pent-up frustration will help re-center my thoughts.

"How's living with Doctor dreamboat?" is the first thing Maddison says on our way to the store.

I giggle, which then turns into a snort. "What made you think of that name?"

"You don't hate it...hmmm...interesting."

I try to bite my lips to prevent a smile, but I can't help it and a small smile breaks through. "It's cute and funny." And totally suits him.

"Are you actually falling for your fake fiancé?"

"No!" I scoff.

But I sound unconvincing, even to my own ears.

Maddison gives me the biggest side-eye.

"I'm not! I just think he's hot, and I'm..." I sigh, not wanting to say the word out loud.

"Horny," she guesses.

"Yeah, that," I mumble, embarrassed.

She laughs. "You can't even say the word. And yet we're about to walk into a sex shop. This will be interesting."

"Maddy, this is embarrassing," I whisper-shout, palming my head.

"Well, we could go to Luxe and find a real guy," she suggests, as if it's just that easy.

I purse my lips. The thought of another guy's hands on me feels completely wrong. "It's not allowed. It's part of our contract," I say.

She snorts. "Fuck, that's such a shit deal. Well, here's to finding the best dildo the shop can offer."

I scrunch my face up, hating the idea. I hope I don't end up regretting this. "This feels strange. I don't know if I want a dildo."

"Why? I have a couple, and they're great. If you can't bring yourself to pleasure, how can you expect someone else to make you orgasm?"

My mind thinks of Alex. If Alex were to touch me, I'd melt into a puddle. He doesn't seem to me like he would have any problems knowing how to please a woman. He's good with his hands at work. And when he's allowed himself to touch me, they've been perfect. Yeah...there's no chance I'd be teaching him how to pleasure me.

He would own me.

With one single caress.

And I'd fucking let him.

Bruised ego be damned.

Hence why I'm here in a sex store, staring at a range of different shapes and sizes of dildos and vibrators. Never in my wildest dreams would I have thought this would be a hard choice. The wedding flowers were easier than this.

I touch a hot pink one Maddison suggested. The ridges on the dildo are so lifelike, but the size of some of these...surely, these aren't lifelike. Having enough of touching the silicone, I remove my hand. Next minute, it's like dominos and one dildo hits the one beside it and they all go tumbling down. To the floor. My heart drops along with them. Dildos scattering the floor like confetti.

I squat and try to pick them up quickly, putting them back upright on the shelf before the worker comes over and sees the mess.

Maddison bursts out laughing. "I thought you meant one. Not the whole shop," she says between laughing at me.

"Please, help me," I beg.

My face is hot, and I bet my cheeks are the color of beetroot. I've never been this mortified in my life.

She starts to pick them up as the store worker comes over. A woman around my mother's age, with brown hair highlighted by her grays, wearing the kindest smile. "Oh no. Are you two okay?"

"Yeah, my friend here just seems a bit touchy," Madison says, erupting in a new fit of laughter.

The worker helps me pick them up, and when she stands, she pushes her glasses back up on her nose.

"I'm really sorry. It was an accident. I'm nervous. This is my first time in a shop like this." My words hang in the air awkwardly. I'm ready to run right out of here, but this lady's face lights up.

"Oh, don't be embarrassed, love. I meet so many people who've never stepped foot in a sex shop before. So, were you looking for a dildo?" she says, casually waving her hand toward the stand.

I swallow the shame and confess to her with a new blush forming. "Looking at them all now, I think it's a little intimidating. Is there something lighter to start off with?" I can't believe those words left my mouth.

The shop assistant beams. "Personally, if you're just starting out, a clit stimulator is a good one. I could show you what's popular for first timers."

"May as well, we're here now," Maddison interrupts, a hint of humor still laced in her voice.

My eyes flick to Maddy in a *please shut up* look. I love her, but right now, I need her quiet until we're out of here. I might need a glass of wine after this.

The woman's eyes flicker to Maddison's, and then back to mine. She waits for my direction.

I nod. "Sure, why not."

The woman wanders off and returns with two boxes.

"These are the two popular ones. Did you want to hold it? See how it feels and how big they are?"

I think I've touched enough for one day. I need to get out of here now. "No, it's fine. I'll grab them both, thanks," I say with a plastered-on smile.

Maddison snorts behind me. My word choices in the store are terrible, but I'm not thinking clearly right now. My mind is a jumbled mess. I just need to drop her home and never venture to a store like that again. Online only from now on.

CHAPTER 25

ALEX

"ARE YOU ON-CALL TONIGHT?" I ask Doctor Damien Gray. We stand side by side, washing our hands at the sink after working on a surgery together. The twenty-five-year-old, with a tumor in the right frontal lobe of her brain we just worked on removing, is being transferred to recovery.

"No, that's all for today. I need to get home to Samuel," he grumbles.

"Is your mom looking after him?" I ask, drying my hands and facing him.

"Yeah. You on call?"

I shake my head, but my mouth quirks at the corner. "No."

His brows draw together. "What are you smiling about?"

We walk toward the locker room to get dressed out of our navy scrubs into our clothes to head home.

Inside the empty lockers, I feel the need to explain. "I have someone at home...it's odd, you know, going home to someone."

I know I'm a selfish prick for holding her all night, but I can't help it. One moment, I was in my room, and the next, I was slipping into her bed, pulling her body close to mine. The caressing of her thigh, and then her sweet spot between her legs, was just an error in judgment. And I should regret everything I did. *Should*, but of course, I don't. How could I regret something that felt so right? I've never felt anything better in my life. In my arms, her soft, smooth, and perfect body snuggled into me was heaven.

"Couldn't think of anything worse," he mumbles as he throws his scrub top into the wash bin, breaking me from my thoughts.

I nod, understanding his reservations with women. His wife left him and his son for no clear reason. Now he's raising Samuel on his own.

"Yeah, I know. After what you've been through, I'd be the same."

We finish dressing in silence, and then I say goodbye. I take the elevator down and pull out my phone to write a text to tell Tahlia to let her know I'm on my way home. But my phone rings in my hand. My mother's name flashes across the screen.

I smile and answer. "Mom?"

"Am I interrupting?"

I exit the elevator and walk to my car. "No. I'm leaving the hospital."

"Finishing a shift?" she asks.

"Yeah, I just finished surgery," I say, driving out of the car lot.

"Are you bringing Tahlia to dinner this weekend?"

Shit. I totally forgot it was Sunday night dinner. We catch up once a month on a Sunday as a family.

"Yeah, I might be a little rough. Mike's throwing me a bachelor party the night before."

"I heard. I can't believe you're getting married." She sounds a little hesitant. I knew she'd be hard to convince this is a real marriage. Can't blame her when I've never brought a woman home before. Unless you count high school relationships that lasted for five months.

Yet Tahlia is meeting my family. I don't even know how to feel about it. My family is the best. I can't complain; everyone will be warm and welcoming. They'll love Tahlia. Fuck, anyone that meets her melts for her sweet and humble nature. And I guess my fear underneath the excitement that I'm bringing her to dinner is that they'll be so happy and get attached. And when our marriage ends, and we separate, I'll disappoint my family. And not to sound cocky, but I've never disappointed them. That sends a heavy feeling in the pit of my stomach.

This was supposed to be an easy fake relationship, but coming to my family Sunday dinner is more serious than I thought. I don't regret it. I know I agreed to this. I suggested the engagement and living together. Seeing and helping Tahlia with Emerald Designs confirms this was the right thing to do. She deserves the direction in life she's craving. This is her fresh start, and it's not my story to share, so I won't be telling my mom the truth.

"Neither can I. Are you proud, Mom? Your bachelor son is finally settling down?" I smile as I say it.

"Love, I'm proud of you. You haven't settled for any woman. You were waiting for the right one."

Gripping the steering wheel tighter with white knuckle force, heavy guilt twists in my gut. She really thinks I've fallen in love. If only she knew her son doesn't have a heart. He can't fall in love. He's fucking broken.

"Yeah. No settling here," I say, pulling up into my driveway, knowing Tahlia's behind my door...waiting.

If only I wasn't so fucked up in the head, I could be with her. Give in to her not-so-subtle hints for sex. I don't know exactly what we're doing; it's not like we're sticking to the friend zone, and yet I can't love her, so where does that leave us? I know I care a lot about her. More than I have about a woman before. I want to protect her and make her happy, but then what does it make us if we're not a real couple and not friends either? I rub my face with my hands. Utterly at a loss.

I put my car in park and push my head back on the headrest, closing my eyes briefly.

"You're at home," Mom says.

"Yeah, I just pulled in," I say and sit up, unbuckling my seatbelt.

"Well, I was just calling to check if she was coming for dinner on Sunday. I'm sure you're tired and just want to get inside to your fiancée." Her voice is lighter now.

Fiancée...

Want to get inside to your fiancée...

I'm waiting for the word to make my stomach roll. But I don't feel that at all. If anything, I'm thrilled to get inside to talk to her about her day. What did she do? What did she learn? What can I help her research tonight?

I've never given a shit about any of that with anyone else.

But with her, I want to hear about the most mundane details.

Things are definitely becoming way more complicated and less simple.

"All right, Mom. Love you."

I hang up on the only woman I've loved. Pushing open the car door, I trail the steps up to my house. I'm grinning as I go inside, ready to see the stunning blonde with the most magnificent green eyes curled up on the sofa, watching trash TV. And I'm going to shower and join her. I don't care what I'm watching, I just want to sit and unwind by listening to her speak about her day.

Except when I walk through my house, she isn't doing that.

The house is quiet, and if it wasn't for her car parked outside, I'd think she was out. Unless a friend came to pick her up?

I pull out my phone, but there's no message from her. My shoulders drop, and I dump my keys on the counter and stroll to the stairs. It's not like she owes me an explanation if she goes out, but I just can't shake the disappointment. In the back of my mind, reality is trying to remind me that this fake marriage will be over before I know it, and I will be back to coming home to no one. And I can't help the way my stomach drops from the knowledge.

A noise comes from upstairs...or should I say, a moan?

I walk upstairs and stride straight to her door when another raspy moan leaves her room. My dick twitches.

She's pleasuring herself.

It's only fair I take a peek after what she did to me, and I know how hot it was when she watched me. Walking the steps to her doorway, I'm hit with her sweet chocolate and strawberry scent. It's so strong and sexy. My mouth waters from the sight in front of me. Her laid out on her bed, her white bed sheets bunched down to the bottom, propped up on pillows, where her blonde hair drapes messily. But the knee-weakening vision is her legs bent, wide open, allowing me to see her pussy. She has a pink toy in her hand and she's rubbing it in lazy circles. The room is dark except for the lamp on her bedside table.

"Alex," she says, her voice strangled.

I step closer. Her chest is heaving from her quick breaths. I curl my fingers as I lower my gaze down to the peaks of her nipples. It makes me thirsty to see how rosy they are and beg for a taste. My legs move on their own accord as I step farther into her room. Crossing the boundaries I put on myself.

She's staring at me with a longing that is making it hard to resist.

"Tahlia..." I say on a ragged breath.

She moans and tips her head back, her eyes rolling as pleasure overtakes her. I'm so hard right now. She's more turned on now that I'm watching. I swallow the lust that's rising and step closer again.

Her hand comes out and wraps around mine. My gaze peers down at it. "Please," she begs, tugging my hand to her. It's almost like she's desperate for me.

"What's wrong with me?" Her eyes flutter open, and they are so bright and beautiful, but the pain of rejection sits heavily in them.

I fucking did that.

I put that pain there.

And I don't want her to feel rejected, because I want her. Fuck, I've wanted her so much, but I'm trying to protect her.

I'm breathing hard and fast now, struggling to get oxygen to my brain to think. But I'm so tired of thinking. I've never felt this way about a woman or sex. I've never wanted it or thought about it as much as I have with her.

"Absolutely nothing. You're perfect."

Her bright green eyes bore into mine. Moving closer to the edge of the bed, I sit on the bed beside her. My hand skims her jaw to tilt her head back, exposing her delicate neck and her heart beating rapidly. I trace my finger along it, admiring her full lips parted, before gripping her head and crashing my lips to hers. She kisses me back ferociously and my tongue skims her lower lip before tangling with hers. Reveling in her taste.

Our lips and tongues move in hard movements. It's desperate without being frantic. The sound of the vibrator hums in the background, and the buzz can be felt on my lips. Moving my lips away from hers, she lets out a whine. I smirk and move my lips to her neck, laying a kiss there and breathing into her ear.

"Can I touch you?" I ask.

"Yes," she says with need.

I have to take a deep, centering breath to take this slow and enjoy every piece of her. Keeping my eyes on my hand, I lay my finger on her lips and bring it over her jaw, down her neck, over to her right nipple. Grazing my finger over the stiff buds, her breath catches, and I flick my gaze to hers to find her watching me. I pinch the nipple lightly, and she arches into my hand. I do it again, but harder, and she moans and arches again. Leaning down, I capture a nipple in my mouth and suck, flicking my tongue over it again and again. Popping off, I bring my mouth to her lips. Her eyes open slowly, revealing heavy lust. I lay a kiss on her lips.

"Do you know how many times I've thought about you?"

"No." Her voice wobbles.

"A fucking lot, Tahlia. But nothing can compare seeing it in real life. No fantasy in my head could prepare me for the way you look. Look at my hand. See how your flushed skin looks with me touching you. You're so beautiful."

My hand skims her stomach, admiring the touch of her silky soft skin, and when I reach the top of her mound, I pause at where her hand has the toy. Her heavy breaths sound in my ear, increasing with despair. She rocks her hips as if she wants my fingers on her clit, and straight into her pussy, so when I move them, her thighs try to close.

"Keep them open," I say, pushing her thigh open, and then taking the stimulator from her hand. Her hand grips the bedsheets as I lower the toy to her swollen clit. Peering briefly up at her face, I find her eyes are heavy lidded and trying to close.

"Watch me touch you," I say gruffly, putting the toy aside. The blood rushes to my cock as soon as my fingers touch her wet pussy. Rubbing her clit in lazy but hard circles, then down to the opening and back up. Her back arches with every stroke, legs shaking, and I love how wet she is. What a sight to come home to.

I slip two fingers in slowly, and the sound of my name erupting from her lips is extraordinary. I move my fingers in and out and she trembles with the need to come. She drops the vibrator from her clit.

"Does this feel good?" I ask, as her hips rock, trying to chase an orgasm.

"Yes," she chokes out. Her hands reach out to clutch my neck and shoulders.

She rides my hand faster, and I pump harder, matching her rides with a pump.

"Good. Because feeling how wet you are and how tight you are is making me fucking crazy."

A deep grumble leaves my chest when one of her hands trails down my neck, digging in, and I'm sure she's leaving marks. It's sexy, knowing I'll walk around with evidence my fiancée is pleasured by me. Thinking of pleasure, my eyes drop to the pink toy beside her, and I can't help but ask, "What other toys do you have?"

"A dildo," she says quietly. "But they are new. I, ugh, just brought them today."

I smirk, loving the fact she's shy about buying toys. It's adorable, but to me, the fact she's purchasing toys is hot. Even though she wouldn't need a dildo with me. I'll happily fuck her anytime she needs, now that I've crossed the line. It would be a fucking honor.

My hand drifts to her thigh as it quivers, and her mouth falls open on a silent pant. As if hating the loss of my fingers inside her and chasing them again.

"What were you thinking about before I walked in?"

"You," she whispers back.

My mouth tips up even more, and I slip my fingers back inside her pussy. Her walls clench down hard on them, and her breaths become whimpers. I return to the slow movements, and she lets out a long, guttural sound. My gaze locks onto the pleasure exploding across her face. I don't stop my fingers from moving along her walls, hitting her G-spot. Her hips ride my hand, and it isn't long before her orgasm slams into her.

It's fucking hot to watch.

She's incredible.

"That was amazing," I say, slipping my fingers gently out, and her whole body shudders.

Her face tilts to the side, and I love the flush on her face. Bringing my lips to hers, I can't help but swipe my tongue along the seam of her lips, and then kiss her passionately with everything I have left.

CHAPTER 26

TAHLIA

I guess we're even now. I found him pleasuring himself, and now he's come home to find me doing it too.

The way he's looking at me, it's like I flipped a switch in him. Turning his brain off and finally allowing himself to give in.

Maybe the purchases today were worth the disaster to get them.

His lips control the deep kiss we've found ourselves in. With a moan, my hands jerk him onto the bed, and his body moves to hover over mine. Closing me in and trapping me under him, he's consuming me, but I'm not scared. No, I'm elated. Soaking in every sight, taste, and smell.

"What are you thinking about?" he whispers over my lips, his warm breath tickling my open mouth.

"Is this real?" I ask.

His boyish grin comes out, and I melt back farther into the bed. "I can't believe it either. I wasn't meant to touch you."

"Ouch." I wince.

He drops his chin so I can't see his eyes and shakes his head. "Sorry, I didn't mean it to come out like that."

Butterflies hit my stomach at the sincerity of his words. He tips his head up, his eyes stare down at me. Taking me in. It's as if he can't believe this feels just as good for him as it does for me.

His face tightens and nerves hit me. Biting my lip between my teeth, I wonder what he's thinking, but I'm giving him the time he needs to speak. The crossing of his own boundaries is clearly weighing heavily on him. His fingers touch my face in soft, slow strokes before he cups the side of my face. "I'm just messed up, and I didn't want you tangled up in it."

A frown creases deep between my brows. "What do you mean?"

He rolls to the side and onto his back. Tucking one arm behind his head, the other pats his chest with a small half smile.

I rise and rest my head on his hard chest, facing him. Enjoying the beat of his heart under my ear, I stay silent, waiting for him to speak. His hand goes to my forehead and then runs through my hair. My eyes flutter from the gentle touch.

"Tell me," I plead softly, trying not to scare him away. I only want him to open up to me. So I can understand him.

His lip quirks, but then he sucks in a deep breath, pushing it out on a heavy exhale. "Whenever I've slept with a woman, I've never felt anything."

I don't understand, but instead of interrupting, I give him the chance to talk. He's watching his hand move through my hair with fascination.

"Afterward, when they leave, my body doesn't react. There're no feelings and no desire for them to stay or see them again."

The pain etched in his face makes it hard for me to watch without encouraging him to continue.

"What do you feel?" I whisper.

His eyes hit mine. There's so much turmoil sitting in them. "Nothing. Kinda numb, to be honest." He looks away for a moment before holding my gaze again. "I didn't want to touch you. Hurt you. But fuck, you made it impossible."

I can't help but giggle at that, knowing what he means, because when I saw him jerking off, I had the same reaction. But we'd only just started to get to know each other. I bet if he was to do it now, I would've been on his bed.

"I know this is an arrangement, so don't feel bad. I wanted this."

I practically forced myself on him so I can't blame him for any hurt feelings. I pushed him into a corner. And he had no option but to sink or swim.

"Yeah," he challenges, and his hand pauses in my hair.

"I want more," I say, my voice dropping seductively, unintentionally.

His brows rise. "Is that so?" he asks with amusement.

I slap his solid chest playfully. "Even though I know you're a broken man," I tease, and his eyes sparkle with humor. His fingers are back combing through my hair, easy smiles on our faces.

I lick my lips. "I still want you, Alex."

Scrunching his shirt in my fingers, I push it up, lifting my head and holding his gaze. His mouth parts, watching every movement, hand slipping from my hair to my body. I want his skin on mine. I want to feel his hot body touch mine.

"I want you too."

We both know where I'm going as I slide his shirt up, enjoying the feel of his powerful body under my palms. He lifts until the shirt is off and tossed to the floor. I lean down and take his lips in a quick kiss, unable to help taking another taste of him. Especially when he looks up at me in awe. Having him look at me like I'm the sexiest woman in the world makes me wet. Plus, he's a damn good kisser. Skillful. It's not like I have much to compare with, but still.

Dropping my gaze to his pants, his dick strains against the fabric. I reach out and trace his waistband, watching his skin prickle in goose-bumps. Loving how he's affected by me, just as much as I am by him.

I want his hands on me, but I also love the act he's watching me and allowing me to explore him. And I already know I want to ride him. I haven't stopped thinking about what it would be like since I saw him on his back. Tonight, I want to own his pleasure.

"I know they call you a player, but I'm not sure you really are."

He narrows his eyes at me. "What do you mean?"

"For a player, I expected you to fuck me already."

His chest rumbles with a loud laugh.

"Why are you holding back?" I ask sheepishly.

"Do you know how badly I want to throw you on this bed, spread you wide, and fuck you until you're screaming my name?" he rasps.

I can hear the struggle in his voice.

I blink rapidly. Well, okay, that's not what I was expecting him to say. My body tingles with new anticipation, and a wolfish grin takes over his face.

"You liked what I said."

My teeth sink into my bottom lip. "Very much."

My fingers drop back to his firm stomach, and I unbutton and slowly unzip him.

"So, you don't want me to be in control?" he asks as his hand comes up to skim along the side of my boob. I suck in a sharp breath at the soft touch on my sensitive skin.

"You're making me want to control now..." he taunts.

"No," I snap. Shuffling my knees over the sheets, I grab his pants and boxer briefs and pull them both down. Then he kicks them off. Both of us are now naked. Flicking my gaze up, I see his breathing has grown labored, and it spurs me on.

"You're enjoying yourself, aren't you?" he asks.

I hold his gaze as my hand touches his thigh, feeling it twitch. "So much."

He growls, and I feel it vibrate through me. Moving my hand to his big hard dick, I enjoy the hot and throbbing length in my hand. I break our eye contact to look down to where my hand has moved to the base of him. But I need...

I quickly move between his thick thighs as the words, "Fucking hell," leave his lips in a strain. "Tahlia."

But my tongue is already out, and I'm taking his dick into my mouth. Wetting him. Enjoying the taste of his pre-cum on my lips. One hand on his thigh holds me up and the other moves along his thick length. My mouth sucks the tip, and he groans.

"I can't see you," he says. His hands rake through my hair to make a ponytail, and he tugs it out of his way.

Peeking up under my lashes, I revel in the way his face is struggling to hold it back. I've only ever gone down on one guy before, and I didn't enjoy it, but here with Alex, I feel sexy and powerful, and I want to do this all the time.

"I want to be able to see you take me deep into your mouth and swallow me."

My core aches from his words, and I squeeze my thighs together to help, but it doesn't work. I try to concentrate on the feel of his smooth skin along my tongue and the swell of his dick. I suck harder and faster on his dick, squeezing the base of him. He moans, and his hand in my hair tightens in response. Pinching my scalp, it causes me to moan around him, sending a vibration through him, and a loud groan leaves his chest.

"Eyes up, T. I need to see your eyes as I come down your throat."

I open my eyes and tilt my head slightly. Our eyes lock. Staring back at me are a pair of blue eyes heavily laced with desire. I can only imagine my lust-filled ones. His hips rock, and I gag. His eyes widen, and a breath rushes out. He liked that, so I try to take more of him, and he thickens. He's close. I suck a little bit harder and squeeze my hand as he rocks his hips, meeting me with each stroke. I groan at the way he's enjoying this as much as me. He's giving me what I want.

"I'm going to come," he warns.

I mumble my approval around him.

"Fuck," he calls out as he jerks inside my mouth and cum spills down my throat.

He moans as I swallow him down. My wrists are sore, my jaw is on fire, and my core is aching, but I wouldn't change it for the world. As I slide my lips off him, his hand drops away from my hair and onto his chest. I sit back on my heels, gasping for air, looking back at him. There's a sparkle in his eyes, and if I didn't know any better, I'd think he's wondering what the fuck just happened. I've never felt that high, but I want it again already. It's addictive.

His mouth twists into a smug grin, and he crooks his finger. "Come here."

A shiver runs up my spine at his demand. I follow. He grabs my head, and I think he's going to kiss me, but he brings his lips to my ear.

"Now it's my turn."

My eyes widen. But I don't get a chance to think. He sits up and grabs me effortlessly, as if I weigh nothing, and lies me propped up on my pillows.

Leaning down, he whispers in my ear, "I'm starving," then bites my lobe.

He drops his lips to my collarbone, nipping it with his teeth, and then soothing it with a kiss. My breath catches at the sight of him moving over to one of my breasts. He blows on my sensitive nipple, and I let out a ragged breath.

I'm desperate to squeeze my legs together, but his large frame sits between them. He lays kisses over my chest, and between the gentle caresses, he nips. The push and pull of sensations is an out-of-body experience. I've never felt anything like it. Moving to one of my nipples, he sucks it hard into his mouth while his hand squeezes my other full breast. I'm close to begging him to hurry up.

Popping off my nipple, he whispers against my torso, "You're desperate, aren't you?" His voice can't hide the satisfaction.

His warm breath sends my body up in flames and goosebumps erupt.

"Yes," I whisper.

"Good, because I've also thought of how sweet you will taste. And just by the smell of you, it's going to be sweeter than fucking nectar."

His words are too much. And I'm about to tell him to shut up, but his mouth lowers down to the top of my mound. It's feather-light and teasing, but he doesn't waste time as he kisses the top of my slit. And when he sneaks his tongue out, touching my clit, my back arches into him.

He chuckles darkly above me. "So fucking ready."

His hand skims my inner thigh as he pushes my legs wider and drops his head lower. His thick tongue swipes in one long motion, and my eyes roll back into my head as I tip my head back and melt into the bed.

I moan loudly as his tongue laps over my clit before dipping down to my core.

"Look how wet you are. Is this all because of me?"

It's not like I can say no. I've been getting hornier and wetter by the second.

Dipping his tongue inside, I arch my hips into his face again. Enjoying his five o'clock shadow brushing me.

"Yes. All you. Oh, God."

"It's Alex," he mumbles over my clit before nipping my sensitive bundles of nerves.

"Smartass," I mutter between sucking in deep breaths.

My lower back heats, letting me know I'm already close. I run my hand through his hair, gripping it tightly. Rocking my hips up and down on his face, I let him feast on me. As the tension builds in my body, I close my eyes and moan.

"Don't close your eyes. Watch me eat you. Like the best meal I've had in years."

I peel my eyes open and meet his stare.

His eyes have the same longing and desire that I feel. It's scary. Onetime thing? He won't have feelings for me after tonight. But will I have feelings for him?

I already do...

Ignoring the little voice in my head that is throwing caution, I focus on the here and now. Enjoy the moment. If this is all I get, it was one hell of a fucking night. The best oral sex of my life. And hopefully sex.

I watch him from under heavy-lidded eyes. But I need more.

"What do you need?" His fingers grip my thigh as he breathes over my pussy.

"More. I bought..." I trail off.

He growls loudly. "You don't need a toy with me. I'll give you all the pleasure you need. Fuck, I want to feel you squeeze my fingers as you come all over them."

I swallow the butterflies. He's adamant he'll give me pleasure, and I'm not going to say no. I'd rather him than a toy anyway, and when he slides his fingers in, my toes curl. Yeah, that's what I needed.

His mouth goes back to my clit, and his tongue rubs in hard circles. I can feel the tension building inside me more and more.

"Alex. I'm—"

"Come."

And the orgasm hits me. He doesn't stop the torturous pace of his fingers or the sweet circles with his tongue. He continues until the waves of pleasure stop wracking my body and I become still under him.

He lifts his mouth off and removes his fingers, and I shudder from the sensation.

"You're so fucking beautiful."

"I thought you don't have feelings. This sounds like the opposite of that," I tease.

"So did I." He crawls over me, pausing to kiss my lips in a soft and surprisingly tender kiss. Not allowing me to respond. But I've been the one who's been actively pursuing him, so this was him telling me he's catching feelings too.

My chest warms as I look at his clear blue eyes.

His panty-melting smirk returns as he bucks his hips into me, and I feel his hard length. "Are you ready for the finale?"

Am I?

CHAPTER 27

ALEX

I've never wanted to be buried deep inside of a woman as much as I do right now.

I want to be surrounded by her and totally consumed until we come and pass out.

Staring into her eyes, I see nerves, shock, and excitement. And I can't help but give her a kiss. My mouth moves with hers, and her tongue skims along the seam of my lips. I tangle my tongue with hers, both of us tasting like the other and now mixing as one. This feels so surreal, and I kiss her harder. My hand is dusting her hip, and I grip it. Pulling her leg up to wrap it over my hip, she understands and follows with ease.

I run my hand up her thigh and over her ass, squeezing her full cheek in my hand. Loving how soft her skin feels, I move my hand to her pussy then give it a slap. It's gentle, and when she whimpers, I do it again, but harder. She tips her head back and moans.

Her hands grab the sheets, her pebbled nipples pointing up at the ceiling, and her mouth parted. She looks heavenly.

"Your body is incredible. So fucking perfect. I can't get enough."

I slap her pussy again, and a louder whimper leaves her mouth this time.

"You love it when I do that, don't you?"

"Yes," she moans.

Totally lost in the euphoria of pre-sex.

She's so fucking responsive to me, but my body is the same. My dick is so fucking hard, it hurts. Her face, her body, her taste, it's all fucking perfect. I can't get enough.

I reach out and graze my thumb over her puckered nipple. Her eyelids open, and she stares back at me hungrily. She fucking wants me just as much as I want her. She's never been as bold as she has tonight.

I slap her pussy one last time before I bend forward and bring my lips to her ear. Her hands snake over my arms, caressing my muscles before gripping onto my shoulders and digging her nails into my back.

"Fuck, your nails."

"Oh, I'm sorry," she mumbles, releasing her fingers.

"Don't be. I want you to mark me. It would be an honor to wear scratches from you."

"Oh…" Her voice wobbles with uncertainty.

But her nails dig in again and run down my back.

"Yeah," I murmur.

"Is this your thing?" she breathes out curiously.

"No. It's a *you* thing."

She bites her lip like she does when she's shy, and her voice is barely above a whisper. "Oh."

"What are you thinking about?" I ask.

Her gaze looks around before meeting mine. "I wanted to ride you."

I smirk, loving that confession. "Is this your thing?"

Her hands come to link behind my head, bringing my lips to hers so she can kiss them. "I don't know what my thing is. I haven't been with a guy in a long time and there wasn't much besides the basics."

Shit.

How the fuck can I say no to that? I want her to use my body to explore kinks. I'd do it proudly. Any position, in any way, I'll pleasure her repeatedly until she's seeing stars. Figuring out what she likes will be fun.

"Fuck, who are you?" I say with a crooked smile.

"Tahlia." She gives me a playful smile.

"You are, and you were made for me," I say, kissing her lips before I try to slide off the bed to grab a condom from my room.

She grabs my arm. "No. I'm on the pill. Please. I want to feel you with nothing between us."

Fuck. How can I argue with that?

I want that too.

"Are you sure?"

She nods.

I sit back and lean against the headboard. She watches me. My dick twitches in appreciation. She comes to sit on top of me, full of confidence. It's sexy as hell.

I lift my hand and drag my thumb over her bottom lip, and her tongue peeks out to graze it. I lower my hands to her waist, marveling at how incredible her hourglass shape is.

I move my hand and spank her ass. She moans, her body gliding over my erection. I grunt from the sensation, repeating the spank.

"Lift your hips."

She follows my instructions, and I grab the base of my dick, but her hands cover mine. "Let me."

I can't argue when she says it in such a husky tone. It's impossible to say no.

My hands drop to her thighs, and she lines herself up at her entrance.

"Are you ready?" I ask, because I'm so fucking ready. I'm barely holding myself back from bucking my hips to enter her already.

She nods and sinks down. The heavens have opened, and fuck, she's so tight. I have to breathe through it.

"Alex," she moans, pausing at my base to adjust to my size. Her head tips back in lust, exposing her neck to me. Her hands on my stomach steady her.

"I know, baby. I know." My hands rest at her hips, and I lower my eyes to her perfect creamy tits that are rising and falling with every breath she takes. Her rosy nipples are in tight peaks.

Her head lifts, and when her eyes meet mine, the air leaves my lungs. Her eyes glow with so much pleasure, I'm not sure how long I'll last.

She rises and sinks down again, and my gaze drops to where we join. I revel in how perfect her pussy takes me and she's watching our union with fascination too. It's hot, and I don't want this to end. I've never felt sex like this. The longing, the anticipation, the holding back, it's all lead up to this.

Now that I've had her, I don't think I'll be able to let her go. I've been attracted to Tahlia since I met her, but nothing prepared me for the way she makes me feel. I thought I was broken beyond repair, but I'm coming to realize I was just with the wrong person.

She rocks her hips, and her nails dig into my stomach, taking away my thoughts for a second. My hands glide up to her waist, and I lift her to help take her harder. Her eyes roll back into her head, and she gasps.

I thrust my hips up as she slams down on my cock. Her pussy clenches tightly around me. I grunt loudly. "Tahlia, fuck!"

Her head tips back as my cock jerks. We continue thrusting, until her legs tremble, and my name leaves her mouth in a whisper. The fact she's shattering on my cock, for me, is the best thing I've experienced in a long time. A cry leaves her mouth, and her body convulses as I keep thrusting up, trying to ride out her orgasm.

No sex will compare.

She's sexy and sedated as she comes down from her high, her body flushed with a just-fucked look. Flipping her onto her back, she squeals in surprise, and I stare down at the most beautiful woman I've ever laid eyes on. She brings me a happiness I never in a million years thought was possible. But here we are...

A sheen of perspiration makes her body glow, and I bring my lips to hers, devouring her. My hips rock into her, finding a rhythm that has her writhing under me. I want her to come again, but this time with me. Her hands grip my shoulders, and I pump my hips harder.

"Told you, you wouldn't need toys with me."

She giggles in the sweetest, breathiest way. And I slam my hips more forcefully, moving her body with each pump. I can't get enough of her. She's like a drug to me. A new addiction. I loved her body, but her heart and soul have crept beneath my skin. I've never felt like this. I'm hers.

"Definitely not."

I can't help but grin. The words every guy wants to hear, but only coming from the right person does it matter. And hearing it from her is everything. I don't even know why the thought of a damn toy being inside her over me made me see red, but it did.

"Good, because you have me now. And I plan on pleasuring my fiancée," I grunt out between thrusts.

Her legs quiver, and she arches her back as she cries out. "I'm coming!"

My orgasm hits me at full force, causing my vision to spot and her name to leave my lips on a groan.

Both of us are gasping and spent as I drop down beside her.

Once I've caught my breath, I press a kiss to her cheek and pull her body flush against mine. And then I sink my face into the crook of her neck, inhaling her scent.

Leaning to kiss the back of her head, I whisper, "Thanks for making me feel something other than numb."

I hold her tightly. I don't want to let her go from this position.

"Who knew you just needed to find the right person," she breathes, laying her arm over mine.

"My person," I say as I tug her even closer.

She tenses briefly before letting her body go lax in my arms.

Her sweet scent drugs me and helps the heaviness in my body drag me under. Not before I realize I'm at fucking peace.

I wake up deliciously hot from holding her all night. I've never thought much about sharing a bed with a woman. But she's changed that. With her body perfectly in front of mine, with my arms wrapped around her middle, I lavish in it.

I see her twirl the ring around her finger, and I can't help but grin proudly. I'm fascinated by the sparkles bouncing off it from the morning light. Going to the venue today doesn't seem so sickening at the moment. I couldn't be fucking happier.

"What are you thinking about?" I ask, watching her drop her hand back to sit on top of mine.

She sinks farther back into me. "How happy I am."

I love how easily that spilt from her lips. No need to hold back how we feel. Last night, our words were raw and honest, and it opened a new door. I'm still grappling with the idea that we're in this new happy bubble.

I growl and bury my head in her neck. Her giggle fills the room. And I love it. Her laugh is everything to me. It lightens up my house. It lightens me. Before she lived here, the only noise came from the TV. It was dull and unfulfilling. I never would have known that if she never moved in. I'd still be living the same life...but now, with her here, my life is different. Better. There is a future with possibilities I never dreamed of. Thanks to her.

"You make me happy too," I say, tugging her so she rolls flat onto her back. My morning erection hits the side of her body. For a split second, I wonder if we have time for a quick round.

"We have to meet my parents today," she says, as if reading my mind, and I give her a crooked grin.

"Yeah, we should get ready." I lean in, kissing her with a hot, demanding caress. My hands trail over her warm bare skin, and my dick twitches with excitement.

She hums in delight and disconnects our lips. "If we shower together, we could help wash each other."

I chuckle gruffly. "Is that code for sex? Because if it is, I'm down for that."

A full smile opens on her face and a flush coats her neck and cheeks. I get out of bed, and scoop her up effortlessly, she gasps.

"Put me down," she says with a wiggle, but there's no fight.

She's secretly enjoying this. And so am I.

"No. I'm practicing for our wedding night," I say, looking at her with a newfound intensity, reminding me that our wedding night is right around the corner.

"Well, I'm not here to stop you," she says as I carry her into the bathroom.

Lowering her in front of the shower, I open the door and turn the water on. Then move to set up our towels for when we step out. Her eyes glow as she watches me.

The room fills with steam. Her body is begging to be touched by me.

She steps in behind me, and I waste no time yanking her to me and locking lips with her. Pushing her back against the tiles, we disappear into the steam of lust.

"If we seat your family at this table and us at this one, would that be okay?" Sonya's eyes flick between mine and Tahlia's.

We're at the restaurant we're getting married in next Friday, looking down at the tables set up as a mock-up, so we can get the seating arrangements and menu decided.

I have my fingers linked tightly with Tahlia's, and it feels natural. To hold her hand and be out as a couple after last night is surprisingly easy.

"Please, take a seat," Gary suggests. He has staff beside him, holding plates of food. We all take a seat, and as the staff lower the plates onto the table, I don't miss the way the young server eyes Tahlia. His eyes drop over her face and then down the low-cut top and to her ample cleavage. My teeth clench. I know what he's thinking, and I don't like it one fucking bit. I'm close to telling him to keep his eyes where they should be and not on Tahlia or her goddamn body. The possessiveness pumping through my veins is foreign, and I'm worried about how fucked I am when it comes to her.

I've never thought of anyone as mine. But with her, I do.

She's fucking mine.

I'm tense until he leaves the room. I'll have to talk with Gary about his staff and let him know that guy will not be here on my wedding day.

No fucking chance.

"Are we going to fight over what we eat, or are we going to compromise?" I smile down at Tahlia before kissing her cheek.

She giggles at my pepper of kisses up her neck. "Depends if you like what I like."

"Oh, I think I like what you do," I whisper into her skin before pulling back and giving her a wink.

"Well, then we won't fight."

I shake my head with a smile and take a bite of my Baklava.

"Honey, try this," I say, holding the spoon up to her mouth. She opens her mouth wide and wraps her luscious lips around the metal. It immediately reminds me of how well she took my dick last night.

Fuck. This isn't the time to be thinking of that. I don't want to be getting an erection around her parents.

"What are the plans for your bachelor party?" her mom asks.

Internally, I groan. I don't want to go, but I know if I don't, it'll be suspicious. I asked for something low-key, but I'm not the one who organized it. Mike, being loved up and married with baby Ethan, should give me something quiet. Like dinner and drinks.

"I don't know. Mike said it's a surprise." I look over to Tahlia's dad, who's nodding between bites of food.

"What are you girls doing?" I ask, peering over to Tahlia, and then her mom, for answers.

"Alice is still breastfeeding and sleep deprived, so I said we'll have it at my house."

My back stiffens. She registers what she said and quickly corrects herself.

"At Madison's, where I used to live." She laughs, but I don't.

She has a new home, and it's with me.

Her mom picks up her wineglass, taking a sip before lowering it to the table. "Yeah, just dinner, some games, drinking, and that's it. Tahlia isn't into clubs and drinking heavily."

This intrigues me, and if my memory serves me correctly, there's been numerous times I've seen her at Luxe with Blake and Maddison. Dancing, drinking, and having fun. I think the person who doesn't like drinking and dancing and going out is her mom. Because the woman she's describing isn't Tahlia.

Touching Tahlia's leg, I squeeze it. I told her to not wear panties under her dress today, and I'm barely keeping my thoughts in check as I touch her.

"No, she's such a respectable woman."

CHAPTER 28

TAHLIA

I FEEL NERVOUS WALKING into the wedding dress store. My wedding with Alex is feeling real. I should hate the fact I'm making Alex marry me—but I don't. In fact, I'm beginning to really fall for him. Every day, I'm going to work, a job that I don't hate, and then coming home to him, and it's changing my life. A life that was so unfulfilling is now filling with a newfound happiness. And I have him and Emerald Designs to thank.

The nervous energy I'm feeling in the shop is about me unable to find a dress he'll like. I want to see his face transform when I walk toward him.

"This brings back so many memories," Alice coos as she touches the fabrics of different wedding dresses.

My heart is in my throat, and I feel too scared to touch them. My mind is spinning in panic. I haven't seen or spoken to any of my friends since I slept with Alex.

I told them to meet me earlier than my mom. I need to get it off my chest. They already know the wedding isn't real, but are happy to participate, but now things aren't so fake. Well, my feelings definitely aren't.

The vulnerability of his confession last night and his soft touches make me admire the man who most people wouldn't know. And I see why Alice always wanted me and Alex together. But it wasn't the right time. Until now...

"Can I tell you guys something before my mom gets here?" I walk toward the center sofa and away from the dresses.

Maybe that's why I can't touch them. Too much turmoil running through me to enjoy the process.

"What's up?" Maddison asks, taking a seat beside me.

"Tell us what's going on," Alice says.

"You fucked him, didn't you?" Blake blurts.

My eyes go wide, but my mouth parts on a laugh. I have missed my friends.

"You so did," Maddison adds.

My eyes look at Alice, who has a funny expression taking over her face. "What?" I ask.

Even though I know it's the *I told you so* face.

"Nothing. I'm waiting to hear what you've got to say," she argues innocently.

"We all are!" Maddison says loudly.

"Shhh! Calm down. For fuck's sake, let her speak." Blake spits.

"So, Maddy, you know how we went to the shop the other day?" I whisper. "A sex shop."

"No," Blake gasps, his hand covering his shocked mouth.

"She did," Maddison says, with a look of pride.

"*We* did," I correct her. But they don't bat an eyelid at me telling them she came. They'd expect that from her.

"Anyway, I bought some stuff. I'm not explaining that in detail, so don't even ask. He came home, and yeah, let's say, we crossed the friendship line." Suddenly, I'm embarrassed about what they're imagining now. This conversation is a lot for me.

"Fucked his brains out, didn't you?" Blake rubs his hands together.

I roll my lips, refusing to spill my dirty secrets. Even as the vision of me riding him flashes in front of my eyes.

"This makes marrying him a little interesting," Alice says with a smug look.

"I don't know how to feel. I'm nauseous being in here." I touch my stomach, trying to ease the flutters.

"Aww, sweetie, that's nerves," Blake says, reaching out to rub my arm.

"I'd say we can cancel, but with the timeline for this, you can't," Alice says with a small shuffle forward to me.

I suck in a deep, cleansing breath and stand, shaking off the strange feeling. "Let's start looking and maybe that'll help?" I say to my friends, who all look at me like I've grown two heads. "Come on." I walk away and hear their steps behind me.

"So what do you like?" Maddison asks, browsing the dresses beside me.

"I don't know. Maybe elegant? Lace?" I move one dress at a time and look over it with care before moving on to the next one. "It would help me if you could each pick a dress for me to try on."

Mom joins us a few minutes later, and chooses one too. Now I have a dressing room full of wedding gowns to try on.

I suck in a breath. Here goes...

"Are you ready?" the associate asks me in the changing room.

Am I?

I don't know. Yes and no.

"Y-yesss," I stammer.

She holds out the dress and I slip my mom's long-sleeve choice on; it has a high neck and flows out at the bottom. As soon as the woman buttons me up, I turn from side to side to look at myself in my first wedding dress. How do I feel trying a wedding dress on, as a fiancée to a man I actually like?

It's crazy. This whole experience is crazy, but a large smile breaks on my face.

"You like this one?" the sales associate says.

I realize by my smile, she must think I do.

"Actually, no, it's seeing myself in a wedding dress. It's kinda surreal," I babble.

"Oh. Well, explain what you don't like about his dress," she prompts, standing behind me, staring at me in the mirror and waiting for my answer.

I run my hands over the dress as I explain. "The sleeves, the high neck, the shape is just too proper."

This dress is my mom's choice, and not me at all. I want to feel sexy. I imagine Alex's blue eyes hitting mine the moment I walk down the aisle, and I love how everything else in the room disappears and I'm all he sees. In this, I won't have that confidence.

Walking out, my mom's eyes immediately well up, and I can't help but smile. This is a moment that feels special for us, even if our relationship has been strained due to the way she believes I should live my life. But with me "growing up," as she calls it, I see the change in how she views me. And God, I've wanted this so much.

My friends grimace, but they all stay quiet. No one likes it—other than my mom.

I try on Blake's choice next. It's way too short and when I walk out, they all admit they don't like the blush color.

I get back to the dressing room, where I decide to try on Madison's choice. But as soon as I put it on. It's all wrong.

There's one more left. Alice's choice. I don't have high hopes, but as I step into it, I know it's the one.

The soft lace feels so soft and feminine, and then the slight dip in the back makes me feel sexy. I imagine his hand on my back during our first dance together. And the front cinches in my waist, which I know is something he loves. His hands found any excuse to touch my waist last night. As the zip is fixed, I gasp at myself in the mirror. My eyes fill with unshed tears. I feel beautiful, and my nerves turn to excitement as I envision his face when I walk toward him in this.

I walk out to my friends and mom. The room is dead silent, but not for long.

Alice is a blubbering mess, and I can't bring my eyes to her because I know the tears I'm holding back will fall down my cheek.

I was so lonely before I met him. And I didn't realize it until recently. Living with him and spending time with him showed me how nice it was to have someone to listen to and talk to. Maddison is great, and I'll love her forever, but it's not the same. I feel different with him. When I slept in his arms, I felt like I had it all. We just clicked. We fit together perfectly.

Blake claps. "This is the dress!"

"It is." I choke on my tears.

My mom's dabbing her eyes with tissues. Maddison's eyes are glassy, Blakes crying, and Alice's damn sobbing hits me.

And my dam of tears releases.

I had a great day out. I've chosen a dress that I love and fits me like a glove. The moment I open the front door to Alex's house, I feel giddy.

Walking through the entry, I find him sprawled out on the sofa, one leg hooked over the back.

His head lifts from the armrest. "Hey." His panty-melting smile hits me at full force.

"That was quick." I say, as I come to stand behind him, kicking off my shoes and rounding the sofa. I enjoy the cold wooden floors on my bare feet. Now the awkward *do I sit straight down, or do I kiss him?* I want to kiss him...

He tugs my hand, and I stumble. Making the decision for me, his hands grab my hips and lower me down onto his lap.

As he kisses me, I melt into him, kissing him ferociously. I've missed him so much today. His hands skim over my waist to touch my lower back and hold me. My heart beats frantically because my body remembers him and wants his hands all over it. It would be so easy to swivel my hips and grind into him, turning this sweet moment into hot sex in a second. But even though I want that, I also just want to eat and rest. Today was mentally exhausting.

I pull away from his sweet kiss, opening my eyes to find his shimmering ones looking at me.

"Did you choose a dress?" he asks softly. His hand reaches out to tuck a piece of hair behind my ear. I lean into it, looking down at my body on top of his. His hand lifts my chin.

I bite the inside of my cheek and nod.

He gives me a lop-sided grin. "What does it look like?"

"I can't tell you." I giggle and then lay a sweet kiss on his lips.

"Why not?" He frowns. He's being such a guy at this moment, oblivious to how special the moment will be when he sees me.

"It's the rule."

His fingers dig into my hips. He shakes his head. "I don't always follow the rules."

The way he's looking at me makes it hard to not give in. But I don't know if I could tell him without crying. It was a dress that made me feel heavy emotion, and he makes me do the same, so it's only going to end up with me looking like a mess.

"Well, bad luck, this is a rule I'm sticking to," I reply and stick out my tongue.

His hand moves to the front of my thigh, as he wears a knowing expression.

"And there's no way I could change your mind?" His husky voice is out, and all the humor leaves me.

His fingers drift down, caressing my inner thigh. My skin prickles with goosebumps from his tempting offer.

"No chance." My voice wavers, totally giving away how affected I am.

"Are you sure?" His tone is deeper now.

"Very," I breathe.

"That's a shame." His fingers stop, and his lips twist with a satisfying smirk.

I sigh. "Unfair."

"I know, honey. I'm such an asshole." He grabs the back of my head and slams his lips to mine, taking the air from my lungs.

I squirm on his lap, trying to rub the ache from my core, using his growing erection, but he pulls back.

"Dinner's ready? Are you hungry?"

Fucking starving for him.

How can he just stop?

He's clearly as turned on as me.

"Yeah, a little."

"Same, I'm famished." He's being such a smartass.

I climb off his lap, and he stands, adjusting his pants. I raise my brow at him. He's actually going to just end it here.

He smacks my ass. "Don't even think about it. You need to eat. I need you to have energy for later."

Oh. Here I was thinking that was it, but he has plans for us, and tonight I want him to take control.

"Did you cook?" I ask, following him.

"Yeah, why's that?"

"No reason," I reply, watching him move around effortlessly in the kitchen.

I didn't think he could cook.

"You cooked that?" I say, dumbfounded, as I stare at a large pastry crust pie.

"Yeah." But the sly smile tells me something different.

Squinting at him, I read his too amused face. A smile escapes my lips, knowing he's not telling me the whole truth. "You did not. You liar."

His lip twitches. "I may have bought it and I put it in the oven."

We laugh. It's so easy being with him. I can't wipe the smile off my face.

CHAPTER 29

TAHLIA

TONIGHT, I'M GETTING READY for my bachelorette party. Alice is coming to pick me up soon. I told her nothing fancy, but she instructed me to wear white. I've chosen a white simple dress, and I'm finishing my hair, choosing a half-up, half-down look. And I kept my makeup simple.

The doorbell rings, and I open it. Alice stands there in a red midi dress, that compliments her bouncy brown hair and matching red lips.

"Alice, you look beautiful. I love the red," I say, standing back and letting her pass me to get inside.

"And look at you. Happy Bachelorette!" she says, hugging me. When we disconnect, she thrusts a bag toward me.

"What's this?" I ask, taking the bag with caution.

"Open it and find out," she encourages.

I smile. Pulling out the tiara and sash, I can't help but be happy she's putting in so much effort. I could argue and say I don't want it, but I'm not. I want this. Everything about this feels right. Just like my feelings toward him.

"Thanks, Alice, it's perfect," I say sheepishly. Taking the tiara out first, I walk to the mirror. Staring at my reflection, I place the tiara on top of my head.

"I just need to put my shoes on, and I'm ready," I say, turning around, where she smiles her approval.

I quickly head upstairs, and a couple of minutes later, I'm wearing my shoes and sash, and I'm in her car, heading to Maddison's.

Walking the path up to my old house, I realize I don't want to leave Alex's. This feels like my old life, and I don't want to go backward.

My new life is a fresh start.

Arriving inside, I walk into a party playing music. All my friends and family are dressed up, waiting for my arrival. The house is decorated with balloons, ribbons, and there's even a life-size picture of Alex.

I'm handed a drink by Maddison, and as soon as I taste it, I recognize the drink as vodka, soda, and lime. But the straw is in the shape of a dick, and I can't help but laugh. I seriously have the best friends ever.

Once we've all had a few drinks, we play one game where Alex had to answer a list of questions. If I got the answer right, they all had to take a sip of their drinks, but if I got it wrong, I did.

"All right, five-minute warning. Everyone pee, touch up, and get ready to party," Blake announces to the room.

"I thought this was supposed to be low key," I say to Alice.

She shrugs. "You know them; you can't rein them in."

True. And so far, my bachelorette party has been fun, so I just want to let go and enjoy the night. Whatever crazy ideas they came up with.

Heading outside, I take in the limousine and my mouth opens into a full smile.

Tonight couldn't get any better.

Sliding into the back, I ask Blake, "Where are we going?"

"Our old stomping ground." He winks.

"Luxe?" I ask.

He nods with a knowing smile.

I smile eagerly.

I do love that club. Private and elite. Fancy and perfect for tonight. It's also where I first met my now fiancé, and that knowledge alone makes me giddy. It'll be like he's with me without being physically there.

I didn't want to go out, but now with some drinks and everyone around me, I can't wait to dance.

Arriving there, we go inside and into a VIP area. This is new, as we've never rented out an exclusive spot before. We even have our own bartender, and we order a round of drinks.

My gaze drifts over the crowd until a familiar set of eyes stare at me from across the room.

Alex.

CHAPTER 30

ALEX

SIPPING MY SCOTCH, I welcome the warmth that spreads through me. Not from the alcohol, but from the woman I'm engaged to. Her eyes hit mine, and they widen before a smile curves her lips. My gaze runs over her, and I can't help but smile. She's wearing a crown and a white sash with gold writing that says *Bride*. Never in my life did I think I'd be here having a bachelor party. Me. Nope, I'm still in shock, but I'm fucking happy we are.

It still doesn't feel real.

Pushing that aside, I look at the vision in white. Pure heart, probably a little too good for me. But I'm selfish and won't give her up. The thought of anyone touching her has me clutching my tumbler a little more tightly than I should.

Her teeth sink down into her soft, pillowy lips. God, I want to march over there and kiss them. I'm about to cross the room when a hand slaps my shoulder.

"You're not meant to see her tonight, you know," Mike's voice says. He's teasing me, and I give him a smirk back.

"I know, but I don't like these rules."

Mike chuckles. "No one fucking does. But considering my wife is there, and if she hadn't just had Ethan, I'd impregnate her tonight."

"Jeez, that's a bit much."

He raises his brow in a challenge. "Let's see what happens when you get married and have—"

"We're not having kids. The agreement was to get married."

"And then what?"

I drain my glass and put it away before coming to stand beside him, my hands in my pockets, watching her swing her hips. I know it's all for me. The way her eyes flick over here to make sure I'm watching. Fuck me, I wouldn't want to watch anyone else. Only her. I'd choose her every single time.

Both of us are enjoying each other and living together has transformed our relationship from friends to lovers.

It was just a game to me, and I thought after we got married, she'd get her inheritance and move out. I don't want that now.

But what if she still wants to leave and move out? Doesn't want me or a relationship?

I shrug. "I don't know. We'll probably talk about that after the wedding."

"But you like her?" Mike asks, rubbing his brow, looking at the girls across the room. All dancing and having fun.

"I don't want her to move out," I confess.

"And are you in a relationship for real now?" he asks.

"I think so...At least, to me, we are. We're going to Mom's tomorrow for dinner as a couple. So, fuck, I hope so." I laugh, but it's without humor.

I need to find out tonight.

"This is why you're single," a familiar voice booms behind me.

I turn and do a double take. Not believing who it is.

It's Doctor Damien Gray.

"You came!" I light up. Happy to see my friend out...in the first time in years.

"I'm regretting listening to you two," he grumbles.

Mike throws back his drink and drains it. "Bullshit. Look at the place. It's a vibe. You don't even have to find a woman. Just come here and relax after work for a few drinks with friends and unwind."

"Kid, remember?" Damien grumbles.

"Oh, we remember," Mike says, being a smartass before grabbing another round for us all.

I don't have kids, so I don't want to get involved, but Mike is on the same level playing field.

"You have a wife and newborn. Let's see how long it lasts," he says as he takes the glass Mike offers.

"Not every woman is your ex-wife," Mike adds, a hint of annoyance in his voice.

"I guess not," Damien says through gritted teeth.

My eyes follow Tahlia and her group onto the dance floor. She's totally lost in the beats of the song and gaining male attention. The sash is adding more eyes to her instead of scaring them away. It's like a magnet to say *one last hurrah*.

Not a fucking chance. Before I watch any guy touch her, and allow for the potential for me to lose my shit, I start walking. "I'd love to stay here, but I have to go see my fiancée."

"You can't," Damien says, trying to stop me.

"When you have a fiancée—" The words die on my lips.

"I've had one," he says with venom, wiping his jaw.

"Well, I want Tahlia, and I'm not following any rules."

Mike's voice chuckles. "You can't leave your own party."

My feet stop moving. I rub the back of my neck, thinking of how I can be in two places at once.

"I'll go dance for one song," I say with a smug grin, knowing I figured out the best of both worlds.

"I'll do the same," Mike adds.

I shrug. "Whatever. I'll be back."

As I push through the crowd of moving bodies, I see her white dress, and the strappy heels make me swallow a growl. Those are staying on tonight. The rest of her will be naked, but those heels stay on.

Her friends' eyes bug out as I approach.

"Hey! You're not supposed to be here!" Blake cries out.

"One dance. Let me have one fucking dance with my fiancée." My tone is husky now, my throat filled with her heavy perfume.

Once again, her presence consumes me.

"Only one," Alice says.

I give her a nod before telling her, "Mike said he gets one next."

Alice's face brightens, and I would normally envy the love they share, but I have a woman looking at me like I'm the only person in her orbit right now. I no longer envy them, because I'm now living that life.

Grabbing Tahlia's hand, she steps over to me, and I move so we're flush against each other. She giggles, and it's a sound I love so much.

Her hands skim up over my biceps and over my shoulders to link together behind my neck. I touch her waist and keep my hands just above her ass, gently pushing her body against mine. We move easily to the music together.

Leaning close to her ear, I whisper, "You look incredible. I simply couldn't resist."

"I'd tell you I'm mad, but I secretly wanted you to come over."

I chuckle at her confession.

"Not so secret now."

I lay a kiss just below her ear. With her hair half up, it exposes her neck, allowing me to get easy access. She winces from my breath tickling her neck, and I release a full smile. I'm so glad I ignored the boys and came over. Moving our hips to the music feels so natural.

I've never had a connection this deep, intimate, all-consuming. But with one touch from her, she takes over me. I welcome the warmth of contact. But the question from earlier enters my mind. I have to ask.

"What are we doing?" I ask, keeping my hands on her hips.

"Dancing," she teases.

"No. I mean, between us."

She hiccups. "We weren't supposed to end up together."

My body tenses before relaxing again. "But we are."

"Are you sure you're not normally into relationships?"

"I'm into you."

"You are?" She pulls back to stare into my eyes, bright and glossy from the alcohol.

"I am."

"I'm into you too. Alex, I really like you. Like, I'm falling hard."

I swallow a groan. There's something about her saying that about me that makes me feral.

"I told you not to fall in love with me," I breathe.

She brings her face closer to mine. "You made it impossible not to."

"Good. Tell me you're mine."

"I'm yours," she whispers.

"You're mine," I repeat in a mumble as we stare at each other, unblinking.

"And Alex...I love you," she whispers, as if scared I'll run. But the opposite emotions rush through me at hearing it. Because I know in this moment, I feel exactly the same.

"Tahlia, I love you too," I repeat back to her, not hesitating.

I dip my head and claim her lips in a sensual kiss. Hoping she can feel my love through my kiss, because I mean every single word.

She kisses me back with equal passion, trying to climb me, and a grumble leaves my chest. I'm overheating from our desire, and I wish I could rip her dress off her right now. A voice interrupts.

"It's been one song. My turn. Go get Mike."

I peel myself off Tahlia, and she's flushed and smiling sheepishly as I stare down at her.

"You better go," she mimes, wearing an amused look.

"I wish I didn't," I grumble, the erection making me edgy.

"Later," she whisper-shouts.

"Definitely. At our house."

She grins, and I think she liked me calling it *our house*.

Taking one last look over my shoulder, I feel settled, as I walk back to the guys.

I tell Mike it's his turn, and he's gone so fast, I barely get the words out.

After another round of drinks, I'm over it. I only want to dance with Tahlia, and because I can't, I tell the guys I'd like to leave.

Mike's happy with that, because he wants to go home and enjoy being with his wife alone while our mom has the baby for the night.

I can't imagine not having Tahlia all the time and having to have a baby around.

I say goodbye and walk to the exit, but a voice stops me. I suck in a frustrated breath. Fucking hell. I just want to get out of here.

"Where are you going?" she purrs. I stare back at the woman I slept with once after we met here. I can't even remember her fucking name.

Why does the sound of her voice now irritate me?

"Home," I reply. I don't want to lead her on, so I try to word it in a direct but kind tone.

"Why? I just got here. Why don't you come and have a drink with me? I'm sure you won't want to leave then."

You mean, buy you a drink? But I don't say that.

"No, I'm going home."

She bats her eyelashes and whines about joining me, but I'm distracted. In the corner of my eye, I see Damien talking to a woman. His face still wears the same thin lips and grumpy expression, but from the way he's giving her dopey eyes, I think he knows her. How? I don't know. Right now, though, I don't give a fuck.

I walk to the exit on a mission. I can't stop. I have a date with my fiancée, in my bed, and I'm not staying here for anyone. I only want to go home to her.

CHAPTER 31

ALEX

"YOU DROVE ME CRAZY wearing this sexy little dress tonight."

My eyes travel slowly over every inch of Tahlia while my fingers twitch to touch her. Only, I don't know where to start.

"I'm sorry," she purrs.

"Don't be sorry. It's fucking perfect," I say. My gaze drops to her mouth, and then back to her eyes as I lick my lips.

"It is?" she asks.

I don't answer her with words, instead I do what I want. I kiss her.

My eyes shut, and I lean in, capturing her whimper with my lips. I try to take this slowly and enjoy every swipe of my tongue and every move against her lips, but that one caress of her lips on my own sent me into a frenzy. I've never been this desperate to kiss a woman. She feels amazing on my lips and between my hands.

We take a breath and I trail a finger down her chest. "This sash and bachelorette dress tells the world you're marrying me. That I get to have you in every way possible, including your body. All those guys wanted you."

"I don't want them," she rasps.

The knowledge makes my dick twitch. She wants me. I want her.

"Oh, I know. You belong with me. That ring on your finger is to tell them you're mine."

She moans. "Alex."

My mouth drops to hers again, and I swallow another one of her moans.

Her hands grab my shirt, clutching it and keeping me close. I swipe my tongue over her lips seeking entry, and she parts them easily. She tastes a mix of sweet and spicy, and I can taste the mix of drinks.

When we pull apart, I stare at her swollen pink lips, her hooded lids, and her rosy cheeks. This look is hot, but it gets me remembering what she looks like when I've just fucked her. Yeah, she's an angel with the just-fucked glow.

"That was nice." She hiccups.

I chuckle, but it turns dark. "Nice?"

She hiccups again. "Well, more than nice, but I don't need your head bigger than it already is."

"I'm going to do something un-nice and rip this dress off your body," I gruff. "That's what you want, isn't it?"

"Jesus, just do it already. You're killing me," she whimpers.

A sly smile spreads on my face. "You're desperate," I grunt. "That means you're achy, clenching, and so fucking wet."

"Yes," she moans, but I'm quick to swallow it with my mouth.

I do what I promised and bunch the soft white fabric in my hands and rip and it down the middle. Revealing her bra and panties, all white and fucking edible.

Tossing her dress on the floor, I don't move my eyes from devouring her body.

"I thought I liked the dress. But I prefer it on the floor."

"Please, Alex," she begs urgently.

I lay a kiss on her collarbone, and then on her plump breast. "These tits are begging to be freed."

Her head tips back and her hands find my hair as I pepper her chest with kisses. Then pushing the fabric of the lacey bra down, I tease her nipple with the slightest dusting of my tongue.

"God, Alex," she calls out.

Her desperation makes me want to draw this out. Make her release so much harder.

I unclasp her bra, and when my fingers skim her skin to remove it, her body shivers. Now those pink pebbles beg for attention.

I growl, "So fucking beautiful." I suck a nipple into my mouth hard, enjoying her cries of my name.

Twirling my tongue, I drag my teeth along the nipple as I pull off and kiss my way to the other, giving the same attention. When I pull back, I can see them glistening from my mouth.

I bring my hands to the sides of her panties and slide them down over her curves.

"Keep them around your ankles, but part your legs," I instruct.

"Why?" she breathes.

"You'll see," I murmur, and bring my fingers to her swollen clit, rubbing it in circles. She groans again, and her hands are on my shoulders.

I know I haven't gotten her to the edge yet, because I want her digging her claws in, begging for a release.

I press down harder on her clit, and she jerks.

Sliding my fingers to her opening, I suck in a sharp breath. "Already soaked for me. Good girl. Now, what will I do to you tonight?"

"Everything," she asks quietly.

Her eyes hold mine in a bold stare. "You are a dirty girl. That could be dangerous."

I move my fingers around the opening of her pussy, teasing her. Her breath hitches. I try to take it slow and not rush, but without warning, I enter two fingers into her snug pussy, welcoming the way her walls clamp down on the intrusion.

"I can't open my legs."

"That's the point. It's so tight. Can you feel how tight it is? I can rub your clit and have you coming in minutes."

Her nails dig into my skin, body shuddering.

"You liked the sound of that?"

"Yes," she breathes.

I move my fingers quicker to mimic a thrust.

"Ride my fingers. Ride them as if it's my cock and come all over my hand."

She's so close, I can feel the bruising pressure of her nails piercing my skin.

"Alex, I need to—"

"I know, and I'm not stopping you. Come for me," I rasp, struggling to speak.

A moment later, she's calling out my name as her body shakes and her walls clench down as she climaxes.

When her body slacks, and I know she's come down from her post orgasm high, I carry her to the bed and lay her down.

I pull her panties off and then grab both of her wrists in mine and pin them above her head. "You okay?"

"Alex, please fuck me," she begs.

I almost cave, but my mouth is watering to taste her. I want her to come on my tongue first.

"I know, honey, but I want you to come again, just as much as you do. Just not yet. I have one more orgasm coming out of you before I fuck you."

"Oh." Her voice hitches.

The pleasure staring back at me through her eyes matches my own.

"Spread those legs," I command and settle between her thighs.

"I can't," she tries to say.

I shake my head.

"You can and you will. It will feel amazing."

"Has sex always been like this for you?" she asks.

"Never. But with you, I want to pleasure you and make you come in every way possible before I fuck you."

I don't bother asking if sex has been like this for her, because the surprise on her face as I told her she's getting multiple orgasms before I fuck her answered it for me. There's something thrilling about knowing I'm the only man to please her so much.

Lowering, I take one long swipe from the opening of her pussy, all the way up to her swollen clit. I grunt like a starved man. I continue to lick and swallow her flavor. My tongue is strong and slow, and the movements are controlled. Her body becomes a quivering mess under me.

Her hands touch my head, gripping my hair as she moans.

"Keep your hands above your head. No touching," I say hoarsely.

"I can't—"

"You can. Relax and breathe. Ride my face until you come. I'm right here waiting—"

I don't even finish talking, as she does exactly that. The smell and taste of her pussy riding my face makes me feral. I fuck her pussy with my tongue and my hands find her ass and give it a squeeze, lifting her hips to smother me.

As her thighs tighten around my head, I'm in heaven. Goosebumps prickle on her skin before she shudders uncontrollably.

I can't breathe as she tightens around me, but I could happily die like this. I murmur into her pussy, "How good," she is.

She's panting.

I climb over her, and my hands sit on either side of her head, caging her in. She stares back at me with heavy lids and so much desire it makes me feel complete. I've never felt like I do when I'm with her. She makes me get lost in all the little moments with her. She looks at me like I'm the only man for her, and she's the only one for me.

Her breathy voice tries to speak, but no words are needed right now. I understand this is different for her too.

I kiss her lips and ease my hips forward, my cock jerking at her wet entrance. When her eyes hold mine, I get lost in the dreamy look. Thrusting forward, I enter her in one swift motion, and as I move, she meets me thrust for thrust. As we always do. We meet each other in the middle, sometimes communicating without words.

I thrust again, and I'm all the way in, not a gap between us. Her back arches and pushes her pretty tits up high.

I reach out and squeeze one in my hand.

"God, Alex," she moans from my touch.

"You have the best tits."

"I'm glad you approve. But shut up and fuck me."

My eyes widen, and a smirk takes over my face. Her cursing is very rare, so I know she's desperate to be thoroughly fucked. It's so fucking hot.

"You better hold on. I'm about to fuck you so hard, you'll remember me between your thighs all day tomorrow."

Her eyes flare.

With no other warning, I slam my hips, and I expect her to regret her words.

Instead, she calls out, "Please. Harder."

Her words unhinge me, and I snap.

My name falls from her lips in a cry, and at the same time, I jerk as I grunt. My own climax slams into me. I come so hard, I lie down immediately after and hold her tightly. And to think I was scared of love. One affectionate hold, and she makes me feel worthy of it.

CHAPTER 32

TAHLIA

SUNLIGHT FILTERING THROUGH THE drapes wake me. My head is laying on top of Alex's warm chest. His soft chest hair reminds me just how much of a man he is. I can't help but smile.

"Morning, beautiful," he says gruffly. His morning voice is so thick, and if I wasn't sore from him fucking me hard last night, I'd be climbing up on top of him and using his morning wood to relieve me.

"Morning," I say, smiling before turning to him. God, he's even more beautiful in the morning.

He smiles softly at me, pushing the hair off my face. "What are your plans today?"

I lift my head. "I'm planning to finish studying the finance book I got from work...but I'd love some company."

"I have to work today."

"Boo," I say and push my bottom lip out in a pout.

Reading my sad face, he chuckles and brings my chin to him so he can kiss me briefly.

"Don't sulk. I'll make it up to you later. We've got dinner at my parents' house, remember?"

I nod and lay my head down for another minute before he heads for a shower. Meeting his family is exciting, but I won't lie. It's also a little nerve-wracking. I haven't met a boyfriend's parents in a long time, and I just hope I don't make a fool of myself.

I lie here, enjoying the scent left on his pillow, thinking about what I should wear that would not look like I'm trying too hard, but still pretty enough to impress them.

His phone goes off beside me, distracting me. I peer at the message and think it's work, so when I read part of the message, dread freezes me.

Unknown number: It was nice seeing you last night. Wish we repeated...

I can't read the full message, but last night meant at the club. Repeat what?

I can't pick up his phone and open the message to read it in full. It's not something I feel comfortable doing. Instead, I let the dread sit heavy in my stomach as I peel myself out of his bed and walk to my room and get changed. Purely for something to do.

I decide a workout will keep me busy until he leaves, and then I need to go to Maddison's to talk to her. The dull ache of the hangover has been replaced with the pain of confusion.

I thought we were in a relationship. I thought I could trust him. I thought he changed. But that message tells me he's still a playboy and I'm an idiot for believing him. I'm due for my period, so maybe I'm extra paranoid, but before I accuse him, I need Maddison's advice.

Is this all part of his charm? Am I a fool?

Downstairs, I move to the treadmill and begin walking slowly. His shape stands in the doorway, and I hate the way my traitorous body is enjoying the way he watches me.

My heart constricts as he walks toward me. I don't want to appear rattled by the text, so I hold on to the sides of the treadmill, so I don't trip or fall.

"You're back in here. I clearly didn't wear you out enough." He gives me one of his crooked smiles, and if I wasn't so numb, I'd feel hot from his suggestion, but every muscle is still tense.

I need to let this go for now. I can feel him staring at my profile beside me, so I turn to face him and look over him. Yeah, he's a delicious man. Bringing my gaze to his amused one, I answer honestly. "I'm definitely sore."

He frowns with deep concern. "I wasn't too rough, was I?"

I soften slightly and offer a small smile. "No, it was hot." And that's the truth.

"Good. My parents' house for dinner tonight?"

"Yeah, what time?" I ask, knowing I need to get my shit sorted before then and to make sure I'm ready on time.

"Six-thirty?"

"Sounds good," I say, and he kisses my cheek, lingering a little too long. My heart aches from the gesture.

When he leaves the room, I let out a heavy sigh and text Maddison to tell her I'll be around in a couple of hours.

I hit stop on the treadmill and walk into the kitchen to find he's made me a coffee. Damn him. Why does he have to mess with my head? I need to get out of here and think seriously about what we'll do after the wedding. I take the coffee and see the heart design on top, and I sigh. He's definitely trying to kill me.

I drink the delicious coffee he made me, and then hit the shower. My mind is still in a bad way when I get to Maddison's. I tried to eat breakfast, but the knots in my stomach wouldn't ease up. So, I skipped it and brought some snacks for us to have with tea.

"Is everything all right?" Maddison asks, opening the door and seeing the bag of food I'm carrying.

"Not really, but let me sit down and explain. I need to pick your brain," I mumble.

"Let's talk quietly. My head isn't 100 percent today." She gives me a knowing smile and closes the door behind me.

"Hungover? I didn't think you drank more than me," I question with a frown.

We take a seat on the sofa. She sinks low and throws a blanket over her legs.

"I brought snacks," I say, waving the bag between us.

"I wondered what you brought. Gimme." She curls her fingers into grabby hands.

I hand over the bag, and she pulls the bag of chips out and tears the packet open.

"Talk to me," she says before eating a chip.

I exhale deeply. "He got a text this morning."

"Mm," she encourages.

"From an unknown number, but it was clearly a woman. It said *it was nice seeing you last night, and wish we repeated*...but I didn't read the rest because I didn't want to open his phone—it felt wrong."

Her mouth twists in an unsure look. "Did you ask him about it?"

I grab some chips and munch on them.

My stomach welcomes the food.

"No, I was shocked, and he was in the shower for work. I wanted to think about it and then talk to you. I don't want to be a paranoid girlfriend, so if I come to him, I need to be controlling the situation, not emotionally driven."

She shuffles off the sofa to stand. "Soda?"

"Please." I smile back. I need the sugar to stay awake today.

"Be honest with him and say you saw part of a text on his phone, and you want to know if he's seeing other people. Just be casual, and I think it'll be fine." Her voice is soft as she walks farther away, but I catch the rest of what she's saying.

"Yeah, I was so shocked this morning, my heart couldn't have asked him about it."

"That's fair, but when he gets home, ask him." She arrives back in the living room and hands me a bottle.

"Tonight, I'm meeting his parents, so I'm also nervous about that," I say and gulp some of the drink, welcoming the bubbles.

"Meeting the parents is always nerve-wracking, but you'll be fine. Just be yourself."

"You're always so calm about everything. The text and now the parents," I say.

"Remember, it's easy to tell someone else how to be calm, but if it were me, I'd be losing my shit."

We laugh, and even though she didn't have much to say about the text, I just needed some time to digest it. Feeling much better now, I sit back on the sofa, and we watch a few old *Friends* episodes, eating chips and drinking soda until it's time for me to leave and get ready.

We arrive at the edge of a gated area, where we are buzzed in. Alex drives through the set of gates, following a long driveway up to his parents' house. It's a white, two-story building, surrounded by a beautiful garden full of flowers.

He opens the car door, and I step out on my shaky legs, grateful I decided on flats instead of heels. But butterflies hit my stomach, and I second guess my outfit. Is it too simple?

"Do I look too casual?" I ask, running my hands over my white blouse and light blue jeans. I look down, analyzing them before looking up.

He approaches with a genuine grin. "No. You look breathtaking," he replies.

"Please, be serious," I beg. How can such a basic causal outfit be breathtaking?

"I am," he answers. His blue eyes soften, and he grabs both of my hands in his. His thumbs circle the skin on the back of my hands in a caress. He's trying to pull my thoughts away by his touch. And of course, it's totally working. One single touch, and I'm weakening. Forgetting about any text or any other problem I have.

He leans into the side of my neck, and I wait for his next move, biting my lips together to prevent a sound, or worse, a moan. His mouth hits below my ear, and he kisses it. Breathing in my perfume, as if he needs to taste it. "Let's go inside."

I'm sure once I meet them, my nerves will settle. The longer I stand outside in this unfamiliar environment, the worse I'll feel. Holding hands, we walk up to the door. Alex opens the door, and I tug his arm.

"You didn't ring the doorbell?" I mutter.

His face transforms with humor. "I don't need to. It's my parents."

So different from my parents. They wouldn't accept me barging into their house.

I follow his lead, keeping my hand firmly in his.

"Mom. Dad. We're here," he calls out loudly as we step inside.

My eyes widen, unable to believe he just did that.

A gray-haired man a little shorter than Alex appears from around the corner. He wears the same smile as Alex too. If I hadn't already guessed it was his dad, this just confirmed it.

"Hi, welcome. You must be Tahlia?" he asks kindly.

"Yes." I smile nervously, offering my hand.

He shakes it. "Paul."

"It's lovely to meet you, Paul."

I hear shuffling as we wander farther into the house.

His mom walks toward me with a wide grin. Her bouncing gray hair that sits just above her shoulders is perfectly styled, and her emerald pants and white blouse make me feel settled about my outfit. "Hi, love. I'm Margaret. It's great to finally meet you. I'm grateful you could join family dinner, even though I'm sorry to say, Mike isn't able to come, and neither is Stephanie."

My eyebrows shoot up in surprise. Does that mean...

"It's just us. Sweet," Alex beams down at me. His hand disconnects from mine, sitting on the small of my back. I love how he always finds a way to touch me. As if he needs the constant connection as much as me.

I draw in a long breath and just try to enjoy the moment.

If he's happy, I should be too.

"Dinner is almost ready, but the starters are on the table. Come and help yourselves." Margaret walks us into the dining room, where a table is set up with lots of food, ranging from bread and dips, to fruit and meats.

"Would you like a glass of wine?" Alex asks.

"That sounds great," I reply quietly.

"Mom, Dad, would you both like wine as well?" Alex asks, turning his attention to them.

"Sure, let me help you," his dad offers.

Alex's hand drops away from my back, and he strolls into the kitchen with Paul to grab drinks.

"I'll have a small glass. They're in the fridge," Margaret calls out.

A moment later, Alex yells, "Mom, did you buy the whole store?"

I peer at her as I grab an olive to pop into my mouth. She smiles at me. "Maybe..."

I take a seat and nod, laughing lightly.

Alex and Paul arrive back with four glasses of wine. Alex lowers a glass in front of me, and Paul does the same with Margaret before they sit beside us.

We nibble on the food.

"Did you make the charcuterie board?"

"Yes, love. But wait until you eat dinner. It's going to melt into your mouth. It's Alex's favorite dish."

"Oh, is it?" I ask, getting my first piece of information out of her.

"What was Alex like as a kid?" I ask, just to be funny.

"Great, here we go. The next hour of mom spilling my secrets," Alex says.

I can't help but love it. I want all the details. I grab some bread and tear it apart as she speaks, her face lighting up with happiness.

"He was always so outgoing, but he's also the softest, most gentle soul. He'd always take care of Mike and Stephanie. When he loves you, he will protect you with everything he can." She meets my gaze before looking at Alex, who winks at her.

"We're incredibly proud of the man he's grown to be. We're glad to have met someone who means so much to him," Paul says.

"Yes, we've never met—"

Alex clears his throat beside me. "Mom, please. Now this is embarrassing."

"Oh, is it? Sorry, my love," his mom says, chuckling to herself.

"I don't think so; it's all the good stuff I came here for," I say, elbowing his side playfully.

His hand grabs my thigh, and I suck in a sharp breath at the sudden unexpected contact. Leaning into my ear, he whispers so only I can hear. "You know everything about me...more than they do, trust me."

His hidden meaning makes me close my thighs, but he slides his hand up farther. I excuse myself to the bathroom, needing a moment alone to take a cleansing breath as the dinner is brought out. Over dinner, we fall into more easy conversation. We talk about Mike, Alice, and baby Ethan, and I learn more about his sister Stephanie, her husband Chris, and their baby girl Ellie.

"Dinner was amazing. I wish I could cook this," I say as I eat the chicken potpie.

"I could teach you sometime. I learned it at cooking school."

Alex's chuckle pulls me. I look at him, confused.

"She finds any way to discuss cooking school," he answers me.

"What's wrong with that?" Margaret asks, offended.

He shakes his head, looking at her. "Nothing, Mom. I love how passionate you are about it," Alex replies, finishing his dinner.

I bring the wineglass to my mouth and enjoy the moment of being around his family. I think it was better just to meet the parents first. I don't know how I would've gone meeting the huge family at once. It would've been too much. Now I know more about them, and I feel more comfortable about the next Sunday dinner with everyone here.

My phone rings with my mom's name on it. "Sorry, I have to answer this. I won't be long," I say with a wince. I hope they don't think I'm rude.

"Go ahead. I'll get a start on dessert," Margaret replies as Alex's pager goes off.

I answer and quickly realize when Mom sneers "Tahlia Adams". That my world is going to be ripped apart.

CHAPTER 33

TAHLIA

"How dare you lie to me to get your inheritance." Her icy tone freezes my veins through the line.

I swear I stop breathing.

"Mom. I'm sorry, I can explain. I'm coming over right now," I say in a hurry.

"You better have a good excuse. I'm extremely disappointed in you."

I swallow the sickness threatening to spill. Everything around me is falling apart.

When I hang up the phone, Alex is looking at me, confused.

Mom knows I lied about our engagement is sitting at the end of my tongue. But they don't come out, because I'm in a state of disbelief. And I need more details before I tell him. Especially now that work is paging him with an emergency. I don't want to take him away from that. From his patients. They need him.

"I need to go to my parents' house," I say in the most composed voice I can muster.

His eyes widen as he dusts his hands of crumbs. "Now?" he asks.

I stand up, shaking my head and collecting my stuff. "Yeah, sorry. They. Ah. Need me for something."

Margaret smiles and steps forward to hug me, and I didn't realize how much I needed it.

"Thanks for dinner, and I'm sorry to cut this short," I whisper as I take a step back. I was having such a good time. I could see how easy it would be to be a part of his life, his family. But now—

"It's fine. Family first," she says.

I swallow the guilt bubbling in my throat. "Thanks."

"Just be sure to join us for next Sunday dinner, and at least you'll meet the whole gang."

I give her a warm smile. "That sounds nice."

We say goodbye and on the drive, he gets another urgent call from the hospital.

He drops me off after some persuading not to come in. But he knows he has no choice when I remind him about work.

I walk up the steps to the house, and I don't even need to bang on the door.

"Tahlia," Mom's cold voice says as she opens the door. My dad's anger is radiating off him in waves.

I step inside, and we walk to the kitchen.

"Do you want a drink?" Mom asks. Even angry, she won't stop being polite.

"No. I just had one at Alex's parents' house."

"Do they know?" my dad asks with a bite.

I nervously moisten my dry lips with my tongue before answering. "No. Only Maddison, Blake—"

"Everyone knows but us?" Mom asks curtly.

"Let me clarify what part," I reply, holding on to hope they might be talking about something else.

A muscle flicks angrily in my dad's jaw before he scoffs. "You know exactly what I mean, young lady."

"I'm dating Alex, that's not a lie—"

"You two are not engaged?" Mom cuts me off.

"Not really. He asked me, but technically, no," I confess. I can't expect the truth from others if I don't speak the truth. No matter what it costs me.

I shouldn't have lied, but I wouldn't be with Alex if I hadn't, so I can't say I regret it.

"I'm glad your father is close friends with the jeweler Alex brought the ring from. Imagine if he didn't tell us that Alex had come in buying the ring but asked about returning it in a few months, or what happens if you divorce. It wasn't hard to figure out this was set up for your inheritance. But I have to know why you lied?"

That's how they found out...

"I wanted to get my stake in Emerald Designs," I admit. Unable to stand anymore, I pull out a dining chair and sit down.

They sit in front of me.

"You've wasted so much of your life. You should've finished college and listened to us and now you lie. Who are you?" my mom says with a loathing expression before looking away.

My dad's hands are clasped together as he leans forward and speaks in a cold tone. "We raised you better than this. We gave you the freedom you wanted, even if we didn't like it. We thought as you grew older, you'd settle down, but it went the other way. You went the other way."

"I'm sorry," I plead.

"I can't believe you would come up with a sick and twisted plan to deceive us." My dad's voice drips with disbelief.

"It wasn't a plan. The will said I need to settle down. So, I made it happen, but I should've been more honest about our relationship status. Again, I'm sorry. I really am," I beg, trying to get them both to understand it wasn't a disturbing plan, but more of a life raft for me.

"I don't know what to think." My mother dabs under her lashes with a tissue.

I hate how I hurt them.

"You will not inherit the business if you don't marry for love. No daughter of mine will get a business we've worked hard for after lying and cheating to get it."

"Please—" I cry, tears trailing down my cheeks. I feel my future slipping before he says it and my heart shatters.

"No. Tahlia. Your tears will not help. You cannot change the will. Emerald Designs will be sold to an investor, not to you, end of discussion." My dad rises from his chair and leaves to head upstairs, probably to his office.

I can't blame him. I just wish I was honest from the start. Now what do I do?

Leaving my parents' house feels like a blur. I can't even cry anymore because my body is in such a state of shock.

Alex's name flashes on my phone screen. For a moment, I just simply stare at it.

I can't answer it in this taxi. I'm too scared that between the mysterious text I saw and the deal being off, he won't want to be with me.

Alex: Where are you? Is everything okay?

The backs of my eyes prick with more incoming tears. Why can't everything stay the way it was? I was so happy, feeling like my life was finally having direction.

Now I have no inheritance.

No direction.

And maybe a relationship over.

What a damn mess.

The look of disappointment in my parents' eyes killed me. We haven't had the best relationship, and being with Alex gave it a new life. But now they think the worst of him and me.

I'm upset with myself. And at life.

Why can't it give me a break?

As I sit in the silence of the taxi, I think over how this is the first time in a while I've felt alone again, and I hate it. But I deserve it.

I deserve this soul-crushing feeling.

With only myself to blame.

I pick up my phone and try to write a message. The heaviness hits me and a tear leaks as I type.

Tahlia: My parents found out about the fake engagement, and they are selling my stake of the business. I'm going to my own place. I'm so sorry for dragging you through this mess. I bet you hate me.

He's reading it already, and the dots bounce.

Alex: Don't be sorry. I'm not sorry. It got me a girlfriend. I could never hate you. I love you. You've brought me so much joy. What time will you be home? I'm still at work but when I get home from the hospital we can talk then. I don't want to talk through texts.

More tears roll down my cheeks. What time will you be home? As if it's my house, too. One I don't deserve. God, I have fallen head over heels in love with Alex, and it's all going to be over.

I can't face him right now. I'm too fragile. I don't want to look into another pair of disappointed eyes. I also don't want to have a discussion about the text message either. I'm too exhausted from the emotional rollercoaster day.

Tahlia: I love you too. I'm here with Maddy so I'm going to crash at my old place tonight.

I don't see any dots bouncing, and I'm about to close my phone, when he finally replies. And my heart drops.

Alex: Ok.

But I asked for this. I just need to get my head right and figure out my next steps. I drop my phone into my bag and sob into my hands until the driver tells me we've arrived. Looking out the window, I sniffle and hand over the cash, then I drag myself up the path to my old place again. I open the door, and Maddison calls out.

"Hello? T, I hope that's you."

"It is." I close the door behind me and kick off my shoes, walking directly to the kitchen. I need wine and TV.

Neither is going to help me figure out any future steps, but I just want to relax and zone out and stop mulling over Alex and my parents.

"By looking at you and the fact you're getting wine and you're not at Alex's, shit has gone wrong."

I pour myself a glass. And then lift the bottle in her direction.

She nods. "Drinking alone is sad. And you look like someone already told you Santa isn't real."

I pour her a good helping before walking to the sofa and sitting down.

"Are you going to talk, or am I mind reading?" she says, taking her spot on the sofa.

Flicking my gaze to her, I take a gulp of the wine. "So, to keep this short, my parents are selling my stake of the business to an investor. I can't go through with the wedding if they won't support it. It doesn't feel right. I want my parents to be there."

"They're upset I get it. Sheesh. Like, I kinda get it, but it's your parents; they're supposed to be there for you."

"I know, but it's not like we've had a great relationship. They wanted to control my life. And everything had a hidden agenda. Well, until recently. Until I had a stake and interest in Emerald Designs, and I had a fiancé."

"It had to benefit them," Maddison adds.

"Exactly. This was the first time it worked in my favor...until it didn't."

"But you and Alex are dating now. Did you tell them?"

"Yep, but they didn't care. They said they can't believe I would come up with a twisted plan to deceive them," I say, the image of my dad's icy gaze flashing through my mind. He didn't believe a word I said. I broke their trust.

"Now what?" she asks.

I exhale. "We sit and watch TV and drink wine."

"Lots of wine," Maddison adds.

"And after that, I'll sleep in my own room...and tomorrow, I don't know," I admit easily.

"This isn't like you, T. I've known you forever, and you never avoid or dig your head in the sand about a problem. You're honest."

I sigh. "I know. I just need to do the opposite for once."

"I think you need to talk to Alex," she deadpans.

"I will," I say.

"When?" she asks.

"Soon," I lie.

"When is soon?" She smirks accusingly.

"Tomorrow?" I say, but it isn't convincing.

But instead of pushing me further, she drops it. Snuggling back into the sofa, I drink my wine and watch TV, but I can't escape it all, as he sends me a text.

Alex: *I miss you. The house feels lonely without you.*

Tears fill my eyes as I type back a response.

Tahlia: *I miss you too.*

CHAPTER 34

ALEX

I BARELY SLEPT LAST night. When I woke up after a couple of hours, I got up to make my morning coffee, figuring I may as well work out.

Instead of helping her learn or making us both one, I'm here alone like it used to be. Without her.

I run my hand through my hair as I look around me. This fucking house is filled with memories of her. Everywhere I look, I see her.

I can't have her walk away. That's what she's doing. I'm fucking crazy about her. I need to get her back. This is so unlike me to fight for a woman, but this feels right. For the first time in my life, I know what it feels like to be in love, and even with my stomach bottoming out with nerves, I want to be in love. I fucking miss it. I miss her.

The best way to do that is to talk to her parents. I need to figure out what was said. If I'm going to go to her and force her to talk to me, I need to know what happened between them.

I pick up the phone and call Sonya Adams.

"Doctor Alex Taylor, you lied to me." Her anger and hurt seep through her words.

"I'm sorry. I'd love to come and talk to you and your husband face to face," I say in a pleading tone I hope makes her give in.

It's quiet for a moment before she agrees.

"Fine. We're home. I don't want to be seen in public talking about this."

"Fair enough. I'll be around soon."

I hang up and suck in a breath.

I'm going to fix this.

With new determination, I grab my keys and get in my car.

Arriving at the house without Tahlia doesn't feel right. But I push it aside. Both of her parents wear thin lips and angry expressions, but they still act polite, asking if I need a drink or anything.

The nice act reminds me of her. She's always so kind and puts others first.

And here I am, putting her first. I like that I'm fighting for her. I've never done that for any woman. I've never been compelled to, but Tahlia is different.

Sitting down at a table opposite my girlfriend's parents should be good, but it's intense.

I clear my throat and start.

The quicker I do this, the quicker I can go to her.

"I want to know what happened. And why she can't get her stake in the family business?"

"Because your engagement and upcoming wedding was a sham," Hector spits angrily.

"But the business was on a hard-to-get clause. She was single and didn't have a boyfriend, so what did you expect her to do?" I ask.

"We had a husband she could have married," Sonya adds.

"She doesn't want him," I argue, my words cold, hating the idea of another man with her.

Fuck no, she's my girlfriend and my future wife.

"And what? She wants you?" Hector all but laughs.

I grind my teeth together, taking a moment to let the anger wash over me.

"Yes," I answer, my voice controlled.

"The relationship was fake," Hector scoffs.

I shake my head vigorously. "You're wrong. We've always been attracted to each other. This opportunity—"

Her dad snorts, and I crack my neck.

I remind myself this is her dad, and I need to be here for her today.

"Set-up, you mean," he argues.

Her mom stays silent. She's watching me. Listening.

"Yes, I told her to marry me. But the way she spoke about hating her current life, this fashion business was going to give her the direction she desperately craves."

Her mom moves. I bet she didn't know that.

I need to win them over. The next words that leave my mouth remind me of the little talks and moments we shared. I miss them already. I want her back.

"She was so excited to take the business on. We often spoke about the wedding. We were actually happy, and we started dating for real."

"It doesn't change the fact you two lied," Hector adds, as if my words don't affect him.

My body goes tense at the mention of lying.

"I admit that was wrong. My own parents would be disappointed, but Tahlia is worth it."

I am desperate to make this right. But so far, nothing is helping. No matter what I say or do, it isn't going to get her the business she deserves, or actually...I don't know how she'll take it, but I have no other choice. This is the moment I ask them.

"I want to buy the business as a wedding gift."

"You're going through with the wedding?" her mom asks.

My head shifts to her face. This is the first time she's spoken more than a few sentences since I entered the house.

Buying the business and marrying her is what feels right in my heart. I want to see Tahlia's full smile at home every day as she talks about what she's learned or implemented at work. I want her to tell me what new thing she's organized for our wedding. I want to be with her now regardless of how we got here. I can't apologize anymore. If Hector and Sonya don't accept it, I guess they'll witness it.

"Of course, and if you don't mind, can I do this the right way? Hector and Sonya, could I please have your daughter's hand in marriage?"

Sonya gasps and covers her mouth. A sheen covers her eyes, and she looks at her husband, laying a hand on his shoulder.

Her dad wipes his forehead with his palm. The look of shock hits him at full force. "Well, Alex...this is a lot to take in."

He looks to his wife with his brow raised, as if seeing what she thinks.

I need an answer now.

"I need your answer tonight, because she's upset, and I want to make her happy again. She's so beautiful when she smiles."

Sonya dips her head, and Hector sighs before turning to face me. "Yes, you have our blessing, and you can buy the business for her." His tone isn't warm, but at least it isn't as icy as before.

As I think about her and how to surprise her with this new information, a thought comes to me.

"Please don't tell her about the business. I want to gift it to her next weekend."

They both nod. Sonya cries as Hector speaks. "As you wish."

Checking the time on my watch, I stand. "I must go and talk to her. Thank you for hearing me out. And I'm deeply sorry."

"Please never lie to us again," Hector warns.

"Never, Mr. and Mrs. Adams. Never again," I say, walking to the door.

I kiss Sonya's cheek and shake Hector's hand. "Well, I'll see you both next Saturday for the wedding."

"You will," Hector says.

Sonya nods.

I leave and and pull out my phone to text Maddison.

Alex: *Is she at work, or at your house?*

Maddison: *Actually, at yours. Please sort it out. I want my space back. She's miserable.*

Alex: *She won't be back at yours, mark my words.*

Maddison: *I knew you two were good for each other.*

Alex: *Thanks. See you next Saturday.*

Maddison: *Really?*

Alex: *The wedding...*

Maddison: *That's still going ahead?*

Alex: *Yes. She'll be my wife.*

CHAPTER 35

TAHLIA

I'M EXHAUSTED FROM PACKING up my stuff and from the lack of sleep I had last night. My mind was too busy racing with replays of my conversation with my parents and the text message Alex received. It's strange how I feel more comfortable here than at my old place. I love Maddison's company, but my heart is here.

The front door opens, and my heart rate picks up, knowing I'm about to see him. It's been a day, yet it feels like a week.

"Honey, I'm home," he calls out, closing the front door as he walks in.

His shoes tap the wooden floors, and I peer up over the sofa to see him.

I struggle to find my voice as I sit up.

My nerves are back in full force, because I have to bring up the fact I saw a text on his phone, and I wonder how he'll take it. Will he lose his shit and think I was snooping? We also need to talk about what happens now that the deal is off.

"Hi," I say back.

He leans over the sofa and kisses me unexpectedly on the lips in an all too brief kiss.

"I need to go shower quickly. I had to rush to work. Can we talk after that?" He sounds conflicted, but he always showers after work. It's his routine.

"Yeah, sure," I breathe.

"You won't run away on me, will you?" He winks.

His teasing. Another thing I missed yesterday.

"No, I'll be right here waiting," I reply.

"I'll be quick," he calls out as he jogs up the stairs.

I try to resettle on the sofa, but I can't concentrate on the show I'm watching. My mind is still overthinking, mostly about that text I saw yesterday. I need an answer about who she is. I can't wait. Being here, excited to be around him again, I'm desperate to know.

I walk up the stairs and find him unbuttoning his shirt. I rest my head on the door frame and watch his smooth hands slip the shirt off his shoulders.

It's sensual, and I can't help licking my lips.

"Are you going to stare at me? Or come join?" he asks darkly.

The corner of my lip rises, but it's a half smile. I can't shake the heaviness in my gut.

"I need to ask you something," I say nervously and walk into his room. I watch him pause and turn around, curiously staring at me.

"Yeaaah?" he draws out.

I peer down at my fingernails, picking at the skin beside the nail bed. "Yesterday morning, when you went in the shower, I saw a text from a woman, and it said something about seeing them."

I peer up from under my lashes to see his face soften. He sighs and stalks over to me, taking my hand and leading me to his bed. We both take a seat on the edge. He's looking at me with adoration, and I don't get it.

"It was one stupid hook-up before I met you," he says. "So that's why you were on the treadmill before I left for work? I thought it was strange."

My lips part and I try to act offended. "Are you saying I don't exercise?"

He arches one brow at me. "I've only seen you use it twice."

A loud giggle bubbles out of my chest. "Yeah, I'm not a fan of the gym."

"Well, I can give you more exercise," he grunts huskily, kissing my lips before he pushes me back on the bed and lays kisses over my neck and little nips up to my ear. He bites down on my earlobe, and a shiver runs through me at his promise.

I cry out from his affection, not hating it one bit after being in my head about us.

"I was leaving Luxe when she tried to get me to have a drink with her. Which I declined, because I had a sexy fiancée at home, who I wanted more than anything."

His fingers comb my hair and bring my face close to his. He whispers, "Were you really worried?"

I nod sheepishly, feeling the tears seeping onto my cheeks. I feel better now that it's off my chest. I've never been one to argue and fight. And the fact he was just as mature was surprising, but also a relief.

"Honey, there's no need. I only have eyes for you. In such a short time, I've fallen completely in love with you. Which is making it hard to fake this marriage. How can you fake something that feels so right?" His smile reaches his blue eyes, and up this close, the lines beside them are more evident. "I don't want our marriage to be over, do you?" he asks with so much trepidation, staring back at me. I want to put him out of his misery.

"No. The thought has been twisting me up and causing me so much anxiety," I say as a warm tear leaks and runs over my cheek at his words. I didn't realize how much I wanted to hear him say that until now.

The emotion is clogging my throat, and I can't speak. He takes the opportunity to talk more.

"You were able to love me even when I didn't love or believe that I was worthy of one person. I was always told I was a player and I let myself believe it. But that's not me. I hated myself every single damn time. And fuck, I tried not to let you in, but you barged through, and you took away my numb, hollow self. You have no idea what that means to me. I don't even know if I'm making sense—"

I nod through the stupid tears that fall, but I say through a sob, "You are."

"I thought I was broken. I can't go back to waking up alone without love. So, I'm sorry, but I can't let you go. I still want to go through with our wedding. I even asked your parents today for your hand in marriage."

"You what?" I gasp, trying to digest the fact he spoke to my parents, and on top of that he still wants to marry me. This is a lot to process.

"I asked if they'll let me marry you. But only if you still want to." He smiles down at me.

"You still want to get married?" I should be screaming out *yes, I still want to*, but I can't get my mouth to work.

"I do." He says it with these sincere eyes staring back at me.

This man. His heart. I can't even breathe. He loves me.

I sniff and bat all my tears away, drying my face.

"I love you, Tahlia. You're it for me. Please, say yes," he pleads.

I smile. Those words hit me in the center of my chest, and I feel every word. I believe him and I love how raw and open he is right now. It's time I'm honest with him, too.

"I'm scared," I whisper.

He leans his forehead on mine, our breaths loud. "Do you trust me?"

I don't have to think about it. "Yes, I do."

"Then let me love all of you. Give me your heart and I promise not to break it."

I nod, moving my head against his.

"I want you," he rasps in an authoritative tone.

He wins, because my resolve is melting. I can't say no to him. I'm officially addicted. Running his nose up my neck, he whispers in my ear. "I know you want this too."

"Yes," I breathe, fixing my gaze on his handsome big blues. I want us naked and making love. I know right now that I don't ever want him to let me go.

"Good, because I want to reassure you that you're my woman—my wife. You. No one else. You got it?"

CHAPTER 36

TAHLIA

I'M LYING HERE ON the sofa a few days later at my old house with Maddison. My mom organized for me to have a hair and makeup trial this morning. She's been surprisingly nice since our first argument. I haven't had a moment to dwell on it, because in a week, I'm getting married to a man I love.

"Here. You need to take this." Maddison thrusts out a pregnancy test.

My period is late.

It's never late.

Until now...

I missed my pill the morning after Luxe. I was vomiting and hungover. It slipped my mind. That's never happened to me before.

I grab the box with shaky fingers and sit up. My gaze flicks between the box and her.

"Don't be scared. Just go take it, then you'll know for certain," she says, as if reading my thoughts.

"I know. I'm just scared."

"I'll be here with you," she says softly.

I nod. "Thanks. I guess I'll do it."

She checks her watch. "Yeah, get it done. That way, you have the time to digest the news."

"Are you already predicting I'm pregnant?" I try to muster up a smile, but there's minimal movement on my lips. My nerves taking over, my stomach feels sick.

I stand and walk over to the bathroom, tearing open the box and following the instructions. I don't want to be alone, so as soon as it's done, I open the bathroom door. Maddison is standing right behind it.

I clutch my chest at the fright, but then I giggle. "You're more eager than me."

"Sorry. I didn't mean to scare you. I just want to know you're all right," she replies with a somber expression.

"I'm doing okay. I just can't wait three minutes and look at it by myself. I'm too chicken."

"I'll do it with you," she offers.

"Thanks, Maddy."

We're silent for a few seconds before she blinks and looks around. "Did you check the time?"

Eyes wide, I realize I hadn't. "No. I don't have my phone with me."

"Let's start the three minutes now, just to be sure," she says, tapping her watch face.

I bend my head and study my hands, desperately holding myself from picking my nail beds. "The longest three minutes of my life."

"Come on. Let's sit." She gestures to the sofa. Feeling a little light-headed from the anticipation, I welcome the idea. We leave the test in the bathroom and sit back down. I try to concentrate on the *Friends* episode on the TV to take my mind off the test results.

"It's time," Maddison announces.

"Oh, God. I feel sick," I mumble, staring into her hopeful face.

She holds her hand out, and I accept her invitation to help me up. Standing tall, I stare directly in her eyes, and inhale deeply.

She gives me her friendly smile before spinning on her heel and tugging me along. "You've got this. Let's go see. You might be overreacting," she says as she walks us over to the bathroom.

"Jeez, thanks," I mutter.

"You know what I mean."

Inside the bathroom, she steps back from the counter, and it reveals the test stick. Immediately, I see the two pink lines.

I'm pregnant.

There're no tears. No nothing. I'm stunned. I'm waiting for it to hit me. I wander back to the sofa on trembling legs.

"I can't believe you're pregnant," Maddison says with a disbelieving voice from the other end of the sofa.

"Same. This was not in my plan." I rub my eyes, feeling the exhaustion hitting, but I can't lie here all day.

She twists on the sofa to grab the remote and play the next episode of *Friends*. "Nothing ever goes to plan. You should know that by now."

I sigh. "I know, but I feel like a burden to Alex."

I'm grateful for how he makes me feel and how he loves me, but I don't want him to think I'm taking advantage. He's had a lot of change already. Playboy to marriage and now baby. It's too much to ask. It's a lot for me, let alone him.

"He wouldn't. Have you seen him with baby Ethan? My ovaries flutter," she says, resting a hand on her heart.

I giggle at her dramatics. But she's right.

"Yeah, he loves him. How do I tell him?" I ask, trying to think of a special way.

Those pink lines on the stick are confirmation. Whether or not the timing is right, this is our baby, and I'll love it so much.

"Give him the stick," Maddison suggests.

"I don't know," I say, lost in thoughts. My brain already feels like it's not working. "I need to see him. He deserves to know." Standing up, I walk to grab my car keys.

"Are you sure? You could wait and gift it to him as his wedding gift?"

"I know, and that would've been a nice gesture, but my gut says to tell him now. I'll be back, but, Maddy, please, not a word to anyone," I plead.

"You got it. It's your news to share," she says with an understanding smile.

"I'll be back soon. Wish me luck," I say, spinning around and striding out the door.

"You don't need luck, silly," she calls out, and I leave, making the nervous drive over to his house.

At his door, I'm basically shaking like a leaf. The door opens before I can unlock it, and I see him wearing navy pants, no tie and an open white shirt. He was in the middle of getting undressed from work.

"Tahlia," he says, with his irresistibly devastating grin.

I drop my chin and swallow the lump in my throat as I look to the ground, trying to gain the strength to tell him the news. "I—"

He lifts my chin up with his hand, so I'm looking at him. He stares back longingly, and it cuts me up. "What's wrong?" he breathes.

My first attempt at talking just has my mouth opening and closing. I swallow the fear knotting inside me and speak the words in a whisper. "I'm pregnant."

His eyebrows draw up in surprise as his mouth slackens. I watch the wheels turning in his head as he tries to process the information. "What?" he replies coolly. He drops his hand from my chin and dives it into his hair, and he leans back, staring at the ceiling, mumbling under his breath, "Fuck."

Not the reaction I wanted. Any hope of happiness has been removed by him in one second. Why did I think he'd be happy? It was a lot for him to commit and love me, and now I'm pregnant. I've pushed him. But it wasn't on purpose.

Long silence looms between us, making me more uncomfortable.

"How...What...When?" Now he can't even form a sentence.

"What do you mean?" I ask shakily, looking up at him, disorientated. Hearing the fear in his voice is adding to my anxiety.

His eyes are wild. It's like the news has shaken him, and the next words cut deep. "I'm not ready to be a father."

My body tenses. I'm not ready to parent either. But it's happening.

It's silent again, and all I can hear is the blood rushing to my ears. So much turmoil pulsing through me. "I thought you loved me?" I ask in a broken whisper.

"I do..." he says in an odd, yet gentle, tone.

"This is a funny way of showing it," I mutter hastily.

His hurt eyes look around, as if he's seeking answers. I wish he'd hug me. Hold me. But I shouldn't have to ask for those things; he should want to comfort me. Fear is causing him to retreat. Withdraw in on himself.

"This wasn't planned," I say quietly, as tears fill my eyes, but I will not let them fall. Now is my time to be honest with him, even though my heart is splintering. I say the next words with as much conviction as possible. "I thought you'd be happy."

He drops his head and doesn't say anything, so anger seeps into my veins and replaces the sadness. I need to get out of here. But just as I'm about to move, he speaks, reaching out for me before pulling his hands back and tucking them deep inside his pockets. "I'm sorry. But I don't know what to think or feel right now."

I take slow, deep breaths, trying to calm my racing heart. "The first step would be to accept it," I choke out in a broken voice, wrapping my arms around myself. "If you knew me, you'd know I didn't want a kid right now. But look, it's here, so it's bad luck we both need to accept. No tricks, no nothing. It's what happens when you have sex. We need to talk about it."

His jaw ticks. "No. I can't talk right now," he says, before his mouth flattens into a thin line. He's holding himself back. Not saying anything else. We glare at each other. Both hurt, scared, upset, and confused.

I wait for him to change his mind. But it never comes. The quiet only inflicts more pain on me.

As my breath catches in my lungs, I mumble, "I need to leave." I turn and don't look back. He remains silent.

I jog up the stairs and grab my case and begin to pack.

"For how long?" he asks, entering my room.

I flick my gaze up, noticing his pained eyes stay on mine. My bottom lip quivers as I feel my eyes brimming with tears. It won't be long before I'm sobbing uncontrollably. I can't do that here.

"I don't know. What are you doing anyway? Get the fuck out and stop watching me."

I can't believe I swore at him. It's so not me. I'll blame the emotions of having my heart ripped out by the man I love.

He doesn't move, watching me continue packing my clothes into the case. Then suddenly, he sighs and spins around, leaving me alone. His heavy feet disappear down the stairs, and the front door opens. When the door slams behind him, I can finally breathe.

Sadness hits me deep inside the chest. The despair rips me apart, as deep sobs rack my insides. I'm sucking in breaths, trying to pull myself together, but they fall harder. Burying my face in my hands, I let myself cry, until I have no more tears left.

And then I suck up in one last calming breath and wipe my face with both hands. Standing, I walk over to my clothes and finish packing. As I drive back to Maddison's, I'm sad, angry and, of course, I stupidly miss him.

CHAPTER 37

ALEX

THOSE TWO WORDS "I'M pregnant" made something snap inside me. I can't be a father. I've just accepted I'm worthy of a relationship. A father is just too much.

Fuck. I need a second to think.

To breathe.

When I came back home from a long drive, she was gone.

I pour a good three fingers of whiskey. Bringing it to the television, I take a big sip and sit on the sofa. The stupid sofa reminds me of all the times we laid here. Watching TV, talking, and hanging out. My eyes drift to my pool. My stomach hardens as I remember the time I hadn't touched her yet, but the way her body looked submerged in the water naked...she made me hard.

Made me question things.

God, I wanted her so much.

Now I sit alone with my thoughts. I watched her pack her bags and said nothing to stop her. I let her go, even though it killed me.

I want to go one way, and my life pulls me in another.

How the hell did I get here?

I shake my head in disbelief. Where the hell did my life go? It seems to have spiraled. I pushed her away and shouldn't I be glad?

I should...

But fuck, I'm not.

Bringing the glass to my lips, I tip my head back and drain it.

I need to drink until I can't feel the fear thrumming through me anymore. I get up and grab the bottle and escape to one of the rooms that she's never been in, so I don't have to see her beautiful face when I close my eyes.

Visions of her blur the more I drink.

I wish I could be happy, but I'm fucking shit scared.

What if I suck at being a dad?

What if I revert back to my old ways?

I wake up delirious in one of my spare rooms the next day. It's the first time I've ever been in here.

It's for guests only.

To think now I'm a guest in my own house.

I peel myself up and stroll to my bathroom, ignoring the way my head is yelling at me for drinking last night. Nothing coffee and food can't fix.

I shower and dress and do the only thing that will allow me to run away from visions of her...work.

Before I think about hitting my office, I walk directly to the barista and order a coffee and a bagel.

But before I join the line, I hear my name.

"Alex," a familiar deep voice bellows.

"Damien, man, how are you?" I step forward and shake his hand.

He shakes mine back firmly. "Busy, but good," he says, stuffing his hands in his suit pockets after our exchange.

"Freshly shaven," I say, noticing his beard is gone.

"You could do with a shave," he says through a chuckle.

I rub my jaw, feeling the stubble under my palm, and with a smug grin, I say, "Nope, the wi—woman digs it."

I almost said *the wife*. Like the word just rolls off my damn tongue and we're not even married yet. If we even do get married now that I've made a mess of things.

My temple throbs. I can't think about it right now. The headache will form into a migraine if I don't stop with the running thoughts of Tahlia.

He laughs and shakes his head at me.

I ignore his tease and get away from my own shit to ask about him. "Talking ladies, how're the chicks loving the single dad tag?"

He pulls out a hand to scratch his brow before answering. "What women? I've been with none since—"

"Now you're really pulling my leg," I say, cutting him off, shocked.

He fires back quickly. "I'm a plastic surgeon with a young son. Not attractive to women at all."

My brows rise to my hairline. "You're kidding. You're a chick magnet. You just don't put yourself out there."

He snorts, as if I'm the one being ridiculous. "And how would you like me to do that?"

"Go out to Luxe with some friends."

He clicks his tongue on the roof of his mouth. "Son, remember?"

Think, Alex...

"Online," I say with a jackpot smile.

Damien scrunches up his face with disdain. "That's even worse. I suck at talking, especially small talk, and particularly about myself."

I can't argue with that, as he isn't as easy-going or as talkative as me. Hmmm.

"Well, I'm out of ideas. Let me grab us a coffee." I shrug and tilt my head to the barista.

He grins as if he's won. "Told you it's impossible."

I hate losing, so I shake my head and say, "Not impossible, but definitely not easy. Let me think about it and see if I can come up with any ideas. I'm running on a few hours of sleep."

"Were you on call?" He frowns.

"No. I was—" I stop speaking, not knowing what to say. I can't tell him Tahlia's pregnant and that I drank until I passed out.

"Was wha—" His pager goes off, cutting him off.

"Did you want a takeaway coffee, or is it urgent?" I ask, watching him.

He reads the message on the pager. I'm grateful that mine hasn't gone off, and I'm able to get in a much-needed caffeine kick.

Tucking his pager away, he looks back at me. "No, I gotta get back upstairs now. I'll have to catch you soon."

I nod, knowing I should start the mountain of paperwork I have let build up and get to visiting some patients. But I can't function properly right now without a hit of caffeine. "All right. Catch you later."

He wanders off toward the elevator, and I walk over to order my coffee. My phone rings, and I see Mike's name. I hit decline. I'm not ready to answer it. He will be angry. I don't blame him. I just don't have any answers.

Carrying my latte and bagel to the elevators, I become instantly awake without even taking a sip of my coffee.

Tahlia is walking with Blake toward the elevators. She's here. But why?

Is she okay?

Or has she come to confront me?

The glum look on her face tells me she's not here for me. I never got a text or call.

Suddenly a rush of panic hits my chest, and I press my lips together and stride closer.

Her eyes widen when she sees me.

"Tahlia."

Blake clears his throat.

I flick my eyes to his and nod. "Hi, Blake."

"Hi," he says curtly, but my eyes are already back on the captivating greens I've missed. Just now, she stares back at me with bold defiance. I know Blake probably wants to chop my balls off, but I don't care. I need to see why Tahlia's here. My hand grabs her waist instinctively, but she steps back, forcing my hand to slip.

She doesn't want me to touch her. And I can't stop the selfish way that hurts me.

I stuff my hand into my pocket to stop it from happening again.

"Why are you here?" I ask.

She winces, as if I wounded her by not wanting her to come here. But that's not it. If anything, seeing her now makes me miss her more. I've not felt myself without her.

"A doctor's appointment," she says matter-of-factly.

"Are you and the baby okay?" I ask.

"Routine one. Calm down, Daddy," Blake cuts in, the word making a wrinkle between my brows.

"Blake. Do you mind?" She turns to face her friend, whose eyes are still narrowed on me.

"You want me to leave you with him?" he asks.

Inside, I'm hoping she says yes.

"Please."

He blows out his cheeks in a frustrated breath, then turns to face her. "Okay but call me if you need me. I'll sit here and wait for you."

"Thanks." She gives him a small smile.

He snaps his gaze to me. Shaking his head in dismay, he strides to the tables and chairs in the cafeteria. He's not happy.

When her eyes return to mine, I patiently wait for her to tell me what's going on.

"Did you want to come with me? It won't be long. It will be a chat and blood test to confirm..."

"Confirm the pregnancy?"

"Yes," she replies sadly.

I nod. I'm still confused about how to feel, but the way I can't let her do this without me tells me to suck it up and go.

"Yeah, I'll come, if you'll have me."

Her mouth parts, as if she wants to speak, but she walks off, and I follow.

I stay silent the whole elevator ride, and even sitting in the obstetrician's office, listening to Doctor Paddock talk, I can't find my voice.

I'm confused, shocked, wondering when it'll wear off.

I can't believe we're doing this.

A baby.

Chapter 38

Alex

After the appointment, I walked her down to Blake. She quickly said goodbye and left. My head has been spinning ever since. I couldn't concentrate on work, so I left and drove myself home. I've been lying on the sofa, wondering what to do. A part of me wants to go to her place and throw her over my shoulder and bring her home. This place doesn't feel right without her. But also, after the way I reacted, I don't feel worthy of her.

I rub my hand over my face just as the doorbell rings. I get up slowly, knowing deep down it's not her, so what's the rush?

The bell rings again, and it irritates me. No one is meant to be here. I need more time to be alone.

I stride to the door and open it.

Mike stands in my entry. I shouldn't be surprised. I ignored his call earlier.

I clench my jaw.

He knows.

"Mike," I answer, keeping my voice emotionless.

"Alex." He steps inside, and I walk to my kitchen to make some food. I need to eat.

I know why he's here, and I know I'm being a man child, but I don't want to talk about it. Because it'll mean I have to be vulnerable and that's not me. I'm the easy-going guy, not the talk-my-feelings-out guy.

Seeing Tahlia today has me feeling more restless.

I move to the kitchen and grab an apple. Mike stares at me. If he wants to talk to me standing up, then go for it. I don't have the energy.

"What happened? he asks.

I lower the apple with a sigh. "She told me she was pregnant."

He rubs his jaw in thought. "And what's so bad about that?"

"I'm not ready for a kid, Mike. Fuck."

He snorts. "No one is."

Staring at him, I ask, "How did you know you were ready for a kid?"

"I didn't," he says with a shrug, pulling out a stool and sitting down. "It wasn't planned either."

"So, you just accepted it happily?" I ask.

"It was either accept it, or lose her and the baby," he deadpans.

I nod. Understanding his difficult decision. I don't want to lose Tahlia, but a baby is a lot to take on. Listening to the doctor talk today cemented that.

"Do you want to cancel the wedding?" he asks, pulling me right out of my thoughts.

Cancel the wedding?

Looking down at my hand, where soon I'm supposed to be wearing a gold wedding ring, my answer is immediate. "No."

His firm grip grabs my shoulder, and he meets my eyes head on. "Do you want to lose her, dumbass?"

"Fuck no. I love her. I'm shit scared now that the things I imagined in a fantasy with her are coming true. Like having a kid and teaching him or her how to swim or playing with Ethan. I pictured it all, but now it's happening. I'm freaking out."

"I thought so. So, pull your head out of your ass, stop being scared, and go get her. Figure it all out together."

Mike leaves me sitting there without another word.

I love Tahlia. I need her. She's everything to me. I run my hand through my hair, pondering how to fix this.

I pull my phone out of my pocket and bring up her name to call her. But as I stare at the screen, I can't pull the trigger, as something inside me stops me. Even if it destroys me, I can't call her. I have to see her. I rush to grab my keys and run for the door to drive to her old house.

During the drive, my heart is pounding as I worry that I've fucked up the greatest thing in my life. Her.

CHAPTER 39

ALEX

WHEN I GO TO her house, Maddison opens the door. Her face is tight and her lips thin. I deserve the hatred. I hurt her best friend.

"I know I fucked up. Let me talk to her," I beg with a shaky voice.

She twists her head, looking inside the house, before bringing her icy gaze to meet mine. I'm slightly scared of this pocket-sized woman.

"If she wasn't so sad, I'd tell you to stick it where the sun doesn't shine, but because she needs you, loves you for some reason, I'm going to go out for a little bit. And when I get back, if you've hurt her more...watch out." She purses her lips, and I like how protective she is of her friends.

"I promise. I won't. I'm really sorry."

"Let's see if she'll accept it. I can't blame her if she kicks your ass out of the house."

I nod. She barges past me and straight toward her car.

I stand there for a second, a wave of guilt hitting me. I'm such an asshole.

Not wasting another second, I stride inside and close the door. Walking through the house, I follow the blaring noise of the TV, knowing it's an episode of *Friends*. I'm secretly happy she isn't watching our reality show without me.

Catching sight of her on the sofa, my heart lurches. I take in her appearance. Her blonde hair is messily tied up in a loose bun on top of her head. She's wearing a cream sweater and pants. Her knees are brought up to her chest...giving herself a hug.

And the sight of that makes me want to give her a hug and tell her I'm so fucking sorry. Even sad, she's fucking perfect.

"Hey," I say, staring down into her red-rimmed eyes.

The puffy bags under her eyes make me feel worse. She didn't look like this yesterday.

I keep hurting her. She deserves better than me.

But I remember what Mike said, and I don't want to lose her, or the baby, all because I'm scared.

"Hi," she says hesitantly. I can't blame her for being quiet. She probably thinks I'm going to storm off and have a tantrum, or stay silent, because that's how I've been acting.

Sitting down beside her, I inhale her scent deep into my lungs. I've missed the smell of her.

I just missed everything about her.

"What are you doing here?" she asks, keeping her voice low.

I shift closer to her, but she stiffens. My heart sinks. I did this. And I hate myself for it. I need to be completely honest with her.

"I'm so sorry for the way I reacted. I just needed time to process. Before you, I never wanted kids, but since being with you, falling in love, and wanting what my brother has...it's what I want too. To be honest, I don't know if I'm ready, and that's what's scaring me."

"I'm not ready either," she sniffles.

I nod. "I don't want to let you down. I'm scared. So, fucking scared. But Mike said something before we got together that's stuck with me."

Her head tilts up at me, curiosity etched in her face.

"He said you'll know she's the one because she feels like home. Keeping you safe, warm, and loved. And that's you. You feel like home."

Her eyes meet mine, and a flicker of deep emotion stares back. The cavernous pain from her makes my chest squeeze, and I have to look away for a moment before returning to her green eyes.

"I trusted you to be there for me..." she says, her voice husky with unshed tears. "And you broke my heart." She swallows and opens her mouth as she cries. "I don't..."

The blood pumps in my ears. Her hands covering her face make her ring unmissable. My own damn eyes sting.

Seeing my engagement ring still on her hand makes my heart pump harder. I reach out, unable to stop myself from touching it. She looks down at me touching the ring on her finger.

"I needed you," she adds, her voice broken and barely above a whisper.

Needing to touch her, I rest my hand over hers and speak the truth, no matter how painful. "I know, and I fucked up the best thing that has ever happened to me. I asked the world for one thing, and I got it. Yet I pushed it away from fear. Loving you scares me so much, but losing you would be worse. Fuck, no, even saying that out loud crushes me."

She stays silent. Tears still sprinkle down her cheeks as anguish looks back at me. With my other hand, I brush the tears away as I continue to beg. I'd rather give everything to at least know I tried, because I need her in my life, and I won't let her walk away from me. She's going to be my wife.

"Always getting accused of being promiscuous and a player, I guess I believed that to be true. That love wasn't in my future, let alone a family," I say in a panic. Pulling my hand away from her face, I hit my chest. I remember the numbness. It was so debilitating and so hollowing. "Tahlia, before you, I was so fucking numb inside."

"Alex," she sniffs, and there is a softness in her expression now.

"I swear to love you all my life," I say, grabbing her hand and turning it so I can lace my fingers with hers, admiring how perfectly we fit together. I squeeze her hand as my eyes hold hers. "You're my person. And without you, my life isn't worth living. I want a family. I want to fill my house with love, laughter, and happiness. I promise I'll make it up to you every day for the rest of our lives. Just give me a chance to prove how sorry I am."

Her green eyes fill with new tears, and my own finally trail down my cheeks.

CHAPTER 40

TAHLIA

THIS BEAUTIFUL, BROKEN MAN. As he swallows hard, clearly trying to hold back his struggle, I can't stop the tears that spill down my face from his words. I understand his freakout and that he needed a moment to digest. Staring at his solemn face, I know in this moment, my heart is his. The words he spoke were so vulnerable and honest, begging me for another chance. My heart aches as I look at the torment in his eyes. He's deeply sorry, and it's evident. I grab his hands in mine, calming from the heat of his skin. Entwining our fingers, I stare down at them. Everything is right when he's with me.

"I know you're sorry. I forgive you. But I'm sorry too, for not giving you a chance to digest things or talk it out when you were ready."

"Don't be sorry. I'm the fucking idiot. But do you really forgive me? Can we be a family? I so badly want to deserve this life with you." He speaks as if he can't quite believe it.

"Of course. I love you," I explain.

"I love you too. I want nothing more than to be your husband and a father to our baby. But I might need you to be patient as I ease into the fatherhood part."

"Why, Alex?"

He drops his gaze to our tangled fingers, as if looking for answers. I don't press him. I wait patiently.

"I'm not worthy," he whispers, like he's too scared to say them too loud. I catch it, and with those words, I feel his deep-rooted apprehension in all this.

It's my turn to be delicate and offer him comfort the same way he has given to me. Grabbing the sides of his face, I welcome the rough texture of his scruff on my palms. The familiarity soothes me. His blue eyes are so bright and his pupils grow bolder with worry.

"You are, Alex. Look at the way you love and care for me. I can already tell you're going to be amazing. All a baby needs is love," I say tenderly, as if he may break if I speak too loudly.

He nods in my grip. "I can do that. I already do love our baby."

I smile, leaning up to kiss him. I lay my head on his chest, and he wraps his arms around me.

"I need to ask you something," he says, getting off the sofa. He drops to one knee and the dam of tears spill again.

"Tahlia Adams. I never would have believed we would be here today. What started as friends and then turned to a fake engagement to a real loving relationship is beyond my wildest dreams. It doesn't feel real that I get to come home to you. Me before you was so different that I would never have believed I could feel like this. This deep, earth-moving love everyone dreams about. But you make me feel every type of emotion, and I thank you."

"Oh, Alex." Clutching his hand that's holding mine, I inch forward.

"I was a shell of a man before I met you. I believed bad things about myself and couldn't see the good. You've been there every time I think I'm not worthy enough. I want to spend every day showing you and our baby how I'm worthy of both of you. That I am a better man. I promise to love you and our baby with everything that I am. I'll be there now and forever. Will you do me the honor and become my wife?"

"Yes, yes, yes!" I say, sealing my lips to his. He's mine, and I've never been surer of something in my life.

"Fuck yes! Let's get married then."

Chapter 41

Alex

Alex: *Did you take your pregnancy vitamins I had delivered to you?*

Tahlia: *Yes, Doctor Daddy.*

Alex: *Good girl. I can't wait to marry you today.*

"Let's go, people," Blake's voice booms loudly over the music playing.

I quickly reply to Alex before getting in the car.

Tahlia: *I can't wait to marry you.*

Blake, Alice, and Maddison are in my bridal party. Mom and Dad are here too. Mom smiles kindly, and there's a twinkle in her eye. I think she's pleased I'm following through with the wedding to Alex, even though my stake of the business was sold to someone else.

Alex and I sat down with them and chatted about our relationship. We had the chance to explain what our honest plans were going forward with the relationship and the wedding. We haven't mentioned the pregnancy yet, but they were happy with our answers to all their questions. We aren't the warm and fuzzy family. But I'm fine with the relationship. I accept it for what it is, without expectations. It's better now than ever, and I'm excited to see how a baby will change the dynamic more. I do hope it brings us closer.

I'm still unsure about work and where I'll go from here. I'm disappointed. The business would've been great, but having Alex and the baby are more important.

Today is such a surreal moment. It finally feels real. I can't wait to marry him and start our new life as a family. I never thought this is where my life would've ended up in a short amount of time, but I'm extremely happy it's turned out this way.

"Come on, let's get you to him. Looking at your face makes me jealous," Blake murmurs.

I giggle and walk outside. There's no more time to daydream. I'm about to live my fantasy in real life. I'm extra nauseas as I watch everyone climb inside the limo after me. I just want to see him already.

The drive isn't long, and once I get out of the car, I gaze at my dad. My dad's eyes are misty, and I can tell he's holding back emotion. He smiles at me before his elbow pushes out in encouragement, and I thread my hand through his arm.

"You've got this. You two love each other. The rest will come in time."

I give him as much of a smile as I can through my wobbly chin. "Thanks, Dad," I say, kissing his cheek.

The music sounds, and my heart thrums inside my chest.

When it's my time to walk, my breath catches. Alex is waiting for me at the end of the aisle.

His black suit and bowtie show off his broad frame and tapered waist. I try hard not to drool. Alex in a tuxedo is scorching. But the most beautiful thing about my soon-to-be husband has to be his smile.

Today it's full and bright.

He's happy.

Which makes me happy.

We're both ready to take the next step toward making us permanent.

I walk on shaky feet, keeping my arm firmly holding on to my dad. Ignoring all the noise around me to just focus on those soft blue eyes drawing me closer.

My dad lifts my veil, and I hear Alex exhale.

When our hands touch, and we are standing face to face, he says, "You look beautiful."

His eyes drop over my dress appreciatively. When his gaze reaches mine again, they're full of silent approval. "I love the dress," he breathes.

My nerves fade away at the look in his eyes. I want to hurry up and officially be his wife.

I want to be Mrs. Alex Taylor.

We exchange vows and kiss at our ceremony full of our closest friends and families.

Later at the reception I'm sober and, of course, my husband doesn't drink because I can't. Instead, he takes my hand, and we move onto the dance floor for our first dance.

"This is nice, but I can't wait to get my wife home. And be alone with her."

"Is that a promise?" I challenge.

"Are you talking code, Mrs. Taylor? I was talking about running a bath and tucking you into bed."

I giggle. "It was code, but clearly you have much better ideas."

"Hey, now. I think you need all of it."

"It sounds like the best way to end a perfect day."

Our dance ends and we return to our seats.

A tapping sounds on a glass, drawing the crowd and us to a silence. It's Blake.

"Thank you, everyone, for being here for my good friends, Alex and Tahlia. I always knew these two had something going on. A spark that they grew to figure out. Can we all raise our glasses up and cheer for the new Mr. and Mrs. Taylor?"

The crowd erupts in clapping and whoops.

Alex stands, and I know what's coming, and that makes waves of butterflies swarm my stomach.

"Thank you, Blake. And thank you all for joining me and my beautiful wife, Tahlia, on this special day. We hope you enjoy the night. We thank you for your gifts. We have one to give back to you...I'd like to announce our pregnancy. Not only do I have a beautiful wife today, but also a beautiful mother-to-be."

The room applauds loudly.

I stare at Alex, lost in his adoring words. He peers down at me and kisses my lips.

"You guys surprised us." My mom's voice pulls me away from him.

Looking at my parents' faces makes me smile. Their proud and watery eyes have me getting up and giving them a hug. Alex's parents have also come over to congratulate us too. We spend the next couple of hours eating, cutting the cake and when we go around to the whole room and say our thanks and goodbyes, Alex leans into my ear.

"My beautiful wife, are you ready to go home?"

"Please," I exhale.

He nods. But before we leave, Alex pulls me aside for a moment. I can't help but kiss him.

He stops, smiling down at me, and I moan. "More."

"Soon. I need to give you your present," he says.

The nerves are kicking in, and my heart is in my throat. What is it now?

"Here you are," he says excitedly.

I take the envelope with deep concentration and open it. Reading its contents, I blurt, "No, you didn't."

He smirks at my reaction. "I did."

I drop my hand and hold the letter. My name is the majority stake owner of Emerald Designs.

"How?" I ask.

"Your parents like me. What can I say?" He laughs.

"You charmed them. And paid how much? How much do I have to pay you back?"

"Nothing. This was a gift to my wife. You gave me the most magical gift." He taps his chest before continuing. "To feel anything but numb, and you did that. No present will ever be enough of a thank you. I'll always be indebted to you."

I grab his hand and we exit, my heart warm and my body ready for him.

Back at our house, he carries me up the stairs to our bedroom and stares at me with a fire I've not seen before.

He carefully lowers me to the bed, and my stomach is in a wild swirl of anticipation. When our lips touch, my eyes flutter closed, and I sink deep into it. His strong hand is on the back of my head while the other roams over my back and rests above the curve of my ass. My hands move from his broad shoulders up his thick neck, and I rake my fingers through his hair before curling my grip.

I feel everything, and our closeness is like a drug that brings me closer to euphoria.

He parts our lips, and his tongue runs over my bottom lip, seeking entry. I groan from the feeling of his tongue inside my mouth. Sweet and warm and captivating. I want more.

I need more.

And it's safe to say, he's feeling the same. The way his hand grips my ass and brings me flush against his hard erection. There is no mistaking the sparks.

Our tongues move in fluid strokes. I lap up his taste, and when he teases my mouth with his tongue, a whimper leaves my chest. No time to be embarrassed or silent. I can't hold myself back, even if I wanted to.

Every sweep of his tongue, I match it with my own in perfect rhythm. He's such a good kisser. Kissing him has fast become an addiction.

When we pull apart, both of us are gasping for oxygen. I bring my eyes to his and hold them, seeing the same struggle and confliction I feel, but he has a little...excitement.

"Let me worship you."

Chapter 42

Alex

"I don't think I've seen a better dress," I rasp, touching her hot skin that's exposed from the dip in her wedding dress.

The lace is a mix of soft and rough against my fingers.

"You like it?" she asks in a sexy purr.

"No, honey. I love it. Knowing you picked this to wear for me as we become one. My wife. My future. My love for now and forever," I murmur.

The green in her eyes glows brighter. I don't miss the misty look, though.

"Honey..." I start.

She shakes her head. "I'm okay. Just extra emotional."

I lay my hand on her cheek. She nuzzles into it.

"Are you sure? I can run you a bath and make you tea."

Her lips twitch. "No, Doctor, even though that sounds nice. I don't want nice right now."

My eyebrows draw together. "You don't?"

"No. I want my husband." She gives me a sexy smile, and I don't miss the hint of mischief in her eyes.

"My wife needs her husband to fuck her, worship her, and make love to her," I whisper, leaning in and bringing my lips to hers in a hot kiss.

Her lips part to breathe out, "Yes."

I drop my hand from her face. "Good. Because the look of you as my wife makes me want to come," I murmur darkly, before adding, "Turn around."

She spins slowly until her back is facing me. I take a steady breath and admire her curves, then my hand reaches out to unzip her in an unhurried movement.

My fingers grip the metal, and I pull down steadily, exposing her skin. No matter how hard my body screams at me to do it faster, I don't. The moment I make love to her as my wife will be worth it.

I finish unzipping her dress, and take it off. She turns to face me again.

"Something blue," I mutter as I look at her pretty panties.

"You know about that?" she asks, surprise dripping from her voice.

"Of course. The moment we were getting married, I wanted to know every single detail about weddings. And when the lines became blurry between fake and real, I knew the reason for my research was to please you. Because ultimately, I want to give you everything."

"I want to please you too." She drops to her knees and my eyes widen at her sweet offer.

I cup her face, staring adoringly at her. My dick is throbbing behind my black pants, begging for her hot mouth.

"How am I meant to worship you, if you're on your knees?" I grind out. I fight back with how much I want this, but also struggle to accept the pleasure she's offering.

"You letting me suck your cock will make me feel incredibly powerful. To watch you struggle and give me the power to bring you to your knees with just my mouth, that is better than anything you could do to me right now," she says, licking her lips.

She's fighting hard. My world is spinning. I'm so conflicted. She's on her knees, with her bright green eyes begging to suck me off.

"Fine but afterward, I'm going to make you come so much, you won't remember sucking my cock."

She smirks dryly at me. "I'll always remember. I don't want to forget the look on your face as you come down my throat."

Fucking hell.

"Suck my cock, my beautiful wife. Own me, as if you don't already," I murmur.

She swiftly works on my button and zipper. I'm so hard, transfixed, watching her pull me out of my briefs and trying to wrap her dainty hands around me. My dick jerks in her hands as she gets ready to take me into her mouth.

"You're already leak—"

I thrust my dick between her parted lips. I can't hear another word, otherwise I'm going to come all over her pretty face.

She takes me as far back as she can, humming around me. The vibration causes me to grow harder. The feel of her wet, warm mouth is incredible.

My hands fly to her hair, grateful her hair is pinned in a neat bun, so I don't have anything blocking my view. I force my eyes to stay open. I don't want to miss a second of her taking me deep. As if checking I'm still there, her eyes snap to mine, and a little pre-cum spills before breathing through it and holding myself back.

She pulls back, giving me a second, which allows me to collect myself. "You taste so good," she pants.

I shake my head. "You're too good at this," I grind out.

"What?" she asks, confused.

"Your mouth is wicked. Now the only sounds I want to hear soon are you moaning," I say, bending down to lift her to her feet. I need her wrapped around me.

"You like my dirty talk?" she asks, dazed.

I swallow the growl threatening to leave my throat. "Too much." I move my hands up the middle of her back, enjoying the softness of her skin and the heat of her. Slipping the dress from her shoulders, I watch the dress fall to the floor. Now standing in only the panties and heels, I soak in every part of her.

The sight of her pebbled nipples and her quickened breaths are the only giveaways she's holding back.

I bring my lips to her in a passionate kiss, only breaking it to lean my forehead on hers.

Needing more, I sink to my knees and look up.

"I'm yours, and you're mine."

She nods.

"Forever," I say.

"Forever," she repeats.

I grab the sides of her panties and slip them down. She steps out of them, and I lower a kiss to her stomach in a gentle caress. Just over our baby.

My world, right here.

I kiss the top of her apex. She gasps, and her hands immediately find my hair.

"Kneeling for you is my greatest pleasure," I say through a moan. Grabbing her leg, I lift it onto my shoulder.

"Ah. Alex," she gasps.

I lean in and suck her swollen clit, hard. Her hands tighten in my hair, urging me to go harder. When I lick her opening, her legs buckle. My hands fly up to her hips to hold her up. I'm not ready to let go of her yet. I need to devour her on my knees. So, I don't stop eating her pussy until she's coming in a quivering mess on my face.

Once she does, she lowers her leg, and I stand. I remove my tie, ripping it off and tossing it to the side before I remove my shirt as fast as I can.

Walking to the bed, I take a seat and pat my leg. "Tonight is all about you. So, sit on my cock in your favorite position and ride me. Ride me as hard and as fast as you want."

She doesn't hesitate. She hovers, just as urgent and as eager as me. Sinking down, her pussy takes my cock deep inside of her. She's right, warm, and perfect.

My hands grab her waist, and I admire the way she lifts and lowers on me. Watching myself be swallowed up by her pussy sends me wild. I tilt my hips up every time she slams down. I know she's climbing, so I help her. Reaching around, I touch her swollen clit.

"Alex. Yes," she cries, a breathless tone that I love.

I rub her clit harder and faster, and when I feel her pussy tighten around my dick, I grunt. "Good girl, use my cock to get off."

She moans louder as she continues to fuck me. Chasing her orgasm. "You feel amazing."

Her hips rock when she's fully seated again. She tightens and pulses from the intrusion. "Alex, I want to come."

"I know, honey, and you can." I slide my hands up her stomach to grab both her tits. Squeezing them both at the same time, I find her peaked nipples and pinch them. Feeling her around me as husband and wife makes my chest swell.

The loud feral moan she lets out is erotic.

"Alex," she cries out through her orgasm.

As she rides me through her aftereffects, I come the hardest I have in my life.

I lift her up and spin her around to face me, and I hold her against me. Our perspiring bodies moving together, our breaths are fast and hot.

Fuck. I love her so much.

"Are you okay?" I ask when I can catch my breath.

She nods. "Yeah."

I kiss her temple. "Let me run a bath for my wife."

CHAPTER 43

ALEX

"COME BACK TO BED," Tahlia begs with a purr.

From the side of the bed, I look over my shoulder at her. She's giving me her best *come fuck me* eyes, seducing me again.

And I can't resist.

I grin, rolling back under the blankets. "Ten more minutes, but after that, we've gotta get up. We need to go to your appointment on time."

My hand slides over her waist and I scoot so her ass is flush with my groin. My hand strokes her belly. I love holding her, sleeping next to her, and waking up with her.

"Someone's eager..."

"You have no idea," I say, laying a kiss to her bare shoulder. "I want to meet our baby already."

"We're way too early."

"I know. I know. I'm just excited to find out who he or she will look like. I hope it's you. You're so beautiful."

Her hand settles over mine, holding it still. "You have to say that. I'm your wife."

"I'm saying it because it's true." I pepper kisses over her shoulder.

I continue to hold her in my arms. I wish she could feel what I feel inside. Everything is hot, electric, and beating. I'm no longer the same person I once was.

No, I feel so much for this woman. Love, happiness, laughter. The list is endless, just like my love for her. I don't feel deserving of everything, but Tahlia reminds me every day she loves me and that's she's here for me. Heck, she even irons my shirts topless. I don't know why that happened, but I don't ask questions. I simply enjoy the fucking view of my wife ironing nude. That's my fucking life. A life I love.

"I love you," I whisper into her skin.

"I love you too."

I caress her bump. "We have to get up now." She turns in my arms to face me, and I kiss her lips. "Let's go see our baby."

She nods with a smile. "Let's."

We walk into the hospital holding hands. It's strange for me to come to work for a non-work activity, but today's all about our baby. The last time I was here, I didn't take anything in. It was all a blur. But now, I'm ready.

Ready to be a father.

We take a seat in the waiting area of our obstetrician's office. Doctor Paddock is one of the oldest and wisest ob-gyns working here. Tahlia chose well. She has great instincts, and I can't wait to see her as a mother.

While we wait, Tahlia pulls out her phone to reply to a work email. I'd tell her to stop working, just relax, but she'll be on maternity leave soon, and it's nice to see how much she's loving her job. I know the rewarding feeling of being passionate about your job, so I want to support her in any way I can.

"Welcome guys," Doctor Paddock says, standing at the entrance to the waiting room. "Come with me."

Tahlia tucks away her phone, and I put my hand on her lower back as we follow the doctor into the exam room.

"How is everything going with your pregnancy?" Dr. Paddock asks Tahlia as we take a seat.

I sit back and let them talk, taking it all in. I feel lost, like I'm waiting for direction. It's strange being on the other side of the table.

"I'm a little tired at night, but otherwise, it's easy," Tahlia says.

"Make sure you don't overdo it," Doctor Paddock replies.

Tahlia throws a thumb in my direction. "As if he would let that happen."

"I'm glad your husband is looking out for you. I wish more were like him."

I shift in my seat, suddenly feeling awkward and unsure why that was unusual. Not only has Tahlia got my heart, but she has another piece of me growing inside of her. Both are equally important to me. They are my reason.

"I will check your blood pressure before I do a small scan for you. You can book your twenty-week scan with my receptionist when you leave. I need you to get more bloodwork done then, too."

He stands, and Tahlia does too, walking to the exam table. Once she's situated, he takes her vitals.

"Did you guys find out the sex?" he asks as he finishes removing the blood pressure cuff.

"Not yet. I thought they were going to call, but they didn't," Tahlia replies, her brows furrowed.

"That's unusual. Well, I have the results here. Did you want to know?"

My stomach bottoms out, and I stand in a rush to move beside Tahlia. I want to be near her when we find this out. We've been waiting for this moment. I've guessed girl, and she has guessed boy.

I want another *her*.

A mini-Tahlia. Bringing me joy.

I hold her hand, caressing the soft skin in circles.

Her gaze stays fixed on the doctor, but mine is on her.

Her glassy eyes are already emotional as we wait for the results.

"Congratulations, Mr. and Mrs. Taylor, you're having a girl."

My smile nearly splits my face, and emotion hits me hard and fierce. I'll admit, my eyes sting.

Tahlia's lip quivers, and a tear slips down her cheek. "You were right," she says to me through sniffs.

"Are you happy? I ask worried she's disappointed she didn't get a boy.

She nods rapidly. "Yes. I'm so happy. Are you?"

"Over the fucking moon. I have two queens to take care of now. My heart has never beat so fucking fast in its whole life."

She smiles as more tears spill onto her cheeks. I remove my hand from hers and swipe away the tears with my thumbs before kissing her lips. "Are you ready to see our princess?"

A choke of a sob sounds out of her mouth as she says, "Yes."

She lies back on the table, and the doctor preps her stomach with gel and scans Tahlia's belly. The little baby girl comes onto the screen and a tear leaks from my eye. My world. These two beautiful women are mine. I'll do whatever it takes to make sure they know how much I love them.

"Do we have a name?"

"Not yet," I say in a shaky voice.

When he's finished the scan, while he wipes the gel from Tahlia's belly, I grab my phone and order something for her.

We move back to the chairs and discuss the next few weeks in detail. Dr. Paddock answers all Tahlia's questions and once we're done, he hands over forms for the upcoming scans and tests. Tahlia takes a detour to the bathroom, and I head to the reception desk to check out.

The receptionist hands me the box I had delivered for Tahlia. "This came for you."

"Thank you," I say, just as Tahlia enters the room.

Her eyes widen, and a grin transforms her face when she sees what I'm holding. "You didn't."

I smile. "I did."

She walks closer and lifts the lid to peek inside the box. The same bakery box I brought the time she dropped Mike and Alice's downstairs.

Cupcakes with pink icing. At least if she chooses to wear it, I'll happily help clean it up. Right now, seeing her carrying my child makes me want to fill her with another baby. Why? I don't know. But the thought and now seeing her pregnant is sending me feral.

"Get me home so we can enjoy these." Her eyes are no longer glassy with tears. No. They are full of wickedness. My wife's going to wear icing on her body, and I'm going to enjoy licking it off her. She's mine, and I am hers. I never thought I could have feelings for a woman, but every day I spend with her, I'm certain I couldn't switch them off. Tahlia fulfills me. My person.

EPILOGUE 1

TAHLIA

Months later

I LOOK OUT MY new office window. The pool and city views as my backdrop are something out of a magazine. Alex wanted to move us into a bigger house, but there were too many good memories here that I wasn't ready to part ways with.

I like his house. It's loving, and everywhere I turn, I think of us. I want our baby to be welcomed and brought to this home.

Alex argues it's too small. Which is ridiculous. She will have her own room, and the house is modern, with more than enough accessories. Kids don't need all this. They simply need us. I know we're already going to shower the baby with love. The way Alex pampers me, you'd think I was the queen. The cooked food, medication, massages, and the coffee. I had to make the switch to decaf because I couldn't deal with his doctor's comments anymore. I just want the taste anyway.

I get it, he loves the baby and me, but damn, sometimes him being a doctor is a lot. I have to remind him I'm his wife, not a patient. On the positive, it always ends up in hot sex.

Since the wedding, life has been busy. The complete move here, with not a single item left at my rental with Maddison. The home office has only just been finished being built. It needed an upgrade to accommodate what I'll need to work from home.

Speaking of...my phone rings.

"Mom. Hi," I answer.

"I'm just popping over. Alex said you were working from home today," she says, and I can tell she's driving.

"I am. I have a new sample of the fall line. Did you want to come to help me approve it?" I ask with a smile, peering around the room to look for the box of samples. It just arrived.

I have accepted their help as a way of continuing our new relationship. Plus, I don't have time to train anyone new right now. I'm twenty-eight weeks pregnant, so to hire and train a new person to add to the business all while I'm still adjusting, is silly. This way, they help me, and I can still learn all from my house. The office and warehouse are not too far away if I need to go there for any reason.

The door rings, so I wander down and open the door.

"Hi, Mom," I say with a pinched brow when I notice she's holding something. "What's that?"

"Oh, it's for you." She hands me a white gift bag, and I take it as I close the door behind her.

"What is it?" I ask, unable to help myself.

She chuckles. "Open it and find out."

I walk to the table and lower the bag and open it. I pull out a long, white, flowy dress. The little flowers are beautiful.

I'm so confused.

"It's beautiful, and thanks..." I trail off, still not understanding. There's nothing else inside the bag.

"Your father and I designed it, and had it made," she replies softly.

Now I'm even more confused. "Why?"

"Your friends, me, and Alex decided if you weren't going to organize a baby shower, we would."

My hand flies to smother my gasp.

It dawns on me, my parents made this special dress for me to wear to my very own surprise baby shower.

"No," I mumble into my hand.

"Yes. It starts in one hour, and any minute, a team will arrive to do your hair and makeup. Also, to set the house up for guests."

I drop my hand and look down at myself in my Lululemon leggings and shirt. "Do I have time for a shower?"

I hope so.

"Of course," she replies.

"Oh," I say, as a wave of disappointment washes over me. I know it's not traditional, but I wish Alex could come and celebrate with me today.

"Alex needed to pick up a couple of things, but he'll come near the end," she says, smiling.

"The end?" I ask.

"Your friends didn't want him to hover and not let you have fun."

I giggle. "He's a little protective of us," I say, touching my bump.

"Who can blame him? I'm grateful you have him."

"I know he's taking extra caution, but...it's early for a baby shower. I'm only twenty-eight weeks."

We had our big scan recently. I received the all-clear and, finally, I feel like I can breathe. But realistically, I don't know if I will fully relax until I hold her in my arms.

"Again, he wanted you to rest in the final stretch not party."

I snort. "Mom, it's a baby shower. I'm not clubbing."

Her lips lift, and I know she agrees.

"You know Alex," she adds.

"I do. And I love him. My helicopter husband."

"Helicopter husband?" she asks, perplexed.

"Just a phrase, Mom."

"Okay—" she's cut off when the door sounds.

My eyes widen.

"Go shower. Take your time. I'll let them in and set up," she says, shooing me away.

I exhale and smile. "Thanks, Mom."

I grab my dress and head to the bathroom, but not before sending Alex a thank you text. I love him so much it hurts to be without him, even for a moment.

EPILOGUE 2

ALEX

One Year Later

I WAKE TO A cold bed. Rubbing my eyes, I stretch and get up. It's just before seven in the morning. I stroll down to the kitchen, following the delicious smell.

A wide smile takes over my face as I see Tahlia making coffee. I come up behind her and wrap my arms around her middle. Touching her growing bump is my favorite thing to do. Resting my hands there, I murmur into her neck, "Smells good."

"Yeah, I've finished making your coffee. Sit down, and I'll serve breakfast."

"I'll help."

"I'm fine. You always cook me breakfast and coffee. It's my turn," she says with an odd twinkle in her eye. The curve in her lips makes me think something up.

Looking around the kitchen, I take a seat. I can't help but notice there are no dishes.

"Where're the dishes?"

"Ah. I cleaned up."

My mouth purses, trying to contain a laugh.

But she bursts out laughing first.

"Fine, you got me. I ordered delivery."

"That's still thoughtful, thank you." As I look at the array of food, my mouth salivates. "Looks like we have a bit of everything."

"Yeah, I couldn't decide on what to get, so figured I'll get everything."

"Maybe he's growing."

"It might be a she..."

"It might. I wish we could find out."

She shakes her head. "Nope. I want a surprise."

"We didn't have a surprise with Elsie," I mumble.

The sound of the monitor goes, letting us know our little blonde angel is awake.

"I've got it," I jump up, leaving Tahlia laughing to herself.

I walk into her nursery, finding Elsie talking loudly to her hanging mobile. She notices me over the side of her cot and she kicks her feet. I smile at her messy short hair from the night's sleep. It's grown patchy and in the cutest mullet style. It's damn adorable.

"How's my baby feeling?" I coo as I pick her up and lay her down on the changing room table. I take her out of her sleeper and change her diaper.

Elsie's eyes are a darker green, and they remind me so much of her mom. She's a gentle and quiet soul. Not like other babies. Well, I only have Ethan to compare to, but he's now two years old, with the funniest temperament. He's like a little Mike, with the same scowl set between his brows. It's hilarious.

Except when I tickle her, she becomes loud. I rub her ribs gently to tickle and the sound out of her mouth has me smiling brightly down at her. I love her laugh as much as I love her mom's.

"Are you ready to go stay at gramps and grams for the night?" I ask.

Elsie smiles happily with no care in the world. Her rosy cheeks from her laughing make me want to cuddle her.

I swoop her up in my arms, and it's funny how much I'm wrapped around her little finger, and she doesn't even know it. Her mom owns me and she does too.

After hanging out with my whole family and leaving Elsie there, I drive Tahlia and me home. Parking the car, we step out and make our way to the door. I'm ready to spend some time alone with her before our second baby arrives.

"Sorry, what did you say?" She blinks rapidly, meeting my gaze.

"Are you okay?" I ask louder.

Her face softens. "Yeah, just tired."

"Too tired for that shoulder massage?" I ask her. Having my hands on her is always a risk, because I get visions of touching her intimately. Stroking her breasts and down to her sweetness between her thighs. I shake my head, needing to clear the dirty thoughts before an erection tents my pants.

"Never," she says back with a half-amused smile.

"I thought so." I wink, happy she is lighter now.

I open the door, and she brushes past me.

"I'll go put my sweats on," she calls out over her shoulder, practically racing through the house and skipping every second step.

The door closes behind me, and I flick the lock. Her dressed up is one thing, but there's something uber-sexy about Tahlia dressed down. Her natural freckles, tousled messy hair, and sweats are my kryptonite.

Moving through the house, I flick on the TV and scroll to find our show. I've been forced to watch with her, but it's not half bad. I'm just keeping that secret to myself. Otherwise, after this season, she may expect me to endure more. The reason I watch it is to be with her.

I pause the show and walk into the kitchen. Her light footsteps sound down the stairs, and as I finish grabbing us a bottle of water, I smile to myself as she's clearly looking for the remote. I hit play and her face lifts. Her eyes meet mine. I come to a halt in front of her. She straightens and grabs the bottle from my outstretched hand.

"Thanks," she says and takes a seat, unscrewing the lid and taking a sip.

I lower my bottle to the coffee table and lay my hands on her shoulders. Her body jumps a little with shock from my sudden touch. I move my thumbs in deep, sweeping movements.

As she eases back, I watch her eyes flutter closed, and I can't help but move my lips to her ear. "You're missing the show."

She grumbles and waves me off. Her shampoo hits me at full force, and I bite back a groan.

"Does this feel good?" I ask, my voice deep with arousal.

"Yes," she says as she eases farther into my touch.

"Good. Now just relax."

She takes a big intake of breath, and she tries to open her eyes. But fails.

I grin and move my hands to either side of her neck. Stroking up and down and finding her pulse. I love how hard and fast it goes underneath me. The rhythm matches my own. As I draw my touch in harder and slower, a whimper escapes her lips. My sole focus is on her and to make her feel good.

Her breathing picks up as she mumbles, "You really are a doctor, aren't you?"

Chuckling from above her, I tease, "Didn't believe me before?"

Her eyes snap open. "I did, I just...I've never been your patient before."

My hands freeze. I'm unable to massage for the moment. Thinking of her as my patient wouldn't be good. "I don't want you as my patient. Ever."

I curse at my tone. It's too clipped; I sound almost angry. And I instantly regret it. It's just the dread of a loved one getting ill scares me. "I didn't mean to be rude to you, but the patients I treat are not healthy. And I can't bear—" I swallow past the lump in my throat from my thoughts.

She tries to turn, and it snaps me back to reality. My hands hold her still so she can't turn around and see the pain I know that's etched into my face. I return to the massage, trying to distract her.

"Sorry," she whispers.

"Don't be sorry."

She opens her mouth to add something, but when she closes it, I'm kind of relieved.

Tahlia and my kids are my whole universe. I don't want to imagine anything ever happening to them.

She stays silent as my fingers dig into her knots and ease the tension that's built.

"Your hands are seriously magic, Doc."

"Magic?" I repeat, chuckling at her analogy.

I shake my head. "And you calling me Doc?" I smirk.

"Can I call you that?" She looks away, returning to watch the TV.

I lean down to whisper, and it comes out huskier than I mean for it to. I blame her intoxicating scent for being inches away from her skin.

"You can call me anything you want. I love all the nicknames you give me."

She nods her head, but I can't read her expression. My mouth doesn't move from her ear. My finger twitches to touch her, and on instinct, I do. Moving my finger along the front of her neck, I stroke it delicately, feeling her pulse ricochet up and then her swallow.

And I imagine her swallowing me, my dick coming to life just from the imagery. It's one hell of a vision I wouldn't mind having for real right now. But I don't want to ruin this sweet moment.

"All right, Doc," she whispers hoarsely, licking her lips, and my dick twitches at the sight.

I can't help but lean in and kiss her temple slowly before pulling back.

I don't know what's coming over me. I'd like to think I know exactly what I'm doing, yet my body isn't syncing with my brain. But she didn't say to stop it, so I inch closer.

She turns and her lust-filled eyes drink me in. I want to say fuck the massage and haul her upstairs to our bedroom.

My eyes drop down to her pouty pink lips, and they are wet from her just licking them. Teasing and taunting me some more. She's letting out these cute pants, and I want to just lean in and kiss her.

I clear my throat and pull away, leaning my forehead on the back of her head. My eyes slam shut tight, and I'm telling myself I'm doing the right thing. Let myself enjoy the peace of us doing something so mundane and then ravish her in our bed later.

When I'm finally off the ledge of kissing her, I slide her silky blonde hair to one side and return to giving her a massage. She hasn't moved or said a word. Only our heavy breaths can be heard. I don't even know if she's paying any attention to the show. I know I'm not. I'm still focused on every inch of her and how I'm struggling to rein myself in. Being sexually frustrated will make later so much better.

We continue until the episode ends, and she yawns. I stop massaging but keep my hands on her. I'm not ready to remove them; I feel closer to her like this.

"I think it's bedtime," I growl, knowing I can't hold on a second longer. I need my wife now.

I hear a cute gasp, and then her giggle. God, the sound is like music to my ears, soft, sweet, and so her.

"Ladies first."

That wins me a snort. "That's so kind of you."

She rolls her eyes at me with a smirk, and gets off the sofa, before turning to take the stairs.

I follow her until we're upstairs then I smack her ass. "Hey. No teasing."

She stares for a second, completely baffled, and I don't even know what came over me. But she's giving me a look I know so well.

"Did you want more of that, honey?"

We stare at each other. I'm drowning with desire. The chemistry is thicker up here than it was downstairs, and it causes me to sweat. I run a hand through my hair as I stare back at her. Her alluring eyes are bringing me closer.

When we are toe to toe, her sexy pants leaving her mouth are back. The sound through those parted pink lips is so sexy, and I just want those lips screaming out my name. Fucking hell, this woman is a force to be reckoned with. As I stand, taking in her begging eyes, her mouth parts, giving me a glimpse of her tongue. Without another thought, I lick my lips and dip my head down and capture her mouth. When I pull back for air, I watch as her eyes flutter, matching the beat in my chest.

"Yes. I want more," she breathes.

I bend down and lift her up, walking her into our bedroom. I need to take her now.

Bonus Scene

Tahlia

The house is awfully quiet, and I haven't heard him leave, so I'm wondering if he had an early call out before we have to see my parents.

I get up and amble down the stairs, rubbing the sleep from my eyes. When I make it downstairs, I scrunch up my face as the morning sun hits me. It's bright and letting me know it will be a nice sunny day.

When I step into the kitchen, I pause. He hasn't left for work. A smile spreads on my face at him flipping pancakes on the stove.

"Is that the first time you've ever used the stove?" I move toward the stool, and when I sit, I prop my head in my hands, watching him cook breakfast.

It's sexy. A handsome, intelligent man cooking is a weakness I didn't know I had until right now.

His deep chuckle echoes through the house, and I can't stop myself from how happy he makes me. I don't think I could wipe the smile off my face if I tried.

Eyeing me over his shoulder with an amused cheeky smirk, he returns his focus to the stove. "You behave."

"Why? I'm right, aren't I?" I tease as I check him out openly. His sweatpants hang low, but it's his lack of t-shirt that I struggle with. His naked muscled back straining with every movement. I gulp down some air into my constricted throat, trying to get more oxygen in to breathe better.

My mind flashes back to last night and how every ripple and curve is too perfect to be real. He's ridiculously hot.

"Maybe, but I wanted to make you breakfast."

"You didn't have to because I did," I argue and go to get up and make us both a cup of coffee, but he interrupts.

"I've got it."

He carries the plate of pancakes, lowering them down on the counter. There is more than enough, and they look fluffy and perfect. I'm salivating and excited to taste them. But not as much as I'm dying to taste him. My mind and body want something else entirely to feast on.

"I need the practice," I say, hating how hard it was to use the machine last time. I got more coffee out of the machine than in it.

"And I need a decent coffee," he announces playfully.

My mouth opens wide before I form the words to speak, "It wasn't that bad, was it?"

I scratch my head, unable to believe he drank the whole cup, even though he thought it tasted like crap.

What does that mean?

I don't know, other than it makes my heart thrum faster.

I sit up and hold my hands up, shaking my head. "Wait, don't answer, I get it. But I promise you, I'll work on it without you having to succumb to trying it until I've perfected it."

He walks to his pantry, and then the fridge, pulling out topping options for the pancakes. Bringing them to the counter, he pushes them toward me. "I'll drink whatever you make me."

When he's finished, I take a sip. It looks and tastes much better than mine.

"Good, right?"

"Stop it. You're making me feel bad."

His hand covers mine in a second as his face pales. "Sorry. I don't mean it to be hurtful. I'll stop. Let's eat before the food gets cold."

Flicking my eyes to the pancakes, I'm reminded I'm hungry. "Please, these look so good. I think I might need the recipe."

He frowns as he stares down at me. "Why? Anytime you want them, I'll make them."

Alex is not only hot but so kind. Kinder than I ever gave him credit for.

As he takes his hand away, I clamp my mouth shut to prevent a whimper from slipping. I mourn the loss of his heat. I pick up the syrup and coat my stack.

"Do you have butter?" I ask curiously.

He snorts. "Your pancakes are drowning in syrup, and you want to stick butter on top?" He shakes his head but moves to the fridge and steps back to me.

I shrug. "And. Have you tasted it?"

"High cholesterol? No. I haven't. But as a doctor, I strongly recommend you don't do this."

My lips quirk, and I challenge him. "The doctor isn't allowed to work when he's at home. And how about, before you judge me, you taste it?"

I open the butter and layer a decent amount on top, and as it melts, I hear his grumbling.

"This is so bad for you."

I smirk as I cut a piece off, and then thrust the piece to those full lips. I lift a brow at him. A simple dare. He looks at the pancake, and then holds my gaze as he licks his lips and opens his mouth. Wrapping those hot lips around the fork, he drags it back, chewing the piece, and it's so sensual and hot, my own mouth drops open. I close my mouth and swallow.

"Good, isn't it?" I ask excitedly.

"It's all right." He shrugs.

I gasp and point at him with amusement written across my face. "Liar."

His face breaks out into the biggest panty-melting grin.

I cut off a piece and bring it to my mouth, not caring how many calories or how high of a cholesterol meal this is. But he made it, so I have to eat properly.

"How did you know I can't back down from a dare?"

I roll my lips and think, before blurting out, "You wanted to know what I tasted like—"

He leans in and his breath hit my cheek. "You have no idea." Those words tickle my skin, and I shiver with desire. I bite down on my lip, preventing a moan.

"Wrong word. Not happening. I've got work soon," I reply, but with little conviction. It was way too breathy, and I'm sure he heard the wobble in my voice. I know I heard it.

He pulls back and picks up his coffee, takes a sip, and looks at me over the cup. I swear he's drinking me in. And already, I know this is going to be a long day.

A hell of a long day.

The End.

DOCTOR GRAY

SHARON WOODS

CHAPTER 1

DAMIEN

"SAMUEL, IT'S TIME TO get up," I whisper as I enter my son's room. It's 7 a.m. He needs to get up for school, and I need to get to the hospital because I have a full day of patients. My mom will be here to drive him to school, but I need to get him moving or he'll be late.

He snuggled his little body under his red Lightning McQueen blankets that match his red racing car bed, so all I can see is the top of his messy brown hair and forehead.

The morning light seeps through his curtains. I walk toward them and push the fabric wide open, trying to let the natural sunlight wake him up, but it doesn't work. He's still fast asleep.

A deep sigh leaves me, as I know I'm waking him from his favorite hobby: sleeping. The total opposite of me who thrives off very little sleep. I've been lucky he's always been a great sleeper. Even as a baby.

I walk closer to him. "Come on. Get up, bud," I plead, adjusting my navy work tie. I'm already dressed in my navy dress suit and black work shoes. After my early morning home-gym workout and shower.

Samuel grumbles and rolls onto his other side. "I don't want to go to school," he mumbles sleepily into his pillow.

I smile, finding his grumpy side amusing. I know he gets that gruffness from me. And I don't think it's a good thing as an adult, but as a child, it's adorable.

If I didn't have to be at work already, I'd let him stay home. But it's a workday and I have a long list of patients and doctors who are depending on me.

"You've gotta. I need to go to work, and you need to go to school." I rub his soft, short hair. His hand comes out from under the blanket, and he tries to swat my hand away.

"Fine." He huffs and pushes his blankets off him.

He sits up lazily, his blue eyes hitting mine. Everyone says he's my mini-me, which I can see. Not only is he a spitting image of me, but the scowl between his brows and the way his lips thin are a dead giveaway.

I can't help but chuckle as I stand. "Let me fix you some Lucky Charms," I say, walking away. I'm pulling out the bribery today. That's how desperate I am. I ignore my thoughts on how bad the cereal is for him and remember it's not like this every day. Some days are just harder than others. Heck, parenting is hard. I'm surviving here.

"Nana said they're not good for me," he says, causing me to stop moving and spin around at his doorway. He swings his legs off the bed, getting ready to stand, and rubs his eyes.

I walk back over to him and squat down in front of him, so my eyes are at his level. "Well, she's not here yet, so you have to hurry and eat them, so she won't know." I wink and poke his nose.

His nose wrinkles in response, and that one look reminds me of my ex. The one who walked out on us one year ago. Having my mom help me raise a kid was never in my plans. But shit happens, and now I'm going to be the best mom and dad I can be to Samuel. He deserves to know he's enough. The smartest, most handsome, and kindest little boy I've ever met. I know I'm biased, but fuck, what do you expect? He's mine.

He runs past me in his car-themed PJs, and all I can do is shake my head, stand up, and follow him into the kitchen, where I make him breakfast.

"Are you picking me up from school?" he asks, watching me from his seat at the counter. I grab the milk and pour it into his cereal bowl.

The guilt of disappointing him is always so hard to swallow, but sometimes I've gotta do it. I'd love not to work as a plastic surgeon and be the only one to pick him up and drop him off, but that's not an option. I've got to work and parent. I can't do both without some extra help.

"No, buddy. I've gotta work late today. Nana is," I explain, pushing the bowl in front of him.

"Yay! Nana!" he replies, grabbing his spoon and eating.

Fifteen minutes later, the doorbell rings and I check my watch to see she's right on time.

When my ex-wife Lucy left, she gave me full custody of Samuel. Which is hard when I work and my schedule isn't great, but I make it work. With the help of my parents, I can manage both. It leaves minimal free time for me, but when time permits, I see my friends. Like my best friend Elijah, who is hosting a BBQ this weekend as a housewarming party.

"Where's my favorite people?" Mom calls out as she enters the house, her words echoing throughout it.

Samuel giggles as if he's never heard her say that before.

The sound of her shoes lets me know she is getting closer to us. "There they are!" she exclaims, and Samuel beams at her.

She moves to him first and smothers him with kisses and hugs. His arms and hands hug her back in a warm embrace.

"Eaten your breakfast, I see. Now you're ready to brush your teeth and wash your face." She pulls away from Samuel and moves over to me. She kisses my cheek and greets me, "Son."

"Mom," I reply, before grabbing my briefcase, phone, and wallet.

I'm about to leave when I remember I need to ask her for a favor. "Before I go, I need to ask if you're free on Saturday. I've got a barbecue at Elijah's new house."

She winces. "I'm sorry this Saturday I'm meeting my friends. But maybe—"

I shake my head. "Mom, it's fine. I'll take him with me."

"Eli has games for me. I want to go too, Dad," Samuel interrupts.

"Are you sure?" she asks.

"Yes. I'd miss it if it wasn't for Elijah," I admit.

Elijah's been my friend since high school. I don't want to let him down. He's been there for me in the difficulties of the last few years. And between work and Samuel, there's little time for me. It would be nice to have a little downtime with my friends.

"No. Go. You need to have some fun. Maybe even find—"

"Not happening," I say, cutting her off. I know exactly what she was going to say. And there's no chance. I'm a single dad. My needs are not important. Love isn't worth the pain. I loved a woman once and look how well that turned out.

It didn't...

"I hate how bitter and angry she's made you. You need more fun in your life. It's time."

I'm bitter and angry because I didn't see the red flags. I should've known she didn't want to be a mother. She didn't want that life. She wanted to be free. I can't understand why she could easily leave us or, more specifically, leave him. Hurt me as much as you want, but to hurt your child, how could you do that?

I'll never understand.

"I'm happy and also late for work," I reply. My eyes shift to those big blues still sitting at the counter. I walk over and kiss and hug Samuel before I leave. I know he won't ask me anything about his mom today. Samuel stopped asking me about Lucy when every time he did, I didn't have answers. I know one day I'm going to have to explain the truth to him. But how do I explain something I don't even know myself?

No clue, but I'll at least have to try.

He deserves that whenever the day comes.

I just hope it's not anytime soon.

Half an hour later, I'm supposed to be pulling up to the hospital building. But I detoured in need of a strong caffeine hit, because ever since I left my house, my mind has been in overdrive.

It happens every time I think about my past.

My mistakes.

I avoid the cafeteria at work, knowing colleagues will stop me, and I'm not ready to chat.

I'm never really chatty, but today is even worse. This is why I'm not going there now. I stride into the coffeehouse, where I'm hit with heat and the smell of coffee beans. It's busy with the morning rush of people on their way to work. A mix of takeaway and eat-in patrons.

I get in line to order takeout and grab my phone to respond to a few emails while waiting for my turn. As I'm reading, the sound of a familiar laugh pulls my gaze to the front counter. I spot Marigold, my best friend Elijah's little sister, and she laughs again.

It's a light, wholesome laugh. No fake or forced hints in the tone.

The green sweater and tight blue Levi's sit nicely over Marigold's curves. She's pulled her hair up in a tight ponytail and she's holding textbooks in one hand and paying with the other.

A book slips down and drops to the floor. I'm moving to pick it up before I've thought about it and holding it out for her to take.

"Hey!" she says brightly. "Give me a sec." She spins to finish paying and then we stand to the side.

"How are you?" she asks with a smile.

I try to not get lost in her brown eyes and answer her. "All right. And you?" Even without the black makeup on her eyes, they stand out.

"I'm well. Are you about to start work?" Her eyes drop over my suit, and I don't miss the slight widening.

I run my hand down the front of my suit, smoothing it, wondering for a second if I look okay. I clear my throat. "Yeah. I just needed coffee first," I say dumbly. *Like, why else would I be in a coffeehouse?*

Her brow lifts. "Don't you have a cafeteria?"

"I didn't want to be annoyed," I mutter honestly.

"And here you find me," she says, biting her lip and trying to hold back a smile.

"You're not annoying," I reply easily. Because honestly, she never has been. If anything, she's always been quiet. She never really hung around Elijah and me over the years. Less so since I became a dad. I haven't had as much time with Elijah at his place as I used to.

Her cheeks flush a shade of pink. "Thanks."

Her name is called out. Relief floods her face, and she turns, grabbing the cup and taking a sip. She moans before meeting my gaze. "I needed this today. It was a late night."

I remember being twenty-five, living off caffeine and no sleep just to work and study. Now my college and residency days are long gone.

"You're in your second year of law school, right?"

"Yes. Thank God. Almost at the end now."

She takes another sip and then licks her lips. I follow the movement with my eyes. For a split second, I wonder what her lips would taste like.

What is wrong with me?

"I need to order," I rush out.

"Yes. Sorry. Go, go." She waves.

I get in line, and she stands to the side. My eyes keep drifting her way. She's wearing a tiny smile, but there's this glow about her. Like even tired, she looks radiant.

I order my Americano with a dash of cream and move to stand next to her.

"Did you get my invite for my birthday dinner?" she asks.

"I did."

"And you never responded..." She looks around before meeting my eyes.

Shit.

"I didn't?"

She shakes her head. "No, but you got the text?"

"Yeah. Sorry." I rub the back of my neck. "I'll be there."

Her birthday is so close to Elijah's; it's hard to forget. I must've been at work when she texted and thought I'd reply later. But I didn't.

My name is called out.

She waits as I go to the counter and grab it before we walk side by side to the door. I open it and hold it out for her. The corner of her lip lifts, and she dips her head as she passes me. I step outside after her. She crosses her arm over her due to the cool morning breeze.

We stand in front of each other, holding our hot drinks, when my phone rings.

"You can get it," she says, sipping her drink.

I check my phone. It's Doctor Natasha Blackwood. We've known each other since college. She's working for the NFL team, the Chicago Eels. I don't know what she could be calling for. Unless it's about a player from her team.

"It's not urgent. I'll call *her* back," I say, tucking the phone back into my pocket.

Her heavy lashes that shadow her cheek fly up, and complete surprise sits on her face. "It's okay. You should call *her* back."

I take a sip of my drink and glance at the time. "Yeah, I probably should get going. I have a big day."

"I bet. Well, have a good day. Don't work too hard," she says with a sparkle of humor in her eyes.

"You try to get some sleep," I say.

"I'll try."

A gush of wind picks up, and she covers her eye with the few fingers she can with her cup and books filling her hands.

"Ah," she mutters.

"You okay?"

She's blinking rapidly. Her dark lashes flutter as she tries to remove something that's blown in there.

I step forward and give her my cup to hold. "Let me look."

"Okay," she breathes.

I lay my hands on the side of her face and tilt her head back. The touch sends a buzz of electricity through my hand that I don't understand, so I ignore it and focus on the task at hand.

But as I stare down at her this close-up, I really take her in. Fuck. She's beautiful. Which is making it hard for me to concentrate. The bow of her full pink lips, the slope of her button nose, and those long black lashes blinking are causing my desire to re-spark. Even more so when her eyes hit mine. But it helps me spot the problem.

"Hold still," I grit out, picking out the particle sitting in her eye.

Once it's out, I drop my hands and step back.

"Better?" I ask.

She bites her lip. "Much. Thanks, I better go. I'll see you Saturday?"

My brows pinch together.

"Elijah's," she replies.

I nod a thanks. I almost forgot. "Right. Yes. See you then."

She gives me a small smile and wanders off. I follow her until she's completely out of my sight. Unable to help the way my eyes drop over her curves one last time.

I unlock my phone to call Natasha back. I'm in urgent need of a healthy distraction. And work is the best one I have.

My head is down, reading an email before I see my first patient of the day, when a knock on my office door sounds. Without lifting my head away from the email I've almost finished, I call out, "Come in."

The door swings open and Doctor Alex Taylor strolls in and plops himself down in the patient's chair.

My eyes dart to him before I return my focus back to the email. The guy is so laid back about work and life, I don't know how he does it.

"Do you actually get any work done?" I ask.

"All the time."

I snort and hit send on the email before facing him. "I doubt that." I lean my elbows on the desk.

His brow lifts curiously. "Why do you say that?"

Other than the fact he's not wearing a tie at work...

"You're always talking to people and avoiding being in your office. Doing actual work."

He waves his hand in front of him. "Paperwork isn't my strong suit, but I actually get shit done, you know."

I stare blankly at him, doubting that.

"I dictate," he answers my silent question.

I push my glasses up.

He pulls out a little black rectangular box and waves it toward me. "I talk into this, and I pay someone to type up my notes."

I nod.

My desk phone rings. "Damien," I answer gruffly.

"Your first patient is here, Doctor Gray," my receptionist informs me.

"Give me five minutes. Doctor Alex Taylor is here," I say, intrigued by the dictation that could save time and allow me to spend more of it with my son instead of being buried in paperwork.

"Okay, she's filling in her paperwork anyway," she replies.

I hang up.

My eyes are back on Alex's. "Send me the details. I'll look into buying one. Might give me more time at home."

His brows reach his hairline. "Oh, some new girl, huh?"

"I'm thirty-eight. I wouldn't date a girl. I date women..."

Well, I did. Past tense.

"Sooo, it is a woman," he drawls, sitting up eagerly in his chair.

I cross my arms. "No. My son. I want to be home with him more."

"And you've never thought about dating again since Lucy?"

Her name makes my stomach harden. I hate hearing it. It's always an unwelcome reminder.

"I don't need someone. I'm happy," I argue, through clenched teeth.

He chuckles loudly, shaking his head. "Fuck, if you're happy, I'd hate to see you actually in love."

"Never going to happen," I growl. I don't intend to repeat my mistake.

"Well, don't you miss pussy?"

I pinch the bridge of my nose. I'm not even sure how to respond to him. I've not been with a woman since...well, fuck. Since Lucy.

"No. When you're busy with a kid, you don't have time—"

"Bullshit," he cuts me off, sitting up in his chair so he's closer to my desk.

I look down at my watch. Five minutes have passed already, and I don't want to keep my patient waiting any longer. "I don't have time for this. My first patient's out there. I'll catch up with you later."

"I can't," he states matter-of-factly.

I sit back in my chair, ready to spin around, but I pause midway. "Why?" I ask.

He wiggles his brows at me excitedly. "I'm heading home to Tahlia."

"Right." I grunt back and swivel to face my computer. Bringing up the new patient's notes. Alex looks like he has no intention of leaving.

A soft tap on my door sounds.

Alex finally gets up. Thank fuck.

"Come in," I call out, taking my glasses off and putting them on my desk. I don't have any idea who this could be now. But I really need to get a start on work and not already be thirty minutes behind.

A door opens and a throat clears. "Sorry." I hear Marigold's voice.

I twist in my chair to see Alex standing in the doorway. His eyebrow arched, his finger pointing at Marigold, and he's miming. *Who's this?* Alex has a look of amusement written across his face.

I flick my gaze to hers, ignoring Alex.

"You left your coffee," she says sheepishly, and she's still juggling her coffee and books. I push my chair away from my desk and stand. I stride around the desk to take my cup from her. My fingers brush hers, causing her to suck in a sharp breath and jerk. A splash of her coffee spills from the lid onto my suit sleeve.

She winces. Embarrassed.

I touch her arm gently, ignoring the way she feels beneath my palm and the stain that the coffee leaves. "Are you alright?" I ask.

"Yes. I'm sorry. I didn't mean to ruin your suit," she replies in an apologetic tone.

"It's fine. I'll be in scrubs soon."

Her shoulders drop away from her ears, and I know Alex is still watching us. But I don't care right now. My focus is on Marigold.

"I always wondered what your office looked like," she mumbles, looking around at my basic modern office.

"You did?" I ask, unsure why she'd want to see it. It's nothing exciting; it's bland just like me.

"Yeah, and it's what I imagined."

I am intrigued now. "It is? How?"

I never cared about what anyone thought of me or my office, but suddenly, her opinion matters.

"Modern brown timber and white." She laughs and says, "You have organized everything perfectly. Seriously, not a paper or pen out of line."

I look around, noticing for the first time that I have an impeccably clean office. But I prefer no mess, no clutter, and simple furniture pieces because it all makes me feel less stressed.

She peers down before meeting my gaze again.

"I better get to college. I just wanted to drop off your coffee."

"Thanks."

"You're welcome." She dips her chin and turns around, offering Alex a goodbye on her way out.

I stare at the door she just left through for another moment before I walk back to my desk. I take my seat in my office chair and put my glasses back on.

Alex steps toward me, and I immediately shake my head. "Don't get any ideas. She's off-limits."

"What? I was just going to say that you two look cozy."

I roll my eyes. "You're imagining things."

He shakes his head. "No chance. You're not grumpy or snappy with her. You're different. Happier."

Now I'm sure he's making things up.

I groan. "Go away and work," I say, the need to bring my first patient in and get to work taking over.

Alex steps away, laughing. He walks to the door, opening it but not before calling out, "Ignoring it won't make it go away. Trust me."

When he closes the door behind him, I sit back and take a sip of my now cold coffee, but I welcome the way it cools down my overheated body. Marigold brings out a reaction that I haven't felt for a very long time. And I'm unsure what to think about that.

CHAPTER 2

MARIGOLD

I GET HOME FROM college and grab the mail from my mailbox. A letter from the University of Chicago is one of them. I drop my bag on top of the counter and begin opening it.

"Oh. Hi. I didn't hear you get in," my mom says.

As soon as I see the word *urgent*, I quickly put the letter back in the envelope and throw it in my bag. I'll read it later. I know what it is, and I can't pay for it right now, so it's not a big deal if I don't read it right this second.

My eyes flick up to meet hers. "Yeah, I just got home."

My stomach growls, reminding me I haven't eaten since lunch. I walk to the cupboard to grab a snack and find mom has baked today. My mouth waters at my mom's famous fresh banana bread.

"What do you feel like for dinner?" Mom asks, opening the fridge and handing me the butter.

"Anything," I answer, grabbing a slice of banana bread and putting it on a plate to add a decent layer of butter. It melts when I take a bite.

Mom sighs. "That's not much help."

I swallow the bread before replying, "Sorry, Mom. I love anything you cook."

She turns to find me moaning and eating the bread way too quickly.

"I can see that."

"I need to study, so maybe something quick and easy?"

"What about a stir fry? Your dad will be on his way home from work now."

I pop the last bite of banana bread in my mouth and swallow it before answering.

"Sounds good. I'm going to chill out in my room and call Clara. Unless you need a hand?"

She grabs some beef strips out of the fridge, then closes it and turns to me. "No. You go relax and I'll call you when dinner is ready."

"Thanks." I take my plate to the dishwasher, then I grab my bag off the counter and take the path to the guest house.

It's just me and my parents living here now. My brother moved out in his early twenties.

I plan to move out as soon as I've got a full-time job at a law firm.

It's not bad living here, though. They live in the main house, and I live in the guest house.

Thankfully, they don't come over to the guest house too often and not when I work, which is at night, as a cam girl, which means I always keep my door locked. Just in case.

When I get inside my house, I head to my room, grab the letter out of my bag, and collapse on my unmade bed to read it.

It's a reminder notice for tuition.

I grab my phone out of my bag and check my bank account. There's currently not enough money to cover it. However, after this week's work, there should be enough to pay for it. I just need a couple of new subscribers to join my page or one subscriber to join my premium where we live chat.

Obviously, I'm risking my law career if I were to get caught, which is why I always wear a mask and hide my face. No one can find out it's me. I know that means I'm walking a fine line, but I'm so close to finishing school and right now, that's my goal. Pay my tuition without owing my family.

My parents barely check on me. I'm twenty-five, so they give me the space I want—to do things like online apps. Of course, they don't know about it, but it means I've never had to worry about them barging in. They're happy that I'm doing law. They see me as their innocent daughter. I am, but I desperately need money for school that I can't ask for.

I only just started the online work this month. After I used all my savings on my last semester's tuition, I knew I had to find a job. That night, I stumbled across an online article. I thought it was too good to be true. The figures the girls were getting on the app Mysterious Fan would cover my college tuition and more. Plus, it doesn't require eight hours on my feet. My studies have to come first and getting a degree in law, there's a lot of studying involved. I figured I could try it out. If I didn't like it, I could quit. It's not as bad as I thought. I'm still nervous when I first get on with someone new. But luckily, I haven't met too many weirdos that I've had to block. A few subscribers just want to talk or ask for a picture. It's been easy money so far.

Putting the letter away in a drawer, knowing I'll take care of it later this week, I take a seat on my bed with my books ready to read.

I start, but I'm too restless, and I can't stop thinking about bumping into Damien today. He has always had this effect on me. I'm always hoping to see him. Anytime he and my brother are together, I'm there watching him. It's been like that for years and I'm aware I'll never be able to have him...unless it's in my dreams. And I have many dreams about him. Now seeing him today, I know for sure that I'll have a new one tonight.

The memory of him keeps replaying in my mind. His hot breath on my face. His close proximity. The darkened eyes. His soft touch. And finally, his strong spicy pear scent. It's all making me hot and bothered. I rub my head, trying to clear it, but it's no help.

I get up and grab my phone to call Clara. Maybe talking about today will get me to concentrate again.

She answers on the first ring. "Hey!"

"Hey, can you talk?"

"Yeah, why?"

"Guess who I bumped into this morning?"

"I dunno. Who?"

"Damien," I whisper.

"You've always had a crush on him."

I laugh as I imagine her rolling her eyes. I sit down to remove my old nail polish.

"I do. He's hot." I sigh, remembering how he looked in his suit today.

She makes a disapproving noise before replying, "He seems like a grumpy old dude to me."

I get why she says that. And I've explained to her how his wife left him and his son. For reasons we don't know. Which has made him different. But she also doesn't see the soft side of him like I do. I hope it's just for me, but I'm not stupid. He doesn't look at me the way I look at him. I'm his best friend's little sister. He'll never look at me as anything more than that.

"You haven't known him for as long as I have. He's so sweet under the hard exterior," I argue.

"He's all hard."

I know she's being dirty and heck, I wish I knew if he was hard or not.

"I wouldn't know, but he was sweet today."

"What happened today?"

I finish removing the nail polish and throw the rubbish in the bin. Then I retake my seat.

"I bumped into him at the coffeehouse close to his work and he chatted with me."

"Sounds romantic," she teases.

"Hey! He is. Something blew into my eye, and he held my face and removed it."

She snorts. "Look out. Next, he'll kiss you."

I grab my favorite purple polish and paint my nails.

"God, I wish. The number of dirty dreams I've had about him is so unfair. He was so close to my face today. Those hands on my face felt amazing."

"Your brother will lose his shit if you go there," she reminds me.

I breathe out heavily. "I know. But it's not about that. I'm hesitant because I don't want to put myself out there to be humiliated. It's only been a year since Lucy."

I finish painting my nails and let them dry.

"Didn't you say they had issues before she walked out on him?"

"And Samuel. But yeah, that's what my brother said. Oh, and I'm seeing him Saturday at my brother's new house for a barbecue."

The image of him out of his suit and in casual clothes enters my mind.

"You need to look hot!"

I grin, totally agreeing with her. "I was just thinking about what I'll wear. Can't be too dressy though..." Looking over my closet, I try to remember what I have.

"That yellow sundress."

I know the one she's talking about. "Yes, it brings out my eyes."

"I'd say your tits, and isn't that what you want?"

I laugh and when I recover, I say, "Yes, but I'm not as blunt as you."

"What? You need to up the seduction, woman. He doesn't even know you exist."

"He does," I argue.

"Yeah. As Eli's little sister, not as a woman."

I look out my window into the cloudy sky. "Hmm."

She's right.

"Lucky I'm working all week. I can work on my confidence and pay my overdue college tuition."

I'm honest about my money issues with Clara. But with everyone else, I hide it. I don't want people feeling bad for me.

"Why don't you ask your parents or your brother for money? He's loaded."

It's the exact reason I don't want to ask them. I want to earn it.

"No. I want to do this. I enjoy being online. It's helping me grow confident."

"You're insanely beautiful. I don't know why you aren't confident."

I don't feel beautiful. Guys have never treated me right. So over time, I've never felt good enough. "Not with guys."

"That's because your ex was a dick."

A loud giggle leaves my mouth at her honesty. "That he was..."

"Well, if it can bring the kitten out in you, I'm all for it. And do your homework because I expect a good story about Saturday."

My intercom buzzes. I check my nails and they're dry, so I stand.

"I'll try, but I better go now. My mom's calling me to come eat dinner and then I need to shower."

"Better get yourself prepared for work," she replies.

"Exactly. Call you tomorrow," I say and hang up after she says bye.

There's a fresh spring in my step now that I've got a plan for the weekend. I just have to get through this week first.

CHAPTER 3

DAMIEN

"HOW WAS SCHOOL?" I ask, tugging at my tie to remove it as I enter the living room.

"Alright," Samuel answers.

I walk up to him and rub his damp hair.

"Just alright?" I ask with a frown.

He shrugs his little shoulders. "Yeah."

"Did you need help with your homework?" I ask. I'm wiped from the long day at work, but always find the energy to help him.

"No, I've just done it, darling," my mom calls from behind me. She'll be tidying the bathroom just how I like it.

I exhale a deep breath, grateful for her help. "Thanks. Do you want to stay for dinner?"

"No, we ate already. Samuel was hungry earlier today, so I cooked and ate with him. There're heaps in the fridge."

I'm just not up to cooking right now, so to hear that she's cooked is like music to my ears.

Elijah enters the kitchen. "Hey!" he says, coming to kiss my mom on the cheek.

She says hi back with a smile. She adores Elijah.

"I really need to take back my key," I mumble.

He smirks. "Don't be like that. You love me coming over to hang with you. I bet you were sad I couldn't do it last night."

He usually comes every Sunday, but he had a conference this weekend.

"You're not my girlfriend. But you have one that probably wants you to spend time with her."

Jackie is nice and I hate the guilt I feel from him being here instead of being with her. Yes, our weekly hangouts started when Lucy left. We never had a conversation; it just happened. He kept coming over every week, usually on Sundays, and one day, he was here before me, so I gave him a spare key to let himself in if he did again.

"Nah, she understands I like hanging out with my asshole of a best friend."

I roll my eyes. "Smartass," I murmur and move to the fridge. There's a big plate of lasagna. I take it out, cut it in half, and set it on two plates before heating them up. Elijah wanders off in the direction of Samuel.

"How was work?" Mom asks, joining me in the kitchen.

"Fine. How did it go with Samuel?"

I don't like to talk about my work. It's a mix of pure exhaustion from the long day, and I don't want to bore people with my work talk.

"I picked him up from school. We went to the park to play and then came home."

"Thanks," I say, taking the plates from the microwave.

Samuel is setting up Mario Kart with Elijah, ready for us to play. It's becoming our thing. Before bed, we play together. Usually, I cook, shower, and put him in his PJs, but tonight, I was on call after my shift, so Mom's already done it all.

Elijah comes and eats his food.

"I'll let you go. I better get home to your father and cook him his dinner," Mom announces.

Elijah says goodbye and puts his plate in the dishwasher.

I swallow the last bite of food, along with the guilt of taking my mom away from him.

"He's fine. Don't worry about him," she says, reaching over to rub her hand over mine.

I nod, not knowing what else to say. They've been married for over forty-five years and have two kids, me and my sister Kylie. And they still like each other.

I used to want that.

Now I don't believe in marriage.

I follow her to the living room, where she hugs Samuel goodbye. I walk her out and head back to watch Elijah play with Samuel for twenty minutes before Samuel yawns.

"Time for bed," I say.

"One more race?" he pleads.

"Yeah, I want to beat him," Elijah argues, as if he's actually been trying to beat him. I know he purposefully has been losing. I never win either, because I love to watch the pure joy on Samuel's face when he beats me. And Elijah is the same.

My resolve falls. I can't seem to say no to Samuel. Because if playing one more round means I'm making him happy, then I'll take it. He deserves a little happiness.

So, we all play one more race before I'm reading a book and tucking Samuel into bed. I sit on the end of his bed until he's sound asleep. He knows I'm there. This is more about me than him. I need him to know I'll always be there for him. Need him to know I'll never leave him. He's never alone.

Being alone sucks.

I return to the living room where Elijah and I watch a basketball game, grateful that Elijah doesn't want to talk too much tonight because I'm wrecked. He leaves after the game, and after checking on Samuel, I head to my room to shower. I remove my suit and step in, welcoming how the water washes the stress from the day. Back-to-back patients and being on call meant a lot of talking and I wouldn't say I'm good at that. It's forced, but I do my best. I don't need to have the best bedside manner to have a long waitlist. I just need to do my job well. And I do. My schedule is jam-packed, and I'm booked out for the next five months.

Going to sleep should be easy tonight. I succeeded in another day of being the best dad I can be and being the best plastic surgeon. So then why is it that when I curl into bed, I can't sleep?

I toss and turn for an hour. My mind drifts to Marigold and then to Alex and our conversation. Back to Marigold and her ass in her jeans, her big, kind smile, genuine laugh, and the sexy flush on her cheeks after I touched her face.

I pinch the bridge of my nose and stifle a groan. I shouldn't be thinking about her. And definitely not imagining what she would sound like under me, which reminds me that I haven't been with a woman...Fuck! I haven't seen a woman naked in over twelve months. I wouldn't even know where to start. That thought alone makes me want to see Marigold.

How would I feel seeing a woman naked again? Would I still be angry and hurt? Or could I actually enjoy myself?

Today, when I touched Marigold, I enjoyed it. However, I can't help but wonder if I would be less myself if it had been someone else. I need to ignore these silly feelings because fuck, I can't go there. It's so fucked up. Like, why am I suddenly thinking about her? I'm having these wayward thoughts, and I don't want to date a woman. I'm simply horny.

Then why am I thinking of her?

Then it clicks...Marigold is familiar, a friend, so it makes sense I would think of her.

I just didn't expect her to stir feelings I haven't felt in a long time.

I glance around my dimly lit bedroom, wondering if Samuel can somehow hear my thoughts. I get out of bed and see that he's still sleeping soundly. Relieved, I walk back to my bedroom and shut the door. There's no way I'm going to sleep without relieving some of the tension. I lie on my mattress and scroll through the web for something to stimulate me. Some sites I stumble upon are cringy and gross and they definitely don't turn me on. The noises and faces of the women look fake. Just like their tits. I want to see a real woman.

I'm embarrassed at myself for doing this, but before I hook up with someone, I want to see if I still work. Near the end of my relationship with Lucy, we stopped bothering. Sex was a chore, not only for her but for me, too. I swear she faked most of her orgasms, but pretended she didn't. So, this is definitely a better way to ease into getting back out there.

I type different words into the search bar. I find a website that looks okay. But I need to sign up.

I groan in defeat. Entering my details, I officially sign up and click around until I find a username that doesn't make me feel creepy.

Finding one called Wild West 25, I click on it and flick through all her pictures and videos that she's already posted on the site.

I can't help but admire her long brown hair with soft highlights and the way it contrasts against her pale skin. One particular image captures my attention. It makes me hard instantly. She's wearing a black glitter mask and a black bodysuit that hugs her in all the right places. I can see she's curvy, yet she has a more athletic build. She has me utterly transfixed and I accidentally hit the like button.

A message pops up, interrupting my runaway thoughts. My eyes widen and I quickly open it.

> **Wildwest25:** *Hi, how are you doing tonight?*

Nervous. Like I wanna fucking vomit. I shake my head. I can't write that. Her message is simple yet polite.

I haven't answered, still feeling guilty about doing this. Here I am, acting like she's asking me on a date. I'm a fucking teenager all over again. I'm considering bailing, but then what? I'll remain in the same space I was in. What if this helps me figure out if I'm ready to be with a woman again?

I'm already here...way past my comfort zone. What's the harm in talking to her? Nothing!

Nothing bad can come from simply messaging her.

Before I can type a message, another one pops up on my screen.

> **Wildwest25:** *Do you want to do a live?*

I stare at the message for a second.
Do I?

> **Wildwest25:** *Would it make you feel more comfortable?*

I think nothing right now could calm the tsunami of nerves in my stomach right now. The last time I felt like this was when Samuel was being born. The whole unknown and lack of control messes with me. I wipe my hand over my perspiring forehead.

She doesn't give me any more time to think because there's a pop up alerting me to the fact she wants me to join her in a live video chat.

I stare at the tempting button, wondering if the woman will be just as sinful. Based on the photos, I'm going to say yes.

My mind flicks between yes and no. Before I decide, fuck it.

She's hot. And if I can get hard from looking at her photo, imagine a video. I will definitely make a mess. But at least I'll walk away with answers.

With nothing else to lose, I hold my breath and I hit...accept.

CHAPTER 4

MARIGOLD

I LET OUT THE breath I was holding the moment his body comes onto my screen.

Finally, a guy is willing to do a live. I thought he was going to decline, and I'd have to accept a dreadful night's pay.

I take him in. He's lying in bed. I assume it's his. A pile of plush white pillows propped behind him. I can't help but notice all the bedding surrounding him is white. The way he's tilting the phone screen, I can only make out from his lips down. He has dark day-old scruff on his jaw. He's wearing a gray t-shirt that he must sleep in, and I can't see lower because his torso is long and takes up the whole camera.

The outline of his stomach and chest make me run hot. There's ab definition on his solid body. The dark hair on his toned free arm makes me think he works out.

"Hi," I say, using a slight accent.

When I turn the camera on, I play a different person. One who doesn't have to do this to pay for college. Instead, I play an older, sexy and desirable woman. Free from money worries. I know my bedroom lights complement the shape of my body. Enhances my features and focuses more on my body and less on my face. Knowing they don't know me makes it easier, and it adds to my self-confidence.

His lips stay thin, and he says nothing back.

"You've never done this before, have you, sir?" I say with a purr of seduction. I don't know if he's a guy who likes names, so I start with the simple "sir" instead of "Daddy" or something that can have him turning off his camera.

"No," he grunts.

And the sound of his voice is deep and sexy, scattering goosebumps all over my skin.

"It's okay. I'll take care of you," I breathe. "Is what I'm wearing pleasing to you?"

I watch his Adam's apple bob as he swallows hard.

"Yes," he replies, his voice thick with desire.

And that causes a flame of heat to take over my body. I love the idea of pleasing a man. And after the way my ex and I broke up, I'm ready to feel needed again.

"Good. What do you want to see?" I say, staring at his image in front of me. Wondering where his head is at.

I expect him to think about it, but he doesn't.

"Your body," he grunts, and it's barely above a whisper.

The heat now hits between my thighs, something that hasn't happened with a client before. This is just for him. I smile into the camera, loving how direct he is, but I can't help but wonder if he's shy. He doesn't speak much, but there's something about him that has me intrigued.

And it makes me playful. "You mean naked?" I ask curiously.

He clears his throat and shuffles on the bed, trying to get comfortable.

"Yes."

He adds nothing else, but taking in his body makes my lip catch between my teeth. Before I can stop myself, the words, "Will you take your shirt off for me?" leave the tip of my tongue.

As soon as they leave my mouth, I don't regret them, even though it could make him log off. Because, technically, he's paying to see me naked. But I desperately want to see what's under that gray top of his. It's already lifted in the corner of his hip since he shuffled around in bed. He's teasing me with his firm, tanned skin.

He doesn't speak. And my heart beats frantically as I curse myself for asking. For sure, I've scared him away, but just as I'm about to apologize, he lowers the phone and lays it on the bed so it's staring up at his white ceiling. I automatically step closer to the camera and soon see his torso on display. I have to swallow a moan because he's just as I suspected...hot.

He has a tanned and toned body with just the right amount of muscle and soft edges. The dark hair on his chest makes my hand curl, wondering what it would feel like under my palms. I've never come on here and met a guy like him. Not that I've been on here long, but I've seen a few to know they're at least double my age. Hairier, rounder, and lonelier, too. So, I wonder why a guy like him would need me. Surely, he wouldn't have trouble finding a woman to please him. I know I haven't seen his full face, but the jawline, lips and nose are causing my stomach to flip.

My gut tells me he's handsome. And it's never wrong.

His chest is rapidly rising and falling. I can't help but pause and take it all in, holding on to this moment.

"You're beautiful," I say with a husky voice. My whole body is overheating now.

He chuckles deeply. The sound is so soothing and real. It's as if he's never heard those words before. And it makes me want him to know it.

I step closer to the camera. "It's true. I haven't seen anyone on here like you before," I explain.

He licks his lips and my sex clenches at the sight. His wet tongue has me dreaming about how good it would feel between my thighs with that scruff adding a roughness to my pussy that I've never felt before. The thought alone causes my pussy to ache. I shuffle on my feet, trying to rub the ache. It won't take me long to orgasm with him tonight.

"That's sad," he mumbles, pulling my thoughts back to the conversation.

"Is it? I'm on here as a cam girl so I can't exactly choose a specific type of look. Can I? It's not a dating app," I say, glancing down at my freshly polished purple toes.

"Yet I'm here." His voice pulls my gaze back up.

"And I'm glad." I stand straighter and pop my chest out. A new rush of arousal hits my core when my hands skim softly over my thighs, all the way up to my shoulders. "Enough about me. Let me give you what you came here for."

I'm watching him intently, and I don't miss the way his lips part as my hand moves to the strap on my left shoulder.

I slip it off, then do the other side before slowly pushing it down to my waist. Exposing my full round breasts. His breathing is now faster and louder.

My nipples pebble into stiff peaks under his gaze.

I reach up and touch both of my breasts and moan. With one in each hand, I alternate in squeezing them. Then roll my nipples between my fingers. I imagine it's his firm hands on me instead of my own.

"I wish these were your hands," I breathe.

"So do I." He grunts.

My head rolls back as I succumb to the euphoria pulsing through me.

"Would you be rough or gentle?" I ask.

"Rough," he rasps straight back.

Knowing he's aroused too makes me wild. I straighten my head, desperate for more. I push the lingerie off my body slowly as I sway my hips sensually. It drops to the floor with a faint thump, and I push it away with my foot. I'm standing completely naked for him. My breathing hitches and I suddenly feel nervous. But instead of showing him nerves, I own my desire.

"Beautiful," he murmurs, but I catch it.

He asked to see a woman, and I'm going to open myself wide for him.

"I'm going to lie down for you and touch myself. You're making me horny." I give the camera a flirty expression.

He exhales heavily.

I move the camera to tilt it toward the bed. I lie myself down on the mattress before checking if the way I'm lying is giving him the best view of me.

I part my legs and he audibly sucks in a sharp breath. "Incredible," he says in a gravelly tone. Heat pools in my already-soaked sex and I suddenly find it hard to swallow. One word and I'm getting more turned on than ever before.

I slide my hand over my stomach and straight to my pussy, but as I touch the top of my mound, he says, "Look at me," his control snapping.

I bite the corner of my lip and bend up on one elbow. I've propped myself up enough to stare into the camera. He adjusts the camera angle. My view of him suddenly increases, allowing me to see more of him. His sloped, crooked nose is now on display, and I can see him wearing navy shorts; I also don't miss the massive bulge he's sporting. But movement catches my eye. His hand slips down and I'm breathless with anticipation, watching his hand slip beneath the waistband of his shorts.

He's going to get off with me and with that knowledge, I skim my fingers over my body until they touch my clit. I rub circles around the swollen, achy nub. The pressure has me gasping loudly and arching my back for more. His hand moves rapidly as he gets himself off. I assume it's all for me and that is incredibly hot. I lower my fingers through my wet pussy and when they hit my hole, I hum in pleasure. My knees cave in.

"Open wider," he gruffs out.

Spreading my feet wider earns me a deep sensual growl, and my pussy tingles from the sound.

My fingers move faster.

"Show me how hard you are," I beg.

His hand ceases moving, and I'm worried this is the end.

"I just want to see what seeing my body did to you," I explain. I'm hoping with a little honesty it might get his walls to come down.

Unexpectedly, he tilts the camera. I can see his hand inside his shorts but not his dick. He shuffles the shorts down so I can see his fingers wrapped around his thick cock.

"Yes," I breathe out as my fingers move faster in my pussy. The sight of his slick precum leaking on the tip of his erection causes my tongue to slide over my bottom lip. I keep fingering as I stare at him, transfixed. He's slowly stroking himself. The muscles in his arms flex as he squeezes hard, and imagine it's me doing it for him. As if he can hear my thoughts he begins pumping his cock.

Heat spreads over my lower back. I'm trying to keep my legs open as I chase my orgasm.

"Tell me you're close," I whisper. "I want to come with you."

He pumps his dick faster, and the grunts out of his mouth are too much to bear. But thankfully, after a few more strokes, he rasps out, "Fuck. I'm coming."

My head tilts back and my legs quiver intensely as my orgasm takes over.

I ride the wave until I'm utterly spent. That was the best orgasm I've ever had. What a shame it was through a camera. I shiver at the thought of his cock pumping hard into me until I shatter around it. Imagine...

As my mind and body calm, I suck deep breaths, trying to settle my beating heart. Then I peel my eyes open and sit up on the edge of the bed. He covered his tanned abdomen in his mess. His cum gleams all over himself, and hell, if I thought he was hot before, he's sweltering now.

He's going to want to clean up, so I have little time to talk to him...

"Did you enjoy yourself tonight?" I ask with a cheeky grin.

"Yes. Thank you. You were perfect," he says in a deep voice.

I get full-blown butterflies from hearing those words.

My cheeks flush and I plead, "Please show me your face. I want to see the only man that has made me come that hard."

I bite down on my full bottom lip as anticipation turns to surprise when he tilts the camera to show me his face. Before he quickly turns his camera off.

I blink rapidly, thinking I'm dreaming.

But I'm not.

My dream is real. Because the guy on the other side of the camera was Damien Gray, my brother's best friend.

Chapter 5

Marigold

After a couple of minutes, I get a notification on my phone from the app. My heart rate picks up as I quickly open it. I see it's from *grays_online* which is Damien's username, and I nibble on my lip as I read his message.

> **Damien:** *You are beautiful. Thank you.*

I stare stupidly at my phone with a giddy smile. I knew he was sweet, but those words turn me to mush.

It should disgust me. I just orgasmed in front of my brother's best friend...who's thirty-eight.

Thirteen years older, to be exact.

But I'm not.

The quiet, intriguing guy ended up being him. Surprised is an understatement of how I'm feeling inside right now. As I sit on my bed in shock, I drop my phone on my bed and put my face in my hands, shaking my head.

The memory of his body flashes in front of my eyes. He's broad, athletic, and masculine.

I need to write something back. After taking a moment to collect myself, I sit back up and grab my phone to type out a response.

> **Wildwest25:** *Thanks! And you're very hot. :)*

I shouldn't be encouraging this, but I can't help myself. There's something about him that has me being completely honest. If he was in front of me right now, I couldn't say it. I like the fact I can hide behind the mask and my phone. It allows me to speak freely.

I've been fantasizing about him for a long time, so finally seeing him naked in all his glory was a dream come true.

A message alert tone breaks my trance.

> **Damien:** *Can we do this again tomorrow night?*

All rational thought escapes. I grin stupidly as I type back.

> **Wildwest25:** *Bit keen, are we?*

He responds instantly.

> **Damien:** *You have no idea.*

> **Wildwest25:** *For me, only, I hope?*

> **Damien:** *Only you.*

I stare at those two words. Simple yet powerful. Should I confess it's me?

If I do, will this arrangement end? Because I don't want it to.

I decide to keep it to myself for a little longer.

> **Wildwest25:** *Am I corrupting you?*

Damien: Yes. If I'm being honest, I never thought I'd want to talk or see a woman again. I was burnt in the past. Yet. Somehow, you make me change my mind. There's something about you.

Wildwest25: I'm glad I can be the one to show you not all women are bad.

Damien: Oh, you're definitely bad. But in the best way.

Wildwest25: I'm an angel.

Damien: You definitely are. Although I don't want to go, I need to take a shower. I know what I want for tomorrow's video. I'll send it to you now.

I scrunch up my nose, wondering what it could be. Luckily, I don't have to wait very long because I get a new message explaining exactly what he wants.

I open the message and my mouth drops at the elegant and sexy see-through, expensive lingerie and fuck. A toy...

I message back quickly.

Wildwest25: I love them.

> *Damien: I'll send you the money for them now so you can buy them. I can't wait to see them on you. Night.*

I can't argue about him buying them because the 199-dollar set is way out of my budget.

I stare at the messages. I wonder what to do. My mind is reeling.

I text Clara and beg her to come over and debrief. While I wait, I distract myself by showering. An hour later, I usher her inside my guest house.

"You're sure it's him?" Clara, my best friend of ten years, says.

She sits down beside me on my sofa. I lie back with my hands covering my face.

"I saw his cock, for fuck's sake."

She laughs so hard it turns into a snort. "Hopefully it was worth it. Tell me it was. Please."

I stay silent a moment too long, thinking just how perfect he was.

"It was. You fucking liked it." She slaps my upper arm.

I drop my hands beside me and tilt to face her, frowning. "Ouch. What'd you do that for?"

"Sorry. I'm excited," she exclaims.

"Why?" I ask, sitting up.

"This is so interesting. Did he know it was you?"

I shake my head. "No. I'm lucky that I wear a mask as part of the outfit," I say, as I walk over to the mask I was wearing.

She follows and takes it from me and touches it.

"You say it's good money?" she says while deliberating it.

"Mmm," I hum, wondering where she's going with this.

"I think I might join. I'm struggling with cash right now. Bills are getting higher and God, the gas is shocking." She drops the mask back in my drawer and stands back.

"Yeah, you're telling me." I wander over to my sofa, sitting down again. "If you sign up, make sure you tell me how it goes."

"I'm sure my story wouldn't be as juicy as yours." She raises her brows at me.

It sure is something else...just like him.

I keep that to myself.

"I reckon."

"What're you going to do about it?" she asks.

The million-dollar question.

"No idea. And of course, he wants to chat again tomorrow night."
I rub my eyes.

"Yeah?" She looks at me brightly.

"He requested a turquoise set and a toy." A hint of a smile lifts on
the side of my lip as I remember how stunning it was. I'm excited to
try it on but nervous to show him. I hope I live up to what he expects
it to look like.

I show her my phone with the picture of the items. "You have to
buy that?" she asks, grabbing my phone to inspect.

"It's the good stuff from Honey Birdette, but he's buying it. He
transferred the money before you came," I explain.

She hands over my phone. "Why didn't he buy them and ship them
to you?"

"I didn't want to give him my address."

"Oh yeah, duh!"

I smile at her. I'm glad I can guide her if she wants to do this. At least
I can keep her safe and talk stuff out with her. It would be more than
what I had. Mine was researching online and a lot of trial and error.

"So, how do you plan to stay anonymous?" she asks.

"I'll wear the mask and if he hasn't recognized my voice by now, I'm
safe. Luckily, he's quiet, so we don't speak too much."

She looks at me, puzzled. "That's odd."

I shrug. "Not really. I feel strangely at peace with him other than
also being extremely turned on." As I openly admit that, I feel a flush
hit my cheeks.

"Isn't that part of why you're online?"

"Unfortunately, most guys who come on are not like him. They're
definitely not as hot. Don't get your hopes up. It's a job. But tonight,
well, that was a surprise."

"This is so interesting. How long will you play this out?"

A deep breath escapes me. "I don't know. I just want to get to know
him."

Her eyes narrow. "I know that look." She waves her finger around
my face with a humorous expression.

"What?" I ask, not understanding what she's seeing on my face
other than a flush from talking about him.

"Don't go falling in love with him."

I grimace. "Not happening. He has a kid and an ex-wife, remember? Oh, and add to the fact my brother will kill me when he finds out."

She narrows her eyes at me. "I know, but I also know you."

I tilt my head, not understanding. I wait for her to finish.

"You fall in love too easily."

"Pfft," I say, waving her off, "I do not."

"Yes. You. Do."

As I think about my past boyfriends, I can't help but bite the side of my cheek and dissect how every single one of them left me hurt. I loved them more than they loved me. Take my ex, for instance. Our relationship lasted for two years. I fell head over heels in love with him. Looking back, I realize I loved him more than he loved me. I would constantly message and call him. Try to make plans with him. All he wanted was his friends and to party. He cheated on me with a co-worker because he said I was too vanilla.

I'm not so vanilla now.

I sigh, defeatedly. I can't argue. All I can say is, "I won't fall in love with him. I promise."

She dips her chin. "Good because you have too much to lose, and I don't want my best friend in pieces again."

I smile at her kind words.

I lean forward to wrap my arms around her and hug her. Her arms reach around my back and hug me back harder.

At this moment, I wish I could find someone dependable, like my best friend.

The next day, when I return home from school, I see a package on the counter in my parents' house. I look and it's addressed to me. I grab it and carry it to the guest house with a spring in my step, knowing it's the stuff I ordered.

Inside my room, I rip open the package and examine my purchases. I also see they added some free chocolate sauce.

My face drops in surprise.

Seems Damien is going to be in for some fun tonight. I'm giddier seeing this stuff in person and I can't wait to try on the lingerie.

I snap a picture and send it to him through the app. Along with a message.

Wildwest25: Look what arrived.

He doesn't respond straight away. So, I go about getting ready for later and then study.

I'm reading a case at my desk as my phone sounds.

I pick it up and see a notification from the app. I open it and read the message.

> **Damien:** *Chocolate sauce?*

> **Wildwest25:** *Damn it. I forgot about leaving that as a surprise. Bad luck now.*

> **Damien:** *I'll tell you a secret about myself. I don't like mess. Like at all.*

> **Wildwest25:** *I'll get really messy then.*

> **Damien:** *Wish I could lick you clean.*

I shiver from reading those words. What would it be like to have him licking my body?

I force myself not to think too long about it and type back.

> **Wildwest25:** *I wish too…*

> **Damien:** Same time tonight?

> **Wildwest25:** Yes. I've got studying to do.

> **Damien:** Good girl. Study hard, and I'll see your pretty face later.

I nibble on my lip as I think about being his good girl. And how that would sound coming from his lips.

I refocus on my case.

The next few hours pass and when it's finally time to dress and get ready, I become a little nervous. But I ignore the nerves and finish dressing.

Butterflies fill my stomach as I wait for him to come online.

When the green light flicks on, letting me know he is, in fact, on, I shift on my bed, getting the angle just right.

> **Damien:** Are you ready?

I adjust my mask and take a big steadying breath. I send him an invitation to join my live as an answer.

"Hi," I breathe. My playful voice is in full force.

"Hi," he darkly replies.

My body tingles in response to him. He's topless tonight. Again, only from the nose down to the top of a black waistband. His five-o'clock shadow comes through and how I'd love to feel it against my face.

His toned abdomen contracts from the way he's sitting tonight.

I imagine his gaze running over me. Admiring what he bought me. I stand and turn slowly. My hands touching my thighs and hips to settle on my waist.

"What do you think?" I ask in a sultry voice.

I feel sexy in the satin fabric. The way it pushes my breasts up and compliments my skin. I can imagine him growing hard from just looking at me.

"Beautiful."

My lips part into an open smile.

"It would be a shame to ruin it." I skim my hands over my hips again and then down across my stomach, pausing on my outer thighs. "But then I don't want to take it off."

I bring my finger to my lip and tap. Deliberating it.

"Take it off." The strain in his voice tells me he's affected by me.

"Already?" I ask teasingly.

"Actually, no. Get on the bed and on your hands and knees. Ass in the air and face me," he orders gruffly.

It sends a thrill through me as I take a breath to calm my excitement and strut to the bed, purposefully pushing my hips out. When I'm in front of my made bed, I follow his instructions. I keep my knees closed just to get him to order me around.

I usually take charge in my lives, but with him, I'm living out my fantasy and letting him give out the orders.

"No. Part your knees. Wide."

I do, and he groans with appreciation.

"Perfect. Now reach between those pretty thighs and tell me if you're wet."

I slide my hand over my stomach slowly and then slip my hand under the waistband of my thong. My fingers hit my warm, wet pussy.

I mumble incoherently.

"I want to see. Bring your hands out so I can see how wet you are for me."

I do it, and it earns me another loud groan.

I decide I can't be the only one getting hot right now. I want to make him equally horny, so I take over.

I sit back on my heels, reach around, and remove my bra with one swift motion. Then I scoot off the bed, slip my thong off, and stand in just black stilettos before I grab the chocolate sauce.

"Dirty girl," he rasps.

"So dirty," I whisper as I look into the camera and pour sauce over my tits until it drips down over my body, and I smear it everywhere.

I make the biggest mess I can.

"Fuck." He barks.

I bring my fingers to my mouth and suck hard.

"Look at me as you do that."

My eyes flutter open, and I stare at him through the camera. I move my fingers in and out and I know he's picturing me sucking his cock like this. I grunt and hollow out my cheeks with every stroke and suck. Everything with a purpose to bring him closer to climaxing. Because I bet if I put my fingers back on my pussy, I'd find myself dripping.

"I'm all messy. I wish you were here to help clean it up, sir."

"Me too," he mutters.

I grab the pink vibrating dildo from my bedside table. It's soft to touch and close to lifelike with all the ridges.

I spread my legs. My eyes are closed as I bring the toy to my wet pussy. The vibrations make me moan.

"Show me," he says.

I grab a chair and lower the camera down so that I can lift a leg and let him see what he's so clearly desperate to see.

"Better?" I ask.

"Much. Now fuck that toy as if it was my cock."

Who knew Damien had this dirty mouth?

Not me, that's for sure. But I enjoy knowing this secret side of him. As if it's something special that only I know about.

"I'd much prefer it was you," I say, pouting.

As the words leave my lips, I'm shocked at how much those words ring true. It's not like I haven't had similar words spoken to me, and every time bile rises to my throat and I have to fake every word. But with him, I don't feel repulsed.

I feel turned on.

What's happening to me?

I close my eyes and imagine the toy is him and the hum through my body takes over. I glide the toy in and out slowly. Then I pull the toy out to slide it over my clit before easing it back inside me.

The heat in my lower back quickly becomes unbearable and I know that I'm climbing.

My legs quake. "I'm close."

I peel my eyes open and look straight into the camera and I'm pleasantly surprised to find his eyes boring intensely into the camera. Dark, broody and so much heat.

Yep. I will not last with him looking at me like that. Why him? What's so different about him? Even though I know I shouldn't, I am attracted to him, and it will end in disaster. I can't help it; I'm like a moth to a flame.

I don't close my eyes because I want to keep the image of his face as I come.

I pick up the pace. I fuck the toy with his eyes on me and before I know it, I'm coming.

"Fuck, you're incredible." He grunts.

I lick my lips and remove the toy before standing up.

"Seems you have good taste in lingerie and toys."

"I'll have to buy you more. So much more."

The idea has me smiling.

If that's what I'll feel like if he does, I can't say no.

I know Damien has money, so I don't feel guilty. Well, not for that. The only guilt I feel is about me hiding my identity when I know him. But he'll end this when he finds out, and I don't want him to.

"What are you thinking?" I ask.

"Red and a—"

He's cut off by a knock and a faint voice. "Dad, why's the door locked?"

I know it's Samuel, but before he can speak, the screen goes black and I'm blinking at a blank screen.

I think Samuel just interrupted us.

Shit. That was close. A little too close.

CHAPTER 6

DAMIEN

I ADJUST MY ERECTION back into my sweats. Another one for the day if you count waking up hard this morning. I rub my face roughly with my hands as I get off my bed, quickly unlocking my bedroom door. Grateful, I added a lock today.

Samuel walking in to see his father masturbating would scar the poor kid.

I'm still worked up by seeing her fucking herself with the dildo, so I take a deep breath before I open the door to find Samuel screwing up his sleepy face.

"Hey, what are you doing up?" I ask.

"I had a bad dream," he mumbles, looking up at me with glossy eyes.

I rub his head and then pick him up.

"Let me sit on your bed until you fall asleep again."

He nods, but his head lowers to my shoulder. I grip him. And it's moments like these that remind me I shouldn't think about myself or a woman. I should remain focused on being there for him.

I carry him down to his room, lower him onto his bed, and tuck him in.

"You'll stay here until I fall asleep?" Samuel asks with a wobble in his voice.

"I promise." I squeeze his hand.

Samuel nudges his head into the pillow, getting back to sleep. I take a seat at the end of his bed and drop my head in my hands.

And for the next ten minutes, all I see is her.

She won't leave my brain. What is it about her that has me wanting more? I know it's more than just seeing her naked. Even if that's why I was on the app. In fact, she has the sweetest pussy I've ever seen. But if that was all it was, I wouldn't be constantly thinking about her. She's consuming every spare moment. Even now at work, I daydream about a woman with rosy lips and a mask. Which is rather odd to me. I haven't dreamt about a woman in many years.

I sit up and look across at Samuel, who's fast asleep again. Getting up, I kiss his forehead and make my way to my room. I spot my phone on my bed and I immediately pick it up. There's a message notification on the app. It's her...

> **Wildwest25:** *Is everything okay?*

Reading that message makes me tense. I hate how she thought she did something when it's all me. I need to make her feel better, so I respond.

> **Damien:** *Yes, perfect.*

I stare at my phone, thinking it wasn't enough. What should I say? I'm a single dad?

I shake my head. No, I can't say that. I don't know her enough to share that piece of information about myself. This is only about satisfying my needs, and I did that. So what am I doing?

> **Wildwest25:** *Did you want to see me again?*

I should say no...

> **Damien:** *Yes.*

I'm so screwed over this woman I barely know. Why couldn't I type the word no? I can say the word just fine usually, but I can't with her.

> **Wildwest25:** *I have a late-night class tomorrow, but I could do it the following?*

I check my work schedule and see that I'm on call.

> **Damien:** *It should be good. I'm on call, so if I bail, don't think it's because I don't want to see you!*

> **Wildwest25:** *What do you do?*

To make her feel at ease and trust I really am on call, I'll answer. She won't know exactly what type of doctor I am, and there's plenty in the state that I won't get found out.

> **Damien:** *I'm a doctor.*

> **Wildwest25:** *Wow, impressive :)*

> **Damien:** *Yeah, it's pretty cool.*

My job is one thing I'm proud of. I love it. Other than Samuel, it fulfills something in me. Maybe it's the helper in me. Which I've never admitted out loud.

> **Wildwest25:** *I better shower. I'm a sticky mess.*

The chocolate sauce smeared over her sexy body. She's still covered in it, and yet, it doesn't repulse me or make me overwhelmed. No, I was harder than I've ever been in my life.

> **Damien:** You're making me change my mind about messes.

> **Wildwest25:** Am I?

> **Damien:** Only if it involves you.

> **Wildwest25:** I'll hold you to that. :)

> **Damien:** Night.

I exit the app and take a shower, where I jerk off until I come. If I don't, there's no way I'd be sleeping tonight.

Thursday night arrives, and I've put Samuel to bed. I'm reclining in my bed with one of my arms folded behind my head.

I don't bother switching the TV on because I know she'll be waiting for me. I've never had a woman wait for me so...eagerly. And God, to have such a beautiful one actually look forward to pleasing me is unfathomable.

However, I get it. I am paying her so that could be a good enough reason for her to be on before me. I've paid for all of her time. So, she doesn't need to have any other clients. I made the payment above the usual requirement. And I tip well for her services. Not just sexual services, which she is fulfilling. But for the ones I never imagined I'd like. The comfortable nature I've found myself in around her is worth every cent. It feels like this is more than money. Dumb, I know. But there's something I can't quite put my finger on that seems so familiar about her.

I close my eyes briefly as she comes onto the screen and my heart races.

"Hi," she says quickly, beating me to talk. "No callout?"

I shake my head, my body agreeing with my head that it's not ready for me to be called in. "Hi. Not yet."

If I do get one, I have to drop Samuel off at Mom's on my way. Or she'll come here. It all depends on the hour and the callout.

"That's good." Her pink lips part into a seductive smile.

"It is," I mutter, trying to keep my mind from picturing those lips wrapped around my cock.

"Have you had a good day so far?" she asks in a way that makes me believe she genuinely wants to know and isn't just asking to be polite.

Not wanting to discuss Samuel still, I stick to everything else.

"Yeah, gym, paperwork and emails. Riveting." A deep chuckle rumbles from my chest. Even to my own ears, that sounds depressing, but I can't explain any further.

I dropped off and picked Samuel up, too. But I obviously don't tell her that.

"Always working."

Isn't that the truth...

"Yep. How about you?" I ask, wanting to know what she's done all day. This is probably unusual, but I don't want to dive into sexual activities straight away. Don't get me wrong, I'm damn excited to see her delicious body again, but I also just want to talk for a minute or two. I want to savor these moments that normally give me the ick in real life.

"I had college all day, and I went to the gym too."

I shuffle in bed, working to get more comfortable. "What do you like to train?"

"Weight training or attend a Pilates class."

"Not only smart, but you work out. You're my weakness."

"I'm sorry." She hums with a mischievous look.

"Are you?"

"No, because you're becoming my weakness. Talking to you has made my week."

"What happened?" I ask. Her tone is suddenly familiar, but I can't put my finger on it.

She hesitates, adjusting the mask on her face.

"Tell me," I encourage her. But it comes out as a command, and I can't help but feel relief when she spills. "I'm drowning in college debt. Hence why I'm on here." Her gaze drops from the camera.

"You wouldn't do this if you didn't have the debt?" I ask.

Her head lifts to stare into the camera to answer. "No, but I have it, and this job pays well. Well, better than any other job I could get. I don't have a lot of free time to work after my classes and studying, so this works well."

I grunt, and we fall silent. But not for long. Her mouth twists and I know we're done discussing heavy life topics for tonight.

There's a new, determined sparkle in her eye as she asks, "Do you like what I'm wearing?" She steps back so I can view her whole body through the camera. She's wearing a mask with lace and a nightdress to match. The dress has see-through pieces on the sides of her body. I love how she wears heels, even with lingerie. She can wear gym shoes by day and heels at night. The woman is becoming my weak spot or my newest addiction. I was already hard at the sight of her. Now it's damn painful.

"Yes. But I can't see much of your body," I say.

Her hands skim her hips and she bunches it to the side. "You want this off?" she asks, but it's not really a question because she's lifting it over her head, exposing her naked body.

"Fuck." I growl. "Get on the bed."

She turns and her full round ass sashays to the bed and she bends so her ass is in the air.

"I'd give anything to fuck you from behind."

Her head lifts over her shoulder, batting her eyelashes at me. She pauses in that position, allowing me to take in every little detail. I know she's teasing me because it's written all over her face.

"You enjoying pleasing me?" I grab my dick tightly in my hand and work it over.

"I want you," she breathes as she wiggles her hips and then rolls onto her back and opens her legs.

The words *I want you too* are stuck in my throat with air. I'm struggling to breathe.

"Are you always this wet?" I ask in a rasp, working my dick harder and faster.

She peers down and then looks bashfully up into the camera. "Never. It seems only for you."

Those words are my undoing; my balls draw up, and when her knees cave in, I can't see her sweet pussy as clear.

"Spread wider. I need to see you wet and swollen for me." She follows my order with a groan. "Good girl." I praise, my dick throbbing. "Now touch those pretty tits."

Her hand reaches up, and she touches her breast. And man, do I wish I could feel how amazing they are. They look gorgeous. The right amount to play with. She moves her fingers to her nipples and tweaks them. She whimpers at the same time her hips move up. It's as if she needs more. Her eyes stay on mine through the camera.

"You need to fuck, don't you?"

"Ye...yesss," she stammers.

"Bring your fingers to that swollen pussy and rub your clit."

She follows my instructions and I'm lost in the way she tips her head back and moans as she pleasures herself. I watch every rub as if it's important to know just how she likes it.

I keep stroking my cock, chasing my climax. "Put your fi—" I'm cut off by my phone ringing. "Fuck." I bark and thrust my hand through my hair. "It's work." I close my eyes and count to ten. I need to answer the call without sounding like I'm coming down from an almost explosive orgasm.

"It's okay, get it." She pants.

I want to say, *It's not okay. I want to watch you come so hard that I come too and make a mess of myself.* But I grumble, "I'll talk to you soon. I'm sorry."

I hang up with a heavy sigh, taking one last look at her lying there with her legs spread wide and her fingers on her clit.

I exit the app and drag my hand over my face as I answer the call.

I've been called into the hospital, so I quickly shower. Afterwards, I find a notification from the app. I open to see she's messaged. But this time, it's not just a typed message. There's a video message attached.

> **Wildwest25:** *I recorded myself coming for you. Watch me later (kiss emoji). Have fun at work.*

CHAPTER 7

MARIGOLD

WHILE OTHER TWENTY-FIVE-YEAR-OLDS ARE getting ready to party on a Friday night, I'm here drowning in my studies. There's a pile of textbooks and papers scattered in my living room. I'm deep into reading about a case containing gray-area ethical issues when my phone rings.

I smile, reading Clara's name. "Hey—"

She cuts me off with her panicked voice. "Please come. I've somehow flooded the rental."

I stand and look around for my bag and keys.

"Alright, I'll be there in five."

I hang up and before I leave, I grab a bucket and my emergency tool kit and as many towels that I have in my linen closet.

I drive to hers and dash to her door. I don't have a spare hand to knock, but she must've been waiting for me because the door opens as soon as I hit the top stair.

"Thank god you're here." She exhales and grabs some towels from my hands.

"What happened?"

"I decided to do some laundry, and it's leaking water, and I can't get it to stop."

"Did you turn the water off at the main?"

Clara looks at me, confused. "Did I do what?"

"Don't worry. You put the towels down and I'll turn it off," I instruct in a calm, confident voice.

Clara doesn't get frazzled easily, so in times like these, I take over.

"Okay." She walks off in the direction of the laundry room and I head to turn the water off.

Afterwards, I meet her in front of the washing machine and roll up my sleeve, cursing myself I didn't choose a short-sleeve shirt. I have my leggings on at least.

Clara's trying to mop up the water that's pouring out from under the machine still. It should stop soon, though, because the mains are off.

"Can you help me move the washing machine?"

"Yeah, but...do you know what you're doing?"

"You called me, remember? I'll take a look and see if I can find the culprit. If not, I'll call someone to help."

"I can't afford to. Neither can you."

I can use the money I made from Mysterious Fan this week. My student loans can wait. My friend is more important.

"I've got it, don't worry. Let's see if I can work it out first. Let's worry about money if we need to."

She steps over to the other side of the washing machine. And we zigzag, pulling each side until it's away from the wall.

The problem is obvious, and I can't help the bubble of laughter pouring out of my mouth. My elbows lean on the top of the machine as I stare at the hose on the floor.

"What?" Clara asks.

I point to the wall. "Have a look and tell me if you can spot the problem. I bet you do."

She peers down and then softly shakes her head as she straightens. "Are you kidding me?"

I roll my lips together, trying to hold back from laughing hysterically. This was a nice distraction from the hours of studying and assignments I've been doing. Even though I still have hours more.

"At least we can fix that. For free."

"Except my dignity. I don't even know how the stupid thing fell out of the wall."

"I'll put it back and secure it, so it never happens again."

"You're a lifesaver. I'm sorry to pull you away from your studies. I owe you."

"Clara, shut up. We're friends. I'm here anytime you need me. Let me fix this and clean up. How about you give me one of your cookies you make, and we'll call it even?"

"I wouldn't say that's even but deal. And don't clean up. I can order us dinner and I can do it later."

"I'd normally say yes, but I have an assignment to hand in tomorrow."

She heads to the kitchen, and I go about fixing the pipe. Ignoring how wet my socks are from all the water. I really should've changed, but I didn't think about it when she called me. I fix the hose and add tape around it to secure it.

We clean up the floor of the laundry room and she insists on washing my towels and returning them clean and dry. I don't argue, because by the stress on her face, I know she wants to do this as a repayment. And truthfully, I'd be the same if I were her.

I turn the water back on and while we wait and test the towels in a wash cycle, she hands me a bag of her freshly baked chocolate chip cookies.

After a few more minutes, I speak. "It all looks to be working. I'll go now, but if something happens, call me and I'll come back."

"Thanks. I do hope I don't have to call. Hopefully, one of my roommates will be home soon, so they can help."

"I don't mind. Call me if you need me."

I leave her house after a hug on her steps, and with my bag of cookies, I trek to my car in soaked socks and shoes.

As soon as I reach my house, I put my shoes outside to dry and take a shower.

After a warm shower, I feel clean and refreshed. Ready to sit back down in my living room and continue studying. I take a bite of a cookie and read over the last paragraph I was on before I left.

Time passes, and before I know it, I've eaten three.

My phone chimes with a message. I see it's from the app. I shouldn't check it because I need to hand this assignment in tomorrow and I'm already going to be up all night.

But I need to know if it's him...

It'll be quick and I will return to my studies.

He's on a late shift at work. I know because my brother told me.

I open it.

Damien: *What do you do on a Friday night?*

Wildwest25: *Not what other people my age do. No partying here.*

I take a picture of my living room and send it with the message attached.

Damien: *I remember those days. Long nights. Red Bull and sugary foods.*

Wildwest25: *It sucks. I can't wait to work.*

Damien: *Your drive is alluring.*

Wildwest25: *You mean boring?*

Damien: *No. I find you anything but boring.*

Wildwest25: *:) What's a word you would use to describe me?*

Damien: *Addictive.*

Wildwest25: *Don't hold back now…*

I type it out as a joke. Thinking he would give me more. I want to hear him call me beautiful again. This is so dangerous. What is going to happen when he finds out it's me?

When I wait but he doesn't text back, I return to my assignment. I haven't got much more to do when I finally get a new message.

Of course, I have zero restraint and I need to read it. I pick up my phone and open it at lightning speed.

> **Damien:** *Beautiful. Intelligent. Just to name a few.*

> **Wildwest25:** *Thanks :) And just so you know, I feel the same about you!*

> **Damien:** *Have you finished your assignment yet?*

> **Wildwest25:** *Just about. Maybe a paragraph left.*

> **Damien:** *Finish it now and message me when you're going to sleep. You need sleep.*

> **Wildwest25:** *Bossy, aren't you?*

> **Damien:** *You have no idea...*

Wildwest25: *I'd have to argue with you and say you have bossed me around once before ;) and I liked it. I liked it a lot.*

Damien: *That's because you're a good girl. Now go to bed.*

Chapter 8

Damien

I PULL UP TO Elijah's new house for his afternoon barbecue. Walking up the path, I know I'm walking into a house full of adults. Out of all my friends, I'm the only person with a kid, other than my friends from work, Mike and Alex, who have babies. I feel out of place and like the odd man out. But mainly, I feel sorry for Samuel as he has no one to play with. He's a good sport though and I always give him the option not to come, but he says he wants to.

My friend's shower Samuel with love, but it's not the same. It's not like I'll be having another kid, so he's going to be an only child. Which makes me sad for him. Growing up with my sister, Kylie, was definitely a highlight of my childhood. I think of all the laughs, pranks, and fights we shared. The love you share with a sibling is special, and I know Samuel won't get that. Which is why I need to be the best dad I can. Shower him with all the love so he won't feel like he's missing out. Not just on a sibling, but a mother, too.

Samuel presses the doorbell and I open the door, knowing they're all probably out back with music playing. They are probably out enjoying the weather since it's a sunny day.

The door opens and I step back.

"Hi!" Samuel says to Marigold.

Her eyes are wide as she holds the door open. Her eyes flick between me and Samuel. It's as if she didn't expect us.

"Hi, Marigold," I say.

"Ah. Hi," she says and clears her throat. "Come in, everyone's out back." She steps to the side, pulling the wooden door wider, and Samuel enters the house, pulling me along behind him.

I look straight ahead, spotting a backyard full of people standing around clutching beers and talking and laughing. The door closes behind us, but I continue walking farther inside, following Samuel.

"Hey! Glad you could come," Elijah calls out. He walks into his house to meet us.

"Of course. Congratulations. Nice house," I say, looking around at the white walls and spotless furniture; the kind of furniture you have when you don't have kids.

"Let me take you on a tour," Elijah adds.

I nod. Samuel and I follow him as he walks around explaining the house. Outside, I stop and say a quick hello before we finish the tour and return to his kitchen.

"Samuel, did you want your iPad and toys set up in the living room?" I ask.

"I can put a movie on for you," Elijah says.

"Can I play Nintendo?" Samuel pleads, looking up at Elijah with bright, hopeful eyes. Elijah bought one for his old house when he knew it kept Samuel happy and entertained. Allowing me to hang out with him and not miss out on boys' catch-ups.

"Samuel, just settle down for a second. We just walked in," I say, embarrassed at how excited Samuel is.

"Of course, I can set that up for you, little man," Elijah says with a grin.

I love how my son can make so many of the quiet and big men of this place turn to jelly. There's something about kids that brings us to our knees.

"Did you want to eat first?" I ask.

"Mmm. I am a little hungry," he mumbles, as his eyes look over at the food spread out on the table.

"Let's get you something to eat and drink then," I say and move to the table. I grab a plate as Samuel tells me the food he wants to eat. He knows it's a party, so he can eat whatever he wants. So, to my horror, it's all greasy or packet food. But I hold my tongue and let him go. It's a once-off. We don't attend many parties, so I want him to be comfortable, even if that includes a sugar high.

"You eat and I'll set up Nintendo and you can play after you eat. Sound good?" Elijah asks Samuel.

Samuel nods his head vehemently.

We sit down and eat. After we're done, I clean up and take him to Elijah's living room. I settle him in, surrounded with toys and games, before it's my turn to relax. I head to the fridge to grab a drink when I see Marigold already grabbing one.

"Can you grab me a beer?" I ask.

She jumps and spins around to look at me.

"You snuck up on me," she breathes, holding her hand on her chest. She dips her head and leans forward in her yellow sundress, her cleavage practically eyeballing me. I dart my eyes away. Suddenly feeling uncomfortable. I shouldn't be looking at her breasts, despite them being a good handful and spilling out of her dress at this angle.

She stands and I can't help but notice she looks different.

More dressed up?

More makeup maybe?

But I guess it's a party. I shake it off and take the beer. "Thanks." I remove the cap, cheer the air, and walk off.

"You're welcome," she says cheerily behind me.

"Glad you and Samuel could make it," Elijah says as I walk outside to join him and his friend, Jeremy. There's another group swimming in the pool. I lift my beer in a hi. They wave back. I've known them all for years now. Any time Elijah has a boys' night or catches up, it's with the same people.

"Thanks for having us," I say as I take a sip of my drink.

He elbows me, and I fold forward, wincing. "Where've you been?"

"Working." I groan back.

"I don't believe you. You're hiding something," he accuses with a significant lifting of his brows.

I know he can't read anything on my face. I'm stone. He's just trying to poke me.

"There's nothing to tell."

"I have a friend of Jackie's—"

"Not happening," I cut him off. "You and I don't have the same taste."

Jeremy chuckles beside us. "I have to agree with Damien."

I quirk my eyebrow at Elijah. "See."

"You two suck. I'll be back and we'll continue this conversation, but I need to grab more meat to cook up." Elijah strides off into the house.

Jeremy faces the barbeque and I stare out into the backyard, watching the game of volleyball in the pool. My shoulders drop away from my ears the second Elijah walks away. The way Elijah stared at me; it was as if he knows I'm holding something back.

Which is impossible. I won't say anything. My online life is for me and my masked friend. I also know I'd be the laughingstock of the group if I explained my little crush on an online girl. Hell, I'm paying for her time and for her sweet words. Yet...I can't help the stupid way I wish for a beautiful and confident woman to want me and my son.

"Are you getting ready to move?" I ask Jeremy.

He's tall, dark, and successful. I'm sure Elijah doesn't know how to hang out with anyone who isn't a minimum seven-figure salary earner.

"I've had the house in New York the whole time, but my Grams is sick."

I nod, totally understanding. The thought of losing my mom is unbearable. I'm so grateful for her. And it's not just me. Samuel only has her as a woman's role model. I don't want that taken away from him. My mom is teaching him motherly things like washing, cooking, and saving. It's what she taught me growing up.

"I'd do the same. Is she terminal?" I take a sip of the beer.

"No, but I just want to be around my family now with her diagnosis."

"Fair enough," I reply.

We both sip our drinks.

"What did I miss?" Elijah's voice cuts in. He's carrying a tray of meat.

"Do you need to cook all that? Are you expecting more people?"

I was hoping to keep it less like a party with Samuel here. If it gets out of control, I'll leave.

"No. Everyone's here, but the meats are almost gone."

"I'll cook it," Jeremy says, taking the tray from Elijah's hands.

We're standing under the shade near the barbeque.

Jackie slides up beside Elijah, her hand coming around his waist to snuggle in. I swallow a whine because PDA makes me sick. But for some stupid reason, I can't stop watching. He looks down at her. A softness takes over his face as he stares down at her. Jackie stares longingly back, her head tilted up at him.

Jackie's not what you'd expect from Elijah. She's not a Barbie doll, or a self-centered woman, or a seven-figure boss bitch. She's just a nice, kind-hearted woman.

"I don't know what you see in Elijah, Jackie," I say, shaking my head.

"I have to agree. You're too good for him," Jeremy adds.

Jackie and Elijah share this look. Full of—dare I say it—love.

"That I have to agree with." Elijah smirks and leans in to kiss her.

I look away and take a big drink of my beer. This is the first time in a while I've had fun with my friends. I've missed it. There's something about being surrounded by my friends that relaxes me. Maybe it's the fact I can trust them. I've had a hard time trusting anyone this past year.

The sunshine surrounding us and the stereo playing good tunes add to my enjoyment.

After a while, I get up to check on Samuel. As I enter the doorway to the living room, I pause mid-step with my half-drunk beer midway to my mouth.

Not wanting to interrupt, I lean my shoulder against the door frame. I can't help but soak in the happiness in front of me. My son's face is lit up as he kneels on the cream-colored carpet. Marigold is cross-legged next to him in her pretty yellow sundress. They're playing Mario Kart.

His face is hard as he concentrates on the game. He's winning, but Marigold is gunning for him. She's not letting him win. And I love that.

"I'm catching you," she yells excitedly.

His face suggests he is comfortable with it. No, he's loving every second. The competitive nature in him is coming out.

There's a strange jealous pang in my gut that I can't quite understand. Is it because she's playing with him and not me?

But why?

It's Marigold.

The sweet, intelligent, pretty, and much younger woman.

Yet, I want to join them.

I don't know what's pulling this emotion from me.

But also, if I do, will I interrupt their happiness?

The push and pull of emotions is fucking with me.

Instead, I decide to stay quiet and watch, sipping my beer. Samuel wins and he throws his hands in the air like a champion before jumping into her arms and wrapping his arms around her neck.

I suck in a sharp breath.

I'm taken aback.

I haven't seen him with another woman before...well, not since his mother. But it's been a while since he's had a hug from anyone other than my mother.

There's a warmth that pierces through my heart. It clogs my throat for air at how big of a moment this is.

But also that Samuel instigated it. He's clearly comfortable with her to dive into her arms and hug her.

Does he miss having a woman around?

I don't miss the way Marigold's eyes shimmer with softness. Someone else caring for him and giving him this attention means the world to me. Her arms cover his back, and she hugs him. It causes my breath to catch. I want to thank her, but I don't want Samuel to hear. I don't want him to know how rattled I am by his actions.

When he pulls away, I push off the door frame, ready to turn around and rejoin my friends when Samuel calls out. "Dad. Did you see me win?" he says proudly.

I turn back around and clear my throat to keep my voice even as I say, "I did. Well done."

My gaze drops to Marigold. Whose nose is flushed a cute shade of pink and she's nibbling on her bottom lip. "Seems I suck at Mario Kart."

My lips twitch at her words. "I'm sure you're good at other things."

"Is that a challenge?" she asks, and I know she wants me to play.

"I'll win," I reply.

She wiggles over, making room between her and Samuel. With her eyes locked on mine, she pats the empty spot on the carpet. "Show me what you've got," she says, giving me a challenging look.

I stare back, sipping my drink, debating what to do. I don't want to interrupt them playing so well together because he clearly needs one-on-one time with a woman. But the jealous part of me is pulling me in, so when Samuel says, "Dad, come play with us please," with those damn eyes, I can't say no to him.

I push off the door frame, crossing the line. "Fine. One game. But I'm going to beat you both." I walk into the room, put my beer bottle on the tv cabinet, and sit down between them.

"Come on Mari, we have to beat him," Samuel says, gripping the controller in his hands.

"Don't worry, I've got this," she says as her eyes stare at the screen.

Her side profile is so pretty. Even in her competitive streak, the woman is graceful. Her eyes are wide with the black makeup on her lashes, making her brown eyes stand out. Her skin is glowing and soft, with the flush of her cheeks making her look youthful yet so damn beautiful.

"Are you going to stare at me the whole time or actually play?" She tilts her head and lifts her brow.

I swallow hard and rather than admit I was staring at her, I say, "I'm ready. I was just checking if you are."

I'm lying through my teeth, and I can see the corner of her lips lift. I know she doesn't buy it, but she says nothing else, which I'm grateful for.

The game begins, and so much adrenaline pulses through my veins from playing Mario Kart. It's a high I've not felt in a very long time. Both Marigold and I are actually trying to beat each other as Samuel watches on, ready to play whoever wins.

Usually I'm easy on Samuel, but Marigold is elbowing my arm and I lean her way. We both shuffle on the spot until the last lap. I drop the control as she crosses the finish line.

Her lips part with a wide smile. "I won."

"You did," I reply in awe. I've not seen this fun yet competitive side to Marigold.

"My turn and I'm going to beat you Mari," Samuel says.

"You wish," she replies, and I can't help but notice how wet and plump her lips are.

Why is my mind thinking about her like this?

For fuck's sake, ever since I joined that damn app my mind can't leave sex. I'm now constantly thinking about it. And how much I just want to go back online and talk to Wildwest25.

And maybe Marigold's lips just remind me of the girl online and that's the confusion. Because I keep imagining the online woman's luscious lips wrapped tightly around my cock. Her cheeks hollowing out as she swallows everything as I come down her pretty throat. Yeah, surely, I just associate every woman's lips now with a fucking fantasy. It doesn't stop me from feeling disgusted with myself, though. I get up and grab my drink.

"I'll leave you two," I grumble and head back out of the room.

But her voice stops me. "Wait up."

CHAPTER 9

MARIGOLD

I DON'T KNOW WHAT I'm going to say. All I know is I didn't want him to leave the room. I wanted to have him around longer. Something about knowing him online and now in person has me wanting more. It's risky as hell. He could figure me out. But I'm willing to risk it...just to know more about him.

In real life, we've always had basic conversations. Nothing too deep, but now I want to know more.

"Did you want another beer?" I ask, leaving the living room and ambling to the kitchen.

He shakes his head, following. "I'm driving."

"You've only had one."

His brow rises. "You counting?"

My cheek twitches as I hold back a smile. "No."

He stares at me for a moment, and I expect him to say no, but, of course, he surprises me. "Well, I guess I can have another one."

I dip my chin and grab him one out of the fridge. This time I twist the cap off for him. But the bottle breaks.

"Crap!" I curse.

"What?" he questions with a look of concern.

I open my clenched hand to show him my palm and the blood leaking from the deep cut.

Without hesitation, he grabs my hand in his. His fingers touch the area. Scrutinizing it.

His eyes peer up into mine. They're bright with a deep-set frown between them. "Does this hurt?"

My lungs constrict at him being so close. I can feel the air leave his lips as he asks.

I have to concentrate on what he asked.

"A little," I rasp, unable to speak properly. His spicy pear aftershave is so strong, I'm getting dizzy. I miss what he says the first time he grumbles.

"What did you say?" I ask.

"Let me clean it up," he exclaims.

"I'm fine. I'll wash it under the tap and put a Band-Aid on it."

I try to pull my hand away and out of his grip, so I can take the few steps over to the sink. He winces and keeps a firm grip on me.

"No, it needs pressure." He applies it to stop the bleeding. He clearly doesn't trust me to do it. And I don't want to stop him from touching me. I like this caring and nurturing side of him. It's different to the quieter, grumpier one that I've grown up with or his new, sexier side. But it's also more than that; it's the zap of electricity I feel from his touch. I wonder if he feels it too.

"Are you going all Doctor Gray on me now?" I smile through the nerves. Thankful no one interrupts us in the kitchen. This moment alone is nice, and I don't want anyone to put a stop to it.

He growls. "Yeah. So let me clean it up."

The thrill of his voice sends a shiver through me. It reminds me of the commands he gives me online. It's so freaking hot.

"You're cold," he grinds out.

I want to say no, but before I know it, I'm being taken to a chair where he drapes a blanket over my shoulders.

"I won't hurt you," he says as he stands over me, leaning over to check the wound again.

Those words are like a promise, and I want to say, *But I'll hurt you when you find out the truth.*

I blink away the dread of fear that's filling me.

"You need stitches," he mutters.

Again, I try to tug my hand back, but he holds me firmly in place. His gaze flicks to mine and under the intense stare, I drop my gaze to his hands. Those same hands that have stroked his thick cock on camera.

What would it be like to see him do that in real life? Incredibly hot. The thought is making me flustered. I force my eyes back to his.

"No, I'm sure it will be fine soon. I just need to hold pressure on it longer."

"Are you the doctor now?" his cool voice asks.

"No," I drop my gaze away from his hard one. Not before enjoying how good his jaw looks from this angle. The powerful urge to reach up and touch his day-old scruff is fierce, but I shrug it off and pull myself together. No more daydreaming.

My brother is just outside, and Damien's son is in the room nearby.

"You need stitches." He grunts as he shows me how the blood is still trickling out and is that b—

Everything goes black.

I blink my eyes open. Looking around, I see I'm lying in a bed in my brother's spare room. The last thing I remember was being in the kitchen with Damien.

"Hey, you're awake," Damien's deep voice says.

"Seems so. What happened?" I ask, confused. I sit up on the edge of the bed and he comes to stand in front of me. He's reading my face. The intensity is unnerving. Is this what he's like at the hospital?

"You fainted."

"Oh God, how embarrassing." I cover my open mouth with my good hand. I wish I could remember him catching me and carrying me in here because how else did I get here?

I'm mortified I fainted from a stupid cut on my hand. I drop my hand away from my face.

"That's never happened to me before," I say, as if to justify my behavior. There's something in me that wants to impress him. Even though I have done the complete opposite.

"Is it sore?" he asks.

"A little." I shrug, knowing it doesn't hurt as much as the embarrassment does.

"Let me take you back to my house, where I can stitch and bandage it. I can give you some painkillers, too."

"You sound like a serial killer," I say, trying to joke to take away the thought of him taking care of me.

"You know me," he deadpans, unamused.

I do...*A lot more than you realize.*

"I know. I just don't think I need all that."

I try to focus on anything but the feeling of embarrassment. Him caring for me will only make me feel worse.

"Come on Mari, listen to Damien." My eyes fly up to my brother. I didn't hear him come in.

"Fine," I say, glaring at my brother. I'm agitated and nervous about going to Damien's place alone. We may not be technically alone when Samuel is there; nevertheless, I'll be in his space. I wonder what his place is like. I know what his bedsheets and pillows look like...

"Let's go," he says and follows my brother out.

His gruffness bothers me. I know I've seen snippets of his tender side in moments when we're alone. But right now, he's reverted back to being aloof.

I sit stunned momentarily on the bed, giving myself a mental pep talk before I get up and get this over with. The quicker I go to his house, the faster I'm back here.

I'm holding a pathetic makeshift bandage made of whatever they could find here. Clearly, my brother needs an emergency kit for times like this.

I walk out to grab my bag and pass the living room, where Damien is talking to Samuel.

"Samuel, we need to go. Please pack up your toys."

"Why?" he asks with his little face screwed up, not understanding. Guilt washes over me as I know he's leaving early because of me.

"I cut myself, Sammy, and your dad wants to stitch me up. But maybe I could go to the emergency room."

"No." Damien cuts me off with a hurt look. It completely unnerves me. "You'll come with us, and I'll fix it."

I swallow hard.

"Yeah, let Dad, he's great at fixing stuff," Samuel's soft sweet innocent voice cuts in.

I flick my gaze from Samuel to Damien, who's now wearing a small smirk on the side of his mouth. I haven't seen Damien smile much, and when he does, it makes my chest ache. His eyes stare at me with a challenging look to say something else. Something I can't read.

"Looks like I don't really have a choice," I say, trying to keep my voice as even as possible. I move out and walk on shaky legs to grab my bag and leave with Damien and Samuel. My brother sees us off outside on his front porch. I tell him I'll see him as soon as I'm fixed.

The drive in Damien's black Porsche isn't quiet, and it's not from Damien. No, he's still and quiet. He's completely focused on the road. Samuel is the chatterbox in the car, replaying his fun on the games he played.

"I love Eli's house," Samuel says, sitting beside me in the back seat.

"What's wrong with yours?" I ask curiously because I can imagine his place is just as nice as my brother's. The glimpse of his bedroom looked nice...Real nice.

"It doesn't have as many games," Samuel recalls.

"You can get your dad to buy more." I twist in the leather seat to give Samuel a wink, and he beams excitedly.

"Hey. Dad's right here," he grumbles from the driver's seat.

As if I didn't know he is sitting there. Inside this car is almost combustible with him in it.

He's hard to miss.

My gaze drops over his olive-green shirt and blue jeans. The green makes his blue eyes stand out more, but what has my mouth watering is the way he grips the steering wheel. It makes the fabric tight on his arm, showing off how toned they are.

"He has this arcade game that I really want."

"Show me and I'll get it for you," Damien replies instantly.

I pinch my lips together to prevent myself from laughing.

He doesn't want Elijah to outdo him. Also, he wants to prove how much he loves Samuel by giving him anything he wants.

"Then we can play it, Mari," Samuel says excitedly.

Samuel's lit-up face makes me smile. "Sounds like a plan."

And for the rest of the drive, Samuel talks about the game, and I nod and reply when needed, but otherwise, I stay pretty silent. My mind is reeling about what to expect next.

Damien pulls up to black gates. They open to reveal a two-story cream house. He opens the dark wooden garage door and then drives into the parking spot under the house. My pulse is racing as I try to focus on breathing to calm myself down.

I follow him and Samuel into an elevator and into their house.

"Nice place," I mumble to no one in particular as I enter. It's a large open house with dark wooden floors and white walls. Gray feature walls warm up the place.

I wonder if this is the house he shared with his ex-wife. It's not like I can ask. My brother and I don't talk about things like this. And I don't recall him ever mentioning Damien moving.

I amble through the house, following the direction they both went. I scan the house as I make my way into the kitchen. My jaw drops at the marble granite wall behind the oven.

"Wow," I breathe in awe.

This is a kitchen.

Gosh, how I would love to cook in a kitchen like this. I'm actually not a terrible cook. My mom taught me well. Plus, I loved learning and well...eating too.

Damien is pulling boxes out of a walk-in pantry and putting them on the counter before looking around for more.

"You keep medical supplies in your food cupboards?" I ask baffled.

"Not all of it. Just some basics," he answers nonchalantly.

I stand by the marble island and watch him move around. I run my good hand through my hair and clasp my hands together to prevent further fidgeting.

He wanders off to another room for a minute. For a second, I wonder if I was supposed to follow. But the thought vanishes the moment he steps back in the kitchen. He lowers a box to the countertop. I look on until he unexpectedly stands in front of me, grabs my waist and lifts me onto the counter.

I audibly gasp in surprise.

What's he doing?

That one slight movement means so much more to me than he realizes. He, however, doesn't seem bothered that his large hands were on my waist hoisting me up effortlessly. It's as if I weigh nothing at all.

I'm shaking all over from the nerves, desire, and pain.

"Painkillers?" he asks.

I nod. "Please."

I think about how my cut feels stingy and uncomfortable now. So, I can imagine how badly it will hurt when he stitches it up with a needle if I don't have pain relief in my system.

He strolls over to one of his kitchen cupboards and looks over his shoulder at me. "Do you have any allergies?"

I shake my head. "Not that I know of."

He opens the door and retrieves a box. My gaze drops over his toned wide back down across his tapered waist and ass. He's ridiculously hot and after seeing what his abdomen looks like naked, I can't imagine what the rest of him would be like...

He stands directly between my legs again. My breath hitches as his face lines up with mine at this height. If I moved my head a couple of inches forward, I could capture those lips.

His touch on my hand shakes me. I look down as he places a glass of water into my free hand. My parched throat is grateful for it, but between my thighs, I'm definitely growing wet. There's something about him standing between my legs, with a look of concern on his face, caring for me that leaves me flustered. Imagine my shock when he brings a tablet to my lips. His fingers brush them and suddenly, I wonder how I'm going to pull off not crossing a line tonight.

Chapter 10

Damien

Her pink pouty lips have the cutest defined bow. Like they were made for kissing.

The way her mouth is parted, I can see her wet tongue. It makes me hard. Fuck. I shouldn't be thinking of my best friend's sister in this way.

I feel her lips touch my fingers and my heart thumps. What the fuck is wrong with me.

I pull my hand away after I drop the pill in her eagerly awaiting mouth. And I step back.

I drop my gaze to my kitchen counter. My mind is on overdrive.

Why do I feel like she's different with me tonight?

Is she playing me?

She must be. Because all women play me.

I peer back up at her and watch her swallow the tablet before I prepare to suture her hand. I give myself a moment of silence and space; I need to collect myself.

Once prepped with the equipment on the counter, I'm pleased to see she hasn't moved from her position. She's stayed directly where I put her.

I take her hand and wash it with a cleansing solution. Ignoring the way my body is responding to touching her small delicate hand. How soft they look and the cute purple nail polish she wears. Youthful and out of bounds, I remind myself.

Now and then, I peer up and see her watching me with heavy eyes.

I drop my gaze, not missing the way her chest rises and falls slowly. Unable to stop myself from catching sight of her cleavage I saw earlier. *Nice handful...*

I refocus on the task. I grab my glasses and put them on.

"You wear glasses?" she asks.

I look up at her surprised face "Yeah. Why?"

"Nothing. You look cute," she says matter-of-factly.

I exhale heavily. Cute?

Who calls a thirty-eight-year-old man cute?

A twenty-five-year-old woman.

See...this is why I can't be thinking dumb-ass shit.

I'm a father for fuck's sake.

I have responsibilities.

I give her some local anesthetic and begin suturing with dissolvable stitches. It'll only need a couple to close the gap. She won't have a big scar.

She squeezes her eyes shut.

A sense of dread runs cold through me. "Can you feel that?" I ask, immediately stopping what I'm doing. I am about to grab some more local. The thought of her in pain is unbearable.

"No, it just feels like pressure."

I exhale my relief. The tense feeling in my body withdrawing. "Good. I was worried I was hurting you. Pressure is normal. I'm almost done. Will you be okay for me to finish?"

A flush hit her cheeks. "You're not hurting me. Finish whatever you need to."

I push my glasses up my nose and step closer again. My hand touches her hand again. I try to ignore the way touching her skin startles me. I bite back a groan and get back to work mode. A safe zone for me. Her presence has disrupted my usual ability to hone in and focus on work. Her breathing, her sweet perfume I'm breathing in, and the way her ample cleavage is in my face taunting me. They are a perfect pair of breasts. But still breasts I have no right looking at. Even though they are at my eye level if I tilt my head back a fraction.

She's pushing past my boundaries that I normally can control. Why can't I control the way I'm feeling right now?

When I finish the final suture, I drop the needle into the safety bin. "There, all done."

She lifts her hand to her face. "Neat."

"I'll bandage it," I say, looking around for the correct-sized bandage.

"Sure. But then can I lie down for a second," she mumbles.

Panic fills me. She's going to faint again.

Fuck the bandage.

"I'll lay you down now," I say, whisking her into my arms, ignoring the weird hum my body produces as I hold her.

"Oh," she gasps from the unexpected movement, but she doesn't fight me. Her arms wrap around my neck and her face moves in close to mine in this position. The hum is much stronger now. Her athletic curves in my arms are playing push and pull with my body. I hold my breath, not wanting to inhale any more of her sweet honey scent.

Who smells like honey?

It's so odd.

Yet...so her.

Her breath fans over my cheek. I grit my teeth and take the last step toward the sofa and lay her down gently. She sinks into my cream sofa. It looks so big compared to her.

I stare down at her while leaning over her.

She gives me a small smile. It's genuine, but I stand, needing to put distance between us. I grab her a blanket. And drape it over her body, tucking her in carefully and pausing my hands beside her hips.

She's watching me with lust-filled eyes.

Why did I pause, and why is she giving me this look? I need to get out of this room before I do something stupid like kiss her. Because kissing her would be stupid, right?

"Let me know if you need anything else," I grunt out. I turn around and make my way to the kitchen to clean up. Then I get her a glass of water in case she needs it. But by the time I return to the living room, holding the glass, I find her fast asleep. Her pretty brown hair with flecks of gold falling over her face. She's tucked up on her side, looking every bit enticing.

My legs move on their own accord. Before I can stop myself, I reach over and tuck the loose strand of hair behind her ear. Admiring her openly while she's asleep because I'm sure if she was awake, she'd think I'm weird.

And fuck, I can't blame her.

This is wrong. Yet, despite that, I stare openly a moment longer before I decide a cold shower is in order.

I check in on Samuel who's in his playroom. He's at his table happily coloring. I join him.

"Is Mari okay?" he asks, his brows furrowed. He's clearly worried about her.

I reach out and touch the top of his head. "She's all better. I stitched the cut in her hand."

"Where is she?" He looks around.

I drop my hand from his head. The image of her sleeping soundly hitting me.

"She's resting bud."

His face relaxes and his eyes drop back to his book, and he starts coloring again.

I color with him. But I find some of his pencils dull, so I sharpen them.

After I color a page, I decide it's time for a shower and some time alone. So when he's settled, I go.

I stand under that shower for longer than needed as punishment.

After putting on sweats, I call Elijah.

"Hey! How's Mari?" he asks when he picks up.

"Yeah, her hand is fine. I gave her some painkillers and stitched it up. She's lying on the sofa fast asleep." I walk from my room to the living room, raking my hand through my damp hair.

"Let her sleep," he says casually. As if it's no big deal.

As soon as I hit my living room, my feet stop moving on the cream plush carpet. She's still out cold. She hasn't moved at all.

Panic fills me. "What if she doesn't wake up? Do you want me to wake her and drop her home?" I ask with hope. Having her under my roof while I have some strange connection with her feels wrong.

"Nah. Let her crash on your sofa. If you don't mind."

It's not like I can say no. He'll ask why and I don't want to admit his sister turns me on.

Fuck. He'll punch my head in.

I know I would if I had a little sister.

"Sure," I mutter in defeat.

"Sweet. I'll let you go. Call me if you need anything."

"Will do," I say and hang up.

I stare at the phone, cursing under my breath.

I can't have her sleeping on my sofa all night. No matter if it's comfortable, she needs a bed. But her hand catches my eye. First, I need to bandage her hand. I grab the bandage from the counter and return to her and gently wrap it up.

I take my time, and she doesn't stir at all.

Once I'm finished, I pick her up again, but this time, she snuggles into my neck. The tip of her nose running along the side of my neck as she murmurs, "Mmm, yummy."

I freeze momentarily. Surely, she's not talking about me?

No, don't be fucking stupid. I shake off the silly thought and walk carefully to the spare bedroom.

With her in my arms, I carefully pull back the blanket and lower her down. Her arms still locked around my neck. My cheek against hers. Reaching behind me, I peel her arms from around my neck and stand up. She snuggles into the pillow. For a minute I stare and wonder if I should dress her? Change her into what? A shirt of mine?

But I scratch that idea straight away. Seeing her naked skin would make the situation worse. There'd be no good from me changing her.

I tuck the blankets in and move to step out, but not before hearing a soft whimper. "Damien."

My name on her lips in a sleepy yet sultry way stills me.

I run my hand over my face with a deep sigh; I take a second and walk out. I need to put Samuel to bed and then have another cold shower. The new tension from being close and touching her is too much. I close my bedroom door when I get back to it.

Lying down on my bed with a deep exhale, I message Wildwest25, thinking she'll help me release tonight and get Marigold out of my head. But after ten minutes, I receive nothing back. I sigh heavily and tuck myself into bed and try to sleep. Despite, my best efforts, I quickly realize there's zero chance I'll be sleeping tonight. Not with the constant images of Marigold in my arms, or my name leaving her lips.

There's a banging noise followed by a fit of giggling.

I groan.

I feel like I've only been asleep for five minutes.

Which is probably exactly what happened.

I never heard from Wildwest25 last night, so I'm grumpy about that too.

Another crash sounds and I wince. This time it was louder. I curse and shove the stupid blankets off me. I rip open my bedroom door and stomp down until I hit the kitchen.

I rub my eyes and try to focus on the vision in front of me. Marigold has found a white mug, but she's opening all my cupboards to find something. I should ask what she needs, but my jaw hits the floor when I find her wearing one of my white shirts. It barely covers her ass. Her toned legs are on display as she reaches up to scour my cupboard.

I wonder if she's wearing panties...

"I'm sorry. I hope you don't mind that I borrowed one of your shirts. The dress has blood on it. So Samuel found the shirt and gave it to me," she rambles before chewing on her lip. Her gaze peers around before her eyes meet mine again.

I don't mind...

But I should because it looks better on her than on me.

And my mind is straight back to how her body looks in it.

"It's fine," I mumble out, but my eyes continue to stare at her legs.

"She's trying to find tea," Samuel explains. Totally interrupting my perv session. Which I'm a mix of grateful and bummed about.

Tea. Right.

I don't even remember owning any.

But my housekeeper might've bought it on one of her weekly shopping trips.

"Let me look," I grumble in my rough morning voice.

I open the cupboards one by one.

"We looked in all of them," she states, pointing to the same ones I'm opening and closing.

"Have you checked the pantry?" I ask.

She turns to face me, and I drop my gaze, which was a terrible idea because I struggle to not stare at her erect nipples.

Is she trying to fuck with me?

I swipe my forehead with my hand and walk into the pantry. Not finding any tea. I wouldn't even have a clue what type to buy.

"I don't get why you wouldn't drink coffee. It's weird," I grunt as my eyes take in those taunting buds.

She raises her brows and crosses her arms over her chest. She caught me. "You're weird," she argues.

Samuel laughs.

"What are you laughing at?" I question him with a smile. No matter what, he can always turn my mood around.

"She called you weird," he answers with a goofy grin.

"And?" I ask, grabbing him and giving him a hug as he wriggles in my arms.

"It's funny," he replies as he tries to get out of my grip.

"She's weird too. She drinks tea and not coffee," I say as I tickle him under his arms.

He stops thrashing and stands. He's screwing up his face. "I'm weird too because I don't drink coffee either."

I smile at his innocence and peer over at her. She's pinching her lips together.

"You're a kid. You don't drink coffee, it's not good for you," I say, roughing up his hair with my hand.

He ducks his head, getting away and laughing. "But you drink it."

Marigold giggles, and a twitch forms in the corner of my mouth as a smile starts to form.

I flick my gaze to her. She covers her mouth with her free hand. It reminds me of why she stayed last night.

"How's your hand this morning?" I ask, stepping forward to inspect the bandage.

She bites the corner of her lip. "Good, but I must've passed out from the tablet."

"Seems so," I mumble.

"I'm sorry," she whispers.

"It's fine. I spoke to Eli and told him you fell asleep here."

Her brows rise. "Yeah, and what did he say?"

"He told me to let you stay," I mumble.

She nods but says nothing else.

The air is strange between us. Samuel is watching in fascination. I take her hand and inspect it.

"Looks fine. But I'll write you a script for some antibiotics. You're not going to pass out from them, are you?" I ask with a slight tease in my voice.

She shoves my shoulder playfully. "Ha. Ha. Smart as—" She looks at Samuel and then me. "Pants."

My body relaxes from all the tension of the last twenty-four hours. Her morning energy is addictive. And normally, other than my son, nothing can make me smile. Especially not a woman.

I drop her hand and step away to make a coffee. She turns to the kettle to make hot water?

"You're going to have hot water over a coffee?"

She shrugs. "Yeah, well, you don't have tea." She grabs the kettle and pours water into the white mug.

I watch on in shock before sipping on my latte and moving toward the fridge. I grab some eggs, sausages, and turkey bacon from the fridge.

"Are you making that for us?" she asks, looking at me over the rim of her cup.

"Are you hungry?"

"Starving," she replies eagerly.

"Well then, I'm cooking."

She lowers her cup to the counter and steps closer to me in the kitchen. "How can I help?"

I stare dumbly as thoughts pop into my brain.

Let me kiss those damn sexy lips or let me feed you breakfast while you sit on my counter with your legs spread.

Fuck! I can't say any of that.

I clear my throat that's tightening with arousal. I need space. "Just hang out with Samuel, and I'll call you two when it's ready."

She beams. "I'd love to."

My stupid heart flips at her reaction to hanging out with my kid.

She spins and reaches for her cup, but she spills it on her hand.

"Crap," she mutters.

I hiss and move instantly, grabbing her hand and bringing my mouth to her skin to suck the water off.

My brain clearly disappeared because why didn't I grab a cloth?

Why my mouth?

Where the hell has Doctor Gray gone?

Because I'd been thinking of my mouth on her. The sweet, unusual taste hits my tongue.

I remove my mouth from her hand. Her hand is slightly pink, but it's not too bad; it won't blister.

"How was the water?" she asks.

I swallow hard as I meet her dark eyes that are now filled with heat.

"Delicious," I gruff out.

I meant her, not the water.

"Play with Samuel and I'll cook," I add.

It'll give me a second to breathe and find my brain.

"You don't have to. I promise I can cook." Her lips twitch with a hint of a smile forming.

"Thanks for the offer. I believe you, but I want to cook for you...two," I say as my eyes hold hers. She dips her chin and walks away, carrying her cup, and I see her and Samuel head to his playroom.

When I'm alone, I rub my face with my hands, knowing right now I'm in over my head.

CHAPTER 11

MARIGOLD

I WALK AWAY IN his shirt, not missing the way his eyes roamed hungrily over my body. He loved me wearing his shirt and no bra.

I wanted to tell him I'm Wildwest25, but I had Samuel right beside me, eagerly awaiting to play. I'll take care of it before I leave today, so his little ears won't hear. I survey the room. The playroom is in order. All the boxes are neatly labeled and completely different from how I remember a toy room being as a kid.

Toys were everywhere, but here, it's neatly organized. Samuel walks to one box in particular.

"What did you want to play?" I ask.

"Legos?"

He glances up at me as he tips the box of Legos out.

"Sure," I say and sip more water.

"What do you like to build, Sammy?" I take a seat at his little table and chairs as he brings a box over.

"Buildings or a police station," he says eagerly.

"Got it. Let's build this together."

"I like this," he states.

"What?" I ask, not understanding.

"Playing with someone."

My heart drops. "No one plays with you?"

But Damien seemed good with him before...I don't get it.

"No, my dad works a lot and Nana doesn't like to."

I blink rapidly as I digest this information and find the best way to respond.

"Have you asked your dad to play?"

He scrunches up his nose and shakes his head. "No."

"Well, maybe ask him next time. Your dad seems pretty cool."

"He is. It's just he's been sad."

I frown. "Why?"

"My mom left," he states matter-of-factly.

Building blocks together seemed easy, but now I'm not so sure. I feel like he's unloading all his feelings on me. Which on one hand I love, but on the other, I'm not sure how to properly handle the questions. I'm only twenty-five and not a parent. But he's opening up to me and I don't want to shut him down.

"That must be hard. Are you sad?"

He lifts his little shoulder. "A little. At school when they talk about moms and dads. I don't have one."

I continue stacking little colored blocks on top of each other. "That would make me sad, too."

"But it's okay."

"It sounds like your dad and nana love you dearly."

"Mmm," he mumbles, but he's too focused on his building to answer.

I blow out a breath in relief. He understands he has no mom, but his dad is doing a great job at being both. The only issue is the playtime. It seems Sammy needs more time with Damien.

I continue stacking.

"Woah. Cool. Look how awesome your building is," Samuel exclaims.

"Yeah, good work, Marigold," Damien says from the doorway.

I side-eye him and enjoy the view of him only wearing sweatpants. "Thanks."

His naked torso is burning me up with memories on the camera. But seeing it in real life is something else.

My fingers twitch, wishing I could touch him.

"Food is ready," Damien announces.

Samuel jumps up and runs out of the room.

I laugh.

"Thanks for playing with him," Damien grits out.

"Anytime. It was actually kind of fun." I hold his eyes as I answer.

His brow lifts. "I doubt that."

"Try it. Legos are actually fun and sorta relaxing."

"You and I have different versions of relaxing."

I swallow the words, *but Sammy wants you to play with him*. Not wanting to overstep. Did Samuel say that to me in secrecy, or should I share it?

I don't know Damien enough as a dad to know how much I can say. It's not my place. I'm just a visitor....

We're sitting around the table eating breakfast as a family. Both Damien and me sit next to Samuel, who's at the end of the table. Every so often, I look up and into Damien's eyes. I soak in the hard lines around his eyes and his morning scruff over his jaw. I try to remember all the little quirks and this relaxed version of him before this ends. Because it will.

The only other side I'll see of him is online.

However, that side is more for sexual relief. There's no friendship, fun or relaxed Damien.

Samuel finishes breakfast and runs back to his playroom to finish our building.

Damien stands to clean up the plates. I follow to help him clear the table.

"You're good with him," I say quietly, not wanting Samuel to hear.

"Thanks," he replies. But it's gruff and I feel like I've said something I shouldn't have.

I stay quiet and pack up before I ask to take a shower. Even if I have to put on yesterday's dress, it'll still feel better when I'm clean.

In the shower, I grab the body soap and the moment I open the lid, a waft of pear hits me. It's his scent. There's something about using his soap and walking out smelling like him that makes me bathe in it. I make a mental note of the label, planning to order a few bottles once I'm back home. Stepping out of the shower makes me feel and smell better. I wonder if he'll mind if I keep his top. I want to...

I decide that it's too much, so I'll give his shirt back. I walk out to the living room and find him reclined and watching TV.

"Is it okay if I go? I have studying to get back to," I say, biting the corner of my lip.

He switches the TV off and climbs off the sofa before he calls out, "Samuel. We need to take Marigold home."

"I can grab a taxi," I say quickly, not wanting to disrupt their morning any more than I already have.

"Nonsense. I'll drive you," he says it with the commanding voice I love.

I'll admit wasting money on a taxi isn't ideal, so I keep my mouth shut and just nod.

Samuel comes running out. "Do you have to leave?" He moans.

"I'm sorry I do," I say, giving him a sad look back.

He steps forward and hugs my waist. I'm momentarily stunned. I look at Damien, who looks pale and shocked himself.

I rub Samuel's back. "What if I promise to come back one time and finish playing Legos?"

"Yes. Tomorrow?"

"Not tomorrow, but soon." Damien's voice cuts in.

I thrust out the top for Damien to take. "Here, thanks for letting me borrow it."

It was nice catching his eyes on my legs a few times. But other than that, I do not know what he thinks about me. I know he likes my body online, so it would have been nice to see his responses in real life. Would he suck in a breath?

Hiss?

Groan?

Yeah, I'd love to hear what I do to him.

"Keep it. It looked better on you."

I stare at him at a loss for words.

He clears his throat and grabs his keys.

"Ah. Thanks," I mumble, not knowing what else to say.

I squeeze his shirt in my hand and bring it to my stomach. He just gave me his shirt and said it looked better on me...what does that even mean?

I wave goodbye to Damien and Samuel, wishing I didn't have to walk away from them. Instead, I want to stay inside my bubble at their house, but reality settles in now that I've arrived at my house. It's like a cloud lifts. I need to forget the fantasy of what life would be like if Damien and I were together, because when he finds out who I am, he'll end us.

I open the door to my house with a heavy heart. When I close it behind me, a gush of air leaves my lungs. As if I closed the door on us, I drag my feet to my room and collapse onto my bed.

After a couple of minutes moaning to myself in my bedroom, I call Clara.

"Hey!" she answers, out of breath.

I sit up on my bed. "What are you doing?"

"Cleaning my room."

"Why?"

"I'm preparing to start…" she trails off.

"Oh, I get you. Do you need any help?" I ask. Even though I have to study, I know I won't concentrate if my mind is still thinking about Damien.

"Not if you don't want to," she replies.

"I want to. I need a distraction and to tell you something."

"A Damien something," she asks curiously.

I can't help but perk up; talking out loud about him makes me happy. "Yep."

"Get your ass over here and spill. But then you can't sit and watch me," she warns.

"I promise to help," I say enthusiastically.

I hang up and get dressed. Driving the five minutes to her house.

Inside her room, my eyes bulge. "Clara, this is a mess."

"I know, but I'm cleaning behind everything and then I'm moving my furniture."

I rub my temples, wondering where to even start.

"I want the camera here so they can't see my desk."

"Let's do the furniture pieces first, and then I'll help you set up the camera. Did you get new lingerie?"

This should be the perfect distraction, but it also brings up the memory of Damien and I meeting online.

I miss that.

After the sparks flying last night, I know I want to go online to see him.

"Yes," she beams. "Come look." She waves me over to her drawers.

She pulls out a beautiful blue set and I gush. "That's gorgeous," I say as I reach out and touch it. Admiring the silk and I know already I need to buy a silk set to show Damien.

"Oh, and I copied you. I hope you don't mind." She pulls out a blue mask.

"No, of course not. This is smart. Hide your identity."

"Speaking of..." She narrows her eyes at me.

"Can we at least make tea for this?" I say with a strangled laugh.

She huffs. "Okay."

We head into her kitchen. She shares this house with two room-mates who are both out today.

I help her make tea rather than stand around watching. I need to do something with my hands as I tell her.

"Yesterday I went to his house," I whisper.

"What?" she screeches. And I know the shock. But also, it's not what she thinks.

"It wasn't like that. I wish," I admit.

"Ah, dammit."

We carry the tea to her table, and I clutch it in my hands. I stare down at the milky liquid.

"I cut my hand at my brother's, and it needed stitches, so he took me to his place to do that."

"The handy doctor." She wriggles her brows at me.

"He has excellent hands." I giggle.

She leans forward a bit, smirking. "And you know what they say about hands."

"I do. And I'd say they match."

"God damn. You lucky bitch!"

"Hey, you might find your guy," I say with a wide grin.

Her face falls a bit.

"What?" I ask.

"You need to be careful. Remember, he's a lot older, has a son and is—"

"My brother's best friend," I finish.

"Yes, but you're so in love with the idea of love. I feel like you could go all-in and get hurt. Again," she says with a worried look.

"I'm so bad at love, but you can't blame me for trying. Maybe an older guy is the answer," I say with a shrug.

"I wouldn't get your hopes up. He's got a lot of baggage."

"I'm already in too deep. I wanted to tell him who I was yesterday and even this morning, but I couldn't."

"This morning?" she asks.

"Yeah, I ended up passing out from the painkillers he gave me."

"It gets worse, doesn't it?" she says, shaking her head and lifting her tea to take a sip.

"I don't think it's bad. I did, however, wear his shirt this morning."

"He changed you?" she asks with a slacked jaw.

I shrug and sip my tea before answering. "No. My dress had blood on it, so Samuel found one of his dad's shirts. And then this morning, I tried to give his shirt back to him and he said it looked better on me and insisted I should keep it."

"Fuck," she mumbles, sitting back in her chair.

"I know. I know. I should've told him who I was, but I was scared," I say.

"Of him not wanting you? Man, your ex is a massive douchebag."

I laugh. "I can't argue with that."

"What about the kid? You're not even finished with school yourself."

"Sammy is so sweet. He told me no one plays with him. His dad works all the time, and his nana doesn't like it."

"It doesn't mean you need to do it. He's not your problem."

I wince. "Ouch, that's harsh."

"I'm trying not to be. More of a realist. You're always so kind and you look at life as an opportunity. And sometimes we can't fix everything."

I sip my tea, taking a moment to sit with her words. "Who in the world leaves their kid?"

"I don't have the answer, but it still doesn't mean you should dive in without thinking about the pain you could inflict if the relationship crumbles. Sammy then gets hurt again."

"Shit. You're right."

"Just go slow, and I think you need to tell him soon. Before it's too late."

"I will. I promise I was going to yesterday. Believe me, I had every intention. But when he's around, I can't think clearly."

She gets up from the table and puts her cup in the sink, and I drain my cup and follow her.

"Come on, help me finish my room. I want to do this tonight."

CHAPTER 12

DAMIEN

Wildwest25: Why did I think by being a lawyer I could change the world?

Damien: You will change the world.

Wildwest25: I like your optimism, but I'm not feeling it. :(

Damien: Would it help if I told you that was one of the reasons I wanted to be a doctor?

Wildwest25: To change the world?

Damien: Yes. And now that I am. I do think I'm changing the world.

Wildwest25: Please tell me you're not full of yourself. I did like you…

> **Damien:** *I'm not cocky. I promise. And I like you too. I just love my job and I see how it changes people's lives.*

I walk back to my office from surgery the next day. My hand digs through my pocket in my scrubs to pull out my phone. I scroll through my phone, checking emails, and I notice a missed call from Elijah. I hit redial. He answers on the second ring.

"I just left surgery. I missed your call," I say as I continue moving through the corridor toward my office.

"All good. I just left your place. Your mom said you're working."

"Yeah. I'll be here for a little while longer," I reply.

"I'll see you next Sunday? Or are you working?"

I wish I was home right now. I'm spent. I barely slept last night with Marigold in my house.

"I'm off next Sunday," I reply, after checking my calendar.

"Cool. And how did Mari get on?"

I swallow the lump that's formed at the mention of his sister. My hand grips the phone tighter.

"Yeah, great. I put her in the spare room to sleep," I say as casually as I can.

I feel like I had to mention the fact it was a spare bedroom. Which was dumb because why would he think I'd let her sleep in my bed?

Because I wanted that.

But why her?

Why am I so drawn to her?

Why the fuck do I have to think about his little sister in this way? It's going to end badly.

I'm just glad we've done nothing sexual. Christ, no. That can't happen, because going deeper would give her false hope.

I can't introduce a woman to my son, especially one who's thirteen years younger than me.

Every way you look at this, someone winds up getting hurt, or my friendship with Elijah will end.

"Thanks. I really appreciate it."

He appreciates me ogling his sister.

Appreciates how I loved seeing her wear my shirt. Or how I soaked in every sliver of delicate skin on her body, admiring her freckles and the touch of her buttery soft skin as I carried her.

And then, to make matters worse, I tried and failed to jerk off with a woman online. Fuck. I'm so fucked up.

I scrub my scalp frustratedly.

How am I a doctor?

I seem to have lost all of my brain cells. Women seem to take over and turn it to mush. If I were to be with a woman, I know that I'll get hurt again, because that's what happens when you fall in love.

"Anytime," I reply.

"Do the stitches come out?" he asks.

Arriving at my office door, I yank it open and close it behind me, as I think about his question.

"Uh. Yeah," I mutter, knowing I didn't think about that when I sutured her last night. "I'll have to take them out," I add.

After how tempted I was last night, I know I'd have to remove them in my office. Away from my house. Away from the memories. And way away from dangerous territory.

"I have to drop off your birthday present on the weekend," I say, not wanting to forget. Samuel's been begging every day to drop it off. I've had to explain that we'll do it on the weekend.

His deep chuckle sounds in my ear. "Yeah, come. I don't have any plans. I'm staying low key."

I snort, taking a seat in my office chair. "Bout time."

"Hey, someone needs to have fun," he says. He's clearly making a dig at me. It's not the first time. He just wants me to live a little. It's something I'm hearing from everyone—my parents, friends and work colleagues. Everyone seems to be saying the same thing to me right now.

"I have fun...sometimes," I clip.

"Whatever you say," he mumbles. "You could come out this weekend to The Players' Club."

I've heard only great things about this club from both Alex and other friends, but the idea of going out takes time away from my son, and frankly, I don't want to pick anyone up, so I don't see the point.

"I don't know..." I say, leaning my elbow on my mahogany desk and leaning my head into my hand.

"Are you seeing someone?" he asks, amusement lacing his voice.

The internet girl...no.

His sister...no.

"No," I sigh.

"So, come. Even just for an hour," he says mischievously. He's trying to persuade me.

"It's never just an hour, though, is it?" I say, reclining back into my office chair.

"Not with Jackie and Marigold together. It will be hard to get them out of there." He laughs.

My molars grind together as he continues, "Those two are the same and when they drink, they let loose. They have every guy drooling. I'm going to have to watch them all night, so come help me."

I shouldn't care that his sister will be drunk and have guys drooling over her all night. I can't. I shouldn't. So why the fuck do I then?

Why does the very thought of her being looked at piss me off?

This needs to stop. Including this stupid boner that's tenting in my scrubs now.

"No," my voice breaks, so I clear it to add, "I already have a child, remember?"

"Touché, man. But it would be nice to have a drink together. Out. You know, away from our houses."

I know exactly what he means, but I simply can't. Between work and Samuel, I have minimal spare time, and I'm too tired to do that for fun.

I put my glasses on to check the time on my computer screen. I need to wrap up work fast and make it home before the nighttime routine is done. I'd hate to miss it.

"I gotta go. I want to finish up my notes and then head home. Mom's looking after Samuel for me, and I don't want to be here longer than I need to," I say, typing my notes to finish them.

"Alright. I'll catch you on the weekend."

I hang up and return to my notes.

After I've finished them, I send the final email. I pack up my desk, but when I go to leave, the sunset catches my eye. It draws me in closer to the window. The golden hues remind me of Marigold. I should've asked if his sister would be there over the weekend, but I probably would've made it a bigger deal than it needed to be. It's just that I don't want to fuck up my friendship with Elijah. No woman is worth that.

I made it in time to tuck Samuel in and read him a book. After a shower, I turn the TV on in my bedroom, but there's nothing interesting, so I turn to my phone and begin scrolling through social media. I spend the next hour doing that, but I'm bored again. As I flick the home page of icons, I see the Mysterious Fan app. I hover my thumb over it.

Do I?

Don't I?

I do it. Holding my breath.

Once inside, I see she's online. The deep exhale leaves my chest shaking.

When I'm about to click off, thinking this is a dumb idea and I need to stop it...she messages.

> **Wildwest25:** *Hey! I've been waiting for you.*

I squeeze my eyes shut. She's so fucking sweet, it hurts. I'm such a miserable user. But, of course, that doesn't stop me from typing.

> **Damien:** *You have?*

> **Wildwest25:** *Yes. For an hour.*

At the same time, I was scrolling.

> **Damien:** *Sorry...*

I trail off with nothing else because I don't know this woman and I was so close to confessing to her about my night.

My son.

I was going to tell a stranger about my son.

I've officially lost it.

Wildwest25: *You can make it up to me :)*

I hesitate. Do I want to know what she's thinking? Like, the dirty bastard that I've become, I type back.

Damien: *How?*

A message for a video call pops up. I pause a second, looking around my dark room lit up by the TV screen. I hit accept, unable to deny myself tonight. Maybe this will help me get my mind off Marigold.

Yeah. Anything to help with that.

When she comes into view, I see a pretty gold lingerie set against her flushed skin.

"You look breathtaking in gold." My voice is gritter than I've ever heard, and breathier. She literally stole my breath with that color on her luscious body. So unusual and yet so elegant at the same time.

"Thank you," she says with a blush that begins on her chest and runs upward onto her neck. "How was your day?" she adds, wringing her hands in front of her.

A small smile tips at the corner of my mouth. She's endearing too. "Tiring. I got called into work and it took longer than usual," I answer honestly.

It's strange for someone to ask me about my day. Not even my ex-wife asked. She only cared about spending my money. She didn't care if I was barely home, as long as I gave her the lifestyle she wanted. I felt more like a bank than a husband. And even after giving her everything, she walked away.

"Let me help you forget about it," she whispers with a knowing grin.

"What about your day?" I ask, genuinely wanting to know how her day was. It's probably unusual, considering the app we're on, but this feels like a friendship, at least to me it does. She feels less of a stranger now.

She smiles at my question before answering lightly. "I hung out with a friend and then came home to finish an assignment."

Her high-pitched tone makes me understand the importance of completing college and how proud she is of that.

"Good girl," I say with my own praise. I know what it feels like to achieve and to graduate from college, so to find her just as happy hits me differently in the chest. Like it adds another connection to this online stranger. One where work and careers are important. You're in control of your future, but you ultimately have to put the work in.

She's putting the work in. I'm proud of her.

Her teeth catch on her bottom lip. "I like being your good girl. But did you want me to show you how bad I can be?"

I sit up in surprise. The purr in the way she said *bad* has my attention.

"Of course."

A soft, adorable smile overtakes her lips. "I got you a present."

My brows rise, but I stay silent. I've never received a present from a woman. Well, unless you count when you're ten and you have a girlfriend and think she's your forever girl. So a woman buying me a present seems too good to be true.

And we barely know each other, so what could it be...

"A new toy."

That has my attention. "Yeah?" I say with a wicked grin.

"Do you want to see it?" She bats her eyelashes, totally seducing me, and it's working. Of course, it's fucking working.

"It actually matches my outfit."

My curiosity peaks.

She crawls over the bed to her bedside drawer, and my dick jerks. I get the vision of her crawling toward me.

Would she be down for that? Because fuck, that would be hot. I could ask her for it after she shows me the toy.

She grabs it and slides off the bed and comes to the screen to show me. Instantly, a deep growl leaves my chest at the butt plug. She moves it around, so I get all angles in the camera and really appreciate its beauty. The small rose jeweled end is gold. Fuck, that's hot. My dick is painfully hard now. Tonight is going to be wicked. But when she inches closer to the camera, I freeze.

Fuck, no way.

She's wearing the same purple nail polish as Marigold does, and when I catch those brown eyes, I instantly wonder how I missed them.

My stomach hardens, and I end the video.

It's Marigold...

CHAPTER 13

MARIGOLD

A few days later

"How's it feel to be thirty-five?" I tease as soon as Elijah opens his front door.

He laughs. "The same as thirty-four."

I step inside his two-story brick house. He closes the door behind us.

"Figured. It's just a number," I say, walking through the house. Damien is a couple of years older than my brother.

"I feel like I did in my twenties," he mutters from behind me.

I walk into his living room and make my way to his gray sofa. "Just with a few extra lines and bags under your eyes," I say with amusement.

He smacks his chest. "Ouch."

I shrug casually at him. "It's fine. We all get there." I take a seat on his sofa.

"You're way off it, lil sister."

Normally, the little sister comments don't bother me, but today it hits different. I want to be seen as a woman. I push the disappointment aside and pull out my phone, ready to order our lunch. "What does the birthday boy want to eat?"

"Jackie is taking me out for dinner, so nothing heavy," he says casually.

That has me smiling. I'm so happy my brother met his one. He's been career focused for way too long. Yes, he's a successful billionaire, but he's worked every day for years. It's surprising she wasn't his PA or someone that works for him. Don't get me wrong, there's nothing wrong with that. But to me, that's him finding something convenient and not finding the right one.

So, with Jackie, it was a complete surprise.

I feel like she's the sister I never had. We're so alike, it's uncanny. She used to be a bartender for The Players' Club but recently stopped. Well, I'm going to blame my controlling brother. Not that she'd have to give up her job. I don't see my brother putting too many rules in place. He can, however, be persuasive. People listen to him.

"So, things are good with Jackie?" I ask excitedly. I turn my head as he takes a seat on the other sofa, flicking the TV channel from sports.

"So far," he answers nonchalantly.

I smile. It's those minor details of knowing I don't really like sports that make me wonder what he's like as a boyfriend. He's a typical guy, so me asking too many questions will have him closing up. I pick and choose my questions each time I see him.

"I'm happy for you. I like her. Well, I'll order a sandwich from the deli. That's lighter."

"Yeah." He shrugs, not bothered.

I order our food. When it arrives, we move to his dining and kitchen area.

I'm sitting eating lunch with Elijah at his table when the door sounds.

Jackie must be here.

He pushes his chair out to answer it as I take a bite of my sandwich.

"Hey, Damo, come in," my brother says happily.

I almost choke on my food.

"Thanks. Happy Birthday," Damien replies as their heavy footsteps sound.

Coming closer and closer to me.

"Thanks man. Catching up to you in the old age." He laughs.

Damien's deep chuckle sounds.

I squeeze my eyes and scrunch my face up tight. The age topic makes me sick.

My throat tightens and I force myself to swallow the piece of bread that's in my mouth. I lower the rest of the sandwich back to my plate and push it from me. I put my hands on my thighs and rub them up and down. The butterflies somersaulting in my stomach are making me too nervous to eat.

The last time I spoke to Damien, I was showing him a toy online. A blush hit my cheeks at the mere thought.

How embarrassing.

He messaged after a couple of minutes, saying the line disconnected the other night and he said he had internet problems. So he could not get back on. But he hasn't been back on since, leaving me to believe the opposite.

Maybe I'd pushed him too far. Maybe he's not interested in different toys? Even though he initially seemed excited, he quickly became wide-eyed, and then he disappeared.

To see him today is uncomfortable. He doesn't know it's me. I've kept my identity a secret, but I know how uncomfortable I'll feel. The only savior will be Samuel. I'll just play games with him the whole time to avoid Damien.

They come into view, and my flush deepens. I focus on my brother, who sits down at the table. Then I move my gaze to Damien. He's face is hard today. The line between his brow is deeper. When his eyes catch mine, his body stiffens.

"Hi," I say in an uneven voice.

He nods. But he doesn't talk back.

"Take a seat," Elijah encourages, but he just shakes his head and stands in the doorway to the kitchen. He's refusing to sit down at the table, as if he doesn't want to be here.

What's with him today?

He's back to being grumpy and quiet. I hate it. The online version and the one I saw at his house are much more relaxed.

"Where's Samuel?" Elijah asks. I wondered too, but with the cool exterior he's giving me, I remained silent.

"He's got a cold, so my mom is watching him. I told her I wouldn't be long. Hope you don't mind."

My brother shakes his head. "No biggie. Hope the little bugger feels better soon."

"Me too," Damien mumbles, stuffing his hands deeper into his tight acid-wash jeans. The black biker jacket and his black top scream moody. It's a shame he's hot and I have a stupid major crush on him. I purse my lips and wish he wasn't frowning at me. Instead, I imagine him giving me one of those crooked smiles from our night chats. I'm coming to crave the rare smiles. Which is dumb. Clearly, he'll never be interested in me.

He has no problem replying to my brother, but with me, I get the silent treatment.

"Did you want a drink?" Elijah asks.

"No, I'm good," he replies.

"What about something to eat? We just finished lunch, but I got snacks." Elijah pushes out his chair and grabs a bag of crisps. He holds them out to Damien.

His lips twist slightly, but if you weren't watching them, you would have missed it because his mask is already back in place. "No. Seriously, just relax. I'm here to see you."

My brother lets out a sigh. "Well, sit down. You're making me nervous. Did you want to watch some of the basketball game?"

My brother moves toward the other room, but his phone rings, and he answers it.

"Hey," he talks, but the way his face wears a stupid look, I'm guessing it's Jackie. Ugh. He walks away to talk, leaving Damien and me alone.

The silence in the air is too uncomfortable. He doesn't look like he'll speak to me. His thin lips, hunched shoulders and crossed arms definitely tell me he's in a mood.

Maybe something happened with his ex-wife?

"Are you okay?" I whisper.

He doesn't answer, just stares for a moment. His gaze drops to my hands and then back up. Something is definitely up. His jaw is tight and his muscles twitch.

The silence returns, and it's deafening. I can't sit here any longer like this. I push back on my chair, rising to walk to use the bathroom.

I need a moment alone to wrap my head around this awkwardness.

The layout of my brother's house means I need to step past him. So I suck in a breath and hold it. I ignore the way my body hums being close to him and move past him.

But just as I think I'm safe, he grabs my wrist and grits out. "It's you."

Panic swirls in my gut. His angry face inches from mine. "What are you talking about?" I ask, my heart beating wildly in my chest. A sense of dread washes over me.

I want him to say the words in case I'm wrong. But of course, I'm not.

"You're Wildwest25," he spits under his breath. I drop my hand. He pushes off the frame and stares down at me with wild eyes. "Fuck, how stupid am I?" He shakes his head and drags a hand over it. "Your name, for fuck's sake. And I never realized. I must be a joke to you!" he sneers. The words drip like venom from his mouth and it tears me apart.

My heart is thumping so hard inside my ears. "No, you're not." I rush out in a panic.

"Then why trick me?" The hurt staring back at me pierces my heart.

"I didn't," I plead. My voice cracking just like my heart. I wish he believed me. I didn't know it was him. Yes, when I did, I should have come clean. I tried to, but I just...Jesus, I couldn't do it.

He laughs, but it's scary.

"West. Twenty-five. Like fuck, why didn't I think more?" he says with disdain as he scrunches up his nose, causing a wrinkle there.

"I'm sorry," I say, twisting to walk off, but he grabs my hand and I spin back around. He leans into my hair. His nose touching my head and he sucks in a deep breath. Normally, this position is romantic, but right now, it's painful. My heart is already cracking. I just want to go and be alone to cry. I've made a huge fucking mess. And I do not know how to fix it.

"You smell like my soap," he grunts.

I shudder. Even to myself, the fact I bought his soap to smell like him is insane.

The words slip out from my lips. "I wanted to have you around me all the time," I stupidly admit.

He pulls his head back, his eyes frantically looking into my eyes. "Fuck. No. This is a bad idea," he adds, pinching the bridge of his nose.

"What the fuck is going on?" My brother's icy voice cuts in.

CHAPTER 14

DAMIEN

HER LAST NAME IS West, and she's twenty-five. Why was I so fucking stupid? I should've put two and two together. Now, with Elijah catching us, I step back. To put some much-needed distance between Marigold and me.

"I said what the fuck is going on," Elijah roars.

"Nothing," I say, keeping my cool.

"It doesn't sound or fucking look like nothing," he accuses as his icy gaze flicks from mine to Marigold's.

Marigold stays still and all the color has drained from her face. A part of me worries she's going to faint, but I'm too hurt to ask. She manipulated me. She knew who I was and kept going. I feel so fucking stupid.

"Someone better tell me what the fuck's going on. Now!" Elijah yells again.

Marigold stares at me. My frustration gets the better of me.

"Ask your sister." My voice vibrates with anger.

The fact another woman has purposefully hurt me sends me seeing red.

Her sharp intake of breath stills me. And for a second, I wince, but no, I can't feel sorry for her.

She did this, so she needs to explain.

"Eli...I need to tell you something." Her soft voice wavers from emotion.

"Both of you sit at the table now and start explaining why the fuck you two are acting like you're hooking up." He says those last few words through gritted teeth.

He turns and storms to his table, dragging the chair out and sitting down with a huff. It's not hard to know he's pissed. He's making it abundantly clear.

I still follow with heavy feet, but less anger than him.

His face is murderous, and it's all directed at me. His hand propped under his tight jaw.

I cross my arms and sit up in my chair, not sinking in from his stare. I've done nothing wrong.

Yes, my mind and body haven't been a hundred percent pure, but I never said or acted on them. I've never had feelings or thoughts about Marigold. But suddenly, they've just started out of the blue. I always thought she was good looking, but I thought nothing more of it.

The sound of her chair squeaking has his gaze finally tearing from mine.

"Start talking, Marigold." Elijah's voice is firm, but he's slightly more in control now.

"I need money for...that's not your business. None of this is so after I explain myself, don't think you can change my mind. This is my choice. You cannot take that away from me," she says.

I bite down so hard the taste of metallic hits my tongue. I hate the thought of her working online.

The other men staring at her body, her tits, her pussy. Her brown eyes looking flirty at them. Fuck, even talking to them, not even sexually...but emotionally is making my body turn to stone.

"I don't like the sound of this," Elijah warns.

She sits up and there is this powerful aura around her as the next words pour from her lips. Loud and proud. "I work online for money."

Elijah frowns. "I'm not following. How is Damien involved?"

My full name leaving his lips shows he's hiding his anger from us. Which is way more powerful than his sneering words.

"I met him online," she says, and her lip catches quickly on her bottom lip.

She enjoyed meeting me there just as much as I did. But that's when I did not know who she was. Now that I do, I should feel regret. But I don't. Which makes me angry again, but this time at myself.

Glad it's all coming out now and this can be out in the open. Elijah will never approve of Marigold and me.

"Online dating?" he asks, totally dumbstruck. He drops back in his chair as his eyes flick between mine and Marigold, waiting for answers.

"Yes and no," she mutters, her gaze dropping to the table and I watch the wheels turning in her head. Will she say what she's been doing or won't she?

I hope she doesn't—

"It's not dating. It's an app where I get nak—"

"No!" Elijah slams his hands on the table. It's loud, and it causes me to jump, and Marigold gasps. "You do not need to do that for a job. I'll give you the money. How much do you need?"

He digs into his pocket and grabs his black Amex. He throws it at the table in front of her. "You use that. I don't care how much you use. Pay all your fucking debts. No sister of mine lowers herself—" His words catch on the last word. He's struggling to comprehend this.

"I'm not taking it. Your girlfriend worked at The Players' Club, remember? That's how you met. Don't be a hypocrite, Eli," Marigold says with anger, pushing the card back to him. Then her arms cross over her chest, and she purses her lips. Challenging him head-on. I've never seen this side of her toward her brother.

Now it's my turn to be stunned silent.

"We will talk about this later," he sneers, and then his eyes snap to mine. "You won't come out to The Players' Club, or any club for that matter, but you'll pay for her?" He flings his arm out toward Marigold.

"Don't speak to her like she's trash, Elijah. She's your sister," I say, trying not to snap. I know he's shocked and hurt. Fuck. So am I.

"She's selling herself. What would you like me to say? I'm calling a spade a spade," he argues.

I lean forward, narrowing my eyes. "No, you're acting like a fucking prick. You know Marigold. Don't be like this. You're hurt, I get it, but don't do this." My words come out low, controlled, and cold.

"You two are hooking up! That's why you're sticking up for her." He claps and lets out a strained laugh. He's being a total asshole.

"No, it wasn't like that. We both hid our identity. Well, I didn't know it was her. I swear to you, Elijah, I did not know. I'd never do that. If I had known—"

"What, you would've stopped?" He says in a disbelieving tone. His brow raised at me.

"I figured it out the other night and I stopped," I confess, refusing to look her way as she realizes what happened.

"You two did that shit the other night. Fuck you're thirteen years older. You have a kid. You're not supposed to be with my baby sister, for fuck's sake."

An audible exhale escapes me. "I get it. I'm sorry and I promise you I didn't do this on purpose."

"Neither did I," Marigold says, interrupting me.

My lips pinch together, and my chest is rising and falling rapidly.

Where do we go from here?

"I think you better go," Elijah says angrily to me.

I nod and push back my chair to stand. My eyes flick to hers briefly, and they are frightened and sad. My gaze diverts. I can't look at them anymore. I can't help her.

I don't even know what to think or feel. I'm so fucking lost. How do I move past this with Elijah?

I need to get him to believe that I never sought her out.

I walk to the front door slowly. I pull the door open and step outside. He follows closely behind me.

"I swear I want to punch you in the face right now."

I can't stop myself from smiling. "I would too, but I promise you I didn't go on there for her." Shaking my head, I wince. "I didn't know she did that."

"Then why were you on there?" he asks.

He's standing tall in front of me, his hands stuffed in his jeans, kicking the floor in front of him.

"Honestly, I'm not ready to commit to another woman. But I'm fucking lonely," I say and I expect a hit, but it never comes. I feel like I need to open up more to get him to understand and forgive me. "It's been a long time. I work long hours, and I have a kid. I can't exactly go out and meet anyone."

He stays quiet for a moment.

"It's my fucking baby sister. You two aren't even on the same wavelength in life. She's in law school and you need to heal from your ex-wife."

I swallow the hard words he delivers, and I am at a loss. What he's saying is true.

"Go back inside and talk to her. Be gentle, she might be open to you if you're not the overbearing older brother."

He snaps. "Don't tell me what to do. I know how to talk to her."

With that, I turn and leave his house, heading for the nearest bar.

I spend hours there drinking alone. Which isn't making me feel any better because on top of the shitshow already going on in my head, I feel like a shit dad. I needed a breather, so I left him with my mom and headed to this bar. Despite only having time alone at work, my guilt still overwhelms me as I drink more. I love my son. He's my whole fucking world. And I hate that I'm not there with him right now. But I need some time to think and process what I've just found out. I'm a jumbled mess.

I sit in the corner, unmoving. My head sits in my hands on the sticky wooden surface until it is time to leave. I didn't want to talk unless I was ordering another drink.

I want to drink until I can't think about her anymore. Or the mess of my relationship with Elijah. It's now fractured, and I just hope it's not broken beyond repair. I've known him for far too long for this honest mistake to ruin our friendship.

By the time I get home, Mom has put Samuel to bed. I thank her, and, of course, she asks if everything's okay. I'm sure the look on my face and the state I've come home in doesn't take a rocket scientist to figure out something is wrong.

I'm not able to speak a word about my problem. I answer with a simple, "Yes," and tell her "I'll be fine," before she leaves. After she drives away, I close the door. Then my feet move to check on Samuel. I stand in the doorframe, swaying side to side as I watch his little body breathe. He's fast asleep. And I can't help thinking how simple life is when you're five and you have no troubles in the world.

I take a few moments to soak him in before I leave his room and head to mine, where I shower and crawl into bed. I check my phone to silence it and find a notification that there's a message...

I know it's her, and I shouldn't bother reading it, but I can't help myself. I'm a sucker for her. Opening it, I read.

> **Marigold:** I'm really sorry, Damien. I swear I wanted to tell you the time I was at your house, but I couldn't. Please forgive me :(

I stare at unfamiliar words...

Sorry.

Please forgive me.

Words my ex-wife never said. Not even once. She hurt me, and she simply left without a care for either Samuel or me. No sorry, no nothing, just a closed door and silence ever since.

The sides of my head pound in slow beats of pain as I stare at her message. I decide it's best that I don't respond when I'm drunk, so I don't message her back. Instead, I lie my head down on my pillow and close my eyes. In my dreams, she's wearing her gold lingerie set.

CHAPTER 15

MARIGOLD

"YOU CAN'T MOPE ABOUT him and your brother all weekend," Clara says, sitting down on the edge of my unmade bed beside me.

I haven't been making my bed or cleaning my room because I don't see the point. He hasn't been online. And he never responded to my text, either.

I've had zero desire to get back online and talk to other guys. So, there's been no point in making my bed or tidying for Clara's sake. She takes me as I am.

I won't last very long because I need the money, but I refuse to take it from my brother. He keeps trying to give me the money every time we speak, so I've started avoiding his calls. I tell him I'm at college or studying.

I'm sure he sees through my bullshit, but I'm grateful he's not pushing me right now. I need to find my happy self again.

"We had this connection, I'm telling you." I sigh. She thinks I'm doing my usual fall too hard and fast, but I don't think so. I've known Damien for many years now and I trust we've always had a connection. His marriage troubles were obvious to onlookers. But I also had insider information from my brother. Damien's ex-wife sounded like a user who wanted the lifestyle and not the family. Which is a shame for poor Samuel and Damien. She left two people very hurt.

"I'm not in the mood to do anything. And I don't have money," I complain, lying back on my bed.

"I have some money. How about we drink before we go, so we don't spend so much when we're out?" she suggests.

It's not a bad idea, but I don't want to take any money from her. "I don't want to do that to you," I say, turning my head to give her a sad smile.

"I know, but I want my happy friend back. This here," she runs her finger through the air over me as she speaks, "is not her and it's dreadful to be around this version if I'm honest."

I wince, laying my hand over my chest. "Oh."

She twists further on the bed to face me properly and shrugs. "It's true. Get up and show me some outfits and then we'll go to mine and get ready and drink."

I stare at my white painted ceiling, thinking I could lie here and sulk. Or I can get up and go drink with her and forget about him.

I get up. I've made my decision. Alcohol and a night of dancing with my girlfriend sounds like the perfect way to forget about Damien.

"Yes!" She claps excitedly.

"Skirt or dress?" I ask, walking toward my closet.

"Let's go to Luxe. Less chance we'll bump into anyone we know there," she says as she stands and walks over to me.

"Dress it is," I mutter to myself, looking through each dress I own. I pull out all my nightclub dresses and put them on the bed.

Clara helps by choosing ones she likes too. We both make a pile, and after I've gone through everything I own, we then narrow it down.

Unable to decide between the last five, I take them all and two pairs of heels as options and we make our way to her house in her car. Her housemates have already left to go out to a party, so we're alone.

She orders us a pizza to be delivered while we make our vodka and soda drinks. When it arrives, we carry our food and drinks to her room and get ready. After trying on all five options, I decide on a classic little black dress. I want to keep it simple. My hair's straight and I've done a warm brown makeup look. We've had a couple of drinks, so we're slightly buzzed. Not too bad that we can't walk straight. The bouncers at Luxe are ruthless and if you're looking tipsy or drunk, they'll deny you entry.

We head to the club and don't have to wait in line for very long. Lucky it's a warm night because we didn't bring jackets. Once inside, the club's music vibrates through me. It's so loud. The dark-gray walls are softly lit by lights; 3D sculptures are popping from the ceiling. I haven't been here for a long time, but I love it whenever I come. It's nice and clean, but most of all, we always leave having had the best night. The DJ is the best in Chicago.

"Let's grab another drink and then we can stay on the dance floor all night," Clara says, slipping her arm through mine. I squeeze it and don't object because the line isn't too long at the bar, so we're served pretty quickly.

We order our drinks at the gunmetal bar, and even though Clara was hoping someone would pay for them, no rich men took the bait tonight. Sometimes these guys are the tightest people. Hence why they're so filthy rich.

But I'm not going to lie, I'd love a guy to look after me. I want to feel special and loved. I just haven't met someone who loves me back.

It's always one-sided.

Me loving them.

They always end up loving someone else.

We grab our drinks and move away from the bar to stand together and look over at the crowded dance floor.

"Cheers for a good night." Clara beams as we clink our glasses together.

"Cheers." I clink it and we both take a decent sip. I welcome the burn down my throat from the vodka. These are strong. A moment later and I'm warm again.

"Did you want to talk to me more about D—"

I shake my head. "No." I don't want to talk about Damien. I'm here to forget him. "Tell me about you," I say, giving her a fake smile.

"You sure?" she asks, narrowing her eyes at me.

"Yes," I chuckle. "Talk to me."

She steps closer, clearly not wanting anyone else to hear. "My second night of the cam girl stuff was amazing," she says with a twinkle in her eye.

"Yeah? Why's that?" I ask, knowing her first night was a little awkward. The guys were a little weird or pushy with their kinks. I've told her to only do what she feels comfortable with. It's all about us being in control. We don't have to do everything. She has more than enough rights to say no.

Boundaries are important. And if they're abusive, block them.

I have zero tolerance for that, and I want her to as well.

Our purpose for being there is to pay our bills. We don't want to be treated poorly. We didn't sign up for that.

I sip my drink as she explains.

"Last night, this guy came on and he wanted to talk. He paid me just to talk," she says, astounded. Like it was a waste of money. But when I first started and realized it was common, I understood. Some guys are super lonely. They've either lost their wives, are divorced, or their wives don't listen to them. It doesn't matter what the circumstances are; it's important that we sit and listen. Essentially be their friend. It's what they want.

"That's all?" I ask, wondering why this one seems different.

"Yeah, but it was just the way he wore his work suit. He's so hot. Dark wavy hair, honey eyes and this model-like chiseled jaw. And God, his voice was so deep, and I actually wished he wanted more than talking."

I giggle, but it turns into a sigh. I know exactly where her mind is going. "Doesn't mean you get to see him naked."

"Damn it," she says.

We laugh together.

"How did you know I thought that?" she asks, squinting at me.

I smile. "By the way you described him. Anyone would've wanted to see what was underneath his suit."

"Maybe next time?" she asks with a hopeful look. She sips the last of her drink. Her glass is now completely empty.

"When do you talk to him again?" I ask, stirring my drink with the straw to mix the last of the soda and vodka together.

"Sunday night," she says, all giddy.

I roll my eyes. "Don't fall in love with him."

"I won't," she replies in a huff like I'm being ridiculous.

"He could turn out to be your brother's older best friend," I say, teasing my own situation.

I laugh at myself. Now that I've had a few drinks, I can do it. I see the humor in it.

"Yeah, what a nightmare," she mutters. "Let's forget about the online world and go find some real-life candy."

I nod and finish my drink. I grab her empty one from her hand. After locating the nearest table, I place them on it. She grabs my hand, and we head onto the dance floor.

The music is the latest radio pop and I'm happy I came. Sitting in my room tonight with all my studies up to date would have meant I would've thought about him all night. As we dance, I peer around at the mix of guys and girls. A guy bumps me, and I turn around. He excuses himself, and I smile at his apology. He's kinda cute and definitely closer to my age, maybe thirty?

He leans into my ear. "Wanna dance?" he asks in a slightly drunk tone.

"I can't, my friend—" I cut off my words when my gaze lands on Clara, who is currently kissing a guy.

Far out, that was fast.

"Your friend seems to be having fun," he comments.

I'm still staring at her as I answer. "Seems so," I mumble.

"How about we dance?" he asks again.

I want to but also, I don't.

The only thing I want to do is try to forget about Damien. To do that, I need to push myself past my comfort zone.

"Sure," I say with a forced smile.

"You sound so enthused," he hesitates.

I shake my head. God, how awful am I that he noticed. "Sorry it's not you. You're great," I say, hoping that's true because I don't have a clue about him. Not even his name, but I'm hoping for the best.

We dance and his pine soap smell does nothing for me. His hand on my lower back doesn't send a tingle up my spine. Right now, I feel nothing, and the alcohol is wearing off. I miss the warm buzz. I want another drink.

As soon as the song ends, I look over at Clara, but she's still kissing the guy. I don't want to interrupt her, so I decide to grab another drink. Not saying bye to the other guy I was with, I squeeze my way through the crowd, to the opposite side of where the guy I was dancing with is. As I turn around, I notice him watching. I mouth, *Sorry*. Spinning around, I pinch my lips and make my way through the crowd of people. Out of the dance floor, I pass all the VIP areas and their cream chairs. I'm passing the final one, where a quiet part of the bar is, when a hand snakes around my waist.

"Oh," I squeal from the unexpected touch. My heart is in my throat, and I'm scared the dance floor guy has followed me. Shit. He was fast.

"What are you doing here?" Damien's voice grumbles in my ear, making the hair on my arms stand on end.

Chapter 16

Damien

Her thick honey scent hits me as I speak into her ear. The touch of her body in my palm feels incredible. I flex my hands to savor the moment before she turns. I stay exactly where I am and stare into her eyes. They're very heavy from alcohol. I grind down on my molars.

I'm here with Alex and Mike because it was for work. One surgeon is moving to another state. Alex dragged me here, bitching and moaning, but why is she here?

I hope she hasn't drunk too much.

"I'm here with friends," she says, her gaze snapping away from me to the crowded dance floor. She's clearly looking for them. My head turns and I follow her gaze, but I don't spot anyone familiar.

"Who?" I ask, knowing I have no place to ask, but I can't help myself. I want to know if there's a guy...

"Just me and Clara. Girls' night," she answers with a hiccup.

I nod. My gaze drops over her luscious full breasts that are hugged by the smallest black dress I've ever seen. It barely covers her ass. I'm holding myself back from ordering her home.

Her hand sits on her hip, and she has a challenging look on her face.

I hold back a smirk. Even when she tries to be confident, she cannot hide her kind side.

Her pure, whole heart draws me to her. She's like the sun to my darkness.

Although life has thrown me into a shitty hole, her energy pulls me out of it, and it should repulse me. But I'm not. Samuel needs more lightness. I don't want him to grow up miserable like me.

"You look…" I know I shouldn't say this, but seeing her here sets me off. "Incredible."

A small lift to her lips and a wriggle of her nose make her so damn cute I'm struggling not to cross the line. I'm holding on to the little restraint I can. Running my hand up my neck, I squeeze the tension building. I remind myself she's off-limits. Even though her brother is not here, so technically I'm safe, it still feels wrong to be talking to her behind his back. So why am I?

Because I'm fucking stupid.

"Thanks," she says sweetly. Her eyes close as she sways herself forward. I know she wants to kiss me, and fuck, I want that too, but I can't. I fucking can't.

"I need to go," I mutter to myself. Both of us have been drinking tonight, and she's wearing a killer outfit that's not helping me make any smart decisions. She's clouding my better judgment and fuck, I'm so out of control. And I like control in my life. No, I need it. It keeps me calm. Her carefree attitude rattles me.

As I turn, she grabs my wrist. I gaze down at her delicate small hand, encasing as much of my arm as she can. It doesn't close though. I'm too thick for her hand. Her fingernails catch the light and sparkle. The damn purple nail polish haunting me.

"You haven't been online," she says.

I tilt my head back and bring my eyes to hers.

I stay silent. Internally battling myself not to answer and just leave. She's holding my gaze firmly, making it impossible to walk away. Her face is so beautiful, it's so unfair.

"I can't." It falls out of my mouth in a sigh.

Her eyebrows pinch together. "Why? Are you scared?"

"Of your brother?" I ask.

She nods.

I shake my head. "No. But he's important to me and so are you. I don't want to risk it."

Her eyes flash open in surprise before a smirk takes over her mouth. "He'll get over it," she says, but it's husky with desire.

"He wouldn't. Fuck, I wouldn't," I say, inhaling deeply. "He's still mad."

"You're not him," she whispers. Her hand reaches out and touches my jaw up to my cheek, and she moves closer. My heart stops. The alcohol is definitely making her bolder tonight. But I'm not ready for a woman to be in control of me again. I can never give that up for a woman.

"He'll forgive us," she says with a voice dripping in a plea, which makes it hard to say no.

I close my eyes to gain my control back. If I look at her while I try to explain, it could undo me. "I won't forgive myself. And your brother is one part of the problem."

There's a gleam in her eyes. Or am I imagining it? "You're reading way too far into this. Why can't we have a little fun?" she says.

"That's all you want? Fun?" I ask, trying to keep my composure. Does she really believe we could just fuck once and it would be enough?

I know once I touch her, I'll want more. That's the fucking problem. I'll need her in ways I haven't needed a woman in years.

Her hand drops over my stubble jaw to the side of my neck, where she can feel my beating pulse. She comes to rest her hand on my shoulder. Her hands feel way too right on me.

"I don't get to have fun anymore," I remind her.

"Dating seems too much for Sammy," she says brightly.

The nickname for my kid sends my heart thumping. He's fond of her. The amount of times he mentioned her name after she stayed over was a constant reminder how much I might not be enough. And I'm at a loss on how to give him more. More of what I don't know.

"We're not dating. We're not doing anything. You're drunk and not thinking clearly," I reply.

Her hand drops from my shoulder over my pec and stays there. "I'm fine. Maybe you should have another drink. Seems you need to loosen up."

I don't need to loosen up. I can't think clearly; the heat of her hand mixed with her touch is too much right now. "Don't drink anymore." I grunt through my clenched jaw.

She spins around and says over her shoulder, "I'm not yours to boss around."

I'm about to reply, but she winks and saunters away before I get the chance. But how can I argue with her? We aren't together, so I can't tell her how to behave, even if I want to.

When she's out of view, I exhale a deep breath and head back to the VIP area. The group I came here with is pouring fresh drinks.

"Pour me one," I shout.

"Where did you go?" Alex asks, doing a double take.

"For a walk," I lie.

He nods, and he hands me over a fresh drink. I take a sip and stay quiet while they go back to talking about today's game. I twist my body slightly to see if I can see where she's gone. My eyes scan all the brown hair women with black dresses, but when I can't locate her, I try to engage in their conversation again.

The next hour passes slowly. I'm leaving the bathroom to wander back through the crowd when I spot her talking to a guy. Her face seems tight, as if she's slightly panicked. My spine straightens and I pause, watching them for a second. He grabs her arm. She shakes her head and says *no*, but he doesn't remove his grip. I see red and storm over, yelling, "Get your hands off her."

"Who are you?" the guy asks when I approach him. The prick wears a smug smile, and it pisses me off further.

"None of your fucking business, but if you want to keep your face intact, wipe the smirk off your face and remove your hands off her. She doesn't want you touching her. You can clearly see that. And did she not say no?"

"She didn't say no earlier," he replies.

I stiffen.

"What are you talking about? We danced for one song," Marigold argues.

I'm breathing so hard, my nostrils flare. I'm trying to rein in my anger. His dirty hands on her. I fucking can't think about it.

"You two are weird. You're too old for her, you creep," the guy slurs.

My jaw ticks with annoyance. He's either drunk or high and calling me a creep adds more fuel to the fire.

"I'm warning you, if you say one more thing, I will not hold myself back."

I can't believe I haven't hit the smug prick. The only thing stopping me has to be how I'm trying to teach Samuel how to deal with problems, and fists aren't the answer. Even though he's not here, I feel like I owe it to him and myself not to do things I don't want him to do. This guy isn't worth it.

The dickhead says nothing. He just drops his hand and walks off.

I look at Marigold, who's shaking her head. She doesn't seem bothered now, but I still can't help it. I need to know.

"Are you okay?" I ask, stepping closer to her, close enough to hold her gaze.

There's no reply from her. She just blinks up at me in a daze. She's definitely had more to drink. Which irritates me.

"Marigold," I call out louder.

"Yes." She closes her eyes before opening them with a huff. "Will you ever call me Mari? I don't like Marigold."

"No. I don't like Mari," I answer honestly.

I never thought it suited her. It's tacky. She is anything but that.

She opens and closes her mouth repeatedly before saying, "Of course you don't." She giggles.

"Why are you laughing?" I say, frowning at her amused face. Nothing is funny right now.

"Nothing makes you happy. Yet..." she says, tilting her chin up defiantly. She steps toward me, closing even more distance between us.

"Online, you seemed happy," she says, and her breath tickles my face.

I groan, embarrassed.

"You were, weren't you?" A flicker of fear stares back at me.

"Yes," I reluctantly admit.

Why is it so hard to admit that? Because I've told myself, I won't go there with her. Yet, she's making it impossible not to want her.

"I knew it. But I wanted to hear you say it," she says with a full smile.

I rub a hand over my face. "Why do you want me? Fuck, Marigold. I'm old, grumpy and a single dad. You don't want this life."

She looks down briefly before looking back at me from under her dark lashes. "I've never felt so attracted to someone like I do with you. I looked forward to our chats, and you're obviously hot."

I shake my head. Not obvious to me. I don't see what's good about the gray flecks in my hair or the hard lines in my face or the tiredness I feel. I don't have the same energy she does.

"Chats? I'm not a talkative person," I say, confused.

"You have slowly opened up every time. With you, it takes time. It takes trust. I'm also not going to give up on you. I've finally gotten those nervous butterflies in my stomach that every movie talks about."

The words coming out of her mouth. The way she's breathing. All the words have left my lungs as I gaze down at her with wonder.

She won't give up on me.

I'm overwhelmed by her beauty. I'm done fighting.

Under the club lights, she glows, and I can't seem to stop myself from crushing my lips against hers. She gasps and kisses me back fiercely. Her body climbing mine. Her hands skim my chest, over my neck, and up through my hair. She pushes my head down toward hers. I grunt from her apparent desire. I've never felt a woman want me as passionately and obviously as she does. It's like she can't get enough of me. And that spurs me on.

My hands slide over her hips and down over that ass I've jerked myself over and dreamed about even more. I give her round ass a rough squeeze. I push her hips against mine. She gasps in my mouth, and I swallow it. I know she can probably feel my erection that I've had since I spotted her stalking across the dance floor in that tight black dress.

Our lips move in a frantic rhythm, and I press my tongue against her soft lips, needing more. She instantly parts them, and I slip in my tongue and taste her sweetness. A deep groan leaves my chest. Our tongues glide over each other, exchanging breaths. Her hand curls tighter in my hair, gripping me hard so I can't move. Her hips grind up and down over me and fuck, it snaps me back to the present...to what we're doing and where we are.

I pull my mouth reluctantly from hers. She flutters her lashes, and her heavy lust-filled eyes stare back in confusion.

"We shouldn't." I sigh.

Chapter 17

Marigold

He steps back abruptly. "Fuck, this is a mistake," he mutters, closing his eyes and pinching the bridge of his nose.

"Why?" I ask, stepping forward to reach out and run my hand down his arm. He watches the movement but says nothing.

"Didn't you enjoy it?" I ask, staring into his eyes. They're so full of the same longing and lust I feel, but his swirl with so much pain and torture. Is this all because of my brother?

"Of course, I did. Doesn't make it right," he mumbles. "And what your brother said to us is true."

Disappointment floods me, and I drop my hand to hug myself.

I'm so done with the whiplash. He's ruining my night. I'm here to forget about him. So, I need to do just that. I spin around and keep my head up as I storm out. It's time to go home and sleep.

I squeeze past all the people in the club to make my way to the exit. I pull out my phone to text Clara and let her know I'm leaving and if she wants to come too, she needs to meet me outside.

I'm shaking, but it's not from the cold. It's all because of him.

"Wait," he calls out.

I know it's him because his voice cuts through any noise and silences it.

I keep going without stopping. As soon as I pass the bouncers and step outside, I suck in a deep lungful of air.

My overheated body welcomes the chill of the night air. The streets are lit up by all the buildings and lamps.

While waiting for a message back from Clara, a hand grabs my arm. I jump from the sudden touch. But the spicy pear scent surrounds me again, so I spin on my heel and stare into Damien's hard gaze.

His eyes show a mix of torment and confliction, which adds to the hardness in my stomach.

"I said wait," he grumbles. Clearly unimpressed.

"I didn't tell you to follow me," I argue.

His other hand grabs the back of my other arm.

He exhales a deep breath. "I know it's just—"

He looks away for a moment. Probably to gather his thoughts, but it annoys me.

"Just what? You're hurting me. I can't deal with you kissing me and then pulling away," I say.

His hard features soften. "I'm sorry. I don't mean to be like this. This isn't how I usually act. You seem to bring this side out of me," he says.

"It's not a very good one," I mutter, letting myself admire his lips that I kissed moments ago.

I've dreamed of us kissing for a very long time. Now that we have, I want to do it again. His stubble is rough and sexy against my face. My lips swollen from our rough and passionate kiss. The way he sucked in my breath made me believe he wanted me just as much as I want him. Like he wanted more, too. Until he snapped back to reality and pulled back. I feel like a joke. As if he's treating me like a child and I'm not having it. He has to make a choice. Either we do it or we don't because these games hurt. I don't want to keep letting people walk over me. My past relationships hurt me, and I refuse to keep the same cycle going. The online job helped me feel empowered. I wish I'd use it more offline.

How I wish I didn't need to be loved. But I love the all-consuming feeling. And as I stare at his full, kissable lips, it reminds me of how it feels to like someone. The beating of my heart when I can't get enough of them. I want to talk to them and be with them as much as I can. And with Damien, I want all of that. But he's not showing he wants it too. And if he doesn't, I need to accept it and find a way to move on. But if he does, then he needs to give us a chance. And no more push and pull.

His hands on my arms drop to catch my hand. The movement causes my eyes to peer down and watch him hold my hand in his.

He does the same and our faces are so close; he leans his forehead on mine and we stay like this for a beat. I soak in the city's noise from the traffic and the drunk patrons around us. But I cherish this moment of us holding each other.

"I'm sorry," he says, moving his head off mine and he lays a single kiss on my forehead. I expect him to end us.

"I can't let you go. I fucking should, but I can't. There's this ability to trust with you that I haven't truly felt in years. And I'm not ready to leave it before it's began..." He trails off.

My heart thumps so hard I can hear it in my ears.

"So, you're going to give us a shot even though my brother will kill us?" I ask, my voice shaking. But I need to confirm it before I get excited about the possibilities. I need to be on the same page as him.

"I think we need to sleep and talk about Samuel and Elijah tomorrow. You've been drinking and I want to discuss this when we're both clear-headed."

I grumble loudly. I don't like the sound of it because I just want to jump in his arms and sail off into the sunset, but what he's saying makes sense.

I need to think about Samuel and Elijah. And then we both need to discuss how it's going to go.

"I'll call a cab after I see if my friend is leaving, too."

My phone chimes when I take it out. I see it's a text message from Clara.

> **Clara:** I'm having fun and I want to stay. Come back in.

I quickly type out.

> **Marigold:** I'm out of here, but I'll speak to you tomorrow. x

"Is she leaving?" Damien asks.

"No, she's staying. I'll call a cab now." I swipe my thumb over the screen, but that's as far as I get before he removes my phone from my hand.

I tip my head back, frowning. "Hey, why'd you do that?"

"You're not grabbing a taxi."

"No?" I ask, totally confused.

"You're coming with me, and my driver will drop you home." He grabs my hand, and he walks us toward a side street.

I curl my fingers tighter, enjoying the way his hand feels in mine.

We walk to a black car that's parked waiting. He opens the door and I meet his eyes in a silent thank you, before ducking my head and getting inside.

He sits down beside me and buckles in. I sit nervously beside him. As if sensing my uneasiness, he grabs my hand in his and I tilt my head to look at him. Seeing a hint of a smile on his usually tight lips makes butterflies return to my belly.

We drive off and I ease back into the black leather and enjoy the radio tunes while he directs the driver to my house.

The drive isn't long and when we park outside my parents' house, Damien gets out to open the door for me. Standing outside the car, we both stare at each other.

His gaze drops to my mouth, and I wonder if he's going to kiss me, but when his eyes lift to the house, I know he doesn't want to.

But I don't care what anyone thinks. I meant it when said I was all-in. Well, it's not like anyone's awake at one in the morning.

"Do you want me to walk you to the door?"

"Depends," I challenge with a smirk.

His head quirks. "On?"

"If you'll come inside," I ask, but I know he'll turn me down before he even says the words.

"No chance. You live with your parents, and I'd like to stay alive."

I giggle. "I live in their guest house."

My hand lifts to his face, needing to touch him as a reminder he's real. The mix of scruff and soft skin is beyond delicious.

"They won't care. I promise. Elijah will, but we'll deal with him," I plea.

He drops his chin with a groan. The movement makes my hand slip from his face. I hold my bag instead, to give my hands something to do.

"It'll be fine. Stop stressing," I say.

"Is that the answer?"

I nod and step closer to him, so my open-toe black heels hit his black dress shoes. I press my chest against his and he sucks in an audible breath.

"Marigold," he growls.

I press my index finger to his lips. "Shhh, unless you call me something else." I ignore the excitement my body feels when I have my finger on his lips.

But I don't let him utter another word because I close the distance between us. There was no way I was walking inside without another kiss before bed. This is my dream coming true.

This kiss is just as frantic as the first, but the fact my bed's not far away makes me hornier. The bed he's seen in my videos.

I pull back, breathless.

"We'll talk tomorrow," he says, his voice husky and interrupting.

"What time?" I ask.

"I have to work, but after that?" He kisses my lips for a moment longer, prohibiting me from speaking.

I bite the corner of my lip. "Yes. I'd like that very much."

"Okay, Goldie, get upstairs and dream of me." He winks. I don't know if it's the alcohol or the high of us that makes him carefree right now. But I'm loving it.

"Not full of yourself, are you now?" I tip my head back and laugh. His mouth moves to my exposed neck, and he kisses the sensitive flesh there, which causes me to erupt with a loud moan.

"Shhh," he mumbles into my neck.

I pinch my lips together.

When he pulls back, I hold his gaze. "You called me Goldie."

"I did," he replies matter-of-factly.

"Why?" I breathe.

"You really want to know?"

I roll my eyes and shove his chest gently. "Duh."

He shakes his head. "You can find out tomorrow."

I groan and get annoyed. "Unfair."

He chuckles before stepping back. And I know it's time to end tonight.

He pecks my lips and I go to head off, but he grabs my hand and I frown, confused.

"I'm walking you to the door."

I want to argue and let him know it's only a few steps away, but the other part of me loves him caring for me. Making sure I'm safe. So, I nod.

We wander over until I get right up to my parents' wooden door. I grab my keys and unlock it. When I'm inside, he walks back to the car and waits beside it until I close the door. I rush to the living room window and push back the curtain to look out. He stands beside his car door with a smug expression. It's as if he knew I would do it. I feel like a princess in a castle, looking out at this grumpy dad who is turning out to be my knight in shining armor. I wave and he blows me a kiss and mouths, *Goodnight, Goldie.*

CHAPTER 18

DAMIEN

> **Marigold:** Thanks for the best kiss of my life.

I blink. Surely not. She's just trying to make me feel good about defying her brother and giving into the kiss we both have been longing for. I text her back.

> **Damien:** You can't be serious.

> **Marigold:** Deadly. No guy has kissed me the way you have. Like you were destined to kiss me.

I stare at her words. How true they ring. I'm addicted to her. One taste wasn't enough. A twenty-five-year-old woman who's my best friend's little sister is totally consuming any rational thoughts when I should be fucking disgusted with myself. Yet I already long to hold her in my arms and kiss her again.

And I type out the words like a confession.

> **Damien:** I was. Even though I shouldn't.

Her brother was there for me when my wife left. He helped me pick up the pieces and now I want his sister. Fuck. I'm addicted to her. Like messaging now, I can't stop myself.

When she walked off in the club, I couldn't help myself. I had to go after her. Consequences be damned and I've now said yes.

> **Marigold:** We should…

> **Damien:** In secret?

> **Marigold:** Is that the only way I can have you? Because that's unfair. I'm not a dirty little secret.

She's right; it's not fair, but I can't sing it from the rooftops when people could get hurt, if and when she leaves. Because what if we're not really a match? We're better off as friends?

I selfishly ask her…

> **Damien:** Just for a few weeks?

> **Marigold:** And then we tell him?

> **Damien:** Then we tell all.

I bought myself a few weeks. She'll probably get sick of me by then. But if not, it gives me the time to figure out how to tell her brother and enjoy some alone time with her with no outside noise.

"I've been sick all morning," my mom coughs down the line. "I can—"

"No," I say, cutting her off. "Stay home. I'll figure something out." I run my hand through my hair aggressively, trying to figure something out quickly. I'm meant to be in surgery in a couple of hours.

I hang up and call work to reschedule as much as I can.

I receive a message and it's Marigold. It gets me wondering...

Marigold wouldn't mind, but I don't want to.

Fuck, I can't ask this of her...Can I?

I lean back on my kitchen counter and read her message.

> **Marigold:** Hey handsome, what're you doing?

"Dad, can we go play some basketball out back?" Samuel asks, coming to stand next to me in the kitchen.

I lower the phone to the countertop to talk to him.

With a heavy heart, knowing I have to say no, I gently explain. "I've gotta find someone to look after you. I'm supposed to be working soon."

"Nana will come," he replies.

I shake my head. "She can't, bud. She's sick."

"What about Mari? She was heaps of fun," he says, nodding excitedly. The way his face lights up makes it hard for me to ignore the obvious.

What's the harm in asking? She can always say no.

"I'll ask her." I suck in a breath and pick up my phone.

> **Damien:** Any chance you're free today? I need a favor.

Marigold: *What type of favor? ;)*

I pinch my lips together, knowing where her mind is going. And as much as I want to touch her again, I have to get to work.

"Did she say yes?" Samuel yells, walking off to the toy room.

"I haven't asked her yet," I call back.

With the clock ticking and no other options, I type a reply.

Damien: *My mom's sick and I need to go to work in two hours.*

Marigold: *You need me to look after Sammy?*

Damien: *I don't want to make you do this. We're only just seeing each other. You didn't agree to this. But I'm desperate. I've canceled and rescheduled as much as I can, but I'm stuck with a few hours of work. I can't move. It's an emergency.*

Marigold: *I'd love to.*

Damien: *Seriously?*

Marigold: *Seriously. Sammy and I will have the best time.*

Damien: *Thank you. I owe you one now.*

Marigold: You can owe me...

Damien: What are you thinking?

Marigold: Something fun for me, but torturous for you.

Damien: I don't agree!

Marigold: You won't have a choice.

Damien: Payback will be twice as hard, Goldie.

Marigold: I'm twitching thinking about it. Who said mine's dirty? I could make you drink tea with me.

Damien: Not happening.

"Is she coming?" Samuel asks again.

"Yes, bud." I say, and the way the corner of my lip lifts tells me I'm in trouble. Not only is my son obsessed, but I am too.

"Yes!" He claps. "Now?" he asks.

"Very soon."

Marigold: *Dirty is better, then?*

Damien: *Way better than tea.*

Marigold: *What time do you need me to be there?*

Damien: *Latest, two hours.*

Marigold: *I'll be there in an hour.*

I tuck my phone away and head to my room and get dressed for work.

An hour later, the doorbell rings and Samuel sprints to the door.

I open the door when Samuel pounces on her.

"Mari, I've set the Legos up. Come play." He grabs her hand and pulls her along through the house.

My throat constricts at the sight. He's so at ease with her.

"Hang on a sec. Meet me there. Let me talk to your dad before he leaves."

"Don't be long." He gives her a sad look and I shake my head. He's so much like me it's scary.

"Samuel, she'll be there when we're done," I say with my low and controlled dad voice.

He runs off.

"You're such a wonderful dad." She smiles.

I look at her, frowning before blurting, "Me working on a weekend and calling you to babysit doesn't seem good to me."

I'm not used to compliments about me being a father. I try my best and give Samuel everything I can. She wouldn't fake the compliment, though...would she?

"You're a single father who needs to work. There's nothing wrong with that," she replies with a shrug.

"You're too nice."

She wiggles her brows. "Not a bad thing."

"People can take advantage of you," I mumble.

"Like you?" A wicked grin appears, and I can't help but grin back.

I lean forward in her ear. "You have no idea. The things I want to do to you."

Her whole body shivers before she clears her throat.

"You owe me."

"Mmm, and?" My mouth moves slowly toward hers.

"I might not want that." Her voice cracks, betraying her.

My eyes drop to her full breasts and hard nipples. "Your body says otherwise."

"I can say no."

"Is that a challenge?" I ask darkly.

I may not have been with a woman in a while, but it doesn't mean I don't know how to pleasure one.

A challenge with her would be fun. The way we met online was part of the spark. Speaking of buying her outfits and toys...my body hums with desire.

She sucks her lip into her mouth while my head stays close to hers.

"I need to go," I whisper.

I hear a whoosh of air leave her lungs.

It snaps something in her. "Yep, I'll go to Sammy," she says in a prominent voice, walking away from me.

I stay like that, and when she turns to look over her shoulder at me, she finds me staring back. She dips her head and walks into the room and out of my sight. I'm in over my head with her.

I need some thinking space, so I grab my keys and walk out of the house.

This is the first woman, other than my mother, that has looked after Samuel all on their own since my ex left.

What's strange to me is that there's no panic or fear pulsing through my veins. Only excitement for me to get home to them.

Six hours later, I finally arrive home. I'm beat. When I step through the door, I'm hit with a smell. I frown, strolling through the hall, and when I enter the kitchen, I'm surprised to see she's cooked. Except for the mess. Walking around, I grimace at the state of the counter. There are splatters and dirty dishes. Despite the shitshow it is, I try to figure out the sweet and sour smell. My mouth waters and my stomach grumbles, remembering I haven't eaten since lunch. I tidy the counter and stack the dishwasher. Her soft voice talking causes me to pause my wipe down of the counter.

I try to return to cleaning, but I'm too distracted. I need to know what they're doing.

I quietly head toward Samuel's room. It's seven thirty and I'm surprised she knew to put him to bed. I failed to tell her what time he goes to bed. Somehow, she just knew.

I stand in the doorway, admiring her lying beside Samuel, reading. His big, heavy lids drop every so often. He's tired. But also, stubborn. He'd happily fight to go to bed. So how did she do it? Or is he being good because it's her?

I do hope they had a good time...

"Are you going to come in and say hi or just watch us?" She taunts with an amused expression.

"Dad. Hi," Samuel's excited voice calls.

I move to his side of the bed to give him a cuddle.

"Hey, you're in bed?" I say, surprised.

"Mari said I should get some sleep and that she'd read me books until I fell asleep."

In the corner of my eye, I see her sitting up and swinging her legs off his bed.

"I need a shower. Did you want Mari to finish reading the books while I do that?"

He nods excitedly.

She swivels and kicks her legs back up. I catch her button nose turn slightly pink, but I don't ask why.

My phone rings, and it's the hospital. I say goodnight to Samuel and then walk out of his room to answer it. I wander through the house, giving the nurse phone orders. When I get off the phone, I kick off my shoes and strip.

I turn the shower hot and stand under it. Enjoying the way the heat melts away my tension. A creak of a door has me tipping my head forward and swatting away water from my eyes.

I wipe my eyes again, thinking I'm seeing things.

Marigold leans against the bathroom counter, watching me. She's flushed in the face, and I haven't moved.

I have so many questions.

"What are you doing?" I whisper-shout.

"You owe me," she says with a mischievous expression.

My jaw drops. Marigold was always the good girl. But this new side I keep seeing is bolder. More direct. Pure dynamite.

"I do. This is an easy repayment. I'm going to hope Samuel is asleep."

She dips her chin. "Out like a light." She clicks her finger.

"How?" Mom and I always struggle. He fights for at least half an hour, but more like an hour. Marigold did it in ten minutes? How?

"Back tickles," she says proudly.

"He's going to expect that every night now," I grumble, shaking the water from my face.

"Stop being such a party pooper. If I want to do it, let me. Or are you jealous because you want some?"

"No one would ever turn down back tickles."

"You already owe me..."

"I'm paying for it now. You're watching me."

"That's not enough."

A brow lifts. "What do you want?"

"I want to watch you jerk off," she says with such ease.

I shake my head. "Come in here and join me. Make us both feel better."

"No. You gave me a challenge and I will withhold until I've claimed my prize."

I'm stunned. I didn't think she'd stay true to her word, but here we are.

"I haven't done this before," I mumble, grabbing the conditioner. "Sure you can't help? You're going to get too excited."

"It's okay. It's the same as if you didn't have me watching."

"But I do..."

"Don't worry about me." She waves her finger over my lower body. "Get pumping."

"I can't believe you're not helping me," I mutter.

She crosses her arms over her chest. "Stop whining. You'll sleep like a baby once you come and I tickle your back."

I hum. "That does sound good."

"But you're not horny?" I ask curiously.

"I'm wet and achy for you, but I have control."

My dick jerks at the knowledge she's needy for me. "So do I. I have the best control. Well, normally I do. With certain situations, though, you seem to break down that wall."

I hate that I'm losing control and it's even worse now that I know I can't stop it. I'm fighting a losing battle. The way Marigold has a hold on me is unlike anything I've ever felt before. It's a mix of relief and anxiety. Will giving her control end up with me getting hurt?

"I know. I'd say I'm sorry, but I'm not. In all aspects of your life, you're in control. Hence why I want to control your actions now."

I stay silent and read her face. My dick has been hard since the moment I spotted her in here.

I lather the soap on my hand and lower my hand onto my throbbing dick. I hold her gaze the whole time in hopes she'll crack and join me in here, because surely, she will.

CHAPTER 19

MARIGOLD

MY EYES SOAK IN every droplet of water running over his naked body. It's erotic and I've never done this before...seen a guy bring himself to pleasure while I watched.

I feel naughty, but I can't stop...

His solid chest is bigger than the videos and his dark hair is short, and it sticks to his chest. That wide chest would feel nice to lay my head on and have his strong arms wrap around me.

As I think of all the possibilities, his abs contract, pulling my eyes lower. I follow every muscle in his stomach until I stop on his hand. Which is wrapped tightly around his thick cock and he's pumping slowly.

I fix my gaze on his movements. That it takes a moment to register he's talking to me until he repeats his question.

"Did you want to join me?" he rasps out.

"You owe me, remember? And I don't see how me getting in there will end up in my favor." My voice is weak and breathy.

"I can give you the best orgasm," he tries to coax me.

That I can guarantee.

He's already shown he could definitely blow all my previous sexual experiences out of the water.

He screams experience and pleasure.

Definitely the second.

His happy trail of dark hair from his belly button to his dick is my favorite part. It's like an arrow to his cock. As if anyone could miss it.

He's also the biggest I've been with, which sends my nerves up.

"I know you can, but you could give yourself one." I jut my chin out toward his stroking hand.

"I intend to. If you don't want to help."

"I do, but I want to watch you more," I admit, feeling my cheeks turn pink.

"You like to watch," he states. It's not a question, more an observation.

"I do."

"Are you wet?" He grunts out.

I nod and bite down on my lip. "Yes."

"Good girl. Did you want to come together?" His voice is thick, and it sends a shiver down my spine.

"I told you—"

He cuts me off. "No. I mean, you stay there and touch yourself while I touch myself here."

The tingle between my thighs is too much to bear. "Sure."

"Touch yourself and tell me how tight, wet, and warm your cunt is."

My lips part and the steam of the bathroom and how horny he's made me make this room combustible. I can't breathe when he talks dirty. It's such a turn-on. A part of me wants to say no. To push back, but I can't. There's something about him telling me what to do that leaves a promise of an orgasm.

And I want that.

I want that so badly.

My sex pulses at the thought of a hard orgasm.

I keep my gaze on his dick as I slip my hand in my jeans, but I struggle. They're too restrictive.

"Take your jeans off," he barks, as if annoyed by them.

I unbutton and wiggle as I slide the jeans over my hips until they pool at my ankles. I kick them away, then I peek up at his face and whimper at the sight.

He's breathing rapidly with his brows furrowed and lips parted. Droplets of water run over his lips. I lick my own as I imagine kissing the water off his full lips.

"Get rid of the panties. I want to see all of you."

I push them down easily and now I'm naked from the waist down. I stand staring at the God-like man in the shower. His eyes on my pussy.

He stares like he wants to feast on me. If he didn't challenge me, I'd let him.

"Touch yourself," he instructs with a growl.

I slip my hand down to my pussy, feeling my wet, swollen bud and causing me to moan. I close my eyes and enjoy the way my fingers draw circles around my hot clit.

"Tell me what you're doing." His guttural voice causes me to flutter my eyes open.

I look at him in a daze.

"I...I touched my clit," I stammer.

A rumble in his chest sounds. "Rub it in hard circles."

I do, and my body suddenly feels heavy. Leaning back on his bathroom counter, I welcome the support as I widen my legs.

I'm panting as I feel the ache increase. I need more.

My fingers touch my soaking entrance.

"Put your fingers inside of you and fuck them," he says, as if reading my mind.

I let out a relieved breath and enter two digits inside and move them in and out.

"Faster," he yells out.

My eyes snap to him and he's fucking his fist so fast that the sight unhinges me, and I meet his pumps with my own. Both of us are chasing a release. I want us to come together.

The tingles in my sex tell me I'm close. I'm gasping for more air and a release.

I do as he asked and I'm fucking my fingers hard until the pressure becomes too much and my legs quiver.

"Come now." He groans.

My eyes drop from his heavy lids to his flexing bicep and tight forearm, all the way to down to the tip of his dick, where I watch the stream of his cum burst onto the shower floor and over his hand.

"Fuck." He grunts loudly.

I moan and come apart. My whole body shakes from the intensity.

The water turns off. I peel my eyes open and he's rubbing his body roughly with a towel.

His head quirks. "You want more?"

"Not yet," I reply, but it's more like a pant. I'm still coming down from the high.

He smiles. "Soon?"

"Definitely, I just need a second to recover."

He steps forward, closing the distance between us. All the air leaves my lungs. I'm face to face with the chest I've been dreaming about, that I've only seen on camera.

I drop my gaze to his chest, watching my hand touch his warm body. The softness of his chest hair against the hardness of his chest is incredible. I curl my fingers, enjoying the feel of the hair between them. His pec moves underneath my palm. I gasp and retract my hand.

"You're even better than the video," I breathe, staring into his heavily hooded eyes.

The air is still thick and wet from the steamy long shower, but also filled with the soap that I now use on my body. But it still hits differently when he wears it.

"If you don't want me to fuck you right now, you need to stop looking and touching me like that," he rasps out.

My skin prickles with excitement, but I don't get to speak because he adds.

"But don't get me wrong. I love it. I must admit, it's a little strange to hear." He sighs and steps back.

Immediately, I miss his body close to mine. But his words confuse me. He's withdrawing. "Why?" I ask.

He runs his hand through his damp brown hair. "My ex and I weren't very..." He clears his throat and his forehead creases. "Close sexually."

My mouth drops. "Oh."

I'm taken aback. How could she not want to have sex with him every chance she got?

"Me and my body repulsed her." He looks down at his body.

I throw my hands up, completely lost. "You must be joking."

"I wish I was." The pain etched in his dark eyes crushes me.

"Her loss," I say with a small lift of my shoulder.

He stares at me so intensely and his nostrils flare with every exhale that I feel like I've upset him.

"How could I be so lucky? Why would you want an—"

I cover his mouth with my hand. His eyes widen with shock at my response.

"Don't talk badly about yourself. You're a catch and I'm sick of the ex-talk. Fuck her and her dumb ass."

I feel movement behind my hand and his eyes soften. I drop my hand slowly away from his mouth and he grabs my head, slamming his mouth on mine. He kisses me with such hunger that I can't help but match the ferocity. I grab his head and wiggle my ass so I can sit on the edge of his bathroom counter.

"I believe you said you needed time..."

"You can't blame me," I say between kisses. "I need you."

He pushes his hips into my open legs. His hard dick hitting my aching pussy.

His white fluffy towel has long gone somewhere on the floor. My fingers grip his damp hair, tugging his head closer to me as he rewards me with a grunt.

My legs lock behind his back, and I grip him tighter to me. My pussy and his dick flush against each other.

"Dad, I can't sleep." The door rattles, but thankfully, it's locked.

Samuel's voice sends a panic rushing through me, and our lips instantly pull apart.

"I'll be right there. Just got out of the shower," Damien says calmly to him. I don't know how he did that; I'm still shaking all over.

Our position remains unchanged. We haven't moved yet. "Okay," Samuel's footsteps patter away. He's gone back to his bedroom. I let out a deep exhale, full of relief.

Damien holds my eyes again and leans forward to whisper over my lips. "I'll tuck him back in. Wait for me in my bed. Please don't go." The last three words are hoarse, like it was painful for him to say.

"Of course." I peck his lips and watch him step away, his bare ass walking into his closet. I slip off the counter, turning around to look at myself in the mirror. My face is flushed with arousal. I wash it under cold water to cool myself down until a smack to my ass has me jolting and standing back up to see a smirking Damien.

He whispers in my ear, "I'll be back."

I stand and dry my face and then I step out of his bathroom and slip into his bed, and I hold back a moan. His bed is soft, but the way I can smell his scent everywhere feels so heavenly, and I just want to sleep here tonight.

Not wanting to put the TV on and make noise, I turn on the bedside lamp and wait.

When he walks in ten minutes later, I can't help but feel giddy.

He dives toward me on his stomach. With his elbows propping him up, he looks at me. "He wanted more of your tickles," he grumbles, but I see a hint of a smile.

"Are you jealous? Do you want some so you can see why they're the best?" I ask.

"What makes them so good?" he asks with a scrunch of his nose.

"My nails," I say, wiggling my fingers in front of his face.

"You know, that's how I knew it was you."

I frown. What's he talking about?

"Your purple nails. You wear the same color." He lifts my hand and threads it through his, staring at our interlocked fingers.

"Maybe I should change them," I say as I look at the purple sparkling in the warm lamplight.

"No. It's you. Girly, sweet and fun."

My heart skips at how he can say the nicest of words to me when no one's around.

I run my hand over his shoulder. "Come closer. I can't reach your back."

He shuffles up the bed. And his head lies down on my stomach, and he drapes his arm over my legs.

I run my nails over his back, and he sinks further into the bed. "Incredible."

I continue moving them across his shoulder and back. Enjoying the planes of muscles there. His breathing slows as he groans here and there. "Fuck. I love your nails."

I dig harder and he grunts. "Mark me, Goldie."

He sounds delirious. But I draw over his back repeatedly. Words like I like you. But, of course, he doesn't get it. I'll have to tell him with words. Even if it may seem too fast to Clara.

This is me.

I don't want to change.

"So now you'll have to tickle Sammy to sleep. Now you know how good they are."

Silence.

I lean forward and take in his beautiful face.

He's fast asleep.

I look over at the time on his alarm clock and I realize I have to go. I've got classes tomorrow. Reluctantly, I slip out from under him and slide off the bed. I walk over to his side and bend down, kissing his lips softly.

"Goldie, I need you." He muffles into the blanket.

I freeze. My heart is beating frantically.

"Shhh. I'm here," I hush into his ear and tickle his back again. He goes back to sleep. I slip out of his room and into my car. God, how I wish we were out in the open and I could crawl into bed with him and sleep over.

CHAPTER 20

DAMIEN

"Dad, am I going to school today?" Samuel's voice pulls me from my sleep.

I rub my face into my pillow. A soft honey scent makes me sigh.

I lay my head to the side and see Samuel standing over me. He's watching me. I jerk in bed. It scares the crap out of me.

"Yeah, bud, just give me a second and I'll get up and get you breakfast."

A sudden thought hits me. I frantically look around the bed. Is she hiding out in the bathroom?

I scramble out of bed and usher him out of the room. I rub my hand over my face, move to the kitchen, and see the time.

Double fuck.

Did I sleep in?

I never sleep in. My natural lack of sleep means I haven't used an alarm clock in over ten years. And yet today, I slept in. I don't even have time to think about what this means and why this happened. I just know I need to get him to school and my ass into work.

"We don't have much time, so you need to be fast like Superman today, okay," I say, trying to get him to move faster without him panicking.

I grab his breakfast in record speed.

"Here's your cereal. I'm going to have a quick shower and then I'll get you dressed. Stay here and eat."

I rush off to see Marigold in the bathroom, but when I walk in, it's quiet. "Marigold?" I whisper-shout. No answer.

I walk into the closet and it's dark and empty. There's no sign of her here.

Did she go home last night?

She left in the dark and drove home. What if something happened to her? I wouldn't have known.

I walk to my phone that's on charge and swipe it open.

A message sits there.

But when I open it, I sigh. It's not from her. Mom texts to say she's still off.

My day is going from bad to worse.

I run a hand through my hair and wander to the bathroom and text her.

> **Damien:** *Did you get home safe?*

Despite my desire to wait for a text, I don't have the time to check my phone. I shower as fast as possible and get dressed. I start with my boxers and socks, then my white shirt, and finally my navy suit pants. I multitask by checking my phone while fastening my buttons.

She texted back. I tuck my shirt in and zip, then button up my pants and read it.

> **Marigold:** *I did. You were out cold. I didn't want to wake you.*

I type out a response.

> **Damien:** *You should have woken me. I don't know how I didn't hear you. I'm normally a light sleeper.*

I put the phone on the counter and walk back into my wardrobe, grabbing my jacket and shoes. Before slipping them on, my phone dings again. I pick it up.

> **Marigold:** *It must've been those back tickles...*

I can't help but wear a stupid, lopsided grin.

> **Damien:** *Those nails are a good and bad thing.*

> **Marigold:** *Just like me.*

> **Damien:** *Just like you. A lethal combo for me.*

Why is she so different? What is it about Marigold that makes me feel something new? Is it because we've been around each other for years that I feel comfortable with her? Fuck, am I settling for a woman who's giving me the attention my ex never gave me? I hope fucking not. Surely, it's because we're attracted to each other, even though we're so opposite. It just seems to work.

> **Marigold:** *You're perfect for me, too.*

I brush my teeth and style my hair. I'm leaving my bed unmade because my maid will be here soon. I get out to Samuel and hurry him along. I don't want to hire a nanny. My goal is to fulfill both the mother and father roles to the best of my ability. It feels like he deserves that, at the very least. I'm just wearing myself down little by little, but it won't last forever. He'll grow old and not want to know me, so I'll enjoy this for as long as possible.

I drop Samuel at school and drive to work. When I ride the elevator to the hospital, I text her back.

> **Damien:** *Are you talking to anyone else online?*

> **Marigold:** *No. I haven't responded to anyone else since I met you.*

I read her message and grip my phone tighter. A mix of happiness and jealousy pulses through me. On one hand, I'm grateful it's just me, but on the other, I'm hating the knowledge she was speaking to other guys before me.

> **Damien:** *Do you miss it?*

> **Marigold:** *Miss what?*

I open my office door, walk straight to my seat, sit down, and text her back.

> **Damien:** *Being online?*

> **Marigold:** *I haven't really thought about it. I need to get a job soon, though.*

I stare at the words, and I know I can't have her with anyone else. She needs a job. Maybe I could give her two?

> **Damien:** *I have a proposition for you.*

> **Marigold:** *I'm listening…*

I turn my computer on and rub my jaw. I should think about this. Can I ask for both? Is this a good idea?

I put my glasses on and stare at my screen. I can't concentrate on a single word. Not when I need to answer her text. Fuck it. I'll ask her. The worst that can happen is she says no. Emails can wait. I won't be long.

> **Damien:** *First, we could do a night a week where we go online. I pay you as normal, but I'm your only client.*

> **Marigold:** *I feel like there's an and...*

> **Damien:** *There is. Could you babysit Samuel when my mom can't? I don't want to hire a nanny; I don't know. I want to be there for him as much as possible, but Mom's still sick and it made me think about how I have no back-up. Would you be interested if I get stuck?*

> **Marigold:** *You'd pay me to do both?*

Her message seems like she's not keen on the idea. I quickly type.

> **Damien:** *You don't have to do either. Don't feel obligated to say yes.*

I don't hit send because a message comes through from her first.

> **Marigold:** *It sounds too easy.*

> **Damien:** *But is it too much with your studies?*

I know how important college is to her. She went online because of that.

> **Marigold:** *But why online when you can have me in real life?*

I think about our time in my bathroom last night. Her fingers were deep in her pussy, fucking them until we both came. I've never come as hard as that. Watching her come apart from looking at me fuck my fist. I think I've found something I enjoy. To have her come undone from my words without a single touch from me was incredible. The power it gives me is something I crave. It makes me feel desired for the first time in a long time. Deep in my gut, I feel true want, genuine desire, and a deep need. And fuck, every time we do something together, it's hotter than the previous time.

I want her every way I can. One way is not enough. I'll take everything she's willing to give me.

> **Damien:** *I want both.*

I'm addicted to her in every way. And why choose one when we can both get off when we're together and when we're apart? I still connect to her when we're online and we can play.

> **Marigold:** *Oh.*

> **Damien:** *I love watching you. You're sexy and confident on camera, but I love how you sub-*

mit to me when we're together. It's the best of both worlds. What do you think?

Marigold: *Deal. What night is the online chat?*

Damien: *Eager? To come or for me?*

Marigold: *I miss you.*

Those three words make my chest tight. No one misses me. Well, except for my parents and Samuel. A knock on my door breaks me from my bubble of lust.

"Doctor Gray." My nurse comes in and drops off a list of typed patient notes and new charts for me to look over. We talk for a couple of minutes about a patient, and I explain I'll be there to visit the patient soon.

"Thanks," I mutter and pretend to be reading an email on my computer. As soon as she leaves and my office door closes, I grab my phone and type out a quick response. I need to get back to work. Marigold's totally consuming my every waking moment.

Damien: *Wednesday? Get me through the week.*

Marigold: *And I'll be with you this weekend?*

Damien: *Exactly. But mom's still sick tonight. Any chance the babysitting can start today?*

Marigold: *You owe me again.*

I smile as I reply.

Damien: *I'll make it up to you tonight, I promise.*

I know exactly what I want to do to her tonight. My mouth is salivating, thinking about it.

Marigold: *Like, fall asleep again?*

I chuckle to myself. The sound leaving my throat and that feeling of warmth spreading across my chest are unfamiliar. Yet, it's a feeling I want more of.

Damien: *Cheeky! Just don't tickle me.*

Marigold: *Deal.*

Damien: *I'll see you at about six. Here is the code to get into my house 1234 and Samuel's school is on Bell's Road. He finishes at three. If you need anything, call me.*

I get to answering all of my emails while I wait for the patient to come in. But before I do, I tuck my phone into my desk drawer, so I don't get tempted to message her again.

CHAPTER 21

MARIGOLD

I'M WAITING TO PICK up Samuel from school. I get a few odd looks from the other moms. Their eyes scan my black leggings and crop sweater. I'm sure they are comparing me to their designer pants, tops, and bags. They even look like they have stepped out of the hair salon.

They whisper into each other's ears. I manage to catch a few words.

"Who is she?"

"She's young."

"Surely not a girlfriend?"

"Must be a new nanny."

"To whose kid?"

I internally roll my eyes as I kick the ground in front of me. They're all so cliquey. I thought high school was over.

I guess not.

Adult women seem to be worse.

I've been feeling extremely insecure since he messaged. His offer for me to do one online worries me he just wants sex. Maybe all he wants is the online fantasy girl. The one he can control. He can pay for. And maybe he isn't ready for a relationship. I've always been a little this way because of my past boyfriends.

How can I not?

Being cheated on, or not being fully committed to, wounds me a little.

So, in the back of my mind, a warning bell is going off. But I forget about it the moment I see Samuel exit the classroom.

"Mari," Samuel yells. He comes running over and cuddles my legs with such force, I almost topple over.

"Hey, Sammy. Are you ready to grab an ice cream or cookie before we go home?"

The shriek of a woman near me pulls my attention. I peer up and find her horrified expression. I remember I said home. It didn't even cross my mind to say his house. It slipped out naturally. I'm sure I'll be the talking point of the women now. Great...

"A cookie?" he asks, his face lighting up with pure excitement. I forget about the moms and focus on Samuel.

I squat down to his level and speak. "Yeah, and then we need to do homework while I cook some dinner. I might grab some items from the store."

"Okay," he says, but he's lost the spark in his voice.

"What's wrong?"

I want to know what I said that seems to have upset him. It won't make a good impression if I upset his son.

"I wanted to play Legos," he mumbles.

I smile, understanding his mood shift. "Oh, we will. First, we need to get the cookie, then do the boring but super important things like homework and dinner, but the quicker we do them, the quicker we can play. Does that sound like a deal?"

He frantically nods.

"Let's get the cookie first," I say as I grab his bag and sling it on my back. He grabs my hand and I look down and see his smiling face.

"My dad says I shouldn't have too many sweets," he says as we walk along holding hands.

"Why's that?" I ask.

"He says it's not good for me."

"He's a doctor, so I guess he would want to protect you."

"That's boring," he mumbles.

I try not to laugh at his words. I agree it's not fun, but luckily, Damien didn't tell me I couldn't give him sweets.

"It is, but I'm sure he'll be fine with one cookie if you eat your dinner. And maybe if we buy him a cookie, he won't be so grumpy."

"Good idea," he replies excitedly.

"Who can be grumpy when you eat a cookie?" I add as we walk into the shop.

Fifteen minutes later, we walk out with many cookies because Samuel couldn't decide which one to pick. It was difficult for me to choose one for Damien, too. I don't know what flavor he would like. I'm a little embarrassed, I don't know. But all the times I've seen him at my brother's place, I've never seen him eat sweets. My mission tonight when he gets home is to find out what his favorite flavor is.

At eight o'clock, I tucked Samuel into bed already. Checking my phone, Damien still hasn't checked in. Where is he?

I'll give him until 8:30 and then I'll message him. Luckily, I brought my studies. I spread out my work over his coffee table with the TV on. I find a lamp to turn on and begin. I don't know how long I'm there for, but when the door clicks, my body jerks up. He's home.

My eyes train on the entry to the room. I wait for him to come to find me. The thrill of that is something I've never felt before.

The keys drop to the bench and his loud feet stomp down toward this room.

His large body stops in the doorway, his hands deep in his pocket. "Hey, is the little man asleep?"

Damien's silhouette is huge and the way the lamp hits him, I can see his brown hair is free of his usual styling gel. He's clearly had a rough day. His hands have been raking through it.

I nod and stand up with a struggle. My legs are numb from being in one position for too long. I need a study break. I've been going hard since Samuel went to bed.

"He sure is. Out like a light. Let me heat you some dinner," I whisper, coming toward him and pausing in front of him to meet his dark and curious eyes.

"You cooked for me?" His face softens as his hand reaches out at the same time to trace a finger lightly along the side of my face.

My heart beats wildly from the awe in his eyes. "Yeah, it's no big deal. Just tacos," I reply.

He leans in and kisses my lips. Completely surprising me.

He pulls back an inch and breathes. "Thank you."

I lick my lips, savoring his taste. I take his hand in mine and drag him into the kitchen and get him to sit down on the stool.

I lay out the taco shells, chopped lettuce, tomato, cheese, salsa, and a clean plate. I heat the meat and let him make his own. Then make one of my own.

"You haven't eaten?" he asks, as if he's angry at me for waiting.

"I did with Sammy, but I only had one so I could eat with you."

He stares at me oddly. "Where did you come from?"

"I've been around you for years. It's only now that you've taken notice." I wink.

"Hard not to when you masked up and seduced me," he teases. Then takes a bite of his taco.

He moans like he hasn't eaten in years.

"I didn't plan for it. But I'm glad it happened. I'm glad you went on."

"Guess I've got to thank my buddies for peer pressuring me."

"To be on the app?" I ask.

"No, for pushing me to try dating."

"Oh," I mumble.

"Yeah, they know nothing about the app."

"I see." He's naturally always been quieter, like my brother. Not sharing much.

I want to hear about what happened tonight and where he was.

"How was work? I'm assuming bad if you're coming home late," I ask as I take a bite of my taco.

He wipes his hands of crumbs. "It was. I had an emergency surgery."

The mix of conflict and pain written on his face tells me something isn't good. I keep quiet to let him know I want to hear more when he's ready.

"I don't normally talk about my day. Good or bad, and today was definitely fucking bad."

"I'm here. And I want to hear about your day every day." The corner of my lip pulls up in a half smile.

He stares at me for three seconds with trepidation before sadness washes over him, as if getting pulled back to work. "The surgery was on a child who had been bitten on the face by her family dog."

"What?" I choke. I can't imagine what's running through his head as he performs those surgeries.

He looks down at his plate and spins it, speaking to it rather than to me.

"It was awful. She's seven and now needs multiple surgeries for the rest of her life."

"Christ, I can't imagine," I mumble as I reach out to cover his hand with mine. His gaze fixes on it and we stay silent.

Staring down at the hands that help others, I can't help but admire him more.

"How was your day?" he asks, the question surprising me. And I'm sure an unusual question to ask anyone when he gets home. I'm sure he's used to only asking Samuel how his day went, so to ask an adult, a woman, I'm sure is unusual. It is for me. But I surprisingly like it.

"I think you have a few fans," I say as I remember those women today. The whispers, the outfits, and God, when they registered I was there for Samuel. I can't help but laugh.

"What do you mean?" He tilts his head, meeting my gaze with a wrinkle on his forehead.

"You should've seen the whispers I got picking up, Sammy. I think they thought their shot with you was over."

He grimaces. "I'd never touch any of them. And half of them are married, anyway."

"Are they?" My eyes widen with horror, and I add, "I didn't check for wedding rings."

His eyes darken. "Were you jealous?"

"No. I was more worried about you. They look like they might hit on you."

"They do and I run away every time," he grumbles.

I try to imagine the scene in my head. What they would look like flocking around him and him trying to escape. A deep scowl in place as he grabs Sammy and runs.

"Did he have a good day?" he asks.

"Yeah, Sammy said he's got show and tell this week."

"I'll have to text Mom and remind her."

He goes to make another taco.

"Save room for dessert. We bought you a cookie today. Sammy will be sad if you don't have it. Speaking of, what's your favorite flavor?"

He pulls his hand back and doesn't make another one. Instead, he gets up to take his dirty plate to the dishwasher, but he stops behind me. He leans in and breathes. "The only flavor I want is yours. I know that will be my new favorite." His voice tickles my neck. And his words send a tingle running from my head to my toes. It's not a flavor I want to say, but my imagination runs wild with the vision of his hungry mouth on me. I can't think clearly when he oozes confidence and talks about sex. It has me wanting it even more.

I go to get up and make some tea, realizing he doesn't have any, and I forgot to get some at the store. I'll have to remember to bring some next time.

But will there be a next time?

I need to remember I'm only filling in while his mom is sick.

"Were you looking for this?"

He opens a cupboard above the kettle, and my mouth drops open at the sight: a mass selection of every type of tea imaginable.

"You bought the entire store."

"I didn't know which flavor you liked, so I got one of everything."

Chapter 22

Damien

After she drinks her tea, I come to stand beside her and reach for her hand. She slips off the stool and stands face to face with me. Right now, I don't even know my name. I've been dying to have her. I've thought of nothing else.

I lock my eyes on hers. She emits warmth that has me lost. I inch forward. Our lips are almost touching. Our breaths tickle each other's mouths.

"I hope Samuel doesn't wake this time," she breathes.

I suck in air, desperate for my next breath.

"Same, because the things I want to do to you requires no interruptions."

The quiver in her chin makes me close the distance between us. As soon as our lips join, she grips me with urgency. I groan and kiss her back with equal passion. I'm so different with her. More desperate.

"It's not my birthday yet. For this thing you want to do to me," she rushes out between our kiss.

"I'm going to have to think of a birthday gift," I mumble between peppering her with kisses.

"Just come to my dinner. That will be enough."

"No, that's not a gift. That's a given. But what are you going to say when your brother asks about us?"

It's probably unfair to ask her to do this, but it's either that or this ends. And I don't want this to end yet. We've only just begun.

"Lie." She moans.

"Good girl," I say and kiss her.

She pulls back, her lashes fluttering open. I gaze down at her adorable face, waiting for her to express her thoughts. She's so easy to read.

"I wish I didn't have to. It's only a dinner with my closest friends and family," she says.

It makes me reach out and stroke her face. I wish I wasn't so fucked up and could give her what she wants now.

"I know, but it won't be forever. Just until we figure us out."

She opens her mouth, but I can't give her anymore, so I selfishly shut her up with my mouth. I run my tongue over her bottom lip. She parts them easily. I want to be tender, but I also want to ravish her like a starved man. Which I am. I haven't had a woman in a long time, especially one that cares for me and my son. Well, I'm fucking desperate for that.

I pull back and suck in a deep breath as I stare at her. I know I'm going to have to beg her to stay. And fuck, I'd just do that if she wants to leave my house right now.

"My bedroom?" I rasp out. Unable to hide my desire.

"Is that a trick question?" she whispers.

"Don't be cheeky. Meet me in my room in five. I want to check on Samuel...Say goodnight."

I felt like I owed her a reason for not throwing her over my shoulder and into my bed. But even though I want to be a caveman, I haven't seen Samuel since this morning and even sleeping, I just need to check in on him. And after today's case, I just want a moment where I sit on his bed and look at him and count my lucky stars that he's here and healthy. And how lucky I am and how sorry I am for being late tonight.

That part sucks, and it's also time I can't get back, but I also can't throw away my job. It's what keeps me feeling in control and provides his education. He can do whatever he wants to do with his life, and I love how I can provide that for him. My parents could do that for me, and I want to do that for him.

Marigold kisses me, and I watch her stroll toward my room. My heart is so full right now. To have someone in my room waiting for me. Who wants and needs what I can offer?

When I can't see her anymore. I head off toward Samuel's room.

Inside, I take the moments I need there before walking into my room. The instant I see her in my bed wearing one of my white work shirts with the light of the lamp highlighting her, I almost choke on my tongue.

She's delectable, and I never want her to wear anything else.

"Is something wrong?" she asks with a wicked smirk. She knows exactly how hard I am. And I know how ready she is for me. Her tight nipples evident through my shirt.

"You know damn well there's nothing wrong. Everything is right." I close the door softly behind me, locking it, and then walk over to her.

She's grinning sheepishly at me.

"This shirt is yours. It looks way better on you." I reach out and touch the collar of the shirt, feeling the heat of her skin. I trace my finger from her neck down to her collarbone.

Her breath hitches. And it makes my dick jerk. I love all the sounds she makes.

I drop my hand on the blanket and rip it off her. I lick my lips as I take in her bare legs uncovered by my shirt.

"Are you wearing any panties?" I rasp.

She bites her bottom lip and shakes her head.

"Fucking perfect. You know how to please me."

"Yes, sir."

A deep grumble leaves my chest. I haven't heard that word since we met online. And I love it. I've never been called it before, but it's so hot coming from her lips. And with her, it feels special.

"Good girls need to be rewarded."

She nods frantically.

I crawl between her legs. Her eyelids heavy as she watches me come toward her. I hope it's as hot as she looked crawling over the bed that day online. And one night I'll get her to do that. But tonight is all about her. I'll crawl to her any fucking day. When I reach her, I push her thighs apart.

She hitches a breath.

"I've got you," I say, as if to remind her. Promising only pleasure.

She sinks back into the pillows. She looks so dreamy in my white plush pillows.

I settle my body between her legs. My fingers skim over her thighs. They prickle with goosebumps, and I don't stop even as I watch her clutch the blanket beside her.

It excites me, and as I push her shirt up, I growl.

"You're dripping. Fuck, Goldie, so wet so—" I run my tongue over my teeth and move closer, my hands gripping her thighs. Unable to speak anymore. I just need to taste her already. Unable to hold back, I lean in and take one large swipe of my tongue over her opening and up over her swollen bud. Her back arching and her mouth moaning.

Her hands clutch my head and I open my eyes, watching her face light up in ecstasy.

My tongue enters her pussy. I feel her tighten and I can't help but fuck her with it. Slowly at first, but then, she tips her head back, exposing her neck, and the fast beat of her pulse on the side of her neck spurs me on to fuck her hard.

She rewards me with a clench of her thighs, and I let her do what she wants with me. Suffocate me with her delicious pussy. I'd happily die this way. Her thighs are tight on my head as her ankles cross on my shoulder blades and she rocks her hips up and down. And I'm officially the hardest I've ever been. I can feel precum leaking from my tip without a single touch. I'm on the verge of coming in my pants if she doesn't come soon. She rides my face faster and harder. My name leaves her lips, and this is heaven. She's heaven. The taste of her pussy. Her clutching at me as if I'd come up for air.

I don't let up as she writhes on the bed as I try to go deeper. She continues to arch into my face, and I keep my eyes trained on hers. Lost in the moment. It's incredible.

"If you don't stop, I'll come." She struggles for air, and it's hot as hell hearing her try to talk.

"Come. Come on me. I want to taste what I do to you," I say that to her between her bucking her hips. It's muffled by her pussy encasing me, but I don't care. I don't want to move until she comes apart on my tongue and with that, she lets out an, "Oh my god."

And I know she's close. I thrust my tongue in harder and fuck her with it.

She moans and comes hard on my tongue. Her whole body shudders beneath me. When her body relaxes, her thighs dropping away from my head, I slowly withdraw my tongue and sit up to hover over her. With my hands on either side of her head, I take in her flushed post-orgasm face. Her eyes flutter open, and she stares at me with adoration, making my heart pound harder. As if it wasn't already beating madly from the thrill of pleasuring her. I stare at her intensely with hooded eyes, her brown eyes a lot brighter now.

"You're so beautiful when you come."

I'm so ready to just hold her. Something I've never wanted to do before; yet, right now, I want to wrap my arms around her and sleep.

Chapter 23

Marigold

I saw stars. The intensity of my orgasm sedates me. The lust staring back at me when I open my eyes makes my heart pound.

He crawls up over my body and licks his lips, and the sight is my undoing.

He lies beside me, and grabs hold of my waist. Then pulls my body in front of him. The hardness between his thighs alerts me to an important fact. "You didn't come."

"Later, Goldie, for now, you need rest, and I just want to hold you."

We haven't had sex and I'm worrying why? Old demons come up. Am I not enough?

His arms tighten around me and I don't want to be insecure and drag the night down by overthinking. So, I snuggle my head into him with a sigh. He lays a chaste kiss on my cheek and then props his chin on my head. The closeness I feel is something I've not felt before. I'm wondering if he was like this with his wife.

I don't think so based on what he's told me.

The thought makes me sad.

Don't you go into a marriage for love? I've always loved the idea of getting married and wearing a big poofy princess dress. With a sequined bodice with so much tulle, I look small in comparison.

I want to look like a real-life princess. I've always wanted a big wedding. And as I close my eyes, I get lost in a dream that Damien is waiting at the end of the aisle with an actual smile. No scowl, just utter longing and awe.

A deep exhale in my ear and the heaviness of his arms tell me he's fallen asleep.

After his day, I can understand. I need to leave in five minutes; otherwise, I will fall asleep. Samuel isn't supposed to know about us. At the moment, no one's meant to know.

The tug on my heart hurts. I hate this secret. I get it, but I don't like it.

I just need to remind myself it's not forever. He just needs a few weeks.

I soak in the last couple of minutes of cuddling him. I finally find the energy to slip out into the darkness, making my way to my cold bed, wondering if he'll notice I've gone. Secretly, I hope he does.

"You look like shit," Clara announces the next day as I step into her apartment. The smell of baked goods hit my nose.

"Thanks," I reply with a sarcastic tone.

"What? I'm just telling you what I see," she says, closing the door behind me.

Walking into her kitchen, I scan the counter. I spot the bread cooling on the wire rack. I take a seat, ready for a cup of tea, and to talk her ear off about Damien.

I need some neutral advice.

She doesn't ask if I want tea; she just goes about grabbing out cups.

"Tell me what's wrong," she encourages, while dropping a bag in each cup. Then fills them with water and cream.

I push the humiliation away and speak. "I went to help Damien out with Samuel again because his mom's still unwell. And when we went to bed that night, he didn't want sex."

"At all?" she asks, bringing the cups to the table and sliding mine over toward me.

"Thanks," I mutter and grab the handle, but don't sip yet, knowing it'll be too hot.

"No. We...sorry." I shake my head. "He did stuff but not that," I say, hoping she won't ask exactly what the stuff we did was because I'd rather not say. That's just between him and me.

"And you want to have sex with him?"

"Yes," I say quietly, "But it's more the fact I worry he doesn't want me sexually, and it's messing with my head."

"When are you seeing him again?"

I blow on the tea, trying to cool it before I take a sip. Enjoying the warm, sweet liquid. Comfort in a cup. I take a moment before I answer. "So, we agreed we'd do an online chat during the week and on weekends, I'll go over to his house. I'm due to see him online tonight." I explain and sip my tea again.

Clara gets up and opens her cupboard and pulls out some home-made cookies. She returns and slides the plate between us. "Maybe ask him tonight."

"I want to, but then I say it in my head, and it makes me sound crazy. I'm too scared I'll sound stupid."

She grabs my hand and squeezes it. "You're not stupid. Guys have mistreated you in the past, so you're needing extra reassurance. A real man will give you that."

Oh, he's a real man alright. There's nothing unmanly about Damien.

"And another thing," I say, "Something about being online with him feels off. It's less exciting now."

"How come?" She asks, puzzled.

"I want him in person. Not online."

She lifts a brow.

"Don't give me that look."

"What?" she fires back.

"Yes. I'm comparing him to my exes. Totally unfair, but I can't shake it. I just want to be with him. Talk to him. Hang out with him. Normal relationship stuff. Online makes me feel like he isn't really into me. Like he's only into the other version of me."

Why was that so hard to admit?

She bites into a cookie. I follow her lead and grab one, taking a bite of the white chocolate chip cookie, enjoying the butter taste on my tongue.

"Yeah, I guess I can see that. But online is fun," she adds with a smug grin.

"It was fun until I had it in real life. Now I want him offline every time."

"I need to take note. Never meet a guy offline."

I nod. "Exactly. Well, how's it going? Are you enjoying it?"

"Yeah, it's good. I've been talking to this one guy a lot."

I sip my tea. "Don't meet him," I add too fast.

"Jesus, woman, say it, don't spray it." She wipes her face, laughing.

"I didn't spit," I argue, feeling heat tickle my cheeks.

"You did. Anyway, I get it. I don't need complicated anyway, so online works for me." We drink our tea before she speaks again. "What are you wearing for your birthday dinner?"

I groan. I'm not as thrilled to go, so I haven't given it much thought. "I don't know, but he'll be there. And so will my brother."

She whistles. "Well, this should be interesting."

"Yeah, we're keeping it quiet for a few weeks. Trying to get to know each other. We still need to figure out the best way to tell Eli and Sammy."

She snorts, but then it turns into a laugh. "Good luck with that. Not Sammy, I mean your brother."

I grumble. "I wish I could sit next to him and be a couple at my birthday dinner."

She offers me a sad smile. "Maybe you should make it difficult for him."

My eyes brows pull together. "What do you mean?"

She leans in. "Let's go find a new outfit that's sure to piss him off."

A part of me likes the idea. Make me too tempting to resist and see what he'll do.

"I can't spend money."

She eases back into her chair, frowning. "Isn't he paying you?"

"Too much," I mutter, remembering the money that he transferred into my bank account for looking after Samuel.

"What do you mean?" she asks.

"He transferred one thousand dollars," I admit reluctantly.

"Are you kidding me?"

I shake my head. "Nope. Ridiculous right."

"Ridiculously good. If I got that for babysitting, I'd do it all the time."

"I know it was a shock to see it in my savings this morning."

"Well, let's go spend a little on an outfit. Treat yourself. Make him struggle all night. Or better yet. Have him hard all night. Payback's a bitch. I bet he'll take you back home and you'll get the sex you want."

I stare at her, contemplating her offer. My brain is trying to think if there's any other way. But when I realize there isn't, I answer her with a sigh.

"Why not?"

It's our Wednesday night online date. And I'm nervous.

Why? It's not like I haven't done this with Damien before. Hell, I've come on camera for him. Then why can't I shake the flutters in my stomach away?

I decide to take a photo and send it to him. With the hope it makes me feel more comfortable before we start.

I turn my lamp on and light a candle that I love and then slip the new baby blue lingerie on. I pose in the mirror, so my body is hiding any insecurities, and snap a photo and text a message.

> **Marigold:** *I'm ready, sir.*

Before I can over-analyze it, I hit send, not wanting to attack any of my flaws.

I don't have to wait longer than a minute to get a reply.

> **Damien:** *You're incredible. I'm going on now.*

I swallow the lump in my throat and wait for him to come on the app.

When he comes on screen, I can't help but give him a small smile.

"Hey," I whisper.

"What's wrong?" he asks, not even waiting a full minute.

"Nothing." I wave it off, not wanting to ruin the start of the night with my concern. I wanted to bring it up in the end. Or better yet, on the weekend when I see him. I wonder if I'll see him after my birthday dinner this Saturday.

"It's not nothing. You've lost that sparkle in your eye and you're not smiling the same."

I swallow hard at his keen eye. Am I really less smiley today? It's sweet he notices these parts of me, but I really don't want to confess the silly, childish thought. I think deep down it's because I want confirmation there's nothing wrong with me.

I've been obsessed with this man for so long, I don't want to screw it up now. I need to keep my mouth shut. Let him change the subject. Or better yet, distract him so he forgets. Maybe after tonight, I'll feel better. I'm probably just in my head.

"It's nothing," I whisper, running my hands over my exposed skin, along my stomach and the curve of my hips. My movements are slow and controlled. I'm trying to tease him and turn myself on. "So, you like the blue?"

"I love it," he replies.

On his bed, he looks effortlessly handsome. It helps me to get in the mood a little more. His eyes drinking me in. His upper body is naked, hard and hot. No shirt, just a pair of gray sweats. He loves my body just as much as I adore his. We could get lost in each other's bodies for hours.

My fingers continue to skim over my feverish body. His chest rises and falls the longer I tease. I imagine it's his fingers trailing over my skin. Not mine. I close my eyes and allow my head to roll onto my shoulders. The teasing of my warm, soft skin helping ease the tension. I trail my finger to my bra strap and push it off my shoulder. My pebbled nipple is now exposed to him. I part my lips, and my tongue skims my bottom lip. My fingers move to the other strap and push it off.

When I open my eyes to see him, his parted lips and messy hair make me want him more. I can't get enough of him. But in this moment, my façade drops and his face changes into a tortured expression.

"Goldie, please," he murmurs.

The endearing name and the plea are hard to ignore.

I sigh heavily and wander toward the camera. I lift the straps back onto my shoulders to recover myself. My fingers are twisting, but my eyes are trained on him.

He's now sitting on the end of his plush mattress. A bed and a room I remember so well.

His top is still off, but he's closer in the viewfinder. It all makes me wish I was beside him...or better yet, on top of him. His arms around me, holding me and then pleasuring me.

He noticed I'm not feeling this, so I should feel satisfied, but I'm consumed with stress. Why does he have to read me so well? Even through the damn camera, he knew I was faking enjoyment. I tried too hard.

"Why won't you have sex with me?" I ask quietly.

"Is that what's bothering you?"

I tug my lip into my mouth and nod. "I know it's lame, but I can't help it."

He sits up in his bed. "Hey, listen. I definitely want to have sex with you."

"You do?"

"Of course." He gives me a sexy smirk. "It's just...to be honest, it's been a long time since I had sex. I want to take my time and savor all these moments between us. Rather than rush in and do it all quickly."

I think about what he's saying, and it's more thoughtful and sweeter than I realized.

But while I'm being honest, I want to get everything off my chest. "So, it's got nothing to do with me?"

"Of course not. You please me so much."

My body relaxes for the first time tonight. A small smile appears on my face, knowing it was the right decision to admit my concern.

"How about tonight we just talk for a while?" he says.

My heart thunders in my chest. "I'd like that very much."

I don't change. Instead, I stay in my sexy blue set.

He leans back on one elbow. "You should've seen the moms at school today."

My lips twist into a full smile. "What did they do now?"

He shivers visibly, and I giggle. Whatever he's about to say clearly is in the forefront of his mind in a disturbing way.

"They surrounded me and fired me with questions about you."

"Yeah?" I smirk, picturing the scene in my mind.

"Don't smirk. You're the cause."

"I am. They think I'm competition."

"They're dreaming. I only have eyes for one woman."

"Really."

"Yeah, she's five-four and fucking edible in baby blue."

My finger runs along my lip. "What else is so good about her?"

"She's intelligent. Studying law."

"And that helps how?"

"Good lawyers always want to be on top of things."

I roll my eyes and laugh at his dirty joke. "I do."

"But the worst was Samuel. He comes running out after the school bell with the words 'Where's Mari?'" he explains, running a hand through his hair. "And I said it was only me and the cheek on him to tell me 'Oh, I miss Mari.'"

"You're not his favorite anymore. That's gotta hurt," I tease.

"I can't blame him. You're too..." He trails off, as if not knowing the word. "Adorable."

As dumb as it is, I needed to hear those words. I should be content with how our relationship is progressing, but the little voices in my head were there with my ex too. I ignored them and look where that got me. No, this time I want to ask the questions. As difficult as they are. I may have fallen fast again, but this time, it's different. I've known Damien for years. Everything with him feels different—including me.

We spend all night talking about a variety of things, from his work to Samuel, then life in general, and my classes. Even the moments of silence are relaxing and I'm glad I asked the burning questions. And I'm happy we did nothing sexual tonight.

After, I say goodbye and get changed for the night.

I walk out of the bathroom when my message tone goes off. I reach over, thinking he sent me a text, but it's the money for the online chat. Staring sadly at the screen, my heart feels heavy. He's paid me for tonight. While I stare at the money in my bank account, I realize I don't want that. I want the feeling that he's falling for me, because my crush has turned to me falling for him.

I need the money, and we agreed. But something about this makes it seem more like a transaction. I'm going to have to tell him on the weekend I can't do the app anymore. That it doesn't sit right with me.

CHAPTER 24

DAMIEN

I WALK INTO THE Guild Restaurant searching around in the dim lights for those brown eyes. It's Marigold's birthday dinner and I can't shake the sudden nerves. I know I'm going to have Elijah drill me with questions. Every time we've spoken, he asks me elusive questions, which is his way of checking to see if me and his sister are still hooking up.

And every time I lie through my teeth. I need to figure out a plan soon. It'll be worse if he finds out by walking in on us again. God, I can't even imagine how he'll react.

The restaurant has a mix of dark brown leather chairs and booths with dark wooden tables. It's the opposite of how Marigold is. This is moody and dark. The only commonality is that the darkness adds sexiness, and she has that in abundance.

As I'm waiting to be served, it's as if everything disappears and it's like a spotlight shines directly on Marigold.

All the air has left my lungs and I force myself to move. I stride to the table. As I come closer, I see her family and friends have already sat down. Checking my watch, I'm on time—just. I had to wait for my mom to come and watch Samuel before I could leave.

My eyes drop over her outfit. She's wearing a black satin V-cut dress that makes my mouth dry. It molds perfectly to her body in the most delicious way. The sexy slit in the already short dress makes me think how easy it would be to rip that dress in two.

As I've been strolling closer and soaking in all her beauty, I've found myself in front of her.

"Goldie, you look breathtaking," I say hoarsely.

She bats her lashes and gives me a sweet smile. "Thanks." I don't miss the way her eyes run over my black suit and my heart beats faster, hoping she likes it. I bought it just for tonight. Just for her.

"You look handsome," she responds, her eyes gleaming with happiness. Her hand reaches out to run her fingers over my black checkered tie.

Feeling eyes on me, I clear my throat and hold out her gift. It causes her to drop her fingers away from my body. "Happy Birthday," I say with a hint of a smile.

"You didn't have to," she replies with a grin, but takes the bag and the touch of her fingers feels all too much, but not enough when they leave. I push my hands inside my pockets and watch her peek inside the bag.

"Don't open it here," I whisper as I lean in so no one else can hear.

She closes the bag and peeks up at me from under her black lashes. "Now I really want to know what it is," she whispers back.

"Later," I say with a wink.

Just then, one of Marigold's friends comes over to join us.

"Hey, I'm Clara," she says, sticking out her hand.

I dip my head and shake her hand softly. "Damien."

"Oh, I know who you are," she deadpans.

A sense of dread hits me.

What has Marigold been saying?

I look around and I've got two choices: either I go to the table, or I go to the bar, and see if I can get five minutes more without seeming suspicious.

"Let me buy you a drink," I say to Marigold.

"That would be amazing. We just finished our drinks," Clara interrupts. Even though I want Marigold to myself, having Clara there might look better to the other eyes. Mainly Elijah.

Marigold's sympathetic eyes meet mine. I dip my chin and stroll to the bar. The click of their heels tells me they're following.

When I reach the bar, I rest my elbows on top. I tilt my head, and I'm relieved to see Marigold next to me. "What are you girls drinking?" I ask.

"Grasshoppers," Clara calls out.

I frown, thinking of the bugs. "What are those?"

"They taste like a thin mint cookie," Marigold says and the way her gaze drops to my mouth, I can't help but lick my lips.

When the bartender arrives, I order two of those and an old-fashioned drink for me.

"I wish I could kiss you," Marigold breathes.

I look back at her friend, finding her busy talking to another friend at the bar. I'm relieved because I can talk without worrying about Clara overhearing.

"You have no idea how much I want that too," I say in a low voice. My eyes stare at her plump, glossy lips. Before I bring them back to her eyes.

"I have to admit something," she says, looking away from me.

"Mmm. What's that?" I probe with a little concern at her uneasiness.

"I don't want to be online anymore."

I sigh in relief. "I'm not going to complain. The thought of sharing you makes me murderous."

She's about to reply when the drinks arrive, and she picks hers up and takes a sip while I pay.

I pick up my glass and raise it to hers. She copies. "Happy Birthday, Goldie. May your wishes come true."

We clink glasses. Our eyes never leave each other's as we both take a sip of our drinks.

"My wish came true," she says as she lowers her drink.

I lift my brows. "Oh, really."

"Mm-hmm. I finally got you," she says with a wide smile.

I'm stunned. No words are forming. She must see it, so she asks an unrelated question.

"Do you want a taste?" she asks, holding out her cocktail glass. My mind wants to say yes from your mouth, but it's not an option. Even though I wish it was.

"No thanks. I've got mine," I murmur, holding up my glass as I take a drink. "Do you want a taste?"

She screws up her face. "I don't know. That looks strong."

"It's alcohol," I tease.

"Duh. I know that. But I'm a lightweight. I also have had little to eat tonight," she admits, taking the glass and wincing as she sips. "Ah."

"You don't like it?" I hold back a laugh.

"No, it's foul. I'll stick to this." She sips her green cocktail, clearly trying to wash away the taste of my old fashion.

"You need to eat if you're drinking," I say.

"I don't want to bloat. This dress isn't forgiving." She drops her hand over the front of her stomach.

I groan. "Are you serious? You're the most beautiful woman in the room."

She blushes. "Thanks."

"It's true. Listen to me." I reach out and grab her chin and lift it with my finger. I want those shimmering eyes on mine as I speak. "Do not worry about what you look like. To me, you're perfect. Hot, smart, and kind. Every guy in this place has looked at you at least once tonight and is probably jealous of me right now." I reluctantly drop my hand from her face.

"Except my brother," she adds.

I grimace. "Yeah, minus family. But every other guy has wished they were with you and that's only from the outside. If they knew you in here," I touch her chest briefly, "they'd want to date you."

She doesn't speak for a while. She just blinks.

"I don't want to date anyone else," she replies.

"No?"

She shakes her head. "No. The one person I want is you."

Bold Marigold is so hot. I stare wordlessly at her, trying to figure out a response. We're still a secret, so is that dating if no one knows? I don't think so. She deserves better, but I'm selfish and I can't fucking let her go.

"Going back to what I was saying. I didn't mean just with others..." she trails off nervously.

I go to reach out with my hand to touch her arm, but I curl my fingers back in and grab my glass. Hopefully, it will prevent any additional near misses. I need to keep my control in check. Otherwise, Elijah will breathe down our necks or cut my dick off.

"I don't want to do the online night with you on the app anymore," she deadpans.

My jaw slacks. "You don't?"

I almost want to say you don't want me anymore, but I am quick to close my mouth.

She moves her head and her perfume from her hair hits me, causing me to suck in a deeper breath. I notice she still uses my soap, which is adorable.

"I want you in real life. It wasn't the same the other night," she adds quietly, as if embarrassed.

"Did I make you uncomfortable?" I ask, trying to think back. I never asked her to do anything sexual. We just ended up chatting for a couple of hours.

She shakes her head. "No, never. It's just now that I've had you in real life, that's all I want."

My chest expands from her words.

"What about your college bills? How will you get by?" I ask worriedly. "Are you going to take the money Eli offered you?"

"No way. I'd never take his money. I'd feel like I owe him something. Life is about opportunities, and I'll see when the next one comes along."

I take a sip of my drink. "No plans will lead to failure."

"Listen, I'll figure it out. You don't have to worry about me," she replies with a hint of frustration in her voice.

Is she joking?

"I do and I always will," I say.

She stares at me, bemused. "See, so online doesn't work. You act protective and yet we're a dirty little secret. We need to come out and tell people."

I exhale a heavy breath. "Soon, I promise."

A wave of disappointment hits her face. But she picks up her drink before I can speak again. "I better get back to the table." She saunters off toward her family and friends and since I can't ogle her, I turn back to the bar and sip my drink, lost in deep thought.

CHAPTER 25

DAMIEN

AFTER ORDERING ANOTHER OLD-FASHIONED, I wander back over to the table.

"Hey. Over here." Elijah waves me over. I nod and approach the empty chair beside him. I lower my glass to the table and sit.

"Hey, Jackie," I say, tipping my head. It's hard to miss the large dimple on her cheek when she smiles, and her youthfulness reminds me of Marigold. Probably because they're similar in age.

She finishes sipping her drink to say hello. Her cheeks have a new flush, probably from the alcohol.

"Nice for you to finally come over and say hi," Elijah says, squinting his eyes at me. He's pissed.

"I had to say happy birthday," I reply.

"And you came with a gift," Jackie adds. I don't miss the twinkle in her hazel eyes.

"I did," I answer.

"What is it?" Elijah asks. "Ah. What did you do that for?" Elijah rubs along the side of his navy suit.

Jackie glares at him, wearing a scornful look. "Don't ask him that. It's rude," she replies.

I exhale a sigh of relief. I didn't want to lie to him about what I bought her. It's not something he'd appreciate.

"Sorry," he grumbles.

Well, this is new.

Elijah apologizing and following a woman's orders. Here I was, thinking he'd need a feisty woman to keep him in line. Turns out we both have a soft spot for sweet, young, and determined women.

They quickly share a private conversation, making me feel like a third wheel.

I turn to grab my glass, but I pause it midway to my mouth. Marigold is sitting directly across from me. And I have to swallow the groan bubbling in my throat from the way the boning of her dress pushes her beautiful full breasts up.

My erection is becoming harder to handle. I'm sitting next to her goddamn brother hard as a rock. I have no control over my body when it comes to her. It has a mind of its own. And right now, it wants to be buried deep inside her.

Her eyes flick to mine when she grabs her drink before turning to her friend and whispering something. She gets up and walks off alone, and I follow her with my eyes. Enjoying the way her hips sway with each step.

I lower my glass and stand.

"I'll be back," I mumble to Elijah without looking at him and walk off in the same direction Marigold went.

I peer around the dark hallway and see no one else. Before I'm noticed, I slip inside the bathroom. The door closes with a thud behind me, causing an echo inside the bathroom.

Inside, a door is moving, so I step closer and hold my hand out. I catch the door before it closes. She gasps when I push it open before she can lock it. The fear instantly drops from her face the second she realizes it's me. Now there's the sexy as fuck challenging look. Since we've hooked up, she's found her voice. Less of the quiet, scared Marigold. Now she's the woman she wants to be.

Confident, empowered, sexy, and downright irresistible.

"What are you doing here?" she asks, lifting a brow. "It's the ladies' bathroom. The men's is next door."

I close the door behind me as I smirk at her smart-ass comment and stalk closer to her. She steps back until she's backed against the stall wall. She sucks in a breath. Her reaction to me is clear, and I have to control the ache in my chest.

I dip my head, bringing my face to the side of hers.

"Damien," she pants.

I run my nose from her ear to her collarbone, whispering over her warm skin. "I know exactly where I am. And I know you wanted me to come find you. Didn't you?"

She nods lazily. "Yesss."

"You wear this short, tight, barely there fucking dress for what? To get my attention?"

"Yes. I wanted to drive you crazy."

"It fucking worked. This dress. Fuck, this dress shouldn't be seen by anyone else but me. But fuck, I love it. I love it so fucking much." I lay a kiss under her ear, feeling her pulse beating wildly against my lips. "So now you've got me. What do you want, Goldie?" I ask against her skin before pulling back to stare into her magnificent eyes.

She exhales with a shudder. Her arms trail up over my arms, all the way up over my neck until her fingers grip my hair tightly. She brings those plump lips to my ear.

"I want you," she purrs.

My dick strains against my pants and I can feel precum leaking from my cock. I want her so badly.

She blinks slowly.

"What part of me do you want?" I ask.

"All of you."

I swallow hard, knowing her lust-filled brown eyes are telling the truth.

"You want me to fuck you here in this bathroom and not romantic on a bed?"

She nods her head with a cheeky smile. "Yes. I'm sick of waiting."

"Are you wet right now? Are you making a mess in your panties?" I ask, as my hand drops to her ass and then to the tops of her thighs, where I pull up her dress and find her bare pussy.

"I'm not wearing any—"

She's too fucking hot. I can't hold back any longer; she's making it impossible.

"Fuck! Goldie. Tell me you really want this here and now," I beg.

"Yes! Fuck me, Damien. Fuck me so hard, I'll walk out of here feeling sore. Every step reminds me you were there," she says huskily.

A growl rumbles from my chest. I snap. My mouth comes down hard on hers and I kiss her with all the night's worth of pent-up passion. Fuck, her lips. They feel so soft and plush against mine. I've missed this. Missed her.

My tongue touches hers and a deep, guttural growl leaves my chest. She's so fucking perfect. I'm trying to ignore the gnawing ache in the center of my chest. This is too good to be true. People like me aren't worthy of a woman like her. She's kind, pure and intelligent. When she figures it out, she'll leave me, but right here, I'm savoring this moment.

Our bodies tangle in limbs going everywhere. I push her dress up to her hips as she fumbles with my jeans, belt, and button. When her hand dips in with no warning and grabs my length, I choke on my breath. "Fuck."

I grab both of her legs and lift her by her thighs. I push my erect cock over her wet pussy and roll my hips around. She tips her head back and a loud moan leaves her chest.

I bury my face into the base of her neck and rasp, "Shhh. Otherwise, someone might hear you."

She hums. My lips trail up her hot neck, nipping at it until I reach the shell of her ear. Enjoying her heavy perfume. She shivers under me. "Your brother will kill me if he finds my cock buried deep inside you," I add.

"Oh." She whimpers as I rub my cock through her pussy. "Please, Damien."

I'm so hard for her. I've never wanted anything as much as I want Marigold right now. The online foreplay, the desire of her body and this new intimacy we share, they all make me excited to have her shatter on my cock.

"Condom. Hang—" I say, pulling away. Her legs drop from my waist so she's standing again.

"No! I'm clean. I want nothing between us. I want to feel all of you," she cuts me off, gasping. Her hands grabbing my shoulders. Yanking me back to her. She's desperate and so fucking sexy.

"Fuck, Goldie. You're too fucking good for me."

I want to tell her I haven't been with anyone since my ex, but I don't want to bring up her name and ruin the moment.

My hand grabs the side of her face, the other gripping her hip. With our eyes locked, I ask, "Are you sure?"

She answers me by trying to grab my cock. But I'm quick and I grab her hand, lacing our fingers and pinning them to the wall. "Don't move them."

She closes her eyes, expecting me to kiss her, but I bend down and lick up her neck, over her beating pulse. Her head falls to the side until my mouth lifts off her skin. I grab her hips again and lift her, so her legs wrap around my back.

Her warm heat is at the perfect angle now. Her breath quivers.

I line up my cock and slowly enter her. The tightness steals my breath. "You're so tight. Fuck."

I slide in and out of her slowly, stretching her.

"You're big," she says with a pinch to her tone that has me pausing.

I stare at her. "Are you okay? Do you want me to stop?"

"Don't you fucking dare," she replies.

I close my eyes briefly and my grip on her tightens with approval.

"I better give the birthday girl what she wants. And it sounds like she wants to be fucked hard."

I slide farther in until I'm buried as deep as I can go. Her head drops back and her parted lips gasp for air. "Yes."

When I thrust the rest of the way in, I still, waiting for her to adjust and then when her body softens, I fuck her hard. My lips return to hers in a punishing kiss.

The way her walls tighten tells me she's close. She pulls her lips away and cries out as she orgasms. My name leaving her lips in the sexiest pant. I feel the way my climax hits me, and I can't form the words to tell her to be quiet. I don't think I could. The way she looks shattering on my cock is hot. Her body sags and she whimpers. We both are breathing heavily as we come down from the high. She was better than I could've imagined, responsive, eager, with the most perfect pussy. I just wish I wasn't here right now so I could hold her.

"You're exquisite," I rasp, enjoying the way her cheeks are a darker shade of red.

She smiles groggily back at me, unable to answer. She's still riding high from her orgasm. It reminds me of her statement earlier about lack of eating.

"When we get back out there, you need to eat something. You need your energy."

She nibbles her lip. "Why?"

"Because I want to fuck you again, but this time, I want to take my time, and in my bed, where you can scream as loud as you want."

"I love the sound of that," she replies.

"So you'll eat?" I ask.

"Yes, sir." She gives me a smug look.

"Fuck. I love it when you call me that."

"Good to know." Her eyes have a mischievous look about them. And I want to ask what she's thinking. But I'm aware of the time and that we both need to get back out there before they notice she's missing.

"I better get back out there."

"Yeah," she replies, the same disappointment lacing her voice. We both don't want this to end.

We redress and then I lay one last lingering kiss on her swollen lips. They're extra pink from my five-o'clock shadow, which is hot. I can't stay, so I reluctantly drag myself out of the bathroom and back into the hall. Marigold is back at the table, so I head to the bar.

I'm waiting to order a drink when Clara's voice sounds behind me.

"You know she's falling, right?"

I turn my head to see Clara moving closer to me. She mirrors my stance on the bar. Her grasshopper cocktail in front of her.

"Sorry?" I ask.

She rolls her eyes. "She's falling in love with you."

"She is?"

She sighs heavily. "This is what she always does. She falls too hard, too fast, and then the guys don't feel the same."

Her eyes twitch and I can see she wants me to talk. Only I'm not a talker. Well, normally, I'm not. Unless it's Marigold and I can't seem to stop talking. Our conversations are always so effortless. Different from anyone else.

"Okay." I'm at a loss for words. What else should I say?

I'm not falling in love with Marigold.

I can't.

"So please, let her go if you don't feel the same. I can't see her in pain again. If you break it off now, it won't be as bad."

My mouth opens and closes, but no words move past my lips. She takes that as if I've given her an answer.

"I thought so. Do the right thing, Damien," Clara adds, picking up her drink and walking off. She leaves me there goggle-eyed and open-mouthed.

If I don't love Marigold, I have to set her free, because she's already fallen?

I rub my hand over my face. I can't even think about this right now.

No.

I'll talk to Marigold later.

I'm sure she hasn't fallen, and Clara has it all wrong...right?

I walk back to the table and sit.

"Where'd you go?" Elijah asks.

"Bathroom and then to the bar," I reply.

Elijah is about to speak to me. "Where's your dr—"

My phone vibrates in my pocket. Slipping it out, I look at the caller ID. Fuck!

It's work. I can't ignore it.

"Sorry, it's work. Let me grab this really quick."

He nods. I slip out from the table and walk away to answer it. Five minutes later, I'm walking back to the table with my head hanging low. My eyes catch hers and I see the concern etched on her face.

"Everything alright?" Elijah questions. "Is it Samuel?"

I sigh. "No, it's work. I've been called into the hospital for an emergency."

"You'll miss a good night, but with the way she's looking at you, I think it might be for the best."

I don't have to look very far to know he's referring to Marigold.

Has she been watching me all night?

We've held each other's gazes a couple of times, but that's it. However, I guess Elijah would be watching us closely.

I'm glad he didn't catch us in the bathroom a couple of minutes ago.

I'm reluctant to leave. I don't like the fact we just had sex for the first time, and now I'm running away. I feel like a dick. Maybe she could still come by after I get off? But when her friend brings her another cocktail, I'm reminded that it's her night. She's here with friends and she'll be drunk later. I grind my teeth, hating her drunk and out of control at God knows where they end up later. I imagine someone taking advantage of her, so it's difficult for me to leave now. I just want to...watch her?

Fuck, seriously, what's wrong with me? No, that's not fair. I have to trust her.

"I'm off, but have a good one. Sorry I had to skip out early," I say to Elijah and shake his hand.

He slaps my shoulder. "Don't sweat it. It's your job."

I walk around the table and stand behind her seat. She stands and I'm well aware of Elijah and Clara's eyes on us.

There's a decent amount of distance and I keep it that way.

Marigold's cheeks have the cutest shade of pink. I wonder if it was the mind-blowing bathroom sex or the alcohol.

I hope it's the first reason.

"I've been called into work. I'm sorry, I've gotta leave your dinner early."

Why is it so hard to say the words?

Maybe because the way she looks at me with sad doe eyes makes me feel remorseful for leaving.

A strand of hair is in her face, and I clench my hand to refrain myself from tucking it behind her ear.

"Oh right. Work. I get it," she replies with a quiet voice. "Thanks for coming," she adds, forcing a smile afterwards.

Fuck, if I didn't already feel horrible for leaving, she goes and kills me with one look. The alcohol is not masking her feelings.

"I'm sorry," I whisper.

"So am I."

I stand there gobsmacked at this beautiful woman whose birthday dinner I'm leaving.

CHAPTER 26

MARIGOLD

WATCHING HIM WALK AWAY was hard. As I stare toward the exit, I swallow the disappointment.

It's my birthday, and he left for work. I know he works hard, but damn, on my birthday, that sucks.

I know it's not his fault and the work he does helps so many people. It just hurts when it affects you. Like we aren't even able to spend as much time together as it is.

"He's not coming back," Elijah deadpans coldly.

I tear my gaze from the exit and face him.

"I know." My voice cannot hide the disappointment.

"You're not still fixated on him, are you?" he asks. I take my seat again.

Jackie tugs on his arm. "Don't do this here."

"Exactly," I reply, avoiding his comment because I'm not just fixated. I'm utterly obsessed and head over heels for Damien. I don't think he'd want to hear that, though.

His lips thin, but he says nothing else, thankfully.

I turn to Clara. "I need another drink."

"Yes, you do!" She squeals.

We stand and amble to the bar. Where we order our grasshoppers.

"You seem down," Clara states with a curious expression.

"I am. We hooked up in the bathroom and then he left," I murmur, so no one around can hear.

Her eyes widened. "You mean hooked up, hooked up?"

I nod. "Yep. It was incredible. I've never been with any guy that's made me feel this good."

"I can hear a but coming."

I huff, knowing she's right. "He left and I feel a mix of dirty and bummed. He said I was going to go back to his place. But then work called."

The bartender arrives with our drinks. After paying, we clink our glasses together and take a sip.

"You're not going back to his. We're gonna go dancing until we can't feel our feet anymore."

I giggle and it helps lift my spirits a little. "You know what? I don't want to feel down. I want to still have a good night. We're dressed up and I will not waste it."

"That's the spirit. Let's drink and play nice until the party leaves and then let's head out."

I lift my glass to my lips with a wicked grin. I love how Clara knows me so well. Maybe better than I know myself. I'm ready to have some fun. Even if I wish I was going back to his place, I know Clara and I can still make this a great night.

The next morning, I wake with the worst hangover.

"Fuck, my head feels like it's going to explode." Clara rolls in bed beside me.

I check the time on my phone and see a message. My head feels just as bad.

"I'll order some MacDonald's. I need greasy food stat." I groan.

"Mmm. Good idea," Clara mumbles.

I prop myself up on pillows and order some food quickly as Clara rolls back over to go back to sleep.

I can't sleep, so as I wait for the food to be delivered, I open the message. It's from Damien.

> **Damien:** *Finally made it home. My bed feels empty without you. How was the rest of your night?*

He messaged at 4 a.m.

I don't know what time we got home, but I didn't see this message.

> **Marigold:** *Sorry, I just woke up. I must've passed out last night.*

> **Damien:** *That's okay. I didn't get home until late. How was it?*

> **Marigold:** *Great. We went to Luxe. I drank and danced until I don't know what time. I'm paying for it today.*

> **Damien:** *Did you eat?*

> **Marigold:** *No, sir.*

> **Damien:** *I told you to eat.*

> **Marigold:** *I didn't feel like eating.*

> **Damien:** *Why?*

I kept my feelings to myself about him leaving and feeling hurt and angry, so I change the subject.

> **Marigold:** *Thanks for my gift. It's too much though, I can't accept it.*

I snap a pic and send it to him. But I cut out my head because I look like a hot mess. I need to shower after I've eaten.

> **Damien:** *So beautiful. And it's not too much. I should've done something better. I just know you aren't into materialistic things. Which makes it hard to buy you a gift.*

> **Marigold:** *These are perfect.*

I stare down at his white shirt and touch the gold G necklace. G and gold. Fitting for the nickname he uses for me...Goldie.

> **Damien:** *Are you mad I left?*

Here's my chance to admit how I honestly felt. Normally, I'd want to be the happy-go-lucky partner and not say anything to make the guy mad, but with Damien, I feel like I can be myself and maybe he won't run.

> **Marigold:** *I understand it's your job, and it's important, but I'm sad you left. It was my birthday.*

I hit send and wait to see how he reacts. I'm proud that I expressed my feelings without toning them down. This is another step in striving to become the newly empowered Marigold. I've always toned myself down for men and look where that's left me.

> **Damien:** I'm so sorry. I'll make it up to you, I promise.

I don't know what to reply. So when the door sounds, I rush to it and grab our food. Along the way, I get some painkillers for our pounding heads.

I return and lower the food on the bed. Straight away, grabbing a fry and chewing it. The salt is exactly what I need right now. My belly is churning from finally getting food. I definitely should've listened to him and ate something and I definitely would've if I didn't feel sick when he left.

My phone chimes and I see it's another text from him.

> **Damien:** What are you doing this weekend?

> **Marigold:** I'll be doing assignments or studying. Why?

> **Damien:** I'm taking you away. You can bring your books with you.

> **Marigold:** Is this to make up for leaving?

> **Damien:** Yes. I fucked up big time. Let me make up for what I did. I'll give you just-me time all weekend.

God, I want that so much. Before I can type a reply, he sends another text.

> **Damien:** I should've made other arrangements.

I'm not fighting this offer. I'm desperate for alone time.

> **Marigold:** I'll pack a bag. What's the weather?

> **Damien:** Bring a mix. I want to surprise you with the destination.

> **Marigold:** So many surprises.

> **Damien:** You have no idea.

It's finally Friday. I go straight home after college. I have been adding items to my open suitcase as I think of them. With us not doing our Wednesday night video chat, it means I miss his face and voice more than normal. We still text, but that's it for the week. So, I'm excited to have all his attention on me.

I pull all my clothes onto the bed and begin with the lingerie when I hear a knock on my door.

"Come in," I call out.

"You told your mom you're going away with me?" Clara announces as she wanders into my room.

I wince at her from my kneeling position on the floor. And with an apologetic smile, I say, "I'm sorry. I just can't tell them it's with Damien, they'll tell Eli."

"Why does he have a problem with it?" she asks.

I shrug. "He thinks Damien needs to heal from his ex, and I need to focus on school."

She shoves clothes aside from a section of the bed, so she can take a seat.

"Listen, I'm not a huge fan of this. I worry if this is really what you want?" Clara says, which totally surprises me.

"Him, of course. He's different," I reply.

She purses her lips. "I'm not sold."

I huff. Emotions bubble through me. I feel like I'm on the verge of crying. How can I convince everyone he's not like any of the 'ones' before him?

"Why?" I ask.

"He's older and a single dad. He's set in his ways. You're a carefree, single young woman, living the best years of your life. Whereas he's living a quiet and busy work and dad life." She leans her elbows on her knees.

"I know we sound so opposite, and yes, I've seen his hectic life and his controlling ways, but I've found my voice with him. I've started speaking up. That's something I've never done before. Have I?"

She shakes her head. "No, but I don't want you to change for him."

"I won't and if I'm changing, it's because I've found myself and my voice. If things don't work out, I'll deal with it then, but at the moment, we can't officially date because so many people frown upon us. Our relationship with strangers commenting will be hard enough. I need support right now."

She stands up from the bed and drops to her knees in front of me. "Don't think I'm not supporting you. I love and care about you. Since I've been through a few breakups with you, I just want to protect you."

"I get that, but sometimes I need to be hurt to grow. And I've gotten stronger. I finally realize my worth."

She hugs me and asks, "How can I help you?"

We break out of our hug, and I turn to the mess on the bed.

"Could you pass me clothes and tell me yes or no? I have to take a bit of everything because he won't tell me where we're going."

That's what's adding to my nerves. I wish I had an idea if it's cold or hot. Jackets take up way more room than thin summer dresses.

"You have no idea?" she asks.

I shake my head. "Nope."

"Okay. Well, that's a bit cute."

He's more than a bit cute.

I exhale a breath. "Let's start with lingerie, socks, bikinis."

A new knock sounds at my door.

"It's open," I yell out.

The door opens and closes. Footsteps come until my mom appears in my room.

"Marigold, this just arrived for you."

I stand and grab it from her. "Thanks."

"Do you girls need anything?" Mom asks.

I shake my head. "No, thanks, Mom. We'll be over at the main house soon for a cup of tea."

She smiles. "I baked a chocolate cake, so that will be good timing."

I nod. She closes the door as she leaves.

I open the package and laugh. Bikinis.

"He just gave away that he's taking me to somewhere warm!"

I pull it out and she laughs.

"Guys are so dumb sometimes," Clara adds.

I giggle. "But so thoughtful. Him buying me stuff is odd. I'm not used to it. Is it bad that I like it?"

"No, silly. It makes you normal. I'd like it if a guy did that for me," she admits with a long sigh.

"What's happening with the online guy?"

"Still good, don't get me wrong, he's hot. But he will not be taking me away. And if he buys me a gift, it'll be dirty, not sweet." She laughs and I laugh too.

"I guess a gift is a gift," she adds.

"That's true. And are you still enjoying it though?" I ask.

"Yeah, I like the extra confidence it brings."

I smile at the memories. "That's what I loved."

"Do you miss it?" she asks.

"Not at all. I just worry about money, but I'll figure something out."

I don't know what yet. But I'll need something soon.

CHAPTER 27

MARIGOLD

LATER THAT DAY, I step outside, where I expect a taxi to be waiting. But I falter mid-step when I see an older gentleman in a black suit standing beside the same black car as the night after Luxe.

"Miss West," he asks.

"Y-yeah," I stammer.

What in the world is going on?

"I'm here to take you to the airport." He steps back, pulling open the door for me to go in. "Mr. Gray is waiting," he adds.

Excitement bubbles inside me at the thought of Damien being inside.

I'm moving quickly now. I duck my head in and look around for him, landing on his awaiting gaze.

"Hi," I say, trying to ignore the butterflies in my stomach.

His eyes are brighter, and he's wearing a sexy grin. I can't help but smile back. I take my seat next to him.

"Goldie, come here," he says, patting the seat beside him.

His deep, smooth voice runs over my skin, warming me up. I dip my head and move. When I'm close, he wastes no time locking his lips onto mine. The touch of his heated skin on mine causes my sex to ache.

"I've missed you," he adds between kisses.

I whimper as he nips on my lip. It sends desperation through me. There's a privacy screen between us and the driver. I climb onto his lap, and he grabs my hips roughly. He pushes me into his groin. I don't miss the hardness in his pants. I rock my hips over him, and he grunts.

My hands grab the sides of his face and I hold him tight and kiss him hard at the same time as I rock my hips. I tell him with actions just how much I've missed him, too.

I know he's allowing me to control what we do right now.

And he does nothing when I run my tongue over his, tasting him. He explores my mouth just as hungrily.

Inside I'm building and I increase my speed to chase a release. His fingers dig harder into my hips, and I love how much he's enjoying this.

"Use me. Get yourself off," he rasps between kisses.

I rock faster and grind down harder.

"Oh, Damien." I moan.

"Leave a stain on my pants, baby. Let everyone know I'm yours. That's what you want, right?"

I clench at his words. My pussy is so hot, and I feel my lower back tingle.

"Yes. You're mine," I choke out.

"And you're mine," he says with such a deep, low voice, it sends me over the edge.

I shudder as the orgasm rips through me.

I collapse in his arms.

He catches me, and I suck in deep, heavy breaths. I soak in his spicy pear smell. It's comforting. His warm arms hold me and his scent relaxes me. I feel as if I could drift off to sleep. I was too excited to get much sleep last night, so I'm paying for it today.

One of his hands moves up over my back, where he rubs up and down in a soothing manner. He encourages me to stay right where I am.

His cock is still hard, and I make a note to help him as soon as I've recovered.

I just want to stay in the bliss of my post-orgasm state. Even though I can't believe I just dry-humped him like a teenager, but honestly, I'm not even sorry. He let me take charge and use him. And I know that's a big step for him. Control is something he likes; yet, he let me. No. He assisted me in controlling what I wanted.

That's why I know deep down we have something special. That's worth fighting for.

We stay like this for the entire drive. With me safely in his arms and the car in total silence.

The car stops, so I reluctantly pull away from his body and gaze into his soft brown hues. Something passes between us. I lean forward and peck his lips. "Thank you," I breathe.

"What are you thanking me for?" he asks.

"Being you."

We exit the car when we arrive at the airport. I hitch my handbag higher on my shoulder. As we walk in, he taps my tricep and I tilt my head to the side. He's waving his hand near mine. My pinched brows drop. He wants to hold my hand.

I try not to react too much on the outside, even though inside I'm dancing.

The walls are down now. We're away from home. This will show me exactly what he'd be like as a boyfriend. And maybe after this trip, I can convince him to be exactly that.

With our fingers interlocked, we waltz through security and to the gates.

"Let's grab snacks." I tug him along to the shop before the gate.

"You want snacks before boarding?" he asks, puzzled.

"Why do I get the feeling you've never had airport snacks?"

"Probably because I haven't."

"Ever?" I ask, mortified.

He shakes his head and says, "Nope. A couple of times when my flight got delayed, I grabbed a coffee, but that's it."

"Well, I'm about to blow your mind."

His brows rise. "With sugary, unhealthy snacks."

"Mm-hmm. Don't knock it till you've tried it." I playfully poke out my tongue and add, "The doctor cannot come along on this trip."

"We'll see about that. Lead the way."

My heart swells. The way he just allows me to choose what I want to do without a fight. I'm trying to wrap my head around why he's been single for so long. But then I remember his usual cold, quiet stance with others is to protect himself. With me, he doesn't hide away. I don't even think he's realized; it's just happened naturally.

I stand in front of the chips, grabbing a few Doritos and Pringles and then move to the chocolate and grab an Almond Joy and Reese's.

With snacks in toe, we move to the gate, and the first class is already boarding. Before I get to sit down on the black leather airport seat, he's pulling me. "We have to go board now."

"But that—" I trail off, my mouth wide open as I realize he's paid for us to fly first class.

"Seems I'm about to blow your mind." He smirks at my stunned reaction.

"My snacks seem stupid compared to this...this is too much, Damien," I mutter.

As we step onto the plane, the flight attendant offer refreshments and I take the champagne because I need something to kill the nerves.

"Nothing is too much for you. It's your birthday."

I look at him with a frown. "You've already given me a present." I touch my necklace as if he needed a reminder.

He sighs, and a tight expression sits on his face. "I left your night early and I hate that I hurt you."

"I-I..." I stumble, trying to talk.

What should I say?

His desire to make it up to me after hurting me makes me feel appreciated. However, this is way more than a simple apology and trust me, I'd have forgiven him with that.

I'm totally overwhelmed by this.

I peer around the space. There's so much leg room. My own TV and being waited on, this is seriously a pinch-me moment.

"Where are these snacks?" he asks, pulling me away from my first-class inspection.

"Ah. Here." I pull the bag up from the floor.

Once the plane's completely boarded, the pilot talks and mentions Santa Barbara. I knew it was warm but I didn't know the exact location.

"Are you kidding?" I whisper, turning to face Damien.

His brow knits. "Never been?"

"No. But I've always wanted to," I admit.

"I can't wait to take you then," he replies, grabbing my hand in his and squeezing it.

"So you've been?" I ask.

"Yes, once with my family, but I've always wanted to come back with someone."

The way he says it with a gleam in his eye makes it obvious he means me.

Getting off the flight feeling refreshed is a novelty. I could get used to it. Once again, we're hand in hand and walking to get our bags.

It isn't long before we're ushered into a private car and on our way to our hotel.

But when the car pulls into this large house, I wonder exactly what we're doing. Lush landscape surrounds an old Victorian bed-and-breakfast. It gives me a warm and inviting feeling. Pure relaxation, and yet again, I'm surprised he's taken me here.

When we check in, it makes me feel like royalty. The service is unlike anything I've experienced. We're shown around privately, and I try to absorb everything that I'm seeing. Then they leave us alone to explore.

"Wow." I exhale. "This place is beautiful."

He kisses my temple. "We have this whole place to ourselves, so you can choose whichever room or cottage you want to sleep in."

"You rented this whole place?" I ask, perplexed.

I don't even know why I did because I know the answer before he says it.

"Yeah. I wanted us to spend time alone. I want to block out the noise for a while and just be with you. Spend time with you for a couple of days."

"You could have done that with one of the private rooms."

"No. I want you alone. I'm selfish." The deeper tone hinting at exactly where his mind was. It sends a shiver through my body, causing all the hairs to stand up on my body.

I try to ignore my body's reaction and focus on walking through the gardens. Admiring each cottage. First stop, we walk into a more traditional cottage room. Then an orange painted one, followed by one with crazy green and white patterned wallpaper. The last one is simple in fresh white paint. All the rooms have a king-sized bed and a fireplace.

I'm unsure which one to choose because of how unique they all are. I want to stay in them all. The last few are nice too, but the cottage that catches my eye has a traditional four-foot bath and a four-poster dark wooden bed.

"This one." I turn to him.

"It's nice. What part do you like most?" His voice is low and thick. *He likes this one too.*

"Ah. The bath and the, um, the bed."

"Mmm," he mumbles as his hands grab my waist. He turns me around to face him. His eyes are darker. He dips his head and kisses me. I sink against him, feeling his hard muscles against the softness of my breasts. He grabs my ass in a hard squeeze, thrusting my hips into his large, hard erection. I moan into his mouth, reveling in the feel of him. My palms move from his chest to his cheeks, enjoying the roughness of his beard against my hand. Our tongues tangle in a hard kiss. He tastes of whiskey and peanut butter from the plane and it's delicious. I can't wait to have him in every way tonight. To taste him and have him deep in my mouth. I've not done it before and the thought of me bringing him to his knees at the sight of me on mine is a dream come true.

"Definitely this room. I can tie you up and fuck you hard before getting in that tub and soaking in it for hours with you in my arms."

"Oh, Damien," I rasp against his lips. That sounds like heaven.

My grip is tighter on him, and he edges me back to the bed.

"You'd like that, wouldn't you?"

"Yes," I choke out.

"The thought of you spread out on that bed, unable to move your arms and at my mercy, is so fucking hot."

"Oh God. Please, Damien," I beg. Not caring how desperate I sound. I want that now.

"Please what? Tell me what you want," he rasps.

"You," I beg.

"You have me."

"I want you to tie me up and fuck me," I admit.

"Fuck, those words leaving your mouth are sexy. And fuck. Get on that bed now!"

With a grin, I step back and obey his commands. I kneel on the bed in my sweats. I wonder if I should remove them or leave them.

"Good girl." He steps toward me.

I'm about to take my gray sweater off, but he shakes his head.

"Leave it on. I want to peel the clothes off you. It's like a present to me. Your body is mine." He grunts, all his control disappearing.

The sound of his phone ringing breaks our moment. He runs his hand through his hair. "Fuck," he spits, pulling his phone from his pocket. He checks the caller ID, his eyes softening, and then glances back at me with an apologetic face.

"I better grab this. Mom is trying to FaceTime. I have to take it."

I nod. "Of course. I'll have a quick shower."

But as soon as I slip off the bed and he turns to answer it in the small living room where the fireplace is, I can't help but admire his firm body. I'm all hot and bothered.

I smile as an idea hits me. His hands and mouth are busy, but mine aren't.

CHAPTER 28

MARIGOLD

"WHAT ARE YOU DOING with Samuel today?" he asks his mom.

She thinks he's away at a work conference and I told my family I was going away with Clara.

I amble closer. His brows pinch; he's probably worried I'm going to say hello, even though I know I'm still a secret. I don't dwell on that now. Right now, I want to control his pleasure. When I stand in front of him and unexpectedly drop to my knees, his eyes widen.

He braces his hand on the back of the large armchair in front of the fireplace. As if he needs the support.

I've taken him by surprise.

I'm about to see how controlled he can be.

I shuffle my knees closer on the cold wooden floor until my face is at eye level with his bulge.

Reaching out, I unbutton the top of his pants. I keep my innocent eyes on his hungry ones. I can see his breathing quicken, but he doesn't remove his eyes from me. My fingers push his pants and briefs down at the same time until they pool at his feet, leaving his big, hard dick exposed.

"O-Okay," he stumbles, trying to answer his mom. "The line's terrible. I gotta go. I'll phone you right back," he adds, throwing the phone to the side.

"Oh God," I mutter as I take in his muscular thighs covered in that same dark hair and make my way to his dick and stare at it. He's huge. I don't know how my hand will even wrap around him, let alone how much will fit in my mouth, but I'm going to try. I'm eager to try it. I flick my eyes up at him. His wide, dark brown eyes fix on me, and I can't help but lick my lips. I'm excited about doing this. The thrill is becoming too much to wait. I'm salivating.

He swallows and I watch the bob of his Adam's apple. "Fuck. You're eager to suck me, aren't you, Goldie?" He grunts.

His thumb reaches down to rub my lips roughly. I tip my head back and hum in response. My core aches. I'm savoring the way he looks at me with adoring eyes. As if he can't quite believe this is happening. Hell, I'm the one that's dreaming. I've wanted this for so long. And it's finally happening.

My lips part, and I open my mouth wide. He guides his thick cock to my mouth. But instead of pushing his dick inside, he traces my lips in a tease. My tongue darts out to try to catch him.

"Fuck." He chokes out as a drop of precum leaks and I lean forward, catching it. I swallow the unique salty taste.

Another hum leaves my chest.

"Those noises you're making are killing me. I need to fill your mouth and hear what sounds you make when your mouth is full of my cock." His voice is husky. It makes me desperate, to the point I'm almost feral with the need for him to come undone. To make his knees buckle and quiver as he comes just from my mouth.

He guides his dick into my mouth, and I wrap my lips eagerly around him. Loving his hot skin and more of his salty taste on my tongue. A hiss leaves his mouth. His cool composure is falling.

He likes it, and it encourages me to keep going. I twirl my tongue around the head of his cock and then suck hard, hollowing my cheeks. I'm moving my head slowly up and down his cock. Holding onto the base of his thick cock with one hand and gripping his ass with the other, I'm in control. A hand touches my hair and I peek up from under my lashes to see his heavy eyes watching me.

"Keep your eyes up. I want to see you."

I do. Not only because he tells me, but because of the way he's staring at me. I'm in control of him and I think he needs this. I need to take more control and he needs to give in. The perfect combination.

He's growing thicker in my mouth, so I try to take more of him. He thrusts his hips at the same time I take him down my throat. I'm loving the fact that he's really close right now. He fucks my mouth like an unhinged man.

I don't want this to end. His fingers curl in my hair, and I try to suck back, but he holds my head still. I flutter my lashes as I see him close his eyes and his dick jerks and hot cum spurts down my throat. I try to swallow as much as I can, but some leaks out of my mouth. He drops his tight grip from my hair, and he pets my head in a silent thank you.

"Better?" I ask.

He brushes his thumb over my lips and then cheek. "Yes. Thank you," he whispers hoarsely.

I sit back on my heels, my hands on my knees, staring up at him as he looks down in a daze.

He holds out his palm. I put my fingers in his and push up to my feet. My hands land on his solid chest. His heart beats wildly under my hand. I'm grateful I'm not the only one rattled by what just happened. It was better than I could have imagined. I feel powerful and unstoppable.

He presses his lips to mine. We kiss until I need air.

"You better call your mom back." I wink.

He looks down at his pants and briefs still around his ankle. "You're something else, you know that?"

"I'm yours," I say, biting the corner of my lip and strolling toward the bathroom. My jaw is aching in the best way. It's a reminder for me. I just gave him the best blow job I've ever given a man. I take a peek over my shoulder to find his eyes on me. A wash of disbelief and awe.

Inside the bathroom, I turn on the shower and shave and refresh my body. Then I step out, finding a robe, and slip the white fluffy warm robe on and walk out. He's on the phone walking around half-naked, so I go to the white-sheeted bed to enjoy the show. I'm probably going to pay for earlier, but the thrill of his punishment makes me wet.

A few minutes later, he's saying goodbye, and his eyes hold mine. He stalks over to the bed. I'm propped up on pillows with the soft sheets under me. My pulse speeds up with anticipation growing.

"Was that fun?" he asks with a voice still full of arousal.

"Yes," I breathe triumphantly.

"Did you enjoy sucking my cock?"

I nod. "So much."

He removes his shirt, tossing it to the floor.

He's standing completely naked. I was going to ask if he enjoyed it, but he beats me to it.

"That was the best fucking blowjob I've ever had," he says, climbing onto the bed and crawling to me. The way his biceps flex with each movement causes a whimper to leave my parted mouth.

"Really?" I say coyly, fluttering my lashes because I know full well he loved every second.

"Yeah, really. Watching you take me deep into that tight mouth and then eagerly suck me until I came down your throat was fucking hot." He looks at me with delight. "But I should punish you for trying to give me head while on the phone with my mother."

I drop back on the bed when he gets closer. "How?" I whisper. My brain went blank at what he could do to punish me because tying me up and fucking me are things I'm craving right now. There's no punishment in sex.

"How about I bring you so close to the edge of orgasm but then don't let you come?" he says, looking torn. His gaze drifts seductively down my body as if he doesn't know where to start. When his gaze holds mine, I lose my breath. There's so much desire and lust swimming in his eyes, but his words finally hit me. Sinking in.

What?

I gasp. "No!"

"But then that would punish me if I was to do that," he murmurs as he touches the tie holding my robe together. "I want to feel you come apart from my cock being buried deep inside you."

He yanks at the tie hard until it comes apart and the robe opens. The middle of my body on display for him.

"You're naked," he mutters in fascination. His eyes drop hungrily over me. It makes me feel adored.

"I had a shower," I reply.

His finger touches my stomach, and I shiver from the rough pad of his finger. "Without me."

"Sorry, sir." I whimper.

My nipples tighten to hard desperate peaks. He trails his finger up to my mouth in a straight line, avoiding my begging nipples. He traces slowly down. I arch into his tender touch. He doesn't stop until he touches the top of my mound.

"Are you wet?" he asks in a gravelly tone.

I close my eyes briefly and nod. "Yes."

His gaze is dark and hot on my core while my gaze is on him. His fingers slide down over my swollen clit to my opening.

I moan.

"You're so wet for me, Goldie." He growls. "How am I so lucky? Is this all for me?"

His finger strokes over my clit in lazy circles. Slow at first, then circling a little faster.

"Yes. Damien." I pant.

"Damien?"

"Yes, sir."

He grunts. "Better."

My core muscles tighten in response. The heat between my legs is becoming an inferno with every slow stroke.

"Oh, God,"[PD1] I mumble, desperate for his thick fingers to enter me. And it's as if he can read my mind because he eases his fingers inside me. Moving them in and out slowly. I moan loudly. My walls tighten around his fingers, encouraging him to go deeper. He doesn't need help to find the spot. He knows exactly where it is. There's no need to introduce him to a woman's body. No, he reads my body so well. As if my pleasure means more to him than his own.

His fingers feel so good. I never want this to end.

"Yes," I breathe. "Just like that."

Our eyes meet and I swallow a moan at the mirroring sight. His gaze is full of arousal.

He adds another finger and more pressure to my clit at the same time. The pleasure building inside me is almost too much.

"Don't stop," I cry out.

"Never." He growls. "I'm going to make you come like this. And then again on my cock."

"Yes." I whimper loudly.

His thumb rubs at me harder as he keeps a solid pace. My core losing control and my orgasm pulsing through me in hard, delicious waves.

I blink, trying to focus on him under the post-orgasm haze.

He's breathing hard when his hand pulls on the robe. "I need to see all of you. Take this off."

I slip off the bed and drop the robe, then turn to face him. He's lying on the bed with an elbow propping his head up. "You're so beautiful. Come here."

As I do, my phone rings this time. For God's sake, will the phones stop ringing? I want to ignore it, but I need to see who it is before I turn the stupid thing off.

"Elijah," I say, showing Damien my phone with my brother's name flashing across the front.

"Answer it," he says with a sexy grin.

I don't have time to ask him what the looks for, [PD2] otherwise, I'll miss the call.

"Hey!" I answer.

"How's your trip?" Elijah asks.

"I just arrived, but the place is—"

"Is what?" he pushes at the same time Damien picks me up.

"Breathtaking." My voice wavers from the nerves and excitement running through it.

"Where did you end up?" Elijah asks through the phone.

I stare down into the wicked brown eyes kneeling between my thighs, and I clear my throat to talk.

"Santa Barbara. I thought I told you," I lie. Since I did not know where, I kept it from him.

"You didn't, but it's a brilliant spot for a few days. How are you paying for this? I thought you weren't online anymore."

I squeeze my eyes shut. This trip and this moment are too precious to be ruined by my brother. "I'm not, but I'm about to have lunch. Can I talk to you after?"

He grumbles, clearly not happy with my answer, but I speak before he can. "Okay good. I'll call back soon. Bye."

I hang up and toss the phone. I'm met with Damien's dark eyes.

"The only person eating lunch is me," he says with a wide grin as he spreads my legs.

Suddenly, I'm shy about him going down on me. I've showered and shaved; yet, I feel nervous.

He leans into my pussy and inhales. "God, you smell incredible."

My heart is beating wildly in my chest. He kisses the top of my apex, and the sweet gesture is too much to bear. I close my eyes and tilt my head back.

"Don't be nervous. I'll look after you. Open your eyes as you watch me enjoy every inch of you."

I open my eyes and meet his head on. I ask the question playing havoc in my mind. "How did you know?"

"I'm good at reading people. You're not relaxed at all."

I suck in a deep breath, trying to calm my body down. "Guys don't like to do this."

The last time Damien went down, I didn't have time to stop and think. But today is different and I'm feeling vulnerable. My exes hated going down on me.

"I'm not all guys. And I fucking love it. You'll see. I'm already painfully hard from the smell and sight of your pussy. One taste and I'll have to hold myself from coming in my pants like a teenager."

My sex clenches and my fears trail off when I feel that first lick of his tongue on my pussy. And that one lick causes me to cry out with need. He continues to lick and fuck my pussy with his tongue, making these sweet grunting noises from the back of his throat.

"More," I beg, forgetting about everything other than how this feels.

"Your taste is addictive," he says, barely removing his mouth from me so it's muffled.

He circles my swollen clit with a swirl of his tongue, and I whimper.

"This is so good." I pant. He sucks on my clit hard, and I buck my hips. "Ah." My fingers slide through his brown hair, and I push his head to my pussy, not wanting him to stop. The building intensity in my lower body becomes unbearable. I buck my hips again when he circles his tongue, fucking me hard with it.

"Damien!" I cry out. My orgasm slams into me.

He doesn't stop devouring me until I'm completely spent. When I sink further into the mattress, I try to catch my breath. His body moves to lie beside me. One of his arms grabs my waist to hold me tight. We both lie there naked, totally exposed, yet closer than ever.

Chapter 29

Damien

I LAY A KISS on her forehead, soaking in the scent of her shampoo. "I'm going to run a bath for us."

She moans in pleasure. I hold her in my arms, but struggle to let her go. I know I'm becoming addicted, and I don't see how this weekend will not have me craving her more.

I reluctantly pull away and walk toward the bathroom. I wonder if we'll venture out of this house in the next forty-eight hours or if we'll stay here ordering food in.

I wouldn't say no. The thought of waking up, fucking, eating, talking, and relaxing with her is the perfect break.

Come to think of it, when was the last proper break I had?

I have an annual vacation with Samuel during spring break, but one-on-one with an adult...with a woman. Never.

Now I want to plan another trip as soon as I get back home.

I switch on the faucet on the bath, then look around to find bath salts and rose petals. I put a scoop of the salts in the water, then sprinkle the roses around the bath.

The room is full of steam, and I walk back into the bedroom and pause. Marigold is lying naked on the bed. My gaze runs over her curves. The ones I touched recently and I'm currently obsessed over. She's stunning as always, but there's a sparkle in her eye that makes her a whole other level of incredible.

"Don't look at me like that. Bath first. Food and then sex," she mutters.

"How did you know?" I ask with a crooked grin.

She goes to sit up, but I move closer to the bed and scoop her up in my arms. I don't want her to walk.

Her arms come around my neck and gently hold on as I wander into the bathroom.

"The look in your eyes."

I remember I asked how she knew my mind was on sex.

"What look?" I ask.

"They dilate and the brown is almost black. Like you're—"

"Hungry," I finish her sentence. "I'm more than hungry. I'm famished."

Her breath hitches and I lower her into the white tub. She grabs the sides of the bath and looks up at me. I go to pull back when she speaks.

"Aren't you coming in?" she asks with a disappointed tone.

My lips twitch at her eagerness. I kiss her briefly. "I'll order us food and then I will. I wouldn't miss this for the world."

No. The way her body looks submerged in the water and her doe eyes look at me with a silent beg. I wouldn't miss one second.

Fuck. I need to feed her before I fuck her and God, I want to fuck her again.

"What do you want to eat?" I ask, squatting beside the tub. Leaning my arms on the side. My chin resting on my hands.

Her head drops back to lean against the white edge.

"Noodles or a burger," she replies after a minute. Her eyes try to suck me in, but I stay strong.

"Alright, let me see what I can do." I rise halfway and kiss her lips before walking out of the bathroom.

I find a noodle bar not too far away. "What noodles do you like?"

"I'm easy. Surprise me," she calls out.

I read the menu and find something with beef, and it sounds somewhat healthy, so I order that and a chicken dish, just in case she doesn't want beef.

"What did you want to drink?" I ask, moving to the bathroom. I find her totally relaxed in the bath with her eyes closed.

"Pepsi," she replies.

I screw up my face. "That stuff is bad for you. It's full of chemicals," I argue.

She tilts her head and opens one eye. "But it's also tasty," she says with a smile before closing her eyes again.

I order her a Pepsi and myself water.

"Dessert?"

"Is that a trick question? Of course, I want dessert."

I shake my head. "What artery-clogging item do you want?"

She shakes her head. "You need to live, Doctor Gray. You're way too serious."

I stay silent for a second before I lift my eyes to her soft facial features. Admiring how brutal honesty just rolls off her tongue.

I swallow hard because fuck, I know I'm set in my ways. Health is my life. But it's also stopping me from enjoying it too. And that's a tougher pill to swallow.

"That wasn't the question," I call back as I scan the menu.

"Fine. Give me ice cream or pudding. Yeah, yum, chocolate pudding." She moans.

I rub the side of my temple as I read over our list before I hit order and pay. It'll be here in thirty minutes. Plenty of time to bathe together and with those noises and sinful curves, I want to soak in our time together every spare second I can.

I put the phone away and then move closer to the tub.

"It says it'll be here in thirty."

A smile plays on her lips, and she shuffles in the bath. "Well, what are you waiting for?"

"Nothing. You've been a good girl. Patiently waiting. You deserve a reward."

I carefully get in behind her. There's not a lot of room for both of us when I lie down but having her on top of me was the plan, anyway. My fingers automatically grab her waist and lay her on me. Enjoying the way she fits perfectly in front of me.

"Are you always hard?" she asks, obviously feeling my semi on her back.

"I can't help it. You're naked in here and the soft touch of your skin against mine is too good. I want more."

"Well, we can fix that," she says as she tries to spin around. Her ass grinds along my cock. I swallow a growl and tighten my grip on her so she can't move. "No, let's stay here. You need to eat first." I say it out loud to remind myself that she needs food for energy.

"I am pretty hungry," she teases.

I chuckle. I know exactly where her mind is, but I need to care for her first. "I'll be happy to fuck your face after you eat. Which means you'll have plenty of energy for sex and you'll need it."

She twists her head and lifts her chin to look up at me as she drawls, "Oh, really?"

"Mm-hmm," I mumble, pulling her close again, not leaving any space between us. My hands fold over her waist. "Yes. All fucking night. But for now, let me hold you."

"I can't argue with that," she whispers, lying her head back on my chest. Her whole body relaxes on top of me. Our relaxed state causes me to close my eyes and rest. Something I do with her. From someone barely getting a full night's sleep to nodding off in a bath, who am I?

The buzz of my phone wakes me. Food's here.

"Let's get out and eat," I whisper into her ear.

"Mmm. I am getting wrinkly skin on my fingers from being in the water too long."

I release a deep laugh and whisper in her ear, "I love your wrinkly skin."

"I love your wrinkles too." I know she genuinely is speaking about the lines on my face. The fact she loves them soothes the worry I'm feeling about our age gap. The fact she knows we are so different, yet she still wants me, makes my chest swell.

She peels herself away and gets out of the bath, and I follow her.

We eat our late lunch in silence. Now we're both dressed in robes. I can't believe I'm wearing a white bathrobe. I've never worn one of these in all my hotels and holiday stays.

Yet here we are, matching each other like an old married couple. And that thought should send me running for the hills, but it doesn't.

"What did you want to do before dinner?" I ask when she's finished her bowl of noodles and Pepsi. As much as I'd love to lie around in here, I also want to check in and see what she wants to do.

This trip can't just be all about me.

Her comment about me living a little has been playing on my mind since she said it.

"Let's go for a walk. The gardens here look beautiful."

She tucks her legs up onto the chair and hugs her knees.

"Are you planning to garden?" I tease.

A light giggle leaves her. "No, but it would just be nice to go for a walk around here with you."

She gazes away from me, but I get out of my chair and grab her chin softly. I gaze into her soft eyes.

"I'd love to do that, but, also," I lean in to kiss her lips, thinking of a great idea, "did you want to watch the sunset?"

Her eyes flutter open, and she gives me a giddy smile. "That would be nice. I'll see if I can find a picnic blanket or something we can sit on."

I kiss her lips again as if it would never be enough. Then I step back. "I'll get changed and flick through the information booklet and see what trails I can find." I walk toward my bag to grab a change of clothes.

"No. Let's just walk and explore. No thought-out plan. Let's just see where we end up."

"I don't like that. What if we get lost?" I ask, horrified. This property is enormous, and we could easily get off track.

"What if we don't? You're so controlled and organized. Why don't we just relax here?" She sighs.

"We don't know this place. If we get disorientated..."

She quirks her eyebrow at me. "What? What are you gonna do?"

The humor in her face makes me laugh out loud.

"Nothing," I say as I walk over to her and kiss her again. "Nothing at all. I guess if I have you, I'm not lost, am I?"

"Exactly, Mr Cute. Let's go on an adventure." She beams.

"You realize I'm thirty-eight and not eight?" I tease.

"I'm well aware of how old you are. That's the difference between guys I've been with previously."

"I don't like thinking of you with other men. It pisses me off," I grumble, pulling her up into my arms and holding her tightly.

"We all have a past..." she adds.

"I'm well aware." Not wanting to talk negatively about my ex right now, I steer the question around. "What's the difference with me?"

"So much. I'll start with the fact you're generous, kind, thoughtful, and sexy. Oh, and you know your way around a woman's body. No need to tell you what I like. It's as if you can read my body better than I do."

"I love your body and the way it responds to me and my touch. It's addictive. Your body is beautiful. I can't get enough." The tone in my voice drops.

"Nah. Ah. Mr. Gray, we need to get ready to explore." She wags a finger at me and steps out of my reach.

I grumble. "I'll be happy to explore you."

"You're insatiable." She shakes her head as she spins to open the cupboards, and I turn around to get changed. I can't believe I'm about to go out there without a map.

We step out of the cottage and into the cool air. Wind gushes and she quickly zips up her jacket before I grab her hand.

"Which way?" I ask, taking in all the trees and flowers. A lot of it looks so alike, I try not to worry about getting astray and finding our way back in the darkness.

"This way. I want to see the flowers with the light we have left."

We amble through the garden, which is surprisingly fun. Seeing many flowers and trees I've never seen before. The way Marigold's face lights up with a flower that's unique makes me want to plant all of them in my yard. Her radiant face deserves to be there all the time.

"What would happen if your ex-wife wanted you back?" she asks in the dead silence of our walk, which takes me off guard.

I grind down on my teeth. The mention of Lucy irks me. But it's not Marigold's fault.

"No chance," I say through gritted teeth.

"For her or you?" she replies.

I stare out into the greenery, soaking in the peaceful place. The sounds of bugs and nature puts me at ease. Or is it her? Because isn't she always the thing that grounds me? It's why I'm sneaking behind her brother's back. I know I'm doing something forbidden in his eyes and maybe everyone's eyes, but I can't help it. She draws me in with her whole being. I just want to stay close to her warmth. I'm pushing aside how fucked I'll be when Elijah finds out. But as I think about my ex and then Marigold, I see how vastly different they are.

"I begged her to not leave me...us," I exhale, unable to believe I'm spilling it all to her. "But she didn't choose us. She chose herself."

It's silent for a beat before she asks, "Did she cheat?"

"I don't know. Well, I should say not that I'm aware of."

She touches an orange rose. "Ouch." She winces, shaking her finger where a thorn has pricked her.

Immediately grabbing her hand, I turn it over, and blood is trickling. I suck her finger and then look at it in the crappy night sky. It looks okay, but I need to ask her to be sure. "Better?"

"Ah. Yeah," she breathes. "How do patients not hit on you?"

I chuckle. "Oh, they do, but I'm very firm about my no-dating rule."

"You've never dated a nurse or staff member?"

"No, remember I have an ex-wife..."

"Yes, but between her and now. You have needs," she adds, in a tone that's a little unsure.

I stop in front of her and lean forward, rubbing my thumb over her bottom lip. "I do. But you fulfill them perfectly."

She opens and closes her mouth. And I can see her struggle to form words.

"Why don't you believe me?"

"You're hot and a doctor. I just assumed."

"Wrong," I add.

There's a softness in her face and a lift in the corner of her mouth that tells me she enjoyed hearing that.

"Let's set up the blanket and look at the stars."

She scrunches her face up. "Why do I feel like there's something I'm not getting?"

I shake the blanket in a hidden spot that gives the best views of the garden and the sky. The moon is so bright tonight.

I move closer to her and run my finger over the zipper on her jacket. She sucks in a sharp breath.

Her eyes widen. "Here?"

"Yes. Here. I want to fuck you under the stars. So every time I look up, all I think about is you."

CHAPTER 30

MARIGOLD

I DON'T SPEAK. WORDS aren't forming. Only a sudden swelling in my chest from his words. I clutch his head in my hands and reach up on my tiptoes, smashing my lips and body to his. He grabs my ass with a firm squeeze and a deep grunt. His hard erection hits my stomach. In a frenzied mess, I run my hands down to push his sweater up. He breaks our kiss to help lift it over his head. I stare at his white shirt that fits tight over his muscled chest. I'm quick to remove that, too. He tosses it on the grass, and I soak in his familiar muscles. I reach out to touch him, enjoying the feeling of his hot skin on my hands. I make my way down to the top of his sweats. He grabs my hands and lays them on either side of my thighs.

"Let me peel these clothes off you. I want you naked on that blanket now."

His hands expertly remove my clothes in no time. Leaving me panting. There's something about the way his eyes watch me that makes my core ache.

"Lie down."

I don't hesitate, fearlessly lowering my naked body down. I want this more than I want my next breath. The cold blanket on my feverish body is a welcomed surprise. My nipples are tighter buds as I stare up at his broad frame hovering over me. His aftershave fills my nostrils with a familiar warmth. A promise that I'll remember this moment for a long time.

"Stunning," he rasps with a look of adoration. It's always something I've longed for, and I see it in his eyes whenever he looks at me.

He lays a kiss on my neck. "You're so beautiful," he adds, kissing down to my chest.

He moves to kiss my nipple with an opened mouth and a sweep of his tongue. It's warm and wet with added pressure that has my back arching for more.

"Oh." I gasp, clenching my thighs together to ease the tension that's becoming borderline painful.

He moves his mouth to my stomach, continuing to lay hot kisses over my body. With the cool night air and the warmth of his breath, I shiver. When he drops to his knees and lays a trail of kisses from my stomach to the top of my mound, I moan from the intensity. My eyes never leaving his. Seeing his large frame between my legs is something I'll never get sick of looking at.

"You ready?"

I nod frantically. I want his mouth on me again, but I also just want to be fucked under the stars like he promised. But the slow way he's kissing me tells me he's not rushing tonight. Even though the thought drives me to the edge, I want him whatever way I can get him, because I know I'll love every second.

With a firm grip on my hands, he spreads my legs on the blanket. "Keep them open."

I don't answer. My words get lost when he pushes his sweats and briefs down and then off and I get to see his thick cock sitting hard and ready between his thighs. My fingers twitch to lean forward and grab him, but he crawls and hovers over me. His hands settle on either side of my head. I'm sitting with my legs wide open and he's kneeling between them.

Looking at his face and then between our bodies, I see how close his thick cock is to my opening. I rock my hips up, trying to get him inside me.

"You're eager tonight."

"I need you, Damien," I reply desperately. Unbothered, I'm doing so. My gaze returns to his lustful ones.

"Fuck. I need you too, Goldie, so fucking much."

"D—" but the words fall from my lips when he enters me.

The tight way he fits inside me steals my words.

"You're pussy fits over my cock so perfectly. Do you see how well we fit? Look at us," he commands.

I lift my head and look at where his cock enters me. And Christ, it is perfect.

"It's made for me. This pussy is mine to take as hard or as slow as I want."

"Yes. Don't stop," I breathe as I drop my head back down.

"Oh, Goldie, I don't plan to. I'm about to fill you so full of my cum that it will drip down your legs on our walk back."

"Yes-s," I stutter. His filthy words are everything I've wanted.

He wants me. This is not a one-sided relationship. The knowledge sends another flutter in my heart.

There's sweat forming on his brow as he thrusts his hips in and out in a deliciously slow rhythm.

He fills me all the way as deep as he can go and then pulls all the way out just so his tip is in. It's a lot and yet I need more.

"Harder," I cry out. I grab his shoulders and tilt my hips up as he enters me, trying to get more friction. He must read me because, on his next thrust, he slams into me. The tingle in my lower body lets me know I won't last much longer.

"Yes. Don't stop."

"This pussy is so greedy for me," he says with a grunt. Slamming even harder into me. Our skin slapping together is the only loud sound to be heard. It adds to my growing orgasm.

"I'm so close."

As the words leave my lips, the ripple of an intense orgasm slams into me. I cry out into the still air. My toes curl until the wave of climax eases. I sink back down into the blanket and watch his hard face turn to pleasure as his own orgasm takes over. I feel the jerk of his cock, knowing he's coming hard, and I enjoy every minute.

Afterward, he stays inside me, sucking in deep breaths of air as he stares at me, bewildered.

"Incredible," he says as if he's shocked it keeps getting better too.

"You're probably going to have to carry me back. I don't think I'll be able to walk."

He chuckles. "I like the sound of that. As long as I can fuck you again later?" he adds, licking his lips.

"You're serious?"

His eyes roam my body. "I'm already half hard again."

"Seriously?"

"Yeah. Your body is addictive. I can't get enough."

"I feel like a teenager."

He pulls out and aftershocks have me shuddering. I'm spent. "You're all woman to me."

He lays a kiss to my lips and then my temple before he lies beside me, and we hold each other. Our heavy breathing in sync, I stare at the stars and thank them for bringing him to me. I'll never look at the night sky without thinking of this special night.

Even if we're not boyfriend and girlfriend yet. Well, we can't be until we're not a secret anymore. Despite that, the way he shows me he cares is keeping me hanging on. Our connection is real. These moments are glimpses of what I know could be our life together. They are everything and yet more than I could have ever asked for.

A cold, wet droplet hits my face. It's raining.

"Are you ready to sit by the fire and study?" he asks as more rain sprinkles down on us.

I twist in his arms to face him. He pecks my lips.

"That sounds nice," I reply, picturing the evening snuggled up together, listening to the rain outside.

It sounds relaxing and carefree. So different from our lives at home.

He stands up and holds out his hand. I grab it and stand up. Ignoring the heavy, cold splashes hitting me. He grabs the blanket and folds it.

"I should've checked the weather," he complains.

"Why? It's nice feeling the rain on my skin."

He blinks, and a pinched look hits his face.

"What?" I ask.

"You're unlike any woman I've ever met. And in my line of work, I've met a lot."

"Don't remind me," I mumble as I peer down at the grass.

He lifts my chin to bring my eyes back to his. He strokes my cheek with his thumb in a reassuring way. "Don't be jealous. They don't hold a candle to you."

"Are you saying I don't need any work done?"

"Never. I wouldn't touch you. You're perfect the way you are."

"But I like the look of fake bo—"

"No," he cuts me off.

His free hand touches my breast and squeezes. I moan. The unexpected touch stirs me up again. "These are the right size and feel. I don't want plastic. I love how real you are."

"Are you just saying that to get into my pants?" I grin in the darkness.

He chuckles lightly. "I've already been in them tonight."

"True. You love your job, right?" I ask as the rain comes down harder on us, but we don't walk any faster. Instead, we keep the same pace.

"I do. I've always wanted to be a doctor and then I became fascinated with plastics."

"You've done nothing else?"

"No."

"You don't want to?"

He's quiet a second longer this time before answering. "No. And enough about me, it's your turn."

I bump my shoulder into his arm. "You never want to talk about yourself."

"I did for what felt like the last ten minutes."

"Fine. Ask away,' I reply.

"Have you thought about what you'll do after college?"

"You mean other than get a job," I tease.

"Cheeky."

I blow out a deep sigh. "I want to work with one of the top three firms in Chicago."

My voice lacks conviction, and of course, he doesn't miss a beat. "But..."

I look down at the paved path as we stroll back to our cottage. I explain my fear. A fear I've told no one. Not even Clara.

"I don't know if I'm good enough."

"What makes you say that?"

A jerk on my arm spins me. He stopped walking.

I frown, not understanding.

He tugs on my hand, and I move closer to him.

"Tell me. Why don't you feel good enough?"

His brown eyes glow in the night. The warmth of his body radiates through me.

"I wasn't accepted for a scholarship, and I believe in signs. This feels like just maybe I should choose a different career path."

I bite down on my bottom lip nervously.

The gentle stroke of his finger around my neck pulls me closer and he whispers across my lips. "You're more than deserving. It's a business, remember? If you didn't qualify for a reason, it's because of their rules. They aren't signs; I promise. A sign. You want to know a fucking sign?"

I nod.

"You were on Mysterious Fan the night I joined. Of all the people I met, I met you. My ray of sweet golden sunshine."

I can't help but smile widely. "It was a scary coincidence."

"It was destiny, and I want you to never doubt yourself. I know what it's like to feel unworthy."

And before I can ask him why in the world he would ever feel unworthy of love, he brings my head closer to his to kiss him. He makes me forget my name. His kiss is so strong that the rawness of opening up pours through my lips. As the rain continues to pour down on us.

CHAPTER 31

DAMIEN

I WAKE TO THE shallow breathing of the brunette lying next to me. A soft curve lifts on my lips as her honey scent lingers. I snuggle her closer to me. My morning wood pressing into her side. I can't get enough of her; I seem to have a constant erection.

I wish we didn't have to leave today and go back to reality. But that's in fact what we have to do in the next two hours. Even as I lie here after a night full of sex, studying, and a sleep-in I never had. The thought of the amount of work that's piled up since being here makes me not want to return.

Rather than focus on the negative, I kiss her cheek and try to wake her gently. I want to soak in this time before we land back in Chicago and go back to barely seeing each other.

My fault. I know.

She's made it clear what she wants and that it's me who needs to pull the trigger and make us official and fuck the consequences. But the fear of losing my best friend is what's holding me back. I've been risking it ever since Marigold and I began hooking up. But telling Elijah, when I know he's already warned me away from her, is tougher than I thought.

I run my fingers over her delicate, warm skin. Starting from her hand to her shoulder in soft, lazy strokes. The purple on her fingernails is so soft and feminine...so her.

I drag my lips along her neck and onto her cheek where I lay a kiss on the side of her face and she rolls over. The morning sun glows on her. Like a spotlight. My Goldie.

She's not ready to wake up. I'm the eager one. She's flicked a switch in me and made me find extra energy. It's as if I'm twenty-five again. So, I slip out of bed, go to the bathroom, and then go search in the cupboards for breakfast.

Minutes later. I'm buttering toast when a warm body comes up behind me. Marigold's arms circle around my waist. My abs contract from the touch. Her head lies on my back as she cuddles me from behind. "Good morning," she mutters in a sexy morning whisper.

"Morning, how'd you sleep?"

"Mmm. Really well," she replies.

"Not too sore?" I ask eagerly, lowering the knife when I finish buttering.

Her head lifts from my back and her arms drop. "Tender, but not sore. Did you make this for me?"

I twist to face her. She scans the tea and toast before glancing back at me with wide eyes.

"I fucked it up, didn't I? I was supposed to dip the tea bag in and throw it out. Stupid Google said either that or leave the tea bag in. I left it in." I run a hand through my hair, frustrated.

"No, I'm shocked because you made me tea." She smiles, stepping in to hug me. "And you haven't complained that it's not coffee and how I should be drinking that."

"There's still time," I joke, as I wrap my arms around her and kiss the top of her head.

She tips her head back to look up at me. "But no, this is great. I love my tea strong. Thank you."

I kiss her lips in a slow I-can't-get-enough-of-you kiss. "Anything for you."

She opens her mouth but then closes it.

It's been a long time since I waited on a woman, but for her, I'd do it every day. I'd do anything to make Marigold happy. I make coffee as she lifts the cup to her mouth and blows on the steam.

My phone rings and it's Mom, so I know it'll be Samuel. I miss him. I know this break is good for me because I haven't had one since Lucy left. Any time my mom has cared for him, it's been for work. Never for pleasure. And here I am, away for pleasure. I try not to drown in the guilt because if I do, I'll close back up on Marigold and jump back on the plane. I need to remember taking time away will make me happier and a better parent. He can spend some special time with his nana, making memories he'll treasure forever. I swallow the lump of guilt and answer the call. I take the brown chair in the lounge room and talk to them for a few minutes.

After I get off the phone, I see we have two hours before our car comes to take us to the airport. I walk into the kitchen but find it empty. The dirty tea cup and empty plate are making me twitch. I should clean it.

"Goldie?" I call out.

"In here waiting."

I frown. Waiting? For what?

I step into the bedroom and fuck. She's standing at the foot of the bed waiting for me. She's wearing the same outfit I saw her online in. My favorite one. The gold lingerie that made my mouth water and is again. I don't miss the gem she's holding. The same one I saw on that video.

She bites her bottom lip. "You're staring."

"Goldie. Fuck, you're so beautiful," I say as a groan slips out. I can't believe she's so giving to me. Am I worthy of her and how perfect she is? I can try. Fuck, I can try right now.

"Yeah?"

"Mmm, so sexy. And I saw you brought the plug. Do you want to play?" I ask hoarsely.

She nods with a wicked smile.

"Have you used a plug before?"

She shakes her head softly. I don't miss the way she flushes up her neck and onto her cheeks. Her brown hair flows messily over her shoulders with the movement.

"Lets warm you up first then. I don't want to hurt you." Those words ring true in so many ways.

"I brought lube." Her teeth catch on her pillowy bottom lip. The way she wants to try this new thing with me is hot. She trusts me. What is strange about that is…I trust her too. I haven't trusted a woman in forever. But with Goldie, I openly trust her, and it doesn't even scare me.

I smile. "Good girl. But come here." I curl my finger in.

She takes a step.

"No. Stop." I hold up my hand, still wearing a wicked smile. "On your hands and knees. Crawl to me."

Her face transforms and her lips part. She's eager and I bet already fucking dripping wet.

I'm hard as stone watching her move slowly, purposefully, licking those pouty pink lips.

"Fuck. Goldie. You're so sexy. You like this, don't you?"

She nods slowly.

"Yes, sir." She pants.

My cock jerks and I'm already leaking. "Jesus Christ," I mumble under my breath. She's going to be the death of me. And if I'm not careful, I'll be coming way too fast and I don't want to. I want to enjoy fucking her with the plug deep inside her. Even the thought is driving me wild. I'm going to come so hard inside her.

She stops at my feet and sits back on her heels. Looking up at me with heavy, longing eyes.

"Are you wet?"

"Yes-s," she stammers.

"Show me," I say in a controlled voice, even though I'm shaking from holding myself back. I'm not touching her until she begs.

"Slip your fingers into that thong and show me how wet you are." My eyes lock onto hers. My fingers twitching to touch her. But I can't. Not yet.

She follows the command, and her slickness covers her fingers.

I suck in a sharp breath.

Fucking hell.

"Taste it. Tell me how sweet you are."

She doesn't hesitate; instead, she keeps her eyes on me and her wet, pink tongue slips out and she licks at her wetness. Her eyelashes flutter, and she moans. "Mmm."

I'm throbbing with need. But she has to come at least once first.

"Do you taste good?"

"Hmm-mm, so sweet."

I lose it. "Don't tease me."

Her eyes open wide, and she gives me a look. "Sir, do you want a taste?" she purrs as her hand lifts toward me.

I don't want just a taste; I want to devour her.

She knows exactly what she's doing, but I'm in charge today. I want her to have all the pleasure.

"Soon. First, I want you to get on that bed, spread your legs and fuck yourself with two fingers until you come all over your hand."

Her brows pull together. "What will you do?"

"Watch."

She hesitates, wondering if she can walk or if she has to crawl.

"You can walk," I say and hold out a hand, which she takes and then walks to the bed.

"Do you want my thong off?"

"Yes," I answer in a low growl. I stand at the end of the bed perfectly between her spread thighs and Goddamn. Her beautiful pink glistening center is too much.

"You're soaked."

"I'm horny," she breathes, biting down on her bottom lip as her hands slide over her stomach and slip through her wet pussy. She circles her clit with her two fingers and moans.

This is torture. I want to fuck her already. My eyes are locked on her slow and controlled movements. It's hypnotizing.

"Are you hard?"

"So hard, Goldie, it hurts," I answer honestly.

"Let me help you." She begs in that seductive tone. Killing me more.

I shake my head. "No. Fuck your fingers now."

And she does. She slips two fingers deep inside her pussy and I lose my breath. She fucks them slow at first and then she picks up the pace to where her toes curl, her neck on display, because she tipped her head all the way back. I know she's close.

She continues pumping until the words, *I'm coming*, fall from her lips.

My heart is hammering inside my chest. "Good girl. Come for me."

"Ahhh." Her body shudders in shock waves as she comes hard.

I move and then crawl until I'm hovering over her, breathing hard and fast. "Incredible."

"Now roll over. Let me warm your other hole up."

"Oh," she flips over eagerly.

I unclasp her bra and skim my hand over her back down the dip just above her butt. Her skin erupts in goosebumps.

I touch her full ass and smack it gently. She moans. I love how fucking responsive she is to me. Both my words and touch make her putty in my hands.

I enter her pussy with two fingers.

"Ah, Damien. Yes."

She's so fucking wet.

"Is this mess all for me?" I ask hoarsely.

"Yes," she pants.

I move my fingers and when she tightens her walls against them and her breathing picks up, I slide her wetness up over her tight hole.

I press a single finger inside and she cries out. In a feral way. A mix of a moan and pain. Her puckered hole so hungry for me.

"Are you okay?" I ask, holding back how hot this is making me.

"Yes. Don't stop." She whimpers.

I'm going to come apart inside her when it's my turn. I can't wait.

"I can't wait for your ass to take the plug."

"Yes-s," she stammers again.

"I'm going to stretch you first. You like this, don't you?"

She nods.

I move my finger in and out. When she takes it easily, I ease a second one in. She moans more. "Do you like the way this feels?"

"Yes. So much."

I move my fingers in a rhythm that has her wriggling and writhing in pleasure.

"Fuck!" My dick jerks just from watching how much she loves this. I love this.

She's ready...

"Where's the plug and lube?"

"In my bag."

I remove my finger and she groans.

I smirk. "I'll be back."

"I got the smallest one," she answers in a hurry.

"Goldie, relax, I won't be long. You need the lube, even if it's the smallest size."

She exhales and slumps down as I quickly grab the plug off the floor and the lube from her bag.

I climb back on the bed and open the lube and squeeze a generous amount down her crease. She squirms from the coldness.

I return my finger and rub the puckered hole for a second. She writhes and tries to encourage me to enter her. I do and she moans loudly. "Damien, fuck."

"So good." I encourage her as I pick up the pace and continue to press around the edges. When she feels stretched enough, I work to insert the metal plug.

"Are you ready?" I ask, even though I know the answer.

"Yes!"

I add more lube and slip my finger out and grab the toy, rubbing the tip over her hole. She rocks her hips back. And I dip it slightly inside. "Oh, that's tight."

"Tight but good?"

"Yes." She breathes.

I push more inside and she takes a deep breath and then I push the rest in. She groans and grips the bed sheets tightly. "You should see how beautiful it looks."

"Mmm." She rocks.

She's so fucking beautiful I can't hold back anymore. I need to fuck her. Fill her.

"Roll onto your back." I grunt.

She does and cute noises leave her mouth, and I know it's because the plug hits differently when she moves around.

I settle my hands next to her head. The sunlight beams on us through the window. She's beautiful all lit up.

My cock jerks, knowing it's so close to fucking her tight, wet cunt. "I'm going to fuck you now."

She nods frantically. "Okay."

I sink my hips and enter her tight hole.

The gem in her ass is making me crazy, and I have to control the urge not to fuck her hard.

I thrust, and when I hit all the way in, she cries out.

"I'm not going to last long. You feel too good and those fucking sounds are making me crazy."

She has the nerve to side-eye me and I cock a brow.

"Are you challenging me to fuck you hard? Because I wouldn't tempt me."

"Give it to me hard, sir." And the way she says sir is like she's playing me and she's so fucking hot.

"You are going to be the death of me," I say as I slam into her hard and only my name leaves her lips.

I pull back and thrust inside her again. The tightness is torture but the best fucking kind. I continue to thrust repeatedly. Picking up my pace, I feel her walls clamp down before she spills her next words.

"I'm going to come." She moans.

I thrust a little harder now. When I feel that she's stretched and on edge, I reach around and gently wiggle it in and out. Before removing it, she cries in pleasure as she violently shudders from an orgasm. Unable to hold back any longer, I come hard. Emptying myself inside her. I watch her flushed face gasping for air. I'm breathless too. That was the most intense fuck of my life. The best fuck of my entire life. Nothing and no one will compare. She's ruined me.

When I somewhat recover, I pull gently out and collapse beside her and hold her to me. When I find my breath again, I get up and carry her to the bathroom.

"What are you doing? I can walk."

"No, I'll carry you. We need to shower before our ride gets here," I answer as I turn on the shower. We stand under it for a lot longer than we should, but both of us are still coming down from the peaks of our orgasms.

We quietly shower, pack our bags, and get inside the taxi then onto the plane.

Both of us are quiet, deep in thought. I keep my hand in hers and watch as she's engrossed in a movie. I reflect on our weekend and it makes me realize something about her.

The fact is, truthfully, she scares me. I worry Marigold could choose herself too just like my ex-wife did because, why not?

My life is in a different stage to hers, but I have to remember she's not my ex and she has only shown me how much she wants me and a relationship.

She chose us.

Me and Samuel.

I need to choose her and face the consequences that will come my way from this decision. But she deserves all of me.

No more secrets. No more hiding.

Chapter 32

Damien

SHE UNBUCKLES HER SEAT belt, but I reach out to stop her. I'm not ready for her to leave. My hand on hers has her brows pulling together.

"What are you doing?" she asks, threading her fingers in mine.

My gaze looks down at our joined hands. Admiring how small and perfect her hands fit in mine.

"I don't want to end our weekend yet." My voice cracks, giving away how sad I am to have this end.

Her exhale and soft expression make me think she was wishing this wasn't ending either.

But it is and there's nothing either of us can do.

Her lips part, but I speak first, wanting to turn this sad talk around.

"And I know a five-year-old who keeps asking for you to come over."

Her face brightens at the mention of Samuel. "We can't have him upset, can we?"

This weekend would have cost her a lot of important study time. She tried doing it on the plane rides and once at the cottage, but as a past student, I know it's not enough. I see her tired, puffy eyes and I would hate to think she'll be up all night studying tonight because of me. I can't be selfish. So as much as it pains me, I think even though I want her to come to my place now, I need to look after her.

I sigh heavily. "No. But I know you need to study. You didn't get a lot done the last two days."

She smirks. "We were busy. And I needed a break."

My mouth tips up at her insinuation. "We did. But I know this is a big year for you."

She nods, unable to disagree with me.

"I have an interview with Lincoln LLP firm," she announces, straightening up in her seat.

"Congratulations. Where is it?"

She hesitates, nibbling on her lip, and I'm not looking forward to what she'll say based on her body language.

"New York."

I swallow the disappointment I feel and think about how important this is for her. "Which division?"

"I chose criminal."

"How long will you be gone for?"

She swallows and glances down at our hands again before meeting my gaze. "Eight to ten weeks."

That feels like a kick in the gut. The thought of not having her around is unbearable. "How will I live not having you with me?" I blurt, moving my other hand to the back of her head to bring her face closer to mine.

"Lucky, we have phones," she breathes.

I groan and tip my head back. The woman who was made for me thinks I will be fine without her. I don't think she understands how much she means to me. "It's not the same. Now that I've had you, going online for that long won't be the same."

"I know but it won't be forever."

"What if they offer you a full-time job?" I ask in disbelief. She wouldn't be able to turn down a good offer. And I couldn't let her give up her life for me. I don't want to hold her back, even if it kills me.

She shakes her head. "I won't take it. I'll find a job here."

The way she says it makes me believe her. But it doesn't sit right. "Don't give up your dreams for me."

"I'll get a job here. I won't give up my dreams, but I won't give you up either." She reaches up and touches my cheek with her palm. Her thumb dusts along in a soft, reassuring way.

My heart pounds harder in my chest. "You make it hard to fight."

"It's why I'll make a good lawyer."

I chuckle before I turn serious. "You will. You'll be unstoppable."

She smiles bashfully at the compliment.

I move my face closer to hers to lay a kiss on the tip of her button nose, where it's flushed. "Will you come to my place after you unpack and study?"

She tugs her lip into her mouth as if contemplating something. "What if I promise to study for an hour before I come?"

I gaze into her bright eyes and she looks so happy. "How can I say no?"

"You can't."

I lay my forehead on hers. I'm not ready for her to leave the car, but I have to let her go. And the quicker she gets into the house, the quicker she'll be back in my arms.

"Go and I will see you soon," I whisper sadly.

We kiss one last time and she slips out and enters the house, but not before looking into the car as if she knows I'm watching her. After she's fully inside, I tell my driver to take me home.

As much as I'm disappointed to let her go, I'm excited to see Samuel. I've missed him. I can't wait to hug and kiss him.

And it always makes me wonder how Lucy just left and never missed him.

But just as I'm confused, it quickly changes to anger.

Samuel deserves a woman who wants him and loves him. And Marigold does.

I can't wait to get home and tell him she's coming over.

As soon as the driver parks, I'm out of the car striding to the door to look for my son.

There's clashing in the kitchen, so I can bet my mom is cooking or cleaning.

"Hey, Mom," I say, finding her putting dishes away.

"Son. How was your trip?"

"Good. Where's Samuel?"

"In his playroom. We just finished lunch. Did you want me to make you something?"

"No, I've eaten. Thanks for looking after him."

"I'll let you go and spend time with Samuel. He missed you."

I know she doesn't mean to say that to make me feel guilty. But it does. Will I ever be able to do something for myself without drowning in self-disgust?

"Thanks." I kiss her cheek and head toward the playroom.

I step into the doorway, and I can finally breathe.

"Hey!" I say, moving closer to him.

Samuel's head tips up and a huge smile erupts on his face.

"Dad!" he replies, dropping the Legos he was holding as he stands. I squat and open my arms wide in time for him to jump into them. I clutch him close and stand.

"I've missed you. Did you have a good time with Nana?"

"Yeah. Can I go play now?"

"Yes. I'll shower and then I have a surprise for you." I lower him down. But he doesn't walk away from me to sit back with his Legos.

"What surprise?"

I hand him a souvenir, it's a puzzle of Santa Barbara. "This is one. But there's also someone you've been asking to see."

Samuel's brows lift. "Mari!" he yells.

I can't help the grin that forms on my face. Yeah, I'm definitely not the only one smitten with her.

I shower and turn the TV on in the living room. I've put on a movie for Samuel and me.

Samuel said he didn't feel well when I got out of the shower. I checked his temperature, and he had a fever, so I gave him some Tylenol and told him to rest.

The door sounds and Samuel's little head tries to lift, but he struggles. I slip out from under him.

"Let me open the door for her and she can come here and watch the movie with us."

His head moves up and down slowly, but he doesn't speak. This isn't him.

I stride to the door. I open the door and find her in jeans and a sweater. Fucking adorable.

"What's wrong?"

I tried to muster up a grin for her but I feel pretty grim, so I guess I look like it. I hate it when Samuel's sick. I want to make it better for him.

"Samuel's sick. Fever and just not himself."

"Do you want me to go?"

"No," I reply quickly. "He wants you. You should've seen when I got home and told him you were coming over. I'm pretty sure he's more excited to see you than he was to see me."

She steps in and I grab her waist and yank her to me. I need a kiss from her. Even though I had so much of her mouth and body already, it's just never enough. I can't get my fill of her. All day and night with her is still not enough.

We separate and I take her hand and lead her to the living room where Samuel is resting.

He shifts on the sofa. "Mari."

"Hey, Sammy, your dad says you're not feeling well." She moves closer to him and squats beside the sofa.

His hand reaches out from under the blanket, and he wraps an arm around her neck.

My chest feels like it could burst. She puts an arm around him and rubs his upper back so softly.

"Do you want some back tickles?"

He nods.

She moves to sit beside his head, where she puts the pillow on her lap, and he lays his head down. Her purple nails going on his back.

I take a seat at Samuel's feet, momentarily rebuffed.

My mind is a jumbled mess of emotions and thoughts. I try so hard to focus on the car movie, but I zone out. Samuel sleeps and I expect him to wake up better, but just before the movie ends, he wakes up and vomits all over the rug.

Marigold gets up and I grab Samuel and take him to clean him up. But he wants to vomit again. Marigold asks where the bucket is and gets it.

He's sick again and then I go about cleaning him up and getting him fresh clothes.

This time, I take him to his bed. He snuggles in and falls asleep.

I go to clean the bucket, but she's already washed it.

When I move to deal with the living room, I find her on her hands and knees cleaning the carpet.

I stare at her for a moment before I join her. I've never had help. My mother, yes. A partner, no. And Marigold doesn't seem bothered by tonight. It's not sexy at all. Yet this is why she's so different. I don't have to tell her what to do. We're a team. I've not been a part of a fucking team in a long time. I shake my head because if I think about it, tears will form and I'm not crying about it. Even if they're happy tears.

After we clean up, I go to the kitchen to make her tea.

It's the least I can do.

Her hands circle my waist.

"Thanks for your help. You know I don't expect it."

"I know. But I want to. I want this."

I turn in her arms, and our faces are close. I'm lost in her eyes when footsteps sound and I'm too late when it dawns on me. Fuck. It's a Sunday afternoon. I got so caught up with Samuel, it slipped my mind. Here I am, standing in the middle of my kitchen, embracing Marigold with my hand on the top of her sexy ass. Her hands hold my head close to hers. I'm too late and I stare at my best friend Elijah's disappointed gaze.

CHAPTER 33

MARIGOLD

ELIJAH STRIDES TOWARD US. Damien drops his arms from me instantly. My brother doesn't miss it though, and he scowls harder. He flicks his narrowed gaze between our hands and our faces.

He knows.

Elijah reaches us head-on. He marches straight up into Damien's face. I can practically see steam coming from his ears. He grabs onto Damien's shoulder, and I gasp, thinking he's about to hit Damien. "What the fuck? I thought I made it clear I didn't want you with her."

"Elijah, stop," I interrupt with a desperate plea.

He drops his hands from Damien's shoulder. My brother's upset gaze is fixed on me now. "No. I'm mad at you, too. Damien was hurt by his ex and he needs time to heal." He squeezes the back of his neck. "And fuck, are you really ready to take on someone else's kid?"

I wince. His words slice my heart layer by layer.

But it not only hurts, it also angers me. Something I've never felt. And it lights a fire in my belly. "That's not your business. I'm happy. We're seeing each other."

"Like fuck you are," Elijah spits back, cutting me off from further talking.

I see red. My eyes narrow at him and there's so much tension inside of me that my words come out in a snarl. "I'm an intelligent woman who can make her own damn choices!"

Elijah snorts. "Seems to me you can't. Acting like a child. Going behind my back when I said focus on school and let him focus on healing."

I grind down hard on my teeth. Thinking about my next words carefully.

"You need to accept our decision. You have Jackie. And remember she's younger," I argue. I try to get him to see he's happy, so why can't he let us be? Stay out of my business. I know he loves me and it's fair to be shocked, but he's the one acting like a child.

He wipes roughly over his face and whisper-shouts, "I was there when Lucy left him. She ripped his and Samuel's fucking hearts out."

Elijah's eyes flick between mine and Damien's. "You two had a nice little vacation together, didn't you?"

"We did until now," I snap.

He ignores me, of course. "It's all a lie, you get that? Holidays are a fake sense of happiness. Reality is you're in college and he's a workaholic dad."

"I'm well aware, Eli," I sneer. He acts like I haven't given this much thought. I can't help the way I feel about Damien. My heart wants what it wants. And I want Damien.

"Fuck!" Elijah yells and his hands curl into fists.

"Eli," Damien warns.

Elijah's hard gaze whips back to Damien.

"We need to talk. Alone," Elijah demands coldly.

I've never heard him speak to a friend this way. Damien's eyes hold mine and they turn from cold and detached to fury before they flick to Elijah's. "Okay. But first, Elijah, don't fucking speak to your sister like that. Angry or not. She doesn't deserve it. She's done nothing wrong."

Elijah's jaw is twitching. He knows it's true, but he's upset I betrayed him. I didn't listen and give Damien space to heal. I won't get a sorry from him right now. He's enraged. He needs to calm down and realize that Damien and I are adults, and this is our choice. I get he cares for both of us. But fuck, let us work it out.

I run my hand through my hair. My magical weekend is now ruined. This is not the end. "I'm not going anywhere. This involves me and I'm not—"

"Listen to your brother." Damien's voice cuts through and silences me.

My mouth opens and I go to talk, but it feels like razor blades. I swallow the pain and use my firm voice. "You have five minutes and then I want to talk to Damien." I'm proud of myself at how controlled

I sound, even though inside I'm shaking. I'm on the verge of crying. I concentrate on breathing in through my nose and out through my mouth as Damien glances away.

Neither of them answers. Elijah turns and grips Damien's arm and pulls him to the side.

I standalone in the kitchen. My body is shaking with a mix of hurt and anger.

I pull out my phone from my bag and text Clara. I ask if she's busy tonight because I might need to come over. She asks why, but I see movement and the boys are walking back, so I tuck my phone into my pocket. Elijah's face still looks angry as they stand in front of me. I turn my face to Damien, who looks at me with pity-filled eyes.

No...

I grab Damien's arm, ignoring the way his hot skin feels in my hand. The tingles won't help the turmoil I'm feeling. Only his words tell me he's still with me. We're still an *us*.

When we're out of Elijah's earshot, I look away from the asshole who's going to watch us with angry eyes.

I grip the necklace he gave me. As much as I love it and its meaning. If I'm his Goldie, he needs to choose me.

"What's going on?" I ask in a hushed voice.

He looks at me with sad eyes, but I don't like the way he's not touching me. With his hands in his pockets, he keeps avoiding my gaze. The body language is closed off and I'm scared.

Scared my world is falling apart right now.

"Your brother is right. I'm carrying trauma with me. I'll hold you back in life. There's no way for me to answer him with one hundred percent certainty whether I want to have kids or get married again. And as he reminded me, that's totally unfair to you." His voice is so quiet and detached. As if he's already decided.

"I feel like you're punishing me for your ex," I grit out.

My heart is breaking. He's making all these assumptions without talking to me. We never spoke about marriage and kids because we only just started seeing each other. And now he's already shutting me out.

"Your brother, he's important," he says. As if I don't know. He doesn't have many friends and my brother was there for him. I get it. I really fucking do, but Elijah will get over it. I won't. I'm sick of people hurting me and never speaking up. Not today. Today he's getting my honesty.

"And I'm not?" My voice is loud and shaking. The amount of adrenaline pumping through me is like a million shots of coffee. I'm so fucking angry.

"You know you are. I just need time to think...to heal...like Elijah said."

"Fuck my brother. If he can't get on board with our relationship, then that's his problem. But let's get real, Damien. Deep down you haven't completely let me in."

I'm sick of being the girl that gets hurt. I'm so fucking done with falling, only for the other to not fall too.

I want to be loved wholeheartedly in return. Hell, I deserve it.

He brings a hand up to the back of his neck, squeezing it. "I've given you more than I've ever given a woman before. I've known your brother for years and I'm struggling with...I'm fucking broken. No matter how much I want you."

"You're not. You just have to let go of the past and open your heart to love. For a future. Saying you want me and doing it are two different things."

He drops his head, and his hand returns to his pocket. Silence. That's all I get back.

No, I'm so fucking done.

"I choose me," I snap and storm off, ignoring my brother calling out my name in his stupid, authoritative voice.

I grab my phone and unlock it. Through blurry vision, I scroll to find Clara's name and call her. As soon as she picks up, I choke on a sob.

"I'm coming over," I cry.

"Of course. See you soon."

I hang up without another word, swipe the fat drops of tears that are rolling down my cheeks away and get in my car. Not once do I bother looking back to see if either of the guys has followed because a part of me knows they didn't, and I cry harder.

"What a dick!" Clara interjects. "And your brother is an asshole."

"Yep and yep," I say in a raspy voice. The sobbing has changed the sound of my voice.

I cried my heart out on the way to Clara's; I barely remember the drive except for how shaky my body was.

"I seriously can't believe he said nothing." She made us tea, but instead of sitting in her dining area, we're sitting in her room in case her roommates come home. I'm not in the mood to see anyone.

I sip my tea. Grateful for the warm liquid soothing my dry throat.

"And I warned him," she mumbles.

My brows pinch together. "You did what?"

"On your birthday, I told him to not hurt you."

I reach over and squeeze her hand. "Thanks for looking after me."

"Anytime. I'm sorry. I should have told him to break it off with you."

I shake my head. "No. Our weekend was so special I never want to forget it."

"Yeah?"

Memories of the weekend flood my mind. The chats, sex, and sweet moments. "He even made me tea. He looked up on Google how to make it and thought he screwed it up. It was cute," I say with a sigh, but it doesn't help my heavy heart when I think of how blissfully happy we were.

Clara crosses her arms. "It's cute, but I'm still angry."

My lip twitches, but even with her kindness, I can't smile.

Clara continues to stare at me.

I don't know what else to say. My soul feels shattered.

I blow on my tea and take a sip.

"I've never seen you look so sad," Clara whispers.

I try to put a smile on my face, but it's fake.

"I'll be okay," I say, as if to convince myself as well as her.

"I need to find a job. Because keeping myself busy will do the trick."

She takes a big sip of tea. "Distractions work well. Are you thinking about going back online?"

I shake my head. "No."

God no. I couldn't think of anything worse. All the good memories we shared are there and I'll end up a blubbering mess, rehashing them.

"Do you need help with looking?"

I sigh. "Not yet. I'll see what I can find in law, maybe a secretary? I don't really know. I can't think properly, but something fresh."

She nods. "New is good."

I leave Clara's house after we watch a trashy old movie, which I can't even remember the name of. As soon as I get home, I strip for a nice shower. The necklace he bought me shines under my bathroom light. I stare at myself wearing it in the mirror and fresh tears fill my eyes. I touch the metal and tears fall as I take off the necklace. And with trembling hands, I put it away in a drawer.

Out of sight, out of mind.

Just not out of my heart.

CHAPTER 34

DAMIEN

I WAKE UP IN a cold sweat. Sitting up in my bed, frantically looking around. I'm gasping for air. I rub my face when I realize I was dreaming.

I'm back to barely sleeping because every time I try to sleep, I have a fucking nightmare.

I feel like I'm drowning. I need her air like I need to get to the water's surface. This longing for Marigold is an out-of-body experience.

I can't blame her for wanting more than what I was giving her. What kind of man doesn't stand his ground and fight for her?

Me. I didn't.

I let her down. And every day it's been eating away at me.

I'm a big fucking coward. Who doesn't deserve her.

She never once made me feel unworthy, yet I made her feel that way. I know what that pain feels like. And it fucking sucks.

Elijah hasn't spoken to me since telling me to stay away from his sister. He left me standing in my kitchen.

It's been a few days since I saw her last, and I'm back at home with a now healthy Samuel and work.

Like, before...

Before she came into my life.

I've finished writing notes for a patient I discharged this morning. Leaving my office, I head to the theater changing rooms. I've got a case with Doctor Alex Taylor.

"Here's the man," Alex booms as he walks in and I'm putting my scrub top on.

"HI," I reply.

Definitely not in a cheerful mood because now I have to confess what a shitshow my life is.

"And you come back quieter and grumpier than ever. What happened?" he asks, changing into his pair of navy scrubs.

"It just didn't work out," I mumble. He doesn't know who she is or any of the finer details.

"Bummer. But hey, plenty more fish in the sea," he says with a shrug and a cocky smile.

I shake my head in disbelief. Women weren't in my plan. However, Marigold was different and there'll be no one like her. I want to throw myself into work and forget about the heaviness in my chest.

"I'll see you at the sink," I say as I leave the room and find my way to the waiting patient. I introduce myself to the young woman with a benign tumor that Alex will remove. I will close it up, so she doesn't have a large ugly scar. It will take us the rest of the day.

At least here, I can make one person happy, even if it's not me.

After hours of surgery, Alex and I return to the changing rooms. I shower and dress in silence. I'm still struggling with the idea of going home to another restless night of sleep. I want to reach out to her, but I don't want to betray Elijah.

"You're really down about the girl, aren't you?"

My head whips around to see Alex staring at me from the seat where he's putting on his work shoes.

"Yeah, we only just got together," I confess. Not really understanding why I feel the sudden need to tell him, but it feels good to talk. My mom and Samuel aren't the right people to unload this information on, and Elijah is a major problem, which leaves me with a few work colleagues.

I sit forward in my seat, my hands clasped together, and talk. "I was actually dating Elijah's sister."

"The brunette? Young? In college?"

"Yep. That's her."

He whistles. "Nice."

"It was…"

He shuffles in his seat. "But?"

"Elijah told me not to go there."

"Listen, I wouldn't love it if any of my friends were with my sister, either."

"See," I say.

"But I'd get over it. Eventually. Because seeing her happy is more important."

I rub my hands over my face as I remember Elijah's words. "You don't know Elijah like I do."

"He seems easy going every time I've met him."

"Yeah, he usually is. Just not about this," I say with a sigh.

I get it, I do, but it's harder to accept when your heart gets involved. It makes it difficult to listen.

"Have you told him you love her?"

Staying silent, I blink slowly in his direction. I can't deny it. I've been falling in love with Marigold from the second we met online. We connected on a sexual and mental level.

"No."

"Sounds like she's worth fighting for. Tell him you love her."

"Would that seriously change his mind?"

I doubt it.

He shrugs and stands to lean forward, slapping my shoulder. "It's worth a shot. I need the less grumpy version of you back. It's way too quiet now."

A pathetic laugh leaves me.

And as I wave, it's also a silent thank you. He nods and leaves the room. I sit by myself, grabbing my phone, defeated. There's still no call or texts from either Marigold or Elijah. I wonder if I should message her. But what do I say? Nothing has changed.

I stand, shoving it away in my pocket and leave to confront Elijah.

I stand at my best and oldest friend's modern front door.

There's a small part of me that knows he'll probably want to punch me as soon as he sees who's standing on his front porch. But first, I need to explain how sorry I am. Then second, how deeply in love I am with Marigold.

I suck in a deep breath and bring my fist down on the door, banging hard on it.

The door opens and I twist back and come face to face with one of my only friends.

A tightness settles on his face as soon as he realizes it's me.

"What are you doing here?" he asks as his gaze travels around me, looking to see if I'm alone.

"To talk."

He snorts. "You should've done that ages ago."

"I know. I know, and I'm sorry. I just needed time to see if it wasn't a phase."

He scrunches up his face and I realize it's probably appearing if I only wanted casual sex with her.

"She might've not wanted anything serious," I explain.

"And you did?"

Oh, no. I'm going to have to be open and he's going to hate me, but it's the truth. If I want to mend our friendship, I need to be honest.

"I didn't think I was capable."

"Capable of what?" he spits as if I'm being ridiculous.

I'm messing up my words from the nerves.

"Of being in a committed relationship again."

He crosses his arms. "She's thirteen years younger. I'm still struggling with that."

I jut my chin up, not backing down. "I know. But I can't help it."

"You can't control your dick?" He sneers and I understand his frustration.

"I can and I did. I haven't been with anyone since my ex."

Elijah's silent for a beat before he replies. "You two are so opposite." He rubs the back of his neck." I don't get it."

"Oh, I know. I think that's why it works. She has this easy-going nature that calms me. For the first time in a very long time, I feel happy."

His features soften slightly. He knows my past and how dark I've been, so I'm sure he understands how big of a deal it is for me to confess my happiness.

"Jackie said she could see something between you two," he mutters to himself.

"I'm in love with her," I say boldly.

He stares at me with a bewildered expression before it finally sinks in.

"Hold up." He thrusts out a hand. "You're in love with my sister?"

My heart is racing as I finally say it out loud. Those words I haven't uttered to a soul, but now that I have, they feel good leaving my lips. Like the weight of the world just lifted off my shoulders.

"And she loves you for some reason. Does she know you love her?"

I stare wide-eyed and my heart is thumping wildly inside my chest. *She loves me?*

The feeling of knowing that information is overwhelming. My mind is spinning. I didn't fucking know she loved me.

I exhale heavily. I wish I could go back and tell her. "No."

"Hence why you look like shit."

I choke out a laugh. I've barely slept since she stormed out of my house.

"Have you spoken to her?" I ask.

"Nope, she won't answer me. She's being damn stubborn."

I smother a smirk. I'm proud of her. She's standing up for herself. Finding her worth and not wasting a second falling in love with someone who doesn't love her back. Only she doesn't know I do. I love her so fucking much.

"I hate that she's blocked me from her life when all I want is for her to be safe and happy," Elijah says.

"She'll forgive you. She probably wants a little time to think."

He seems to mull over those words. "Are you sure about this?"

"I've never been more sure about anything."

"If you break her heart, I won't forgive you." His eyes turn hard as he hits me with a piercing look. The warning. It warms my heart. I love how protective of her he is because it's how I feel.

"I promise you I won't."

"Now good luck figuring out how to get her to forgive you because I sure as shit have zero chance right now."

I wink. "I'll put in a good word for you."

CHAPTER 35

DAMIEN

THE NEXT DAY, I enter the school grounds to pick up Samuel after school. I don't even get five minutes before I'm mobbed by the moms.

I grit my teeth together as the flutter of eyelashes and shoulder touches begin. My body freezes at the unwanted attention. I know being a single dad is attractive to some, but there's only one woman on my mind.

"Who was that brown-haired woman picking up Samuel?" the bleach-blonde mom asks.

I rub my jaw that's beginning to ache from clenching too tightly.
"A friend."

Her red lips part into a wide smile, and she turns to her friends to say, "Told you." Before she faces me again. "I said she was too young to be your girlfriend."

I say nothing. My life isn't up for discussion, and if I was with Marigold, I don't care what they say. It's not up to them.

"Dad!" Samuel calls as he runs with his school bag that's still way too big for him.

Glad he's here and I can get away from the women.

I catch him in a hug. "Hey. How was your day?"

He pulls back and rolls his eyes like the thought exacerbates him. "I don't want to talk about it."

If I didn't think this kid was mine, those words are how I feel when I think about my day. The only time I've ever wanted to open up was with Marigold. Which gets me asking Samuel. "Did you tell Mari about your day?"

"You called her Mari!" he says, shocked, as I walk with him to the car.

"I did. Did you tell her about school?"

"Yes." He exhales again, not happy with my question. But inside I know why he would've opened up to her. She just draws it out of you, without feeling like you're rehashing, but more she wants to hear about it. That she cares about how your day was. Her kind heart is one thing I love about her.

We stop at the car, and I turn to hold him. I wrap my arms around him a little bit tighter. Missing her sucks.

"How about we go past the arcade on the way home?" I ask, not ready to get into the car.

"Yes!" He claps.

I take his bag off him, and he helps so fast I can't help but laugh at his enthusiasm.

We spend a few hours playing and laughing together. The arcade was the fun I needed to pull me out of my bad funk.

Watching Samuel wear a smile and play games was the highlight. I helped him with a few games to get him to win more tokens to get a big prize at the end.

As we step out of the Arcade, Samuel squeals. "Mari." He's waving frantically.

My heart beats harder in my chest from the anticipation of seeing her again. I've not laid eyes on her since...she left me standing in my kitchen with her brother.

"Hi, Sammy," her soft voice says back.

He hugs her, and it's unexpected and makes her stumble. I reach out and grab her. The electricity shoots up my arm from the touch of her warm, familiar skin. The way my body hums to hers is something else. I don't get time to figure it out. She shakes me off. And I let her go, even if my fingers tingle with disagreement.

Samuel lets go of her leg. "Are you coming to my house to play with Legos?" His hopeful face beams.

My stomach bottoms out with the situation we're in. It's my fault and Samuel doesn't know. The way he is with her is so unlike anything I've ever seen before. It's ripping my heart out. A part of me wants to beg for forgiveness, but the other part knows I have to sort myself out first. I need to think of her happiness over my own. She deserves to be loved unconditionally and lately, I've been selfish and asked her to hide. I should never have done that.

Her eyes hold mine and I don't miss the mix of sadness and anger swirling through them. She's not happy to see me.

"Hey," I give her a small grin.

"Hi," she says, but it's not her usual happy self. It's snappy, short, and angry.

She squats down and lays a hand on Samuel's shoulder.

I've decided I hate her being angry and upset. It's making me rattled. I usually feel a sense of calm, but right now, I'm getting panicky. I scratch the back of my neck and I look over her all-black activewear.

I try to concentrate on breathing and not how much of a fuck-up I am.

"Not tonight. I'm sorry I have work," she says with a genuine smile. What work?

Horror dawns on me...no, she wouldn't be back online...would she?

"Soon?" Samuel asks.

"Yeah, I can do that." She straightens and her hand goes to her throat.

"Are you going back online?" I ask, even though I have no right. It falls out of my mouth like I need to know.

She stares at me for a good second, not saying a word. I see the wheels turning and I hate the waiting.

"No. Not that it's any of your business, but I'm an admin for a legal firm."

My shoulders drop as relief hits me.

"Congratulations. I'm happy for you."

She dips her chin, watching Samuel play with the toys he won at the arcade.

She swept her hair up into a ponytail and it shows off her exposed delicate neck and it reminds me. "Where's your necklace?"

"I put it away just like you did with our relationship," she mutters, without looking at me. Her focus is still on Samuel. Who's distracted playing with the toys.

"That's unfair..." I trail off.

"Is it?" Her head whips around to look me in the eye. She cuts me off angrily. The hurt talking now.

I look at her pinched face. It pains me deeply. I stand there with my mouth open until the words, "I'm sorry," slip out.

A tear sits on her lashes. But she blinks it away as if she can't let it fall. She doesn't want me to see her weak. I don't think that at all. I see her only as strong and beautiful.

"Mari." The sound of Samuel's voice shakes me.

She blinks, sniffing away the sad evidence, and puts on a smile for him.

"Yes, Sammy?"

"Would you have dinner with us too when you come next time?"

She clears her throat while mine is closing up from his words.

"Ah. Sure. That sounds nice. What would we eat?"

"Hmm, pizza!" He beams at her with a twinkle in his eye.

"My favorite. Well, I better get home now, but I'll see you soon, okay?"

"Kay," he says back and hugs her again. This time, she expects it, so she doesn't tumble backward.

"Bye," I say.

She waves and quickly looks away. I sigh. "Are you ready to go home and I'll cook us some pasta?"

"Yep. No sauce, just cheese."

"Just cheese," I repeat and grab his hand and walk back to the car in a daze. Seeing her again should have cemented that her leaving me was the right decision. That she's better off without me. But it didn't. In fact, it did the opposite.

Later that night, I'm cooking dinner when Samuel walks in holding a piece of paper.

"What have you drawn, bud?" I ask.

"A picture for you," he replies.

I grab hold of the paper. Leaning in closer, I draw my brows together. "Who's that?"

The woman with long brown hair isn't my mother....

"Mari," he replies as if it's no big deal and completely natural.

I stare at the three of us. Samuel's holding each of our hands.

"I'm in the middle of Marigold and you," he says.

"I see. I love it. Look at our smiling faces."

"Yeah, let's put it on the fridge."

"Good idea," I say, acting like I'm happy and nothing is wrong.

Yet. Inside, I'm fucking sad. I miss her. And it's clear he misses her, too.

I put it on the fridge with magnets and step back, unable to stop looking at it. When Samuel runs away, I sigh and start making dinner.

I stare at the ceiling later that night, unable to sleep. I lie there thinking about everything that's happened between Marigold and me. How she acted toward me today. The kindness evaporated and was replaced with hurt. I keep expecting her to come to fight for me. As if she's my ex-wife.

She's not.

In fact, she's done nothing but beg for me to risk everything for her. And yet I'm still asking her to fight for me. Who's fighting for her?

Fuck, who's fighting for us?

She has been fighting alone.

No more. I'm going to fight for her. Show her I'll give her all of me if she gives me another chance.

Will she?

I shake my head. Don't think. Like she always pointed out. I'm controlled and planned and fuck so unhappy.

I'm going to find her tomorrow and talk to her. No plan, just see what comes. And if I give her everything and she doesn't want me, I'll have to walk away. I won't like it, but I have to understand.

Chapter 36

Marigold

It's the third missed call from Elijah in a row. I find it hard to ignore and not pick it up to know what he wants.

I'm not ready for his opinion. He doesn't want to listen.

I return to my class before I head to my new job for a couple of hours.

I've only been here a couple of days and the team seems nice. Knowing the terminology and being able to ask questions are helping my studies immensely. Later that night, I don't miss my brother's car in the drive.

Seriously?

What the hell could he want so badly?

I'm tired from college and work. The last thing I want to deal with tonight is Elijah. He got what he wanted, so I don't need to see his gloating face. He thinks he did the best thing for me, but he's trying to control me. I knew what I was getting into with Damien. If it was to fall apart, then that was for me to discover. Life lessons are from some of our greatest pains.

I storm up the drive and enter my parents house. I'm ready to go to war with him. The smell of a roast dinner fills my nose. My stomach grumbles, reminding me I haven't eaten in a while.

My eyes flick to see my parents talking to Elijah, who's sitting in his navy suit in one of my parents' dining chairs. He's eased back as if he hasn't been blowing up my phone all day.

"Hi, love, how was your day?" my mom says, but her face seems a little too happy.

Now my worry peaks. I'm not used to surprises or secrets, so I have this unsettling feeling sinking in my lower stomach.

I kiss my mom's cheek and look at my dad, who looks no different. I move over and kiss his cheek.

"It was good."

"Hi, sis." Elijah smirks.

His face annoys me, and I can't hold myself back a second longer. "What's going on? You've been persistent."

"And you never called me back," he replies, staring at me with a blank expression. He gives nothing away.

"I had college and then work."

He sits up in his chair. "And no time to reply to me?"

"I'm still angry at you."

"Please don't fight. He was only protecting you," Mom interrupts.

I get up and grab a bottle of water for each of us before sitting down and drinking some.

"You're my parents. I expect lectures from you." My eyes flick from my parents to Elijah. "You warning me that Damien's not right. Too old. Too grumpy...what else am I missing Elijah?"

He stares coldly back with a tick in his jaw.

"He loves you," Mom cuts in.

"Listen, I'm glad he asked. I've been concerned since your mother told me about you and Damien," my dad speaks.

I twist to meet my dad's eyes head-on. "Well, why didn't you speak to me?" I ask with a frown.

"I didn't want me, your mom, and Elijah all to say the same thing. I don't want to hurt you, or worse, push you away, so I figured one could speak for all of us."

"Oh," I mumble. My dad's right. How would I feel having them all gang up on me?

I wanted support and I guess they have, as well as being honest with me. They want me to go in with my eyes open.

"Now I've heard you and I'm sorry I upset you, Mari. Let me make it up to you," Elijah says.

"What do you mean? How?" I ask, skeptical.

"Let's catch up on Saturday, and I promise we won't talk about Damien."

Even hearing his name hurts. The pain in the center of my chest is turning into an ache.

"Only if you bring Jackie," I say, knowing she'll make this more bearable. I don't want to hang out with just Elijah yet. I'm still upset about how he's handled the situation at Damien's.

"Fine," he grumbles.

"Okay, I'm glad you two sorted everything out, but can I serve dinner now?" Mom says, slipping on her oven mitts.

"Yes, please, I'm starving." I sit up in my chair and finally a little bit of my appetite is back.

My mom comes over, lowering a plate, and kisses the top of my head. I turn my head, and she gives me a smile and I return a genuine back. The first bit of calmness returning. Let's hope it helps me sleep tonight.

Elijah texted me this morning and asked if I could meet him at the teahouse. I know what he's talking about because it's where I get my tea from.

And the thrill I'm going to a favorite place of mine makes me slip on my favorite blue jeans and a green top. I pop my mascara and gloss on and have my hair in a natural wave. The drive only takes me ten minutes. I look around for Elijah's sports car, but it's not here yet. I don't wait. I'm going to browse the tea. I'm curious to know what new flavors they've got in.

I step inside and smile at the store assistant who's serving someone else at the moment. But the lavender and mint hit me, and I move over to the pots.

I'm about to pour myself a cup when she comes over. "Good morning, Mari." She smiles, standing with her hands joined in front of her. "They're new flavors. I'll get you a cup. Let me sit you down where your booking is."

I glance at my phone to see where Elijah is, but no missed call or anything. Hmm, this is strange. He's never late.

I'll have a cup while I wait for him and Jackie.

She shows me out back where the tables are, and we go to the very back. My walk falters when I see the man with his heavy, lust-filled gaze running over me.

All emotions are hitting me at once. A mix of excitement down to fear. What's going on? Are Elijah and Jackie coming? Or is this a setup? But why?

I don't get to think any longer because Damien stands to his full height, and I suck in a sharp breath. His dark gray suit and a white shirt but no tie with his hair perfectly swept in gel are making my heart flutter and my lower body come alive.

A white shirt still sits at home buried deep in a drawer with fun memories of how sexy they can be.

No need to imagine what's under his suit because that memory is seared into my brain. His sculpted yet dark sprinkling of hair reminds me just how manly he is. I wish I could have it all again. Rewind to the time we were happy.

A brow quirks up high on his face, and I know he has caught me thinking about him in a filthy way.

"Marigold," he says in his low, deep voice. I'm not the only one affected by our reunion.

"Damien," I say, and it's breathier than I want it to be. I don't miss the lift in the corner of his mouth.

He walks around and I inhale his spicy pear scent. And it's so strong I don't smell lavender or mint anymore. I only smell him. It's heavenly. I threw out the body soap the moment I got home from Damien's house. I cried, stepping into the shower and seeing the bottle mocking me.

Not having it for a while and now having it so close reminds me how much I love it. I love him.

I sit down and drag the chair close to the table that's set up for lunch. He steps over and takes a seat opposite me. His gaze fixed on me with so much warmth.

Where's the sadness gone?

I don't want to get my hopes up.

The assistant brings me a cup of tea and I thank her and don't waste a second before I pick up the cup and drink it. The warm fluid hits my parched throat perfectly.

I lower it down.

His brows pull together. "You changed your nail polish."

I peek down at the green color matching my top.

"Yeah, I wasn't feeling the purple anymore." I shrug.

"I love the purple, it was you," he says in a sad tone.

I pick up the cup again. His gaze still holds mine.

He picks up his cup and sips it before he lowers it.

He winces.

I lower my cup.

"It's unusual," he mutters.

"You're drinking tea?"

"We're at a teahouse." He gives me a lopsided grin.

"I know, but you hate tea."

"But you love it."

I flick my hair off my shoulder. "You're drinking it for me," I whisper in disbelief.

"You're worth drinking dishwater for," he grumbles, clearly disliking the taste.

My heartbeat skips at his meaning, though. But I can't get too excited. He still hurt me.

"It's not that bad," I argue. Secretly, it's not my favorite either, but it's not that awful.

His eyes flick around as if to make sure the assistant isn't around. "Are you saying you like this?" He gestures to the cup.

"Not my favorite," I admit.

He waves and calls the assistant over.

"Can we get different tea and then get the cake of the day?"

"Sure. What tea did you want?" she asks.

He peers over at me. I understand he's looking at me for guidance.

"Can we get black tea and maybe some sweetener, sugar and honey?" I say.

I know she'll understand I'm getting him to try the tea with different sweeteners because he's bound to find one combination he likes.

She leaves and I sit staring at him, waiting for him to talk. Did he organize this...date?

"I spoke to Elijah," he starts.

Does he forget I was there? "I know. I was at your place too, remember?"

He shakes his head. "Not then. This week."

"Oh."

I try not to show any reaction, even though I'm on the edge of my seat waiting for him to spill what they spoke about.

"Elijah said nothing to you yesterday?"

I shake my head. "Only to meet him here."

"I got him to help me."

I blink rapidly, not understanding how Elijah switched so easily.

"Okay..." I say, still confused by everything. I'm waiting desperately for him to explain himself.

He grabs my hands and encases them with his. "I missed you."

I want to say *I miss you too*, but I need to stay quiet and let him speak.

"Seeing you but not being yours ruined me. I never wanted to try again. To be fair, I was bitter and angry about women. Then you, my Goldie. From that very first online meeting, I knew you were different."

I nod slowly, letting him know I'm listening. A wobble of my chin has him shuffling in his seat, edging closer to the table. His grip is tight on mine. His eyes reflect so much anguish that I have to bite the inside of my cheek to prevent myself from speaking.

"The scar running through my heart I thought was unfixable. But slowly, you threaded the needle and stitched me whole. I'll never let you go. I'll do whatever it takes to make you happy. Tell me what to do and I'll do it. Just please don't let this be the end. I'm not good at this, but I'll try."

A tear leaks from my eye, and it rolls down. He's my wounded man who's telling me I'm healing him. Words I've hoped to hear, but never thought he'd say. And now he's finally saying them, and I can't speak through my tight windpipe.

"I love you, Goldie. You're everything to me."

Words a man has never said back to me break me. A dam of tears breaks, and I pull my hand out of his grip to cover my face and cry hard into my palms.

A chair sounds on the floor and the touch of a hand on my back makes me cry harder.

"I'm so sorry. I don't mean to upset you. If you don't want me, I'll respect that. No matter how much that hurts me, I'll let you go. Your happiness is more important."

Is he kidding?

I rub under my eyes with my fingers and gaze at him lovingly through the blurry vision.

I sniff. My hands drop to clasp together on my thighs. "You idiot, of course I love you. I've been waiting forever to hear those words and hearing them from you means everything to me."

He gives me a deep exhale and then a lopsided grin.

"Well, nothing is stopping us now."

"Elijah?" I ask, double checking he's no longer going to be a barrier for us.

"Is onboard."

Which means no one is holding us back from being together now.

Those two words hang in the air between us. I try to wrap my head around the fact this is really happening.

"So, can we start again? This time with nothing holding us back? Will you be my girlfriend?" he asks with a longing look.

"Definitely." I choke on another tear as more fall, but this time, happy ones.

CHAPTER 37

MARIGOLD

"What happens now?" I ask Damien.

His hand holds mine across the table. He's barely touched his tea. I know I won't get him to convert to tea. But I'm happy he tried for me. His willingness to try was so sweet.

As long as I get it, that's all that matters.

"Let's go back to my place and see Samuel."

My smile widens at seeing Sammy. "I was hoping you would say that. But..."

My voice lowers, and I cast my eyes down at the table.

"But?"

I sigh and slowly bring my gaze to meet his gentle one. "I wanted to mention something."

"Hmm. Tell me. Anything." He runs his hand over his jaw before reaching out and clutching my hand.

My heart beats wildly inside my chest. I keep my eyes on Damien's. "Sammy told me he wishes you'd play with him. He thinks you don't have time. I feel bad for breaking his trust and telling you, but I'm not sure you're aware."

He sits back slightly. His hand is still firmly on mine. "I wasn't aware. My life is highly structured and organized. But it's something I need to change."

The conflict on his face is hard to watch. It's like he's riddled with shame. There's no need. Just like he is with me, he needs to change his life for Sammy, too.

"Listen, just play some Legos with us. Then here and there, do it, just you two."

He nods. "And I might buy more Nintendo controllers so we can all play."

My lips tremble with the need to smile. "You liked playing Mario Kart with me that much?"

"I loved it. And now you're a part of my life. We will all hang out more," he says, the warmth of his smile echoed in his voice.

A fear knots inside my stomach. "Speaking of. Are we going to tell Sammy?"

Damien leans forward, and I sip the rest of my tea. "I'm going to just hang out and see how he seems. If it feels right, I'll tell him today, but if not, I'll give him another day or so, but not too long. I don't want to keep secrets."

My mind battles with a crazy mix of hope and fear. "Me either. I'm nervous."

"Why?" he asks, an eyebrow rising a fraction.

"Because I love Sammy and I hope he accepts us."

A sympathetic, curved smile settles on his face. "He loves you, I'm sure of it. I'd be shocked if he doesn't accept us, but if he doesn't, we can figure out our next step together."

My smile falters but then with his confidence I draw in a breath, more determined we can do this. Everything will be okay. "Alright, well, let's do this."

"No time like the present." He winks, removing his hand from mine and pushing out his chair. He strides over to me. I look up and without hesitation, I stand and take his outstretched hand and we leave the teahouse.

"Leave your car here. We can come back later and grab it. I'll drive us."

We get in his car for the quick trip to his house. I sit in silence, holding back the apprehension that sweeps through me.

Arriving at Damien's, I follow his lead from his car into the house, and he grabs my hand and walks us through the house.

I can hear the television on and noises in the kitchen. We enter the kitchen, and his mom is busy cooking.

"Mom. This is Marigold. Marigold, my mom."

I smile through the anxiety spurting through me.

"Hi. Can I help?" I ask, looking at the pots on the stove and the bowls on the counter. The mess in the kitchen makes me feel more settled. Maybe his mom is less organized and more organized chaos like me.

Her face brightens at the suggestion. "No, thanks, dear. I'm done now."

"Dad! Mari?" Samuel's voice calls from the living room's direction.

His tiny form comes running into the room and barrelling into his dad's legs for a hug.

"Hey, bud. You watching TV?" Damien responds, bending down to hug him.

Samuel lifts his head away from Damien and peels his body away from him. "Yeah."

Samuel walks over and hugs my leg. I melt on the spot. I didn't realize how much I needed that until now. Though I feel my heartbeat racing from his welcome arms, I keep my composure.

"Hey, Sammy. Do you wanna play something?" I ask, peering down at him.

He pulls back slightly, tipping his head back, wearing the cutest grin. "Like Legos or a game?"

He pulls back, tipping his head back with the biggest, cutest grin. "Yeah."

"Only if I can join in, too."

Samuel's head twists to look at his dad. "Yeah." He turns to me, his eyes brighter. "Right, Mari?"

My mouth curves with tenderness. "Of course. It will be way more fun with the three of us."

"I've always wanted a mom," he replies. His entire face spreads into a smile.

A spoon hits the pot in the kitchen, causing a loud bang. In the corner of my eye, I see his mom scrambling to pick up the spoon. She's clearly shocked, too.

"I always wanted a son," I say with a calm smile. Those words feel as natural as breathing. I never knew I needed him and Damien. But once I fell for them, I can't see my life without them.

Samuel peels off my leg and runs off to his playroom, yelling as he goes. "Come on, let's play."

I'm still shell-shocked, wrapping my head around the bomb Samuel just dropped.

I peer at Damien, finding him staring with luminous eyes widened in astonishment.

"I can't thank you for what you just said. It wouldn't be enough. But just know those words mean everything to not only Samuel, but to me. The fact you could love my son like your own..." He looks away, running his hand through his hair and down to the ground. Appearing to take a second. He looks back up. "I thought I loved you before, but it's immeasurable now."

He steps forward, grabbing the sides of my face, and presses his lips to mine in a slow, seductive kiss. It's full of so much passion it makes my knees buckle. I sink into him. When we pull apart, he whispers, "Meet me when you're ready."

He turns to go and play with Samuel, and I realize he needs a few moments with his son alone.

I watch his sexy figure leave the room and when I turn around, I find his mom staring on with tears leaking from her eyes.

She wipes them away. "These are happy." She sniffs.

I break into an open, friendly smile.

"I've not seen my son smile in a long time. Or seen him tell a woman how he feels. To see this change in him is every mom's dream. He deserves to be loved, and so does Samuel. Thank you, Marigold, for choosing them. Because they've chosen you and I know you'll be very happy together."

She wipes away more tears. I swallow hard and bite back my own.

"He's a good man and I'm lucky to have him and Sammy in my life," I say in a shaky whisper.

"Did you want a cup of tea? I noticed Damien's selection. I figured it was you." The corner of her mouth lifts. No more tears leave her eyes.

"Yes. I'd love one. No sugar or cream. Actually, we were just at a teahouse."

"How lovely," she says, moving around the kitchen to make us tea.

"I got Damien to try tea."

"You did?" She gasps.

I giggle at her shock. "I did."

"And?"

I shake my head. "Hates it. Sugar, honey, or sweetener. He still won't drink it."

She laughs and pours water into the cups. "You're definitely pushing him out of his comfort zone. I love it. Come sit and have some tea. Let's give the boys some time alone and we can catch up."

She lowers a cup in front of me. "Thanks. I think that would be good. Samuel needs time with his dad."

"He hasn't allowed himself to do anything other than work. He's been on autopilot for so long," she says.

I nod and blow on the tea before taking a sip, excited to spend some alone time with his mom. Until I hear my name being called out by Samuel.

"I'm coming," I call out. "Sorry. I better go in there and play."

She reaches out and rubs my arm. Her face is gentle and understanding. "Don't be sorry, go to your boys."

I smile at the words, *your boys*.

I walk into the room and find them both eagerly looking at me standing in the doorway. It feels like a dream. To have them both stare at me like I'm important to them. They do not know how much I need them. My life is now filled with so much love. Love that's reciprocated.

"What took you so long?" Damien winks.

They are playing a game of Trouble.

"I was letting you boys warm up." I step into the room, rubbing my palms together and walking to sit between them. "Now I'm going to win."

"Nuh-uh," Samuel replies. "I'm gonna win."

A light laugh leaves me at his competitiveness. He's definitely like Damien. But I'm also super-competitive too, so I know this game will be fun.

"Nope. I am," I say back, screwing up my nose at Samuel, who is trying to mimic me, and it's adorable.

"I'll beat the both of you," Damien states.

Samuel groans.

"Come on, let's start. Sammy, you go first," I say.

Samuel begins, and I watch with interest. But I can feel the heat of Damien's gaze on me. But it's his soft touch on my knee that has my head tilting up.

I love you, he mouths.

I love you too, I mouth back.

EPILOGUE

MARIGOLD

"YOU'RE AN EXCELLENT PAINTER, Sammy," I say, staring down at my nails. He's painting them, using his dad's favorite color on me. Purple. It's been our new thing. We hang out, play Legos, Trouble, or his favorite, Nintendo.

It's been so easy slipping into their life.

"I'm done," Samuel says, putting the brush back in the polish. And screwing the lid.

"Thank you. Now I need to wait for them to dry before I get dressed," I reply, blowing on the thick layer.

"Are you Daddy's mommy?"

"Do you mean girlfriend?"

I roll my lips as I wait for his answer.

My heart is in my throat at his direct questioning. Damien's not in the room, so I'm going to go with what I think is the right thing to do.

"Yeah."

My lip lifts at what he's trying to ask me.

"Would that be okay?"

He gets up and moves to his box of Legos.

"Yeah," he replies.

I think that's the end of the discussion when he carry's the box over. We both pull out blocks when he speaks again.

"Will you live with us?"

Seriously, where is Damien?

I don't want to answer these questions wrong.

"Would you like that?"

"Yeah."

"Maybe we can ask Da-Daddy."

"What are we asking?" his voice calls from the doorway.

My gaze flicks over to him. He stands effortlessly in gray sweats and a gray shirt.

His face is pinched lightly. Is he laughing at me? I still feel panicked and he's laughing.

"Samuel asked if I will live with you two."

My gaze doesn't leave Damien's. And I expect some fleeting change. But he doesn't even flinch.

"Yeah, I think that's a great idea," he replies smoothly.

"Today?" Samuel asks.

"Not today, bud. We have to celebrate Mari's graduation."

"Oh." He moans.

I turn to face Samuel. "I'll start moving stuff tomorrow. How does that sound?"

He builds his house out of Legos with his brows pulled together. "Good. Now will you play Legos?"

My lips part into an easy smile. Samuel is the sweet, easy-going kid I never knew I needed. The only sign that he's cranky is either in the mornings when he wakes up or when something doesn't go his way. Damien's expressions sit on his face. And on a five-year-old, it's hilarious.

Since we officially started dating, Damien works less. And refuses to be on call on any important dates—like birthdays.

I told him I have a job at a local firm starting soon, so I'll be busy and not to worry about me. But, of course, he won't.

My whole life finally feels settled. Even picking up Samuel from school, the whispers are slowly disappearing. The women, initially finding out I'm Damien's girlfriend, sent them into a tailspin. Now I'm becoming old news. But ultimately, I don't care what anyone thinks. I've fallen in love with the man, not his age, or the fact he's a single father. His heart is what matters, and he's treated me better than anyone ever has.

Samuel still hasn't heard from his mother. He has never asked, but I ask Damien. I still can't understand her reasons and wish I'd get to speak to her to ask why. But I'm sure I wouldn't like the answer, anyway.

The love Damien and I give Samuel is hopefully enough that he doesn't feel like he misses out on anything compared to his peers.

"How about you get ready, bud," Damien says.

"I'm almost done." He moans.

I sit, watching him finish up the last pieces before Samuel jumps off the chair and runs to the bathroom.

Damien comes closer to me. He lays a lazy kiss on my lips. And a sweep of his tongue along my bottom lip. A promise of what's coming later.

"I love that color," he says in a gravelly tone as he looks down at my nails.

I smirk. "I know."

"I'll get Samuel ready, and then will you be ready?"

I bite my lip, knowing he's trying not to push me, but the way he glances at his watch, I know he wants to leave on time. Some things haven't changed, but they aren't relationship breakers. They're his quirks. His acceptance of me into his life without reservation or worries about anyone else has been all that I needed, so I need to accept all of him.

For my graduation, we have dinner booked as a big family. Mine and Damien's family are all together in one room tonight. It's our first big catch up and I'm excited to have everyone together. No one has had any reservations about our relationship since we made it official. Samuel looks at us with so much love and happiness that it doesn't matter what the world thinks.

An hour later, we leave the house, and our driver drops us off at the Ivory Tower. We are a trio now. I'm holding both my boy's hands as we celebrate. It's not something I'm used to, but I also don't hate it. I worked hard to finish and the excitement both Damien and Samuel have shown me has made me want to throw this dinner party.

"I love your purple dress," Damien whispers in my ear, so Samuel can't hear. "I can see the outline of your nipples."

I touch my Goldie necklace and look down at my pale silk lavender dress with a smile before running my gaze over them.

"And my boys look so handsome in their matching suits." The sense of pride in my heart explodes. I've never been so full of reciprocated love. But these two boys have given me it in abundance.

"I love this suit. Do I get to keep it?" Samuel asks. I love the black suits with the lavender shirts. The matching family is my new favorite thing.

"Yeah, bud, it's all yours," Damien says back to him.

"Yesss!" Samuel says loudly, clearly excited by that information.

We step out of the elevator and onto the dark floors. Everyone is already sitting down at the long candle-lit table. I come over and say hello to every person. I notice a few friends are here too.

"Elijah. Jackie, how are you?" I say with a smile.

"Mari. Congratulations. We're so proud of you," Jackie says, handing over a bag.

My gaze slides to my brother, who looks at me, smiling. "Congratulations, sis." He stands and hugs me.

At first, I'm shocked, but then I hug him back.

I next say hello to my parents and then over to Damien's parents.

I finally sit down. Samuel between Damien and me.

We eat a mix of meat, chicken, and fish with an array of side dishes.

Before I know it, two hours have passed, and we need to get Samuel to bed.

As I'm getting ready to leave, Damien's hand slips over my lower back.

"Are you ready?"

I frown. "To go where?" I ask.

"I'm taking you away for the weekend."

I twist to face him. "Sa—"

"Will be fine with my mom. She's taking over from here. We need to celebrate you graduating properly." He wiggles his eyebrows and I know exactly what he's thinking.

"Where are we going?" I ask, totally ignoring the sexual innuendo.

"A surprise."

I groan. "Unfair, but I will not beg because I know you won't tell me."

"Listening to you begging is definitely persuasive."

I lift a brow, wondering if I should start begging.

He shakes his head. "But no, it won't get me to spill. I want to surprise you."

"Damn it!"

We say goodbye to everyone, leave the tower and the driver takes us to the airport.

We board the plane, and the pilot announces Santa Barbara. I side-eye Damien, who looks annoyed by the fact it's no longer a surprise.

I'm buzzing about going back to the same place. It holds special memories for me, and I totally relax there and get the one-on-one time I crave with Damien.

We arrive late, and the sun is already down. I expect to go to bed, but he finds the blanket and ushers me outside. I'm about to lie down on the blanket to watch the stars, but he speaks.

"Open your graduation present," he whispers.

I open the envelope to find a set of keys.

I frown, not understanding.

"Keys?"

They don't look like they are at his house. So what else could they be for?

"This place is ours."

I blink and look around. "You're serious."

He nods with a smug smirk. "I think you like to call my gifts excessive. So here is another one you deserve."

I shake my head. And before I can say anything else, he speaks again.

"I never want this moment to end."

"Mmm, me either." I smile.

"The stars shine just as bright as you. You can't help but smile as you stare at it. Goldie..." He shuffles to get comfortable before he drops to his left knee.

He removes a large solitaire ring in gold from his pocket and slips it on my finger.

"Oh my God," I splutter as the back of my eyes prick with tears.

"You are the woman of my dreams. I never want you to doubt my love for you. Wearing this ring would be a symbol of how far we've come and how serious I am about our future. I want a future with you until my very last breath."

"Damien," I choke as tears spill over my cheeks.

"Marigold, will you marry me?"

"Yes! Yes, of course," I sob, leaning forward to kiss him.

His Goldie.

We kiss and I tear off his jacket. There's so many emotions pouring through me, but right now, I need him. All of him.

"I love you Goldie," he says between kissing me hard.

"I love you too," I rasp between another passionate kiss. "My excessive fiancé."

Bonus Scene

Marigold

I STARE AT MY reflection with tears filling my eyes.

I've always loved the idea of getting married and wearing a big poofy princess dress. And today is finally that day. With a sequined bodice and so much tulle, I feel like a real princess. I've always wanted a big wedding. And as I stare at the woman in front of me, I realize I'm living that dream right now. Damien is waiting at the end of the aisle for me.

With one last breath, I run my hands over the tulle bottom. I'm happy with how I look. My purple nails are on both my hands and feet. I haven't changed them again since he pointed out that the purple was his favorite.

I adjust the tiara in my hair, loving the way I swept my hair into a sleek bun. I wanted the total fairytale vibe and I have it. Everything has been a literal dream.

I can't wait to see Samuel waiting next to his dad. He didn't know who he wanted to spend the morning with. A part of him wanted to see me look like a princess, but the other wanted to look after his dad.

I think he knew his dad needed him today. This step is huge for both of us. Something I dreamed about, but also something he never thought he'd do again, so I guess that would play havoc with him.

"Are you ready?" My dad comes into the room with Elijah.

"Hey, you're not supposed to be here." I shoo my brother away.

"I know but Damien insisted I come and give you something, sis." Elijah steps forward, holding out a bag for me to take.

My brows lift to my forehead, wondering what present he's bought me today. Damien is definitely a giver, and it's always the most meaningful gifts.

"I need a moment, Dad," I say.

"Of course. Take your time."

I take the present into my room and open it up. There're beautiful blue panties and a matching bra. He wants me to wear this while I say my vows?

Something blue...

I don't waste a single second before I slip off my other lingerie and pull these panties on. I'm not wearing a bra with my wedding dress because the top is like a corset.

I check myself in the mirror. My mouth curves into the widest grin. I'm ready to see my boys.

I walk out and my dad stands.

"Are you ready?"

"Yeah."

"Let's go get you married."

We walk out and climb into the car. The drive isn't long, and when I arrive, I don't feel nervous. The butterflies swarming my stomach are from excitement.

Those steps to Damien and Samuel can't come quick enough. Luckily, my dad keeps the pace and prevents me running to them.

The vow exchange to the first kiss is way too slow. I just wanted to hear *I now pronounce you husband and wife.*

"You may kiss your bride."

After a quick peck, we head to the reception. After food, dancing, speeches, and cake, it's time for our honeymoon. Inside the car, I kiss him like I did the first time on my way to the airport. In his lap with pure love and excitement.

"Wait," I say, needing to tell him something important.

He's breathing heavily as he stares at me with confusion.

"I'm off the pill," I confess nervously.

"Goldie," he says. "Are you saying you want a baby?"

I bite my lip and nod my head.

"Yeah, I'm ready if you are," I say.

I didn't expect him to be ready so soon, but I need to be honest with him.

"The thought of you carrying my baby inside of you is hot, and fuck, seeing you pregnant is going to be even hotter."

"Truthfully, I was worried you wouldn't want me sexually anymore if I was pregnant." I laugh as happy tears now spill from my eyes.

"No, Goldie. The opposite. It's a turn-on like nothing else."

I smile with pure happiness seeping out of me. "Well, Mr. Gray, you better get moving and fill me with so much cum I'll be sure to get pregnant."

He growls. "You got it Mrs. Gray."

Mrs. Gray.